THE NEW ANNOTATED
FRANKENSTEIN

The Annotated Peter Pan
by J. M. Barrie, edited with an introduction and notes by Maria Tatar

The New Annotated H. P. Lovecraft
with an introduction by Alan Moore,
edited with a foreword and notes by Leslie S. Klinger

The Annotated African American Folktales
edited with an introduction and notes
by Henry Louis Gates Jr. and Maria Tatar

ALSO BY LESLIE S. KLINGER

Anatomy of Innocence: Testimonies of the Wrongfully Convicted
edited with Laura Caldwell, with an introduction by
Barry Scheck and Scott Turow

"The Date Being—?": A Compendium of Chronological Data
with Andrew Jay Peck

The Sherlock Holmes Reference Library
a ten-volume scholarly edition of the Sherlock Holmes stories

Baker Street Rambles

Conan Doyle, Sherlock Holmes, and The Bookman: *Pastiches,
Parodies, Letters, Columns & Commentary (1895–1933)*
with S. E. Dahlinger

The Grand Game: A Celebration of Sherlockian Scholarship
with Laurie R. King

A Study in Sherlock: Stories Inspired by the Holmes Canon
with Laurie R. King

*In the Company of Sherlock Holmes: Stories Inspired
by the Holmes Canon*
with Laurie R. King

Echoes of Sherlock Holmes: Stories Inspired by the Holmes Canon
With Laurie R. King

The Annotated Sandman
with Neil Gaiman

The Annotated Watchmen
with Alan Moore and Dave Gibbons

FRANKENSTEIN.

"By the glimmer of the half-extinguished
light, I saw the dull, yellow eye, of the
creature open: it breathed hard, and a
convulsive motion agitated its limbs.
*** I rushed out of the room."

Page 43.

London, Published by H. Colburn and R. Bentley, 1831.

LIVERIGHT PUBLISHING CORPORATION
A DIVISION OF W. W. NORTON & COMPANY
Independent Publishers Since 1923
NEW YORK | LONDON

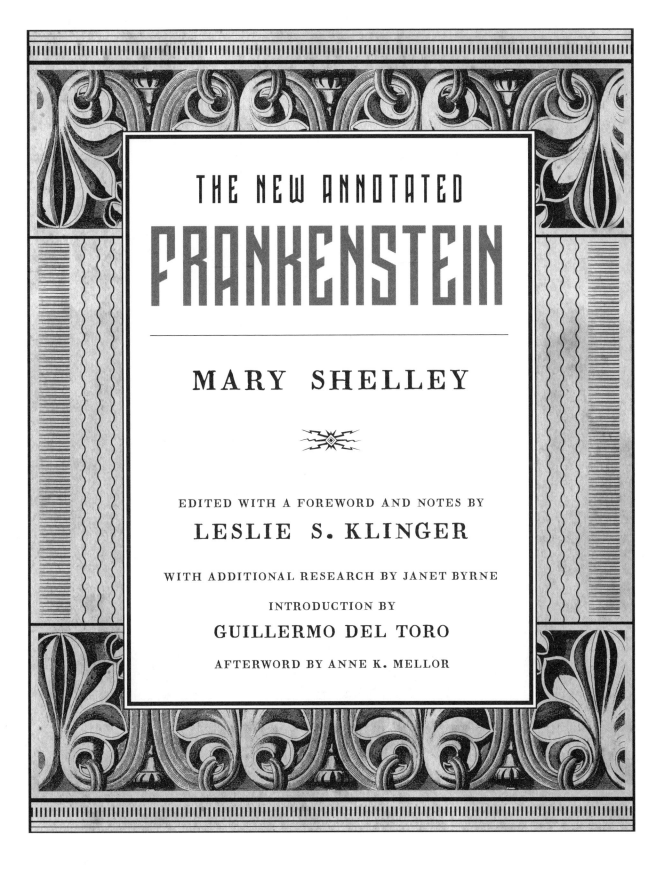

THE NEW ANNOTATED
FRANKENSTEIN

MARY SHELLEY

EDITED WITH A FOREWORD AND NOTES BY
LESLIE S. KLINGER

WITH ADDITIONAL RESEARCH BY JANET BYRNE

INTRODUCTION BY
GUILLERMO DEL TORO

AFTERWORD BY ANNE K. MELLOR

Frontispiece: From Volume I of the 1831 edition of *Frankenstein*.

For information about permission to reproduce selections from this book,
write to Permissions, Liveright Publishing Corporation, a division of
W. W. Norton & Company, Inc., 500 Fifth Avenue, New York, NY 10110

For information about special discounts for bulk purchases, please contact
W. W. Norton Special Sales at specialsales@wwnorton.com or 800-233-4830

Manufacturing by LSC Communications, Kendallville
Book design by JAM Design
Production manager: Anna Oler

ISBN 978-0-87140-949-2

Liveright Publishing Corporation, 500 Fifth Avenue, New York, N.Y. 10110
www.wwnorton.com

W. W. Norton & Company Ltd., 15 Carlisle Street, London W1D 3BS

1 2 3 4 5 6 7 8 9 0

Behold: I live and will continue to live . . .

—MARY SHELLEY, *Valperga*

CONTENTS

INTRODUCTION
Mary Shelley, or the Modern Galatea
BY GUILLERMO DEL TORO

ALL ART IS self-portraiture.

All storytelling is autobiography.

The true North of life is death.

These are some of the truths evidenced by the work of a teenager, writing a piece of fantastic fiction two hundred years ago. A beautiful tale of loss and pain that, by being fantastic, allowed her to reveal her true self.

I have, perhaps, little to add to the scholarly and thorough annotations to be found in this splendid volume Mr. Klinger has assembled. In the volume you have in your hands you will find in equal measure erudition and passion. This may very well be the best presentation of Mary Shelley's book, or at least a touchstone to be consulted time and again.

Knowing this, the only thing I can offer is myself. I can give back some personal observations—love, and a little bit of autobiography—in talking about a book, a character, and a writer who entirely transformed my life.

The monumental achievement of Mary Shelley grows considerably in our eyes the more we know about the context in which the book was created.

Like all great movements, Romanticism was birthed out of rage and need: the need to assert upon the world a new way of looking at things, a way to fight the overbearing certainty of science, to understand the unholy uniformity of mechanization and the need to rescue the numinous, the emotional, above all things. To quote Lord Byron: "The great object of life is sensation—to feel that we exist—even though in pain."

The irony of it all is that Romanticism was considered iconoclastic and rebellious and that, being a movement firmly gazing at the past, it became thoroughly modern.

It was punk rock to the establishment, to academia and the puritan mores of the time because it sought its roots in the provoking intersection of love and death in the poetic balance between loss and passion, damnation and desire.

Romanticism was an exuberant, young movement and it pursued the crossroads of all dichotomies as a source of true art. In ghosts, monsters, and mystery—all essential elements of our past—it found a way to fight against the stodgy narratives and values that dominated socially sanctioned art. It severed any ties with reason and with a rebellious scream gave birth to a world of gods and monsters.

Music, painting, and literature are steeped in outrageous passion and abandon. Graveyard poetry ruminates darkly over death and decay but differentiates itself from the memento mori by finding melancholy and desire in them, perhaps because we innately understand that our permanent state is "not being" and that our ignited state—life—is only transitory and precious. The call of the abyss is the call of Mother Darkness, eternally casting Her shadow over our brief scintillation.

The true North of life is death.

Mary W. Shelley was born in a world of men. Some pernicious and some benign, but all of them firmly in control. In the very best of circumstances, a woman could stumble upon a Pygmalionesque figure that bestowed his benign prejudice upon her and attempted to sculpt her into being.

Shelley was, however, a precious rarity. Being the daughter of an enlightened household and being painfully familiar with true loss, she was shaped by absence as much as she was by knowledge, and, in her solitude, she found her spirit—a spirit that saw no immediate benefit in the raging wound left in her heart by the loss of mother, child, and sibling and the insurmountable distance she felt from her father.

Then, as now, the game was socially and existentially rigged by men: a game of chutes and ladders that was all chutes for her and all ladders for men. Miraculously for us, Mary harnessed her gut-wrenching loneliness and oppression and conjured a book that was destined to outlive and outshine those of most of her male counterparts. This modern Galatea sang louder and clearer and demanded to be let loose from all the modeling hands that surrounded her.

Her questions, like Milton's, became universal, ontological questions. The exquisite Via Crucis she crafted for her creature speaks to all outsiders, and will continue to do so for centuries to come.

For if Hell is others, then the creature experiences it like no other protagonist before him or since. And when he recognizes his true plea and the unforgiving circumstances of his existence, he quests to kill his God, to seek his God and curse him, for in lieu of love he chooses the one emotion he can dispense at will: hatred. But like all art, the final element in this composition is paradox: when you silence your God, when you free yourself of him and realize he was himself a lonely man—simply a man—then you finally find yourself entirely, inescapably alone.

The virtue of this masterwork resides in the fact that it operates purely at various levels. First, it works perfectly as an engrossing yarn by utilizing a shifting narrative: a letter, a testimony, and a plea from three men in a quest for meaning—the captain, the scientist, and the creature. Its plotting and flow are utterly engrossing, and the reader's emotional alliance is usurped time and again by the unforgiving circumstances of all.

At another level, the work is a perfect parable, albeit one that seeks to dispense a most unforgiving truth. Parable is classically used to enlighten the mind, to shine light upon knowledge, but Shelley uses it to gauge the depth of our cosmic despair: the essential loneliness of our existence. Unlike Milton, she doesn't bemoan the loss of a paradise but rather reveals to us that there never was one. In embracing these unforgiving truths and not finding solace in any institutional comforts offered by church, by state, or by faith, Shelley concocts a most contemporary, modern parable that is impossible to outgrow and almost impossible to capture fully in any other medium.

In the popular imagination, and perhaps justly so, the creature and his creator have now fused into a single figure and share a single name. And now "Frankenstein" stands alongside that rarest of breeds—the literary figure that transcends its source. These figures are used colloquially to represent a concept, or many, and become an idiom. Dracula, Tarzan, Holmes, Watson—each of them has now been worshipped in as many mediums as we can consume—illustrated books, comics, film, television, radio, plays, figurines, statues, toys, street names, municipalities—and can be used in our vernacular: "He is a regular _____," we say, and are understood even by those who have only the vaguest notions of the literary source.

If we think of the creature as a shambling assembly of body parts (human and animal alike), and we consider his painful quest into enlightenment, we will come to an interesting question: "Where is the seat of the soul?" or rather "Where did that spark come from?"

Was it lodged in a thorax? The heart? An unmatched forearm? Or was the assembly of these parts an invocation of the ethereal planes—an edifice claiming to be inhabited?

The same can be said about the many parts that animate the novel, for, yes, the woes of the creatures are, somewhat obliquely, an autobiography of Shelley. But then again she speaks not only of her own emotional/spiritual journey and travails—she also serves us a travelogue of sorts, through regions that she became familiar with, and a catalog of notions, both scientific and philosophical, that intrigued her the most. These modern concerns, the uneasy truce between science and religion, machine and man, permeate the work. The soul of the book, then, I believe, resides in the unlikely combination of all these elements that, for the first time in human history, seek to reclaim our awe through a basis in fact and not through atavism and totem. For many, the book births a new genre: science fiction. This can be debated in favor of or against, because to classify is to confine, and like all great works, *Frankenstein* should be unshackled from a single shelf and find its life source as a philosophical meditation, a spiritual tale, a horror story, and a dire warning to science and its limits.

The flame of Shelley's intelligence burned brighter than any of her contemporaries', and the novel surges like an explosion with all the combustible matter available to her. The scorch marks it left behind delineate a perfect portrait of her soul and mind.

It has been oft repeated that of the tales invoked that "Year without a Summer" in Villa Diodati, it is hers that lives on. Polidori's seminal tale of vampirism would transmute into Stoker's *Dracula*, and Byron and Percy Shelley birthed but a barren concept or two.

But her tale found true immortality and it reached me thus.

It is a child of particular disposition that looks at gargoyles while others sing hymns to the Lord at church. I have to believe she felt, like me, more at home with the wretched than with the winners. History is written by the victors, but art is mostly chronicled by the disfranchised.

All of my life, I was in love with monsters; this is a fact. I discovered Frankenstein through the movies—like most people do—and was enraptured by Karloff and Whale's creation.

It was years later, at the start of adolescence, that I stumbled upon a pocket edition of Mary Shelley's work. The first thing that struck me was its literary devices—it was the first epistolary novel I had ever read—and the fact that, in many ways, it bore little resemblance to its filmic counterparts.

Shelley's book moved me to tears. I wept for the monster and admired his thirst for revenge. It spoke to me about the essential contradictions of the spirit and the world. And beyond the tragedy of it all a notion emerged that was demolishing to me: the villain of the piece was life. "Being" was the ultimate punishment and the only blessing we receive. And in the absence of love, it was Hell.

The Romantic essence was there—a notion well expressed by that other Romantic, Chopin, who once stated: "To die is man's finest action—and what might be his worst? To be born."

The fascinating thing for me is that Romanticism was responding to an eminently modern notion: man is alone but for man. We are the plague and the poetry and we are imprisoned by the notions, the gaze of others upon us.

The social misfit, the alienated being, comes to full fruition with the Industrial Revolution and the overcrowded loneliness of the big cities. The birth of the monster coincides socially with these modern concerns—it comes to be at the exact moment at which machines of our own creation usurp our function and surpass our skill and speed, displacing us into anonymity. The death knell of craftsmanship and thus of identity comes hand in hand with mass production of goods and the siphoning of the masses into identically constructed lodging to serve these machines.

The science fiction aspects of *Frankenstein* have always struck me as a byproduct of Shelley's desire to exonerate the existential villains of the past—the devil and sin—and to embrace the rational only as a tool to ask deeper, more urgent questions that are not circumstantial but universal.

Like Goethe, Shelley seems to have an innate grasp of the arrogance of knowledge. She uses surgery, galvanism, and chemistry only to grant an audience to the lonely wretch that is all of us. The impossibility of death is, to me, the greatest of the tragedies for the monster: the fact that his creator made him well and gave him a body that endures in spite of himself—his self, his lonely, desperate self.

There is, in my estimation, no more devastating ending in the history of literature than: "He sprung from the cabin-window, as he said this, upon the ice-raft which lay close to the vessel. He was soon borne away by the waves, and lost in darkness and distance."

I believe that Shelley uses science in order to avoid either divine origin or intercourse as birthing devices for her creature. Trying to avert the usual discourse about good and evil for a larger one: the fact that we are all anomalies—unnatural beings born of spiritually barren parents. And it is very telling that she chooses Nothingness to stage the final dialogue between Father and Child. A frozen hell where warmth is absent and where life seems impossible. She elevates the theater of this encounter by setting it in the most abstract landscape in the whole wide world, and one of the most symbolic.

At her very point of origin, Shelley traded her life with that of her own mother. For less than two weeks she rested in the maternal arms before losing her mother to the grave. Her only visitations were to her grave, and her joy was forever tainted by her pain and that most essential severance. Her origin was death and life her curse. Like her creature, she experienced the pain and steeled herself and found, in the learning of words, the only way to sing about her loneliness.

Much tragedy was to befall her, more than most contemporary minds could bear. It is entirely understandable that she might have believed herself accursed. Most everyone she loved, she lost, and posterity has never offered consolation to the artist. She has always impressed me in a way similar to how the Brontë sisters impress me: Most people would like to travel in time to meet great statesmen or explorers. I would love to travel back to contemplate life with these remarkable women—to hear them speak, to walk by their side on cold beaches or moors and under impossibly steely skies. For I was born in a sunny place in the middle of a sunny country, but within me I had a kinship to the same spirit that animated their melancholy and art.

I had seen Whale's film, and I saw Shelley's novel in the form of a Spanish paperback from Bruguera (my go-to dark fiction publisher in the late sixties, early seventies). Being an import, the book was not cheap. I saved my Sunday allowance for a couple of weeks and bought it. I read it in one sitting, and by the end of it, I was weeping. It was my Road to Damascus. It illuminated the reason I loved monsters, my kinship with them, and showed me how deep, how life-changing, a monster parable could be—how it could function as art and how it could reach across distance and time and become a palliative to solitude and pain.

And here we are, two centuries later, faithfully depositing flowers to this most exquisite storyteller, this extraordinary Galatea who refused to be shaped by her circumstance and gave us all life. And we try, in return, to help her creature stay alive. We strive to turn a curse into a blessing.

We hope that in some way, somehow, our gratitude, our love, can reach him like a whispered prayer, like a distant song. And we dream that perhaps he can stop—amid the frozen tundra and the screaming wind—and can turn his head and look back. At us.

And we hope that then he might recognize in our eyes his own yearning. And that perchance we can walk toward each other and find meager warmth in our embrace.

And then, if only for a moment, we will not feel alone in the world.

FOREWORD

BY LESLIE S. KLINGER

T HREE LITERARY FIGURES loom over the nineteenth century, their shadows extending into the twenty-first century: Sherlock Holmes, Dracula, and the Frankenstein monster. It is easy to describe the simplified, iconic aspects of each: Holmes, the "Great Detective," the supreme rationalist, always in charge, never swerving from his pursuit of justice; Dracula, the "Master Vampire," seductive, immortal, powerful, above the laws of human nature yet fundamentally human; and Frankenstein's "creature," terrific, superhuman, but isolated and innocent, a product of presumption and prejudice. Yet they are far more complex in their original conceptions than these images suggest. Only by considering the sources—the books in which the figures first appeared—can we truly understand them.

While it is beyond the scope of this book to consider Holmes and Dracula,[1] *The New Annotated Frankenstein* allows us to explore Victor Frankenstein and his creature through the text of Mary Shelley's story, *Frankenstein; or, The Modern Prometheus*, as published in 1818. Two hundred years after its original publication, the book's historical and social context, despite the story's cultural familiarity, may be unfamiliar to many readers, and its language, ideas, and events dif-

The Frankenstein Dracula War, No. 1 (Topps Comics, 1995). Roy Thomas, writer; Claude St. Aubin, penciller (cover art by Mike Mignola).

---

1. Fortunately, readers may turn to *The New Annotated Sherlock Holmes: The Short Stories* (W. W. Norton, 2004), *The New Annotated Sherlock Holmes: The Novels* (W. W. Norton, 2005), and *The New Annotated Dracula* (W. W. Norton, 2008), compiled by this editor.

FRANKENSTEIN ;

OR,

THE MODERN PROMETHEUS.

IN THREE VOLUMES.

Did I request thee, Maker, from my clay
To mould me man ?   Did I solicit thee
From darkness to promote me ?——
　　　　　　　　　　　PARADISE LOST.

VOL. I.

London :
PRINTED FOR
LACKINGTON, HUGHES, HARDING, MAVOR, & JONES,
FINSBURY SQUARE.

1818.

Title page, *Frankenstein* (1818).

ficult to readily appreciate; at the same time, two centuries of reinterpretation and reshaping of the work, and of adaptation into film and other media, have only revealed more about the genius of the original material. As biographers and scholars note, Shelley revised her tale in 1823 and 1831, but no previous annotated or scholarly edition of *Frankenstein* has considered the effect of her revisions or the possible reasons for specific changes. Finally, unlike the Sherlock Holmes tales or *Dracula* (which happen to have been written by men), *Frankenstein* surprisingly incorporates a good deal of the personal life of its author, and understanding those linkages enriches the story.

This volume is not specifically intended to add to the existing body of academic scholarship.[2] Beginning in the last quarter of the twentieth century, women's and gender studies gained ascendancy in college curriculums, as did considerations of popular culture; with the convergence of these disciplines, *Frankenstein* shifted from being dismissed as merely early "science fiction" to becoming a regular object of pedagogical scrutiny. An overview of important scholarship is contained in Appendix 5, below. This is also not a catalog of the thousands of reincarnations of *Frankenstein* on the stage, in films, television series, cartoons, comic books, games, and toys, discussed in Appendices IV and VI, below. Instead, this book seeks to show readers that the original text of Mary Shelley's novel, when read thoughtfully, is far more complex and engaging than the simplistic

---

2. For an excellent scholarly view of literary history and the textual allusions of *Frankenstein*, see Susan J. Wolfson and Ronald Levao, *The Annotated Frankenstein* (Cambridge, MA, and London: Belknap/Harvard University Press, 2012).

Poster for *Frankenstein*
(Universal Pictures, 1931),
directed by James Whale.

story that most new readers, who know only the films or comics, expect to find.

It is axiomatic to state that everyone knows the name "Frankenstein." Millions have seen the eponymous 1931 film, loosely based on Shelley's novel, starring Boris Karloff as the monster. A vast amount has been written about *Frankenstein* and continues to proliferate, almost at an exponential rate: Commentary has increased almost tenfold since original publication of the novel.[3] There are nearly 150 films to date bearing the title *Frankenstein* in some form or other.[4] Yet novelist, editor, and literary historian Brian W. Aldiss, who describes Mary Shelley as "the first science-fiction writer," notes that for every thousand who think they are familiar with her tale of a deranged scientist and his ill-begotten creature, only one in fact has read the novel.[5]

Frankenstein is often summarized along the lines of its serving as "a cautionary tale warning of the dangers that can be cast into society by a presuming experimental science."[6] But it is so much more: Remarkably, a nineteen-year-

3. The Google Books Ngram Viewer, which tabulates the appearances of words in the millions of publications scanned by Google, reports that from the mid-1830s, when the revised 1831 edition of *Frankenstein* was first published, to the early 1920s, the word "Frankenstein" appears in about 0.00002 percent of all English-language scanned works. This doubled by the 1940s to about 0.00004 percent and remained steady at this rate of appearance until the 1980s, when Frankenstein became the subject of academic study (see text accompanying note 1, Appendix 5, below), and the rate of appearance again tripled to 0.00012 percent. By 2015, this rate had again climbed steadily and sharply, to about 0.00018 percent, perhaps in anticipation of the two-hundredth anniversary of publication of the 1818 edition of *Frankenstein*. According to Google, the figures are normalized to reflect the number of books actually published in each year. For more on the Ngram Viewer, see Jean-Baptiste Michel, Yuan Kui Shen, Aviva Presser Aiden, Adrian Veres, Matthew K. Gray, William Brockman, the Google Books Team, Joseph P. Pickett, Dale Hoiberg, Dan Clancy, Peter Norvig, Jon Orwant, Steven Pinker, Martin A. Nowak, and Erez Lieberman Aiden, "Quantitative Analysis of Culture Using Millions of Digitized Books," *Science* (published online ahead of print: December 16, 2010).

4. See Appendix 4, below.

5. In *Trillion Year Spree: The History of Science Fiction*, with David Wingrove (New York: Athenaeum, 1986). Aldiss dismisses the arguments of David Ketterer, in *Frankenstein's Creation: The Book, the Monster and Human Reality* (Victoria, Canada: University of Victoria, 1979), who denies "that *Frankenstein* is science fiction at all, on the grounds that it is much else beside. But," Aldiss retorts, "so indeed is all good SF."

6. Maurice Hindle, introduction to *Frankenstein; or, The Modern Prometheus,* by Mary Shelley (London: Penguin Books, 2003).

old, writing her first novel, penned a tale that combines tragedy, morality, social commentary, and a thoughtful examination of the very nature of knowledge. The book is also the offspring of one of the most storied love affairs and collaborations in nineteenth-century literature, that between Mary Wollstonecraft Godwin and Percy Bysshe Shelley, the prodigal daughter of two of the leading English intellectuals of the late eighteenth century and the son of an English aristocrat, destined to sit in Parliament, who turned his back on convention to embrace a wholly original, heretical, and visionary philosophy of life: a pairing of geniuses. And, as already suggested, the work is also deeply autobiographical. The elements of autobiography are so finely calibrated with the book's form and content that the task of deciphering them, as demonstrated in these annotations, rewards effort yet is its own kind of trap; nonetheless, it has always been a vigorous line of research. Among the most obvious factors are, first, that Mary was motherless—her mother, Mary Wollstonecraft, died of puerperal fever, contracted giving birth to her in 1797—and although her father, William Godwin, raised her after his wife's death, their relationship was often strained and distant. Second, in the motherless creature's demonstrations of love and hatred for his "father," Victor Frankenstein, may be found echoes of Mary Shelley's complex relationship with Godwin. Third, like Victor, Percy Shelley was obsessed with the natural and occult sciences, which manifested itself in his keeping "vials, crucibles, 'philosophical instruments,' a solar microscope, a galvanic trough, an air pump, a telescope, and an assortment of electrical devices" in his rooms at college.[7] Fourth, Mary Shelley lost three children in infancy, and her dark feelings about childbirth and child-rearing suffuse the novel. Lastly, she puts into the mouths of the story's principals her own strong feelings about her father's and Percy's pursuit of ideas to the detriment of family.

Too often, *Frankenstein* is dismissed as merely early science fiction, rather than what is truly the first modern myth.[8] Some still view the book as an anomalous product of a youthful author and Mary Shelley herself as a

7. See, for instance, Ashton Nichols, editor of *Romantic Natural Histories: William Wordsworth, Charles Darwin, and Others* (Boston: Houghton Mifflin, 2003), at http://blogs.dickinson.edu/romnat/2011/06/07/percy-bysshe-shelley/.

8. A point made by Nicholas Marsh in *Mary Shelley: Frankenstein* (New York: Palgrave Macmillan, 2009).

Portrait of Mary Wollstonecraft Godwin Shelley, by Richard Rothwell (1840).

Percy Bysshe Shelley, by Alfred Clint (date unknown), after a portrait by Amelia Clint (1819).

freakish prodigy,[9] but it has achieved its place as one of the Romantic period's greatest works of imagination. Its richness and nuance contrast sharply with the reductive, if appealing, story told in stage and film adap-

9. Mary Wollstonecraft Godwin Shelley is referred to in various places below as "Mary Shelley" even though she may have been "Mary Godwin" at the time. She was often called "Mrs. Shelley" or "Mary Shelley" before she and Percy Bysshe Shelley married—see, for example, text accompanying note 53, below. This volume largely uses the simplest and clearest designation, the name by which she is actually known: "Mary Shelley."

Mary Shelley's writing career neither began nor ended with *Frankenstein*. Her first book, a travelogue entitled *History of a Six Weeks' Tour Through a Part of France, Switzerland, Germany and Holland*, co-written with Percy Shelley and discussed further below, was published in 1816, two years before *Frankenstein*. She wrote five other novels, all published initially without naming her but rather by identifying her as "the author of *Frankenstein*," and all largely written after the death of Percy Shelley, as well as numerous essays. All are little remembered today; in this respect, *Frankenstein* is similar to *Dracula*, the story of the other "creature" of the nineteenth century, which greatly overshadows Bram Stoker's other eleven novels, numerous short stories, travelogues, and reminiscences.

tations. For all its antiquarian flavor, it has become a timeless classic, a book that can be read simply and enjoyed as entertainment, but one that can also be parsed and studied for its influence on Western literature—twin purposes that the volume at hand seeks to accomplish. Uniquely, this volume will pay close attention to the changes in the text over the course of its maturation and provide a single-source reference for all of the variant texts.

THE HISTORICAL WORLD OF MARY SHELLEY

Before actually reading *Frankenstein*, it is important to understand the contextual history. The turbulent period between 1772 and 1818, the years encompassed by the events of the book[10] and the date of its publication, included two major political revolutions, the American and the French, as well as "ripple revolutions" the world over. The American and French revolutions, which shifted the tectonic plates of world history, revised drastically the relationship between rulers and the ruled and opened the door to new roles for government.[11] An equally defining series of events was Napoleon's rampage through the European continent, beginning in Italy in 1796, which created a new empire born of war, though one that collapsed by 1821. The period also witnessed revolutions in science, as the fields of chemistry and biology greatly expanded, as did an understanding of electricity. Major advances in theory were accompanied by practical applications, with the introduction of the spinning jenny, the power loom, and gas-lit, steam-driven factories. Roads were built at a growing pace, helping to usher in the Industrial Age and shape the great metropolises we know. Gas mains were laid in London. The first steam locomotives appeared, and then a steamship crossed the Atlantic, these transportation revolutions giving rise to modern cities. As local farms and cottage industries gave way to the Industrial Revolution, lives changed to the rhythms of factory work rather than farm work, and people began to live more distant from their employment. Printing became more efficient

10. See Appendix 2, "A Chronology of the Events of *Frankenstein*," below.

11. Lost among the Terrors of the French Revolution is the fact that in 1793, France established compulsory public education beginning at age six—a rejection of the philosophy of expatriate Jean-Jacques Rousseau, who despised public education and urged parents to provide their offspring with "well-regulated liberty."

Le Serment du Jeu de paume (aka "The Tennis Court Oath"), by Jacques-Louis David (1791).

and less expensive, and reading, once a domain of academics, clergy, and the rich, flourished.

The political events in France stirred a multitude of vocal reactions in England. The great philosopher Edmund Burke wrote *Reflections on the Revolution in France* (1790), beginning a long public debate in England over the role of the aristocracy and the rights of the citizenry. The same year, Mary Shelley's mother, Mary Wollstonecraft (on whom more below), achieved fame when she published a response to Burke, *A Vindication of the Rights of Men*, her defense of the ideals of the French revolution and a repudiation of the aristocracy. (The pamphlet did not actually bear her name until it went into a second edition, the first having sold out in a matter of weeks.) This was followed by the expatriate American Thomas Paine's *Rights of Man*, a radical exploration of liberty that appeared in 1791–92, and by Mary Shelley's father, William Godwin's, *Enquiry Concerning Political Justice* (1793).

In the midst of, and perhaps because of, such changes and political debate,

Entrée de l'Armeé française à Rome le 15 février 1798, by Hippolyte Lecomte, 1798.

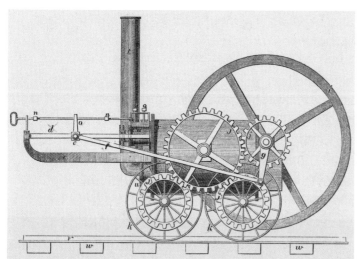

Richard Trevithick's Tramroad Locomotive (1802), artist unknown.

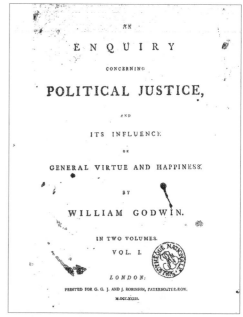

Title page of William Godwin's *Enquiry
Concerning Political Justice* (1793).

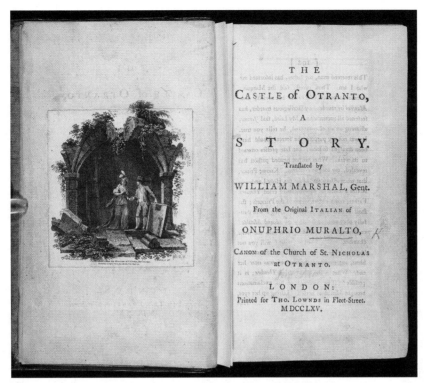

Title page of Horace Walpole's *The Castle of Otranto* (1764).

literature flourished, especially in England. The publication of *The Castle of Otranto* (1764), from the unlikely source of Whig politician Horace Walpole, the son of Robert Walpole, the first prime minister of England, set a new fashion in fiction, called "gothic." Walpole combined the tropes of medieval romance (castles and supernatural beings) with contemporary fiction, striking a balance between the wild fantasies of the former and the strict realism of the latter. *Otranto* was highly popular, and other authors copied Walpole's style, including Clara Reeve (best known for *The Old English Baron*, 1778)[12] and Ann Radcliffe, whose best-known work was *The Mysteries of Udolpho* (1794), though she wrote a half-dozen other novels. Matthew Gregory "Monk" Lewis cashed in on the new genre with a tossed-off but wildly successful scandalous novel, *The Monk* (1796), written before Lewis was twen-

---

12. First published anonymously in 1777 under the title *The Champion of Virtue*, the book was subsequently edited by Mrs. Edward Bridgen, one of four daughters of the successful novelist Samuel Richardson, and republished to great success under this title. (The first name of Richardson's daughter is unknown.)

ty.[13] The book was a favorite of Percy Shelley's. Certainly *Frankenstein,* on its surface, with the nearly supernatural monster and a hero (and heroine) threatened with an apparently implacable doom, displays some gothic elements, but, as will be seen, Mary Shelley's work goes far beyond the tropes of previous books in the genre.

Lewis's work certainly owed a debt to Radcliffe's but also to *Things as They Are; or, The Adventures of Caleb Williams,* a novel by William Godwin, published in 1794, three years before the birth of his first child, Mary. Godwin intended *Things as They Are* to be an exposition of his political principles, as expressed in his 1793 *Enquiry,* but the novel—glorified by his sympathizers and denounced by his detractors as dangerously revolutionary—was successful in its own right, a compelling story of two men in relentless pursuit of each other over a span of years (a theme that recurs in *Frankenstein*). In a preface to the first edition that went unused because

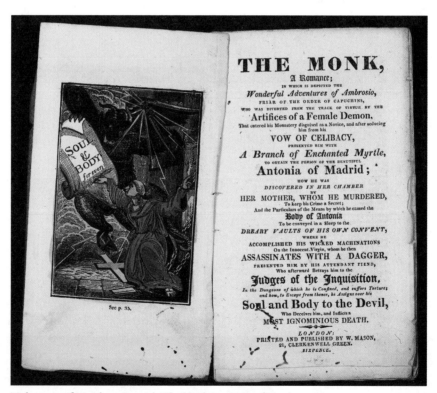

Title page of Matthew Lewis's *The Monk* (ca. 1818 edition).

13. Lewis later visited the Shelleys in Switzerland in 1816, on the eve of the "ghost story" competition discussed below, but he died just two months after publication of *Frankenstein,* in May 1818.

of the reaction of skittish booksellers, Godwin described the novel as a record "of domestic and unrecorded despotism, by which man becomes the destroyer of man." It has been said to have prefigured both the existential novel and noir detective fiction. Mary first read it in 1814, when she was seventeen, and it clearly made a great impression, as is evident not least from the title page of *Frankenstein*.

The gothic movement in literature yielded in the 1780s and 1790s to Romanticism—coinage of the term is usually attributed to Friedrich Schlegel[14]—partly as a reaction to the morbid obsessions of gothicism. It became a complex response to the idealism of the American and French revolutions, with its emphasis on reason, and drew literary sustenance from the sudden onset of the Industrial Revolution and the rise of science, again a crucial and new element of *Frankenstein*.[15] Its adherents rejected classical standards for art and embraced a return to Nature and medievalism. The Romantics extolled the virtues of strong individuals whose heroism and

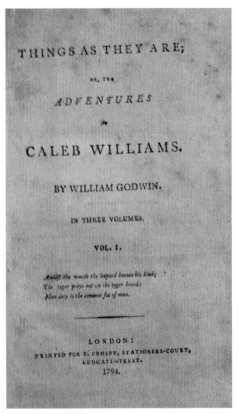

Title page of William Godwin's *Things as They Are; or, The Adventures of Caleb Williams* (1794).

rejection of the strictures of society would by their example lead others to better lives. They also celebrated intense feelings, especially those brought

14. Schlegel (1772–1829) was a writer, critic, and scholar whose work spanned linguistics, philosophy, and other disciplines. For his distinction between the classical and the Romantic, see, for example, Allen Speight, "Friedrich Schlegel," *The Stanford Encyclopedia of Philosophy* (Winter 2012 Edition), edited by Edward N. Zalta,

15. Anne K. Mellor makes the important observation that Mary Shelley was not dependent on Percy to infuse the novel with an understanding of science and the scientific enterprise. "While no scientist herself . . . Mary Shelley nonetheless had a sound grasp of the concepts and implications of some of the most important scientific work of her day. In her novel, she distinguishes between that scientific research which attempts to describe accurately the functionings of the physical universe and that which attempts to *control* or *change* the universe through human intervention" (*Mary Shelley: Her Life, Her Fiction, Her Monsters* [New York and London: Methuen, 1988], 90). In particular, Mary Shelley drew on her understanding of the work of Sir Humphry Davy, Erasmus Darwin, and Luigi Galvani (and his nephew Giovanni Aldani), all discussed in relevant places below.

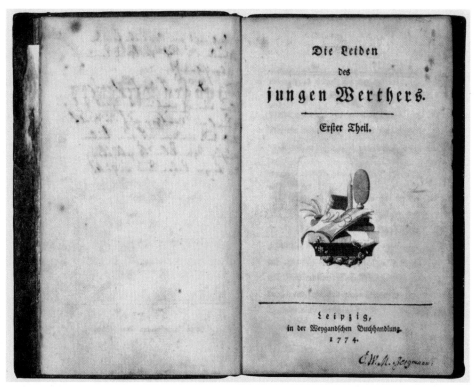

Title page of Wolfgang von Goethe's *Sorrows of Young Werther* (1774).

about by the presence of the sublime—the wonders of the natural world. All of these themes are well in evidence in *Frankenstein.*

Although written during the height of the gothic movement in England, Johann Wolfgang von Goethe's *Sorrows of Young Werther* (first published anonymously in 1774, when Goethe was twenty-five, and revised in 1787) was embraced by the Romantics for its emphasis on sentimentality over sense and may be viewed as the launching point for much of what followed. *Werther* was, to say the least, an incredibly popular novel about a young man driven to suicide by the tortures of love, so successful that not only did readers take to dressing like Werther, but the book appears to have induced "copycat" suicides among its devotees.[16] Another very popular writer of the day was Sir Walter Scott, an early champion of *Frankenstein*, who achieved success with novels and poems dramatizing historical struggles, essentially inventing "historical fiction." His long narrative poem *The Lay of the Last Minstrel* was published anonymously in 1805, when he was thirty-four. This was followed by the epic poem *Marmion* in 1808. *Waverley* (1814, again published anonymously,

16. See note 6, Volume II, Chapter VII, below.

as was all of Scott's fiction until 1827) was the first of twenty "Waverley" novels, and it and others—for example, *Rob Roy* (1817) and *Ivanhoe* (1820)—largely focused on individuals struggling heroically against the confines of their societies.

English poetry began to reflect this change as well, focusing on emotions recollected by the individual rather than consideration of classical or biblical themes. The collection *Lyrical Ballads*, published in 1798 by Samuel Taylor Coleridge and William Wordsworth, truly launched English Romanticism, and succeeding poetry penned by William Blake, Edgar Allan Poe, Robert Burns, Lord Byron, and of course Percy Shelley, Mary's husband, eschewed lofty themes and complex structures such as those in the poetry of Milton and Pope. Instead, the Romantic poets wrote about their experiences, usually in specific locations, recording their personal moods and emotions. Lord Byron, discussed further below, became in many ways virtually the personification of Romanticism, with the "Byronic" hero the ideal.

Sir Walter Scott, by Henry Raeburn (1822).

THE LIFE OF MARY WOLL-STONECRAFT SHELLEY

Mary Wollstonecraft Godwin's biographical details are essential knowledge for anyone reading the novel. She was born on August 30, 1797, in

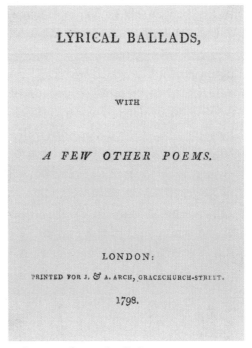

Title page of *Lyrical Ballads* (1798).

London. Her father, William Godwin, a former minister and the son of a Nonconformist minister (that is, a Protestant who elected not to "conform" to the precepts of the Church of England), had achieved a fame equal to or greater than his wife's with publication of his *Enquiry Concerning Public Justice*. It was followed by *Things as They Are*, and he became a central figure among English supporters of the French Revolution—styled as the "English Jacobins"—a group that included Tom Paine and William Blake and, most importantly for our purposes, Mary Wollstonecraft, the mother of Mary Shelley.

Mary Wollstonecraft was the eldest daughter of a once wealthy family, who, as a child, witnessed her father's violence toward her mother and set herself to be the protector of her mother and younger sisters and brothers. Her ministrations were unappreciated and resented by her mother, who, retiring to the sick chamber to nurse both unspecified ailments and at least one very real one (edema, then known as dropsy), would seat Mary in a corner with instructions not to move—a "punishment" that sometimes lasted for four hours. Uncharacteristically for the time, Wollstonecraft left her home at nineteen to make her own way, soon starting a school with her closest friend, Frances (Fanny) Blood. She subsequently served as caretaker of a widow in Bath and as a governess in Ireland for the country's biggest landowners, Robert King and Caroline Fitzgerald King, Lord and Lady Kingsborough—a family once distinguished by its place among the governing elite then known collectively as the Ascendancy, and later disgraced by the elopement of their daughter Mary, one of Mary Wollstonecraft's former charges.[17]

At twenty-eight, after a year in her employ, Mary Wollstonecraft was peremptorily dismissed by Lady Kingsborough. She had grown tired, in any case, of the limited opportunities afforded her and other women, and quite bravely she decided to move to London to try to make her living as an author. Her first novel, *Mary: A Fiction* (1788), written on the job in Ireland, mined her friendship with Fanny Blood; its secondary female character, Ann, is based on Fanny. Wollstonecraft also wrote a 1788 collection of children's tales, *Original Stories from Real Life: With Conversations Calculated to Regulate the Affections and Form the Mind to Truth and Goodness*, centered around her experiences both at the school and in the employ of the Kingsboroughs. In November 1791, the year following the release of *A Vindication of the Rights of Men*, she met

17. Among those blamed for Mary King's impropriety was the "notorious governess": Mary Wollstonecraft, who had quit the premises eleven years earlier. See Janet Todd, *Daughters of Ireland: The Rebellious Kingsborough Sisters and the Making of a Modern Nation* (New York: Ballantine, 2003), 205.

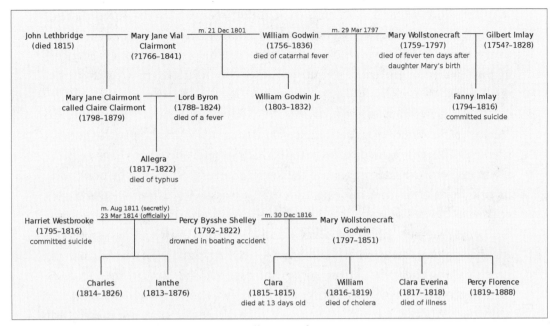

Family tree for William Godwin and Mary Wollstonecraft.

Mary Wollstonecraft, by John Opie (ca. 1797).

William Godwin, by Henry William Pickersgill (date unknown).

William Godwin, and, although their union seemed almost foreordained, this initial contact was a disappointment to both, as they disagreed on nearly everything. Godwin even took umbrage at what he perceived to be "offences, against grammar and other minute points of composition," in *A Vindication of the Rights of Men*.

"The interview was not fortunate," Godwin wrote, seven years later, in *Memoirs of the Author of A Vindication of the Rights of Woman* (1798), a sui generis account of his wife's unconventional life that can safely be said to have no precedent in literature, at least that of the late eighteenth century. The book took its title from Wollstonecraft's proto-feminist classic *A Vindication of the Rights of Woman* (1792). Clearly written from the heart but unsparing in its accounts, Godwin's "memoir" incongruously details Wollstonecraft's affairs—with the married painter Henry Fuseli and others—in the language of a political pamphlet, mixing theory and prurience. "She regarded her sex, in the words of Calista [in Greek mythology, the goddess who was both nymph and, after her seduction by Zeus, a bear], as 'In every state of life the slaves of men.' . . . It is necessary here that I should resume the subject of the friendship that subsisted between Mary and Mr. Fuseli. . . ."[18] Some of Wollstonecraft's sentiments regarding the position of women in society appear in *Frankenstein*, in the mouth of Elizabeth Lavenza, Victor's unfortunate fiancée.

Wollstonecraft had become involved with Fuseli before she met Godwin. Eventually, Sophia Rawlins, Fuseli's wife, not surprisingly, objected to her presence in their lives, and Wollstonecraft removed herself, traveling to Paris. There she had a relationship with an American adventurer, Gilbert Imlay, and became even more highly visible as a writer, publishing, among other works, *A Vindication of the Rights of Woman*. In 1794 she and Imlay had a daughter, Fanny, an event that precipitated a pattern of chronic absences, with Imlay's "ambiguity" and extended business trips to London and elsewhere "the prelude to an eternal separation," according to Godwin's later account.[19] Alone in the midst of the French Revolution, Mary followed Imlay to London, where she apparently attempted suicide. After a second unsuccessful attempt to take her own life, she had begun a slow return to literary circles. Imlay's final

18. William Godwin, *Memoirs of the Author of A Vindication of the Rights of Woman* (London: Printed for J. Johnson, no. 72, St. Paul's Church Yard, and G. G. and J. Robinson, Paternoster Row, 1798), digital edition, loc. 434. An edition of the book edited by Pamela Clemit and Gina Luria Walker, with five appendices containing material such as contemporary reviews, is available from Broadview Press, in Ontario, Canada, at https://www.broadviewpress.com/product.php?productid=236.

19. Ibid., locs. 620, 677, 618.

desertion, in April 1795, had come with the rather cruel implication that he found Wollstonecraft too domesticated for his tastes: "Mr. Imlay," Godwin wrote in *Memoirs of the Author of A Vindication of the Rights of Woman*, ". . . had formed another connexion; as it is said, with a young actress from a strolling company of players."[20]

Wollstonecraft and Godwin met again in January 1796, through writer friends. This time, he took a different view of her. He read her *Letters Written During a Short Residence in Sweden, Norway, and Denmark,* published in late 1795, and he was charmed. Later he wrote, "If ever there was a book calculated to make a man in love with its author, this appears to me to be the book."[21] Although their relationship started slowly—she afraid that she had once again let herself become dependent on a man, he that he was incapable of love—it was to become deeply passionate. "For six and thirty hours," he wrote her, "I could think of nothing else [but you]. I longed inexpressibly to hold you in my arms."[22] Both Wollstonecraft and Godwin publicly vilified the idea of marriage—Godwin described every married man as odiously selfish, treating his wife as a possession—but when Wollstonecraft became pregnant, in order to provide their child the legitimacy that Fanny Imlay lacked, they married. As noted above, five months after the wedding, Mary died of puerperal fever, contracted giving birth to her second child, Godwin's first, their daughter Mary Wollstonecraft Godwin. Wollstonecraft survived for only ten days after Mary's birth.

Godwin, then at the height of his reputation and happiness, was plunged into a period of despair and dissatisfaction from which he never emerged. His state of mind was further compromised by the public's reaction to *Memoirs of the Author of A Vindication of the Rights of Woman*, which was to have the effect, apparently entirely unanticipated by its author, of soiling Wollstonecraft's reputation for nearly a century. It was not until the rise of the New Woman in the late nineteenth century that Wollstonecraft's life and work came to be celebrated as foundation stones of feminist philosophy and writing.

Left not only with Mary but with his late wife's other daughter, Fanny, Godwin declared himself "totally unfitted to educate" the two girls and embarked on a course of child-rearing that was informed by his philoso-

20. Ibid., loc. 643.

21. Ibid., loc. 672.

22. Letter from William Godwin to Mary Wollstonecraft, August 16, 1796, in Ralph M. Wardle, ed., *Godwin & Mary: Letters of William Godwin and Mary Wollstonecraft* (Lincoln: University of Nebraska Press, 1966).

phy but had little practical basis. He was an undemonstrative father, emotionally distant by choice, though later Mary admitted, "I could justly say that he was my God . . . I remember many childish instances of the excess of attachment I bore him."[23] Certainly the relationship between Victor and the monster is colored by Shelley's own feelings about her father. He had hoped for a son by his wife, having chosen the name William, and perhaps out of disappointment, he gave Mary a "masculine" education, exposing her to a broad range of intellectual stimulation and a wide program of reading.[24] This thinking is reflected in the differences between the education of Victor and Elizabeth in the Frankenstein household. In contrast, however, the Godwin household was a focal point for a diverse group of English writers and intellectuals, and there is an oft-told anecdote of an evening in 1806 when the nine-year-old Mary hid behind a sofa to listen to Samuel Taylor Coleridge read aloud his *Rime of the Ancient Mariner*,[25] a work whose themes run throughout *Frankenstein*.

After four years of struggling to succeed as a single parent, Godwin married his neighbor Mary Jane Vial Clairmont, who already had two children of her own, Charles (1795–1850) and Clara Mary Jane (1798–1879). The latter, eight months younger than Mary, first called Jane but later Claire or Clare, would have a significant role in Mary's early life. Mary had no love for her stepmother, writing, in a letter dated September 26, 1817, "As to Mrs. Godwin, something very analogous to disgust arises whenever I mention her."[26] Whatever her deficiencies as a parent, however, Mary Jane was the kind of woman Godwin needed. He described her later as having "great strength and activity of mind." Like many an author, Godwin had struggled to earn money and was frequently in financial straits. Now, with Mary Jane's active partnership, they undertook to publish children's primers on biblical and classical history and such works as Godwin's friends Mary and Charles Lamb's *Tales from Shakespeare*.[27] However, their business, the Juvenile Library, would end in

23. Letter to Maria Gisborne, October 30, 1834, in Betty T. Bennett, ed., *Letters of Mary Wollstonecraft Shelley*, 2 vols. (Baltimore: Johns Hopkins University Press, 1980), Volume II, 215.

24. See Julie Ann Carlson, *England's First Family of Writers: Mary Wollstonecraft, William Godwin, Mary Shelley* (Baltimore: Johns Hopkins University Press, 2007).

25. The anecdote is repeated in Mellor's *Mary Shelley: Her Life. Her Fiction, Her Monsters*, 11, and William St. Clair, *The Godwins and the Shelleys: The Biography of a Family* (London and Boston: Faber & Faber, 1989), 295.

26. The letter was written to Mrs. Julian [Florence A.] Marshall; see *The Life and Letters of Mary Wollstonecraft Shelley*, 2 vols. (London: R. Bentley and Son, 1889), Volume I, 201.

27. Charles Lamb was known as one of the most affable members of the English literary circle of the day. His older sister Mary suffered from mental illness, resulting in frequent

Portrait of Claire Clairmont, by Amelia Curran (1819).

financial disaster, leaving Godwin in constant need of funds. Mary's relationship with Mary Jane and the distance she was to put between herself and her father would later come to shape *Frankenstein*, again reflected in the strained "parental" relationship between Victor and the monster.

Godwin assessed Mary in 1812, in a letter to an unknown correspondent, when Mary was almost fifteen, describing her as "considerably superior in capacity to the [daughter] her mother [Mary Wollstonecraft] had before [that is, Fanny]. Mary . . . is singularly bold, somewhat imperious, and active of mind. Her desire of knowledge is great, and her perseverance in everything she undertakes almost invincible. My own daughter is, I believe, very pretty."

Nevertheless, he must have felt that the family setting was not the right environment for Mary, possibly because of the constant friction with her stepmother. Perhaps arising out of such stress, Mary also displayed a nervous weakness in her arm. Ostensibly for her recuperation, then, on June 7, 1812, Godwin sent her for an extended stay in Dundee, Scotland, with the family of a Scottish friend, William Baxter. The sea air and the warmth of the family, including the presence of the Baxters' two daughters, Christina and Isabella, proved beneficial, and Mary formed her first real friendship with the latter, who was about four years her senior. In her introduction to the substantially revised 1831 edition of *Frankenstein*, she describes the banks of the River Tay near Dundee as "the eyry of freedom, and the pleasant region where unheeded I could commune with the creatures

---

institutionalization. In 1796, when Mary was thirty-two and Charles twenty-one, Mary snapped in the course of an argument and stabbed her mother to death. Charles arranged for private care for her, and after his father died in 1799 brought Mary to live with him, a companionship they shared for the rest of his life. Together, they had an active social and literary life, writing poetry and prose, including at least three books for the Godwins' Juvenile Library. Mary Shelley must have known the Lambs through her father, and they are indirectly referenced in *Frankenstein* (see note 14, Volume I, Chapter II, below).

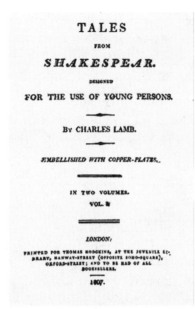

TALES

FROM

SHAKESPEAR.

DESIGNED

FOR THE USE OF YOUNG PERSONS.

By CHARLES LAMB.

EMBELLISHED WITH COPPER-PLATES.

IN TWO VOLUMES.
VOL. I.

LONDON:

PRINTED FOR THOMAS HODGKINS, AT THE JUVENILE LI-
BRARY, HANWAY-STREET (OPPOSITE SOHO-SQUARE),
OXFORD-STREET; AND TO BE HAD OF ALL
BOOKSELLERS.

1807.

Title page of Charles Lamb's *Tales from Shakespeare* (1807).

of my fancy. I wrote then—but in a most common-place style. It was beneath the trees of the grounds belonging to our house, or on the bleak sides of the woodless mountains near, that my true compositions, the airy flights of my imagination, were born and fostered."[28]

While Mary was "recovering" in Scotland, the Godwin household was repeatedly visited by Percy Shelley and his first wife, Harriet. Percy had been born in West Sussex on August 4, 1792, into a life of luxury, the eldest of six children of Sir Timothy Shelley, a member of Parliament, and Lady Elizabeth Pilfold Shelley. With one brother and four sisters (some much younger than he), his early childhood was spent mostly outdoors, hunting and fishing. He began Eton, even then the most elite school in England, in 1804, and refused to engage in sports or the tradition of "fagging" (acting as a quasi-servant for a senior student), making a reputation as "mad Shelley." It was here that he first indulged in the intense interest in science that would last his lifetime, his appetite having been whetted even earlier, at Syon House Academy, the boarding school he attended at ages ten and eleven. At University College, Oxford, in 1810, he plunged into writing. His first publication, identifying its author only as "P.B.S.," was a novel, *Zastrozzi*, with typical gothic elements of an exaggerated character (what John V. Murphy calls the "hero-villain")[29] whose complex motives find him engaged in intricate actions.

Later in 1810, Percy and his oldest sister, Elizabeth, published a collection of verses entitled *Original Poetry by Victor and Cazire*. In 1811, Percy's second novel, *St. Irvyne, or the Rosicrucian*, appeared, as well as a pamphlet called

28. See Appendix 1, below.

29. In *The Dark Angel: Gothic Elements in Shelley's Works* (Plainsboro Township, NJ: Associated University Presses, 1975). The book's eponymous outlaw, Pietro Zastrozzi, pursues his half-brother, Verezzi, whom he is compelled to punish in order to avenge the death of his mother, Olivia Zastrozzi, who was driven to penury and prostitution by the two men's father. He maneuvers his half-brother into suicide to exact full revenge. "[B]y daring boldly, by striving to verge from the beaten path, whilst yet trammelled in the chains of mortality, [thy soul] will gain superior advantages in a future state," Zastrozzi declares to the book's heroine, Matilda di Laurentini, tricked by him into colluding in Verezzi's killing. Tried and convicted, Zastrozzi continues to defy society with smiles of "contemptuous atheism" even as he is stretched upon the rack in the book's closing scene. The text of *Zastrozzi* may be found at https://ebooks.adelaide.edu.au/s/shelley/percy_bysshe/zastrozzi/index.html.

"The Necessity of Atheism." The anti-religious pamphlet landed him in front of the university administration, and when he refused to repudiate its message, he was expelled, less than a year after his matriculation. Sir Timothy intervened, and Percy was offered an opportunity to return to Oxford, but he refused, earning the lifelong enmity of his father.

Shortly after his expulsion from Oxford, the nineteen-year-old Percy met and married his sisters' sixteen-year-old friend Harriet Westbrook, the daughter of a London coffee-house proprietor. Seeking some direction for his career, Percy wrote to William Godwin, whom he idolized, telling Godwin that he wished to become his disciple. Perhaps knowing of Godwin's financial difficulties, Percy introduced himself somewhat immodestly as "the son of a man of fortune in Sussex" and "heir by entail to an estate of 6,000 £ per an." It was actually his second letter to Godwin, and this time the latter took the bait, perhaps seeing a lifeline out of the morass of his financial difficulties.

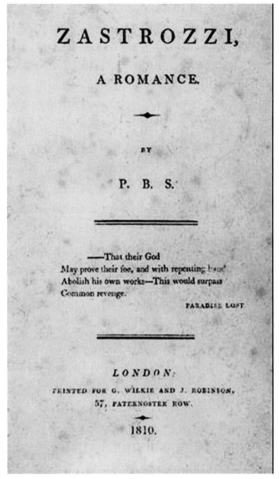

Title page of Percy Shelley's *Zastrozzi* (1810).

He responded, seeking details about Shelley's income. When Godwin learned of the rift between father and son, he counseled reconciliation—and soon began accepting regular financial contributions, in the form of loans, from Percy (who, having exaggerated his father's support, could truthfully little afford to help the Godwins).[30] Percy and Harriet began visiting Godwin, and on November 11, 1812, Percy met Mary for the first time. She was visiting her

30. The precise monetary arrangements made between the two men are not known, but certain details of their relationship in this regard may be found in James Bieri, *Percy Bysshe Shelley: A Biography* (Baltimore: Johns Hopkins University Press, 2008), and Charlotte Gordon, *Romantic Outlaws: The Extraordinary Lives of Mary Wollstonecraft and Her Daughter Mary Shelley* (New York: Random House, 2015). Percy was generally careless about money, and, to his father's displeasure, he frequently borrowed on the strength of his future inheritance, often making gifts that he later resented and perennially finding himself short of funds.

father on a short trip from Scotland in the company of Christina Baxter. Neither wrote about this first meeting.

Mary returned to Dundee for another eighteen months. Percy, by now disappointed that his young bride Harriet was not the intellectual companion he sought, and chafing from the influence her sister Eliza exerted over her, urged both to return to their home and began to spend his time in the company of a circle of London intellectuals that included Godwin. On March 20, 1814, Mary ended her sojourn in Scotland and sailed for London and her father's Skinner Street home, arriving on March 30. On May 5,[31] she met Percy again at Skinner Street, at a dinner at which Godwin and Percy discussed mainly financial matters. Ironically, the romance that developed between Percy and Mary was in part fueled by Percy's financial difficulties, for during these few months, he was dodging bailiffs, staying at an obscure inn, and dining with the Godwins to avoid being seen in public.[32]

Like Harriet when she met Percy, Mary was just sixteen. She felt a range of emotions for the twenty-one-year-old, including, perhaps, gratitude for his largesse: He had become, in her eyes, vitally important to the support of her family. His marriage to Harriet, who was by now pregnant, was clearly a source of not small unhappiness. Percy suggested (but may not have genuinely believed) that Harriet had a lover, one Captain Ryan, and that Ryan was the father of the child she was carrying. In May 1814, he begged Harriet to give up her "remorseless" scorn and offer him pity.[33]

The distraction from such matters afforded by integration into the Godwin household, and the companionship and intellectual stimulation that Shelley found there, influenced him profoundly, setting a new course for his life. Mary was sympathetic to his espoused ideals, which, despite his aristocratic

31. The date is fixed in various biographies, including, for example, Emily Sunstein's *Mary Shelley: Romance and Reality* (Baltimore: Johns Hopkins University Press, 1989) and William A. Walling's *Mary Shelley* (Boston: Twayne Publishers, 1972). William Godwin gives the date as June 18 in a letter dated August 27, 1814, to John Taylor, to whom he wrote to renew a debt (reprinted in *The Elopement of Percy Bysshe Shelley and Mary Wollstonecraft Godwin, as Narrated by William Godwin, with Commentary by H. Buxton Forman, C. B.* [Boston: The Bibliophile Society, 1911], 10). However, there is ample evidence that Percy visited the house frequently between March 30 and June 18.

32. Sunstein, *Mary Shelley: Romance and Reality*, 73. Godwin wrote to Taylor, "He was under apprehension of arrests; & from this consideration I invited him to make my house his principal home, his known haunts being all at the west end of the town. He lodged at an inn in Fleet Street, & took his meals with me" (Godwin, *Elopement*, 11).

33. Sunstein, *Mary Shelley: Romance and Reality*, 69.

ancestry, closely matched her own and her father's. A friendship bloomed, and he often sought her out at her mother's gravesite, to which she and her half-sister Jane retreated to escape the household, particularly Mary Jane. By July 1814, on the occasion of his presentation to her of a copy of *Queen Mab: A Philosophical Poem, with Notes*, his first book of published poetry,[34] she wrote on the flyleaf, "This book is sacred to me and as no other creature shall ever look into it I may write in it what I please—yet what shall I write—that I love the author beyond all powers of expression and that I am parted from him dearest & only love—by that love we have promised to each other although I may not be yours I can never be anothers. But I am thine exclusively thine."[35] Percy reciprocated, declaring his love for her. Mary—scandalously, but in

St. Pancras churchyard, where Mary Wollstonecraft is buried, by Alexander Hogg (1784).

34. First published in 1813, about a year after Percy first introduced himself to William Godwin, the poem is about the perfectability of humankind. It is substantially based on Godwin's writings about "necessity," melded with Percy's own ideas about nature and society. The poem rejects the need for violent revolution and proposes that mankind will improve by reason of inherent virtues and the evolution of society. The actual book is now in the Huntington Library, and some of its nineteenth-century provenance is described in H. Buxton Forman's *The Shelley Library: An Essay in Bibliography* (London: The Shelley Society, 1886).

35. Mary also included remembered lines of Byron's poetry. Huntington Library *Queen Mab*, quoted in Sunstein, *Mary Shelley: Romance and Reality*, 76, and described in detail in Forman's *The Shelley Library*.

keeping with her and Percy's expressed views about marriage—proposed a physical menage à trois, with Harriet as their "sister," which Harriet declined. She urged Godwin to keep them apart, probably imparting the fact of her pregnancy, and Godwin appealed to Mary. In agony, Mary equivocated. Percy likely told her that Harriet was pregnant by another man and in any event urged her to follow the principles of her mother. "He declared unless she joined him as Partner of his Life—he would destroy himself," Jane later recalled.[36] Mary assented, declaring herself persuaded by "love, youth, fear and fearlessness."[37] On July 28, Mary and Percy left for the Continent, aided and joined by Jane, now calling herself Claire.[38]

Mary Jane followed them to Paris. She cared little for Percy or Mary but was anxious to convince Claire to return home. Claire refused, and during the months of July and August, the young trio traveled—a journey recorded in *History of a Six Weeks' Tour Through a Part of France, Switzerland, Germany and Holland*, published as a collaboration between Percy and Mary in 1817. As will be seen, Mary drew heavily on the records of this trip in creating the scenes of *Frankenstein*. However, despite its fruitfulness as a source for many scenes in *Frankenstein*, the trip was miserable. They were friendless, and they had no money. Godwin was furious with both of them,[39] and Mary

36. Claire Clairmont to Edward J. Trelawny, ca. 1870, quoted in Mary Rosalie Glynn Grylls, *Claire Clairmont, Mother of Byron's Allegra* (London: John Murray, 1939), Appendix C, 270. Percy's self-centered view of the relationship with Harriet is evident in his letters to her. For example, in a letter dated approximately October 3, 1814, he wrote, "I am united to another; you are no longer my wife. Perhaps I have done you injury, but surely most innocently and unintentionally, in having commenced any connexion with you. That injury, whatever be its amount, was not to be avoided." He went on, in a postscript to urge Harriet, then far advanced in her pregnancy, to "attend to the preservation of your health. I do not apprehend the slightest danger from your approaching labour" (Leslie Hotson, ed., *Shelley's Lost Letters to Harriet*, with an introduction by Leslie Hotson [London: Faber & Faber, 1930], 41.

37. Frederick L. Jones, ed., *Mary Shelley's Journal* (Norman: University of Oklahoma Press, 1947), October 7, 1822, 183.

38. Jane actually called herself "Clara" at this precise stage; later, indiscriminately, "Claire" or "Clare." While Mary may have had little use for Claire, the latter had enjoined Percy not to leave her behind in "slavery" to her mother.

39. In his letter to John Taylor, written a month after the elopement, Godwin complains, "I felt it . . . my duty . . . to provide, if possible, for the hour of distress (which, I believe, is not far distant) when these unworthy children shall again seek the protection and aid of their father. . . . [T]he poor girls . . . may be brought back to the path of duty, time enough to prevent a stigma from being fastened on their characters . . . When I use the word stigma, I am sure it is wholly unnecessary to say that I apply it in a very different sense to the two girls. Jane [Claire] has been guilty of indiscretion only, & has shown a want of these filial senti-

found Claire's presence almost intolerable. Years later, Mary would write, "Now, I would not go to Paradise with her for a companion—she poisoned my life when young. . . . But years ago my idea of Heaven was a world without Claire—of course these feelings are altered—but she still has the faculty of making me more uncomfortable than any human being."[40] When they returned to England at the end of the summer, Mary was pregnant. The child's father was Percy Shelley.

Born on February 22, 1815, the infant, a girl, survived for two weeks only. In the days and weeks, if not years, after, Mary's thoughts returned repeatedly to the child, whom she had nursed. "['T]is hard, indeed, for a mother to lose a child," she wrote in her journal three days after her daughter's death. On March 13, she wrote, "Stay at home, net,[41] and think of my little dead baby. This

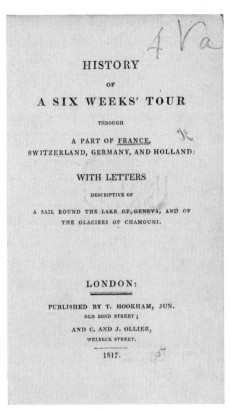

Title page of Percy Shelley and Mary Godwin, *History of a Six Weeks' Tour Through a Part of France, Switzerland, Germany and Holland* (1817).

ments, which it would have been most desirable to us to have discovered in her: Mary has been guilty of a crime" (Godwin and Forman, *The Elopement,* 15–16).

40. In a letter to Edward Trelawny dated May 4, 1836, in Frederick L. Jones, ed., *Letters of Mary W. Shelley,* 2 vols. (Norman: University of Oklahoma Press, 1944), Volume II, 271.

41. An obsolete term meaning the making of small fancywork items of netting, such as a handbag or sachet. This was reportedly one of the only such pastimes Mary Shelley enjoyed. Thomas Love Peacock (1785–1866) wrote a poem, "To a young lady netting," in 1803:

While those bewitching hands combine,
With matchless grace, the silken line,
They also weave, with gentle art,
Those stronger nets that bind the heart.

But soon all earthly things decay:
That net in time must wear away:
E'en Beauty's silken meshes gay
  No lasting hold can take:

But Beauty, Virtue, Sense, combin'd,
(And all these charms in thee are join'd)
Can throw that net upon the mind,
No human art can e'er unbind,
  No human pow'r can break.

is foolish, I suppose; yet, whenever I am left alone to my thoughts, and do not read to divert them, they always come back to the same point—that I was a mother, and am so no longer." On March 19, she recorded: "Dream that my little baby came to life again; that it had only been cold, and that we rubbed it before the fire, and it lived. Awake and find no baby. I think about the little thing all day. Not in good spirits." She mentions another dream of the baby on the twentieth, but never again recorded anything, except as echoes in her fiction, about the child.[42]

The couple spent the rest of 1815 reading and dodging Percy's relentless creditors. In August 1815, they moved to Bishopsgate, Windsor, and on January 24, 1816, a son, William, was born. Godwin continued to shun the couple, and Mary despaired that the relationship could be healed. She made trips to London to see her half-sister Fanny, who had to come outside of the Skinner Street house to talk with her, reinforcing her view that her breach with her father was permanent. She was anxious, too, about Percy's health. They began to plan another trip to the Continent for the summer of 1816, with Claire and their close friend T. Jefferson Hogg.[43]

In March 1816, Claire contrived to introduce herself to the notorious

---

Peacock was a good friend of Percy Shelley's, and in his *Memoirs of Percy Bysshe Shelley*, first published from 1858 to 1862, he defended Shelley's wife, Harriet, recalling her as beautiful, educated, and well spoken: "Her manners were good; and her whole aspect and demeanour such manifest emanations of pure and truthful nature, that to be once in her company was to know her thoroughly. She was fond of her husband, and accommodated herself in every way to his tastes. If they mixed in society, she adorned it; if they lived in retirement, she was satisfied; if they travelled, she enjoyed the change of scene." He admitted that Percy's second wife, Mary, "was intellectually better suited to him than his first, no one who knew them both will deny; and that a man, who lived so totally out of the ordinary world and in a world of ideas, needed such an ever-present sympathy more than the general run of men, must also be admitted . . . ," but he saw no reason to disparage Harriet because of Percy's change of heart (H. F. B. Brett-Smith, ed., *Peacock's Memoirs of Shelley with Shelley's Letters to Peacock* (London: Henry Frowde, 1909), 48, 51–52.

42. See Jones, ed., *Mary Shelley's Journal*, 41. Some suggest that this dream was the true genesis of *Frankenstein*.

43. Thomas Jefferson Hogg (1792–1862) was a friend of Shelley's from his Oxford days, and they collaborated on a collection of burlesque poetry in 1810. Hogg attempted to seduce Harriet Shelley (without Percy Shelley's approval) in 1811, and Percy and Hogg became estranged. By 1812, however, the two men were close again, and within a few short years, Hogg, reprising his earlier effort, declared his love for Mary. Percy encouraged Mary to consummate a relationship with Hogg, but there is no indication that she ever did so, and by March 1817, she wrote, "I do not like [Hogg] and I think he is more disagreeable than ever" (Bennet, ed., *Letters of Mary W. Shelley*, Volume I, 35).

Monument of Mary and Percy Shelley, engraving by George J. Stodard (1853) from a monument by Henry Weekes.

celebrity-poet Lord Byron. Using the pretext of seeking his advice on a theatrical career and, when that failed, on her writing, she obtained an interview with him and apparently sang for him. Byron had been importuned by scores of women, many under false names, and he was not particularly interested. By April 9, she wrote him another note, abandoning all pretense and offering to simply show him that she could "love gently and with affection." She suggested a date, and he acceded. At the same time, she told Mary that Byron was anxious to meet her. Claire arranged a brief meeting in London that left Mary impressed. Claire reported to Byron that Mary had remarked to her, "How mild he is! How gentle! How different from what I expected."[44] Claire had her own agenda as well: In short order, the seventeen-year-old, "prancing" at Byron, became impregnated by him.[45]

44. Letter from Claire Clairmont to Byron, ca. March–April 1816, in the manuscripts of John Murray, publisher of Lord Byron, held by John Murray VI, quoted in Sunstein, *Mary Shelley: Romance and Reality*, 115.

45. Byron described their relationship in a letter of January 20, 1817, to Douglas Kinnaird: "You know—& I believe saw once that odd-headed girl—who introduced herself to me shortly before I left England—but you do not know—that I found her with Shelley and her sister at Geneva—I never loved her nor pretended to love her—but a man is a man—& if a girl of eighteen comes prancing to you at all hours of the night—there is but one way—

Portrait of George Gordon Byron, 6th Baron Byron, by Richard Westall (1813).

Though he showed no further interest in Claire, she urged that later that spring, Percy and Mary accompany her to Lake Geneva, along whose shores Byron was beginning a not entirely voluntary expatriate residence, to effect a reunion with him, in hopes that he would welcome a relationship with her and support their child when born at year's end. In May, leaving Hogg behind, Percy, Mary, and Claire departed for Switzerland, accompanied by William.

Gordon, Lord Byron, was, except for heads of state, perhaps the most famous person of the age, and many today see him as the first celebrity "rock star." He was idolized by young and old and in some ways can be seen to inform the ideals of both Robert Walton, the narrator of *Frankenstein*, and Victor Frankenstein himself. Byron had achieved immense fame with publication of the shockingly self-revelatory first two cantos of his epic poem *Childe Harold's Pilgrimage* in 1812. Born in 1788 to Captain "Mad Jack" Byron and the former Catherine Gordon (his father's second wife), he inherited his title at the age of ten. In intermittent bursts from 1805 to 1807 he attended Cambridge. There he experienced what he later described as a violently passionate relationship with a fellow student, John Edleston, who sang in the Trinity College choir and whose untimely death was said to have later inspired Byron's Thyrza elegies. The relationship continued a pattern of similar earlier infatuations that eventually gave rise in Byron to what one of his biographers has called "a consciousness of sexual differences" that he felt made living in England "untenable."[46] On his subsequent grand tour, Byron visited the Mediterranean, partly, it is said, in

the suite of all this is that she was with *child*—& returned to England to assist in peopling that desolate island. . . . This comes of 'putting it about' (as Jackson calls it) & be dammed to it—and thus people come into the world" (Lesley A. Marchand, ed., *Byron's Letters and Journals*, 12 vols. (Cambridge, MA: Belknap/Harvard University Press, 1973–82), Volume V, 162.

46. Fiona MacCarthy, *Byron: Life and Legend* (New York: Farrar, Straus and Giroux, 2002), 40.

search of further such experiences. This trip initiated his infatuation with the Levant, evident throughout his writing. It was on his return from the Mediterranean that he began to publish his poetry, achieving overnight notoriety that placed him simultaneously as a celebrant of and an exile in London society.

Despite this celebrity and the romantic attentions of women and men, however, Byron was strictly disciplined and kept writing, producing such works as *The Giaour* and *The Bride of Abydos* (both published in 1813), and *Parisina* and *The Siege of Corinth* (1816). He dallied with Lady Caroline Lamb[47] (who famously called him "mad, bad and dangerous to know"), among other lovers, until, pressed by debt, he thought to follow his father's example of marrying wealthy women and began looking for a partner. He had not yet succeeded when, in 1813, he reunited with his half-sister, Augusta Leigh (the product of his father's first marriage), whom he had first met when he was thirteen. They had not seen each other for several years but had kept up a correspondence. The letters laid the groundwork for a deeper affection than they had ever enjoyed face-to-face, and their relationship quickly gave rise to rumors of incest.[48] Indeed, Augusta's daughter Medora,

47. Lady Caroline was married to William Lamb, later Viscount Melbourne, prime minister of England in 1834 and 1835–41, who was unrelated to the Godwins' friends Charles and Mary Lamb (see note 27, above).

48. Lady Byron reportedly made this assertion in her unpublished memoirs and directly to Harriet Beecher Stowe; she also accused Byron of having frequent homosexual relationships. The issue of Byron's sexuality has been controversial for more than a century. Stowe rose to the defense of Lady Byron when the latter was attacked in a memoir published by Lord Byron's last lover, Teresa, Contessa Guiccioli (1800–1873). Stowe's extended analysis of the testimony of witnesses on Byron's conduct, her account of numerous conversations with Lady Byron, and a refutation of Lady Byron's alleged unsupported accusations against her dead husband may be found in *Lady Byron Vindicated* (London: Sampson Low, Son, and Marston, 1870; repr. Teddington, Middlesex, UK: The Echo Library, 2006). Lady Byron's grandson Ralph Milbanke also determined to tell the truth about his grandmother and published a book about her marriage to Lord Byron, *Astarte: A Fragment of Truth about George Gordon Byron, Sixth Lord Byron* (London: Privately printed, 1905), in which he expresses unequivocally that Byron had an incestuous relationship with Augusta and that Medora was Byron's daughter. See Julia Markus's fine *Lady Byron and Her Daughters* (New York: W. W. Norton, 2014).

Henry James wrote a novella, "The Aspern Papers" (1888), about an individual's struggle with a desire for privacy and a conflicting sense of obligation to history. In the story, the aged former lover of a great American poet wavers about whether to publish the poet's revelatory letters and ultimately burns them. In a preface to the 1908 edition, James wrote that he had endeavored, in the work, to summon "the Byronic age" and "a palpable imaginable *visitable* past") (*The Aspern Papers and Other Stories* [Oxford: Oxford University Press, 2009], xxxi). James's notes make clear that the story was based on his interest in the ultimate fate of

Portrait of Lady Caroline Lamb, by Elizabeth H. Trotter (1811–14).

Miniature of Augusta
Leigh, by James Holmes
(nineteenth century).

Steel engraving of Anne
Isabella Milbanke, Lady
Byron, from an original
drawing by Freeman (1833).

born in 1814, was suspected to have been Byron's child. Byron next wooed Anne Isabella (Annabella) Milbanke, the only child of Sir Ralph Milbanke.[49] Byron described Annabella in his journal, after she had rejected his first proposal of marriage: "a very superior woman, and very little spoiled; which is strange in an heiress, a girl of twenty, a peeress that is to be in her own right, an only child, and a savante, who has always had her own way. She is a poetess, a mathematician, a metaphysician; yet, withal, very kind, generous, and gentle, with very little pretension." Byron's fortunes darkened further following her refusal of his proposal, as his debt mounted and the rumors of his relationship with Augusta gained prominence. He pursued Annabella again. Improbably, this time he was successful, and in January 1815 they married.

The marriage was doomed from the beginning, according to Lady Byron. He wanted to lead a profligate life, and she declined to permit him to do so.[50] They had a daughter, Ada, in December 1815,[51] even as Byron continued his

---

Claire Clairmont's Shelley and Byron memorabilia (Claire died in 1879, having been importuned repeatedly to publish her holdings), and he explicitly modeled the lover, Juliana Bordereau, on Claire. But Lady Byron's own unpublished papers also must have been in James's mind. He knew Ralph Milbanke well and observed his obsession with his grandmother's papers. When *Astarte* was published privately by Milbanke, he sent James a copy, perhaps to underline that, unlike Juliana, Lady Byron's grandson felt that setting the historical record straight was more important than family sensitivities.

49. The Milbankes did not have the fortune Byron might have desired, but an uncle of Annabella's—her mother's brother, Viscount Wentworth—left an inheritance, that, however, had to filter through Annabella's parents upon his death, and was never to be enjoyed by the couple for the duration of their very brief marriage.

50. Stowe, in *Lady Byron Vindicated*, records the following interview with Lady Byron: "I said to her, that, even in the days of my childhood, I had heard of something very painful that had passed as they were in the carriage, immediately after marriage. She then said that it was so; that almost his first words, when they were alone, were, that she might once have saved him; that, if she had accepted him when he first offered, she might have made him any thing she pleased; but that, as it was, she would find she had married a devil. . . . At what precise time the idea of an improper connection between her husband and his sister was first forced upon her, she did not say . . ." (90, in the Echo Library edition).

51. Augusta Ada Byron, later Augusta Ada King, Countess of Lovelace and commonly known as Ada Lovelace, who died at the age of thirty-six, was encouraged by her mother to pursue studies in the fields of mathematics and logic, as "insurance" that she would not develop her father's supposed insanity. She later worked with Charles Babbage on his "analytical engine" and is credited as the author of the first computer program. In John Crowley's brilliant novel *Lord Byron's Novel: The Evening Land* (2005), Ada is an unseen character who annotates and attempts to preserve her father's lost novel from her mother's destructive hand by enciphering it. Recently, Ada and Charles Babbage appeared in the charmingly

close relationship with Augusta and indulged openly in sexual adventures with other women. Convinced that Byron was insane, Annabella left him in January 1816, taking their one-month-old daughter with her, and began proceedings for a legal separation. In debt and the object of widespread opprobrium, Byron fled England for Switzerland in April 1816, never to return to the country of his birth.

George Gordon Byron, 6th Baron Byron, by Henry Meyer, after George Henry Harlow stipple engraving (1816).

Much of this strange saga must have been known to the Shelleys before they met Byron; tales of Byron were the stuff of everyday gossip. Despite these lurid stories, or perhaps because Byron seemed to care so little about his reputation, Percy and Mary were anxious to spend time with the exiled poet. Accompanied by baby William, along with Claire, they rented a villa, the Maison Chapuis, in Montalègre, Cologny, quite near to Byron, who occupied a villa, the Diodati, with his physician-companion John Polidori.[52] The parties soon began exchanging visits, spending many days and evenings together. Percy and Byron admired each other's work and became close friends. Byron must have been interested, too, in learning more of the daughter of the celebrated Godwin and Wollstonecraft. Polidori was impressed by Mary (whom he identified as Mary Wollstonecraft Godwin but referred to in his journal as "Mrs. Shelley") but was a bit confused by her irregular company, including—as he perceived—her married lover Percy as well as her sister Claire, "kept" by Percy but also Byron's lover. Rumors soon spread that the Villa Diodati was a hotbed of sexual adventure, with both Godwin daughters sleeping with both men, and the owner of a nearby villa rented primitive telescopes to voyeur-guests, who mistook the villa's tablecloths drying on the line as the women's petticoats.[53]

annotated graphic novel, *The Thrilling Adventures of Lovelace and Babbage* by Sydney Padua (New York: Pantheon Books, 2015).

52. The Maison Chapuis is gone, but the Villa Diodati remains, although it is in private hands.

53. The story is repeated (without attribution) in Dorothy Hoobler and Thomas Hoobler, *The Monsters: Mary Shelley and the Curse of Frankenstein* (New York and Boston: Little, Brown,

Portrait of Ada King, Countess of Lovelace, by Alfred Edward Chalon (1840).

Miniature of Ada Byron Lovelace.

Ada Byron Lovelace at age seventeen.

The Villa Diodati, from *Finden's Landscape and Portrait Illustrations to the Life and Works of Lord Byron*, Vol. 2 (London: John Murray, 1832).

2006), and in Gordon, *Romantic Outlaws*. Some years later, in August 1821, Percy Shelley wrote to the Countess Guiccioli, later the author of *Lord Byron's Life in Italy*, edited by Peter Cochran and translated by Michael Rees (Newark: University of Delaware Press, 2005): "The natives of Geneva and the English people who were living there did not hesitate to affirm that we were leading a life of the most unbridled libertinism. They said that we had formed a pact to outrage all that is regarded as most sacred in human society. Allow me, Madam, to spare you the details. I will only tell you that atheism, incest, and many other things—sometimes ridiculous and sometimes terrible—were imputed to us. The English papers did not delay to spread the scandal, and the people believed it" (Frederick L. Jones, ed., *Letters of Percy Bysshe Shelley* [Oxford: Clarendon Press, 1964], Volume II: *Shelley in Italy*, 328). Mary's journal for Tuesday, August 13, 1816, records, "we all go up to Diodati—war," interpreted by Paula R. Feldman and Diana Scott-Kilvert, the editors of *Journals of Mary Shelley, 1814–1844* (Baltimore and London: Johns Hopkins University Press, 1987), as a reference to the neighborhood gossip. The Hooblers, however, in *The Monsters: Mary Shelley and The Curse of Frankenstein*, suggest that this is just as likely a reference to an argument that broke out among the company, for Mary Shelley never returned to the Villa Diodati afterward.

The seed of *Frankenstein* germinated in this company —the specifics are discussed below—with Mary Shelley beginning work on it sometime in June. There are no materials extant from this period,[54] though she records sharing the "story" with Percy in late June, and with his encouragement, she developed the core of it. In July, Mary and Percy visited the Mer de Glace in Chamonix, the stunning glacier that later became an important setting for *Frankenstein*. They returned to England in September, and Mary began to write what she had now decided would be a novel, only to be faced, in quick succession, by the suicides of her half-sister Fanny Imlay and Percy's wife, Harriet.

Allegra Byron, artist unknown.

Harriet, heavily pregnant with the child that was not Percy's, had drowned herself. Percy took no personal blame for this: He had not abandoned Harriet, she had refused to adapt to his changes. He determined to seek custody of their children contrary to her stated wishes. To improve his case, and despite their principles, he asked Mary to consent to marry him, but they decided that custody was assured without the marriage and put it off. However, Godwin at last relented on his banishment of the lovers and appealed to them to marry; Mary was softened by her father's entreaties, and she and Percy were married on December 30, 1816.

She continued to work on *Frankenstein*, with frequent interruptions, including an interlude to care for Claire, who delivered Byron's baby, a daughter named Allegra. A battle for the custody of Percy's children developed, and Mary alternated working on his case and being immersed in *Frankenstein*. She and Percy left the Villa Diodati and moved to Marlow, a town in south Buckinghamshire, thirty-three miles west of central London, where she continued to work on the manuscript daily for long hours. It was completed on May 14, 1817, eleven months after its conception.

Pregnant again, Mary traveled to London with Percy, where he tried to sell *Frankenstein* to John Murray, Byron's venerable publisher. Percy and Mary agreed that it should be published anonymously, in the tradition of

---

54. Mary apparently recorded her ideas in a notebook, now lost, referred to by scholar Charles Robinson as the "Ur-Text" of *Frankenstein* (see "A Note on the Text," below). The earliest record of her actual writing of the story is a journal entry for July 24, 1816, in which she notes, "I read nouvelles [*sic*: *Nouveaux contes moraux et nouvelles historiques*, a multivolume collection of stories and histories by Stéphanie Félicité du Crest de Saint-Aubin, Comtesse de Genlis, known as Madame de Genlis, published 1802–6] and write my story . . ." (Feldman and Scott-Kilvert, eds., *Journals of Mary Shelley*, 118).

Percy Bysshe Shelley, by William Holl Sr., or by William Holl Jr., after Amelia Curran (1819).

Werther and other important books, both to avoid the attacks that her name, youth, and sex would bring and to allow the book to be judged on its merits, rather than on her heritage and gender. After turndowns from Murray and another publisher, the book was accepted by Percy's booksellers, Lackington, though they requested alterations that she refused to make.

In September 1817, Mary gave birth to a daughter, Clara, and the following weeks were divided between care of the infant and correction of proofs of the novel. Exhausted, she and Percy began planning a trip to Italy, and as 1817 came to a close, she held in her hands the first bound copy of *Frankenstein*, along with a check for £28. There is no record of her emotions on this occasion, and she could have known little of how publication of *Frankenstein* would change her life. Every subsequent book of hers was initially published without her name as author, bearing only the identification "By the author of *Frankenstein*."

Shortly thereafter, the Shelleys (including William and Clara), with Claire accompanying, left for Italy. While there, they visited Byron, whom Percy entreated to care for Claire's daughter, Allegra. Tragically, in September 1818, Clara, just past her first birthday, died in Venice, and nine months later, William, not yet three and a half years old, died in Rome. Remaining in Italy, in 1819 Percy and Mary had a fourth child, Percy Florence, less than half a year after her first son's death. After several relocations in Italy, they settled, with their friends Edward and Jane Williams, near Lerici, in the Bay of Spezia, sixty-five miles from Genoa.

Mary began to write a historical novel, *Valperga*, about a fourteenth-century Italian despot.[55] Her relationship with Percy had by now evolved. Mary's love for him, he felt, had cooled to companionship, as so often hap-

55. *Valperga* is viewed today as a feminist response to Sir Walter Scott's male-oriented historical novels. Though his writing is unfashionable today, Scott's immense output and the quality of his writing made him the rage of the era, so that he became the unquestioned leader of the English and Scottish Romantic movements. Every major composer of nineteenth-century opera seemed to find inspiration in at least one of Scott's works.

pens. In 1820, Percy and Claire had probably become lovers, an intensification of an intimacy that had existed for years. Percy felt that Mary idolized him, but he congratulated himself (to Claire, in a letter) that he had achieved "seclusion" when he and Mary established separate sleeping arrangements. There were other women for Percy, who always seemed to be able to find someone who would understand him and listen to Mary's shortcomings. By 1822, he complained to a friend that he missed "those who can feel, and understand me. Whether from proximity and the continuity of domestic intercourse, Mary does not." A "cloud" hung over their union, he believed. Yet Mary conceived another child, and Percy began work on a major poem.

What had largely been a salacious melodrama, though played out on the highest stage of literary society, soon became a tragedy. The spring of 1822 began badly, again clouded by the catastrophes of infants: Allegra, sent by Byron, without Claire's consent, to be raised in an Italian convent, died suddenly of typhus. Mary's pregnancy was troubled, and on June 16, she had a miscarriage, hemorrhaging so heavily that she was bedridden for two weeks, overcome with weakness and evil premonitions.[56]

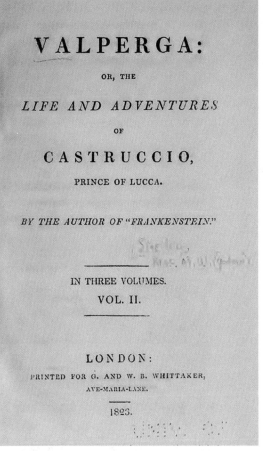

Title page of Mary Shelley's *Valperga* (1823).

56. Uncharacteristically, in Mary's direst straits, Percy took decisive action, probably saving her life. He wrote on June 18, 1822, to John Gisborne (the husband of Maria James Reveley Gisborne, who in her late twenties had cared for Mary in infancy following the death of Mary Wollstonecraft, and who had refused an offer of marriage from William Godwin during the same period): "Mary will write soon; at present she suffers greatly from excess of weakness, produced by a severe miscarriage, from which she is now slowly recovering. Her situation for some hours was alarming, and as she was totally destitute of medical assistance, I took the most decisive resolutions, by dint of making her sit in ice, I succeeded in checking the hemorrhage and the fainting fits, so that when the physician arrived all danger was over, and he had nothing to do but to applaud me for my boldness" (Roger Ingpen, ed., *Letters of Percy Bysshe Shelley*, collected by Roger Ingpen, 2 vols. [London: Sir Isaac Pitman & Sons; New York: Charles Scribner's Sons, 1909], Volume II, 975).

The Allegra Byron memorial stone in Harrow, England (photo by Bob Jones, used with permission).

Then, on July 8, 1822, Percy and Edward Williams, sailing in a small, newly commissioned boat to Leghorn, were lost at sea in a storm. On hearing the news, Mary and Jane, together with their friend Edward Trelawny, a brawny Cornish writer and former midshipman who was to make his mark as a brilliant chronicler of the Romantics, rushed to Leghorn, where they spent fruitless days searching for confirmation of the disaster. Finally, after eleven days of terror alternating with hope, Trelawny—who had helped to design the *Don Juan*, the boat they went down in—reported that he had seen the men's bodies near Viareggio. Italian sanitary laws dictated that the corpses be buried in the sand where they were found. A month later, on August 16, Percy's body was exhumed and burned on a pyre on the beach;[57]

57. The scene was imagined by the painter Louis Edouard Fournier in 1889. He fancifully depicts Mary kneeling on the sand, and Byron, Trelawny, and the Shelleys' friend Leigh Hunt standing before the flames. By custom, Mary would have remained in a carriage. Hunt was not in fact there (though an unsigned review of Shelley's cousin Thomas Medwin's *The Life of Percy Bysshe Shelley* [London, 1847] in the *Eclectic Magazine* [vol. 12, September 1847] puts him in a carriage at the site, an account later hotly disputed by Hunt himself), and Byron left before the fire consumed the corpse. The pyre itself may be reflected in the closing scene of *Frankenstein*.

The Funeral of Percy Shelley, by Louis Edward Fournier (1889).

his ashes, difficult to transport due to quarantine restrictions, were buried in Rome once a chargé d'affaires had signed off on the journey. Percy's death galvanized his critics and admirers alike. While he was not yet well known, his death gave critics the opportunity to score moral points. For example, one newspaper crowed, "Shelley, the writer of some infidel poetry, has been drowned: now he knows whether there is a God or no."[58]

Trelawny's subsequent account of the seaside cremation, particularly the disposition of Shelley's heart, has given rise to two centuries of debate and speculation: Said to resist incineration, the heart was taken from

58. Biographer Richard Holmes reports that the quotation is from the beginning of a "brief obituary" that appeared in *The Courier*, a leading Tory newspaper in London. http://www.theguardian.com/books/2004/jan/24/featuresreviews.guardianreview1

Portrait of Edward John Trelawny, by W. E. West (date unknown).

the flames by the future memoirist himself, fought over, and ultimately claimed by Mary Shelley, who is said to have kept it wrapped in a page from *Adonais*, her husband's elegy to the poet John Keats, a copy of whose *Lamia, Isabella, The Eve of St. Agnes, and Other Poems* had been found in Percy's jacket pocket when his body was exhumed, thus identifying him. Merging literary license and medicine, Arthur M. Z. Norman advanced the theory that "[i]t is not to be doubted that Shelley's heart was actually impregnable to fire. . . . It seems very probable that Shelley suffered from a progressively calcifying heart, which might well have caused diffuse symptoms with its increasing weight of calcium and which indeed would have resisted cremation as readily as a skull, a jaw, or fragments of bone. Shelley's heart, epitome of Romantiism, may well have been a heart of stone" (114).[59]

"I have no friend," Mary recorded in her journal on October 2, 1822, breaking a near-silence of three months, during which she had found herself virtually unable to speak of her loss. "For eight years I communicated, with unlimited freedom, with one whose genius, far transcending mine, awakened and guided my thoughts. I conversed with him; rectified my errors of judgment; obtained new lights from him; and my mind was satisfied. Now I am alone— oh, how alone! . . . I am left to fulfil my task. So be it."[60] The phrase "I have no friend" hauntingly echoes a line written by Robert Walton to his sister, Margaret, in Letter II of *Frankenstein*: "I have no friend, Margaret . . ."

A month following the cremation, Mary left Lerici and settled in Genoa, first taking rooms for herself and Percy Florence, now three years old, at the Croce di Malta inn, and then sharing a house outside the city, in the suburb of Albaro, with Leigh Hunt and his family (he and his wife then had six children,

59. Arthur M. Z. Norman, "Shelley's Heart," *Journal of the History of Medicine and Allied Sciences* 10, no. 1 (January 1955): 114. Norman wrote variously on topics as wide-ranging as references to Plutarch in Shakespeare's *Antony and Cleopatra*, "Linguistic Aspects of the Mores of U.S. Occupation and Security Forces in Japan" (a 1954 piece for the academic journal *American Speech*), and the subclasses of the English nominal.

60. Jones, ed., *Mary Shelley's Journal*, 180–81. She was, of course, speaking metaphorically: Mary was surrounded by friends, as she assured her father in a letter, and Godwin, while he complained that he learned of Percy's death from a stranger, recanted his vow to cease to write to Mary and offered to share her troubles. See St. Clair, *The Godwins and the Shelleys*, 467–68.

all in residence).[61] Byron, who was at the height of his fame, arrived shortly after, and Mary began working with him to transcribe his poetry, also tutoring a few of the Hunt children. Both occupations were sources of either income or rent abatement.

Before Mary returned from Italy, *Valperga* was published, in February 1823. Later that year, a second edition of *Frankenstein* appeared. By now, she was a celebrity in her own right, in no small part because of the success of *Frankenstein* in print and on stage. (See Appendix 4, below.) This 1823 republication, arranged by her father, bore her name at last; although it does not appear that Godwin asked her permission to publish, Mary expressed delight on learning of the event on her return to London. She managed to wrest a

Lord Byron in 1822 (portrait by William West).

small allowance from Percy's father that permitted her to find lodgings near her father.

Sadly, Mary soon lost her friend Lord Byron, who had comforted and supported her in her grief and provided her work. He had traveled to Greece in 1823 to take up the cause of Greek independence. He became quite ill, and on April 19, 1824, at age thirty-six, the most famous poet of the age died in Missolonghi, before the third and final siege of the city.[62] He had been helping to train rebel troops. His death was a great shock, likened by some to an "earthquake." The poet Tennyson remembered the day he heard the news as "a day when the whole world seemed to be in darkness for me." Deeply mourned in England, widely praised by many of his loudest critics, and lionized in Greece, when his body was returned home, he was refused burial at Westminster Abbey alongside other greats of literature. Instead, he was interred in the family vault near Newstead. Not until 1969 was a memorial to Byron finally

61. For more on the Hunts, see note 23, Volume III, Chapter I, below.

62. Although the battle brought about the fall of Missolonghi to the Ottomans, it was a turning point for the rebels in the War of Independence.

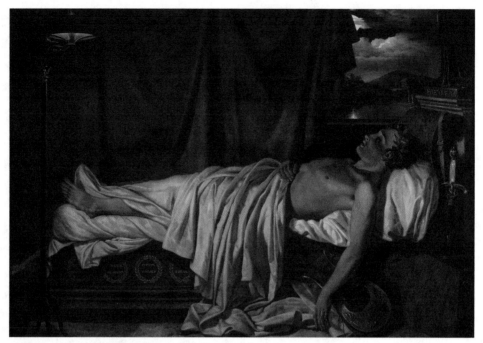

Lord Byron on His Death-Bed, by Joseph Denis Odevaere, ca. 1826.

placed in Poets' Corner of Westminster Abbey. Shunned by the upper classes, he was embraced by the masses.

It was at this critical moment that Mary began her life's work to erect a literary monument to Percy Bysshe Shelley. As early as 1822, she had declared, in her journal for November 11, seven months after Percy's death: "I shall write his life—& thus occupy myself in the only manner from which I can derive consolation." While she often received attention from other men, including several proposals of marriage, she demurred, saying that having been married to one genius, she could only marry another.[63] She began editing her late husband's poetry and

63. Sunstein, in *Mary Shelley: Romance and Reality*, relates that on June 25, 1825, the playwright John Howard Payne gave signs of declaring his love for Mary on a walk home with her from her father's: "She forestalled him by saying, gently but frankly, that in the hypothetical event that devotion to Shelley permitted her a 'second connection' he must be a man whose character and genius approached Shelley's, who 'had drawn her from obscurity'" (267). The actual source of the remarks is revealing: Payne was disappointed to learn that Mary's friendship with him was little more than an opportunity to obtain theater tickets and an introduction to Washington Irving, the American writer who had, by 1825, achieved great success in Europe. Mary apparently placed some hope in initiating a relationship with Irving. Crushed by Mary's rejection of him but determined to remain the "hero," as he put

essays, publishing his *Posthumous Poems* in 1824, a collection that included a short (unsigned) personal introduction, her first public statements on Percy's character. Those who knew the Shelleys understood that the biographical material had been written by her, but, in withholding her name, she sought to conceal her hand in the book from Sir Timothy Shelley, who, the previous year, had grudgingly extended an allowance to her and Percy Florence. The stipend came with strict provisions, one of which was that she refrain from publishing Percy's work or writing about him publicly.

Her effort to remain anonymous failed. After publication of *Posthumous Poems*, Sir Timothy succeeded in having 191 copies of the total print run withdrawn and destroyed. Whether he withdrew her and Percy Florence's stipend in this instance is unclear—there are conflicting accounts—but he was to do so more than once in the coming years, always capriciously. In all, 250 copies of *Posthumous Poems* had been printed—and that only after four writers in their twenties who revered the Shelleys, and who are largely unremembered today, had agreed to stand guarantors.

Mary worked on her novel *The Last Man* (1826), a story of a distant future—

POSTHUMOUS POEMS

OF

PERCY BYSSHE SHELLEY.

In nobil sangue vita umile e queta,
Ed in alto intelletto un puro core;
Frutto senile in sul giovenil fiore,
E in aspetto pensoso anima lieta.
PETRARCA.

LONDON, 1824:
PRINTED FOR JOHN AND HENRY L. HUNT,
TAVISTOCK STREET, COVENT GARDEN.

Title page of Percy Shelley's *Posthumous Poems* (1824).

it, Payne wrote Irving, "There was a long conversation in walking home with Mrs. S. . . . in which she attempted fully but delicately to explain herself upon our sentiments with regard to our correspondence—plainly enough, but very indirectly. She said that she felt herself so placed with the world that she could never expect its distinctions; and that the high feeling she entertained for the memory of her husband forbade the hope of any future connection, which should make the world indifferent to her—or rather the *English* world. Therefore she was desirous of getting to Italy. . . . The conversation then turned upon you. She said you had interested her more than any one she had seen since she left Italy . . . and that she longed for friendship with you. I rallied her a little upon the declaration, and at first she fired at my mentioning that she talked as if she were in love. . . . The scope of her remarks was that whenever she formed any alliance it must be with some one whose high character and mind should be worthy of him who had drawn her from obscurity, and that her selection must not dishonor his choice" (F. B. Sanborn, ed., *The Romance of Mary W. Shelley, John Howard Payne and Washington Irving* [Boston: The Bibliophile Society, 1907], 59–60). In fact, the remarks reported by Payne regarding Percy seem to have been aimed at him, not Irving, but Payne got his subtle revenge: Irving never pursued Mary.

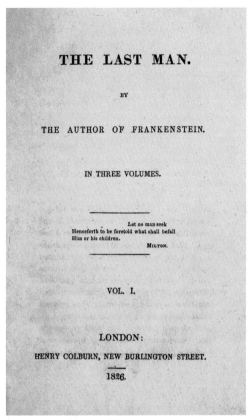

THE LAST MAN.

BY

THE AUTHOR OF FRANKENSTEIN.

IN THREE VOLUMES.

Let no man seek
Henceforth to be foretold what shall befall
Him or his children.
MILTON.

VOL. I.

LONDON:

HENRY COLBURN, NEW BURLINGTON STREET.

1826.

Title page of Mary Shelley's *The Last Man* (1826).

a portion of the second of three volumes is set in the year 2092—wherein the inhabitants of England, Europe, and the Americas are devastated by plague. The book includes thinly veiled portraits of Percy and Byron: The principal character, Adrian, leads his followers in a search for a utopian paradise but drowns when his boat is lost at sea in a storm, and Lord Raymond, another key figure in the tale, leaves England to fight for the Greeks, dying in Constantinople. Predictably, Sir Timothy withheld her allowance temporarily upon publication. The very act of her writing and publishing was anathema to him. In the aggregate, however, the allowance from Sir Timothy increased modestly in 1826, when Percy Florence became his legal heir as a result of the death of Shelley's son Charles (by Harriet).

Mary supplemented her income by writing dozens of articles and stories for a variety of magazines and journals, as well as another historical novel (*The Fortunes of Perkin Warbeck*, 1830, about a pretender to the throne of King Henry VII), and she contributed approximately 1,300 of the 1,757 pages of biographical essays to her father's friend Dionysus Lardner's *Cabinet Cyclopædia*.[64] She continued to see her father and his friends regularly, and they often found writing work for each other. Godwin was the beneficiary of Mary's extraordinary work ethic. As she wrote steadily (if not lucratively) and Sir Timothy Shelley had agreed to pay her (and her son) an allowance of £200 per year so long as she refrained from writing Percy's biography, she was able to support Godwin financially to the end, as Percy had done in his lifetime.

In 1836, William Godwin died, at the age of eighty, forty-three years after publication of his *Enquiry Concerning Political Justice*. His relationship with his daughter had always been complex. She worshipped him, perhaps unnaturally, she feared.[65] Having adopted many of his ideals and principles, Mary

64. Gordon, *Romantic Outlaws*, 505.

65. See note 23, above.

Portrait of Percy Florence Shelley, by George Romney
(from Roger Ingpen, *Shelley in England: New Facts
and Letters from the Shelley-Whitton Press* [Boston:
Houghton Mifflin, 1917]).

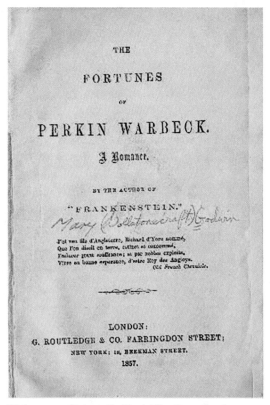

Title page of Mary Shelley's *The Fortunes of
Perkin Warbeck* (1830).

nevertheless felt that he had kept her at arm's length, perhaps seeing her more
as an experimental subject than as a beloved daughter. Her last two novels,
Lodore (1835) and *Falkner* (1837), are about tyrannical fathers and, unsurprisingly, are seen by at least one scholar as scathing criticisms of her father's ideas
on education and parenting.[66]

In 1839, despite Sir Timothy Shelley's continued vocal opposition to a biography of Percy, Mary published a four-volume edition of her late husband's
Poetical Works with extensive notes, including anecdotal biographical material, primarily in the service of the work. Her use of the first person (*"Rosalind
and Helen* was begun at Marlow, and thrown aside until I found it; and at my
request it was completed")[67] clarified her role in the composition and revision

66. Mary Poovey, *The Proper Lady and the Woman Writer: Ideology as Style in the Works of Mary
Wollstonecraft, Mary Shelley and Jane Austen* (Chicago: University of Chicago Press, 1985).

67. For line-by-line comparisons of word substitutions, changes in punctuation, etc., made
by Mary Shelley in her late husband's poems, as well as an overview of her masterful com-
pilation generally of his body of work, see Richard Allen, "Mary Shelley as Editor of the

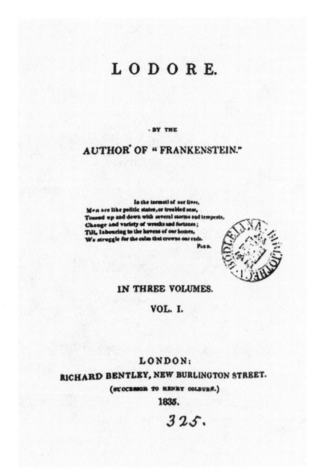

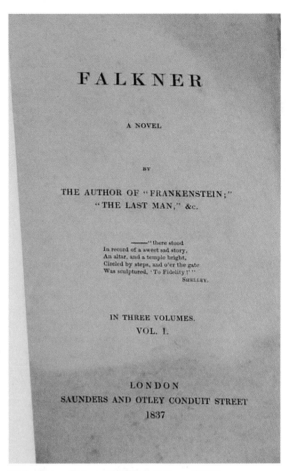

Title page of Mary Shelley's *Lodore* (1835).

Title page of Mary Shelley's *Falkner* (1837).

of many of the poems during their marriage, bringing full circle the collaboration that had defined their marriage. While never reaching the depth of biographical study plied on Percy in the late nineteenth and twentieth centuries, Mary's notes were the first literary biographical study of Percy's work.

Plagued by various illnesses during the months comprised by this massive

Poems of Percy Shelley," http://oro.open.ac.uk/40143/1/MWS%20Finalx.doc; Allen's piece is also included as a chapter in Joan Bellamy, Anne Laurence, and Gill Perry, eds., *Women, Scholarship, and Criticism: Gender and Knowledge c. 1790–1900* (Manchester, UK: Manchester University Press, 2000)—the above remark about Percy's *Rosalind and Helen, a Modern Eclogue* (1818) may be found on page 84 of the book. Editors Kevin Everest and Geoffrey Matthews (*The Poems of Shelley, Volume 2, 1817–1819* [London and New York: Routledge, 2000] further parse Mary Shelley's individual interpretations and elucidations of Percy Shelley's work, maintaining, for instance, in the present case, that "[n]ot all of [Mary Shelley's] statement" with regard to the genesis of *Rosalind and Helen* "is correct" (266).

and emotionally taxing effort, Mary nonetheless managed to travel, and in 1840 and 1842–43, she made extensive European trips with Percy Florence. In 1844, Sir Timothy died, and Percy inherited the baronetcy. In the same year, Mary published her last book, *Rambles in Germany and Italy in 1840, 1842 and 1843*, an account of her travels.

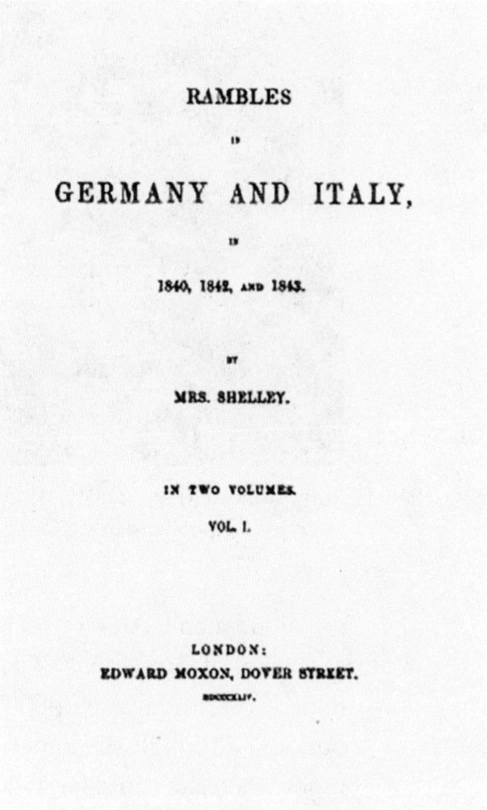

Befriended by many, often courted, cherished by her immediate family (including Percy Florence's wife, Lady Jane Gibson St. John Shelley, whom he married in 1848 and who was deeply attached to Mary), perhaps even reconciled to her nemesis Claire, she lived out her remaining seven years in England. On February 1, 1851, after suffering for almost three years with a brain tumor, she died, at the age of fifty-three. She was buried at St. Peter's Churchyard, Bournemouth, in Dorset, England, thirty-three years after first publication of the book that would make her immortal. Yet her lasting fame was still in the future: In the 1888 edition of the *Encyclopædia Britannica*, for example, while Percy Shelley merited an

RAMBLES

IN

GERMANY AND ITALY,

IN

1840, 1842, AND 1843.

BY

MRS. SHELLEY.

IN TWO VOLUMES.

VOL. I.

LONDON:
EDWARD MOXON, DOVER STREET.
MDCCCXLIV.

Title page of *Rambles through Germany and Italy*, by Mary Shelley (1844).

entry of nine and a half columns, the entry for Mary ran only a half-column and opened with the description, "the second wife of the poet Shelley . . . deserves some notice on her own account, as a writer of romance, chiefly imaginative."

THE GENESIS OF *FRANKENSTEIN*

In her introduction to the 1831 edition of *Frankenstein*, Mary Shelley recounts that on a rainy evening in June 1816[68] at the Villa Diodati, Byron announced to the company—consisting of herself, Percy Shelley, John Polidori, and Claire Clairmont—that they would each write a ghost story. The group had been read-

---

68. Rainy evenings were plentiful in June 1816, the "year without a summer," as the eruption of Tambora caused major climate changes throughout the world. See note 2, Appendix 1, below.

Tombstone of Mary Shelley, Percy Florence Shelley, and his wife, Jane Shelley (St. Peter's churchyard, Bornemouth, Dorset, England).

ing aloud a collection of such stories, and a competition seemed like a natural extension of that activity. Claire seems not to have tried, and the others abandoned their initial attempts. The project foundered, with all but Mary dropping out, and although she persisted, she was devoid of a workable idea until, one night when she could not fall asleep, she had a "waking dream," as she called it, a vivid image of a "pale student of unhallowed arts kneeling beside the thing he had put together." She dreamed that the thing came to life, but its vivification struck terror into the student, who fled.[69] That dream became the basis for the novel that she wrote over the following months. In fact, Mary claimed, "I began that day with the words, *It was on a dreary night of November*, making only a transcript of the grim terrors of my waking dream."

Of course, no book as complex as *Frankenstein* emerges from a single vision. A perusal of the text reveals that the novel does not begin with the phrase "It was on a dreary night of November"—that phrase does not appear until Chapter IV (V in the 1831 edition), almost thirteen thousand words into the story. Clearly, Shelley's vision had evolved and grown, incorporating many other themes and characters. From an examination of the manuscripts that have been preserved (see "A Note on the Text," below), we can deduce that between June and August 1816, she wrote a narrative that may have been twenty to thirty thousand words. By the end of August or the beginning of September, she had begun a revised draft that was likely simultaneously read

69. See Appendix 1 for the introduction to the 1831 edition of *Frankenstein*, in which she gives a fuller account of the conversations that led to the dream.

and edited by Percy Shelley; new passages were more than likely written by him as well. A "fair copy" (that is, a clean copying-over) was made in 1817 by Mary, with further revisions by both Mary and Percy, resulting finally in the text of the 1818 edition. Although, as will be seen, it is possible by careful comparison of handwriting to determine which portions of the draft were written by Mary and which by Percy, the authorship is confused after that stage of the revisions.[70] *The New Annotated Frankenstein* will examine in detail the material written by Mary versus that written by Percy, as well as the revisions made by Mary in later versions of the text.

Elsa Lanchester as Mary Shelley, with Douglas Walton as Percy Shelley and Gavin Gordon as Lord Byron (from *Bride of Frankenstein*, Universal Pictures, 1935).

A few critics have complained that credit for *Frankenstein* should be given almost wholly to Percy.[71] Others are quick to belittle

70. For a more detailed discussion, see "A Note on the Text," below.

71. Much nonsense has been written in support of this thesis. See, for example, John Lauritsen's outrageous *The Man Who Wrote Frankenstein* (New York: Pagan Press, 2007), in which he argues that the book is an encoded hymn to Percy Shelley's secret homosexuality. Germaine Greer, in a 2007 *Guardian* review, trashes Lauritsen's book, arguing that his proposition that only a skilled writer like Percy Bysshe Shelley could have written it bears no consideration: "[Lauritsen's] logic goes something like this: *Frankenstein* is a masterpiece; masterpieces are not written by self-educated girls and therefore *Frankenstein* cannot have been written by Mary Shelley. If *Frankenstein* is not a masterpiece, the thesis collapses. Though millions of people educated in the US have been made to study and write essays about *Frankenstein*, it is not a good, let alone a great novel and hardly merits the attention it has been given, notwithstanding the historic fact that its theme has inspired more than 50 (mostly bad) films." Yet in a 2007 *Salon* review, Camille Paglia defends Lauritsen, taking at face value an anonymous 1824 *Knight's Quarterly* review of *Valperga* that suggests that *Frankenstein* might have been written by Percy Shelley. Paglia incorrectly states that the *Knight's Quarterly* review is evidence that Percy's authorship "seems to have been known in British literary circles." In fact, the review states, "Still I should not, from internal evidence, suppose *Frankenstein* to be the work of [Percy] Shelley. It has much of his poetry and vigour—but it is wholly free from those philosophical opinions from which scarcely any of his *are* free." (The full review appears in the Norton Critical Edition of *Frankenstein* edited by J. Paul Hunter, and as an appendix to Lauritsen's book.) However, Paglia maintains of Lauritsen's work, "This is a funny, wonderful, revelatory book that I hope will inspire ambitious graduate students and young faculty to strike blows for truth in our mired profession, paralyzed by convention and fear."

Lauritsen is not alone in his search for evidence that Percy Shelley was the true author of *Frankenstein*: See, for example, Phyllis Zimmerman's *Shelley's Fiction* (Los Angeles: Darami Press, 1998) and the otherwise thoughtful *Shelley Unbound: Discovering* Frankenstein's *True Creator*, by Scott Douglas de Hart (Port Townsend, WA: Feral House, 2013), both of which conclude that the biographical coincidences of Victor Frankenstein and Percy Shelley are

his contribution.[72] However, this much is clear about the couple's working relationship: First, during the entirety of their companionship, from 1814 till his death in 1822, they collaborated—they read together,[73] conversed endlessly, and together wrote poems, stories, and journals. As Charles E. Robinson writes, in the four-volume *Frankenstein Notebooks: A Facsimile Edition of Mary Shelley's Novel, 1816–17* (New York and London: Garland Publishing, Inc., 1996), "That PBS collaborated on [*Frankenstein*] should come as no surprise to anyone, because the Shelleys left a long history of their shared activities as creative artists. They transcribed and they edited each other's works; they encouraged each other to undertake or to modify major works; and they even collaborated in the publication of *History of a Six Weeks' Tour* at a time when *Frankenstein* was being readied for the press."

Second, after Percy's death, for reasons she never clearly expressed (see her comments in the introduction to the 1831 edition, in Appendix 1, below), Mary began to revise *Frankenstein*, first tentatively in 1823, and then further in 1831. She was an inexperienced writer when, at nineteen, she began her tale; Percy had already published several novels and at least five books of poetry, including *Queen Mab*, one of his major works—and he was five years older, a significant difference, no matter how sophisticated Mary's upbringing. He had an important role in the auctorial process, though scholars argue about the nature and extent of it. If one were to award authorial credit to each of those who strongly influenced Mary Shelley's work, the list would extend to include John Milton, from two centuries before, whose *Paradise Lost* is such an important source for *Frankenstein*, William Godwin, Mary Wollstonecraft, and Samuel Taylor Coleridge, who were vital to the final product, as were Percy's suggestions and revisions and, perhaps most importantly, his encouragement.

---

evidence of Percy's authorship. One may give the conclusion as little credence as the suggestion that Mary Shelley borrowed the entire story from tales she heard while allegedly visiting Castle Frankenstein along the Rhine. See note 18, Volume III, Chapter I, below.

72. See, for example, Betty T. Bennett, "Feminism and Editing Mary Wollstonecraft Shelley: The Editor and/or the Text," in *Palimpsest: Editorial Theory in the Humanities*, ed. George Bornstein and Ralph G. Williams (Ann Arbor: University of Michigan Press, 1993), 67–96. Bennett writes, of her edition of Mary Shelley's letters: "My guiding principle in editing the letters was to credit Mary Shelley, based on the manuscript of the work, with the aesthetic and intellectual mastery that created *Frankenstein* (as opposed to those who still believed that Shelley had either written it or edited it so extensively as to make it his work)" (86).

73. For example, for the year 1817, Mary's journal lists seventy books that she read, fifteen of which she indicated were read by Percy as well. There were also many, many books that they read aloud to each other.

CONTEMPORARY RECEPTION

Readers and critics alike were confused about the authorship of the book from the beginning. Percy Shelley handled the submission of the manuscript to various publishers. The book was published anonymously, as has been noted above, with an unsigned preface by Percy and a dedication to William Godwin.[74] The dedication led many to conclude that Percy had written the text, and the book's initial reception was largely favorable.[75] Among the exceptions was the *Quarterly Review*: "Our taste and our judgment alike revolt at this kind of writing, and the greater the ability with which it may be executed, the worse it is—it inculcates no lesson of conduct, manners, or morality; it cannot mend, and will not even amuse its readers, unless their taste have been deplorably vitiated." One can only imagine the reviewer's comments if he or she had known the true author. The reviewer did manage to praise the "highly terrific" language and the "rationality" of the preface (ironically, wholly from the pen of Percy).[76] The *Edinburgh Magazine* remarked upon the book's "power of fascination" and its "mastery in harsh and savage delineations of passion" but added, "[I]t is one of those works . . . which, when we have read, we do not well see why it should have been written."[77]

Sir Walter Scott, who, by 1818, was already a celebrated Romantic poet and literary lion, assumed, like most reviewers, that the author was Percy Shelley and praised the book highly.

[In] this extraordinary tale . . . the author seems to us to disclose uncommon powers of poetic imagination. . . .

Upon the whole, the work impresses us with a high idea of the author's original genius and happy power of expression. We shall be delighted to hear

---

74. Mary Shelley was not definitively identified as the author until publication of the two-volume 1823 edition of *Frankenstein*, wherein she is Mary Wollstonecraft Shelley. See "A Note about the Text," below, for more on the 1823 edition.

75. Although it is impossible to ascertain accurate sales figures and difficult to make comparisons, Susan Tyler Hitchcock estimates that by 1851 the novel had sold more than seven thousand copies, far more than all the volumes of Percy Shelley's poetry combined (*Frankenstein: A Cultural History* [New York: W. W. Norton, 2007], 101). Indeed, according to Hitchcock, Mary made more from the first printing alone—around £70—than Percy would ever earn from his writing (77).

76. *Quarterly Review*, January 1818.

77. *Edinburgh Magazine*, March 1818.

that he has aspired to the *paullo majora*;[78] and, in the meantime, congratulate our readers upon a novel which excites new reflections and untried sources of emotion.

Other reviewers were put off by the horrific nature of the story, though its contents seem far less shocking than the supernatural terrors of prevailing gothic literature. One wrote:

We need scarcely say, that these volumes have neither principle, object, nor moral; the horror which abounds in them is too grotesque and *bizarre* ever to approach near the sublime, and when we did not hurry over the pages in disgust, we sometimes paused to laugh outright; and yet we suspect, that the diseased and wandering imagination, which has stepped out of all legitimate bounds, to frame these disjointed combinations and unnatural adventures, might be disciplined into something better."[79]

Portrait of Sir Walter Scott, by William Nicholson (1817).

Another reviewer, writing after the second printing of the novel, this time with Mary Shelley's byline, concluded: "Frankenstein is, I think, the best instance of natural passions applied to supernatural events that I ever met with. . . . For my own part, I confess that *my* interest in the book is entirely on the side of the monster. His eloquence and persuasion, of which Frankenstein complains, are so because they are truth. The justice is indisputably on his side, and his sufferings are, to me, touching to the last degree."[80]

Perhaps because of its highly imaginative theme, the book did not achieve the status of a literary classic overnight.[81] As late as 1886, Hugh Reginald

78. More artistically important matters.

79. *The British Critic* (new series) 9 (April 1818): 432–38. The reviewer also commented, "The writer of it is, we understand, a female; this is an aggravation of that which is the prevailing fault of the novel; but if our authoress can forget the gentleness of her sex, it is no reason why we should; and we shall therefore dismiss the novel without further comment." How the critic came to his "understanding" of the true authorship of *Frankenstein* is unknown.

80. Anonymous, *Knight's Quarterly* (August–November 1824): 195–99.

81. Can "classic" ever be more than personal taste and, as such, a product of the time? For example, Arthur Conan Doyle's charming *Through the Magic Door*, a paean to the books Doyle loved, written in 1907, unsurprisingly selects from the nineteenth century the novels of Sir Walter Scott, Charles Dickens, William Thackeray, Tolstoy's *War and Peace*, George

Haweis, the series editor of the Routledge World Library Edition of *Frankenstein*, wrote, "I issue 'Frankenstein' with some degree of hesitation, but after mature reflection. The subject is somewhat revolting, the treatment of it somewhat hideous. The conception is powerful, but the execution very unequal. . . . It is in her natural descriptions, as well as her subtle analysis of moods, that Mrs. Shelley proves herself to be an imaginative writer of no mean order. It is in her construction and plot that she is weak. . . . Still 'Frankenstein' retains its popularity as the first of a class of fiction—not of a very high order—to which the genius of Edgar Allan Poe has given an importance somewhat out of proportion to its merits."[82]

Haweis's opinion was shared by many literary scholars and critics for nearly a century, until, as described in Appendix 5, below, academia discovered Mary Shelley's work in the 1970s, and *Frankenstein* came to be recognized as a deeply nuanced work of genius.

THE LEGACY OF *FRANKENSTEIN*

Joyce Carol Oates writes, "*Frankenstein*'s double significance as a work of prose fiction and a cultural myth—as 'novel' of 1818 and timeless 'metaphor'—makes it a highly difficult story to read directly. A number of popular misconceptions obscure it for most readers: Frankenstein is of course *not* the monster, but his creator; nor is he a mad scientist of genius—he is in fact a highly idealistic and naive youth in the conventional Romantic mode."[83] Oates suggests that the novel melds two archetypal myths: that of the hero who crosses over into unknown realms, as did Odysseus, Jonah, and Beowulf; and that of the cautionary tale of straying beyond the boundary between the

Meredith's *Ordeal of Richard Feverel*, Melville's "Otaheite" novels, and the short stories of Edgar Allan Poe, Bret Harte, Robert Louis Stevenson, Rudyard Kipling, and Guy de Maupassant (notably all men) but includes as the greatest novel ever written Charles Reade's now obscure *The Cloister and the Hearth* and the writing of George Borrow and F. T. Bullen, wholly ignoring anything by Jane Austen, George Sand, George Eliot, Anthony Trollope, or the Brontës and dismissing the writing of Flaubert, Verne, and Wells.

82. Routledge's World Library was, according to advertisements appearing in 1886, intended to make available to the middle class, at a cost of a mere three pence per volume in paperback, works that "the world will not willingly let . . . die." These were initially advertised to include Goethe's *Faust*, Joseph Allen's *Life of Lord Nelson*, a life of Garibaldi, Daniel Defoe's *History of the Great Plague in London*, and Scott's *Marmion*.

83. Joyce Carol Oates, "Frankenstein's Fallen Angel," *Critical Inquiry* 10, no. 3 (March 1984): 543–54.

Sherlock Holmes and the Horror of Frankenstein, by Luke Benjamin Kuhns, writer, and Marcie Klinger, artist (London: MX Publishing, 2013).

Frankenstein: A Monstrous Parody, by Ludworst Bemonster (New York: Scholastic, 2012). Rick Walton, writer; Nathan Hale, artist.

human and the divine, as did Prometheus, Adam and Eve, and Faust. She also identifies a salient cause of the book's enduring currency: "[N]o one in *Frankenstein* is evil—the universe is emptied of God and of theistic assumptions of 'good' and 'evil,' Hence, its modernity." Because Victor is both hero and villain and the creature is both to be feared and pitied, "the ultimate other and . . . a mirror of the deepest self," in Susan Tyler Hitchcock's phrase,[84] the novel both fascinates and repels the reader.

As suggested above, the story of Victor Frankenstein and his creature is the first myth of modern times, an early nineteenth-century version of the epics of more distant times. By focusing on science rather than the gods or the angels, *Frankenstein* could not have been written earlier; it broke new ground and resonated in a way that the classic myths it encompasses no longer do. Certainly the creature was one of the first of the small pantheon of immortals recognizable by virtually all outside of the original work of art, standing alongside the earliest, Don Quixote and Sir John Falstaff, and later Dracula and Sherlock Holmes. If for no other reason than the sheer *indestructibility* of Mary Shelley's creation, we feel we must pay attention to the story and seek to understand its power.

What follows is not a stage play or a film or a comic adaptation of *Frankenstein*: It is the original raw material from which this modern myth emerged, the "hideous progeny" of Mary Wollstonecraft Shelley and her husband, Percy Shelley. This volume supplements the text with notes that illuminate the creative process; it examines the sources and roots of the ideas and characters; and it elucidates the elements of the lives and times of the Shelleys that are interwoven into the narrative. With such material at hand, the contemporary reader may experience *Frankenstein* in all its power.

Sherlock Holmes: The Adventure of the Frankenstein Monster, by Don W. Baranowski (West Conshohocken, PA: Infinity Publishing, 2006).

---

84. Hitchcock, *Frankenstein: A Cultural History,* 5.

A NOTE ON THE TEXT

T HE TEXT USED in this volume is that of the 1818 edition of *Frankenstein*. Scholars have debated for years whether the 1831 edition of the work is "preferable to" or "better than" the 1818 edition. Anne K. Mellor, in "Choosing a Text of *Frankenstein* to Teach," argues that the September 1816 manuscript is the "preferred" text because it permits the reader to discern the intentions of Mary Shelley by ignoring Percy Shelley's revisions.[1] Second best, according to Mellor, is the 1818 text, which espouses the "values" of the original; the 1831 edition is, in Mellor's opinion, fatally compromised by a new pessimism in Mary Shelley's views (see Letter IV, note 53, below). The notes in the volume at hand provide the text of every change made between the 1818 and 1831 editions. The introduction written by Mary Shelley for the 1831 edition is reproduced as Appendix 1, below. Hundreds of editions of *Frankenstein* have been published since 1818,[2] but few identify the text used, although the 1831 text is the most common.

1. In pursuit of Mellor's idea, Charles E. Robinson published *The Original* Frankenstein (Oxford, Bodleian Library, 2008), in which Robinson, using his previous *Frankenstein Notebooks* (1996), teased out Percy's amendments from the 1816 manuscript and edited the remaining text into what he describes as the "original two-volume novel."

2. There were 281 editions in all formats, including foreign, through 2000, according to the Romantic Circles website (https://www.re.umd.edu/editions/frankenstein/textual). Many more have appeared since 2000.

In 1823, a two-volume edition of the novel was published, at last identifying Mary Wollstonecraft Shelley as the author. This was not, as was originally thought, a mere reprinting of the 1818 edition. E. B. Murray observes,[3] "The fact that there are a good many substantive changes . . . seems so far to have escaped editorial scrutiny. M. K. Joseph refers to the 1823 edition as 'simply a page-by-page reprint of the [1818 edition], rearranged in two volumes,' while James Rieger both concurs with Joseph and adds that the volumes were so 'rearranged' by Godwin because Mary was in Italy." Murray went on to tabulate the substantive changes between the 1818 and 1823 editions, mostly word substitutions. Virtually all of the changes would be retained in the 1831 edition, which, in addition, contained often lengthy new passages, reproduced, as noted, in the annotations below. "It is clear that a scrupulous editor was responsible for" the 1823 changes, Murray concludes. Who was that editor? It appears likely that it was William Godwin, who—on the strength of the public's appetite for the play *Presumption*, based on *Frankenstein* (see note 43, Volume I, Chapter VI, below), and the many imitations of *Presumption*—also arranged for publication of the 1823 edition. Godwin applied a similarly liberal editorial hand to the publication of Mary Shelley's novel *Valperga* in 1823. The 1823 changes are not material to understanding *Frankenstein* and are not detailed in the notes below.

However, there is another text that is considered in the notes below. In 1823, while residing in Genoa, Mary Shelley presented to her friend Mrs. Thomas—an Englishwoman whom she met there but who remains otherwise unknown to posterity—a corrected and hand-annotated copy of the 1818 edition. This was apparently created without reference to the Godwin-edited 1823 two-volume edition. Although the Thomas copy is part of the collection of the Morgan Library in New York, it was not until the 1982 edition of the 1818 text, published by the University of Chicago Press and edited by James Rieger, that these emendations were published. Material changes reflected in the Thomas copy (referred to hereinafter as the "Thomas Text") are noted below.

3. In "Changes in the 1823 Edition of Frankenstein," *The Library* 3, no. 4 (December 1981), 320–27, http://knarf.english.upenn.edu/Articles/murray.html. Murray tabulates 117 changes made to the 1818 text. Subsequently, David Ketterer, in "Frankenstein's 'Conversion' from Natural Magic to Modern Science—and a Shifted (and Converted) Last Draft Insert," Science Fiction Studies 71, no. 24, Part 1 (March 1997), describes 8 more, http://www.depauw.edu/sfs/backissues/71/ketterer71art.htm.

prayed with a feeling of bitter tenderness, that she might never suffer ill. Thus we entered the ~~our~~ mansion — and still not speaking, for both our hearts were too full, we went to a balcony that

CHAPTER VI.

IT was eight o'clock when we landed; †
~~we walked for a short time on the shore,~~
~~enjoying the transitory light, and then~~
~~retired to the inn,~~ and contemplated
the lovely scene of waters, woods, and
mountains, obscured in darkness, yet
still displaying their black outlines.

The wind, which had fallen in the
south, now rose with great violence in
the west.   The moon had reached her
summit in the heavens, and was beginning to descend; the clouds swept
across it swifter than the flight of the
vulture, and dimmed her rays, while

× leaving the shore we sought the retreat of our house and garden. Yet Again as I entered the iron gates of the Dimione, an ~~uxxxx~~ un- plainable feeling bade me hold — yet Elizabeth

the lake reflected the scene of the busy
heavens, rendered still busier by the
restless waves that were beginning to
rise.   Suddenly a heavy storm of rain
descended.

I had been calm during the day; but
so soon as night obscured the shapes
of objects, a thousand fears arose in my
mind.   I was anxious and watchful,
while my right hand grasped a pistol
which was hidden in my bosom; every
sound terrified me; but I resolved that
I would sell my life dearly, and not relax the impending conflict until my
own life, or that of my adversary, were
extinguished.

Elizabeth observed my agitation for
some time in timid and fearful silence;
at length she said, " What is it that
agitates you, my dear Victor?   What is
it you fear?"

" Oh! peace, peace, my love," re-

unwarned, and fearless passed on, and I, again half ashamed — & for the first time dreading lest any unholy sight should meet her sense, any shadow of the fiend, should cross her; I hastily walked on, and passing my arm round her

Page from the Thomas Text of *Frankenstein* (1823), from Volume III, Chapter VI of the 1818 edition of *Frankenstein*, with editorial notes by Mary Shelley.

I should listen to the dæmon — my
feelings were against it but the
misery he expressed had already
moved my compassion and I thought
the least justice I could shew would
be to listen to to his tale.
We entered the hut — the monster
lighted a fire and sitting by it he
began thus.

it was Mont Blanc in awful majesty. I re
mained in a recess of the rock gazing on
this wonderful & stupendous scene — My heart
before was swelled with something like
joy I exclaimed Wandering spirit,
if indeed ye wander and do not rest in
your narrow beds, allow me this faint
happiness or take me as your compa
nion away from the joys of life." As I
said this I suddenly beheld the
figure of a man at some distance advancing
towards me with superhuman speed —
He bounded over the crevices in the
ice among which I had walked with caution
his stature also as he approached seem
ed to exceed that of man — I was
troubled a mist covered my eyes and
I felt a faintness seize me. The cold breeze
of the mountains quickly restored me
But I perceived as the shape came nearer

[left margin] the sea or rather the vast river of
ice, wound among its dependant
mountains whose aerial summits
hung over its recesses. Their
icy & glittering peaks shone
in sunlight over the clouds.

Page from Notebook A, the draft of *Frankenstein* by Mary Shelley (Shelfmark MS. Abinger c. 56, fol. 59r, with the permission of The Bodleian Libraries, University of Oxford).

The manuscript of the 1818 edition exists in several versions. The original text written by Mary Shelley, alluded to in her journals (termed the "Ur-Text" by scholars such as Charles E. Robinson), has not survived. It is described by Robinson as a "novella-length narrative written between June and August 1816." A "draft" (hereinafter referred to as the "Draft") in Mary Shelley's handwriting appears to have been begun at the end of August or the beginning of September 1816 and seems to have been in part a copying-over of sections of the Ur-Text.[4] The conclusion that there was significant "copying-over" is supported by several apparent copying errors that appear in the Draft. These are principally of names that Mary Shelley meant to change from the Ur-Text to the Draft but instead copied over and then changed (in strikethroughs in the Draft). Of course, alternatively, she might have changed her mind while writing the Draft. At some point, perhaps even simultaneous with Mary Shelley's editing, the Draft was revised by Percy Shelley, who made numerous handwritten additions, deletions, and emendations.

The Draft is preserved in the form of two notebooks, called A and B by scholars, consisting of 301 pages of text plus a supplement of 8 pages. Unfortunately, the Draft is not complete: The four introductory letters from Robert Walton, whose letters at the beginning and end form a framework for the action, and the first part of Chapter 1 in Volume I and almost half of Chapter 3 and all of Chapter 4 of Volume II are missing. The Draft was followed by a "fair copy," completed in 1817; proofs, with additional changes; revisions, with still more changes; and, finally, the 1818 edition.

Notes below will address Percy Shelley's significant textual changes to the Draft. Although substantial material was added to the work before the final text was published and Percy Shelley largely handled the publishing process, it is not possible to say definitively which portions of that added material were written by Mary Shelley and which by Percy Shelley (as contrasted with the changes to the Draft, where the handwriting of each is readily identifiable). For detailed discussions of Percy Shelley's revisions of the manuscript of *Frankenstein*, see Anne K. Mellor's *Mary Wollstonecraft Shelley: Her Life, Her Fiction,*

---

4. The Draft is at the Bodleian Library in Oxford. It has been published as part of Charles E. Robinson, ed., *The* Frankenstein *Notebooks: A Facsimile Edition of Mary Shelley's Manuscript Novel, 1816–1817 (with alterations in the hand of Percy Bysshe Shelley) as it survives in Draft and Fair Copy deposited by Lord Abinger in the Bodleian Library, Oxford,* and is available online at http://shelleygodwinarchive.org/contents/frankenstein.

Her Monsters and *The Original Frankenstein*, edited by Charles E. Robinson. Also invaluable is Robinson's *The* Frankenstein *Notebooks*, a comprehensive correlation of the notebooks with the published text. That work also contains a complete transcription of the notebooks, of special value because the handwriting is often difficult to decipher.

Page from Notebook C, the "fair copy" of *Frankenstein* by Mary Shelley.

Prometheus Creates Man from Clay, by Constantin Hansen (1845).

Shelley Composing "Prometheus Unbound" in the Baths of Caracalla, by Joseph Severn (1845).

1. E. Cobham Brewer's *Dictionary of Phrase and Fable* (1894) summarizes the myth of Prometheus: "Prometheus made men of clay, and stole fire from heaven to animate them. For this he was chained by Zeus to Mount Caucasus, where an eagle preyed on his liver daily." Note that this is clearly the version of the myth that Shelley had in mind, not the version in which Prometheus gives fire to men to use. Entries in Mary Shelley's journal confirm that in 1815 she was reading Ovid's *Metamorphoses*, in which work she would have found the following passage:

> Whether with particles of Heav'nly fir
> The God of Nature did his Soul
>   inspire,
> Or Earth, but new divided from the
>   Skie,
> And, pliant, still, retain'd the
>   Aethereal Energy:
> Which Wise *Prometheus* temper'd into
>   paste,
> And, mix't with living Streams, the
>   Godlike Image cast . . .
> From such rude Principles our Form
>   began;
> And Earth was Metamorphos'd into
>   Man.
>
> (Garth, Dryden, et al. translation)

Prometheus was evidently very much on the minds of several of the circle of friends at the Villa Diodati in 1816: Not only did Lord Byron write his poem "Prometheus" in July 1816 (the year he also divorced his wife, Anne Isabella Milbanke, whom he had married the previous year); in September he began his Promethean saga *Manfred*; and between 1818 and 1819, Percy Shelley wrote his epic poem *Prometheus Unbound*.

2. Book 10, lines 743–45.

FRANKENSTEIN;

OR,

THE MODERN PROMETHEUS[1]

---❖---

IN THREE VOLUMES

---❖---

Did I request thee, Maker, from my clay
To mould me man? Did I solicit thee
From darkness to promote me?—
PARADISE LOST.[2]

3. Mary Shelley's father and the author, in addition to the works she lists here, of *Enquiry Concerning Political Justice and Its Influence on Modern Morals and Happiness* (1793), hereinafter referred to as *"Political Justice."* This last was one of the prime planks of the platform of the English Jacobins, who not only supported the French Revolution, but raised the possibility of revolution in England. Among these English radicals were prominent artists including Percy Shelley, William Wordsworth, and Samuel Taylor Coleridge. Coleridge in particular admired Godwin's impassioned but reasoned arguments and wrote a sonnet, "To William Godwin, Author of *Political Justice,*" published in 1795, in praise of his outspokenness:

> O! form'd t' illume a sunless world forlorn,
> As o'er the chill and dusky brow of Night,
> In Finland's wintry skies, the Mimic Morn
> Electric pours a stream of rosy light,
> Pleas'd I have mark'd OPPRESSION, terror-pale,
> Since, thro' the windings of her dark machine,
> Thy steady eye has shot its glances keen—
> And bade th' All-lovely "scenes at distance hail."
> Nor will I not thy holy guidance bless,
> And hymn thee, GODWIN! with an arden Lay;
> For that thy voice, in Passion's stormy day,
> When wild I roam'd the bleak Heath of Distress,
> Bade the bright form of JUSTICE meet my way—
> And told me, that her name was HAPPINESS.

Godwin's *Things as They Are, or The Adventures of Caleb Williams,* a novel, was published in 1794. See the Foreword, text following note 13, above.

TO
WILLIAM GODWIN,[3]

AUTHOR OF POLITICAL JUSTICE, CALEB WILLIAMS, *&c.*

THESE VOLUMES

Are Respectfully Inscribed

BY

THE AUTHOR

PREFACE [4]

The event on which this fiction is founded has been supposed, by Dr. Darwin,[5] and some of the physiological writers of Germany,[6] as not of impossible occurrence. I shall not be supposed as according the remotest degree of serious faith to such an imagination; yet, in assuming it as the basis of a work of fancy, I have not considered myself as merely weaving a series of supernatural terrors. The event on which the interest of the story depends is exempt from the disadvantages of a mere tale of spectres or enchantment. It was recommended by the novelty of the situations which it developes; and, however impossible as a physical fact, affords a point of view to the imagination for the delineating of human passions more comprehensive and commanding than any which the ordinary relations of existing events can yield.

I have thus endeavoured to preserve the truth of the elementary principles of human nature, while I have not scrupled to innovate upon their combinations. The *Iliad,* the tragic poetry of Greece,—Shakespeare, in the *Tempest* and *Midsummer Night's Dream,*[7]—and most especially Milton, in *Paradise Lost,* conform to this rule; and the most humble novelist, who seeks to confer or receive amusement from his

Portrait of Erasmus Darwin, by Joseph Wright (1792).

labours, may, without presumption, apply to prose fiction a licence, or rather a rule, from the adoption of which so many exquisite combinations of human feeling have resulted in the highest specimens of poetry.

The circumstance on which my story rests was suggested in casual conversation.[8] It was commenced, partly as a source of amusement, and partly as an expedient for exercising any untried resources of mind. Other motives were mingled with these, as the work proceeded. I am by no means indifferent to the manner in which whatever moral tendencies exist in the sentiments or characters it contains shall affect the reader; yet my chief concern in this respect has been limited to the avoiding of the enervating effects of the novels of the present day,[9] and to the exhibition of the amiableness of domestic affection, and the excellence of universal virtue. The opinions which naturally spring from the character and situa-

4. Notwithstanding the voice of the preface, which implies that it is the author speaking, the preface to the 1818 (anonymous) edition was written by Percy Shelley. In the introduction to the third (signed) edition, Mary Shelley wrote, "As far as I can recollect, it was entirely written by him." The preface also appears in the 1823 two-volume edition, the first to bear the author's name.

5. This refers to Erasmus Darwin (1731–1802). Eminent physician, poet, inventor, natural philosopher, and abolitionist, his grandsons included Charles Darwin and the explorer and anthropologist Francis Galton. He wrote widely on the origins of life, formulating a theory of evolution long before Charles was born. There is no evidence that either Mary Shelley or Percy Shelley actually met Darwin, but it appears that Percy Shelley and Lord Byron knew his work well.

6. According to the *Oxford English Dictionary*, "physiological" at this time referred to the material universe or to natural science; thus the physiological writers were students of nature. The Shelleys' awareness of the physiological writers of Germany likely arose (according to Shelley scholar Marilyn Butler) through friendship with William Lawrence, Percy Shelley's physician. In 1809 Lawrence translated *Comparative Anatomy*, by Johann Friedrich Blumenbach (1752–1840), one of the first to study the natural history of humans. In his *Lectures on Physiology, Zoology and the Natural History of Man* (1819), Lawrence reported on the work of other "recent German zoologists," including Karl Asmund Rudolphi (1771–1832), a Swedish-born German who served as professor of anatomy at the University of Berlin and studied the anatomy of nerves (among countless other topics), and Friedrich Tiedemann (1781–1861), professor of anatomy and physiology at Heidelberg, best remembered for

Portrait of Sir William Lawrence, 1st Baronet (1783–1867), artist unknown (1839).

his pioneering work on the development of the human brain.

7. Each of these plays, which may be said to be Shakespeare's only "fantasies," includes a hideous creature: the monstrous, half-human Caliban, child of Sycorax the witch, appears in *The Tempest*, and Bottom, the (temporarily) ass-headed man, frightens away his friends in *A Midsummer Night's Dream*. Neil Gaiman has revealed in *The Sandman* that both plays were written by Shakespeare at the behest of Morpheus, "Dream" of the Endless.

8. The "casual conversation" is detailed in the Author's Introduction to the 1831 edition, set forth in Appendix 1, below. Of course, no work of fiction can ever be traced to a single source, or to a single moment in an author's life. The author may in fact not recollect all of what influenced her. For example, Mary Shelley may have read an account in the *Edinburgh Review* in September 1814 of a sailor who, having lain in a coma for seven months, was restored to life by physician Henry

tion of the hero are by no means to be conceived as existing always in my own conviction; nor is any inference justly to be drawn from the following pages as prejudicing any philosophical doctrine of whatever kind.

It is a subject also of additional interest to the author, that this story was begun in the majestic region where the scene is principally laid,[10] and in society which cannot cease to be regretted. I passed the summer of 1816 in the environs of Geneva. The season was cold and rainy, and in the evenings we crowded around a blazing wood fire, and occasionally amused ourselves with some German stories of ghosts, which happened to fall into our hands.[11] These tales excited in us a playful desire of imitation. Two other friends (a tale from the pen of one of whom would be far more acceptable to the public than any thing I can ever hope to produce) and myself agreed to write each a story,[12] founded on some supernatural occurrence.

The weather, however, suddenly became serene; and my two friends left me on a journey among the Alps, and lost, in the magnificent scenes which they present, all memory of their ghostly visions. The following tale is the only one which has been completed.[13]

MARLOW, 1817

Cline. The incident is mentioned in an extensive uncredited review of *An Inquiry into the Probability and Rationality of Mr. Hunter's Theory of Life*, by John Abernethy. Abernethy was well known to William Lawrence (see note 6, above), and Lawrence may have pointed out the review—in fact, a long essay on the state of science regarding life and death—to Mary Shelley (who had been Cline's patient).

It is also known that the Shelleys owned Robert John Thornton's *Philosophy of Medicine: Medical Extracts on the Nature of Health and Disease* (1796), which includes extensive material on "the Recovery of Persons Apparently Dead." Several chapters describe methods to be applied to

persons being "recalled to life" from the "silent mansions of the tomb."

The recent death of her own child and a dream of resurrection may well have been another circumstance, though the dream may not have been known to Percy Shelley. See text accompanying note 42, Foreword, above.

The idea that life might be generated by artificial means was of great interest to many people in 1816, when Mary Shelley wrote *Frankenstein*. To which discussions of that idea she was exposed can never be definitively known.

9. The author here seeks to deflect the widespread criticism or "moral panic"

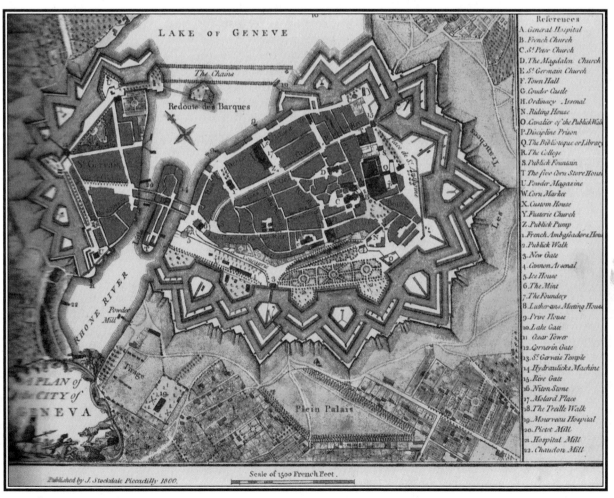

Map of Geneva, ca. 1800.

that had arisen at the end of the eighteenth century as novel-reading spread. Ana Vogrinčič, in "The Novel-Reading Panic in 18th Century in England: An Outline of an Early Moral Media Panic," summarizes the prevailing criticism: "Broadly, one could divide the reproaches into those ascribing to novels the dangerous psychological affects, triggering imitation and inoculating wrong ideas of love and life; and into those referring to the mere habit of novel-reading as a physically harmful waste of time, damaging not only the mind and the morale of readers, but also their eyesight and posture" (*Medij. istraž.* 14, no. 2 [2008]: 103–24, found online at hrcak.srce.hr/file/49661). Circulating or lending libraries were likened to brothels or gin-shops, and the readers of fiction, especially young women, were regarded as debauched and often deluded.

Whether Percy Shelley meant to skewer specific books that bored him is unknown. Popular books of the day that are remembered today include Sir Walter Scott's *Waverley* (1814), Jane Austen's *Mansfield Park* (1814) and *Emma* (1815); less memorable are, for example, Fanny Burney's last work, *The Wanderer: or, Female Difficulties* (1814), a five-volume historical novel that sold poorly, or Maria Edgeworth's four-volume novel *Patronage* (1814), which features two families joined by kinship and inheritance: the Percys, "who demonstrate their worthiness through labor," and their duplicitous cousins the Falconers, who "make their way by patronage into jobs they cannot sustain, homes and social classes for which their taste is deficient, and marriages that are not happy" (Mark Schoenfield, "Novel Marriages, Romantic Labor, and the Quarterly Press," *Romantic Periodicals and Print Culture*, edited by Kim Wheatley [London: Frank Cass and Company, 2003]), 76. As one of twenty-two children of a successful politician

who married four times, Edgeworth was presumably well versed in her subject's complications.

10. Geneva was, at the time of most of the events in *Frankenstein,* an independent city-state, although it was annexed to France by the Directoire in 1798. In 1812, it joined the Swiss Confederation. *Murray's Handbook for Travellers in Switzerland* (hereinafter "*Murray*"), first published in 1838 and a landmark in the history of guidebooks, writes of Geneva,

> Though capital of the smallest of the Swiss Cantons, except Zug, [it] is the most populous town in the Confederation, since it contains 29,960 inhabitants [in 1838]. It is well situated, at the W. Extremity of the lake of Geneva, at the point where 'the blue waters of the arrowy Rhone' issue out of it. The river divides the town into two parts, and the intensely blue colour of its waters, alluded to by Byron, is certainly very remarkable, and resembles nothing so much as the discharge of indigo from a dyer's vat. . . .
>
> Although Geneva is a great focus of attraction for travellers of all nations, 30,000 being the number which is calculated to pass through the town annually, it possesses few objects of interest to the passing stranger. As a town it is not very prepossessing; it has no fine public buildings, and scarcely any *sights*. It is owing to its beautiful environs, its vicinity to Charmouni, to the charming scenery of its lake, and to its position on the high road from Paris to Italy, that it has become a place of so much resort.

Murray goes on to comment on the importance of Geneva as the birthplace of Calvinism and the home of radical thinkers such as Diderot, Voltaire, and Rousseau:

Geneva, if looked at in a historical point of view, may be said to possess an interest for the intelligent traveller far greater than that to be derived from the individual objects of curiosity contained within its walls. The influence which she has exercised, not only over Europe, but over the world, by means of her children, or those whom she has adopted as her citizens, is quite out of proportion to the limited extent of a territory which one may traverse from end to end in a morning's ride. ... Geneva emulated those religious doctrines whence Scotland, Holland, and a large part of France, Germany, and Switzerland derive their form of faith, and which was transported by the pilgrim fathers to the opposite shores of the Atlantic. Here also were sown those political opinions which bore fruit in the English revolution under Charles I., in the American and the French revolutions." (131–33)

The *Encyclopædia Britannica* (3rd ed., 1797) found it equally unprepossessing: "It is handsome, well fortified, and pretty large; the streets in general are clean and well paved, but the principal one is encumbered with a row of shops on each side between the carriage and foot-paths. The latter is very wide, and protected from the weather by great wooden penthouses projecting from the roofs; which, though very convenient, give the street a dark and dull appearance" (Vol. 7, 617).

11. The book appears to have been *Fantasmagoriana; ou Recueil d'Histoires, d'Apparitions, de Spectres, Revenans, Fantomes, etc., traduit de l'allemand, par un amateur*, translated into French anonymously by Jean-Baptiste Benoît Eyriès (1767–1846). It contains a selection of German ghost stories first published in Paris in 1812. The stories included were *"L'Amour Muet,"* ("Foolish Love"), *"Por-*

FANTASMAGORIANA,

ou

RECUEIL

D'HISTOIRES D'APPARITIONS DE SPECTRES,

REVENANS, FANTÔMES, etc.;

Traduit de l'allemand, par un Amateur.

Falsis terroribus implet.
HORAT.

TOME PREMIER.

Title page of *Fantasmagoriana; ou Recueil d'histoires, d'apparitions, de spectres, revenans, fantômes, etc., traduit de l'allemand, par un amateur* (1812).

traits de Famille" ("Family Portraits"), *"La Tête de Mort"* ("The Death-Head"), *"La Morte Fiancée"* ("The Death Bride"), *"L'Heure Fatale"* ("The Fatal Hour"), *"Le Revenant"* ("The Revenant"), *"La Chambre Grise"* ("The Grey Chamber"), and *"La Chambre Noire"* ("The Black Chamber").

12. Actually, of the five (Claire Clairmont, John Polidori, Percy Shelley, Mary Shelley, and Lord Byron composed the group), only Claire Clairmont did not participate, though Percy Shelley's contribution is lost.

13. In 1817, Percy Shelley was correct in this statement. However, in 1819, Dr. John Polidori, another of those present at the Villa Diodati in the summer of 1816, published *The Vampyre* (in the *New Monthly Magazine*, April 1819). Originally heralded as a work of Byron's—and then seen as a satire of Byron—the story recounts some of the activities of the vampire Lord Ruthven, a nobleman marked by his aloof manner and the "deadly hue of his face,

which never gained a warmer tint." In the early part of the nineteenth century, the enigmatic yet strangely compelling Ruthven befriends a gentleman named Aubrey, who finds that even Ruthven's death does not rid him of his deadly companion. When Ruthven returns from death, he rejoins Aubrey, to the latter's horror, and soon attacks and kills Ianthe, the object of Aubrey's affections. Plunged into a breakdown, Aubrey finally recovers, only to find that his beloved sister has also become the victim of the creature, who then vanishes.

Polidori was no great writer—"Lord Ruthven had disappeared, and Aubrey's sister had glutted the thirst of a VAMPYRE!," the book's concluding sentence, is more or less representative of the whole—but his work is credited as the first of the great vampire tales, primarily for its portrayal of a *gentleman* vampire. The character was a far remove from the disgusting, blood-sucking corpses

John Polidori, by F. G. Gainsford (date unknown).

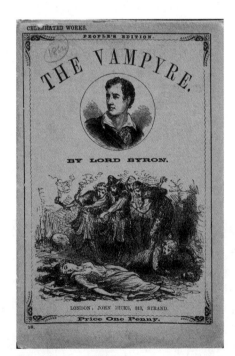

The Vampyre (1816).

detailed in the accounts of the Benedictine Dom Antoine Augustin Calmet (1672–1757), author of *Traité sur les apparitions des esprits et sur les vampires ou les revenans de Hongrie, de Moravie, &c.* (*Treatise on the Apparitions of Spirits and on Vampires or Revenants: of Hungary, Moravia,* et al.) (1752), and other historians. It was immensely successful; within Polidori's lifetime (he died two years after publication), the work was translated into French, German, Spanish, and Swedish and adapted into several stage plays, which played to horror-struck audiences until the early 1850s.

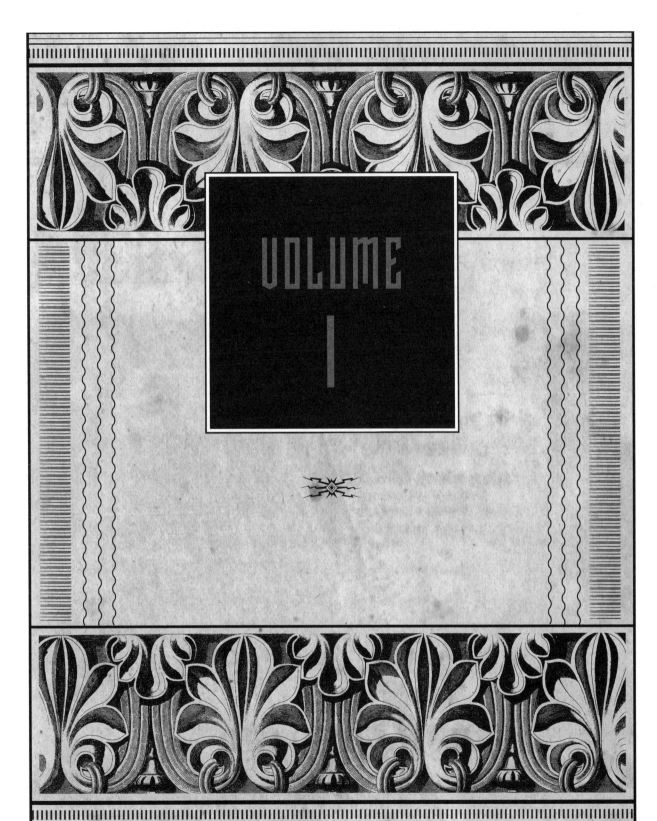

VOLUME

I

St. Petersburg, Nevsky Prospekt, by Benjamin Paterssen (1799).

View of the English Embankment and Galerny Dvor from Vasilievsky Island, by Benjamin Paterssen (1799).

LETTER I[1]

To Mrs. SAVILLE,[2] *England*

St. Petersburgh Dec. 11th, 17—.[3]

YOU will rejoice to hear that no disaster has accompanied the commencement of an enterprise which you have regarded with such evil forebodings. I arrived here yesterday; and my first task is to assure my dear sister of my welfare, and increasing confidence in the success of my undertaking.

I am already far north of London; and as I walk in the streets of Petersburgh, I feel a cold northern breeze play upon my cheeks, which braces my nerves, and fills me with delight.[4] Do you understand this feeling? This breeze, which has travelled from the regions towards which I am advancing, gives me a foretaste of those icy climes. Inspirited by this wind of promise, my day dreams become more fervent and vivid. I try in vain to be persuaded that the pole is the seat of frost and desolation; it ever presents itself to my imagination as the region of beauty and delight. There, Margaret, the sun is for ever visible;[5] its broad disk just skirting the horizon, and diffusing a perpetual splendour. There—for with your leave, my sister, I will put some trust in preceding navigators[6]— there snow and frost are banished; and, sailing over a calm sea, we may be wafted to a land surpassing in wonders and in beauty every region hitherto discovered on the habitable

1. Thus the tale begins in the form of an epistolary novel. The presentation of a collection of letters or other documents organized to tell a story was a form that was widely used in the eighteenth century. Samuel Richardson's *Pamela* (1740) was so successful that it spawned a parody, *Shamela*, by Henry Fielding (1741). Richardson's *Clarissa* (1749) was also widely read. The epistolary format lends a certain verisimilitude to a story that might be less convincing if told as a straight narrative and was revived with great success in Bram Stoker's *Dracula* (1897). As will be seen, however, Mary Shelley quickly discarded the structure for the more complex "Chinese box" of narratives by Victor Frankenstein, the creature, and people with whom the creature interacts, returning to epistolary format only for the conclusion.

2. Note the initials of the recipient of Walton's letters, Margaret Walton Saville: MWS, those of Mary Wollstonecraft Shelley (a point made by Mellor in *Mary Shelley: Her Life, Her Fiction, Her Monsters*, 54), though Mary Shelley had probably written this when she was MWG.

3. As will be seen below, the year appears to be 1798. Why the obfuscation? The elision of the date suggests that the letters have been edited for publication.

4. Edward Jerrmann, in his *Pictures from St. Petersburg*, first published in English in 1852, wrote for German visitors in 1851: "St. Petersburg . . .; which annually receives several hundred German guests, is nevertheless as imperfectly known to us as if it lay beyond the Mountains of the Moon; and the accounts we get of it are so fabulously strange, that when we come to visit it we scarcely dare to trust the evidence of our own eyes. . . . His mind full of such erroneous anticipations, the traveller fancies himself a stage or two beyond Christendom, expects to make acquaintance with a semi-barbarous land, and approaches the City of the Czars with trepidation and anxiety. How startling and agreeable is the contrast, to these gloomy forebodings, of the reality that presents itself on entering the Russian capital . . ." (Edward Jerrmann, *Pictures from St. Petersburg*, trans. Frederick Hardman [New York: G. P. Putnam & Co., 1899], 9).

Petersburg at the time of Walton's visit was a new metropolis, having been built by order of Peter the Great in 1703 by more than 300,000 workers out of a morass of mud and ice. Determined to move the center of his empire from Moscow to Petersburg, Peter demanded that many Muscovites, including nobles, relocate. His aim was to move trade from Archangel (see note 18, below) to Petersburg, in order to establish a Russian fleet that could dominate the Baltic Sea and connect efficiently to the European capitals. After Peter's death, the royal court moved back to Moscow, but it returned to Petersburg when his daughter Elizabeth took the throne as empress in 1741. She spent lavishly on improving the city, building grand structures in the Baroque style. Catherine the Great, who died in

globe.[7] Its productions and features may be without example, as the phænomena of the heavenly bodies undoubtedly are in those undiscovered solitudes. What may not be expected in a country of eternal light? I may there discover the wondrous power which attracts the needle; and may regulate a thousand celestial observations, that require only this voyage to render their seeming eccentricities consistent for ever. I shall satiate my ardent curiosity with the sight of a part of the world never before visited, and may tread a land never before imprinted by the foot of man. These are my enticements, and they are sufficient to conquer all fear of danger or death, and to induce me to commence this laborious voyage with the joy a child feels when he embarks in a little boat, with his holiday mates, on an expedition of discovery up his native river. But, supposing all these conjectures to be false, you cannot contest the inestimable benefit which I shall confer on all mankind to the last generation, by discovering a passage near the pole to those countries,[8] to reach which at present so many months are requisite; or by ascertaining the secret of the magnet,[9] which, if at all possible, can only be effected by an undertaking such as mine.

These reflections have dispelled the agitation with which I began my letter, and I feel my heart glow with an enthusiasm which elevates me to heaven; for nothing contributes so much to tranquillize the mind as a steady purpose,—a point on which the soul may fix its intellectual eye. This expedition has been the favourite dream of my early years. I have read with ardour the accounts of the various voyages which have been made in the prospect of arriving at the North Pacific Ocean through the seas which surround the pole.[10] You may remember, that a history of all the voyages made for purposes of discovery composed the whole of our good uncle Thomas's library. My education was neglected, yet I was passionately fond of reading. These volumes[11] were my study day and night, and my familiarity with them increased that regret which I had felt, as a child, on learning that my father's dying injunction had forbidden my uncle to allow me to embark in a sea-faring life.

These visions faded when I perused, for the first time, those poets whose effusions entranced my soul, and lifted it to heaven. I also became a poet, and for one year lived in a Paradise of my own creation; I imagined that I also might obtain a niche in the temple where the names of Homer and Shakespeare are consecrated. You are well acquainted with my failure, and how heavily I bore the disappointment. But just at that time I inherited the fortune of my cousin, and my thoughts were turned into the channel of their earlier bent.

Six years have passed since I resolved on my present undertaking.[12] I can, even now, remember the hour from which I dedicated myself to this great enterprise. I commenced by inuring my body to hardship. I accompanied the whale-fishers on several expeditions to the North Sea; I voluntarily endured cold, famine, thirst, and want of sleep; I often worked harder than the common sailors during the day, and devoted my nights to the study of mathematics, the theory of medicine, and those branches of physical science from which a naval adventurer might derive the greatest practical advantage. Twice I actually hired myself as an

Map of the Arctic Circle, by Gerhard Mercator ("Septentrionalium Terrarum description," 1595) from his posthumously published atlas, *Atlantis pars altera* (1606).

1796, just shortly before Walton's arrival in Petersburg, made the Russian capital a cultural center as well, establishing a magnificent art collection (now housed in the Hermitage).

5. Corrected in the Thomas Text to "constantly visible for more than half the year," factually correct but far less powerful as a symbol of the appeal of the pole.

6. There were no "preceding navigators" of "the pole," in a strict sense, though by the end of the seventeenth century, many explorers had crossed the Arctic Circle (that arbitrary line at 66° 33' 44" north of the Equator), establishing footholds on places as far north as Bear Island, Spitsbergen, Archangel, and Greenland

The earliest account of Arctic exploration is that of Pytheas, a contemporary of Aristotle and Alexander, who wrote of a voyage north, in about 325 BCE, that led him to an island that he named Thule. It is unknown whether this was the Shetlands, the Faroes, or even Iceland, but regardless, he reportedly continued north, turning back in dismay only when he came upon what he described as a great dark wall, while his ship was seized and held motionless. Arctic historians suggest that he had come across "frost-smoke," dense fog resulting from significant temperature gradients, and quick-freezing ice thick enough to hold his small ship. Pytheas was also disconcerted by the appearance of the heavens, which shifted from eternal daylight to eternal night.

Pytheas's own account is not extant; instead, we must rely on works like Strabo's *Geographica*, first published around 7 BCE, and Pliny's *Natural History* (77–79 CE), which paraphrase Pytheas. Strabo in particular had grave doubts about the veracity of many of Pytheas's claims of discovery, and there is no corroborative evidence of his voyage.

7. The origins of the idea of a "Golden Age" and its primary situs in the antediluvian North are complex and manifold. Jean-Sylvain Bailly (1736–1793), astronomer and mystic, was convinced that the scientific knowledge of ancient Egypt, Chaldea, China, and India—newly discovered by the West—was the half-remembered residue of a superior northern culture that was eradicated by the Flood. This was consistent, he believed, with theories advanced by the Comte de Buffon, who argued that the polar regions were the birthplace of life, because, as the Earth cooled after separating from the Sun, those regions would have been the first to be sufficiently cool enough to sustain it.

Bâl Gangâdhar Tilak (1856–1912), an astronomer and lifelong student of the Vedas (the ancient Sanskrit scriptures, probably first recorded in 1500 BCE), contended that they describe the destruction of an original Arctic home ca. 10,000 to 8000 BCE. Tilak's theory was embraced by John G. Bennett, in his paper "The Hyperborean Origin of the Indo-European Culture," in *Systematics* 1, no. 3 (December 1963), http://www.systematics.org/journal/vol1-3/SJ1-3c.htm. Helena Petrovna Blavatsky, founder of Theosophy, writing in *Isis Unveiled*, claimed, "Tradition says, and the records of the *Great Book* explain, that long before the days of Ad-am and his inquisitive wife, He-va, where now are found but salt lakes and desolate barren deserts, there was a vast inland sea, which extended over Middle Asia, north of the proud Himalayan range, and its western prolongation. An island, which for its unparalleled beauty had no rival in the world, was inhabited by the last remnant of the race which preceded ours . . . the 'Sons of God'" (Blavatsky, *Isis Unveiled: A Master-Key to the Mysteries of Ancient and Modern Science and Theology* [New York: J. W. Bouton, 1877], Vol. 1, *Science*, 589).

Bailly actually believed that Atlantis, queen of all lost realms, was in the far north, probably on the islands of Spitsber-

under-mate in a Greenland whaler,[13] and acquitted myself to admiration. I must own I felt a little proud, when my captain offered me the second dignity in the vessel, and entreated me to remain with the greatest earnestness; so valuable did he consider my services.

And now, dear Margaret, do I not deserve to accomplish some great purpose. My life might have been passed in ease and luxury; but I preferred glory to every enticement that wealth placed in my path. Oh, that some encouraging voice would answer in the affirmative! My courage and my resolution is firm; but my hopes fluctuate, and my spirits are often depressed. I am about to proceed on a long and difficult voyage; the emergencies of which will demand all my fortitude: I am required not only to raise the spirits of others, but sometimes to sustain my own, when theirs are failing.

This is the most favourable period for travelling in Russia. They fly quickly over the snow in their sledges; the motion is pleasant, and, in my opinion, far more agreeable than that of an English stagecoach.[14] The cold is not excessive, if you are wrapt in furs, a dress which I have already adopted; for there is a great difference between walking the deck and remaining seated motionless for hours, when no exercise prevents the blood from actually freezing in your veins. I have no ambition to lose my life on the post-road[15] between St. Petersburgh and Archangel.[16]

I shall depart for the latter town in a fortnight or three weeks; and my intention is to hire a ship there, which can easily be done by paying the insurance for the owner, and to engage as many sailors as I think necessary among those who are accustomed to the whale-fishing. I do not intend to sail until the month of June: and when shall I return? Ah, dear sister, how can I answer this question? If I succeed, many, many months, perhaps years, will pass before you and I may meet. If I fail, you will see me again soon, or never.

Farewell, my dear, excellent, Margaret. Heaven shower down blessings on you, and save me, that I may again and again testify my gratitude for all your love and kindness.

Your affectionate brother,
R. WALTON.[17]

gen and Greenland, and the Novaya Zemlya archipelago (*Letters Upon the Atlantis of Plato, and the Ancient History of Asia: Intended as a Continuation of the Letters Upon the Origin of the Sciences Addressed to M. de Voltaire* [1779; translated by James Jacque, 1801, and published in 2011 by the British Museum]). See Joscelyn Godwin, *Arktos: The Polar Myth in Science, Symbolism, and Nazi Survival* (Kempton, IL: Adventures Unlimited Press, 1996), for a more detailed analysis of Bailly's and Blavatsky's thinking, as well as other sources of the myth of a northern paradise.

8. Polar exploration of the period was largely driven by searches for what were termed the Northwest Passage, a sea route from the Pacific to the Atlantic Ocean along the northern coast of North America, and the Northeast Passage (also known as the Northern Route), a sea route from the Barents Sea to the Bering Strait along the northern coast of Russia. Walton is referring to the latter.

Focused exploration of the Northern Route began in 1553, with an expedition led by Sir Hugh Willoughby and Richard Chancellor along the northern coast of Canada. Willoughby's ships were held fast in the ice off the Kola Peninsula, and all aboard perished; Chancellor's ships landed at Archangel and returned safely to England. It was not until 1556 that Steven Borough, the master of Chancellor's ship, made it as far as the Kara Sea, where he turned back, dismayed by the prospect of a "great and terrible abundance of ice." In 1576–78, Martin Frobisher explored the western parts of the region, and in 1585–88, he discovered and explored the Davis Strait, to the west of Greenland, as well as many other points of interest. In 1610, Henry Hudson sailed into Hudson's Bay, and in 1615, William Baffin explored Baffin's Bay, both areas critical to the fur trade for the next two centuries. Hudson had distinguished himself earlier, when, in 1607, he penetrated to 81° 60' north,

the closest proximity to the North Pole recorded to date. Also noteworthy is the 1596 expedition of the Dutch explorer Willem Barentsz, who discovered Spitsbergen, the 15,000-square-mile island off the northwest coast of the Scandinavian peninsula, and Bear Island.

Czar Michael I closed the Mangazeya seaway in 1619 to limit English and Dutch incursions into Siberia. As a result, most seventeenth-century exploration in the region was carried out by Siberian Cossacks. In 1648 Fedot Alekseev and Semyon Dezhnev explored the entirety of the Chukchi Peninsula by sailing eastward from the mouth of the Kolyma River around the peninsula and into the northern Pacific Ocean. In the process, they demonstrated that there was no land bridge connecting that peninsula (part of Asia) and North America (at what is now called the Seward Peninsula). Eighty years later, Danish-born Vitus Bering voyaged from Kamchatka to the north as far as the Bering Strait, the passage previously found by Dezhnev. The history of many of these expeditions and the stories of the explorers' tragic fates are told in Helen S. Wright's *The Great White North: The Story of Polar Exploration from the Earliest Times to the Discovery of the Pole* (New York: Macmillan, 1910).

The first complete passage of the Northeast Passage, from west to east, did not take place until long after Walton's voyage, in 1878, when Finnish-Swedish explorer Adolf Erik Nordenskiöld and Lieutenant Louis Palander of the Swedish Royal Navy accomplished the trip in the *Vega*.

9. The North Magnetic Pole exists as a function of the Earth's magnetic field, the spot where the field points straight downward, causing a compass needle to do the same. Such a phenomenon was projected by the English physician and natural philosopher William Gilbert in 1600, who also suggested that the planet acted

as a giant magnet. However, the actual spot was not visited until 1831, by British naval officer and explorer James Clark Ross. The location moves over time as the magnetic field varies (as well as traversing a daily elliptical orbit of about 50 miles [80 km]). In 2001, the Geological Survey of Canada sited it near Ellesmere Island in northern Canada at 81.3°N 110.8°W. By 2005, it had moved to 83.1°N 117.8°W; in 2009, its location was 84.9°N 131.0°W, and by 2012, the pole had moved to Russian territory at 85.9°N 147.0°W.

10. See notes 6 and 8, above.

11. Surely the core of Walton's uncle's library was English geographer Richard Hakluyt's *The Principal Navigations, Voyages, Traffiques and Discoveries of the English Nation* (first published in 1582, and expanded in subsequent editions in 1589 and 1600), an extensive work: the 1886–1890 Goldsmid edition is sixteen volumes (see http://www.hakluyt.com/hakluyt_census.htm for a history of the various editions). The library would have also included *Purchas His Pilgrimes* (1625), Samuel Purchas's four-volume collection of travel stories, a continuation of Hakluyt's efforts, which incorporates Robert Juet's journal of Henry Hudson's 1609 voyage, transcribed at http://www.halfmoon.mus .ny.us/Juets-modified.pdf), and accounts of Baffin's travels. Perhaps Uncle Thomas may even have owned—though it was only published in German and was clearly not a "history of all the voyages made for purposes of discovery"—Gerhard Friedrich Müller's *Sammlung Russischer Geschichten* (St. Petersburg: Kayserl. Academie der Wißenschafften, 1758), a pioneering nine-volume account of Russian history that describes Dezhnev's and Bering's voyages.

12. Walton would have inherited his cousin's fortune at age twenty-one. He is unlikely to have taken a whole year to resolve on his undertaking, making him twenty-seven at the time of writing this letter and his later claim to be age twenty-eight a slight exaggeration.

13. As late as 1780 and presumably later, "Greenland" in the context of whaling actually meant Spitsbergen, originally "Spits-bergen" ("pointed mountains"). It was identified with the large island of Greenland to the west and was referred to under that name among the Dutch and English who soon visited it regularly.

Commercial whale fishing off Greenland, as contrasted with what is now termed aboriginal subsistence whaling—that is, the capture of whales by locals for sustenance—can be traced back to the ninth century CE, in the accounts by Alfred the Great of the voyage of Ohthere of Halgoland, in northernmost Norway: "no man abode north of him" (*The Whole Works of King Alfred the Great* [Oxford and Cambridge, UK: Messrs. J. F. Smith and Co., 1852], Vol. 2, Book I, chapter 1, p. 46, https://goo.gl/mRf1sm). The first confirmed English whale hunting (off northeastern Canada) was in 1594, and after Hudson's visit to Spitsbergen in 1607, the merchants of Hull, England, quickly established a vigorous business of it there. The Dutch followed in establishing whale fisheries in Spitsbergen a few years later.

By 1788, according to the Rev. William Scoresby's account of the ebb and flow of British whale fishing in the region, British ships sailed for the whale fishery from over twenty ports. A crew generally consisted of forty to fifty men, "comprising several classes of officers, such as harpooners, boat-steerers, line-managers, carpenters, coopers, etc., together with fore-mast men, landmen, and apprentices" (Scoresby, *The Arctic Regions and the Northern Whale-Fishery* [London: The Religious Tract Society, 1799], 48, https://goo.gl/TNNrrS).

Dutch whalers near Spitsbergen, by Abraham Storck (1690).

The principal tools of the whale-fishers were the harpoon (propelled by hand or gun), the line (rope), and the lance. The whale would be first wounded with harpoons attached to lines, and when the whale was sufficiently exhausted from its attempts to flee, the vitals of the whale would be pierced repeatedly with lances until it expired. The cadaver of the whale would then be secured and typically processed at sea, cut up and reduced to whalebone and oil, the principal commercial products.

Scoresby, to whom references can be found in *Moby-Dick* and Julian Barnes's *Flaubert's Parrot*, among other works, does not flinch from the details of the brutality of whale hunting or the risks to the crew. He cheerily remarks on the providence of God in making the victims so tame and timid and, quoting Genesis, delights in the evidence that God indeed did give man "dominion over the fish of the sea" (72–73). Contrast this with a recent letter issued by Greenland's Ministry of Fisheries, Hunting and Agriculture, discussing the government's policies regarding "aboriginal subsistence whaling": "Cannons with harpoon grenades are used for the main part of the hunted whales. This

ensures a rapid and humane death of the whale. The grenades are very costly—600 to 800 English pounds pr. grenade—so money is a necessity, that is—if animal welfare considerations should be taken into account and that is a requirement according to Greenlandic law." Strict quotas are imposed as well, and whale hunting is justified as follows: "Whale meat is a natural product that does not need any anthropogenic produced fertilizers or pesticides, i.e. it is a 100% environmental-friendly source of 'green food.' The subsistence whaling reduces the need for our import of western food; which also helps in reducing the global CO_2-emissions. By a higher level of utilization and local distribution of our own resources, we will also reduce and limit modern life style diseases that are occurring more often in Greenland" (http://naalakkersuisut .gl/en/About-government-of-greenland/ Whaling-in-Greenland).

William Scoresby, from an engraving by E. Smith (1821).

14. The first coaches in England were simple boxes on wheels, and because the roads were so poor, journeys were extremely uncomfortable, even if the coach box was suspended from leather straps. In the late eighteenth century, C-shaped steel springs were added, and an advertisement could proclaim that a new stagecoach would "for the better accommodation of passengers be altered to a new genteel two-end glass-coach machine being on steel springs and exceedingly light." It was not until the early nineteenth century, however, that elliptical springs were introduced, greatly reducing the jolting, and, as highways improved, the ride became more like that of Walton's sledge.

15. That is, the principal route of mail carriers.

16. On today's highways, this is a distance of 783 miles (1,261 km), requiring about sixteen hours. The Russian postal-road system of St. Petersburg was begun in 1703 by Peter the Great and his advisers. Taxes were imposed on the general population for the upkeep and mainte-nance of roads. John Randolph, associate professor of history at the University of Illinois, describes how the system worked: "[A]t the heart of the day-to-day operation of the system lay a special social group known as the *iamshchiki* ('post riders' or 'coachmen,' we might say in English, although women and children were part of this obliged class as well). These *iamshchiki* were granted agricultural lands and paid small per-trip fees. In return for these wages, their villages were supposed to staff and maintain the postal stations, providing drivers, horses, mounts and wagons in turn. (In the tax jargon of the day, 28 *iamshchik* 'souls,' that is adult males as counted by the census, made up a unit of taxation called a *vyt'*; and each *vyt'* had to provide 3 horses and a driver, for periodic service as managed by an elected elder.)" See http://russianhistoryblog.org/2012/01/imagining-the-petersburg-moscow-road-in-the-late-18th-century/.

17. The signature here is a touch formal for a brother—"R. Walton"—but this may be forgiven as an addition made by Mary Shelley.

LETTER II

To Mrs. Saville, England.

Archangel,[18] 28th March, 17—.[19]

How slowly the time passes here, encompassed as I am by frost and snow; yet a second step is taken towards my enterprise. I have hired a vessel, and am occupied in collecting my sailors; those whom I have already engaged appear to be men on whom I can depend, and are certainly possessed of dauntless courage.[20]

But I have one want which I have never yet been able to satisfy; and the absence of the object of which I now feel as a most severe evil. I have no friend, Margaret: when I am glowing with the enthusiasm of success, there will be none to participate my joy; if I am assailed by disappointment, no one will endeavour to sustain me in dejection. I shall commit my thoughts to paper, it is true; but that is a poor medium for the communication of feeling. I desire the company of a man who could sympathize[21] with me; whose eyes would reply to mine. You may deem me romantic, my dear sister, but I bitterly feel the want of a friend. I have no one near me, gentle yet courageous, possessed of a cultivated as well as of a capacious mind, whose tastes are like my own, to approve or amend my plans. How would such a friend repair the faults of your poor brother! I am too ardent in execution, and too impatient of difficulties. But it

18. Known today as Arkhangelsk, situated on the White Sea, it was the chief seaport of Russia until 1704. In 1693, Peter the Great established a state shipyard there, emphasizing its importance, but in 1704, after conquering territory on the Baltic and realizing that weather conditions severely limited year-round access to Arkhangelsk, he founded St. Petersburg. See note 4, above. In 1722, in order to shift international trade to that port, Peter prohibited Arkhangelsk from importing goods that exceeded its own needs. Although this prohibition lapsed in 1762, by the late eighteenth century, the Baltic trade far exceeded the northern commerce, and Arkhangelsk fell into minor importance until the railways made it a center for the export of timber. Today, with modern ice-breaking, it is again a major seaport.

Tobias George Smollett described Archangel in 1768 as "rich, populous, and built in the modern taste. . . . The houses . . . are generally of wood, but well contrived; and every chamber is provided with a stove, as a fence against the cold, which is here excessive in the winter. The streets are paved with broken pieces of timber and rubbish, disposed so unskillfully, that one cannot walk over it without running the risk of falling, except when the streets are rendered smooth and equal by the snow that falls and freezes in the winter. Notwithstanding the severity of the cold in this place, there is always plenty of good provisions; butcher's meat, poultry, wild fowl, and fish, in great variety, are sold surprisingly cheap" (Smollett, *The Present State of All Nations: A Geographical, Natural, Commercial, and Political History of All the Countries in the Known World* [London, 1768], Vol. 1, 355–57, https://goo.gl/PeV1CI).

19. The year would have been 1799, by our reckoning.

20. How poorly Walton knew his men—see text accompanying note 37, Volume III, Chapter VII, below.

21. "Sympathy" is mentioned more than thirty-five times in *Frankenstein*. Certainly, "sympathy" may mean the capacity to experience the feelings of another, but it also means a magical or mechanical connection. Objects said to be in sympathy with each another (for example, a voodoo doll and subject) share experiences (for example, pinpricks) or move together (iron and a lodestone, or the moon and the tides). Lovers and twins were said to be in "sympathy" with each other as well. As science progressed in the eighteenth century, mechanical explanations for such "sympathy" were proffered.

22. The communal open space of the village.

23. What languages did Walton speak? German, Spanish, French? If he hoped to successfully captain a ship, then certainly a rough vocabulary in the Romance languages so common among the world's commercial sailors and naval crews

is a still greater evil to me that I am self-educated: for the first fourteen years of my life I ran wild on a common,[22] and read nothing but our uncle Thomas's books of voyages. At that age I became acquainted with the celebrated poets of our own country; but it was only when it had ceased to be in my power to derive its most important benefits from such a conviction, that I perceived the necessity of becoming acquainted with more languages than that of my native country.[23] Now I am twenty-eight,[24] and am in reality more illiterate than many school-boys of fifteen. It is true that I have thought more, and that my day dreams are more extended and magnificent; but they want (as the painters call it) keeping;[25] and I greatly need a friend who would have sense enough not to despise me as romantic, and affection enough for me to endeavour to regulate my mind.

Well, these are useless complaints; I shall certainly find no friend on the wide ocean, nor even here in Archangel, among merchants and seamen. Yet some feelings, unallied to the dross of human nature, beat even in these rugged bosoms. My lieutenant, for instance, is a man of wonderful courage and enterprise; he is madly desirous of glory.[26] He is an Englishman, and in the midst of national and professional prejudices, unsoftened by cultivation, retains some of the noblest endowments of humanity. I first became acquainted with him on board a whale vessel: finding that he was unemployed in this city, I easily engaged him to assist in my enterprise.

The master[27] is a person of an excellent disposition, and is remarkable in the ship for his gentleness, and the mildness of his discipline. He is, indeed, of so amiable a nature, that he will not hunt (a favourite, and almost the only amusement here), because he cannot endure to spill blood. He is, moreover, heroically generous.[28] Some years ago he loved a young Russian lady, of moderate fortune; and having amassed a considerable sum in prize-money,[29] the father of the girl consented to the match. He saw his mistress once before the destined ceremony; but she was bathed in tears, and, throwing herself at his feet, entreated him to spare her, confessing at the same time that she loved another, but that he was poor, and that her father would never consent to the union. My generous friend reassured the suppliant, and on being informed of the name of her lover instantly abandoned his pursuit. He had already bought a farm with his money, on which he had designed to pass the remainder of his life; but he bestowed the whole on his rival, together with the remains of his prize-money to purchase stock, and then himself solicited the young woman's father to consent to her marriage with her lover. But the old man decidedly refused, thinking himself bound in honour to my friend; who, when he found the father inexorable, quitted his country, nor returned until he heard that his former mistress was married according to her inclinations. "What a noble fellow!" you will exclaim. He is so; but then[30] he has passed all his life on board a vessel, and has scarcely an idea beyond the rope and the shroud.[31] But do not suppose that, because I complain a little, or because I can conceive a consolation for my toils which I may never know, that I am wavering in my resolutions. Those are as fixed as fate; and my voyage is only now delayed until the weather shall permit my embarkation. The winter has been dreadfully severe; but the spring promises well, and it is considered as a remarkably early season; so that, perhaps, I may sail sooner than I expected. I shall do nothing rashly; you know me sufficiently to confide in my prudence and considerateness whenever the safety of others is committed to my care.[32]

I cannot describe to you my sensations on the near prospect of my undertaking. It is impossible to communicate to you a conception of the trembling sensation, half pleasurable and half fearful, with which I am preparing to depart. I am going to unexplored regions, to "the land of mist and snow"; but I shall kill no albatross,[33] therefore do not be alarmed for my safety.[34]

Shall I meet you again, after having traversed immense seas, and returned by the most southern cape of Africa or America?[35] I dare not expect such success, yet I cannot bear to look on the reverse of the picture. Continue to write to me by every opportunity: I may receive your letters (though the chance is very doubtful) on some occasions when I need them most to support my spirits. I love you very tenderly. Remember me with affection, should you never hear from me again.

Your affectionate brother,
ROBERT WALTON.[36]

would have been useful. Perhaps he also studied Latin and classical Greek, though if he had mastered those, he would not term himself "illiterate." However, it does not appear that he spoke either Russian or any of the Scandinavian languages and so would likely have been isolated from his crew.

24. Walton was born, we calculate, in late 1770 or early 1771.

25. "An attention to the proper subserviency of tone and colour in every part of a picture, so that the general effect is harmonious to the eye. When this is unattended to, a harshness is produced, which gives improper isolation to individual parts, and the picture is said to be *out of keeping*," Frederick William Fairholt, *A Dictionary of Terms in Art* (London: Strahan & Co., ca. 1854).

26. In the 1831 edition, the text continues: "or rather, to word my phrase more characteristically, of advancement in his profession." The lieutenant is only mentioned again in Volume I, Letter IV and apparently plays no part in the eventual near-mutiny of Walton's men. This emendation begins Mary Shelley's seeming though unadmitted efforts, in response to various critics, to make the 1831 edition more of a "moral" tale.

27. Although "master" was common usage for the ship's captain (only military vessels had "captains"), it appears here that the "lieutenant" is the person to whom Walton refers as the "master." This is made evident by the omission of this sentence in the 1831 edition, so that the description of the man's characteristics plainly applies to the "lieutenant."

28. The Thomas Text omits this sentence and replaces it with: "I will relate to you an anecdote of his life, recounted to me by the parties themselves, which

exemplifies the generosity, I had almost said the heroism of his nature." This and the previous sentence have been omitted from the 1831 edition and replaced with the following passage: "This circumstance, added to his well-known integrity and dauntless courage, made me very desirous to engage him. A youth passed in solitude, my best years spent under your gentle and feminine fosterage, has so refined the groundwork of my character that I cannot overcome an intense distaste to the usual brutality exercised on board ship: I have never believed it to be necessary, and when I heard of a mariner equally noted for his kindliness of heart and the respect and obedience paid to him by his crew, I felt myself peculiarly fortunate in being able to secure his services. I heard of him first in rather a romantic manner, from a lady who owes to him the happiness of her life. This, briefly, is his story." By having Walton expand on the virtues of the lieutenant, Mary Shelley softens the picture of him that develops in the 1818 edition, of a young man himself "madly desirous for glory," in sympathy with the obsessed Victor Frankenstein and later seen to be heedless of his crew's desire to return home. Interestingly, the passage emphasizes the mothering that he received from his sister, not unlike the influence of Elizabeth on Victor.

29. "Some years ago" places the events described in Walton's story in the 1780s or early 1790s. The laws of England and most other nations made captured ships of belligerents in war legally the property of the government. As an incentive for capture, it was customary for the value of the ship and its cargo to be given to the captain who had seized the vessel for distribution to his crew. This applied whether the captor was a military vessel or a privateer. The lieutenant, then, was part of the crew of a ship in the 1780s, most likely

Illustration from a German edition of Coleridge's "Rime of the Ancient Mariner" by Gustave Doré (1877).

either a vessel of the British navy or a privateer that captured an American vessel during the Revolutionary War.

30. The phrase following, up to the word "But" that begins the next sentence, is omitted in the 1831 edition, and the following is added: "is wholly uneducated: he is as silent as a Turk, and a kind of ignorant carelessness attends him, which, while it renders his conduct the more astonishing, detracts from the interest and sympathy which otherwise he would command. Yet[.]"

Here Mary Shelley inserts an explanation as to why Walton requires a friendship with Victor, to satisfy needs unsatisfied by this otherwise exemplary crew member.

31. Lines of rope attached to masts to keep them steady. The Thomas Text makes this less obscure, referring to "the ship and the crew."

32. Either Walton is a very poor judge of his own character or suffers a great change in personality, for nothing could be further from the truth with regards to his eventual treatment of his crew. See text accompanying note 37, Volume III, Chapter VII, below.

33. Of course not— the albatross is not found in the North Atlantic.

"The land of mist and snow" is referred to in Coleridge's "The Rime of the Ancient Mariner," first published in 1798; the Mariner kills an albatross and suffers from the curse superstitiously attributed to such slayings. The date of first publication of the poem confirms that Walton is writing in March 1799, as will be seen.

34. In case any reader has missed the subtle allusion to Coleridge's work, the following has been added in the 1831 edition: "or if I should come back to you as worn and woeful as the 'Ancient Mariner.' You will smile at my allusion, but I will disclose a secret. I have often attributed my attachment to, my passionate enthusiasm for, the dangerous mysteries of ocean to that production of the most imaginative of modern poets. There is something at work in my soul which I do not understand. I am practically industrious—painstaking, a workman to execute with perseverance and labour—but besides this there is a love for the marvellous, a belief in the marvellous, intertwined in all my projects, which hurries me out of the common pathways of men, even to the wild sea and unvisited regions I am about to explore. But to return to dearer considerations."

35. This would indeed be quite a voyage, from the northernmost extremes of the globe to the southern passages of Cape of Good Hope or Cape Horn, but Walton is likely being figurative rather than suggesting an actual itinerary.

36. Note the more formal signature, as is appropriate for what Walton believes may be his final letter to his sister.

LETTER III

37. Again, this is 1799.

38. A ship built for commerce rather than warfare.

39. This has been rewritten in the Thomas Text: "the crew is gallant fellows, & I am firm of purpose . . ."

40. The phrase "breaking of a mast" has been replaced with "springing of a leak" in the 1831 edition. Perhaps the image was too painful for Mary Shelley, reminding her of Percy's drowning (see Foreword, text following note 56, above).

To Mrs. SAVILLE, *England*

July 7th, 17—.[37]

MY DEAR SISTER,

I WRITE a few lines in haste, to say that I am safe, and well advanced on my voyage. This letter will reach England by a merchant-man[38] now on its homeward voyage from Archangel; more fortunate than I, who may not see my native land, perhaps, for many years. I am, however, in good spirits: my men are bold, and apparently firm of purpose;[39] nor do the floating sheets of ice that continually pass us, indicating the dangers of the region towards which we are advancing, appear to dismay them. We have already reached a very high latitude; but it is the height of summer, and although not so warm as in England, the southern gales, which blow us speedily towards those shores which I so ardently desire to attain, breathe a degree of renovating warmth which I had not expected.

No incidents have hitherto befallen us, that would make a figure in a letter. One or two stiff gales, and the breaking of a mast,[40] are accidents which experienced navigators scarcely remember to record; and I shall be well content, if nothing worse happen to us during our voyage.

Adieu, my dear Margaret. Be assured, that for my own

sake, as well as yours, I will not rashly encounter danger. I will be cool, persevering, and prudent.

Remember me to all my English friends.[41]

Most affectionately yours,
R. W.[42]

41. This admonition and the signature block of the letter are omitted in the 1831 edition, and the following is substituted:

But success SHALL crown my endeavours. Wherefore not? Thus far I have gone, tracing a secure way over the pathless seas, the very stars themselves being witnesses and testimonies of my triumph. Why not still proceed over the untamed yet obedient element? What can stop the determined heart and resolved will of man?

My swelling heart involuntarily pours itself out thus. But I must finish. Heaven bless my beloved sister!
R.W.

And so Shelley more clearly establishes Walton as a driven adventurer whose hubris resembles that of Victor Frankenstein; he is not a passive recorder of Victor's history.

42. An abbreviated signature, indicating haste.

LETTER IV

43. We will argue that the evidence of various remarks of the protagonists requires that the year is 1799; however, July 31 was not a Monday in that year, and the most proximate year meeting these conditions—1797—is not possible in light of other intervals. Walton must have miscalculated his days. Charles Robinson contends for 1797 on the basis of the chronological match that July 31 was a Monday in that year but dismisses the evidence regarding quotations from works published later.

44. "Sea room" means space for passage. Such incidents, in which a ship is captured by and, if unfortunate, crushed by pack ice, are common in history and frequently occurred during the search for the Northern Route. For example, Henry Hudson's *Discovery* spent the winter trapped by ice in James Bay in 1610–11; William Parry's ships were trapped in 1821; Sir John Ross was stranded for four winters when his ship was crushed in 1829; and Sir John Franklin had to abandon his ships the *Terror* and the *Erebus* in 1848 when they were captured by the Arctic ice. It was not until

To Mrs. Saville, England.

August 5th, 17—.

So strange an accident has happened to us, that I cannot forbear recording it, although it is very probable that you will see me before these papers can come into your possession.

Last Monday (July 31st),[43] we were nearly surrounded by ice, which closed in the ship on all sides, scarcely leaving her the sea room in which she floated.[44] Our situation was somewhat dangerous, especially as we were compassed round by a very thick fog.[45] We accordingly lay to, hoping that some change would take place in the atmosphere and weather.

About two o'clock[46] the mist cleared away, and we beheld, stretched out in every direction, vast and irregular plains of ice, which seemed to have no end. Some of my comrades groaned, and my own mind began to grow watchful with anxious thoughts, when a strange sight suddenly attracted our attention, and diverted our solicitude from our own situation. We perceived a low carriage, fixed on a sledge and drawn by dogs, pass on towards the north, at the distance of half a mile: a being which had the shape of a man, but apparently of gigantic stature, sat in the sledge, and guided the dogs. We watched the rapid progress of the traveller with

The *Endurance* stuck in the ice, 1915, photo by expedition photographer Frank Hurley.

our telescopes, until he was lost among the distant inequalities of the ice.

This appearance excited our unqualified wonder. We were, as we believed, many hundred miles from any land; but this apparition seemed to denote that it was not, in reality, so distant as we had supposed. Shut in, however, by ice, it was impossible to follow his track, which we had observed with the greatest attention.[47]

About two hours after this occurrence, we heard the ground sea;[48] and before night the ice broke, and freed our

1893 that a Norwegian explorer, Fridtjof Nansen, sailed north in a crushproof ship, the *Fram*, deliberately allowed it to be frozen in the Siberian ice pack, and stayed aboard as it drifted to Spitsbergen (where it arrived in 1896), thereby demonstrating the motion of the ice pack.

In later centuries, the Antarctic also claimed many victims. For example, in 1915, Ernest Shackleton's *Endurance* was crushed by ice in the Antarctic's Weddell Sea and sank. As late as 1986, the *New York Times* reported that a British expeditionary vessel was crushed by Antarctic ice, fortunately without loss of life. In January 2014, a Russian research ship and Chinese icebreaker were trapped by Antarctic ice, only to finally break free.

45. Compare the fogs recorded by Pytheas, note 6, above.

46. Ships have for centuries kept time on a schedule of "bells," signifying half-hour intervals in a four-hour duty watch. "Two o'clock" (whether morning or evening) is "four bells." In light of the visibility of the sledge, we must conclude that the time is four bells in the afternoon watch. Walton is evidently translating naval time for the benefit of his sister.

47. The Thomas Text adds the following intriguing sentences: "Are we then near land, and is this unknown wast [*sic*] inhabited by giants, of which the being we saw is a specimen? Such an idea is contrary to all experience, but if what we saw was an optical delusion, it was the most perfect and wonderful recorded in the history of nature."

48. A heavy but temporary swell at sea, with large waves, possibly the result of a distant storm.

49. The dog promptly disappears from the narrative—eaten?

50. As we will see later, the stranger—Victor Frankenstein—also speaks French, German, and Latin.

51. Use of a compound of two parts brandy to one part salt was hailed by William Lee, in a pamphlet published in 1840 (*The Use of Brandy and Salt as a Remedy for Inflammation* [London: Simpkin, Marshall & Co.]), as a remedy for a wide variety of ailments. Lee, who claims to have discovered the compound in France a few years prior to publication of his book, explains in detail how the medicine is to be used, both externally and internally. For cases of dizziness and even insanity (as in an attack of nerves), he recommended rubbing the crown of the head with the preparation and then dosage of a few spoonfuls, diluted with hot water.

ship. We, however, lay to until the morning, fearing to encounter in the dark those large loose masses which float about after the breaking up of the ice. I profited of this time to rest for a few hours.

In the morning, however, as soon as it was light, I went upon deck, and found all the sailors busy on one side of the vessel, apparently talking to some one in the sea. It was, in fact, a sledge, like that we had seen before, which had drifted towards us in the night, on a large fragment of ice. Only one dog remained alive;[49] but there was a human being within it, whom the sailors were persuading to enter the vessel. He was not, as the other traveller seemed to be, a savage inhabitant of some undiscovered island, but an European. When I appeared on deck, the master said, "Here is our captain, and he will not allow you to perish on the open sea."

On perceiving me, the stranger addressed me in English, although with a foreign accent.[50] "Before I come on board your vessel," said he, "will you have the kindness to inform me whither you are bound?"

You may conceive my astonishment on hearing such a question addressed to me from a man on the brink of destruction, and to whom I should have supposed that my vessel would have been a resource which he would not have exchanged for the most precious wealth the earth can afford. I replied, however, that we were on a voyage of discovery towards the northern pole.

Upon hearing this he appeared satisfied, and consented to come on board. Good God! Margaret, if you had seen the man who thus capitulated for his safety, your surprise would have been boundless. His limbs were nearly frozen, and his body dreadfully emaciated by fatigue and suffering. I never saw a man in so wretched a condition. We attempted to carry him into the cabin; but as soon as he had quitted the fresh air, he fainted. We accordingly brought him back to the deck, and restored him to animation by rubbing him with brandy,[51] and forcing him to swallow a small quantity. As soon as he shewed signs of life, we wrapped him up in blankets, and placed him near the chimney of the kitchen-stove. By slow degrees he recovered, and ate a little soup, which restored him wonderfully.

Two days passed in this manner before he was able to speak; and I often feared that his sufferings had deprived him of understanding. When he had in some measure recovered, I removed him to my own cabin, and attended on him as much as my duty would permit. I never saw a more interesting creature: his eyes have generally an expression of wildness, and even madness; but there are moments when, if any one performs an act of kindness towards him, or does him any the most trifling service, his whole countenance is lighted up, as it were, with a beam of benevolence and sweetness that I never saw equalled. But he is generally melancholy and despairing; and sometimes he gnashes his teeth, as if impatient of the weight of woes that oppresses him.

When my guest was a little recovered, I had great trouble to keep off the men, who wished to ask him a thousand questions; but I would not allow him to be tormented by their idle curiosity, in a state of body and mind whose restoration evidently depended upon entire repose. Once, however, the lieutenant asked, Why he had come so far upon the ice in so strange a vehicle?

His countenance instantly assumed an aspect of the deepest gloom; and he replied, "To seek one who fled from me."

"And did the man whom you pursued travel in the same fashion?"

"Yes."

"Then I fancy we have seen him; for, the day before we picked you up, we saw some dogs drawing a sledge, with a man in it, across the ice."

This aroused the stranger's attention; and he asked a multitude of questions concerning the route which the daemon, as he called him, had pursued. Soon after, when he was alone with me, he said, "I have, doubtless, excited your curiosity, as well as that of these good people; but you are too considerate to make inquiries."

"Certainly; it would indeed be very impertinent and inhuman in me to trouble you with any inquisitiveness of mine."

"And yet you rescued me from a strange and perilous situation; you have benevolently restored me to life."

Soon after this he inquired, if I thought that the breaking up of the ice had destroyed the other sledge? I replied, that

52. The preceding phrase is omitted in the 1831 edition, and the following is substituted: "From this time a new spirit of life animated the decaying frame of the stranger. He manifested the greatest eagerness to be upon deck[.]"

53. The balance of this paragraph and the entirety of the next have been substantially revised in the 1831 edition, as follows:

He has frequently conversed with me on mine, which I have communicated to him without disguise. He entered attentively into all my arguments in favour of my eventual success and into every minute detail of the measures I had taken to secure it. I was easily led by the sympathy which he evinced to use the language of my heart, to give utterance to the burning ardour of my soul and to say, with all the fervour that warmed me, how gladly I would sacrifice my fortune, my existence, my every hope, to the furtherance of my enterprise. One man's life or death were but a small price to pay for the acquirement of the knowledge which I sought, for the dominion I should acquire and transmit over the elemental foes of our race. As I spoke, a dark gloom spread over my listener's countenance. At first I perceived that he tried to suppress his emotion; he placed his hands before his eyes, and my voice quivered and failed me as I beheld tears trickle fast from between his fingers; a groan burst from his heaving breast. I paused; at length he spoke, in broken accents: "Unhappy man! Do you share my madness? Have you drunk also of the intoxicating draught? Hear me; let me reveal my tale, and you will dash the cup from your lips!"

Such words, you may imagine, strongly excited my curiosity; but the paroxysm of grief that had seized the stranger overcame his weakened

I could not answer with any degree of certainty; for the ice had not broken until near midnight, and the traveller might have arrived at a place of safety before that time; but of this I could not judge.

From this time the stranger seemed very eager to be upon deck,[52] to watch for the sledge which had before appeared; but I have persuaded him to remain in the cabin, for he is far too weak to sustain the rawness of the atmosphere. But I have promised that some one should watch for him, and give him instant notice if any new object should appear in sight.

Such is my journal of what relates to this strange occurrence up to the present day. The stranger has gradually improved in health, but is very silent, and appears uneasy when any one except myself enters his cabin. Yet his manners are so conciliating and gentle, that the sailors are all interested in him, although they have had very little communication with him. For my own part, I begin to love him as a brother; and his constant and deep grief fills me with sympathy and compassion. He must have been a noble creature in his better days, being even now in wreck so attractive and amiable.

I said in one of my letters, my dear Margaret, that I should find no friend on the wide ocean; yet I have found a man who, before his spirit had been broken by misery, I should have been happy to have possessed as the brother of my heart.

I shall continue my journal concerning the stranger at intervals, should I have any fresh incidents to record.

August 13th, 17—.

My affection for my guest increases every day. He excites at once my admiration and my pity to an astonishing degree. How can I see so noble a creature destroyed by misery without feeling the most poignant grief? He is so gentle, yet so wise; his mind is so cultivated; and when he speaks, although his words are culled with the choicest art, yet they flow with rapidity and unparalleled eloquence. He is now much recovered from his illness, and is continually on the deck, apparently watching for the sledge that preceded his own. Yet, although unhappy, he is not so utterly occupied by his own misery, but that he interests himself deeply in the employments of others.[53] He has asked me many questions concerning my design; and I have related my little history frankly to him. He appeared pleased with the confidence, and suggested several alterations in my plan, which I shall find exceedingly useful. There is no pedantry in his manner; but all he does appears to spring solely from the interest he instinctively takes in the welfare of those who surround him. He is often overcome by gloom, and then he sits by himself, and tries to overcome all that is sullen or unsocial in his humour.[54] These paroxysms pass from him like a cloud from before the sun, though his dejection never leaves him.[55] I have endeavoured to win his confidence; and I trust that I have succeeded. One day I mentioned to him the desire I had always felt of finding a friend who might sympathize with me, and direct me by his counsel. I said, I did not belong to that class of men who are offended by advice. "I am self-educated, and perhaps I hardly rely sufficiently upon my own powers. I wish therefore that my companion should be wiser and more experienced than myself, to confirm and support me; nor have I believed it impossible to find a true friend."

"I agree with you," replied the stranger, "in believing that friendship is not only a desirable, but a possible acquisition. I once had a friend, the most noble of human creatures, and am entitled, therefore, to judge respecting friendship. You have hope, and the world before you, and have no cause for despair. But I—I have lost every thing, and cannot begin life anew."

As he said this, his countenance became expressive of a calm settled grief, that touched me to the heart. But he was silent, and presently retired to his cabin.

Even broken in spirit as he is, no one can feel more deeply than he does the beauties of nature. The starry sky, the sea, and every sight afforded by these wonderful regions, seems still to have the power of elevating his soul from earth. Such a man has a double existence: he may suffer misery, and be overwhelmed by disappointments; yet when he has retired into himself, he will be like a celestial spirit, that has a halo around him, within whose circle no grief or folly ventures.

Will you laugh[56] at the enthusiasm I express concerning this divine wanderer? If you do, you must have certainly lost

powers, and many hours of repose and tranquil conversation were necessary to restore his composure. Having conquered the violence of his feelings, he appeared to despise himself for being the slave of passion; and quelling the dark tyranny of despair, he led me again to converse concerning myself personally. He asked me the history of my earlier years. The tale was quickly told, but it awakened various trains of reflection. I spoke of my desire of finding a friend, of my thirst for a more intimate sympathy with a fellow mind than had ever fallen to my lot, and expressed my conviction that a man could boast of little happiness who did not enjoy this blessing. "I agree with you," replied the stranger, "we are unfashioned creatures, but half made up, if one wiser, better, dearer than ourselves—such a friend ought to be—do[es] not lend his aid to perfectionate our weak and faulty natures. I once had a friend, the most noble of human creatures, and am entitled, therefore, to judge respecting friendship. You have hope, and the world before you, and have no cause for despair. But I—I have lost everything and cannot begin life anew."

In this eloquent disquisition by Walton, beautifully expressed in "the language of [his] heart," the explorer reveals his lofty ideals, only to have them dashed by Victor. In this version, Victor appears to believe that his tale is an important lesson; he reveals the "madness" that drove him to cure Walton of a similar obsession. Yet as will be seen, Mary Shelley altered her original depiction of Victor: In the 1818 edition, he is a man led astray by overly high ambitions, racked with guilt, while in the 1831 edition, he excuses his conduct on the grounds that he was an unfortunate victim of fate, and therefore not responsible for the outcome.

Anne K. Mellor's "Choosing a Text of *Frankenstein*" (in Stephen C. Behrendt's *Approaches to Teaching Shelley's* Frankenstein) makes a compelling case that Mary Shelley's philosophical views themselves changed between 1818 and 1831—the cumulative effect of the deaths of two of her children and Percy Shelley, as well as her difficult financial situation. "These events convinced Mary Shelley that human events are decided not by personal choice or free will but by an indifferent destiny or fate," Mellor writes. "The values implicitly espoused in the first edition of *Frankenstein*—that nature is a nurturing and benevolent life force that punishes only those who transgress against its sacred rights, that Victor is morally responsible for his acts, that the creature is potentially good but driven to evil by social and parental neglect, that a family like the De Laceys that loves all its children equally offers the best hope for human happiness, and that human egotism causes the greatest suffering in the world—are all rejected in the 1831 revisions." Specific instances of these revisions will be noted below. Even the Introduction added to the 1831 edition (see Appendix 1, below) reflects this shift in Mary Shelley's views, as she describes herself as having been "compelled" to write by an imagination that, "unbidden," possessed and guided her.

54. The ancient Greeks posited that a person's outlook and behavior were dictated by the four fluids, or humors, circulating in the body: yellow bile, black bile, phlegm, and blood. Not discredited until the nineteenth century, the philosophy led physicians to attempt cures for physical and mental illnesses through reductions or rebalancing of one or more humors, often through bleeding or purgatives. "Humor" became synonymous with mental condition or temperament.

that simplicity which was once your characteristic charm. Yet, if you will, smile at the warmth of my expressions, while I find every day new causes for repeating them.[57]

August 19th, 17—.

Yesterday the stranger said to me, "You may easily perceive, Captain Walton, that I have suffered great and unparalleled misfortunes. I had determined, once,[58] that the memory of these evils should die with me; but you have won me to alter my determination. You seek for knowledge and wisdom, as I once did; and I ardently hope that the gratification of your wishes may not be a serpent to sting you, as mine has been. I do not know that the relation of my misfortunes will be useful to you, yet, if you are inclined, listen to my tale.[59] I believe that the strange incidents connected with it will afford a view of nature, which may enlarge your faculties and understanding. You will hear of powers and occurrences, such as you have been accustomed to believe impossible: but I do not doubt that my tale conveys in its series internal evidence of the truth of the events of which it is composed."

You may easily conceive[60] that I was much gratified by the offered communication; yet I could not endure that he should renew his grief by a recital of his misfortunes. I felt the greatest eagerness to hear the promised narrative, partly from curiosity and partly from a strong desire to ameliorate his fate, if it were in my power. I expressed these feelings in my answer.

"I thank you," he replied, "for your sympathy, but it is useless; my fate is nearly fulfilled. I wait but for one event, and then I shall repose in peace. I understand your feeling," continued he, perceiving that I wished to interrupt him; "but you are mistaken, my friend, if thus you will allow me to name you; nothing can alter my destiny: listen to my history, and you will perceive how irrevocably it is determined."

He then told me, that he would commence his narrative the next day when I should be at leisure. This promise drew from me the warmest thanks. I have resolved every night, when I am not engaged,[61] to record, as nearly as possible in his own words, what he has related during the day.

If I should be engaged, I will at least make notes. This manuscript will doubtless afford you the greatest pleasure: but to me, who know him, and who hear it from his own lips, with what interest and sympathy shall I read it in some future day![62]

55. This and a portion of the previous sentence (beginning following the word "gloom") are replaced in the Thomas Text with the following: "Which veils his countenance like deep night—he neither speaks or notices anything around him, but sitting on a gun will gaze on the sea and I have sometimes observed his dark eyelash wet with a tear which falls silently in the deep. This unobtrusive sorrow excites in me the most painful interest, and he will at times reward my sympathy by throwing aside this veil of moral woe, and then his ardent looks, his deep toned voice and powerful eloquence entrance me with delight." This florid addition, which, in the view of some critics (see text accompanying note 20, Appendix 5, below), suggests the arousal of homoerotic feelings in Walton, was cast aside in the 1831 edition.

56. The word "laugh" is replaced by "smile" in the 1831 edition.

57. This sentence and the preceding sentence have been replaced in the 1831 edition by the following:

> You would not if you saw him. You have been tutored and refined by books and retirement from the world, and you are therefore somewhat fastidious; but this only renders you the more fit to appreciate the extraordinary merits of this wonderful man. Sometimes I have endeavoured to discover what quality it is which he possesses that elevates him so immeasurably above any other person I ever knew. I believe it to be an intuitive discernment, a quick but never-failing power of judgment, a penetration into the causes of things, unequalled for clearness and precision; add to this a facility of expression and a voice whose varied intonations are soul-subduing music.

Victor here is credited with characteristics not evidenced by his actions—far more so than is the character revealed in the 1818 edition. There, his "power of judgment" regarding the consequences of his own actions is highly questionable, and he is criminally slow to understand that the creature's threats are leveled not at him but at the people around him. Furthermore, this is the only place in either edition in which Victor's voice is described as being pleasing and sonorous. It is also the only place in which observations of Victor are expressed to a listener.

58. The word "once" is replaced by "at one time" in the 1831 edition.

59. This sentence and the two following sentences are replaced in the 1831 edition by the following:

> I do not know that the relation of my disasters will be useful to you; yet, when I reflect that you are pursuing the same course, exposing yourself to the same dangers which have rendered me what I am, I imagine that you may deduce an apt moral from my tale, one that may direct you if you succeed in your undertaking and console you in case of failure. Prepare to hear of occurrences which are usually deemed marvellous. Were we among the tamer scenes of nature I might fear to encounter your unbelief, perhaps your ridicule; but many things will appear possible in these wild and mysterious regions which would provoke the laughter of those unacquainted with the ever-varied powers of nature; nor can I doubt but that my tale conveys in its series internal evidence of the truth of the events of which it is composed.

Here Shelley makes Victor into a moralizer. He tells his tale not to unburden himself but rather to explicitly convey "an apt moral." Frankenstein apparently has learned nothing from his own "disasters": Rather than expressing feelings of guilt regarding his tragedy or attempting to persuade Walton from his course, he hopes only to aid Walton in his endeavors. Shortly—at least in the time frame recounted by Walton's letters—Victor will exhort Walton's men to move ahead recklessly with their expedition.

60. The word "imagine" is used in place of "conceive" in the 1831 edition.

61. The word "engaged" is replaced by "imperatively occupied by my duties" in the 1831 edition, an effort, perhaps, to justify why Walton's record is incomplete.

62. The letter concludes with the following paragraphs in the 1831 edition:

> Even now, as I commence my task, his full-toned voice swells in my ears; his lustrous eyes dwell on me with all their melancholy sweetness; I see his thin hand raised in animation, while the lineaments of his face are irradiated by the soul within.
> Strange and harrowing must be his story, frightful the storm which embraced the gallant vessel on its course and wrecked it—thus!

This depiction of Victor as almost saintlike in mien prepares us for Shelley's revised version of him as a victim of fate.

CHAPTER I.

I AM BY BIRTH a Genevese; and my family is one of the most distinguished of that republic.[1] My ancestors had been for many years counsellors and syndics;[2] and my father had filled several public situations with honour and reputation. He was respected by all who knew him for his integrity and indefatigable attention to public business. He passed his younger days perpetually occupied by the affairs of his country; and it was not until the decline of life that he thought of marrying, and bestowing on the state sons who might carry his virtues and his name down to posterity.[3]

As the circumstances of his marriage illustrate his character, I cannot refrain from relating them. One of his most intimate friends was a merchant, who, from a flourishing state, fell, through numerous mischances, into poverty. This man, whose name was Beaufort,[4] was of a proud and unbending disposition, and could not bear to live in poverty and oblivion in the same country where he had formerly been distinguished for his rank and magnificence. Having paid his debts, therefore, in the most honourable manner, he retreated with his daughter to the town of Lucerne,[5] where he lived unknown and in wretchedness. My father loved Beaufort with the truest friendship, and was deeply grieved by his retreat in these unfortunate circumstances. He grieved also for the loss of his society, and resolved to seek him out and

1. Geneva, the principal French-speaking city of Switzerland, was an independent city-state until the end of the eighteenth century, when it was annexed by France under the Directory (the government of the newly minted French Republic, overthrown by Napoleon in 1799). Its domain extended until 1815, when it was admitted to the Swiss Confederation by the Council of Vienna, the last of the Swiss cantons to join. See note 10, Preface, above, for a discussion of the historical significance of Geneva. As a Genevese and the descendant of Genevese, Victor's native tongue would have been French.

2. In Italy and parts of Switzerland, "syndic," or "sindaco," meant the mayor or head of administration of a commune or canton. In Geneva, the syndics were members of a council appointed to govern the republic. They were ousted by the Directory but resumed power in the nineteenth century.

3. This sentence has been substantially rewritten in the 1831 edition, where it reads as follows: "He passed his younger days perpetually occupied by the affairs

of his country; a variety of circumstances had prevented his marrying early, nor was it until the decline of life that he became a husband and the father of a family."

4. Probably originally "Beaumont"—that name has been corrected several places in the Draft.

5. Lucerne, a cantonal capital, had a population in 1797 of about 100,000, almost exclusively Catholics. Situated in the German-speaking region of Switzerland, it is highly scenic, framed by beautiful lakes and mountains, and was known in the early nineteenth century for the number and length of its bridges.

6. This sentence is substantially rewritten in the 1831 edition to read as follows: "He bitterly deplored the false pride which led his friend to a conduct so little worthy of the affection that united them. He lost no time in endeavouring to seek him out, with the hope of persuading him to begin the world again through his credit and assistance."

7. The fourth longest river in Switzerland, it runs through Lucerne on its way to the Rhine and the North Sea.

8. Straw-plaiting consisted of drying straw and weaving it into strips, used in the manufacture of hats and baskets. It was an industry dominated by women and young children, because the work could be performed at home, and it was said that a woman could earn more from straw-plaiting than could a man working in the fields. See Thomas George Austin, *The Straw Plaiting and Straw Hat and Bonnet Trade* (Luton: Patrick O'Doherty, 1871).

9. The succeeding eight paragraphs have been substantially revised in the 1831 edition; they read as follows:

endeavour to persuade him to begin the world again through his credit and assistance.[6]

Beaufort had taken effectual measures to conceal himself; and it was ten months before my father discovered his abode. Overjoyed at this discovery, he hastened to the house, which was situated in a mean street, near the Reuss.[7] But when he entered, misery and despair alone welcomed him. Beaufort had saved but a very small sum of money from the wreck of his fortunes; but it was sufficient to provide him with sustenance for some months, and in the mean time he hoped to procure some respectable employment in a merchant's house. The interval was consequently spent in inaction; his grief only became more deep and rankling, when he had leisure for reflection; and at length it took so fast hold of his mind, that at the end of three months he lay on a bed of sickness, incapable of any exertion.

His daughter attended him with the greatest tenderness; but she saw with despair that their little fund was rapidly decreasing, and that there was no other prospect of support. But Caroline Beaufort possessed a mind of an uncommon mould; and her courage rose to support her in her adversity. She procured plain work; she plaited straw;[8] and by various means contrived to earn a pittance scarcely sufficient to support life.

Several months passed in this manner. Her father grew worse; her time was more entirely occupied in attending him; her means of subsistence decreased; and in the tenth month her father died in her arms, leaving her an orphan and a beggar. This last blow overcame her; and she knelt by Beaufort's coffin, weeping bitterly, when my father entered the chamber. He came like a protecting spirit to the poor girl, who committed herself to his care, and after the interment of his friend he conducted her to Geneva, and placed her under the protection of a relation. Two years after this event Caroline became his wife.[9]

When my father became a husband and a parent, he found his time so occupied by the duties of his new situation, that he relinquished many of his public employments, and devoted himself to the education of his children. Of these I was the eldest, and the destined successor to all his labours and utility. No creature could have more tender parents than mine. My improvement and health were their constant care, especially as I remained for several years their only child. But before I continue my narrative, I must record an incident which took place when I was four years of age.

My father had a sister, whom he tenderly loved, and who had married early in life an Italian gentleman. Soon after her marriage, she had accompanied her husband into her[10] native country, and for some years my father had very little communication with her. About the time I mentioned she died; and a few months afterwards he received a letter from her husband, acquainting him with his intention of marrying an Italian lady, and requesting my father to take charge of the infant Elizabeth,[11] the only child of his deceased sister. "It is my wish," he said, "that you should consider her as your own daughter, and educate her thus. Her mother's fortune is secured to her, the documents of which I will commit to your keeping. Reflect upon this proposition; and decide whether you would prefer educating your niece yourself to her being brought up by a stepmother."[12]

My father did not hesitate, and immediately went to Italy, that he might accompany the little Elizabeth to her future home. I have often heard my mother say, that she was at that time the most beautiful child she had ever seen, and shewed signs even then of a gentle and affectionate disposition. These indications, and a desire to bind as closely as possible the ties of domestic love, determined my mother to consider Elizabeth as my future wife; a design which she never found reason to repent.

From this time Elizabeth Lavenza became my playfellow, and, as we grew older, my friend. She was docile and good tempered, yet gay and playful as a summer insect. Although she was lively and animated, her feelings were strong and deep, and her disposition uncommonly affectionate. No one could better enjoy liberty, yet no one could submit with more grace than she did to constraint and caprice. Her imagination was luxuriant, yet her capability of application was great. Her person was the image of her mind; her hazel eyes,

There was a considerable difference between the ages of my parents, but this circumstance seemed to unite them only closer in bonds of devoted affection. There was a sense of justice in my father's upright mind which rendered it necessary that he should approve highly to love strongly. Perhaps during former years he had suffered from the late-discovered unworthiness of one beloved and so was disposed to set a greater value on tried worth. There was a show of gratitude and worship in his attachment to my mother, differing wholly from the doting fondness of age, for it was inspired by reverence for her virtues and a desire to be the means of, in some degree, recompensing her for the sorrows she had endured, but which gave inexpressible grace to his behaviour to her. Everything was made to yield to her wishes and her convenience. He strove to shelter her, as a fair exotic is sheltered by the gardener, from every rougher wind and to surround her with all that could tend to excite pleasurable emotion in her soft and benevolent mind. Her health, and even the tranquillity of her hitherto constant spirit, had been shaken by what she had gone through. During the two years that had elapsed previous to their marriage my father had gradually relinquished all his public functions; and immediately after their union they sought the pleasant climate of Italy, and the change of scene and interest attendant on a tour through that land of wonders, as a restorative for her weakened frame.

From Italy they visited Germany and France. I, their eldest child, was born at Naples, and as an infant accompanied them in their rambles. I remained for several years their only child. Much as they were attached to each other, they seemed to draw inexhaustible stores of affection from a very mine of love to bestow them upon me. My mother's tender caresses and my father's smile of benevolent pleasure while regarding me are my first recollections. I was their plaything and their idol, and something better—their child, the innocent and helpless creature bestowed on them by heaven, whom to bring up to good, and whose future lot it was in their hands to direct to happiness or misery, according as they fulfilled their duties towards me. With this deep consciousness of what they owed towards the being to which they had given life, added to the active spirit of tenderness that animated both, it may be imagined that while during every hour of my infant life I received a lesson of patience, of charity, and of self-control, I was so guided by a silken cord that all seemed but one train of enjoyment to me. For a long time I was their only care. My mother had much desired to have a daughter, but I continued their single offspring. When I was about five years old, while making an excursion beyond the frontiers of Italy, they passed a week on the shores of the Lake of Como. Their benevolent disposition often made them enter the cottages of the poor. This, to my mother, was more than a duty; it was a necessity, a passion—remembering what she had suffered, and how she had been relieved—for her to act in her turn the guardian angel to the afflicted. During one of their walks a poor cot [cottage] in the foldings of a vale attracted their notice as being singularly disconsolate, while the number of half-clothed children gathered about it spoke of penury in its worst shape. One day, when my father had gone by himself to Milan, my mother, accompanied by me, visited this abode. She found a peasant and his wife, hard working, bent down by care and labour, distributing a scanty meal to five hungry babes. Among these there

although as lively as a bird's, possessed an attractive softness. Her figure was light and airy; and, though capable of enduring great fatigue, she appeared the most fragile creature in the world. While I admired her understanding and fancy, I loved to tend on her, as I should on a favourite animal; and I never saw so much grace both of person and mind united to so little pretension.

Every one adored Elizabeth. If the servants had any request to make, it was always through her intercession. We were strangers to any species of disunion and dispute; for although there was a great dissimilitude in our characters, there was an harmony in that very dissimilitude.[13] I was more calm and philosophical than my companion; yet my temper was not so yielding. My application was of longer endurance; but it was not so severe whilst it endured. I delighted in investigating the facts relative to the actual world; she busied herself in following the aerial creations of the poets. The world was to me a secret, which I desired to discover; to her it was a vacancy, which she sought to people with imaginations of her own.[14]

My brothers were considerably younger than myself; but I had a friend in one of my schoolfellows, who compensated for this deficiency. Henry Clerval[15] was the son of a merchant of Geneva, an intimate friend of my father. He was a boy of singular talent and fancy. I remember, when he was nine years old, he wrote a fairy tale, which was the delight and amazement of all his companions. His favourite study consisted in books of chivalry and romance; and when very young, I can remember, that we used to act plays composed by him out of these favourite books, the principal characters of which were Orlando,[16] Robin Hood, Amadis,[17] and St. George.[18]

No youth could have passed more happily than mine. My parents were indulgent, and my companions amiable. Our studies were never forced; and by some means we always had an end placed in view, which excited us to ardour in the prosecution of them. It was by this method, and not by emulation, that we were urged to application.[19] Elizabeth was not incited to apply herself to drawing, that her com-

The tale of Orlando (*La Chanson de Roland*) depicted in one illustration, from the *Grandes Chroniques de France*, artist unknown (1274–1422 CE).

panions might not outstrip her; but through the desire of pleasing her aunt, by the representation of some favourite scene done by her own hand. We learned Latin and English, that we might read the writings in those languages;[20] and so far from study being made odious to us through punishment, we loved application, and our amusements would have been the labours of other children. Perhaps we did not read so many books, or learn languages so quickly,[21] as those who are disciplined according to the ordinary methods; but what we learned was impressed the more deeply on our memories.[22]

In this description of our domestic circle I include Henry Clerval; for he was constantly with us. He went to school with me, and generally passed the afternoon at our house; for being an only child, and destitute of companions at home, his father was well pleased that he should find associates at

was one which attracted my mother far above all the rest. She appeared of a different stock. The four others were dark-eyed, hardy little vagrants; this child was thin and very fair. Her hair was the brightest living gold, and despite the poverty of her clothing, seemed to set a crown of distinction on her head. Her brow was clear and ample, her blue eyes cloudless, and her lips and the moulding of her face so expressive of sensibility and sweetness that none could behold her without looking on her as of a distinct species, a being heaven-sent, and bearing a celestial stamp in all her features. The peasant woman, perceiving that my mother fixed eyes of wonder and admiration on this lovely girl, eagerly communicated her history. She was not her child, but the daughter of a Milanese nobleman. Her mother was a German and had died on giving her birth. The infant had been placed with these good people to nurse: they were better off then. They had not been long married, and their eldest child was but just born. The father of their charge was one of those Italians nursed in the memory of the antique glory of Italy— one among the *schiavi ognor frementi* [literally, "slaves forever enraged"— the rebellious intelligentsia who, in the 1820s, inhabited Milan, dissenting from Austrian rule—clearly, long after the events recounted here and an anachronism introduced by Mary Shelley], who exerted himself to obtain the liberty of his country. He became the victim of its weakness. Whether he had died or still lingered in the dungeons of Austria was not known. His property was confiscated; his child became an orphan and a beggar. She continued with her foster parents and bloomed in their rude abode, fairer than a garden rose among dark-leaved brambles. When my father returned from Milan, he found playing with me in the hall

Robin Hood, by N. C. Wyeth (1917).

of our villa a child fairer than pictured cherub—a creature who seemed to shed radiance from her looks and whose form and motions were lighter than the chamois of the hills. The apparition was soon explained. With his permission my mother prevailed on her rustic guardians to yield their charge to her. They were fond of the sweet orphan. Her presence had seemed a blessing to them, but it would be unfair to her to keep her in poverty and want when Providence afforded her such powerful our house; and we were never completely happy when Clerval was absent.

I feel pleasure[23] in dwelling on the recollections of childhood, before misfortune had tainted my mind, and changed its bright visions of extensive usefulness into gloomy and narrow reflections upon self. But,[24] in drawing the picture of my early days, I must not omit to[25] record those events which led, by insensible steps to my after tale of misery: for when I would account to myself for the birth of that passion, which afterwards ruled my destiny, I find it arise, like a mountain river, from ignoble and almost forgotten sources; but, swelling as it proceeded, it became the torrent which, in its course, has swept away all my hopes and joys.

Natural philosophy is the genius that has regulated my fate; I desire therefore, in this narration, to state those facts which led to my predilection for that science. When I was thirteen years of age, we all went on a party of pleasure to the baths near Thonon:[26] the inclemency of the weather obliged us to remain a day confined to the inn.[27] In this house I chanced to find a volume of the works of Cornelius Agrippa.[28] I opened it with apathy; the theory which he attempts to demonstrate, and the wonderful facts which he relates, soon changed this feeling into enthusiasm. A new

Amadis de Gaula, Spanish edition (1533).

protection. They consulted their village priest, and the result was that Elizabeth Lavenza became the inmate of my parents' house—my more than sister—the beautiful and adored companion of all my occupations and my pleasures.

Everyone loved Elizabeth. The passionate and almost reverential attachment with which all regarded her became, while I shared it, my pride and my delight. On the evening previous to her being brought to my home, my mother had said playfully, "I have a pretty present for my Victor—tomorrow he shall have it." And when, on the morrow, she presented Elizabeth to me as her promised gift, I, with childish seriousness, interpreted her words literally and looked upon Elizabeth as mine—mine to protect, love, and cherish. All praises bestowed on her I received as made to a possession of my own. We called each other familiarly by the name of cousin. No word, no expression could body forth the kind of relation in which she stood to me— my more than sister, since till death she was to be mine only.

Chapter 2

We were brought up together; there was not quite a year difference in our ages. I need not say that we were strangers to any species of disunion or dispute. Harmony was the soul of our companionship, and the diversity and contrast that subsisted in our characters drew us nearer together. Elizabeth was of a calmer and more concentrated disposition; but, with all my ardour, I was capable of a more intense application and was more deeply smitten with the thirst for knowledge. She busied herself with following the aerial creations of the poets; and in the majestic and wondrous scenes which surrounded our Swiss home—the sublime shapes of the mountains, the changes of the seasons, tempest and calm, the silence of winter, and the life and turbulence of our Alpine summers—she found ample scope for admiration and delight. While my companion contemplated with a serious and satisfied spirit the magnificent appearances of things, I delighted in investigating their causes. The world was to me a secret, which I desired to divine. Curiosity, earnest research to learn the hidden laws of nature, gladness akin to rapture, as they were unfolded to me, are among the earliest sensations I can remember.

On the birth of a second son, my junior by seven years, my parents gave up entirely their wandering life and fixed themselves in their native country. We possessed a house in Geneva, and a *campagne* [country house] on Belrive [see note 46, below], the eastern shore of the lake, at the distance of rather more than a league from the city. We resided principally in the latter, and the lives of my parents were passed in considerable seclusion. It was my temper to avoid a crowd and to attach myself fervently to a few. I was indifferent, therefore, to my school-fellows in general; but I united myself in the bonds of the closest friendship to one among them. Henry Clerval was the son of a merchant of Geneva. He was a boy of singular talent and fancy. He loved enterprise, hardship, and even danger for its own sake. He was deeply read in books of chivalry and romance. He composed heroic songs and began to write many a tale of enchantment and knightly adventure. He tried to make us act plays and to enter into masquerades, in which the characters were drawn from the heroes of Roncesvalles, of the Round

Heiliger Georg (Saint George), attributed to Hans von Kulmbach, ca. 1510.

light seemed to dawn upon my mind; and, bounding with joy, I communicated my discovery to my father.[29] I cannot help remarking here the many opportunities instructors possess of directing the attention of their pupils to useful knowledge, which they utterly neglect.[30] My father looked carelessly at the title-page of my book, and said, "Ah! Cornelius Agrippa! My dear Victor,[31] do not waste your time upon this; it is sad trash."

If, instead of this remark, my father had taken the pains, to explain to me, that the principles of Agrippa had been entirely exploded, and that a modern system of science had been introduced, which possessed much greater powers than the ancient, because the powers of the latter were chimerical, while those of the former were real and practical; under such circumstances, I should certainly have thrown Agrippa aside, and,[32] with my imagination warmed as it was, should probably have applied myself to the more rational theory of chemistry which has resulted from modern discoveries. It is even possible, that the train of my ideas would never have received the fatal impulse that led to my ruin.[33] But the cursory glance my father had taken of my volume by no means assured me that he was acquainted with its contents; and I continued to read with the greatest avidity.

When I returned home, my first care was to procure the

Image of Heinrich Cornelius Agrippa, artist unknown.

Table of King Arthur, and the chivalrous train who shed their blood to redeem the holy sepulchre from the hands of the infidels.

No human being could have passed a happier childhood than myself. My parents were possessed by the very spirit of kindness and indulgence. We felt that they were not the tyrants to rule our lot according to their caprice, but the agents and creators of all the many delights which we enjoyed. When I mingled with other families I distinctly discerned how peculiarly fortunate my lot was, and gratitude assisted the development of filial love.

My temper was sometimes violent, and my passions vehement; but by some law in my temperature they were turned not towards childish pursuits but to an eager desire to learn, and not to learn all things indiscriminately. I confess that neither the structure of languages, nor the code of governments, nor the politics of various states possessed attractions for me. It was the secrets of heaven and earth that I desired to learn; and whether it was the outward substance of things or the inner spirit of nature and the mysterious soul of man that occupied me, still my inquiries were directed to the metaphysical, or in its highest sense, the physical secrets of the world.

Meanwhile Clerval occupied himself, so to speak, with the moral relations of things. The busy stage of life, the virtues of heroes, and the actions of men were his theme; and his hope and his dream was to become one among those whose names are recorded in story as the gallant and adventurous benefactors of our species. The saintly soul of Elizabeth shone like a shrine-dedicated lamp in our peaceful home. Her sympathy was ours; her smile, her soft voice, the sweet glance of her celestial eyes, were ever there to bless and animate us. She was the living spirit of love to soften and attract; I might have become sullen in my study, rough through the ardour of my nature, but that she was there to subdue me to a semblance of her own gentleness. And Clerval—could aught ill entrench on the noble spirit of Clerval? Yet he might not have been so perfectly humane, so thoughtful in his generosity, so full of kindness and tenderness amidst his passion for adventurous exploit, had she not unfolded to him the real loveliness of beneficence and made the doing good the end and aim of his soaring ambition.

Much is changed in this later version. Victor's parents become more laudable, and the May–September relationship between them is excused. Other changes are noted below.

10. A typographical error for "his," corrected in the Thomas Text and subsequent editions of the 1818 text.

11. Also, coincidentally, the name of Percy Shelley's mother and favorite sister. There are several instances in the Draft where Mary Shelley changed the name Myrtella to Elizabeth, suggesting that the Ur-Text named the character Myrtella. Myrtle is a symbol of love, held sacred by the goddess Venus.

Barbara Johnson observes, in "My Monster/My Self": "All the interesting, complex characters in the book are male . . . the females, on the other hand, are beautiful, gentle, selfless, boring nurturers and victims who never experience inner conflict or true desire." Johnson's criticism notwithstanding, Elizabeth is a fascinating character whose true strength is revealed in the context of the trial of her friend Justine. As will be seen, Elizabeth's

whole works of this author, and afterwards of Paracelsus[34] and Albertus Magnus.[35] I read and studied the wild fancies of these writers with delight; they appeared to me treasures known to few beside myself;[36] and although I often wished to communicate these secret stores of knowledge to my father, yet his indefinite[37] censure of my favourite Agrippa always withheld me. I disclosed my discoveries to Elizabeth, therefore, under a promise of strict secrecy; but she did not interest herself in the subject, and I was left by her to pursue my studies alone.

It may appear very strange, that a disciple of Albertus Magnus should arise in the eighteenth century; but our

Portrait of Paracelsus, copy of a lost work thought to be by Quentin Matsys.

Albertus Magnus, from a fresco by Tommaso da Modena (1352).

family was not scientific, and I had not attended any of the lectures given at the schools of Geneva. My dreams were therefore undisturbed by reality; and I entered with the greatest diligence into the search of the philosopher's stone[38] and the elixir of life.[39] But the latter obtained my most undivided attention: wealth was an inferior object; but what glory would attend the discovery, if I could banish disease from the human frame, and render man invulnerable to any but a violent death!

Nor were these my only visions. The raising of ghosts or devils was a promise liberally accorded by my favourite authors,[40] the fulfilment of which I most eagerly sought; and if my incantations were always unsuccessful, I attributed the failure rather to my own inexperience and mistake, than to a want of skill or fidelity in my instructors.[41]

The natural phenomena that take place every day before

experiences parallel those of Mary Shelley, who endured a stepmother, a female peer introduced into her beloved father's home, and who had a brother named William.

12. In the 1818 edition, we see that Elizabeth is the first cousin of Victor Frankenstein, the daughter of his father's sister. In the 1831 edition, Elizabeth has become the only child of a Milanese nobleman, orphaned and raised by peasants, who is taken away by Victor's parents from this loving family because it would be "unfair to her to keep her in poverty." Elizabeth then becomes a "gift" to Victor from his parents. In both versions, Elizabeth actually kills both her own biological mother (as did Mary Shelley) and her stepmother Caroline; in the 1831 edition, she has *two* stepmothers, the first of whom abandons her (for noble motives) and the second of whom she kills. Is it any wonder that in the later version Victor has so little regard for his own "child"?

13. This sentence was substantially revised and expanded by Percy Shelley.

14. This and the preceding sentence were added by Percy Shelley.

15. This is the first of two places in the Draft where Mary Shelley has corrected the name Carignan to Clerval, suggesting that the name Carignan appeared in the Ur-Text. Clerval is also spelled "Clairval" in early versions, suggesting an identification with Charles Clair*mont*, the stepbrother of Mary Shelley.

16. Orlando, or Roland, was a lieutenant of Charlemagne, celebrated in the eleventh-century *Chanson de Roland* and later in the Italian Renaissance works *Orlando Innamorato* and *Orlando Furioso*. He had

numerous adventures with his famous sword Durendal and horse Veillantif and became one of the chief figures of the literature of knight-errantry. Roland also became the subject of fairy tales, the most popular being a tale of his rescue of his sister from the King of Elfland. Robert Browning's 1855 epic poem *Childe Roland to the Dark Tower Came* was inspired by the fairy tale (and a line in *King Lear*), and Browning's poem in turn formed the framework for Stephen King's eight-volume *Dark Tower* series (1982–2012), with its central figure the gunslinger Roland Deschain. Roland is also echoed as Charles Rowland, one of the Dead Boy Detectives, in Neil Gaiman's *Sandman* epic and his comic series *The Children's Crusade* and *Books of Magic*.

17. Amadís, or Amadís de Gaula, was the son of King Perion of Gaul, and his numerous adventures were recounted in the first great Spanish work of knight-errantry, by Garci Rodríguez de Montalvo, written in the sixteenth century. The books influenced the conquistadores, who grew up reading the adventures of Amadís, as well as subsequent Romantic writers. His story is immortalized in five eponymous operas, by Lully (1684), Destouches (1699), Handel (1715), Johann Christian Bach (1779), and Massenet (1922).

18. St. George, a Roman soldier who lived at the end of the third century CE, is best remembered by the tale "St. George and the Dragon," a legend brought home by the Crusaders and later worked into his hagiography. *The Golden Legend, or Lives of the Saints*, compiled by Jacobus de Voragine, Archbishop of Genoa in 1275, and first published in 1470 (first English edition 1485), recounts the legend. In his journeys, George comes to the city of Silene, where a dragon has ravaged the countryside. The populace soon

our eyes did not escape my examinations. Distillation,[42] and the wonderful effects of steam,[43] processes of which my favourite authors were utterly ignorant, excited my astonishment; but my utmost wonder was engaged by some experiments on an air-pump,[44] which I saw employed by a gentleman whom we were in the habit of visiting.[45]

The ignorance of the early philosophers on these and several other points served to decrease their credit with me: but I could not entirely throw them aside, before some other system should occupy their place in my mind.

When I was about fifteen years old, we had retired to our house near Belrive,[46] when we witnessed a most violent and terrible thunder-storm. It advanced from behind the mountains of Jura;[47] and the thunder burst at once with frightful loudness from various quarters of the heavens. I remained, while the storm lasted, watching its progress with curiosity and delight. As I stood at the door, on a sudden I beheld a stream of fire issue from an old and beautiful oak, which stood about twenty yards from our house; and so soon as the dazzling light vanished, the oak had disappeared, and nothing remained but a blasted stump. When we visited it the next morning, we found the tree shattered in a singular manner. It was not splintered by the shock, but entirely reduced to thin ribbands[48] of wood. I never beheld any thing so utterly destroyed.[49]

The catastrophe of this tree excited my extreme astonishment; and[50] I eagerly inquired of my father the nature

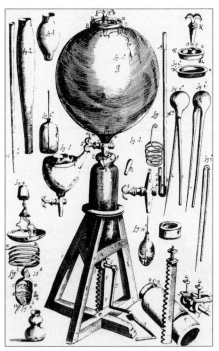

An air pump, constructed for Robert Boyle, from a drawing by Robert Hooke, ca. 1660.

The Château de Bellerive in the nineteenth century.

and origin of thunder and lightning. He replied, "Electricity;" describing at the same time the various effects of that power.[51] He constructed a small electrical machine, and exhibited a few experiments; he made also a kite, with a wire and string, which drew down that fluid from the clouds.[52]

This last stroke completed the overthrow of Cornelius Agrippa, Albertus Magnus, and Paracelsus, who had so long reigned the lords of my imagination. But by some fatality I did not feel inclined to commence the study of any modern system; and this disinclination was influenced by the following circumstance.

My father expressed a wish that I should attend a course of lectures upon natural philosophy, to which I cheerfully consented. Some accident prevented my attending these lectures until the course was nearly finished. The lecture, being therefore one of the last, was entirely incomprehensible to me.[53] The professor discoursed with the greatest fluency of potassium[54] and boron,[55] of sulphates[56] and oxyds,[57] terms to which I could affix no idea; and I became disgusted with the science of natural philosophy, although I still read Pliny[58] and Buffon[59] with delight, authors, in my estimation, of nearly equal interest and utility.

My occupations at this age were principally the mathematics, and most of the branches of study appertaining to that science.[60] I was busily employed in learning languages; Latin was already familiar to me, and I began to read some

tires of appeasing the dragon, especially when their children become the sacrifices. Eventually even the king's daughter is required to be offered to the dragon. George, passing by, learns of her plight and conquers the dragon with his sword and spear, whereupon, according to *The Golden Legend*, he entreats the maid: "Deliver to me your girdle, and bind it about the neck of the dragon and be not afeard." When she has done so, "the dragon followed her as it had been a meek beast and debonair." The couple leads the dragon into town, where George admonishes the townspeople to believe in God; he then slays the dragon. The king and fifteen thousand men were reportedly baptized following this great victory, and a church with a miraculous fountain was established. George went on to become the patron saint of England.

19. In *Politi cal Justice*, Mary Shelley's father, William Godwin, wrote: "Refer them to reading, to conversation, to meditation; but teach them neither creeds nor catechisms, either moral or political. . . . Speak the language of truth and reason to your child, and be under no apprehension for the result. Show him that what you recommend is valuable and desirable, and fear not but he will desire it. Convince his understanding, and you enlist all his powers animal and intellectual in your service."

20. It is possible that Elizabeth already spoke Italian, learning it as an infant, and certainly Victor and Elizabeth would also have been fluent in German, the predominant language of Switzerland; both Italian and German were commonly spoken in Geneva, in addition to the principal language of French. Victor only mentions English and Latin because they were *uncommon* languages to learn, at least for daily use. Victor undoubtedly made extensive use of his Latin in connection

with his studies: Much of the work of the alchemists that he read was published in Latin, and much of his course instruction at Ingolstadt University would have been in Latin. See note 17, Volume I, Chapter II, below.

21. The phrase following was added by Percy Shelley and seems to reflect his approbation of Godwin's methods.

22. The Thomas Text indicates that Mary Shelley determined to strike this entire paragraph and replace it with a less concrete passage: "With what delight do I even now remember the details of our domestic circle, and the happy years of my childhood. Joy attended on my steps— and the ardent affection that attached me to my excellent parents, my beloved Elizabeth, and Henry, the brother of my soul, has given almost a religious and sacred feeling to the recollection of a period passed beneath their eyes, and in their society."

23. The phrase is "exquisite pleasure" in the 1831 edition.

24. The word "But" is changed to "Besides" in the 1831 edition.

25. The phrase "must not admit to" is replaced by "also" in the 1831 edition.

26. Thonon-les-Bains is a town in the Rhône Alps, about twenty miles from Geneva; its population in 1838 was 3,740.

27. *Murray* reports that in 1838 the inn was called Les Balances and that it had been "improved of late."

28. Cornelius Agrippa (1486–1535), German magician-alchemist and philosopher, best known for his book on ritual magic *De Occulta Philosophia libri III* (Three Books of Occult Philosophy),

Benjamin Franklin Drawing Electricity from the Sky, by Benjamin West (1816).

of the easiest Greek authors without the help of a lexicon. I also perfectly understood English and German. This is the list of my accomplishments at the age of seventeen; and you may conceive that my hours were fully employed in acquiring and maintaining a knowledge of this various literature.

Another task also devolved upon me, when I became the instructor of my brothers. Ernest was six years younger than myself, and was my principal pupil. He had been afflicted with ill health from his infancy, through which Elizabeth and I had been his constant nurses: his disposition was gentle, but he was incapable of any severe application. William, the youngest of our family, was yet an infant, and the most beautiful little fellow in the world; his lively blue eyes, dimpled cheeks, and endearing manners, inspired the tenderest affection.

Such was our domestic circle, from which care and pain seemed for ever banished. My father directed our studies, and

Portrait of Georges-Louis Leclerc, Comte de Buffon, by François-Hubert Drouais (1753).

written in 1509 or 1510 and published in 1533. An incantation recorded in the book, said to invoke demonic beings, figures prominently in H. P. Lovecraft's *Case of Charles Dexter Ward*, first published in 1941.

29. This sentence does not appear in the 1831 edition.

30. This didactic comment is stricken in the Thomas Text.

31. This is the first mention of the narrator's first name. Curiously, it was a name frequently adopted by Percy Shelley as a pseudonym.

32. The balance of the sentence is revised in the 1831 edition: "have contented my imagination, warmed as it was, by returning with greater ardour to my former studies."

33. This sentence, the first equivocation by Victor about his measure of blame, was added by Percy Shelley. Psychoanalytic critics of *Frankenstein* point to this passage as a *pretext* (one of many such), a cover-up for Victor's oedipal hostility toward his father and of course a vast overreaction to a father's poor choice of tone of voice at a random moment. See, for example, Morton Kaplan and Robert Kloss's "Fantasy of Paternity and the Doppelgänger: Mary Shelley's *Frankenstein*," from their book *The Unspoken Motive: A Guide to Psychoanalytic Literary Criticism* (New York: Free Press, 1973).

34. Paracelsus, whose real name was Phillip von Hohenheim (1493–1541), was a German-Swiss alchemist and philosopher. He adopted the name Theophrastus Philippus Aureolus Bombastus von Hohenheim and, later, the title Paracelsus: "equal to or greater than Celsus."

(Celsus was a Roman doctor, philosopher, and encyclopedist.) Although most of Paracelsus's ideas and theories have in fact been "overthrown," he stands out in the history of medicine for his rejection of the ancient scholarship and his insistence on building anew on the basis of observation. Paracelsus is also credited with first suggesting that diseases might have a mental cause.

35. Albertus Magnus (ca. 1193–1280), also known as Albert the Great and Albert of Cologne, was a German Dominican friar and a Catholic bishop (and later, saint—today he is the patron saint of natural scientists) whose encyclopedic scholarship won him widespread fame. Among his students was St. Thomas Aquinas. Although alchemy and astrology were two of the subjects that interested him, many works on those topics have been falsely attributed to him, to the detriment of his modern reputation. Although some of his theories, like those of Paracelsus, have been discarded, again like Paracelsus, he is honored today for his stress on experimentation and observation and his rejection of dogmatic acceptance of the classic scholars.

36. The balance of this paragraph and the next are substantially revised in the 1831 edition to read as follows:

> besides myself. I have described myself as always having been imbued with a fervent longing to penetrate the secrets of nature. In spite of the intense labour and wonderful discoveries of modern philosophers, I always came from my studies discontented and unsatisfied. Sir Isaac Newton is said to have avowed that he felt like a child picking up shells beside the great and unexplored ocean of truth. Those of his successors in each branch of natural philosophy with whom I was

my mother partook of our enjoyments. Neither of us possessed the slightest pre-eminence over the other; the voice of command was never heard amongst us; but mutual affection engaged us all to comply with and obey the slightest desire of each other.

acquainted appeared even to my boy's apprehensions as tyros engaged in the same pursuit.

The untaught peasant beheld the elements around him and was acquainted with their practical uses. The most learned philosopher knew little more. He had partially unveiled the face of Nature, but her immortal lineaments were still a wonder and a mystery. He might dissect, anatomise, and give names; but, not to speak of a final cause, causes in their secondary and tertiary grades were utterly unknown to him. I had gazed upon the fortifications and impediments that seemed to keep human beings from entering the citadel of nature, and rashly and ignorantly I had repined.

But here were books, and here were men who had penetrated deeper and knew more. I took their word for all that they averred, and I became their disciple. It may appear strange that such should arise in the eighteenth century; but while I followed the routine of education in the schools of Geneva, I was, to a great degree, self-taught with regard to my favourite studies. My father was not scientific, and I was left to struggle with a child's blindness, added to a student's thirst for knowledge. Under the guidance of my new preceptors I entered with the greatest diligence into the search of the philosopher's stone [see note 38, below] and the elixir of life; but the latter soon obtained my most undivided attention. Wealth was an inferior object, but what glory would attend the discovery, if I could banish disease from the human frame, and render man invulnerable to any but a violent death!

There is little new here; the changes are primarily stylistic, expanding on Victor's seduction by the alchemists.

37. The word is "definite" in the Draft, as seems more apt.

38. The philosopher's stone, the quest for which was termed the "Great Work" of alchemy, was thought to be a substance that had various characteristics, depending on the alchemist: Paracelsus, for example, termed it "alkahest," the universal solvent, with the ability to dissolve anything or to change any substance into another (such as lead to gold). The seventeenth-century alchemist Eirenæus Philalethes, in *The Secret of the Immortal Liquor Called Alkahest, or Ignis-aqua* (1683), wrote: "It is a Catholic and Universal Menstruum, and, in a word, may be called (*Ignis-Aqua*) a Fiery Water, an uncompounded and immortal *ens*, which is penetrative, resolving all things into their first Liquid Matter, nor can anything resist its power, for it acteth without any reaction from the patient, nor doth it suffer from anything but its equal, by which it is brought into subjection; but after it hath dissolved all other things, it remaineth entire in its former nature, and is of the same virtue after a thousand operations as at the first." As late as 1797, it was noted in the *Encyclopædia Britannica* (3rd ed.) that "[t]he third method [of making gold] is by transmutation, or by turning all metals readily into pure gold, by melting them in the fire, and calling a little quantity of a certain preparation into the fused matter; upon which the feces [sediment] retire, are volatilized and burnt, and carried off, and the rest of the mass is turned into pure gold. That which works this change in the metals is called the philosopher's stone. . . . Whether this third method be possible or not, it is difficult to say. We have so many testimonies of it from persons who on all other occasions speak truth that it is hard to say they are guilty of direct falsehood, even when they say that they have been masters of the secret" (Vol. 14, 572).

39. The elixir of life, sometimes actually identified with the philosopher's stone, was said to grant eternal life or eternal youth. Accounts of the search for the elixir—known by hundreds of different names—can be found in ancient Chinese and Indian texts as well as European alchemical works. It was said to be possessed by the Comte de Saint-Germain, an eighteenth-century figure who claimed to be several hundred years old (not to be confused with the four-thousand-year-old vampire whose adventures have been recorded by Chelsea Quinn Yarbro), and Nicholas Flamel, a French scribe who lived in the fourteenth and fifteenth centuries. (Legend has it that Flamel was an alchemist of great skill, and that he is immortal; Michael Scott's fine *Secrets of the Immortal Nicholas Flamel* series sets him in the twentieth and twenty-first centuries.)

Contrary to its attitude toward the philosopher's stone, the 1797 *Encyclopædia Britannica* called the "panacea," the universal medicine, nostrum, or remedy for all diseases, "a thing impossible to be obtained" (Vol. 13, 686).

40. Including Cornelius Agrippa—see note 28, above. The Illuminati, or "the Enlightened" (see note 1, Volume I, Chapter II, below), also searched for a means whereby the initiated could achieve communication with the dead.

41. This passage was substantially expanded in the 1816 manuscript by Percy Shelley to refer to "favourite authors" and "fidelity" to their writings.

42. Distillation—separation of the components of a liquid by vaporization of the liquid and condensation of the vapor—was not new in the eighteenth century. The process was well known to the ancient Greeks; to the Chinese, who are said to have distilled beverages from rice

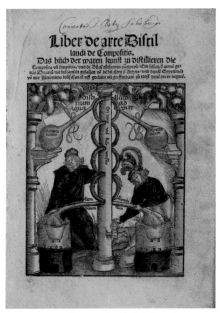

Hieronymus Brunschwig's *Liber de arte Distillandi de Compositis* (Strassburg, 1512).

by 800 BCE; and to Arab alchemists of the eighth and ninth centuries, among other cultures. In 1500, German alchemist Hieronymus Braunschwig published *Liber de arte distillandi (The Book of the Art of Distillation)*, originally written in German but graced with a Latin title, as pointed out by Alasdair A. MacDonald and Michael W. Twomey, the editors of *Schooling and Society: The Ordering and Reordering of Knowledge in the Western Middle Ages* (Dudley, MA: Peeters, 2004), 65, note 15. Braunschwig's work was translated into English in 1527. The first major work on technique and practice composed in English, probably based heavily on the Braunschwig, appeared in 1651 (*The Art of Distillation*, by the British physician John French [London: Printed by Richard Cotes], http://goo.gl/WdBZvK). "I rejoice as at the break of day after a long a tedious night," French wrote, "to see how this solary art of alchemy begins to shine forth out of the clouds of reproach which it has for a long time laid under." He was writing at a time when the use of spagyrical, or alchemical, preparations was being positively reconsidered.

43. It is unclear whether Victor here refers to steam distillation (see note 42, above) or the newly invented steam engine. The use of steam to produce mechanical motion probably dates from prehistoric times. The first patent for a steam engine was granted in 1606, to the Spanish mining administrator Jerónimo de Ayanz y Beaumont, whose invention represented a partial solution to flooded silver mines in Seville. (An entrepreneur, Ayanz also created one of the earliest air conditioners; ovens for domestic and industrial use, including in the metal industry; silver-extraction devices; and nautical pumps.) Nearly a decade later, the Englishman Thomas Savery, adapting the principle of the common pressure cooker (invented by French-British physicist Denis Papin, who was eventually to improve upon Savery's work by substituting a piston for the former's vacuum chamber, to provide better suction), patented the use of steam boilers to devise a continuously operating pump that removed water from mines. Savery's invention worked only in shallow mines, and there were frequent explosions caused by buildup of steam pressure (important to the running of Savery's system), and it was left to the Englishman Thomas Newcomen to create, in 1710, the "atmospheric engine," which used a piston, and whose steam-pressure level nearly matched atmospheric pressure. In 1781, probably around the time of Victor's early schooling (we extrapolate that Victor was born in 1772—see Appendix 2, below), the instrument maker James Watt patented a rotary engine powered by steam that improved still further on Newcomen's invention. Watt fashioned a discrete condenser to cut down on the huge amount of steam used in the process, thus obviating the need for constant cooling and reheating of the steam cylinder.

Eventually teaming up with the visionary and manufacturer (and his backer) Matthew Bouton, Watt coupled the condenser with a double-acting rotary steam engine. Thus the power of the steam cylinder was doubled. Numerous other improvements, including engine speed control and "sun and planet" gears, which made rotary motion out of linear motion, created a machine that was practical, cost effective, and efficient, and which quickly became the engine that literally drove the Industrial Revolution that was to sweep Europe.

44. The English chemist Robert Boyle did extensive work in the seventeenth century with the air pump (manufactured for him by the unsung genius Robert Hooke—for more on both men, see note 30, Volume I, Chapter II, below). *New Experiments Physico-Mechanical, Touching the Spring of the Air, and Its Effects*, an account of Boyle's explorations, was published in 1660. The book had its origins in a letter, composed in 1659, to the Right Honorable Charles Lord Viscount of Dungarvan, later a Fellow of the Royal Society (more formally, the Royal Society of London for Improving Natural Knowledge, established in 1660—not to be confused with the Royal Institution of Great Britain: see note 54, below). In the book Boyle gives full (and rare, in scientific history) credit to the twenty-three-year-old Hooke, and likewise credits the clockmaker's apprentice and instrument maker Ralph Greatorex (spelled variously as Greatrex, Gratorix, etc.), who had attempted to help him develop a prototype; and Otto von Guericke, whose own pneumatic pump had been described in 1657 by the Jesuit scholar and scientist Kaspar Schottus (also known as Gaspar Schott, Gaspare Schotto, etc.), in *Mechanicahydraulica-pneumatica* (*Mechanics of Gas Hydraulics*). The Otto von Geuricke University in Magdeburg, founded in 1993, is named for Guericke, a lawyer, mathema-

tician, and engineer who served as mayor of the city and is perhaps most famous for having paved the way for vacuum technology, in particular for having proven that even two teams of horses could not ("or only with great difficulty") pull apart two vacuum-sealed bronze hemispheres, or spherical shells.

Perhaps Victor simply was privy to a demonstration of the properties of air that Boyle had so thoroughly laid out in his writing. In any event, we can see no connection between his interest in distillation, steam, and air pumps and his later obsession with the study of biology.

45. This paragraph and the following paragraph are replaced in the 1831 edition with the following: "And thus for a time I was occupied by exploded systems, mingling, like an unadept, a thousand contradictory theories and floundering desperately in a very slough of multifarious knowledge, guided by an ardent imagination and childish reasoning, till an accident again changed the current of my ideas."

The "visiting gentleman" is discarded and replaced in a subsequent paragraph by a "man of great research," and Victor's conversion is explained in more detail, although changed from an "accident" to a "caprice" caused by the "guardian angel" in his life.

46. "Belle-rive," as it is more commonly spelled, "beautiful view," is a suburb on the western end of Lake Geneva, northeast of the city, only a few miles from the Villa Diodati (see Foreword, note 52, above).

47. The chain of mountains forming the northwest boundary of Switzerland. The Jurassic geologic period, the age of dinosaurs, is named after the mountain range, where strata of limestone indicative of the period were first found.

48. The word has been modernized to "ribbons" in the 1831 edition.

49. The balance of Chapter I has been replaced in the 1831 edition by the following:

Before this I was not unacquainted with the more obvious laws of electricity. On this occasion a man of great research in natural philosophy was with us, and excited by this catastrophe, he entered on the explanation of a theory which he had formed on the subject of electricity and galvanism, which was at once new and astonishing to me. All that he said threw greatly into the shade Cornelius Agrippa, Albertus Magnus, and Paracelsus, the lords of my imagination; but by some fatality the overthrow of these men disinclined me to pursue my accustomed studies. It seemed to me as if nothing would or could ever be known. All that had so long engaged my attention suddenly grew despicable. By one of those caprices of the mind which we are perhaps most subject to in early youth, I at once gave up my former occupations, set down natural history and all its progeny as a deformed and abortive creation, and entertained the greatest disdain for a would-be science which could never even step within the threshold of real knowledge. In this mood of mind I betook myself to the mathematics [see note 60, below] and the branches of study appertaining to that science as being built upon secure foundations, and so worthy of my consideration.

Thus strangely are our souls constructed, and by such slight ligaments are we bound to prosperity or ruin. When I look back, it seems to me as if this almost miraculous change of inclination and will was the immediate suggestion of the guardian angel of my life—the last effort made by the spirit of preservation to avert the storm that was even then hanging in the stars and ready to envelop me. Her victory was announced by an unusual tranquillity and gladness of soul which followed the relinquishing of my ancient and latterly tormenting studies. It was thus that I was to be taught to associate evil with their prosecution, happiness with their disregard.

It was a strong effort of the spirit of good, but it was ineffectual. Destiny was too potent, and her immutable laws had decreed my utter and terrible destruction.

50. The phrase "Among other questions suggested by natural objects" was suggested by Percy Shelley in the Draft but not used by Mary Shelley. Much of the preceding paragraph does not appear in the extant copy of the Draft, where a page has been torn off.

51. The word "electricity" first appeared in print in the English language in 1646, in Thomas Browne's *Pseudodoxia Epidemica*. Although some work was done in the seventeenth century by Robert Boyle and others, Benjamin Franklin's famous kite experiment in June 1752 demonstrated that lightning was indeed electrical in nature; the Frenchman Thomas François-Dalibard had conducted a similar experiment using different materials a month earlier. Franklin also worked with Leyden jars, used for storing electricity, coining the word "battery" to describe the greater charge held when several of the glass vessels were grouped together. The *Encyclopædia Britannica* (3rd ed., 1797) devotes 127 pages to the history of experimentation with electricity, describing in detail experiments for the reader to conduct. The history makes clear that ongoing research into the effects of electricity on vegetation and animal life (including, of course, humans) was wide-ranging, and an entire section is devoted to the discussion of "medical electricity," though there is no suggestion there that electricity was connected to vitality.

Certainly, the idea that electricity, or something like it, was responsible for life was in the air in the late eighteenth century. The great Scottish surgeon-anatomist John Hunter (1728–1793) wrote, in his posthumously published *Treatise on the Blood, Inflammation and Gunshot Wounds* (1794), "Mere composition of matter does not give life, for the dead body has all the composition it ever had; life is a property we do not understand; we can only see the necessary leading steps towards it." John Abernethy, Hunter's student, in his famous lecture "An Enquiry into the Probability and Rationality of Mr. Hunter's Theory of Life," published in 1814, wrote:

> The phænomena of electricity and of life correspond. Electricity may be attached to, or inhere, in a wire; it may be suddenly dissipated, or have its powers annulled, or it may be removed by degrees or in portions, and the wire may remain less and less strongly electrified, in proportion as it is abstracted. So life inheres in vegetables and animals; it may sometimes be suddenly dissipated, or have its powers abolished, though in general it is lost by degrees, without any apparent change taking place in the structure; and in either case putrefaction begins when life terminates.

Abernethy's views were publicly opposed by William Lawrence, the Shelleys' friend and Percy Shelley's physician, in numerous lectures and his book *Natural History of Man* (1819).

The 1930 play of *Frankenstein* by John L. Balderston and Garrett Fort first made explicit the idea that electricity was used to vivify the "monster" created by Victor Frankenstein, although in that play, it is combined with the "Elixir of Life," the details of which Victor discovered in "old black letter books." (See note 39, above.) In the earliest film, the Thomas Edison production *Frankenstein* (1910), Frankenstein is working with an unidentified alchemical mixture in a cauldron. Leaving the laboratory, he watches through a keyhole as the creature magically materializes, flesh appearing on bones and eyes and limbs taking shape. The iconic 1931 film by James Whale (script by Fort and Francis Edward Faragoh) drops the "Elixir" and uses electricity alone. Other films have used other methodologies—for example, in the 1973 television miniseries *Frankenstein: The True Story*, scripted by Christopher Isherwood and Don Bachardy, the creature is brought to life by solar energy. In Kenneth Branagh's 1994 *Mary Shelley's Frankenstein*, the creature is animated in a copper tank filled with amniotic fluid, into which electric eels are introduced through a long tube, in a scene that one critic said was "supposed to look like sexual intercourse."

Note that Mary Shelley's texts are vague about the means of animation. Bioelectricity—the electrical impulse that passes along nerves in living beings—was in fact not discovered until 1791, by Luigi Galvani. It is not mentioned in the 1797 *Britannica*. If Victor was born in 1772, as seems probable, then in 1787, when he was "about fifteen years old," "galvanism" was a meaningless term, and its introduction into the 1831 text is anachronistic. There is no mention by Clerval of any electrical equipment in Victor's abandoned laboratory, and it surely would have been impracticable to have used substantial electrical equipment on the remote Orkney island on which Victor claimed to have situated his second laboratory.

Portrait of Luigi Galvani, artist unknown.

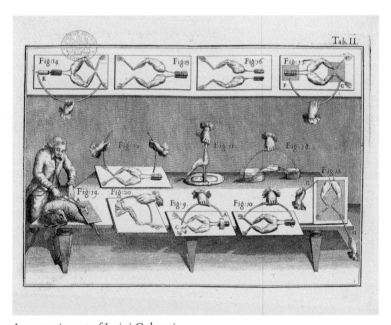

An experiment of Luigi Galvani.

52. This, according to popular belief, is the same experiment conducted by Franklin in June 1752. In a letter written to Peter Collinson on October 19, 1752, Franklin described the experiment:

Make a small cross of two light strips of cedar, the arms so long as to reach to the four corners of a large, thin silk handkerchief when extended; tie the corners of the handkerchief to the extremities of the cross, so you have the body of a kite; which being properly accommodated with a tail, loop, and string, will rise in the air, like those made of paper; but this being of silk, is fitter to bear the wet and wind of a thunder-gust without tearing. To the top of the upright stick of the cross is to be fixed a very sharp-pointed wire, rising a foot or more above the wood. To the end of the twine, next the hand, is to be tied a silk ribbon, and where the silk and twine join, a key may be fastened. This kite is to be raised when a thunder-gust appears to be coming on, and the person who holds the string must stand within a door or window, or under some cover, so that the silk ribbon may not be wet; and care must be taken that the twine does not touch the frame of the door or window. As soon as any of the thunder clouds come over the kite, the pointed wire will draw the electric fire from them, and the kite, with all the twine will be electrified, and the loose filaments of the twine will stand out every way and be attracted by an approaching finger. And when the rain has wet the kite and twine, so that it can conduct the electric fire freely, you will find it stream out plentifully from the key on the approach of your knuckle. At this key the phial may be charged; and from electric fire thus obtained, spirits may be kindled, and all the electric experiments be performed, which are usually done by the help of a rubbed glass globe or tube, and thereby the sameness of the electric matter with that of lightning com-

pletely demonstrated" (*Autobiography of Benjamin Franklin*, appendix [New York: Henry Holt & Company, 1916]).

53. This and the previous sentence are additions made principally by Percy Shelley.

54. Although potash, an alkaline salt containing potassium, was distinguished from the natural alkaline compound, popularly called soda, as early as 1702 by Georg Ernst Stahl, definite experimental proof of the differences between the two caustic substances was not found until 1735, by Henri-Louis Duhamel du Monceau. However, the exact chemical nature of these sodium and potassium compounds was not known, and Antoine Lavoisier's definitive list of simple substances, *Traité Élémentaire de Chimie* (*Elementary Treatise of Chemistry*), published in 1789, did not include potassium. Potassium was not isolated as a metal (and a distinct element) until Sir Humphry Davy used electrolysis in 1807 to refine it. Later that year, Davy also isolated sodium, using the same technique. His discovery of these new "simple substances" (in Lavoisier's terminology) electrified the European scientific community, though the admission that they were *elements* was slow in coming. It seems unlikely that the professor whose lecture Victor attended would have had much to say about potassium, other than noting its mysterious nature.

However, Percy Shelley, who had an intense interest in science, would certainly have been fascinated by the discovery of potassium, and Mary Shelley recorded in her journal (October 1816) that she was reading Sir Humphry Davy's "Chemistry." None of Davy's books bears that specific title, and while the identification is speculative, the text to which she refers is probably his *A Discourse, Intro-*

ductory to A Course of Lectures on Chemistry, the transcription of a lecture presented at the Royal Institution of Great Britain in January 1802 that not only includes many of the scientific ideas reflected in *Frankenstein* but also shares some of Victor's optimism about what science can achieve. See Laura Crouch's essay "Davy's *A Discourse, Introductory to A Course of Lectures on Chemistry*: A Possible Scientific Source of *Frankenstein*," *Keats-Shelley Journal* 27 (1978), 35–44. Davy, who is responsible for having discovered the effect on humans of nitrous oxide, or laughing gas, was appointed laboratory director and professor of chemistry of the Royal Institution in 1801, two years after its establishment in London at 21 Albemarle Street, also its present-day location. The organization is today styled the "Royal Institution" or "RI."

55. By the time of this lecture, around 1788–89, boric acid was a well-known naturally occurring medicinal compound, known as *sal sedativum*, found in hot springs (it was first observed in 1777). Boron itself was as unknown at this time as potassium, except in compounds. It was isolated in 1808 by Sir Humphry Davy, again using electrolysis and, later, potassium to separate it from boric acid. As had been the case with potassium, its recognition as an element was delayed. Again, one wonders what the professor might have said about the substance.

56. "Sulphates," or sulfates, are molecules combining sulfur and oxygen, and the transparent crystals of "vitriol salts," sulfate compounds derived from sulfuric acid, were well-known to alchemists.

57. Oxyds or oxides are molecules containing at least one atom of oxygen as well as one atom of another element. For example, water (H_2O) is an oxide;

Sir Humphry Davy, by Thomas Phillips (date unknown).

the most prevalent oxide is carbon dioxide (CO_2). Oxygen itself was not isolated until 1773–74, by Carl Wilhelm Scheele, Joseph Priestley, and Lavoisier, each working independently. Although carbon dioxide and other oxides, both minerals and gases, had been identified earlier, the modern idea of molecules was not really established until Lavoisier's *Elementary Treatise* in 1789.

58. Gaius Plinius Secundus, popularly known as Pliny the Elder (23–79 CE) was the author of the encyclopedic *Naturalis Historia*. The work was critically important to the development of the science of chemistry, containing a detailed account

Pliny the Elder.

of Roman knowledge of metallurgy and mineralogy. It was widely published, though by the late eighteenth century, the science was largely obsolete.

59. Georges-Louis Leclerc, Comte de Buffon (1707–1788), was a French naturalist, certainly the most important of the second half of the eighteenth century. His influence and work are summed up by Ernst Mayr, one of the twentieth century's leading evolutionary biologists and winner of the Crafoord Prize, awarded by the Royal Swedish Academy of Sciences:

> He was not an evolutionary biologist, yet he was the father of evolutionism. He was the first person to discuss a large number of evolutionary problems, problems that before Buffon had not been raised by anybody.... he brought them to the attention of the scientific world.
>
> Except for Aristotle and Darwin, no other student of organisms [whole animals and plants] has had as far-reaching an influence.
>
> He brought the idea of evolution into the realm of science. He developed a concept of the "unity of type," a precursor of comparative anatomy. More than anyone else, he was responsible for the acceptance of a long-time scale for the history of the earth. He was one of the first to imply that you get inheritance from your parents, in a description based on similarities between elephants and mammoths. And yet, he hindered evolution by his frequent endorsement of the immutability of species. He provided a criterion of species, fertility among members of a species that was thought impregnable. (*The Growth of Biological Thought* [Cambridge, MA: Harvard University Press, 1981])

60. "The mathematics" in the late eighteenth century encompassed many branches of study, including geometry, arithmetic, navigation, astronomy, and optics. In the previous century, planetary motion was intensely studied, and Newton and Leibniz had invented calculus to describe it. Descartes had created a means of graphing the orbits of planetary bodies, and Pascal and Fermat had begun applying mathematics to gambling and probability. The leading eighteenth-century mathematician was probably Leonhard Euler (1707–1783), whose principal fields of work were calculus and complex analysis as well as topology and combinatorics. Although Euler was Swiss and so would have attracted Victor's attention, he lived most of his life in Berlin and Russia. Euler was incredibly prolific, however, with his collected works extending to eighty volumes in some printings, and his work so impressed the mathematician Pierre-Simon, Marquis de Laplace, that he often declaimed, "Read Euler, read Euler, he is the master of us all." Joseph Louis Lagrange (1736–1813) developed number theory, differential calculus, and the calculus of variations, and Laplace (1749–1827) laid down the foundations of statistics and moved celestial mechanics to a science based on calculus.

CHAPTER II.

of Bavaria, the University of Ingolstadt was in the city of Ingolstadt, in the duchy of Bavaria-Ingolstadt (later combined with the duchy of Bavaria-Landshut). With faculties in humanities, sciences, theology, law, and medicine, it was a Christian university, its initial chancellor the Bishop of Eichstätt. The Jesuits arrived in 1549 and, while the order was dissolved in the late 1770s, Jesuit faculty members were not entirely displaced. By the end of the eighteenth century, the university had become a hotbed of intellectual ferment, under the influence of Adam Weishaupt, a professor of law and the founder of the society known as the Illuminati.

Born Jewish and raised by Jesuits after the death of his father when he was six, Weishaupt had converted to Protestantism while reading law at Ingolstadt but subsequently realigned himself with the Jesuits, for reasons that remain somewhat obscure. The announced goals of the Illuminati (or the Order of Perfectibilists, as they were first known) were opposition to superstition, prejudice, religious influence over public life, and abuses of state power: in short, a new, radical Enlightenment. Its

W HEN I HAD attained the age of seventeen, my parents resolved that I should become a student at the university of Ingolstadt.[1] I had hitherto attended the schools of Geneva; but my father thought it necessary for the completion of my education, that I should be made acquainted with other customs than those of my native country.[2] My departure was therefore fixed at an early date; but, before the day resolved upon could arrive, the first misfortune of my life occurred—an omen, as it were, of my future misery.

Elizabeth had caught the scarlet fever;[3] but her illness was not severe, and she quickly recovered. During her confinement, many arguments had been urged to persuade my mother to refrain from attending upon her. She had, at first, yielded to our entreaties; but when she heard that her favourite was recovering, she could no longer debar herself from her society, and entered her chamber long before the danger of infection was past.[4] The consequences of this imprudence were fatal. On the third day my mother sickened; her fever was very malignant, and the looks of her attendants prognosticated the worst event. On her death-bed the fortitude and benignity of this admirable[5] woman did not desert her. She joined the hands of Elizabeth and myself: "My children," she said, "my firmest hopes of future happiness were placed

Map of Ingolstadt, ca. 1700.

on the prospect of your union. This expectation will now be the consolation of your father. Elizabeth, my love, you must supply my place to your younger cousins.[6] Alas! I regret that I am taken from you; and, happy and beloved as I have been, is it not hard to quit you all? But these are not thoughts befitting me; I will endeavour to resign myself cheerfully to death, and will indulge a hope of meeting you in another world."

She died calmly; and her countenance expressed affection even in death. I need not describe the feelings of those whose dearest ties are rent by that most irreparable evil, the void that presents itself to the soul, and the despair that is exhibited on the countenance. It is so long before the mind can persuade itself that she, whom we saw every day, and whose very existence appeared a part of our own, can have departed

leaders were called Aeropagites, from the Greek *Areios pagos* (literally, hill of Ares), where the members of the highest Athenian tribunal, the Aeropagus, convened; the name "Dionysius the Aeropagite" may be found in the Bible (Acts 17:34).

Largely secret, and composed of rationalist freethinkers, the Illuminati exerted an influence at Ingolstadt University and in subsequent popular culture that was far out of proportion to the society's membership. Today, Weishaupt is invoked in comic books and other works (often purposely conflated with George Washington), and the phrase "the Illuminati" is frequently used to refer to presumed masterminds of the world order.

Portrait of Adam Weishaupt, possibly by C. K. Mansinger (1799).

The Illuminati have been credited by conspiracy theorists with fomenting the French Revolution and acting as the force behind many other events. However, historical research suggests that the society effectively disbanded in 1785, with Weishaupt's banishment following dismissal from the university amid accusations of sedition. Said to have nonetheless been offered a pension by school authorities, he refused it, eventually assuming a professorship at the University of Göttingen. Effective 1784, all secret societies were banned in Bavaria by edict of Duke Karl Theodor, the elector palatinate, with membership punishable by death; the Illuminati were specially singled out by further edicts issued over the next several years.

In 1800, the university was shut down, purportedly for financial reasons (one of several preemptive closings in its history), and was moved to Landshut. Two years later it was renamed Ludwig Maximilian

for ever—that the brightness of a beloved eye can have been extinguished, and the sound of a voice so familiar, and dear to the ear, can be hushed, never more to be heard. These are the reflections of the first days; but when the lapse of time proves the reality of the evil, then the actual bitterness of grief commences. Yet from whom has not that rude hand rent away some dear connexion; and why should I describe a sorrow which all have felt, and must feel? The time at length arrives, when grief is rather an indulgence than a necessity; and the smile that plays upon the lips, although it may be deemed a sacrilege, is not banished. My mother was dead, but we had still duties which we ought to perform; we must continue our course with the rest,[7] and learn to think ourselves fortunate, whilst one remains whom the spoiler has not seized.

My journey to[8] Ingolstadt, which had been deferred by these events, was now again determined upon. I obtained from my father a respite of some weeks. This period was spent sadly; my mother's death, and my speedy departure,

The death of Caroline Frankenstein? (*The Dying Mother* by English engraver Thomas Allom, early nineteenth century.)

depressed our spirits; but Elizabeth endeavoured to renew the spirit of cheerfulness in our little society.[9] Since the death of her aunt, her mind had acquired new firmness and vigour. She determined to fulfil her duties with the greatest exactness; and she felt that that most imperious duty, of rendering her uncle and cousins happy, had devolved upon her. She consoled me, amused her uncle, instructed my brothers; and I never beheld her so enchanting as at this time, when she was continually endeavouring to contribute to the happiness of others, entirely forgetful of herself.

The day of my departure at length arrived.[10] I had taken leave of all my friends, excepting Clerval, who spent the last evening with us. He bitterly lamented that he was unable to accompany me: but his father could not be persuaded to part with him, intending that he should become a partner with him in business,[11] in compliance with his favourite theory, that learning was superfluous in the commerce of ordinary life. Henry had a refined mind; he had no desire to be idle, and was well pleased to become his father's partner, but he believed that a man might be a very good trader, and yet possess a cultivated understanding.[12]

We sat late, listening to his complaints, and making many little arrangements for the future. The next morning early I departed. Tears gushed from the eyes of Elizabeth; they proceeded partly from sorrow at my departure, and partly because she reflected that the same journey was to have taken place three months before, when a mother's blessing would have accompanied me.

I threw myself into the chaise[13] that was to convey me away, and indulged in the most melancholy reflections. I, who had ever been surrounded by amiable companions, continually engaged in endeavouring to bestow mutual pleasure, I was now alone. In the university, whither I was going, I must form my own friends, and be my own protector. My life had hitherto been remarkably secluded and domestic; and this had given me invincible repugnance to new countenances. I loved my brothers, Elizabeth, and Clerval; these were "old familiar faces;"[14] but I believed myself totally unfitted for the company of strangers. Such were my reflections

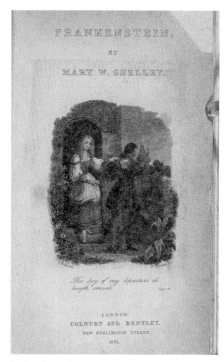

"The day of my departure at length arrived." Illustration from *Frankenstein* (1831), artist unknown.

University, and in 1826 it was moved to Munich, where it is located today, styled LMU.

2. Thus in Victor's mind he is not to blame for departing Geneva—he is forced by his father (with whom his mother sides) to leave the family home.

3. The balance of the sentence and the following three sentences have been replaced in the 1831 edition by the following: "her illness was severe, and she was in the greatest danger. During her illness many arguments had been urged to persuade my mother to refrain from attending upon her. She had, at first, yielded to our entreaties; but when she heard that the life of her favourite was menaced, she could no longer control her anxiety. She attended her sickbed; her watchful atten-

Ingolstadt town hall (photo by Brian Snelson, used under CC-by-SA 2.0 license).

tions triumphed over the malignity of the distemper—Elizabeth was saved, but the consequences of this imprudence were fatal to her preserver. On the third day my mother sickened; her fever was accompanied by the most alarming symptoms, and the looks of her medical attendants prognosticated the worst event."

Thus, because her illness was *severe*, Elizabeth could be viewed by Victor as blameless in the death of Victor's mother. This is a subtle change but important in undermining a psychoanalytic reading of the tale as Victor's unconscious persecution of Elizabeth for depriving him of his mother. This reading is largely based on Victor's post-Creation dream of kissing Elizabeth, who transforms in the dream into his mother's corpse, but interestingly, though Shelley here lessens Elizabeth's blame, she did not later eliminate the strange dream from the text.

Scarlet fever, also historically called scarlatina, was probably known to the Greeks and was first definitively recorded in 1553, in *De Tumoribus praeter Naturam*, by the Sicilian anatomist and

as I commenced my journey; but as I proceeded, my spirits and hopes rose. I ardently desired the acquisition of knowledge. I had often, when at home, thought it hard to remain during my youth cooped up in one place, and had longed to enter the world, and take my station among other human beings. Now my desires were complied with, and it would, indeed, have been folly to repent.

I had sufficient leisure for these and many other reflections during my journey to Ingolstadt, which was long and fatiguing.[15] At length the high white steeple of the town met my eyes. I alighted, and was conducted to my solitary apartment, to spend the evening as I pleased.

The next morning I delivered my letters of introduction, and paid a visit to some of the principal professors,[16] and among others to M.[17] Krempe, professor of natural philosophy. He received me with politeness, and asked me several questions concerning my progress in the different branches of science appertaining to natural philosophy. I mentioned, it is true, with fear and trembling, the only authors I had ever read upon those subjects. The professor stared: "Have you," he said, "really spent your time in studying such nonsense?"

I replied in the affirmative. "Every minute," continued M. Krempe with warmth, "every instant that you have wasted on those books is utterly and entirely lost. You have burdened your memory with exploded systems, and useless names. Good God! in what desert land have you lived, where no one was kind enough to inform you that these fancies, which you have so greedily imbibed, are a thousand years old, and as musty as they are ancient? I little expected in this enlightened and scientific age to find a disciple of Albertus Magnus and Paracelsus. My dear Sir, you must begin your studies entirely anew."

So saying, he stept aside, and wrote down a list of several

books treating of natural philosophy, which he desired me to procure, and dismissed me, after mentioning that in the beginning of the following week he intended to commence a course of lectures upon natural philosophy in its general relations, and that M. Waldman,[18] a fellow-professor, would lecture upon chemistry the alternate days that he missed.[19]

I returned home, not disappointed, for I had long considered those authors useless whom the professor had so strongly reprobated; but I did not feel much inclined to study the books which I procured at his recommendation.[20] M. Krempe was a little squat man, with a gruff voice and repulsive countenance;[21] the teacher, therefore, did not prepossess me in favour of his doctrine.[22] Besides, I had a contempt for the uses of modern natural philosophy. It was very different, when the masters of the science sought immortality and power; such views, although futile, were grand:[23] but now the scene was changed. The ambition of the inquirer seemed to limit itself to the annihilation of those visions on which my interest in science was chiefly founded. I was required to exchange chimeras of boundless grandeur for realities of little worth.

Such were my reflections during the first two or three days[24] spent almost in solitude. But as the ensuing week commenced, I thought of the information which M. Krempe had given me concerning the lectures. And although I could not consent to go and hear that little conceited fellow deliver sentences out of a pulpit, I recollected what he had said of M. Waldman, whom I had never seen, as he had hitherto been out of town.

Partly from curiosity, and partly from idleness, I went into the lecturing room, which M. Waldman entered shortly after. This professor was very unlike his colleague. He appeared about fifty years of age, but with an aspect expressive of the greatest benevolence;[25] a few gray hairs covered his temples, but those at the back of his head were nearly black. His person was short, but remarkably erect; and his voice the sweetest I had ever heard. He began his lecture by a recapitulation of the history of chemistry and the various improvements made by different men of learning, pronouncing with fervour the names of the most distinguished discoverers. He then took a cursory view of the present state

physician Giovanni Filippo Ingrassia, who labeled the disease *rossalia* or *rosania*. It was again observed in an epidemic in Germany in 1564–65 by Dutch physician Johann Weyer, who referred to it as *scalatina* (or *scarlatina*) *anginosa*. Scientists believe that from ancient times until the late eighteenth century, scarlet fever was endemic to every population, that is, present at low levels. When statistically significant numbers of cases occurred, they were relatively benign and widely separated in time. Beginning around 1825, however, outbreaks began to occur regularly and were quite severe, with many fatalities. Scarlet fever was the scourge of mid-Victorian England; countless young children fell victim. After 1885, when the disease was first recognized as the outcome of a streptococcal infection, it appeared far less frequently in developed countries, and by the mid-twentieth century, after serums, vaccines, and eventually penicillin had been developed, fatalities were rare.

4. Percy Shelley added to the Draft the language regarding the danger of infection.

5. The Thomas Text softens the word to "amiable."

6. The word "cousins" is replaced by "children" in the 1831 edition.

7. The Stoic sentiment following was appended by Percy Shelley in the Draft.

8. This phrase is replaced by "My departure for" in the 1831 edition. The psychoanalytic critics contend that Victor now not only feels that his father is banishing him for having killed his mother (or having wished her dead—as is evidenced by his later dream), but that he also irrationally feels that his father's action in eventually making him leave home was the real cause of Caroline's death.

9. This sentence and the balance of the paragraph are replaced in the 1831 edition with the following:

It appeared to me sacrilege so soon to leave the repose, akin to death, of the house of mourning and to rush into the thick of life. I was new to sorrow, but it did not the less alarm me. I was unwilling to quit the sight of those that remained to me, and above all, I desired to see my sweet Elizabeth in some degree consoled.

She indeed veiled her grief and strove to act the comforter to us all. She looked steadily on life and assumed its duties with courage and zeal. She devoted herself to those whom she had been taught to call her uncle and cousins. Never was she so enchanting as at this time, when she recalled the sunshine of her smiles and spent them upon us. She forgot even her own regret in her endeavours to make us forget.

10. The balance of this paragraph and the next paragraph are deleted from the 1831 edition, and the following is substituted:

Clerval spent the last evening with us. He had endeavoured to persuade his father to permit him to accompany me and to become my fellow student, but in vain. His father was a narrow-minded trader and saw idleness and ruin in the aspirations and ambition of his son. Henry deeply felt the misfortune of being debarred from a liberal education. He said little, but when he spoke I read in his kindling eye and in his animated glance a restrained but firm resolve not to be chained to the miserable details of commerce.

We sat late. We could not tear ourselves away from each other nor persuade ourselves to say the word "Farewell!" It was said, and we retired

of the science, and explained many of its elementary terms. After having made a few preparatory experiments, he concluded with a panegyric upon modern chemistry, the terms of which I shall never forget:—

"The ancient teachers of this science," said he, "promised impossibilities, and performed nothing. The modern masters promise very little; they know that metals cannot be transmuted, and that the elixir of life is a chimera. But these philosophers, whose hands seem only made to dabble in dirt, and their eyes to pour over the microscope[26] or crucible,[27] have indeed performed miracles. They penetrate into the recesses of nature, and shew how she works in her hiding places. They ascend into the heavens;[28] they have discovered how the blood circulates,[29] and the nature of the air we breathe.[30] They have acquired new and almost unlimited powers; they can command the thunders of heaven,[31] mimic the earthquake,[32] and even mock the invisible world with its own shadows."[33]

I departed highly pleased with the professor and his lecture, and paid him a visit the same evening.[34] His manners in private were even more mild and attractive than in public; for there was a certain dignity in his mien during his lec-

Chemical lecture at the Surrey Institution, 1808, by Thomas Rowlandson.

ture, which in his own house was replaced by the greatest affability and kindness.[35] He heard with attention my little narration concerning my studies, and smiled at the names of Cornelius Agrippa, and Paracelsus, but without the contempt that M. Krempe had exhibited.[36] He said, that "these were men to whose indefatigable zeal modern philosophers were indebted for most of the foundations of their knowledge. They had left to us, as an easier task, to give new names, and arrange in connected classifications, the facts which they in a great degree had been the instruments of bringing to light. The labours of men of genius, however erroneously directed, scarcely ever fail in ultimately turning to the solid advantage of mankind." I listened to his statement, which was delivered without any presumption or affectation; and then added, that his lecture had removed my prejudices against modern chemists;[37] and I, at the same time, requested his advice concerning the books I ought to procure.

"I am happy," said M. Waldman, "to have gained a disciple; and if your application equals your ability, I have no doubt of your success. Chemistry is that branch of natural philosophy in which the greatest improvements have been and may be made; it is on that account that I have made it my peculiar study; but at the same time I have not neglected the other branches of science. A man would make but a very sorry chemist, if he attended to that department of human knowledge alone. If your wish is to become really a man of science, and not merely a petty[38] experimentalist, I should advise you to apply to every branch of natural philosophy, including mathematics."

He then took me into his laboratory, and explained to me the uses of his various machines; instructing me as to what I ought to procure, and promising me the use of his own, when I should have advanced far enough in the science not to derange their mechanism. He also gave me the list of books which I had requested; and I took my leave.

Thus ended a day memorable to me; it decided my future destiny.[39]

under the pretence of seeking repose, each fancying that the other was deceived; but when at morning's dawn I descended to the carriage which was to convey me away, they were all there—my father again to bless me, Clerval to press my hand once more, my Elizabeth to renew her entreaties that I would write often and to bestow the last feminine attentions on her playmate and friend.

11. The balance of the sentence was added to the Draft by Percy Shelley.

12. The Thomas Text makes a considerable revision to the character of Clerval, striking the two previous sentences and substituting: "Clerval loved poetry and his mind was filled with the imagery and sublime sentiments of the masters of that art. A poet himself, he turned with disgust from the details of ordinary life. His own soul mind was all the possession that he prized, beautiful & majestic thoughts the only wealth he coveted—daring as the eagle and as free, common laws could not be applied to him; and while you gazed on him you felt his soul's spark was more divine—more truly stolen from Apollo's sacred fire, than the glimmering ember that animates other men." Interestingly, Mary Shelley moved in the opposite direction in the 1831 edition, making Clerval into a man of enterprise rather than a poet.

13. A carriage, usually two-wheeled.

14. Victor quotes Charles Lamb's January 1798 poem, "The Old Familiar Faces," which begins:

Where are they gone, the old familiar faces?
I had a mother, but she died, and left me,

Chaise.

Died prematurely in a day of
   horrors—
All, all are gone, the old familiar faces.

The "day of horrors" to which Lamb refers is September 22, 1796, when his sister, Mary (one of only three siblings who survived infancy), killed his mother with a knife in a fit of madness. (Their mother, Elizabeth Field, had borne seven children.) The date of publication of this poem is an important clue to the dates of *Frankenstein*, tending to confirm that Victor's narration to Walton took place in August 1799. Frankenstein left Geneva in January 1798, and he must have read the poem before his hunt took him away from civilized regions and north to the Arctic. Of course, the phrase itself was a commonplace, but the poem seems singularly apt for Frankenstein's recital of the death of his mother, and the phrase is in quotation marks in the narrative, confirming that it is intended to refer to Lamb's poem.

15. Indeed, the distance from Geneva to Ingolstadt is more than 300 miles in a straight line; by road, it was likely over 400 miles, and the journey may have taken as long as two weeks. Today, it is a drive of 409 miles (658 km), taking just over six hours on high-speed toll roads and the Autobahn.

16. In the 1831 edition, the sentence ends here, and the following replaces the balance of the paragraph:

Chance—or rather the evil influence, the Angel of Destruction, which asserted omnipotent sway over me from the moment I turned my reluctant steps from my father's door—led me first to M. Krempe, professor of natural philosophy. He was an uncouth man, but deeply imbued in the secrets of his science. He asked me several questions concerning my progress in the different branches of science appertaining to natural philosophy. I replied carelessly, and partly in contempt, mentioned the names of my alchemists as the principal authors I had studied. The professor stared. "Have you," he said, "really spent your time in studying such nonsense?"

And so Victor is in the hands of his destiny, powerless to resist.

17. "M." must stand for "Monsieur." It seems more likely that at Ingolstadt University, located in the heart of German-speaking Bavaria, Waldman would have been "Herr Doktor" or at least "Herr" Waldman. In the eighteenth century, classes at the university were largely taught in Latin; there were a few German-language courses as well.

18. Originally "W.—" in the Draft, subsequently changed to "Waldham," and finally corrected throughout to "Waldman."

19. The word "missed" is "omitted" in the 1831 edition.

20. This sentence has been revised substantially in the 1831 edition to read as follows: "I returned home, not disappointed, for I have said that I had long considered those authors useless whom the professor reprobated; but I returned not at all the more inclined to recur to these studies in any shape."

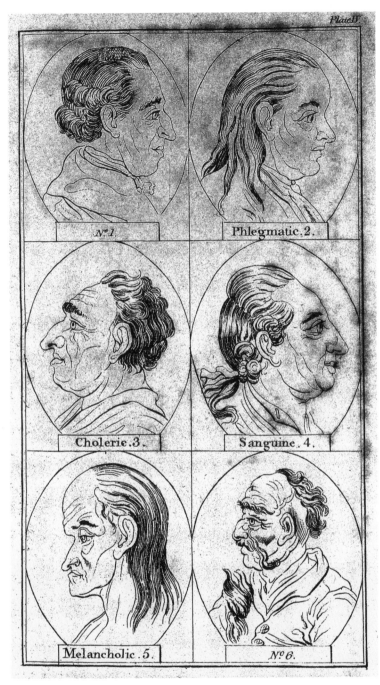

Temperaments, from Lavater, *Essays on Physiognomy* (1793).

21. In thus judging Krempe, Victor falls victim to the supposed science of physiognomy, which discriminated character by outward appearance. Its greatest proponent was Johann Kaspar Lavater (1741–1801), whose eighteenth-century work *Physiognomische Fragmente zur Beförderung der Menschenkenntnis und Menschenliebe* (Leipzig, 1775–78) won considerable adherents. The 1797 *Encyclopædia Britannica* (3rd ed.) vigorously defends the theory, stating, "That there is so intimate relation between the dispositions of the mind and the features of the countenance is a fact which cannot be questioned." The *Britannica* expressed the hope that Lavater's recent publication would "perhaps tend to replace physiognomy in that rank in the circle of the sciences to which it seems to be intitled." By 1888, however, the *Encyclopædia Britannica* (9th ed.) had changed its view:

> The popular style, good illustrations, and pious spirit pervading the writings of Lavater have given to them a popularity they little deserved, as there is really no system in his work, which largely consists of rhapsodical comments upon the several portraits. Having a happy knack of estimating character, especially when acquainted with the histories of the persons in question, the good pastor contrived to write a graphic and readable book, but one much inferior to [Giambattista Della] Porta's or Aristotle's as a systematic treatise. With him the descriptive school of physiognomists may be said to have ended. . . . The few straggling works which have since appeared are scarcely deserving of notice, the rising attraction of phrenology [the determination of character from the shape of the skull] having given to pure physiognomy the *coup de grâce* by taking into itself whatever was likely to live of the older science.

Physiognomy, though now discarded in its broadest precepts, is bound up in the ideas of Victorian criminologist Cesare Lombroso and eventually the ideas of Sigmund Freud relating to the connection of outward manifestations—habits, gestures, facial tics, and the like—and interior neuroses and conditions. Sander L. Gilman, in *Creating Beauty to Cure the Soul: Race and Psychology in the Shaping of Aesthetic Surgery* (Durham: Duke University Press, 1998), lists the following as "three of the major figures in the history of Western theories of physiognomy": della Porta, Franz Josef Gall (1758–1828), and Carl Gustav Carus (1789–1869). According to Carl Jung, it was Carus who identified the role of the unconscious in psychic development. The unconscious functioned on three levels, Carus wrote in *Psyche: On the Development of the Soul; Part I: The Unconscious* (1846), with conscious thoughts acting on the "districts" of the "partial absolute unconscious"—this was the second or middle of his tripartite structure—thereby contributing to one's physiognomy. Gall, who founded phrenology (its practice was once called cranioscopy) with his student Johann Gaspar Spurzheim (1776–1832), cataloged regions of the brain that he said performed specific functions, leading ultimately to the popular theory of right- and left-brain specialization. Among his less enduring propositions was that in each person the brain essentially pushed against the cranium, giving each head its unique contours.

The remnants of the theory of physiognomy persist in modern psychology's categories of "body types," especially the work of American psychologist William Sheldon (1898–1977), who propounded "somatyping" (with the broad categories of ectomorphs, mesomorphs, and endomorphs) and associated physique and personality. Sheldon argued that delin-

quency was caused by a mesomorph physique, but the theory has—like Lombroso's work—been largely discredited as confusing correlation with causation.

22. The word "doctrine" has been replaced by the word "pursuits" in the 1831 edition, and the following sentences added: "In rather a too philosophical and connected a strain, perhaps, I have given an account of the conclusions I had come to concerning them in my early years. As a child I had not been content with the results promised by the modern professors of natural science. With a confusion of ideas only to be accounted for by my extreme youth and my want of a guide on such matters, I had retrod the steps of knowledge along the paths of time and exchanged the discoveries of recent inquirers for the dreams of forgotten alchemists."

23. The balance of the paragraph was added to the Draft by Percy Shelley.

24. The balance of the sentence is replaced in the 1831 edition with the following: "of my residence at Ingolstadt, which were chiefly spent in becoming acquainted with the localities and the principal residents in my new abode."

25. Contrast this description with that of Krempe (see note 21, above), as Victor makes another judgment based on physiognomy.

26. The microscope likely was developed in the sixteenth century by lensmakers in Holland. In the seventeenth century microscopes were used extensively to study the tissue of living things, and Robert Hooke's *Micrographia*, published in 1665, was hugely influential on the basis of its superb illustrations. For more on Hooke, see note 44, Volume I, Chapter I, above.

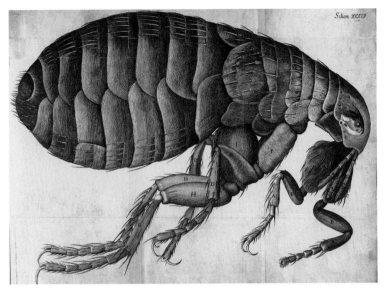

Drawing of a flea, from Robert Hooke's *Micrographia* (1665), by Robert Hooke (though possibly by Sir Christopher Wren).

27. A vessel used to hold heated substances, usually metals; natural philosophers would use a crucible to study the composition of a compound by subjecting it to high heat.

28. The study of planetary motions, as has been noted above, flourished in the sixteenth and seventeenth centuries.

29. William Harvey (1578–1657), an English physician, published *De Motu Cordis* (usually translated as *On the Motion of the Heart and Blood*), the first work to completely describe the mechanism of the circulatory system, in 1628. Harvey did not originate the material but synthesized the studies of others; his book refuted the ideas of Galen (129–ca. 200 CE), which had prevailed for more than thirteen hundred years. Galen had proposed that blood passed through two different systems, the venous and arterial networks, conveyed between them by invisible pores; Harvey explained the network as a single system.

30. This is something of an overstatement. In 1660, Robert Boyle (see notes 44 and 51, Volume I, Chapter I, above) demonstrated that air was essential to both life and combustion. He placed a candle and a small animal in a vessel and used an air pump to create a vacuum. The candle was extinguished and the animal died. This led to Hooke's later work, demonstrating that life could be preserved by artificial respiration, a mechanical device supplying fresh air to motionless lungs. Oxygen, the principal requirement of breathable air, was identified in the late eighteenth century (see note 57, Volume I, Chapter I, above), but it was not until 1878 that oxygen toxicity—caused by breathing pure oxygen—was described, by the French physiologist Paul Bert.

31. The "thunder" of explosions was produced by gunpowder as early as the ninth century in China. Perhaps Waldman refers to the invention in 1742 by Andrew Gordon, a natural philosopher, of the "lightning bell," a device that by converting electrical into mechanical energy could be used to warn of pending thunderstorms, or perhaps he refers to electrical experiments conducted in the 1780s by the Dutch inventor Martinus van Marum (1750–1837) that replicated the undulating motion of water or land caused by an earthquake passing through a body of water or the ground. Compare also the comments of John Abernethy (Preface, note 8, above): "[I]t is electricity which causes the whirlwind, and the water spout, and which 'with its harp and sulphurous bolt splits the unwedgeable and gnarled oak' [*Measure for Measure*], and destroys our most stabile edifices; . . . it is electricity which by its consequences make the firm earth tremble, and throws up subterraneous matter from volcanoes."

32. Again, Waldman seems to be speaking of explosions.

33. The "invisible world" must refer to the microscopic studies of substances, discussed in note 26, above. One hundred years later, the phrase might well refer to the discovery of nuclear radiation and the "invisible world" of the interiors of atoms.

34. This sentence is omitted from the 1831 edition, and the following material is inserted:

> Such were the professor's words—rather let me say such the words of the fate—enounced to destroy me. As he went on I felt as if my soul were grappling with a palpable enemy; one by one the various keys were touched which formed the mechanism of my being; chord after chord was sounded, and soon my mind was filled with one thought, one conception, one purpose. So much has been done, exclaimed the soul of Frankenstein—more, far more, will I achieve; treading in the steps already marked, I will pioneer a new way, explore unknown powers, and unfold to the world the deepest mysteries of creation.
>
> I closed not my eyes that night. My internal being was in a state of insurrection and turmoil; I felt that order would thence arise, but I had no power to produce it. By degrees, after the morning's dawn, sleep came. I awoke, and my yesternight's thoughts were as a dream. There only remained a resolution to return to my ancient studies and to devote myself to a science for which I believed myself to possess a natural talent. On the same day I paid M. Waldman a visit.

Here, too, Mary Shelley emphasizes that Victor had no choice in his destiny—

he was in the hands of fate, and his future actions were not his fault. In *Reproducing Enlightenment: Paradoxes in the Life of the Body Politic—Literature and Philosophy Around 1800* (Berlin: Walter de Gruyter, 2009), Diana K. Reese draws attention to use of the word "enounced," writing that Victor's "quest transforms him into an instrument (by all appearances an organ), or immutable drive, activated by Professor Waldman's enunciation. . . . Dr. Frankenstein is forced to recognize his fate in the work of his own hand, or rather, in what that first work, now alien, continues to effect" (27).

35. The following sentence is inserted here in the 1831 edition: "I gave him pretty nearly the same account of my former pursuits as I had given to his fellow professor."

36. The three sentences following were added to the Draft by Percy Shelley.

37. The balance of the sentence is deleted in the 1831 edition, and the following is substituted: "I expressed myself in measured terms, with the modesty and deference due from a youth to his instructor, without letting escape (inexperience in life would have made me ashamed) any of the enthusiasm which stimulated my intended labours. I requested his advice concerning the books I ought to procure."

38. The word is "pretty" in the Draft, possibly in the largely obsolete meaning of "clever" or "skillful" but more likely an error. ("Petty" was retained in the 1831 text as well.) In 1794, George Adams, in his *Lectures on Natural and Experimental Philosophy* (London: R. Hindmarsh), described the qualities distinguishing "a mere experimentalist" from than "an observer of nature": "The *experimentalist* beholds all nature as particles of dust

disunited from, and *uninfluenced* by, one another; each a world of its own, with properties and qualities peculiar to itself. The *observer* sees all nature as *united*, as actuated and moving upon one common principle, and all the parts as conspiring to form one whole" (Vol. 1, 127).

39. Here Mary Shelley wrote in the Thomas Text, "If there were ever to be another edition of this book, I should re-write these first two chapters. The incidents are tame and ill-arranged—the language sometimes childish— They are unworthy of the rest of the narration."

CHAPTER III.[1]

FROM THIS DAY natural philosophy, and particularly chemistry in the most comprehensive sense of the term, became nearly my sole occupation. I read with ardour those works, so full of genius and discrimination, which modern inquirers have written on these subjects. I attended the lectures, and cultivated the acquaintance, of the men of science of the university; and I found even in M. Krempe a great deal of sound sense and real information, combined, it is true, with a repulsive physiognomy and manners, but not on that account the less valuable. In M. Waldman I found a true friend. His gentleness was never tinged by dogmatism; and his instructions were given with an air of frankness and good nature, that banished every idea of pedantry.[2] It was, perhaps, the amiable character of this man that inclined me more to that branch of natural philosophy which he professed, than an intrinsic love for the science itself. But this state of mind had place only in the first steps towards knowledge: the more fully I entered into the science, the more exclusively I pursued it for its own sake. That application, which at first had been a matter of duty and resolution, now became so ardent and eager, that the stars often disappeared in the light of morning whilst I was yet engaged in my laboratory.

As I applied so closely, it may be easily conceived that I improved rapidly. My ardour was indeed the astonishment

1. Chapter 4 in the 1831 edition.

2. The three sentences following are deleted in the 1831 edition (up to the phrase "became so ardent and eager") and replaced with the following: "In a thousand ways he smoothed for me the path of knowledge and made the most abstruse inquiries clear and facile to my apprehension. My application was at first fluctuating and uncertain; it gained strength as I proceeded and soon"

Old Anatomy building, Ingolstadt (photo by Brian Clontarf, used under CC-by-SA 3.0 license).

of the students; and my proficiency that of the masters. Professor Krempe often asked me, with a sly smile, how Cornelius Agrippa went on? whilst M. Waldman expressed the most heartfelt exultation in my progress.[3] Two years passed in this manner, during which I paid no visit to Geneva, but was engaged, heart and soul, in the pursuit of some discoveries, which I hoped to make. None but those who have experienced them can conceive of the enticements of science. In other studies you go as far as others have gone before you, and there is nothing more to know; but in a scientific pursuit there is continual food for discovery and wonder. A mind of moderate capacity, which closely pursues one study, must infallibly arrive at great proficiency in that study; and I, who continually sought the attainment of one object of pursuit, and was solely wrapt up in this, improved so rapidly, that, at the end of two years, I made some discoveries in the improvement of some chemical instruments, which procured me great esteem and admiration at the university. When I had arrived at this point, and had become as well acquainted with the theory and practice of natural philosophy as depended on the lessons of any of the professors at Ingolstadt, my resi-

4. The Thomas Text adds, "The event of these enquiries interested my understanding, I may say my imagination, until I was exalted to a kind of transport. And indeed [unless I had been animated . . .]"

5. This phrase, beginning with "all the minutiae," was added by Percy Shelley.

dence there being no longer conducive to my improvements, I thought of returning to my friends and my native town, when an incident happened that protracted my stay.

One of the phænonema which had peculiarly attracted my attention was the structure of the human frame, and, indeed, any animal endued with life. Whence, I often asked myself, did the principle of life proceed? It was a bold question, and one which has ever been considered as a mystery; yet with how many things are we upon the brink of becoming acquainted, if cowardice or carelessness did not restrain our inquiries. I revolved these circumstances in my mind, and determined thenceforth to apply myself more particularly to those branches of natural philosophy which relate to physiology.[4] Unless I had been animated by an almost supernatural enthusiasm, my application to this study would have been irksome, and almost intolerable. To examine the causes of life, we must first have recourse to death. I became acquainted with the science of anatomy: but this was not sufficient; I must also observe the natural decay and corruption of the human body. In my education my father had taken the greatest precautions that my mind should be impressed with no supernatural horrors. I do not ever remember to have trembled at a tale of superstition, or to have feared the apparition of a spirit. Darkness had no effect upon my fancy; and a church-yard was to me merely the receptacle of bodies deprived of life, which, from being the seat of beauty and strength, had become food for the worm. Now I was led to examine the cause and progress of this decay, and forced to spend days and nights in vaults and charnel houses. My attention was fixed upon every object the most insupportable to the delicacy of the human feelings. I saw how the fine form of man was degraded and wasted; I beheld the corruption of death succeed to the blooming cheek of life; I saw how the worm inherited the wonders of the eye and brain. I paused, examining and analysing all the minutiae of causation, as exemplified in the change from life to death, and death to life,[5] until from the midst of this darkness a sudden light broke in upon me—a light so brilliant and wondrous, yet so simple, that while I became dizzy with the immensity of the prospect which it illustrated, I was surprised that among so many men of genius, who had directed their inquiries towards the same science, that I alone should be reserved to discover so astonishing a secret.

Remember, I am not recording the vision of a madman. The sun does not more certainly shine in the heavens, than that which I now affirm is true. Some miracle might have produced it, yet the stages of the discovery were distinct and probable. After days and nights of incredible labour and fatigue, I succeeded in discovering the cause of generation and life; nay, more, I became myself capable of bestowing animation upon lifeless matter.[6]

The astonishment which I had at first experienced on this discovery soon gave place to delight and rapture. After so much time spent in painful labour, to arrive at once at the summit of my desires, was the most gratifying consummation of my toils. But this discovery was so great and overwhelming, that all the steps by which I had been progressively led to it were obliterated, and I beheld only the result. What had been the study and desire of the wisest men since the creation of the world, was now within my grasp. Not that, like a magic scene, it all opened upon me at once: the information I had obtained was of a nature rather to direct my endeavours so soon as I should point them towards the object of my search, than to exhibit that object already accomplished. I was like the Arabian who had been buried with the dead, and found a passage to life aided only by one glimmering, and seemingly ineffectual light.[7]

I see by your eagerness, and the wonder and hope which your eyes express, my friend, that you expect to be informed of the secret with which I am acquainted; that cannot be: listen patiently until the end of my story, and you will easily perceive why I am reserved upon that subject.[8] I will not lead you on, unguarded and ardent as I then was, to your destruction and infallible misery. Learn from me, if not by my precepts, at least by my example, how dangerous is the acquirement of knowledge, and how much happier that man is who believes his native town to be the world, than he who aspires to become greater than his nature will allow.[9]

When I found so astonishing a power placed within my hands, I hesitated a long time concerning the manner in

6. As is the case in so many works of speculative fiction that followed *Frankenstein*, the "secret" is never revealed.

7. On his fourth voyage, according to Burton's *One Thousand and One Nights*, the legendary Arabic or Persian sailor Sinbad is presented with a wife by a friendly king. He subsequently learns that it is the custom of the country in which he finds himself that, if one spouse dies, the other is buried alive along with the deceased. When his wife dies suddenly, Sinbad is forcibly entombed with her in a cave. Trapped, he escapes when he sees light admitted through a pinpoint opening in the cave wall, to which he climbs. He enlarges the hole and exits the tomb, fleeing the country. Victor's allusion may also be taken as a commentary on his view of his pending marriage to Elizabeth—he is trapped by his *dead wife*, and only creation—only the creature—will save him from that fate. See William Veeder, *Mary Shelley and Frankenstein: The Fate of Androgyny*, chapter 4, "Woman and the Divided Self." Veeder's book summarizes the view of many psychoanalytic critics of *Frankenstein* and analyzes in some depth how the book attempts to resolve Mary Shelley's personal relationships with "Promethean" men (including Percy Shelley and her father, William Godwin) through the depiction of Victor as well as the proper role of women. "Androgyny," for Veeder, means the harmonious integration of male and female virtues and traits in a single personality, an objective he sees as vital to Mary Shelley in life and literature.

8. Was the "secret" so simple that, if he were so inclined, Victor could whisper a few words to the unschooled Walton and reveal all—to Walton's peril? For example, "Apply a shock of sufficient voltage to the corpse . . ."? Even in the iconic James Whale film of *Frankenstein* (and its successors), although lightning and electric-

ity are *involved* in the germination of life, the "secret" appears to be far more than a simple ignition switch, bringing an electrical spark to compressed gases in an internal combustion engine.

Note that the narrator here breaks the fourth wall, addressing the listener—Walton—and reminding us that we are hearing a *retelling* of Victor's tale by Walton, as transcribed for his sister. This occurs only a few times in the course of a very long narrative.

9. Even at this late stage of his life, on his deathbed, Victor still does not understand that it was not his quest for knowledge that was his downfall—rather, it was his failure to take responsibility for his actions. This is the first instance in the novel in which this theme is sounded—be careful of probing too deeply, don't seek too much knowledge—yet it is the theme on which the popularity of *Frankenstein* seems to be almost wholly founded. Peake's play *Presumption* (see note 43, Volume I, Chapter VI, below), the usage of the creature in the popular press as a symbol of misguided science or invention, and the entire cinematic history of the novel focus on this narrow message and largely ignore Victor's irresponsibility. See the more detailed discussion of this distortion in the Foreword, text accompanying note 6, above, and Appendices 4 and 6, below.

10. The average height of the English soldier ages twenty to twenty-three in 1800 was about five foot five (168.5 cm). See John Komlos, "Shrinking in a Growing Economy? The Mystery of Physical Stature During the Industrial Revolution," *Journal of Economic History* 58, no. 3 (1998): 779–802. Clearly Victor did not intend to be limited to human cadavers for his components.

which I should employ it. Although I possessed the capacity of bestowing animation, yet to prepare a frame for the reception of it, with all its intricacies of fibres, muscles, and veins, still remained a work of inconceivable difficulty and labour. I doubted at first whether I should attempt the creation of a being like myself or one of simpler organization; but my imagination was too much exalted by my first success to permit me to doubt of my ability to give life to an animal as complex and wonderful as man. The materials at present within my command hardly appeared adequate to so arduous an undertaking; but I doubted not that I should ultimately succeed. I prepared myself for a multitude of reverses; my operations might be incessantly baffled, and at last my work be imperfect: yet, when I considered the improvement which every day takes place in science and mechanics, I was encouraged to hope my present attempts would at least lay the foundations of future success. Nor could I consider the magnitude and complexity of my plan as any argument of its impracticability. It was with these feelings that I began the creation of a human being. As the minuteness of the parts formed a great hindrance to my speed, I resolved, contrary to my first intention, to make the being of a gigantic stature; that is to say, about eight feet in height, and proportionably large.[10] After having formed this determination, and having spent some months in successfully collecting and arranging my materials, I began.[11]

No one can conceive the variety of feelings which bore me onwards, like a hurricane, in the first enthusiasm of success. Life and death appeared to me ideal bounds, which I should first break through, and pour a torrent of light into our dark world. A new species[12] would bless me as its creator and source; many happy and excellent natures would owe their being to me. No father could claim the gratitude of his child so completely as I should deserve their's. Pursuing these reflections, I thought, that if I could bestow animation upon lifeless matter, I might in process of time (although I now found it impossible) renew life where death had apparently devoted the body to corruption.

These thoughts supported my spirits, while I pursued my

undertaking with unremitting ardour. My cheek had grown pale with study, and my person had become emaciated with confinement. Sometimes, on the very brink of certainty, I failed; yet still I clung to the hope which the next day or the next hour might realize. One secret which I alone possessed was the hope to which I had dedicated myself; and the moon gazed on my midnight labours, while, with unrelaxed and breathless eagerness, I pursued nature to her hiding places. Who shall conceive the horrors of my secret toil, as I dabbled among the unhallowed damps of the grave, or tortured the

Illustration of resurrectionists at work, accompanying the story of John Holmes and Peter Williams, whipped for stealing dead bodies in 1777, by Hablot Knight Browne (1877).

11. In the late eighteenth and early nineteenth century, students of human anatomy had difficulty finding the cadavers they required. The scarcity was the combined result of the expansion of medical training; a decline in capital punishment due to, among other things, criminal law reform; and the lack of refrigeration. As a result, body snatchers or "resurrectionists" stole corpses from graveyards. In 1827–28 and 1831, Edinburgh serial killers William Burke and William Hare and the copycat London Burkers committed murder for the sole purpose of providing fresh corpses. The Anatomical Act of 1832 in England ended such sprees by widening the pool of corpses available to supply the market.

12. Why did Victor think that assembling parts from human cadavers and animal remains would result in a "new species"? Perhaps he believed that the size of the creature would be inherited by its descendants. The work of Jean-Baptiste Lamarck advocating the theory of inheritance of acquired characteristics was not published until 1809 and so was clearly not known to Victor, but Lamarck's work reflects contemporary thought, including the writing of the Comte de Buffon, who argued for similar notions. The theory was not discredited until the early twentieth century, although Trofim Lysenko, the leading Stalinist agricultural scientist of the 1930s, held on stubbornly to its tenets until his work, too, was discarded.

13. The element of "clay" contains recollections of both Adam, the first man, and, later, golems, creatures of animated clay. In the Babylonian Talmud, Adam is described as having been first a golem (גולם): dust was "kneaded into a shapeless mass," or "husk," resulting in his creation (Tractate Sanhedrin, 38b, Jews' College, London). Rabbi Judah Loew ben Bezazel of Prague (1520–1609) reportedly

created a golem to serve as a defender of the Prague ghetto, to protect its residents from pogroms. In some versions of the legend, the creature is controlled by the rabbi and fulfills its mission; in others, it escapes its master's control and engages in a murderous rampage. Paul Wegener's silent black-and-white Weimar horror classic *The Golem: How He Came into the World* (1920) finds the monster ultimately pacified by Rabbi Loew and an innocent girl, who is seen playing in the streets of the ghetto; the visual depiction of the golem is achieved through the employment of spectacularly grotesque German expressionist sets. In the popular serialized novel *The Golem* (1913–14), by Gustav Meyrink, the creature is presented as the uncontrolled embodiment of the spirit of the ghetto.

Scene from *Der Golem, wie er in die Welt kam* (*The Golem, How He Came into the World*) (Projektions-AG Union, 1920), co-directed by and starring Paul Wegener, from the 1915 novel *The Golem* by Gustav Meyrink.

14. A building for the storage of bones, typically those unearthed in the course of grave digging. In some regions, where suitable burial grounds were limited, the corpse might be interred to decompose and then, after a period of time, the bones disinterred and deposited in a charnel house, allowing the burial site to be reused. Charnel houses persist today in regions such as the Cyclades and in the desert; Saint Catherine's Monastery,

living animal to animate the lifeless clay?[13] My limbs now tremble, and my eyes swim with the remembrance; but then a resistless, and almost frantic impulse, urged me forward; I seemed to have lost all soul or sensation but for this one pursuit. It was indeed but a passing trance, that only made me feel with renewed acuteness so soon as, the unnatural stimulus ceasing to operate, I had returned to my old habits. I collected bones from charnel houses;[14] and disturbed, with profane fingers, the tremendous secrets of the human frame. In a solitary chamber, or rather cell, at the top of the house, and separated from all the other apartments by a gallery and staircase, I kept my workshop of filthy creation; my eyeballs were starting from their sockets in attending to the details of my employment. The dissecting room and the slaughter-house[15] furnished many of my materials; and often did my human nature turn with loathing from my occupation, whilst, still urged on by an eagerness which perpetually increased, I brought my work near to a conclusion.

The summer months passed while I was thus engaged, heart and soul, in one pursuit. It was a most beautiful season; never did the fields bestow a more plentiful harvest, or the vines yield a more luxuriant vintage: but my eyes were insensible to the charms of nature. And the same feelings which made me neglect the scenes around me caused me also to forget those friends who were so many miles absent, and whom I had not seen for so long a time. I knew my silence disquieted them; and I well remembered the words of my father: "I know that while you are pleased with yourself, you will think of us with affection, and we shall hear regularly from you. You must pardon me, if I regard any interruption in your correspondence as a proof that your other duties are equally neglected."

I knew well therefore what would be my father's feelings; but I could not tear my thoughts from my employment, loathsome in itself, but which had taken an irresistible hold of my imagination. I wished, as it were, to procrastinate all that related to my feelings of affection until the great object, which swallowed up every habit of my nature,[16] should be completed.

Ossuary in Valladolid, Spain (photo by Raúl Polanco Montriel, used under CC-by-SA 3.0 license).

at the foot of Mount Sinai, continues to operate its charnel house, which may have been established more than fourteen hundred years ago.

15. The clear implication is that the creature contains parts of the bodies of animals. Eighteenth-century slaughterhouses would have been populated with the carcasses of dead horses, cows, sheep, pigs, and poultry. Beginning in the eighteenth century, reformers argued that, for the production of meat intended for human consumption, public (government-operated or -licensed) slaughterhouses would be preferable to private—for example, a marketplace or butcher's shed. See Amy J. Fitzgerald, "A Social History of the Slaughterhouse: From Inception to Contemporary Implications," *Human Ecology Review* 17, no. 1 (2010), http://www.humanecologyreview.org/pastissues/her171/Fitzgerald.pdf. However, the first such public slaughterhouse was not established until the nineteenth century, in France.

16. This sentence was revised by Percy Shelley from Mary Shelley's more telling "until the great object of my affection was compleated" (Notebooks, 91).

I then thought that my father would be unjust if he ascribed my neglect to vice, or faultiness on my part; but I am now convinced that he was justified in conceiving that I should not be altogether free from blame. A human being in perfection ought always to preserve a calm and peaceful mind, and never to allow passion or a transitory desire to disturb his tranquillity. I do not think that the pursuit of knowledge is an exception to this rule. If the study to which you apply yourself has a tendency to weaken your affections, and to destroy your taste for those simple pleasures in which no alloy can possibly mix, then that study is certainly unlawful,

17. It was common practice in ancient Greece for the conquerors to enslave the entire populace of a conquered nation. Victor here may refer to the conquest of Greece by the Romans in 146 CE, but Turkish rule (from the fifteenth century through 1821) would have been on his mind as well. Lord Byron, in *Childe Harold's Pilgrimage*, bemoaned the Greeks' "[t]rembling beneath the scourge of Turkish hand / [f]rom birth till death enslaved; in word, in deed, unmanned" (Canto I).

18. Which "Caesar" is to blame for the fall of the Roman Empire is a matter of some debate. See, for example, Edward Gibbon's *History of the Decline and Fall of the Roman Empire* (first published 1776–89), which considers the question in depth. Certainly the emperor Constantine (306–337 CE) played a significant role, in allowing Christianity to supplant the Roman gods and in dividing the empire into two parts, with capitals in Rome and Constantinople. Nonetheless, the downfall did not occur for almost one hundred years, when the Visigoths sacked Rome (410 CE).

19. Christopher Columbus made four voyages to the Americas, from 1492 to 1504, seeking a westward passage to the Indian Ocean. His announcement of the discovery of the Caribbean islands set off a frenzy of western exploration by Europeans, though the Caribbean island nations proved to have little to trade or exploit. Subsequent European explorations led to the South American continent itself and the discovery of vast natural resources there. Small groups of Spanish conquistadores, with the aid of forcibly recruited armies of indigenous Americans, along with the devastating pandemics the conquistadores brought from Europe, took over the empires they found in South America. The Aztec empire in Mexico

that is to say, not befitting the human mind. If this rule were always observed; if no man allowed any pursuit whatsoever to interfere with the tranquillity of his domestic affections, Greece had not been enslaved;[17] Caesar would have spared his country;[18] America would have been discovered more gradually; and the empires of Mexico and Peru had not been destroyed.[19]

But I forget that I am moralizing in the most interesting part of my tale; and your looks remind me to proceed.[20]

My father made no reproach in his letters; and only took notice of my silence by inquiring into my occupations more particularly than before. Winter, spring, and summer, passed away during my labours; but I did not watch the blossom or the expanding leaves—sights which before always yielded me supreme delight, so deeply was I engrossed in my occupation. The leaves of that year had withered before my work drew near to a close; and now every day shewed me more plainly how well I had succeeded. But my enthusiasm was checked by my anxiety, and I appeared rather like one doomed by slavery to toil in the mines, or any other unwholesome trade, than an artist occupied by his favourite employment. Every night I was oppressed by a slow fever,[21] and I became nervous to a most painful degree; a disease that I regretted the more because I had hitherto enjoyed most excellent health, and had always boasted of the firmness of my nerves.[22] But I believed that exercise and amusement would soon drive away such symptoms; and I promised myself both of these, when my creation should be complete.

fell in 1521, and the Peruvian Inca empire was conquered in 1532.

Victor chides himself for allowing himself to become obsessed with seeking knowledge rather than enjoying his domestic happiness. Yet he seems to view the sweeping historical changes he lists as the fault of the overthrown, rather than the result of obsessive behavior by the destructive forces—the Romans, the Visigoths, the Spanish explorers—who relentlessly pursued their objectives of conquest. Victor was not alone in this view: Gibbon, for example, propounded the idea that Christianity "weakened" the Roman Empire, introducing pacific ideals and loosening the strong bonds to the official pagan religion, to the point where the Visigoths could overthrow it. Similarly, the success of the conquistadores was seen as the result of the moral decay of the Aztec empire, which crumbled when confronted by the muscular Christianity of the explorers.

20. Another aside to Walton.

21. The balance of the paragraph is substantially revised in the 1831 edition; it reads as follows: "the fall of a leaf startled me, and I shunned my fellow creatures as if I had been guilty of a crime. Sometimes I grew alarmed at the wreck I perceived that I had become; the energy of my purpose alone sustained me: my labours would soon end, and I believed that exercise and amusement would then drive away incipient disease; and I promised myself both of these, when my creation should be complete."

22. The Thomas Text strikes the portion of the sentence beginning with "a disease" and substitutes "my voice became broken, my trembling hands almost refused to accomplish their task; I became as timid as a love-sick girl, and alternate tremor and passionate ardour took the place of wholesome sensation and regulated ambition." That is, Victor suffered all the symptoms of a near-sexual frenzy.

CHAPTER IV.[1]

1. Chapter 5 in the 1831 edition.

2. In the Draft, Mary Shelley wrote, "my man completed."

3. Note the electrical metaphor—a "spark of being"—but note also that there is no specific mention of any sort of electrical apparatus. The phrase "spark of being" does not appear in literature prior to the events Victor describes, though the phrase *flavilla vitae*—literally, the spark of vitality—is used by Erasmus Darwin (see note 5, Preface, above) in *Phytology; or the Philosophy of Agriculture and Gardening* (1800) in his description of how a plant passes vitality to its offspring.

4. Victor's description of the events matches exactly the experience of Professor Giovanni Aldini, who attempted to revive a hanged man by applying electricity. See note 16, Appendix 1, below. Belefant, in *Frankenstein, the Man and the Monster*, concludes that this is no coincidence: Like Aldini, Belefant suggests, Victor *failed* to animate the cadaver, and the balance of his story of the creature is an extended nightmare.

I T WAS ON a dreary night of November, that I beheld the accomplishment of my toils.[2] With an anxiety that almost amounted to agony, I collected the instruments of life around me, that I might infuse a spark of being[3] into the lifeless thing that lay at my feet. It was already one in the morning; the rain pattered dismally against the panes, and my candle was nearly burnt out, when, by the glimmer of the half-extinguished light, I saw the dull yellow eye of the creature open; it breathed hard, and a convulsive motion agitated its limbs.[4]

How can I describe my emotions at this catastrophe, or how delineate the wretch whom with such infinite pains and care I had endeavoured to form? His limbs were in proportion, and I had selected his features as beautiful.[5] Beautiful!—Great God! His yellow skin scarcely covered the work of muscles and arteries beneath; his hair was of a lustrous black, and flowing; his teeth of a pearly whiteness; but these luxuriances only formed a more horrid

Making a monster: a scene from *Frankenstein* (Universal Pictures, 1931), directed by James Whale.

Making a monster: a scene from *Young Frankenstein* (Gruskoff/Venture Films, 1974), directed by Mel Brooks.

contrast with his watery eyes, that seemed almost of the same colour as the dun white sockets in which they were set, his shrivelled complexion, and straight black lips.[6]

The different accidents of life are not so changeable as the feelings of human nature. I had worked hard for nearly two years, for the sole purpose of infusing life into an inanimate body. For this I had deprived myself of rest and health. I had desired it with an ardour that far exceeded moderation; but now that I had finished, the beauty of the dream vanished, and breathless horror and disgust filled my heart. Unable to endure the aspect of the being I had created, I rushed out of the room, and continued a long time traversing my bed-chamber, unable to compose my mind to sleep. At length lassitude succeeded to the tumult I had before endured; and I threw myself on the bed in my clothes, endeavouring to seek a few moments of forgetfulness. But it was in vain: I slept indeed, but I was disturbed by the wildest dreams. I thought I saw Elizabeth, in the bloom of health, walking in the streets of Ingolstadt. Delighted and surprised, I embraced her; but as I imprinted the first kiss on her lips, they became livid[7] with the hue of death; her features appeared to change, and I thought that I held the corpse of my dead mother in my arms; a shroud enveloped her form, and I saw the grave-worms crawling in the folds of the flannel.[8] I started from my sleep with horror; a cold dew covered my forehead, my teeth chattered, and every limb became convulsed; when, by the dim and yellow light of the moon, as it forced its way through the window-shutters, I beheld the wretch—the miserable monster whom I had created.[9] He held up the curtain of the bed; and his eyes, if eyes they may be called, were fixed on me. His jaws opened, and he muttered some inarticulate sounds, while a grin wrinkled his cheeks. He might have spoken, but I did

5. Percy Shelley deleted "handsome" here and in the next sentence and substituted "beautiful" in the Draft.

6. The Thomas Text adds, "And the contortions that ever and anon convulsed & deformed his un-human features." Note that the creature is described as having racial characteristics—black lips, yellow skin—that mark him as alien to the white Genevese.

Psychoanalytic critics of *Frankenstein* have wondered at Victor's superficial response to his marvelous creation. Why is his *ugliness* so off-putting to the genius-scientist? Because it is a pretext, claim the critics: Victor knows full well that he has designed the creature as an instrument with which he will murder his family, and that ultimately his creation objectifies his desire to become a whole person, to end his self-loathing. Another view is that the creature fulfills Victor's oedipal fantasy of fathering a child with his mother, and when the creature is born, Victor is repulsed by his own sexual desires. See especially note 8, Volume I, Chapter II, above, and note 18, Volume III, Chapter VI, below.

7. Rather than "livid," or red, the Draft uses "lurid," a grayish-yellow color comparable to the creature's yellow skin tone.

8. This shocking dream has been the basis for much speculation regarding Victor's incestuous feelings toward his mother and his disgust with an "arranged" incestuous relationship with his cousin/sister Elizabeth. Victor kills Elizabeth and his mother in his dream—with his kiss. It is suggested that Victor wished to kill his women because (a) Elizabeth has killed his mother (infecting her with scarlet fever) and then presumed to replace her, (b) his mother has traitor-

ously died and left him, while naming Elizabeth as her "favourite," and (c) his mother has forced him into an incestuous relationship with Elizabeth, who is also his mother's replacement. See, for example, Martin Tropp's *Mary Shelley's Monster: The Story of* Frankenstein, chapter II, "The Waking Dream," as well as Veeder, *Mary Shelley and Frankenstein*, chapter 4, "The Divided Self and Woman." While Mary Shelley weakened this theory by changes to the 1831 text, making Elizabeth blameless in the death of Victor's mother (see note 3, Volume I, Chapter II, above) and amending the relationship between Victor and Elizabeth from true cousins to mere adopted siblings, the dream remained in the 1831 text.

The conflation of Victor's mother and Elizabeth is paralleled, points out Veeder, by Percy Shelley's courting of Mary Shelley (and perhaps consummation of their love) on the grave of her mother.

Plato, in his *Theaetetus*, ca. 369 BCE, considered the fundamental differences between dreaming and waking and how one might determine *whether* one was dreaming. Although dreams had originally been thought to be messages from the gods, Aristotle (*On Dreams*, 350 BCE) treated them as a psychological phenomenon—that is, individualized, generated from within—reflecting the life of the soul. This idea, that dreams were messages specific to the dreamer's soul, was widely adopted, and dreams were interpreted as symbolic, but the symbols were static—that is, they were common to all dreamers. The first important work recording the meaning of dreams was *Oneirocritica*, by Artemidorus, who lived in the second century CE. First published in English in 1644, it was reprinted many times. Artemidorus posited that dream symbols be interpreted based on the dreamer's circumstances as well as the specific details of the dream. For exam-

not hear; one hand was stretched out, seemingly to detain me, but I escaped, and rushed down stairs.[10] I took refuge in the court-yard belonging to the house which I inhabited; where I remained during the rest of the night, walking up and down in the greatest agitation, listening attentively, catching and fearing each sound as if it were to announce the approach of the dæmoniacal corpse to which I had so miserably given life.

Oh! no mortal could support the horror of that countenance. A mummy again endued with animation could not be so hideous as that wretch. I had gazed on him while unfinished; he was ugly then; but when those muscles and joints were rendered capable of motion, it became a thing such as even Dante could not have conceived.[11]

I passed the night wretchedly. Sometimes my pulse beat so quickly and hardly, that I felt the palpitation of every artery; at others, I nearly sank to the ground through languor and extreme weakness. Mingled with this horror, I felt the bitterness of disappointment: dreams that had been my food and pleasant rest for so long a space, were now become a hell to me; and the change was so rapid, the overthrow so complete!

Morning, dismal and wet, at length dawned, and discovered to my sleepless and aching eyes the church of Ingolstadt, its white steeple and clock, which indicated the sixth hour. The porter opened the gates of the court, which had that night been my asylum, and I issued into the streets, pacing them with quick steps, as if I sought to avoid the wretch whom I feared every turning of the street would present to my view. I did not dare return to the apartment which I inhabited, but felt impelled to hurry on, although wetted by the rain, which poured from a black and comfortless sky.

Boris Karloff as the creature (publicity still for *Bride of Frankenstein*, Universal Pictures, 1935).

I continued walking in this manner for some time, endeavouring, by bodily exercise, to ease the load that weighed upon my mind. I traversed the streets, without any clear conception of where I was, or what I was doing. My heart palpitated in the sickness of fear; and I hurried on with irregular steps, not daring to look about me:

> *Like one who, on a lonely road,*
> *Doth walk in fear and dread,*
> *And, having once turn'd round, walks on,*
> *And turns no more his head;*
> *Because he knows a frightful fiend*
> *Doth close behind him tread.*[12]

Continuing thus, I came at length opposite to the inn at which the various diligences and carriages usually stopped. Here I paused, I knew not why; but I remained some minutes with my eyes fixed on a coach that was coming towards me from the other end of the street. As it drew nearer, I observed that it was the Swiss diligence: it stopped just where I was standing; and, on the door being opened, I perceived Henry Clerval, who, on seeing me, instantly sprung out. "My dear Frankenstein,"[13] exclaimed he, "how glad I am to see you! how fortunate that you should be here at the very moment of my alighting!"

Nothing could equal my delight on seeing Clerval; his presence brought back to my thoughts my father, Elizabeth, and all those scenes of home so dear to my recollection. I grasped his hand, and in a moment forgot my horror and misfortune; I felt suddenly, and for the first time during many months, calm and serene joy. I welcomed my friend, therefore, in the most cordial manner, and we walked towards my college. Clerval continued talking for some time about our mutual friends, and his own good fortune in being permitted to come to Ingolstadt. "You may easily believe," said he, "how great was the difficulty to persuade my father that[14] it was not absolutely necessary for a merchant not to understand any thing except book-keeping; and, indeed, I believe I left him incredulous to

ple, if a slave dreamed of a snake, it was thought to mean something other than what it meant if a priest's wife dreamed of a snake. A dream of sex with a partner—or with one's mother—wherein the individual being dreamed about is in a dominant position was differentiated from a dream featuring that person in a submissive position. Not until the mid-nineteenth century, when French physician Louis Ferdinand Alfred Maury began to experiment with the influences of external stimuli on dreams, did the idea of dreams that arose out of the dreamer's experiences gain wider standing. His results, published in 1865, influenced Freud's monumental *Interpretation of Dreams* (1899), which mentioned Maury's work.

What did the dream of Elizabeth and his mother mean to Victor? Artemidorus interprets dreams of sex (and kissing must be seen as a polite substitute) with a dead mother as symbolic of the dreamer's impending death, with the mother representing the earth to which the dreamer will soon return. Thus, the simple message of the dream would have been: If Victor were to embrace (marry) Elizabeth, he would die. When Victor is later threatened by the creature, he takes the latter's intent to be to slay him on his wedding night. This interpretation would have been confirmed to Victor if he had remembered this dream (as he clearly did, for he recounts it to Walton long after the night of the dream).

9. A very similar scene is shown as having occurred on Victor's wedding night—see note 9, Volume III, Chapter VI, below.

10. How is it possible that the creature, who later describes his struggles to understand the operation of his senses, managed to travel from the solitary chamber in which Victor did his work, located "at the top of the house, and separated from

all of the other apartments by a gallery and staircase," to Victor's apartment—without mishap, and without running into any other tenants? The creature must also have rampaged around the building during the night, trapped in its confines, for Victor later reports that the gates of the courtyard through which he states the creature exited were not unlocked until 6 a.m.

11. Although several species of monsters are described in Dante Alighieri's *Divine Comedy* (1320), none have visages described as "ugly." The *Malebranche*, demons who appear in canto 21 of the *Inferno*, come the closest, with faces described in Italian as "*fero*," translated variously as "savage" or "ferocious." Of course, Victor was not well read and may have simply assumed that in Dante's hell, one would find hideously ugly creatures.

12. Attributed in the 1831 edition to "Coleridge's 'Ancient Mariner.'" Clearly Victor could not have read the poem at the time he is talking about, for it was not published until 1798—this is an addition he makes when telling the story to Walton.

13. We learn at last the family name of the narrator.

14. The phrase ending with "book-keeping" is rewritten in the 1831 edition as "all necessary knowledge was not comprised in the noble art of book-keeping." Whether the art of bookkeeping is "noble" is open to debate, but it has a long history: Records of account for farms and estates were kept in ancient Greece and Rome, and bookkeeping probably traces back even earlier, to before the second millennium BCE, when barter and trade flourished. In *Debt: The First 5,000 Years*

the last, for his constant answer to my unwearied entreaties was the same as that of the Dutch schoolmaster in the *Vicar of Wakefield*: 'I have ten thousand florins a year without Greek, I eat heartily without Greek.'[15] But his affection for me at length overcame his dislike of learning, and he has permitted me to undertake a voyage of discovery to the land of knowledge."[16]

"It gives me the greatest delight to see you; but tell me how you left my father, brothers, and Elizabeth."

"Very well, and very happy, only a little uneasy that they hear from you so seldom. By the bye, I mean to lecture you a little upon their account myself.—But, my dear Frankenstein," continued he, stopping short, and gazing full in my face, "I did not before remark how very ill you appear; so thin and pale; you look as if you had been watching for several nights."

"You have guessed right; I have lately been so deeply engaged in one occupation, that I have not allowed myself sufficient rest, as you see: but I hope, I sincerely hope, that all these employments are now at an end, and that I am at length free."

I trembled excessively; I could not endure to think of, and far less to allude to the occurrences of the preceding night. I walked with a quick pace, and we soon arrived at my college. I then reflected, and the thought made me shiver, that the creature whom I had left in my apartment might still be there, alive, and walking about. I dreaded to behold this monster; but I feared still more that Henry should see him. Entreating him therefore to remain a few minutes at the bottom of the stairs, I darted up towards my own room. My hand was already on the lock of the door before I recollected myself. I then paused; and a cold shivering came over me. I threw the door forcibly open, as children are accustomed to do when they expect a spectre to stand in waiting for them on the other side; but nothing appeared. I stepped fearfully in: the apartment was empty; and my bedroom was also freed from its hideous guest. I could hardly believe that so great a good-fortune could have befallen me; but when I became assured that my enemy had indeed fled, I clapped my hands for joy and ran down to Clerval.

We ascended into my room, and the servant presently brought breakfast; but I was unable to contain myself. It was not joy only that possessed me; I felt my flesh tingle with excess of sensitiveness, and my pulse beat rapidly. I was unable to remain for a single instant in the same place; I jumped over the chairs, clapped my hands, and laughed aloud. Clerval at first attributed my unusual spirits to joy on his arrival; but when he observed me more attentively, he saw a wildness in my eyes for which he could not account; and my loud, unrestrained, heartless laughter, frightened and astonished him.

"My dear Victor," cried he, "what, for God's sake, is the matter? Do not laugh in that manner. How ill you are! What is the cause of all this?"

"Do not ask me," cried I, putting my hands before my eyes, for I thought I saw the dreaded spectre glide into the room; "he[17] can tell.—Oh, save me! save me!" I imagined that the monster seized me; I struggled furiously, and fell down in a fit.

Poor Clerval! what must have been his feelings? A meeting, which he anticipated with such joy, so strangely turned to bitterness. But I was not the witness of his grief; for I was lifeless, and did not recover my senses for a long, long time.

This was the commencement of a nervous fever, which confined me for several months. During all that time Henry was my only nurse. I afterwards learned that, knowing my father's advanced age, and unfitness for so long a journey, and how wretched my sickness would make Elizabeth, he spared them this grief by concealing the extent of my disorder. He knew that I could not have a more kind and attentive nurse than himself; and, firm in the hope he felt of my recovery, he did not doubt that, instead of doing harm, he performed the kindest action that he could towards them.

But I was in reality very ill; and surely nothing but

(New York: Mellville House, 2012), David Graeber writes about medieval "book-keeping techniques for combining compound interest with partial repayments" (431, note 4). An Italian monk, Luca Pacioli, published a book in 1494 lauding the benefits of a double-entry system of book-keeping, and his ideas laid the groundwork for modern accounting.

15. In chapter 20 of Oliver Goldsmith's *Vicar of Wakefield* (1766), the principal of a school whom the narrator hopes to impress with his Greek-language ability responds, "'You see me, young man; I never learned Greek, and I don't find that I ever missed it. I have had a Doctor's cap and gown without Greek: I have ten thousand florins a year without Greek; and I eat heartily without Greek. In short,' continued he, 'I don't know Greek, and I do not believe there is any use in it.'"

Goldsmith's novel, supposedly a memoir written by the vicar himself, presents a comic view of life in the eighteenth century that descends into melodrama in the book's second half. Although dismissed by some critics as overly sentimental, it is now usually seen as a mild parody of the sentimental novel. It was very popular, as its mention here and in other contemporary literature such as Goethe's *Sorrows of Young Werther* attests. Nonetheless, it has only been filmed once, in a silent adaptation in 1916.

16. Does Victor intend this to stand in contrast to the habits of his own overbearing father, who "directed" his studies and whom he blames for banishing him from home? See notes 2 and 8, Volume I, Chapter II, above.

17. The word "he" appears in all capitals in the 1831 edition.

the unbounded and unremitting attentions of my friend could have restored me to life. The form of the monster on whom I had bestowed existence was for ever before my eyes, and I raved incessantly concerning him. Doubtless my words surprised Henry: he at first believed them to be the wanderings of my disturbed imagination; but the pertinacity with which I continually recurred to the same subject persuaded him that my disorder indeed owed its origin to some uncommon and terrible event.

By very slow degrees, and with frequent relapses, that alarmed and grieved my friend, I recovered. I remember the first time I became capable of observing outward objects with any kind of pleasure, I perceived that the fallen leaves had disappeared, and that the young buds were shooting forth from the trees that shaded my window. It was a divine spring; and the season contributed greatly to my convalescence. I felt also sentiments of joy and affection revive in my bosom; my gloom disappeared, and in a short time I became as cheerful as before I was attacked by the fatal passion.

"Dearest Clerval," exclaimed I, "how kind, how very good you are to me. This whole winter, instead of being spent in study, as you promised yourself, has been consumed in my sick room. How shall I ever repay you? I feel the greatest remorse for the disappointment of which I have been the occasion; but you will forgive me."

"You will repay me entirely, if you do not discompose yourself, but get well as fast as you can; and since you appear in such good spirits, I may speak to you on one subject, may I not?"

I trembled. One subject! what could it be? Could he allude to an object on whom I dared not even think?

"Compose yourself," said Clerval, who observed my change of colour, "I will not mention it, if it agitates you; but your father and cousin would be very happy if they received a letter from you in your own handwriting. They hardly know how ill you have been, and are uneasy at your long silence."

"Is that all? my dear Henry. How could you suppose that my first thought would not fly towards those dear, dear friends whom I love, and who are so deserving of my love."

"If this is your present temper, my friend, you will perhaps be glad to see a letter that has been lying here some days for you: it is from your cousin, I believe."

CHAPTER V.[1]

1. Chapter 6 in the 1831 edition.

CLERVAL THEN PUT the following letter into my hands.

"*To* V. FRANKENSTEIN.

"MY DEAR COUSIN,

"I cannot describe to you the uneasiness we have all felt concerning your health. We cannot help imagining that your friend Clerval conceals the extent of your disorder: for it is now several months since we have seen your handwriting; and all this time you have been obliged to dictate your letters to Henry. Surely, Victor, you must have been exceedingly ill; and this makes us all very wretched, as much so nearly as after the death of your dear mother. My uncle was almost persuaded that you were indeed dangerously ill, and could hardly be restrained from undertaking a journey to Ingolstadt. Clerval always writes that you are getting better; I eagerly hope that you will confirm this intelligence soon in your own hand-writing; for indeed, indeed, Victor, we are all very miserable on this account. Relieve us from this fear, and we shall be the happiest creatures in the world. Your father's health is now so vigorous, that he appears ten years younger since last winter. Ernest also is so much improved, that you would hardly know him: he is now nearly sixteen, and has lost that sickly appearance which he had some years ago; he is grown quite robust and active.

"My uncle and I conversed a long time last night about what profession Ernest should follow. His constant illness when young has deprived him of the habits of application; and now that he enjoys good health, he is continually in the open air, climbing the hills, or rowing on the lake. I therefore proposed that he should be a farmer; which you know, Cousin, is a favourite scheme of mine. A farmer's is a very healthy happy life; and the least hurtful, or rather the most beneficial profession of any. My uncle had an idea of his being educated as an advocate, that through his interest[2] he might become a judge. But, besides that he is not at all fitted for such an occupation, it is certainly more creditable to cultivate the earth for the sustenance of man, than to be the confidant, and sometimes the accomplice, of his vices; which is the profession of a lawyer.[3] I said, that the employments of a prosperous farmer, if they were not a more honourable, they were at least a happier species of occupation than that of a judge, whose misfortune it was always to meddle with the dark side of human nature. My uncle smiled, and said, that I ought to be an advocate myself, which put an end to the conversation on that subject.

"And now I must tell you a little story that will please, and perhaps amuse you. Do you not remember Justine Moritz?[4] Probably you do not; I will relate her history, therefore, in a few words. Madame Moritz, her mother, was a widow with four children, of whom Justine was the third. This girl had always been the favourite of her father; but, through a strange perversity, her mother could not endure her, and, after the death of M.[5] Moritz, treated her very ill. My aunt observed this; and, when Justine was twelve years of age, prevailed on her mother to allow her to live at her house.[6] The republican institutions of our country have produced simpler and happier manners than those which prevail in the great monarchies that surround it. Hence there is less distinction between the several classes of its inhabitants; and the lower orders being neither so poor nor so despised, their manners are more refined and moral. A servant in Geneva does not mean the same thing as a servant in France and England.[7] Justine, thus received in our family, learned the duties of a

2. That is, his political influence.

3. This cynical view of lawyers was echoed by writers such as Samuel Johnson, who reportedly remarked that "he did not like to speak ill of any man behind his back, but he believed the gentleman was an *attorney*" (quoted in the *Legal Observer, or Journal of Jurisprudence*, for March 1838, in an article on "Public Opinion of Attorneys"). The article also reported the remarks of one Colonel Stanhope, who, in opposing the nomination of six attorneys to govern a commission, called them members "of a profession in which the public generally had little confidence, and against which many had a decided dislike." Percy Shelley had many dealings with lawyers in the years preceding the publication of *Frankenstein*, as he fought for custody of his two children by his marriage (a marriage that, as we have seen, had ended with the suicide of his wife Harriet). Ultimately, the court found him unfit to assume custody.

4. The name was originally "Martin," not "Moritz," in the Draft.

All of the preceding paragraphs of Elizabeth's letter and the heading "To V. Frankenstein" are replaced in the 1831 edition with the following:

It was from my own Elizabeth:

"My dearest Cousin,
You have been ill, very ill, and even the constant letters of dear kind Henry are not sufficient to reassure me on your account. You are forbidden to write—to hold a pen; yet one word from you, dear Victor, is necessary to calm our apprehensions. For a long time I have thought that each post would bring this line, and my persuasions have restrained my uncle from undertaking a journey to Ingolstadt. I have prevented his encountering the inconveniences and perhaps

dangers of so long a journey, yet how often have I regretted not being able to perform it myself! I figure to myself that the task of attending on your sickbed has devolved on some mercenary old nurse, who could never guess your wishes nor minister to them with the care and affection of your poor cousin. Yet that is over now: Clerval writes that indeed you are getting better; I eagerly hope that you will confirm this intelligence soon in your own handwriting.

"Get well—and return to us. You will find a happy, cheerful home and friends who love you dearly. Your father's health is vigorous, and he asks but to see you, but to be assured that you are well; and not a care will ever cloud his benevolent countenance. How pleased you would be to remark the improvement of our Ernest! He is now sixteen and full of activity and spirit. He is desirous to be a true Swiss and to enter into foreign service, but we cannot part with him, at least until his elder brother returns to us. My uncle is not pleased with the idea of a military career in a distant country, but Ernest never had your powers of application. He looks upon study as an odious fetter; his time is spent in the open air, climbing the hills, or rowing on the lake. I fear that he will become an idler unless we yield the point and permit him to enter on the profession which he has selected.

"Little alteration, except the growth of our dear children, has taken place since you left us. The blue lake and snow-clad mountains—they never change; and I think our placid home and our contented hearts are regulated by the same immutable laws. My trifling occupations take up my time and amuse me, and I am rewarded for any exertions by seeing none but happy, kind faces around me. Since you left us, but one change has taken place in

servant; a condition which, in our fortunate country, does not include the idea of ignorance, and a sacrifice of the dignity of a human being.

"After what I have said, I dare say you well remember the heroine of my little tale: for Justine[8] was a great favourite of your's; and I recollect you once remarked, that if you were in an ill humour, one glance from Justine could dissipate it, for the same reason that Ariosto gives concerning the beauty of Angelica[9]—she looked so frank-hearted and happy. My aunt conceived a great attachment for her, by which she was induced to give her an education superior to that which she had at first intended. This benefit was fully repaid; Justine was the most grateful little creature in the world: I do not mean that she made any professions, I never heard one pass her lips; but you could see by her eyes that she almost adored her protectress. Although her disposition was gay, and in many respects inconsiderate, yet she paid the greatest attention to every gesture of my aunt. She thought her the model of all excellence, and endeavoured to imitate her phraseology and manners, so that even now she often reminds me of her.

"When my dearest aunt died, every one was too much occupied in their own grief to notice poor Justine, who had attended her during her illness with the most anxious affection. Poor Justine was very ill; but other trials were reserved for her.

"One by one, her brothers and sister died; and her mother, with the exception of her neglected daughter, was left childless. The conscience of the woman was troubled; she began to think that the deaths of her favourites was a judgment from heaven to chastise her partiality. She was a Roman Catholic; and I believe her confessor confirmed the idea which she had conceived. Accordingly, a few months after your departure for Ingolstadt, Justine was called home by her repentant mother. Poor girl! she wept when she quitted our house: she was much altered since the death of my aunt; grief had given softness and a winning mildness to her manners, which had before been remarkable for vivacity. Nor was her residence at her mother's house of a nature to restore her gaiety. The poor woman was very vacillating in her repentance. She sometimes begged Justine to forgive her unkindness, but much oftener accused her of having caused the deaths of her brothers and sister. Perpetual fretting at length threw Madame Moritz into a decline, which at first increased her irritability, but she is now at peace for ever. She died on the first approach of cold weather, at the beginning of this last winter. Justine has returned to us; and I assure you I love her tenderly. She is very clever and gentle, and extremely pretty; as I mentioned before, her mien and her expressions continually remind me of my dear aunt.

"I must say also a few words to you, my dear cousin, of little darling William. I wish you could see him; he is very tall of his age, with sweet laughing blue eyes, dark eye-lashes, and curling hair. When he smiles, two little dimples appear on each cheek, which are rosy with health. He has already had one or two little wives,[10] but Louisa Biron is his favourite, a pretty little girl of five years of age.[11]

"Now, dear Victor, I dare say you wish to be indulged in a little gossip concerning the good people of Geneva. The pretty Miss Mansfield has already received the congratulatory visits on her approaching marriage with a young Englishman, John Melbourne, Esq. Her ugly sister, Manon, married M. Duvillard, the rich banker, last autumn. Your favourite schoolfellow, Louis Manoir, has suffered several misfortunes since the departure of Clerval from Geneva. But he has already recovered his spirits, and is reported to be on the point of marrying a very lively pretty Frenchwoman, Madame Tavernier. She is a widow, and much older than Manoir; but she is very much admired, and a favourite with everybody.

"I have written myself into[12] good spirits, dear cousin; yet I cannot conclude without again anxiously inquiring concerning your health. Dear Victor, if you are not very ill, write yourself, and make your father and all of us happy; or—I cannot bear to think of the other side of the question; my tears already flow. Adieu, my dearest cousin."

"ELIZABETH LAVENZA.

"Geneva, March 18th, 17—."[13]

our little household. Do you remember on what occasion Justine Moritz entered our family?"

There are a few subtle changes here: Ernest now desires the "foreign service," a much more public-spirited choice for the son of a respected family than being a farmer. Clerval is no longer blamed for covering up Victor's illness. And tellingly, Elizabeth no longer mentions the death of Victor's mother.

5. Here "M." clearly stands for "Monsieur."

6. The phrase "Where she was taught all the duties of servant & kindly treated" was deleted by Percy Shelley from the draft, and the exaltation of Swiss egalitarianism following was inserted.

7. These observations found their origins in a letter nominally by Percy Shelley in *History of a Six Weeks' Tour* (London: T. Hookham and C. and J. Ollier, 1817), hereinafter "*Six Weeks' Tour.*" The title page of the book credits Percy Shelley as the author, but scholars agree that it was cowritten and significantly edited by Mary Shelley as a record of their trip around France, Switzerland, Holland, and Germany in the summer of 1814. (In a letter written in 1843, she referred to the volume as "my 6 weeks tour.") The book also includes four letters written during a return trip in the summer of 1816 with Claire Clairmont; some were ostensibly written by Percy Shelley and some by Mary Shelley, but all were heavily edited or compiled by the latter from various letters and diary entries. In letter 2, dated June 1, 1816, Percy Shelley commented, "There is more equality of classes here than in England. This occasions a greater freedom and refinement of manners among the lower orders than we meet with in our own country. I fancy the haughty English ladies are greatly dis-

gusted with this consequence of republican institutions, for the Genevese servants complain very much of their *scolding*, an exercise of the tongue, I believe, perfectly unknown here" (108).

8. The prior portion of this sentence is shortened in the 1831 edition to "Justine, you may remember,"[.]

9. Angelica is the heroine of Ludovico Ariosto's epic romance *Orlando Furioso*, "The Mad Roland" (1516–32). There is no passage in which Orlando describes Angelica's beauty as "frank-hearted" or "happy," at least not in the John Harington translation (1591) or the John Hoole translation in couplets (1783), which would have been available to Elizabeth (the popular William Stewart Rose translation was published in 1823–1831), so we must take this remark as Elizabeth's interpretation of the poem.

10. The word "wives" is in all capitals in the 1831 edition.

11. In January 1816, Mary Shelley gave birth to her second child by Percy Shelley, whom she had not yet married. The child, William, died of malaria in 1819.

Many have suggested that the reference to "Biron" and the "two little wives" is no mere coincidence but rather a sly reference to Lord Byron's pending divorce and his two children by his wife. Byron himself jokingly proposed the name "Biron" for his daughter by Claire Clairmont.

12. The balance of the letter, up to Elizabeth's signature, is replaced in the 1831 edition with the following: "better spirits, dear cousin, but my anxiety returns upon me as I conclude. Write, dearest Victor,— one line—one word will be a blessing to us. Ten thousand thanks to Henry for his kindness, his affection, and his many letters; we are sincerely grateful. Adieu!

"Dear, dear Elizabeth!" I exclaimed when I had read her letter, "I will write instantly, and relieve them from the anxiety they must feel." I wrote, and this exertion greatly fatigued me; but my convalescence had commenced, and proceeded regularly. In another fortnight I was able to leave my chamber.[14]

One of my first duties on my recovery was to introduce Clerval to the several professors of the university. In doing this, I underwent a kind of rough usage, ill befitting the wounds that my mind had sustained. Ever since the fatal night, the end of my labours, and the beginning of my misfortunes, I had conceived a violent antipathy even to the name of natural philosophy. When I was otherwise quite restored to health, the sight of a chemical instrument would renew all the agony of my nervous symptoms. Henry saw this, and had removed all my apparatus from my view.[15] He had also changed my apartment; for he perceived that I had acquired a dislike for the room which had previously been my laboratory. But these cares of Clerval were made of no avail when I visited the professors. M. Waldman inflicted torture when he praised, with kindness and warmth, the astonishing progress I had made in the sciences. He soon perceived that I disliked the subject; but, not guessing the real cause, he attributed my feelings to modesty, and changed the subject from my improvement to the science itself, with a desire, as I evidently saw, of drawing me out. What could I do? He meant to please, and he tormented me. I felt as if he had placed carefully, one by one, in my view those instruments which were to be afterwards used in putting me to a slow and cruel death. I writhed under his words, yet dared not exhibit the pain I felt. Clerval, whose eyes and feelings were always quick in discerning the sensations of others, declined the subject, alleging, in excuse, his total ignorance; and the conversation took a more general turn. I thanked my friend from my heart, but I did not speak. I saw plainly that he was surprised, but he never attempted to draw my secret from me; and although I loved him with a mixture of affection and reverence that knew no bounds, yet I could never persuade myself to confide to him that event which was so often present to my recollection, but which I feared the detail to another would only impress more deeply.

M. Krempe was not equally docile; and in my condition at that time, of almost insupportable sensitiveness, his harsh blunt encomiums gave me even more pain than the benevolent approbation of M. Waldman. "D—n the fellow!" cried he; "why, M. Clerval, I assure you he has outstript us all. Aye, stare if you please; but it is nevertheless true. A youngster who, but a few years ago, believed Cornelius Agrippa as firmly as the gospel, has now set himself at the head of the university; and if he is not soon pulled down, we shall all be out of countenance.—Aye, aye," continued he, observing my face expressive of suffering, "M. Frankenstein is modest; an excellent quality in a young man. Young men should be diffident of themselves, you know, M. Clerval; I was myself when young: but that wears out in a very short time."

M. Krempe had now commenced an eulogy on himself, which happily turned the conversation from a subject that was so annoying to me.

Clerval was no natural philosopher. His imagination was too vivid for the minutiae of science. Languages were his principal study; and he sought, by acquiring their elements, to open a field for self-instruction on his return to Geneva. Persian, Arabic, and Hebrew, gained his attention, after he had made himself perfectly master of Greek and Latin. For my own part,[16] idleness had ever been irksome to me; and now that I wished to fly from reflection, and hated my former studies, I felt great relief in being the fellow-pupil with my friend, and found not only instruction but consolation in the works of the orientalists.[17] Their melancholy is soothing, and their joy elevating to a degree I never experienced in studying the authors of any other country. When you read their writings, life appears to consist in a warm sun and garden of roses,—in the smiles and frowns of a fair enemy, and the fire that consumes your own heart. How different from the manly and heroical poetry of Greece and Rome.

Summer passed away in these occupations, and my return to Geneva was fixed for the latter end of autumn; but being delayed by several accidents, winter and snow arrived, the roads were deemed impassable, and my journey was retarded until the ensuing spring. I felt this delay very bitterly; for I

my cousin; take care of your self; and, I entreat you, write!"

13. Mary Shelley notes in the Thomas Text, "This letter ought to be re-written."

14. It is now more than four months since "a dreary night in November" when Frankenstein awakened the creature, yet he spares not a single thought for the latter's whereabouts or what might have happened to him in the interim.

15. Victor makes no mention of having cleaned up his laboratory before passing into a coma. Are we to understand that Clerval found nothing remarkable in a workspace that must have been filled with spare body parts and strange apparatus? As we have seen, Belefant, in *Frankenstein, the Man and the Monster*, suggests that the laboratory (and the creature) are figments of Victor's imagination, which would explain what we take to be Clerval's failure to react.

16. The preceding portion of this paragraph is replaced in the 1831 edition with the following:

Clerval had never sympathised in my tastes for natural science; and his literary pursuits differed wholly from those which had occupied me. He came to the university with the design of making himself complete master of the oriental languages, and thus he should open a field for the plan of life he had marked out for himself. Resolved to pursue no inglorious career, he turned his eyes toward the East, as affording scope for his spirit of enterprise. The Persian, Arabic, and Sanskrit languages engaged his attention, and I was easily induced to enter on the same studies.

Clerval now pursues the languages for *business* purposes, a more conventional reason. By the end of the eighteenth century, trade with Persia and the Arabic-speaking countries was no longer confined to the Dutch, and there would have been ample opportunities for an enterprising young Swiss to develop commercial relationships that would have been facilitated by a knowledge of the local languages.

17. The following is inserted here in the 1831 edition: "I did not, like him, attempt a critical knowledge of their dialects, for I did not contemplate making any other use of them than temporary amusement. I read merely to understand their meaning, and they well repaid my labours."

18. It is now fourteen months after Elizabeth's letter.

longed to see my native town, and my beloved friends. My return had only been delayed so long from an unwillingness to leave Clerval in a strange place, before he had become acquainted with any of its inhabitants. The winter, however, was spent cheerfully; and although the spring was uncommonly late, when it came, its beauty compensated for its dilatoriness.

The month of May had already commenced,[18] and I expected the letter daily which was to fix the date of my departure, when Henry proposed a pedestrian tour in the environs of Ingolstadt that I might bid a personal farewell to the country I had so long inhabited. I acceded with pleasure to this proposition: I was fond of exercise, and Clerval had always been my favourite companion in the rambles of this nature that I had taken among the scenes of my native country.

We passed a fortnight in these perambulations: my health and spirits had long been restored, and they gained additional strength from the salubrious air I breathed, the natural incidents of our progress, and the conversation of my friend. Study had before secluded me from the intercourse of my fellow-creatures, and rendered me unsocial; but Clerval called forth the better feelings of my heart; he again taught me to love the aspect of nature, and the cheerful faces of children. Excellent friend! how sincerely did you love me, and endeavour to elevate my mind, until it was on a level with your own. A selfish pursuit had cramped and narrowed me, until your gentleness and affection warmed and opened my senses; I became the same happy creature who, a few years ago, loving and beloved by all, had no sorrow or care. When happy, inanimate nature had the power of bestowing on me the most delightful sensations. A serene sky and verdant fields filled me with ecstasy. The present season was indeed divine; the flowers of spring bloomed in the hedges, while those of summer were already in bud: I was undisturbed by thoughts which during the preceding year had pressed upon me, notwithstanding my endeavours to throw them off, with an invincible burden.

Henry rejoiced in my gaiety, and sincerely sympathized

in my feelings: he exerted himself to amuse me, while he expressed the sensations that filled his soul. The resources of his mind on this occasion were truly astonishing: his conversation was full of imagination; and very often, in imitation of the Persian and Arabic writers, he invented tales of wonderful fancy and passion.[19] At other times he repeated my favourite poems, or drew me out into arguments, which he supported with great ingenuity.

We returned to our college on a Sunday afternoon: the peasants were dancing, and every one we met appeared gay and happy. My own spirits were high, and I bounded along with feelings of unbridled joy and hilarity.

19. Persian literature was little known in European culture prior to the eighteenth century, its study largely confined to the Zoroastrian liturgical and philosophical texts. A translation into English by William Jones of the poetry of Hafiz (probably the first Persian writer to become known to Westerners) appeared in 1771, and this translation could have come to the attention of Clerval and Frankenstein. Probably the first German translation of his work, by Wahl, was published in 1791, and the famous Purgstall translation appeared in 1812. In 1819, Goethe published a collection of poetry inspired by Hafiz. The poetry of the thirteenth-century mystic Rumi, whose popularity in the twentieth and twenty-first centuries has eclipsed that of Hafiz, was not translated into English until the end of the nineteenth century; French and German translations appeared earlier.

Arabic literature was much better known. For example, *One Thousand and One Nights* was translated by Antoine Galland between 1704 and 1717 and achieved vast popularity. The "philosophical" or "theological" novel or allegory *Al-Risalah al-Kamiliyyah fil Sira al-Nabawiyyah* (*The Treatise of Kamil on the Prophet's Biography*), known in English as *Theologus Autodidactus*, is a tale of an individual spontaneously generated (by unexplained means) on a desert island. By his own reasoning, he develops a system of natural, philosophical, and theological truths. Said to be the inspiration for Daniel Defoe's *Robinson Crusoe*, it was published in English, German, and French around 1708.

CHAPTER VI.[1]

1. Chapter 7 in the 1831 edition.

2. This address does not appear in the 1831 edition.

3. The word "glad" is substituted for "gay" in the 1831 edition.

4. The 1831 edition replaces the phrase "an absent child" with "my long absent son."

5. In the Draft, the date was originally given as the twenty-sixth, but Mary Shelley corrected this to the twenty-eighth. May 7 and May 28 were both Thursdays in 1795. Charles E. Robinson (*The Original Frankenstein*) sees this as suggesting that Mary Shelley was using a perpetual calendar in constructing the chronology of the book and as confirmation of the year 1795. As will be seen, in light of the date of publication of the Lamb poem and other quotations, we must accept this as the year in question. This places the birth of the creature in November 1793.

6. Plainpalais is a neighborhood in Geneva. In July 1794, a group of discon-

ON MY RETURN, I found the following letter from my father:

"To V. FRANKENSTEIN.[2]

"MY DEAR VICTOR,

"You have probably waited impatiently for a letter to fix the date of your return to us; and I was at first tempted to write only a few lines, merely mentioning the day on which I should expect you. But that would be a cruel kindness, and I dare not do it. What would be your surprise, my son, when you expected a happy and gay[3] welcome, to behold, on the contrary, tears and wretchedness? And how, Victor, can I relate our misfortune? Absence cannot have rendered you callous to our joys and griefs; and how shall I inflict pain on an absent child?[4] I wish to prepare you for the woeful news, but I know it is impossible; even now your eye skims over the page, to seek the words which are to convey to you the horrible tidings.

"William is dead!—that sweet child, whose smiles delighted and warmed my heart, who was so gentle, yet so gay! Victor, he is murdered!

"I will not attempt to console you; but will simply relate the circumstances of the transaction.

"Last Thursday (May 7th)[5] I, my niece, and your two brothers, went to walk in Plainpalais.[6] The evening was warm and serene, and we prolonged our walk farther than usual. It was already dusk before we thought of returning; and then we discovered that William and Ernest, who had gone on before, were not to be found. We accordingly rested on a seat until they should return. Presently Ernest came, and inquired if we had seen his brother: he said, that they had been playing together,[7] that William had run away to hide himself, and that he vainly sought for him, and afterwards waited for him[8] a long time, but that he did not return.

"This account rather alarmed us, and we continued to search for him until night fell, when Elizabeth conjectured that he might have returned to the house. He was not there. We returned again, with torches; for I could not rest, when I thought that my sweet boy had lost himself, and was exposed to all the damps and dews of night: Elizabeth also suffered extreme anguish. About five in the morning I discovered my lovely boy, whom the night before I had seen blooming and active in health, stretched on the grass livid and motionless: the print of the murderer's finger was on his neck.

"He was conveyed home, and the anguish that was visible in my countenance betrayed the secret to Elizabeth. She was very earnest to see the corpse. At first I attempted to prevent her; but she persisted, and entering the room where it lay, hastily examined the neck of the victim, and clasping her hands exclaimed, 'O God! I have murdered my darling infant!'[9]

"She fainted, and was restored with extreme difficulty. When she again lived, it was only to weep and sigh. She told me, that that same evening William had teazed her to let him wear a very valuable miniature that she possessed of your mother. This picture is gone, and was doubtless the temptation which urged the murderer to the deed. We have no trace of him at present, although our exertions to discover him are unremitted; but they will not restore my beloved William.

"Come, dearest Victor; you alone can console Elizabeth. She weeps continually, and accuses herself unjustly as the cause of his death; her words pierce my heart. We are all unhappy; but will not that be an additional motive for you, my son, to return and be our comforter? Your dear mother!

tented Swiss rebelled against the Genevese government and, with the support of Robespierre, instituted a "Revolutionary Tribunal." The tribunal ordered the execution of eleven Genevese, including four magistrates, which took place here.

The incident is described in the diary portion of *Six Weeks' Tour*:

> To the south of the town [of Geneva] is the promenade of the Genevese, a grassy plain planted with a few trees, and called Plainpalais. Here a small obelisk is erected to the glory of Rousseau, and here (such is the mutability of human life) the magistrates, the successors of those who exiled him

9 "O God! I have murdered my darling infant! – Elizabeth

> which the willing are wisdom, with such, notwithstanding labour with which have endeavour have rendered lasting benefits to mankind, which all the chicanery of statesmen, nor even the great conspiracy of kings, can entirely render vain. From respect to the memory of their predecessors, none of the present magistrates ever walk in Plainpalais. (161)

Fred V. Randel in his essay "The Political Geography of Horror in Mary Shelley's Frankenstein" (in Harold Bloom's Modern Critical Interpretations: Frankenstein [New York: Infobase Publishing, 2007], 185–212), suggests that Shelley "establishes an equation between the monster's murders and revolutionary violence" and sympathizes with the "monster of revolution" (190).

7. The 1831 edition replaces the phrase "they had been playing together" with "he had been playing with him."

8. The phrase "for him" does not appear here in the 1831 edition.

9. The 1831 edition uses the word "child" in place of "infant."

10. The balance of this sentence and the next sentence are replaced in the 1831 edition by "to say a few words of consolation; he could only express his heartfelt sympathy."

11. The word "lovely" has been added here in the 1831 edition.

12. The concluding period is changed to an exclamation point in the 1831 edition, and the balance of the paragraph is replaced with the following:

Who that had seen him bright and joyous in his young beauty, but must weep over his untimely loss! To die so miserably; to feel the murderer's grasp! How much more a murderer that could destroy such radiant innocence! Poor little fellow! one only consolation have we; his friends mourn and weep, but he is at rest. The pang is over, his sufferings are at an end for ever. A sod covers his gentle form, and he knows no pain. He can no longer be a subject for pity; we must reserve that for his miserable survivors.

Shelley makes Clerval sound more human, less scholarly, in this revision; by 1831, she had already buried three of her own children.

Alas, Victor! I now say, Thank God she did not live to witness the cruel, miserable death of her youngest darling!

"Come, Victor; not brooding thoughts of vengeance against the assassin, but with feelings of peace and gentleness, that will heal, instead of festering the wounds of our minds. Enter the house of mourning, my friend, but with kindness and affection for those who love you, and not with hatred for your enemies.

"*Your affectionate and afflicted father,*
ALPHONSE FRANKENSTEIN.

"Geneva, May 12th, 17—."

Clerval, who had watched my countenance as I read this letter, was surprised to observe the despair that succeeded to the joy I at first expressed on receiving news from my friends. I threw the letter on the table, and covered my face with my hands.

"My dear Frankenstein," exclaimed Henry, when he perceived me weep with bitterness, "are you always to be unhappy? My dear friend, what has happened?"

I motioned to him to take up the letter, while I walked up and down the room in the extremest agitation. Tears also gushed from the eyes of Clerval, as he read the account of my misfortune.

"I can offer you no consolation, my friend," said he; "your disaster is irreparable. What do you intend to do?"

"To go instantly to Geneva: come with me, Henry, to order the horses."

During our walk, Clerval endeavoured[10] to raise my spirits. He did not do this by common topics of consolation, but by exhibiting the truest sympathy. "Poor William!" said he, "that dear[11] child; he now sleeps with his angel mother.[12] His friends mourn and weep, but he is at rest: he does not now feel the murderer's grasp; a sod covers his gentle form, and he knows no pain. He can no longer be a fit subject for pity; the survivors are the greatest sufferers, and for them time is the only consolation. Those maxims of the Stoics, that death was no evil, and that the mind of man ought to be superior to despair on the eternal absence of a beloved object, ought not to be urged.[13] Even Cato wept over the dead body of his brother."[14]

Clerval spoke thus as we hurried through the streets; the words impressed themselves on my mind, and I remembered them afterwards in solitude. But now, as soon as the horses arrived, I hurried into a cabriole,[15] and bade farewell to my friend.

My journey was very melancholy. At first I wished to hurry on, for I longed to console and sympathize with my loved and sorrowing friends; but when I drew near my native town, I slackened my progress. I could hardly sustain the multitude of feelings that crowded into my mind. I passed through scenes familiar to my youth, but which I had not seen for nearly six years. How altered every thing might be during that time? One sudden and desolating change had taken place; but a thousand little circumstances might have by degrees worked other alterations which, although they were done more tranquilly, might not be the less decisive. Fear overcame me; I dared not advance, dreading a thousand nameless evils that made me tremble, although I was unable to define them.

I remained two days at Lausanne, in this painful state of mind. I contemplated the lake: the waters were placid; all around was calm, and the snowy mountains, "the palaces of nature,"[16] were not changed. By degrees the calm and heav-

Cabriolet.

13. Clerval here refers to the philosophers of the later school of Stoicism, principally Seneca (4 BCE–65 CE) and Epictetus (55–135 CE). The Stoics held that external events were determined by fate, not by the actions of individuals, and that the only proper response of the philosopher to good fortune or disaster was calm, passionless acceptance. James Stockdale, who had been a prisoner of war in Vietnam and was later the running mate of H. Ross Perot in 1992, when Perot ran as an independent for the U.S. presidency, gave a remarkable speech, published in 1993 under the title "Courage Under Fire: Testing Epictetus's Doctrines in a Laboratory of Human Behavior" by Stanford University's Hoover Institution on War, Revolution, and Peace, explaining how he survived seven years of imprisonment by relying on the teachings of Epictetus.

14. Cato (95–46 BCE), referred to as the "Younger" (he had been named after his great-grandfather), was a distinguished statesman of the late Roman republic and a Stoic well known for his indifference to pain and suffering, and resolute in character. However, Plutarch, in his *Lives of the Noble Greeks and Romans*, reports that Cato apparently betrayed his philosophy when his beloved brother died, displaying excessive grief and arranging a lavish funeral. The drama of Cato's life was a popular theme; *Cato, a Tragedy*, written by Joseph Addison (1712), was a well-known play concerning his final days.

15. More commonly "cabriolet," a single-horse, two-wheeled vehicle.

16. From the third canto of Byron's *Childe Harold's Pilgrimage* (1812–1818):

ABOVE me are the Alps,
The palaces of nature, whose vast
walls

Have pinnacled in clouds their snowy
   scalps,
And throned eternity in icy halls
Of cold sublimity, where forms and
   falls
The avalanche,—the thunderbolt of
   snow!

Clearly we are not meant to believe that Frankenstein had read Byron's work. Mary Shelley saw the manuscript in 1816.

17. Mont Blanc is the tallest mountain in Europe, rising to a height of 15,781 feet above sea level. The first recorded ascension was in 1786 by the guide Jacques Balmat. *Murray* describes the view, "the first usually enjoyed by travellers from England to Chamouny," as "so impressive as to be generally acknowledged a sufficient reward for the journey." On first seeing the Alps near Chamonix, Percy Shelley wrote, in *Six Weeks' Tour*, "I never knew—I never imagined what mountains were before. The immensity of these ærial summits excited, when they suddenly burst upon the sight, a sentiment of extatic wonder, not unallied to madness" (151–52). He also wrote a four-page hymn to Mont Blanc, included as an appendix to *Six Weeks' Tour*.

18. The custom was certainly still in place by the time Shelley wrote *Frankenstein*. In *Six Weeks' Tour*, she remarks on the gates shutting "exactly at ten o'clock, when no bribery (as in France) can open them" (101). *Murray* observes in 1838, "In former times they finally closed before midnight, and it will be remembered that it was the accident of being shut out one evening, on his return from a walk in the country, that induced Rousseau to fly from his native town and a tyrannical master, whom he, as a truant apprentice, feared to face."

19. The Hotel of Sécheron, about a mile from Geneva, is mentioned in *Murray*.

enly scene restored me, and I continued my journey towards Geneva.

The road ran by the side of the lake, which became narrower as I approached my native town. I discovered more distinctly the black sides of Jura, and the bright summit of Mont Blânc;[17] I wept like a child: "Dear mountains! my own beautiful lake! how do you welcome your wanderer? Your summits are clear; the sky and lake are blue and placid. Is this to prognosticate peace, or to mock at my unhappiness?"

I fear, my friend, that I shall render myself tedious by dwelling on these preliminary circumstances; but they were days of comparative happiness, and I think of them with pleasure. My country, my beloved country! who but a native can tell the delight I took in again beholding thy streams, thy mountains, and, more than all, thy lovely lake.

Yet, as I drew nearer home, grief and fear again overcame me. Night also closed around; and when I could hardly see the dark mountains, I felt still more gloomily. The picture appeared a vast and dim scene of evil, and I foresaw obscurely that I was destined to become the most wretched of human beings. Alas! I prophesied truly, and failed only in one single circumstance, that in all the misery I imagined and dreaded, I did not conceive the hundredth part of the anguish I was destined to endure.

It was completely dark when I arrived in the environs of Geneva; the gates of the town were already shut;[18] and I was obliged to pass the night at Secheron,[19] a village[20] half a league to the east of the city. The sky was serene; and, as I was unable to rest, I resolved to visit the spot where my poor William had been murdered. As I could not pass through the town, I was obliged to cross the lake in a boat to arrive at Plainpalais. During this short voyage I saw the lightnings playing on the summit of Mont Blânc in the most beautiful figures. The storm appeared to approach rapidly; and, on landing, I ascended a low hill, that I might observe its progress. It advanced; the heavens were clouded, and I soon felt the rain coming slowly in large drops, but its violence quickly increased.

I quitted my seat, and walked on, although the darkness and storm increased every minute, and the thunder burst with a terrific crash over my head. It was echoed from Saleve,[21] the Juras, and the Alps of Savoy;[22] vivid flashes of lightning dazzled my eyes, illuminating the lake, making it appear like a vast sheet of fire; then for an instant every thing seemed of a pitchy darkness, until the eye recovered itself from the preceding flash. The storm, as is often the case in Switzerland, appeared at once in various parts of the heavens. The most violent storm hung exactly north of the town, over that part of the lake which lies between the promontory of Belrive and the village of Copet.[23] Another storm enlightened Jura with faint flashes; and another darkened and sometimes disclosed the Môle,[24] a peaked mountain to the east of the lake.

While I watched the storm,[25] so beautiful yet terrific, I wandered on with a hasty step. This noble war in the sky elevated my spirits; I clasped my hands, and exclaimed aloud, "William, dear angel! this is thy funeral, this thy dirge!" As I said these words, I perceived in the gloom a figure which stole from behind a clump of trees near me; I stood fixed, gazing intently: I could not be mistaken. A flash of lightning illuminated the object, and discovered its shape plainly to me; its gigantic stature, and the deformity of its aspect, more hideous than belongs to humanity, instantly informed me that it was the wretch, the filthy daemon to whom I had given life. What did he there? Could he be (I shuddered at the conception) the murderer of my brother? No sooner did that idea cross my imagination, than I became convinced of its truth; my teeth chattered, and I was forced to lean against a tree for support.[26] The figure passed me quickly, and I lost it in the gloom. Nothing in human shape could have destroyed that fair child. He was the murderer![27] I could not doubt it. The mere presence of the idea was an irresistible proof of the fact. I thought of pursuing the devil; but it would have been in vain, for another flash discovered him to me hanging among the rocks of the nearly perpendicular ascent of Mont Salêve, a hill that bounds Plainpalais on the south. He soon reached the summit, and disappeared.

I remained motionless. The thunder ceased; but the rain still continued, and the scene was enveloped in an impenetrable darkness. I revolved in my mind the events which I

20. The phrase "at the distance of" is inserted here in the 1831 edition, and the phrase "to the east of" is replaced with "from."

21. *Murray* describes Mont Salève: "On the S.E. side of Geneva rises the *Mont Salève,* a long line of limestone precipices, seeming to impend over the town, though it is in reality 5 miles off, and within the Sardinian territory. . . . The summit of the Salève, more than 3100 ft. above the lake, is frequently scaled by the inhabitants of Geneva, who make picnic parties to enjoy the view from its summit." Though the Shelleys saw Mont Salève in 1816 and speculated favorably on the quality of the view from the peak, it does not appear that they took the time to climb it.

Frankenstein believes the monster murdered William — no evidence?

such as her mother, the celebrated writer and patron of the arts Suzanne Curchod, also known as Madame Necker; German poet August Wilhelm Schlegel (1767–1845), the older brother of Friedrich Schlegel (see the Foreword, note 14, above); Swiss-French activist-writer Benjamin Constant; and the Genevese historian-economist Jean Charles Léonard de Sismondi.

24. Described by *Murray* as a "sugar-loaf mountain," rising to 5,800 feet above sea level.

25. The "storm" is a "tempest" in the 1831 edition.

26. How can Victor be so certain? Because, answer Morton Kaplan and Robert Kloss, in "Fantasy of Paternity and the Doppelgänger: Mary Shelley's *Frankenstein*," the creature is Victor's doppelgänger, and it was thus Victor himself who murdered the child (psychologically speaking).

> -Frankenstein blames
>   the monster for
> his misery
>
> -2 years since the creation
>   of the monster
>
> - insanity, delirium

30. Vampire lore was not new to the eighteenth century: Accounts of the dead rising and preying upon living victims, often family members or neighbors, have been traced back to the Babylonians and ancient Greeks. As late as the ninth edition (1888), the *Encyclopædia Britannica* reported that the vampire was "supposed to be the soul of a dead man which quits the buried body by night to suck the blood of living persons. Hence, when the vampire's grave is opened, his corpse is found to be fresh and rosy from the

had until now sought to forget: the whole train of my progress towards the creation; the appearance of the work of my own hands alive at my bed side; its departure. Two years had now nearly elapsed since the night on which he first received life;[28] and was this his first crime? Alas! I had turned loose into the world a depraved wretch, whose delight was in carnage and misery; had he not murdered my brother?

No one can conceive the anguish I suffered during the remainder of the night, which I spent, cold and wet, in the open air. But I did not feel the inconvenience of the weather; my imagination was busy in scenes of evil and despair. I considered the being whom I had cast among mankind,[29] and endowed with the will and power to effect purposes of horror, such as the deed which he had now done, nearly in the light of my own vampire,[30] my own spirit let loose from the grave, and forced to destroy all that was dear to me.

Day dawned; and I directed my steps towards the town. The gates were open; and I hastened to my father's house. My first thought was to discover what I knew of the murderer, and cause instant pursuit to be made. But I paused when I reflected on the story that I had to tell. A being whom I myself had formed, and endued with life, had met me at midnight among the precipices of an inaccessible mountain. I remembered also the nervous fever with which I had been seized just at the time that I dated my creation, and which would give an air of delirium to a tale otherwise so utterly improbable. I well knew that if any other had communicated such a relation to me, I should have looked upon it as the ravings of insanity. Besides, the strange nature of the animal would elude all pursuit, even if I were so far credited as to persuade my relatives to commence it. Besides,[31] of what use would be pursuit? Who could arrest a creature capable of scaling the overhanging sides of Mont Salêve? These reflections determined me, and I resolved to remain silent.

It was about five in the morning when I entered my father's house. I told the servants not to disturb the family, and went into the library to attend their usual hour of rising.

Six years had elapsed, passed as a dream but for one indelible trace, and I stood in the same place where I had last embraced my father before my departure for Ingoldstadt. Beloved and respectable[32] parent! He still remained to me. I gazed on the picture of my mother, which stood over the mantle-piece. It was an historical subject, painted at my father's desire, and represented Caroline Beaufort in an agony of despair, kneeling by the coffin of her dead father.[33]

Her garb was rustic, and her cheek pale; but there was an air of dignity and beauty, that hardly permitted the sentiment of pity. Below this picture was a miniature of William; and my tears flowed when I looked upon it. While I was thus engaged, Ernest entered: he had heard me arrive, and hastened to welcome me.[34] He expressed a sorrowful delight to see me: "Welcome, my dearest Victor," said he. "Ah! I wish you had come three months ago, and then you would have found us all joyous and delighted. But we are now unhappy; and, I am afraid, tears instead of smiles will be your welcome. Our father looks so sorrowful: this dreadful event seems to have revived in his mind his grief on the death of Mamma. Poor Elizabeth also is quite inconsolable."[35] Ernest began to weep as he said these words.

"Do not," said I, "welcome me thus; try to be more calm, that I may not be absolutely miserable the moment I enter my father's house after so long an absence. But, tell me, how does my father support his misfortunes? and how is[36] my poor Elizabeth?"

"She indeed[37] requires consolation; she accused herself of having caused the death of my brother,[38] and that made her very wretched. But since the murderer has been discovered—"

"The murderer discovered! Good God! how can that be? who could attempt to pursue him? It is impossible; one might as well try to overtake the winds, or confine a mountain-stream with a straw."[39]

"I do not know what you mean;[40] but we were all very unhappy when she was discovered. No one would believe it at first; and even now Elizabeth will not be convinced, notwithstanding all the evidence. Indeed, who would credit that Justine Moritz, who was so amiable, and fond of all the family, could[41] all at once become so extremely wicked?"

blood which he has thus absorbed. To put a stop to his ravages, a stake is driven through the corpse, or the head cut off, or the heart torn out and the body burned, or boiling water and vinegar are poured on the grave. . . . The belief in vampires chiefly prevails in Slavonic lands, as in Russia (especially White Russia and the Ukraine), Poland, and Servia and among the Czechs of Bohemia and the other Slavonic races of Austria. It became especially prevalent in Hungary between the years 1730 and 1735, whence all Europe was filled with reports of the exploits of vampires. Several treatises were written on the subject, among which may be mentioned Ranft's *De masticatione mortuorum in tumulis* (1734) and Calmet's *Dissertation on the Vampires of Hungary* (1751)" (Vol. XXIV, p. 52).

By 1740, the meme of the vampire was so common that Alexander Pope, in a let- [illegible] he cares not for me now. He never asks after me or sends me word how he is going on. In short, the man I once loved is dead. This is a vampire."

- Justine Moritz is revealed to have murdered William
- Elizabeth's story of Justine

The earliest known poem concerning a vampire, "Der Vampir," was written in 1748 by the German poet Heinrich August Ossenfelder. Goethe, in "Die Braut von Korinth" (1797), tells the story of a bride who, dying prematurely, goes to her betrothed "[s]till to love the bridegroom I have lost, [a]nd the life-blood of his heart to drink . . ." (translated by Edgar Alfred Bowring, 1874). Robert Southey's epic poem *Thalaba the Destroyer* (1801) included a tale of a vampire, and Byron wrote of vampires in his 1813 poem *The Giaour, a Fragment of a Turkish Tale.* However, the most important English writing on the subject, *The Vampyre* (1819), came from the pen of John Polidori, reportedly drawn from the same well of inspiration as *Frankenstein* (see note 5, Appendix 1, and accompanying text, below).

31. Perhaps because the word "Besides" also appears in the prior sentence, the 1831 edition replaces the word with "And then."

—Victor still believes his monster to be the murderer

—Elizabeth also believes Justine is innocent

months ago, and then you would have found us all joyous and delighted. You come to us now to share a misery which nothing can alleviate; yet your presence will, I hope, revive our father, who seems sinking under his misfortune; and your persuasions will induce poor Elizabeth to cease her vain and tormenting self-accusations.—Poor William! he was our darling and our pride!"

"Justine Moritz! Poor, poor girl, is she the accused? But it is wrongfully; every one knows that; no one believes it, surely, Ernest?"

"No one did at first; but several circumstances came out, that have almost forced conviction upon us: and her own behaviour has been so confused, as to add to the evidence of facts a weight that, I fear, leaves no hope for doubt. But she will be tried to-day, and you will then hear all."

He related that, the morning on which the murder of poor William had been discovered, Justine had been taken ill, and confined to her bed[42]; and, after several days, one of the servants, happening to examine the apparel she had worn on the night of the murder, had discovered in her pocket the picture of my mother, which had been judged to be the temptation of the murderer. The servant instantly shewed it to one of the others, who, without saying a word to any of the family, went to a magistrate; and, upon their deposition, Justine was apprehended. On being charged with the fact, the poor girl confirmed the suspicion in a great measure by her extreme confusion of manner.

This was a strange tale, but it did not shake my faith; and I replied earnestly, "You are all mistaken; I know the murderer. Justine, poor, good Justine, is innocent."

At that instant my father entered. I saw unhappiness deeply impressed on his countenance, but he endeavoured to welcome me cheerfully; and, after we had exchanged our mournful greeting, would have introduced some other topic than that of our disaster, had not Ernest exclaimed, "Good God, Papa! Victor says that he knows who was the murderer of poor William."

"We do also, unfortunately," replied my father; "for indeed I had rather have been for ever ignorant than have discovered so much depravity and ingratitude in one I valued so highly."

"My dear father, you are mistaken; Justine is innocent."

"If she is, God forbid that she should suffer as guilty. She is to be tried to-day, and I hope, I sincerely hope, that she will be acquitted."

This speech calmed me. I was firmly convinced in my own mind that Justine, and indeed every human being, was guiltless of this murder. I had no fear, therefore, that any circumstantial evidence could be brought forward strong enough to convict her;[43] and, in this assurance, I calmed myself, expecting the trial with eagerness, but without prognosticating an evil result.

We were soon joined by Elizabeth.[44] Time had made great alterations in her form since I had last beheld her. Six years before she had been a pretty, good-humoured girl, whom every one loved and caressed. She was now a woman in stature and expression of countenance, which was uncommonly lovely. An open and capacious forehead gave indications of a good understanding, joined to great frankness of disposition. Her eyes were hazel, and expressive of mildness, now through recent affliction allied to sadness. Her hair was of a rich, dark auburn, her complexion fair, and her figure slight and graceful. She welcomed me with the greatest affection. "Your arrival, my dear cousin," said she, "fills me with hope. You perhaps will find some means to justify my poor guiltless Justine. Alas! who is safe, if she be convicted of crime? I rely on her innocence as certainly as I do upon my own. Our misfortune is doubly hard to us; we have not only lost that lovely darling boy, but this poor girl, whom I sincerely love, is to be torn away by even a worse fate. If she is condemned, I never shall know joy more. But she will not, I am sure she will not; and then I shall be happy again, even after the sad death of my little William."

"She is innocent, my Elizabeth," said I, "and that shall be proved; fear nothing, but let your spirits be cheered by the assurance of her acquittal."

"How kind[45] you are! every one else believes in her guilt, and that made me wretched; for I knew that it was impossible: and to see every one else prejudiced in so deadly a manner, rendered me hopeless and despairing." She wept.

"Sweet[46] niece," said my father, "dry your tears. If she is, as you believe, innocent, rely on the justice of our judges, and the activity with which I shall prevent the slightest shadow of partiality."

Tears, unrestrained, fell from my brother's eyes; a sense of mortal agony crept over my frame. Before, I had only imagined the wretchedness of my desolated home; the reality came on me as a new, and a not less terrible, disaster. I tried to calm Ernest; I enquired more minutely concerning my father, and her I named my cousin.

This speech, referring to William as "our darling and our pride," seems more suitable for a parent than a seventeen-year-old sibling, but that is perhaps natural in light of the age disparity. How old was William? Victor, at seventeen, describes him as an "infant" (presumably three or four, or even younger), at a time when Ernest was eleven, so William may have been under the age of ten when murdered.

35. The Thomas Text replaces this and the previous sentence with sentiments similar to those expressed in the 1831 edition, again inappropriate for someone of Ernest's age: "the sense of our fortune is yet unalleviated; the silence of our father is uninterrupted, and there is something more distressing than tears in his unaltered sadness—while poor Elizabeth, seeking solitude and for ever weeping, already begins to feel the effects of incessant grief—for her colour is gone, and her eyes are hollow & lusterless."

36. This phrase and the previous sentence are struck in the Thomas Text, and instead, Victor makes the suggestion, "You must assist me in acquiring sufficient calmness to console my father and support my poor Elizabeth." This reliance on Ernest underlines the earlier age of maturity in centuries past; after all, Victor left for Ingolstadt at the same age.

37. The 1831 edition begins this paragraph: "'She, most of all,' said Ernest, 'requires consolation . . .'"

38. Elizabeth—Mary Shelley's counterpart, in the view of the psychoanalytic critics—repeatedly asserts her guilt in William's death, far beyond reasonableness. The critics suggest that not only is this the expression of Mary Shelley's hostility to her half-brother William Godwin, the progeny of her despised stepmother, Mary Jane Clairmont, and the son her father had always craved, but also hostility to her father. This seems farfetched. No evidences suggests that Shelley felt that her father was to blame for the death of her mother or that she had any marked animosity toward her half-brother, a mere age ten when Mary wrote *Frankenstein.* If it must be seen as a personal expression, it seems more likely to be a disguised portrayal of the guilt of a mother who has "allowed" a premature baby to die, as Shelley's own had in early 1816.

39. An additional sentence appears here in the 1831 edition: "I saw him too; he was free last night!"

40. In place of the balance of the sentence, the 1831 edition reads, "replied my brother, in accents of wonder, 'but to us the discovery we have made completes our misery.'" The change was clearly necessitated in order to reflect Ernest's puzzlement at Victor's identification of the murderer as male in the sentence newly added by Mary Shelley.

41. In the 1831 edition, the balance of the sentence reads, "suddenly become capable of so frightful, so appalling a crime."

42. The 1831 text deletes the phrase "and, after" to break up the long sentence to read as follows: ". . . confined to her bed for several days. During this interval one of the servants . . ."

43. The balance of this sentence is replaced in the 1831 edition with the following: "My tale was not one to announce publicly; its astounding horror would be looked upon as madness by the vulgar. Did any one indeed exist, except I, the creator, who would believe, unless his senses convinced him, in the existence of the living monument of presumption and rash ignorance which I had let loose upon the world?" The introduction of the word "presumption," never before used by Victor in connection with his rash actions, may have been inspired by Richard Brinsley Peake's *Presumption: or, the Fate of Frankenstein.* The play, first produced in 1823, ran for many performances and was often restaged during the nineteenth century; it was also widely imitated (see Appendix 4, below). Shelley herself went to see a performance, concluding, "The story is not well managed," though she expressed admiration for the program, which identified the creature only as "————" (letter to Leigh Hunt, September 9, 1823).

44. The six following sentences are replaced in the 1831 edition with the following: "Time had altered her since I last beheld her; it had endowed her with loveliness surpassing the beauty of her childish years. There was the same candour, the same vivacity, but it was allied to an expression more full of sensibility and intellect."

45. The phrase "and generous" is inserted here in the 1831 edition.

46. "Sweet" becomes "dearest" in the 1831 edition, and in the following sentence, "judges" is replaced by "laws."

Program for *Presumption, or the Fate of Frankenstein,* by Richard Brinsley Peake (1823).

CHAPTER VII.[1]

1. Chapter 8 in the 1831 edition.

W E PASSED A few sad hours, until eleven o'clock, when the trial was to commence. My father and the rest of the family being obliged to attend as witnesses, I accompanied them to the court. During the whole of this wretched mockery of justice, I suffered living torture. It was to be decided, whether the result of my curiosity and lawless devices would cause the death of two of my fellow-beings: one a smiling babe, full of innocence and joy;

A trial in 1848 in the Old Bailey in London. Justine's trial might well have looked like this.

the other far more dreadfully murdered, with every aggravation of infamy that could make the murder memorable in horror. Justine also was a girl of merit, and possessed qualities which promised to render her life happy: now all was to be obliterated in an ignominious grave; and I the cause! A thousand times rather would I have confessed myself guilty of the crime ascribed to Justine; but I was absent when it was committed, and such a declaration would have been considered as the ravings of a madman, and would not have exculpated her who suffered through me.

The appearance of Justine was calm. She was dressed in mourning; and her countenance, always engaging, was rendered, by the solemnity of her feelings, exquisitely beautiful. Yet she appeared confident in innocence, and did not tremble, although gazed on and execrated by thousands; for all the kindness which her beauty might otherwise have excited, was obliterated in the minds of the spectators by the imagination of the enormity she was supposed to have committed. She was tranquil, yet her tranquillity was evidently constrained; and as her confusion had before been adduced as a proof of her guilt, she worked up her mind to an appearance of courage. When she entered the court, she threw her eyes round it, and quickly discovered where we were seated. A tear seemed to dim her eye when she saw us; but she quickly recovered herself, and a look of sorrowful affection seemed to attest her utter guiltlessness.

The trial began; and after the advocate against her had stated the charge, several witnesses were called. Several strange facts combined against her, which might have staggered any one who had not such proof of her innocence as I had. She had been out the whole of the night on which the murder had been committed, and towards morning had been perceived by a market-woman not far from the spot where the body of the murdered child had been afterwards found. The woman asked her what she did there; but she looked very strangely, and only returned a confused and unintelligible answer. She returned to the house about eight o'clock; and when one inquired where she had passed the night, she replied, that she had been looking for the child, and

— Victor blames himself for the murder of William and (soon to be) murder of Justine

demanded earnestly, if any thing had been heard concerning him. When shewn the body, she fell into violent hysterics, and kept her bed for several days. The picture was then produced, which the servant had found in her pocket; and when Elizabeth, in a faltering voice, proved that it was the same which, an hour before the child had been missed, she had placed round his neck, a murmur of horror and indignation filled the court.

Justine was called on for her defence. As the trial had proceeded, her countenance had altered. Surprise, horror, and misery, were strongly expressed. Sometimes she struggled with her tears; but when she was desired to plead, she collected her powers, and spoke in an audible although variable voice:—

"God knows," she said, "how entirely I am innocent. But I do not pretend that my protestations should acquit me: I rest my innocence on a plain and simple explanation of the facts which have been adduced against me; and I hope the character I have always borne will incline my judges[2] to a favourable interpretation, where any circumstance appears doubtful or suspicious."

She then related that, by the permission of Elizabeth, she had passed the evening of the night on which the murder had been committed, at the house of an aunt at Chêne,[3] a village situated at about a league from Geneva. On her return, at about nine o'clock, she met a man, who asked her if she had seen any thing of the child who was lost. She was alarmed by this account, and passed several hours in looking for him, when the gates of Geneva were shut, and she was forced to remain several hours of the night in a barn belonging to a cottage, being unwilling to call up the inhabitants, to whom she was well known. Unable to rest or sleep, she quitted her asylum early,[4] that she might again endeavour to find my brother. If she had gone near the spot where his body lay, it was without her knowledge. That she had been bewildered when questioned by the market-woman, was not surprising, since she had passed a sleepless night,[5] and the fate of poor William was yet uncertain. Concerning the picture she could give no account.

2. Multiple judges were uncommon to nonexistent in Swiss courtrooms, other than in a court of appeals. Perhaps Justine, and later Victor, meant the judge and the prosecutor collectively, or perhaps a panel of judges was specially convened out of respect for the victim's father. By the constitution of the Swiss Confederation, crimes against the federal government were tried before juries; the conduct of other criminal trials was governed by cantonal rules. By the early nineteenth century, the canton of Geneva had adopted trial by jury (long a tradition of English law but much less common in other legal systems), and it may be possible to conjecture that Justine's case represents one of the earliest jury trials. In 2009, a referendum in Geneva—the last of the Swiss cantons to use trial by jury—repealed the rule.

3. Chêne, later Chêne–Les Bougeries, and later still Chêne-Bourg and Chêne-Thonex, was about two and a quarter miles outside Geneva, of which it became a part in 1816. *Baedeker's Switzerland and the Adjacent Portions of Italy, Savoy, and the Tyrol* in 1887 terms it a "large village." The economist-historian Sismondi, whose work on the history of Italy was read by Percy Shelley in 1819, died in Chêne in 1842.

4. The preceding portion of this sentence is replaced in the 1831 edition with the following: "Most of the night she spent here watching; towards morning she believed that she slept for a few minutes; some steps disturbed her, and she awoke. It was dawn, and she quitted her asylum . . ."

This change explains how the creature was able to place the broach in Justine's pocket. See note 5, below.

5. The creature testifies later that he approached Justine "unperceived" and deposited the broach into the pocket of

her dress. It is hard to believe that a being of his size could have approached Justine when she was awake without being caught; therefore, she must have dozed off for at least a few minutes. See note 4, above.

6. This sentence is confusing: Did the character witnesses testify or not?

7. Under Greek and Roman law as well as Talmudic rules, women were not allowed to testify except in exceptional circumstances. This injunction prevailed in many Western countries, including the United States, and was one of many deprivations of rights that the suffrage movement sought to correct. The legal silencing of women was dramatized in Mary Wollstonecraft's *The Wrongs of Woman* (1798), also known as *Maria, or the Wrongs of Woman* and *The Wrongs of Woman; or, Mary*.

"I know," continued the unhappy victim, "how heavily and fatally this one circumstance weighs against me, but I have no power of explaining it; and when I have expressed my utter ignorance, I am only left to conjecture concerning the probabilities by which it might have been placed in my pocket. But here also I am checked. I believe that I have no enemy on earth, and none surely would have been so wicked as to destroy me wantonly. Did the murderer place it there? I know of no opportunity afforded him for so doing; or if I had, why should he have stolen the jewel, to part with it again so soon?

"I commit my cause to the justice of my judges, yet I see no room for hope. I beg permission to have a few witnesses examined concerning my character; and if their testimony shall not overweigh my supposed guilt, I must be condemned, although I would pledge my salvation on my innocence."

Several witnesses were called, who had known her for many years, and they spoke well of her; but fear, and hatred of the crime of which they supposed her guilty, rendered them timorous, and unwilling to come forward.[6] Elizabeth saw even this last resource, her excellent dispositions and irreproachable conduct, about to fail the accused, when, although violently agitated, she desired permission to address the court.[7]

"I am," said she, "the cousin of the unhappy child who was murdered, or rather his sister, for I was educated by and have lived with his parents ever since and even long before his birth. It may therefore be judged indecent in me to come forward on this occasion; but when I see a fellow-creature about to perish through the cowardice of her pretended friends, I wish to be allowed to speak, that I may say what I know of her character. I am well acquainted with the accused. I have lived in the same house with her, at one time for five, and at another for nearly two years. During all that period she appeared to me the most amiable and benevolent of human creatures. She nursed Madame Frankenstein, my aunt, in her last illness with the greatest affection and care; and afterwards attended her own mother during a tedious illness, in a manner that excited the admiration of all who knew her. After which she again lived in my uncle's house, where she was beloved by all the family. She was warmly attached to the child who is now dead, and acted towards him like a most affectionate mother. For my own part, I do not hesitate to say, that, notwithstanding all the evidence produced against her, I believe and rely on her perfect innocence. She had no temptation for such an action: as to the bauble on which the chief proof rests, if she had earnestly desired it, I should have willingly given it to her; so much do I esteem and value her."

Excellent Elizabeth! A murmur of approbation was heard;[8] but it was excited by her generous interference, and not in favour of poor Justine, on whom the public indignation was turned with renewed violence, charging her with the blackest ingratitude. She herself wept as Elizabeth spoke, but she did not answer. My own agitation and anguish was extreme during the whole trial. I believed in her innocence; I knew it. Could the daemon, who had (I did not for a minute doubt) murdered my brother, also in his hellish sport have betrayed the innocent to death and ignominy. I could not sustain the horror of my situation; and when I perceived that the popular voice, and the countenances of the judges, had already condemned my unhappy victim, I rushed out of the court in agony. The tortures of the accused did not equal mine; she was sustained by innocence, but the fangs of remorse tore my bosom, and would not forego their hold.

I passed a night of unmingled wretchedness. In the morning I went to the court; my lips and throat were parched. I dared not ask the fatal question; but I was known, and the officer guessed the cause of my visit. The ballots had been thrown; they were all black,[9] and Justine was condemned.

I cannot pretend to describe what I then felt. I had before experienced sensations of horror; and I have endeavoured to bestow upon them adequate expressions, but words cannot convey an idea of the heart-sickening despair that I then endured. The person to whom I addressed myself added, that Justine had already confessed her guilt. "That evidence," he observed, "was hardly required in so glaring a case, but I am

8. The 1831 edition replaces "was heard" with "followed Elizabeth's simple and powerful appeal." The psychoanalytic critics, including in this case Veeder, in *Mary Shelley and Frankenstein*, chapter 6, "The Women of Frankenstein," argue that Elizabeth's advocacy is full of ambiguities, suggesting her deep oedipal connection to Alphonse and her antipathy to Justine, who dared to insert herself into the family and the relationship with Alphonse. Veeder points out that Elizabeth carefully states that Justine is *not* part of the family but a mere servant; therefore, Elizabeth is her superior. Elizabeth also unconsciously expresses possessiveness regarding Caroline—"*my aunt*"—and Alphonse—"*my uncle*"— even though the relationships were perfectly clear without those descriptors. All of this, argues Veeder, reflects Shelley's own feelings about Godwin and her half-sister Claire Clairmont. It is difficult to ignore the many psychological parallels between the relationships in *Frankenstein* and those in the Godwin-Wollstonecraft-Shelley families, but it is very unlikely that, writing at the age of nineteen, the author intended *Frankenstein* as a work of autobiography or a therapeutic exercise. In short, as Sigmund Freud allegedly said, sometimes a cigar is just a cigar.

9. That is, no one among the jury or panel of judges voted for acquittal.

10. The 1831 edition deletes this phrase and replaces it with the following: "This was strange and unexpected intelligence; what could it mean? Had my eyes deceived me? And was I really as mad as the whole world would believe me to be if I disclosed the object of my suspicions? I hastened to return home, and[.]"

11. This is a very cynical view, in sharp contrast to the Declaration of the Rights of Man and of the Citizen (1789), a product of the French Revolution, whose Article IX proclaims: "As every man is presumed innocent until he has been declared guilty, if it should be considered necessary to arrest him, any undue harshness that is not required to secure his person must be severely curbed by law" (translation by Constitutional Council of France). Swiss law followed this principle as well, and therefore this statement must be seen as the personal opinion of Victor.

glad of it; and, indeed, none of our judges like to condemn a criminal upon circumstantial evidence, be it ever so decisive."

When I returned home,[10] Elizabeth eagerly demanded the result.

"My cousin," replied I, "it is decided as you may have expected; all judges had rather that ten innocent should suffer, than that one guilty should escape.[11] But she has confessed."

This was a dire blow to poor Elizabeth, who had relied with firmness upon Justine's innocence. "Alas!" said she, "how shall I ever again believe in human benevolence?[12] Justine, whom I loved and esteemed as my sister, how could she put on those smiles of innocence only to betray; her mild eyes seemed incapable of any severity or ill-humour,[13] and yet she has committed a murder."

Soon after we heard that the poor victim had expressed a wish to see my cousin. My father wished her not to go; but said, that he left it to her own judgment and feelings to decide. "Yes," said Elizabeth, "I will go, although she is guilty; and you, Victor, shall accompany me: I cannot go alone." The idea of this visit was torture to me, yet I could not refuse.

We entered the gloomy prison-chamber, and beheld Justine sitting on some straw at the further end; her hands were manacled, and her head rested on her knees. She rose on seeing us enter; and when we were left alone with her, she threw herself at the feet of Elizabeth, weeping bitterly. My cousin wept also.

"Oh, Justine!" said she, "why did you rob me of my last consolation. I relied on your innocence; and although I was then very wretched, I was not so miserable as I am now."

"And do you also believe that I am so very, very wicked? Do you also join with my enemies to crush me?"[14] Her voice was suffocated with sobs.

"Rise, my poor girl," said Elizabeth, "why do you kneel, if you are innocent? I am not one of your enemies; I believed you guiltless, notwithstanding every evidence, until I heard that you had yourself declared your guilt. That report, you say, is false; and be assured, dear Justine, that nothing can shake my confidence in you for a moment, but your own confession."

"I did confess; but I confessed a lie. I confessed, that I might obtain absolution; but now that falsehood lies heavier at my heart than all my other sins. The God of heaven forgive me! Ever since I was condemned, my confessor has besieged me; he threatened and menaced, until I almost began to think that I was the monster that he said I was. He threatened excommunication and hell fire in my last moments, if I continued obdurate.[15] Dear lady, I had none to support me; all looked on me as a wretch doomed to ignominy and perdition. What could I do? In an evil hour I subscribed to a lie; and now only am I truly miserable."

She paused, weeping, and then continued—"I thought with horror, my sweet lady, that you should believe your Justine, whom your blessed aunt had so highly honoured, and whom you loved, was a creature capable of a crime which none but the devil himself could have perpetrated. Dear William! dearest blessed child! I soon shall see you again in heaven, where we shall all be happy; and that consoles me, going as I am to suffer ignominy and death."

"Oh, Justine! forgive me for having for one moment distrusted you. Why did you confess? But do not mourn, my dear girl;[16] I will every where proclaim your innocence, and force belief. Yet you must die; you, my playfellow, my companion, my more than sister. I never can survive so horrible a misfortune."

"Dear, sweet Elizabeth, do not weep.[17] You ought to raise me with thoughts of a better life, and elevate me from the petty cares of this world of injustice and strife. Do not you, excellent friend, drive me to despair."

"I will try to comfort you; but this, I fear, is an evil too deep and poignant to admit of consolation, for there is no hope. Yet heaven bless thee, my dearest Justine, with resignation, and a confidence elevated beyond this world. Oh! how I hate its shews and mockeries! when one creature is murdered, another is immediately deprived of life in a slow torturing manner; then the executioners, their hands yet reeking with the blood of innocence, believe that they have done a great deed. They call this retribution.[18] Hateful name! When that word is pronounced, I know greater and more

12. In the 1831 edition, the word "benevolence" is replaced with "goodness."

13. The phrase "ill-humour" is replaced with "guile" in the 1831 edition, and in the following sentence, the word "wish" is changed to "desire."

14. The 1831 edition adds the phrase "to condemn me as a murderer?"

15. The French Revolution disenfranchised the Church and subjected it to secular control, and scores of priests and nuns were executed and thousands were deported. Yet the very terror of the revolution apparently led many back to spiritual resources, and some turned to traditional Catholicism. Christopher Dawson, in his essay "Romanticism and Religion," argues that "the most profound expression of the romantic spirit is to be found, not in the Byronic cult of personality or the aesthetic gospel of Keats's 'Ode to a Grecian Urn,' but in Novalis's 'Hymns to the Night,' with their mystical exaltation of death" (*The Tablet [of London]*, 1937). Certainly this much is clear: The revolution did not extinguish the Catholic Church, which gained adherents steadily through the nineteenth century.

The pernicious influence of the Catholic Church as an organization urging conformity and obedience was a popular theme of the day in England. The Church's adherents were perceived as a kind of "fifth column," swearing fealty to the pope rather than the Crown. Although the Roman Catholic Relief Act, enacted in 1791, softened some official views, Matthew Lewis's gothic novel *The Monk* (1796) was a well-received depiction of the wicked clergy. Lewis was acquainted with the Shelleys and visited them on Lake Geneva in the summer of 1816. It was not until 1829 that another Roman Catholic Relief Act extended full religious freedom to English Catholics.

However, as Veeder points out in *Mary Shelley and Frankenstein*, such oppressive behavior by a cleric was hardly to be expected in Calvinist Geneva. Mary Shelley invokes anti-Catholic sentiments here to underline Justine's helplessness, mirroring, according to Veeder, her own understanding of women's vulnerability.

16. The 1831 revises the balance of the paragraph as follows: "Do not fear. I will proclaim, I will prove your innocence. I will melt the stony hearts of your enemies by my tears and prayers. You shall not die! You, my playfellow, my companion, my sister, perish on the scaffold! No! No! I never could survive so horrible a misfortune."

17. This paragraph and the two succeeding paragraphs do not appear in the 1831

[handwritten note:] Victor refers to himself as "the true murderer" he feels guilty

fully, 'I do not wish to die,' she said, that ... is ... weakness and gives me courage ... the worst. I ... said ... bitter world; and if you ... time as of one unjustly condemned, I am resigned to the ... from me, dear lady, to submit in patience to the will of heaven."

Justine's admonition is a far cry from Elizabeth's previous bitter denunciation of the fallibility of the justice system.

18. Already there was popular sentiment against the death penalty. In 1764, Cesare Beccaria, an intellectual and journalist, published *Dei delitti e delle pene* (*On Crimes and Punishments*), which laid out some of the first modern arguments against the death penalty. It advocated reform of the criminal justice system on rational principles. Beccaria reflected the views of Jean-Jacques Rousseau, who wrote, in *The Social Contract* (1762), "There is no man so bad that he cannot be made good

horrid punishments are going to be inflicted than the gloomiest tyrant has ever invented to satiate his utmost revenge. Yet this is not consolation for you, my Justine, unless indeed that you may glory in escaping from so miserable a den. Alas! I would I were in peace with my aunt and my lovely William, escaped from a world which is hateful to me, and the visages of men which I abhor."

Justine smiled languidly. "This, dear lady, is despair, and not resignation. I must not learn the lesson that you would teach me. Talk of something else, something that will bring peace, and not increase of misery."

During this conversation I had retired to a corner of the prison-room, where I could conceal the horrid anguish that possessed me. Despair! Who dared talk of that? The poor victim, who on the morrow was to pass the dreary[19] boundary between life and death, felt not as I did, such deep and bitter agony. I gnashed my teeth, and ground them together, uttering a groan that came from my inmost soul. Justine started. When she saw who it was, she approached me, and said, "Dear Sir, you are very kind to visit me; you, I hope, do not believe that I am guilty."

I could not answer. "No, Justine," said Elizabeth; "he is more convinced of your innocence than I was; for even when he heard that you had confessed, he did not credit it."

"I truly thank him. In these last moments I feel the sheerest[20] gratitude towards those who think of me with kindness. How sweet is the affection of others to such a wretch as I am! It removes more than half my misfortune; and I feel as if I could die in peace, now that my innocence is acknowledged by you, dear lady, and your cousin."

Thus the poor sufferer tried to comfort others and herself. She indeed gained the resignation she desired. But I, the true murderer, felt the never-dying worm alive in my bosom, which allowed of no hope or consolation. Elizabeth also wept, and was unhappy; but her's also was the misery of innocence, which, like a cloud that passes over the fair moon, for a while hides, but cannot tarnish its brightness. Anguish and despair had penetrated into the core of my heart; I bore a hell within me, which nothing could extinguish. We staid several hours with Justine; and it was with great difficulty that Elizabeth could tear herself away. "I wish," cried she, "that I were to die with you; I cannot live in this world of misery."

Justine assumed an air of cheerfulness, while she with difficulty repressed her bitter tears. She embraced Elizabeth, and said, in a voice of half-suppressed emotion, "Farewell, sweet lady, dearest Elizabeth, my beloved and only friend; may heaven in its bounty bless and preserve you; may this be the last misfortune that you will ever suffer. Live, and be happy, and make others so."

As we returned, Elizabeth said, "You know not, my dear Victor, how much I am relieved, now that I trust in the innocence of this unfortunate girl.[21] I never could again have known peace, if I had been deceived in my reliance on her. For the moment that I did believe her guilty, I felt an anguish that I could not have long sustained. Now my heart is lightened. The innocent suffers; but she whom I thought amiable and good has not betrayed the trust I reposed in her, and I am consoled."

Amiable cousin! such were your thoughts, mild and gentle as your own dear eyes and voice. But I—I was a wretch, and none ever conceived of the misery that I then endured.[22]

for something. No man should be put to death, even as an example, if he can be left to live without danger to society." Another vociferous opponent was Basil Montagu (1770–1851), the barrister who represented Percy Shelley in his child custody case. In 1809, Montagu published "'The Opinions of Different Authors upon the Punishment of Death."

19. In the 1831 edition the word is "awful" rather than "dreary."

20. The 1831 edition replaces "sheerest" with "sincerest."

21. This paragraph and the next paragraph are omitted from the 1831 text and replaced with the following:

> And on the morrow Justine died. Elizabeth's heart-rending eloquence failed to move the judges from their settled conviction in the criminality of the saintly sufferer. My passionate and indignant appeals were lost upon them. And when I received their cold answers and heard the harsh, unfeeling reasoning of these men, my purposed avowal died away on my lips. Thus I might proclaim myself a madman, but not revoke the sentence passed upon my wretched victim. She perished on the scaffold as a murderess!
>
> From the tortures of my own heart, I turned to contemplate the deep and voiceless grief of my Elizabeth. This also was my doing! And my father's woe, and the desolation of that late so smiling home all was the work of my thrice-accursed hands! Ye weep, unhappy ones, but these are not your last tears! Again shall you raise the funeral wail, and the sound of your lamentations shall again and again be heard! Frankenstein, your son, your kinsman, your early, much-loved friend; he who would spend each vital

drop of blood for your sakes, who has no thought nor sense of joy except as it is mirrored also in your dear countenances, who would fill the air with blessings and spend his life in serving you—he bids you weep, to shed countless tears; happy beyond his hopes, if thus inexorable fate be satisfied, and if the destruction pause before the peace of the grave have succeeded to your sad torments!

Thus spoke my prophetic soul, as, torn by remorse, horror, and despair, I beheld those I loved spend vain sorrow upon the graves of William and Justine, the first hapless victims to my unhallowed arts.

This characterization of his actions as "unhallowed" is the first suggestion by Mary Shelley that Victor believes that bringing forth the creature was an impious act, and the speech itself is near-biblical in tone. Here also, in this revised text, we see Shelley's decision to foreshadow the further deaths to come.

22. William Godwin wrote, in *Political Justice*, "If there be any sight more humiliating than all others, it is that of a miserable victim acknowledging the justice of a sentence against which every enlightened spectator exclaims with horror."

VOLUME

II

CHAPTER I.[1]

NOTHING IS MORE painful to the human mind, than, after the feelings have been worked up by a quick succession of events, the dead calmness of inaction and certainty which follows, and deprives the soul both of hope and fear. Justine died; she rested; and I was alive. The blood flowed freely in my veins, but a weight of despair and remorse pressed on my heart, which nothing could remove. Sleep fled from my eyes; I wandered like an evil spirit, for I had committed deeds of mischief beyond description horrible, and more, much more, (I persuaded myself) was yet behind. Yet my heart overflowed with kindness, and the love of virtue. I had begun life with benevolent intentions, and thirsted for the moment when I should put them in practice, and make myself useful to my fellow-beings. Now all was blasted: instead of that serenity of conscience, which allowed me to look back upon the past with self-satisfaction, and from thence to gather promise of new hopes, I was seized by remorse and the sense of guilt, which hurried me away to a hell of intense tortures, such as no language can describe.

This state of mind preyed upon my health, which had[2] entirely recovered from the first shock it had sustained. I shunned the face of man; all sound of joy or complacency

1. Chapter 9 in the 1831 edition.

2. The phrase "perhaps never" is inserted here in the 1831 edition.

"a weight of despair and remorse pressed on my heart, which nothing could remove"

3. The Thomas Text replaces the balance of this sentence with the following: "At first he suspected some latent cause for my affliction, but when I assured him that the late events were the causes of my dejection, he called to his aid philosophy and reason, while he endeavoured to restore me to a calmer state of mind." Mary Shelley eventually used a different formulation in the 1831 edition, replacing the balance of the sentence with "by arguments deduced from the feelings of his serene conscience and guiltless life to inspire me with fortitude and awaken in me the courage to dispel the dark cloud which brooded over me."

4. The 1831 edition inserts the phrase "and terror its alarm."

5. See note 18, Volume I, Chapter VI, above.

> Victor felt like jumping into the lake and killing himself but did not want to leave his family with the monster he created

was torture to me; solitude was my only consolation—deep, dark, death-like solitude.

My father observed with pain the alteration perceptible in my disposition and habits, and endeavoured[3] to reason with me on the folly of giving way to immoderate grief. "Do you think, Victor," said he, "that I do not suffer also? No one could love a child more than I loved your brother;" (tears came into his eyes as he spoke); "but is it not a duty to the survivors, that we should refrain from augmenting their unhappiness by an appearance of immoderate grief? It is also a duty owed to yourself; for excessive sorrow prevents improvement or enjoyment, or even the discharge of daily usefulness, without which no man is fit for society."

This advice, although good, was totally inapplicable to my case; I should have been the first to hide my grief, and console my friends, if remorse had not mingled its bitterness[4] with my other sensations. Now I could only answer my father with a look of despair, and endeavour to hide myself from his view.

About this time we retired to our house at Belrive. This change was particularly agreeable to me. The shutting of the gates regularly at ten o'clock,[5] and the impossibility of remaining on the lake after that hour, had rendered our residence within the walls of Geneva very irksome to me. I was now free. Often, after the rest of the family had retired for the night, I took the boat, and passed many hours upon the water. Sometimes, with my sails set, I was carried by the wind; and sometimes, after rowing into the middle of the lake, I left the boat to pursue its own course, and gave way to my own miserable reflections. I was often tempted, when all was at peace around me, and I the only unquiet thing that wandered restless in a scene so beautiful and heavenly, if I except some bat, or the frogs, whose harsh and interrupted croaking was heard only when I approached the shore— often, I say, I was tempted to plunge into the silent lake, that the waters might close over me and my calamities for ever. But I was restrained, when I thought of the heroic and suffering Elizabeth, whom I tenderly loved, and whose existence was bound up in mine. I thought also of my father, and surviving brother: should I by my base desertion leave them exposed and unprotected to the malice of the fiend whom I had let loose among them?

At these moments I wept bitterly, and wished that peace would revisit my mind only that I might afford them consolation and happiness. But that could not be. Remorse extinguished every hope. I had been the author of unalterable evils; and I lived in daily fear, lest the monster whom I had created should perpetrate some new wickedness. I had an obscure feeling that all was not over, and that he would still commit some signal crime, which by its enormity should almost efface the recollection of the past. There was always scope for fear, so long as any thing I loved remained behind.[6] My abhorrence of this fiend cannot be conceived. When I thought of him, I gnashed my teeth, my eyes became inflamed, and I ardently wished to extinguish that life which I had so thoughtlessly bestowed. When I reflected on his crimes and malice, my hatred and revenge burst all bounds of moderation. I would have made a pilgrimage to the highest peak of the Andes,[7] could I, when there, have precipitated him to their base. I wished to see him again, that I might wreak the utmost extent of anger on his head, and avenge the deaths of William and Justine.

Our house was the house of mourning. My father's health

Aconcagua (photo by Albert Backer, used under CC-by-SA 3.0 license).

6. Percy Shelley added this sentence to the Draft.

7. The Andes, the mountain range on the western coast of South America, contains Aconcagua, the highest peak in the Western Hemisphere. The Spanish conquistadores made raids into the mountains, but the first serious exploration took place in 1579–85. In 1735, a French exploratory team investigated the Ecuadorian range, and in 1799, a German geologist landed in Venezuela and explored the mountains there. Aconcagua was not scaled by a European until 1883. Emily W. Sunstein, in *Mary Shelley: Romance and Reality*, writes of the "[p]rodigious tempests" (18) that swept England due to volcanic eruptions in 1797 in the Ecuadorian Andes, whose 250-mile (400-km) southern Central Valley was dubbed "The Avenue of the Volcanoes" by the German explorer Alexander von Humboldt in 1802. Sunstein, William J. Broad (in "A Volcanic Eruption That Reverberates 200 Years Later," *New York Times*, August 24, 2015, on Gillen D'Arcy Wood's *Tambora: The Eruption That Changed the World* [Princeton, NJ: Princeton University Press, 2014], about the April 1815 volcanic blast that shook the Dutch East Indies, present-day Indonesia, and cooled the planet for three

Victor hates and blames the creature.

8. This sentence is replaced in the 1831 edition with the following: "The first of these sorrows which are sent to wean us from the earth had visited her, and its dimming influence quenched her dearest smiles."

This alteration súggests that the trials of Elizabeth and the family are sent by the fates or God as a test, rather different from a mere reflection on the vicissitudes of life. As such, it seems to support Anne K. Mellor's view that the revisions of 1831 reflect deep philosophical changes in Mary Shelley rather than mere artistic choices. See note 53, Volume I, Letter IV, above.

9. "But," not "Yet," in the 1831 edition.

was deeply shaken by the horror of the recent events. Elizabeth was sad and desponding; she no longer took delight in her ordinary occupations; all pleasure seemed to her sacrilege toward the dead; eternal woe and tears she then thought was the just tribute she should pay to innocence so blasted and destroyed. She was no longer that happy creature, who in earlier youth wandered with me on the banks of the lake, and talked with ecstasy of our future prospects. She had become grave, and often conversed of the inconstancy of fortune, and the instability of human life.[8]

"When I reflect, my dear cousin," said she, "on the miserable death of Justine Moritz, I no longer see the world and its works as they before appeared to me. Before, I looked upon the accounts of vice and injustice, that I read in books or heard from others, as tales of ancient days, or imaginary evils; at least they were remote, and more familiar to reason than to the imagination; but now misery has come home, and men appear to me as monsters thirsting for each other's blood. Yet I am certainly unjust. Every body believed that poor girl to be guilty; and if she could have committed the crime for which she suffered, assuredly she would have been the most depraved of human creatures. For the sake of a few jewels, to have murdered the son of her benefactor and friend, a child whom she had nursed from its birth, and appeared to love as if it had been her own! I could not consent to the death of any human being; but certainly I should have thought such a creature unfit to remain in the society of men. Yet[9] she was innocent. I know, I feel she was innocent; you are of the same opinion, and that confirms me. Alas! Victor, when falsehood can look so like the truth, who can assure themselves of certain happiness? I feel as if I were walking on the edge of a precipice, towards which thousands are crowding, and endeavouring to plunge me into the abyss. William and Justine were assassinated, and the murderer escapes; he walks about the world free, and perhaps respected. But even if I were condemned to suffer on the scaffold for the same crimes, I would not change places with such a wretch."

I listened to this discourse with the extremest agony. I, not in deed, but in effect, was the true murderer. Elizabeth read my anguish in my countenance, and kindly taking my hand said, "My dearest cousin,[10] you must calm yourself. These events have affected me, God knows how deeply; but I am not so wretched as you are. There is an expression of despair, and sometimes of revenge, in your countenance, that makes me tremble.[11] Be calm, my dear Victor; I would sacrifice my life to your peace. We surely shall be happy: quiet in our native country, and not mingling in the world, what can disturb our tranquillity?"

She shed tears as she said this, distrusting the very solace that she gave; but at the same time she smiled, that she might chase away the fiend that lurked in my heart. My father, who saw in the unhappiness that was painted in my face only an exaggeration of that sorrow which I might naturally feel, thought that an amusement suited to my taste would be the best means of restoring to me my wonted serenity. It was from this cause that he had removed to the country; and, induced by the same motive, he now proposed that we should all make an excursion to the valley of Chamounix.[12] I had been there before, but Elizabeth and Ernest never had; and both had often expressed an earnest desire to see the scenery of this place, which had been described to them as so wonderful and sublime. Accordingly we departed from Geneva on this tour about the middle of the month of August,[13] nearly two months after the death of Justine.

The weather was uncommonly fine; and if mine had been a sorrow to be chased away by any fleeting circumstance, this excursion would certainly have had the effect intended by my father. As it was, I was somewhat interested in the scene; it sometimes lulled, although it could not extinguish my grief.

During the first day we travelled in a carriage. In the morning we had seen the mountains at a distance, towards which we gradually advanced. We perceived that the valley through which we wound, and which was formed by the river Arve,[14] whose course we followed, closed in upon us by degrees; and when the sun had set, we beheld immense mountains and precipices overhanging us on every side, and

10. The word "cousin" is replaced by "friend" in the 1831 edition.

11. A good deal of the balance of this chapter, up to note 16, below, is replaced

Victors calls himself a murderer, again

~~whom. Remember the friends around~~
~~Have we lost the power of rendering~~
~~you happy? Ah! While we love, while~~
~~we are true to each other, here in this~~
~~land of peace and beauty, your native~~
~~country, we may reap every tran-~~
~~quil blessing—what can disturb our~~
~~peace?~~

~~And could not such words from her~~
~~whom I fondly prized before every~~
~~other gift of fortune suffice to chase~~
~~away the fiend that lurked in my heart?~~
~~Even as she spoke I drew near to her,~~
~~as if in terror, lest at that very moment~~
the destroyer had been near to rob me of her.

Thus not the tenderness of friendship, nor the beauty of earth, nor of heaven, could redeem my soul from woe; the very accents of love were ineffectual. I was encompassed by a cloud which no beneficial influence could penetrate. The wounded deer dragging its fainting limbs to some untrodden brake, there to gaze upon the arrow which had pierced it, and to die, was but a type of me.

Sometimes I could cope with the sullen despair that overwhelmed me, but sometimes the whirlwind passions of my soul drove me to seek, by bodily exercise and by change of place, some relief from my intolerable sensations. It was during an access of this kind that I suddenly left my home, and bending my steps towards the near Alpine valleys, sought in the magnificence, the eternity of such scenes, to forget myself and my ephemeral, because human, sorrows. My wanderings were directed towards the valley of Chamounix. I had visited it frequently during my boyhood. Six years had passed since then: I was a wreck, but nought had changed in those savage and enduring scenes.

I performed the first part of my journey on horseback. I afterwards hired a mule, as the more sure-footed and least liable to receive injury on these rugged roads. The weather was fine; it was about the middle of the month of August, nearly two months after the death of Justine, that miserable epoch from which I dated all my woe.

The weight upon my spirit was sensibly lightened as I plunged yet deeper in the ravine of Arve. The immense mountains and precipices that overhung me on every side, and the sound of the river raging among the rocks, and the dashing of the water-falls around spoke of a power mighty as Omnipotence—and I ceased to fear or to bend before any being less almighty than that which had created and ruled the elements, here displayed in their most terrific guise. Still, as I ascended

In this revision, Shelley heightens the contrast between Victor's pain and the sublime vistas he encounters by having him travel alone, rather than with his family, who function as little more than typical tourists in the 1818 edition. In the Thomas Text, written in 1823, Victor's family is present. By 1831, the author had perhaps come to better appreciate the impact of solitude on the disturbed mind.

12. The village of Chamonix and its vale, in southeastern France, only a short distance from Geneva, is described by *Murray* as "these retired wilds, amidst the most sublime scenery in nature, and at the foot of the loftiest mountain of Europe, where

heard the sound of the river raging among rocks, and the dashing of water-falls around.

The next day we pursued our journey upon mules;[15] and as we ascended[16] still higher, the valley assumed a more magnificent and astonishing character. Ruined castles hanging on the precipices of piny mountains; the impetuous Arve, and cottages every here and there peeping forth from among the trees, formed a scene of singular beauty. But it was augmented and rendered sublime by the mighty Alps, whose white and shining pyramids and domes towered above all, as belonging to another earth, the habitations of another race of beings.

We passed the bridge of Pelissier,[17] where the ravine, which the river forms, opened before us, and we began to ascend the mountain that overhangs it. Soon after we entered the valley of Chamounix. This valley is more wonderful and sublime, but not so beautiful and picturesque as that of Servox,[18] through which we had just passed. The high and snowy mountains were its immediate boundaries; but we saw no more ruined castles and fertile fields. Immense glaciers approached the road; we heard the rumbling thunder of the falling avalanche, and marked the smoke of its passage. Mont Blânc, the supreme and magnificent Mont Blânc,

Valley of Chamonix, ca. 1903.

Mont Blanc (photo by Joe MiGo, used under CC-by-SA 3.0 license).

raised itself from the surrounding *aiguilles*,[19] and its tremendous *dome* overlooked the valley.[20]

During this journey, I sometimes joined Elizabeth, and exerted myself to point out to her the various beauties of the scene. I often suffered my mule to lag behind, and indulged in the misery of reflection. At other times I spurred on the animal before my companions, that I might forget them, the world, and, more than all, myself. When at a distance,

Historic flooding of the Arve (photo by Björn S., used under CC-by-SA 3.0 license).

thousands have made their pilgrimage. Unlike other places, merely fashionable, and crowded by idlers, no extent of participation can lessen the sublime emotions and impressions made by the scenery of the vale of Chamouny." It was the site of the first Winter Olympics in 1924.

Murray warns, "The route from Geneva is so much frequented by strangers in this season, that it is beset by all sorts of vagabonds, who plant themselves in the way openly as beggars, or covertly as dealers in mineral specimens, guides to things which do not require their aid, dealers in echoes, by firing small cannon where its reverberation may be heard two or three times. These idle nuisances should be discountenanced."

13. This confirms that Frankenstein returned to Geneva in June 1795.

14. The Arve River, only 62 miles (100 km) long, flows almost entirely through France, with only a short portion in Switzerland. Its source is the Chamonix glacier, and it eventually becomes a tributary of the Rhône. Because the Arve drains the mountain region, which is often covered with deep snow, it frequently floods. In her journal, Mary Shelley describes the Arve as "dash[ing] against its banks like a wild animal who is furious in constraint." An 1822 travel book mentions "sudden and considerable swellings" in 1570, 1651, 1711, and 1733; another "extraordinary flood" was recorded in 1856. In May 2015, the river reached levels not attained since 1935, when scientific monitoring was introduced.

15. *Murray* comments, "Their sagacity, strength, and sureness of foot are really wonderful." It must have given the Shelleys special pleasure to write this scene only a short time after their own trip to Chamounix on mules (accompanied by two guides and Claire Clairmont) in July

1816, recounted in letter 4 of *Six Weeks' Tour*. Their son William had been born in January of that year and was thriving (he would live for three years), and Mary Shelley had begun the composition of *Frankenstein*. The dark clouds of the suicides of Harriet Shelley and Fanny Imlay did not appear until the late autumn of the year.

16. Here the 1831 edition continues, after the revised text set forth in note 11, above.

17. Pont Pelissier, a bridge over the Arve, "crosses this river a little below the spot where it issues from one of the most striking chasms or gorges in the Alps. On the eastern side are slate rocks of amazing height, nearly perpendicular, their summits and feet ornamented with pine-trees; and, on the western side, there is a granitic mountain over which, the road is carried. The river Arve, a large and impetuous torrent, rushes between these two ranges of rocks, and towering over the whole, the snows of Mont Blânc are seen in dazzling whiteness, which, contrasted with the dark blue of the sky, almost overpowers the sight." The description is drawn from *Travels, Comprising Observations Made During a Residence in the Tarentaise and Various Parts of the Grecian and Pennine Alps, and in Switzerland and Auvergne, in the years 1820, 1821, and 1822*, by Robert Bakewell (London: Longman, Hurst, Rees, Orme, and Brown, 1823).

18. Servox or Servoz, another small village in the Chamonix valley, at the foot of the Fiz Mountains, visited by the Shelleys and noted in *Six Weeks' Tour*. Note the comparison between the "sublime" and the "picturesque." For the Romantics, the "sublime" consisted of grand naturescapes that expressed power and majesty—the mountains, the ocean; the "picturesque" depicted homely scenes,

I alighted, and threw myself on the grass, weighed down by horror and despair. At eight in the evening I arrived at Chamounix. My father and Elizabeth were very much fatigued; Ernest, who accompanied us, was delighted, and in high spirits: the only circumstance that detracted from his pleasure was the south wind, and the rain it seemed to promise for the next day.

We retired early to our apartments,[21] but not to sleep; at least I did not. I remained many hours at the window, watching the pallid lightning that played above Mont Blânc, and listening to the rushing of the Arve, which ran below my window.

focused on man and civilization. Clerval, it will be seen, prefers the picturesque, Victor the sublime.

19. Sharp pinnacles of rock.

20. The balance of the chapter is substantially revised in the 1831 edition to be consistent with Victor's having made the trip alone, and heightening the dreamlike nature of the journey:

> A tingling long-lost sense of pleasure often came across me during this journey. Some turn in the road, some new object suddenly perceived and recognised, reminded me of days gone by, and were associated with the light-hearted gaiety of boyhood. The very winds whispered in soothing accents, and maternal Nature bade me weep no more. Then again the kindly influence ceased to act—I found myself fettered again to grief and indulging in all the misery of reflection. Then I spurred on my animal, striving so to forget the world, my fears, and more than all, myself—or, in more desperate fashion, I alighted, and threw myself on the grass, weighed down by horror and despair.

At length I arrived at the village of Chamounix. Exhaustion succeeded to the extreme fatigue both of body and of mind which I had endured. For a short space of time I remained at the window watching the pallid lightnings that played above Mont Blânc, and listening to the rushing of the Arve, which pursued its noisy way beneath. The same lulling sounds acted as a lullaby to my too keen sensations; when I placed my head upon my pillow, sleep crept over me; I felt it as it came and blessed the giver of oblivion.

21. In letter 4 of *Six Weeks' Tour*, the Shelleys describe staying at various hostels in Chamonix. Percy Shelley was unable to restrain himself from leaving rebellious inscriptions (in Greek) in the registries. He signed himself *atheos* (atheist) in one; in another, he listed their destination as *L'Enfer* (the inferno, or Hell) and described himself thus: "I am a lover of mankind, democrat, and atheist." Byron, encountering one such inscription on a visit a month later, tried to restore his friend's reputation or perhaps spare him future embarrassment by scratching it out.

CHAPTER II.[1]

1. Chapter 10 in the 1831 edition.

2. Arveiron is a glacial tributary of Mont Blanc, its source at Montanvert before it joins the Arve. It was described as "rav[ing] ceaselessly" in Samuel Taylor Coleridge's 1802 poem "Hymn before Sun-rise, in the Vale of Chaumouni." Mary Shelley described it in letter 4 in *Six Weeks' Tour*: "[T]he river rolls forth impetuously from an arch of ice, and spreads itself in many streams over a vast space of the valley, ravaged and laid bare by its inundations" (156).

3. The two preceding sentences do not appear in the 1831 edition and are replaced by the following:

> I spent the following day roaming through the valley. I stood beside the sources of the Arveiron, which take their rise in a glacier, that with slow pace is advancing down from the summit of the hills to barricade the valley. The abrupt sides of vast mountains were before me; the icy wall of the glacier overhung me; a few shattered pines were scattered around; and the solemn silence of this glori-

HE NEXT DAY, contrary to the prognostications of our guides, was fine, although clouded. We visited the source of the Arveiron,[2] and rode about the valley until evening.[3] These sublime and magnificent scenes afforded me the greatest consolation that I was capable of receiving. They elevated me from all littleness of feeling; and although they did not remove my grief, they subdued and tranquillized it. In some degree, also, they diverted my mind from the thoughts over which it had brooded for the last month. I returned in the evening, fatigued, but less unhappy, and conversed with my family with more cheerfulness than had been my custom for some time.[4] My father was pleased, and Elizabeth overjoyed. "My dear cousin," said she, "you see what happiness you diffuse when you are happy; do not relapse again!"[5]

The following morning the rain poured down in torrents, and thick mists hid the summits of the mountains. I rose early, but felt unusually melancholy. The rain depressed me; my old feelings recurred, and I was miserable. I knew how disappointed my father would be at this sudden change, and I wished to avoid him until I had recovered myself so far as to be enabled to conceal those feelings that overpowered me. I knew that they would remain that day at the inn; and as I had ever inured myself to rain, moisture, and cold, I resolved to go alone to the summit of Montanvert.[6] I remembered the effect that the view of the tremendous and ever-moving glacier had produced upon my mind when I first saw it. It had then filled me with a sublime ecstasy that gave wings to the soul, and allowed it to soar from the obscure world to light and joy. The sight of the awful and majestic in nature had indeed always the effect of solemnizing my mind, and causing me to forget the passing cares of life. I determined to go alone,[7] for I was well acquainted with the path, and the presence of another would destroy the solitary grandeur of the scene.

The ascent is precipitous, but the path is cut into continual and short windings, which enable you to surmount the perpendicularity of the mountain. It is a scene terrifically desolate. In a thousand spots the traces of the winter avalanche may be perceived, where trees lie broken and strewed on the ground; some entirely destroyed, others bent, leaning upon the jutting rocks of the mountain, or transversely upon other trees. The path, as you ascend higher, is intersected by ravines of snow, down which stones continually roll from above; one of them is particularly dangerous, as the slightest sound, such as even speaking in a loud voice, produces a concussion of air sufficient to draw destruction upon the head of the speaker. The pines are not tall or luxuriant, but they are sombre, and add an air of severity to the scene. I looked on the valley beneath; vast mists were rising from the rivers which ran through it, and curling in thick wreaths around the opposite mountains, whose summits were hid in the uniform clouds, while rain poured from the dark sky, and added to the melancholy impression I received from the objects around me. Alas! why does man boast of sensibilities superior to those apparent in the brute; it only renders them more necessary[8] beings. If our impulses were confined to hunger, thirst, and desire, we might be nearly free; but now we are moved by every wind that blows, and a chance word or scene that that word[9] may convey to us.

> *We rest; a dream has power to poison sleep.*
> *We rise; one wand'ring thought pollutes the day.*

ous presence-chamber of imperial nature was broken only by the brawling waves or the fall of some vast fragment, the thunder sound of the avalanche or the cracking, reverberated along the mountains, of the accumulated ice, which, through the silent working of immutable laws, was ever and anon rent and torn, as if it had been but a plaything in their hands."

In addition to eliminating the presence of the family, Mary Shelley has removed Victor's commentary on the effect of the scenery on him, leaving only description.

4. This and the following eight sentences are substantially revised in the 1831 edition, as follows:

> I retired to rest at night; my slumbers, as it were, waited on and ministered to by the assemblance of grand shapes which I had contemplated during the day. They congregated round me; the unstained snowy mountain-top, the glittering pinnacle, the pine woods, and ragged bare ravine, the eagle, soaring amidst the clouds—they all gathered round me and bade me be at peace.
>
> Where had they fled when the next morning I awoke? All of soul-inspiring fled with sleep, and dark melancholy clouded every thought. The rain was pouring in torrents, and thick mists hid the summits of the mountains, so that I even saw not the faces of those mighty friends. Still I would penetrate their misty veil and seek them in their cloudy retreats. What were rain and storm to me? My mule was brought to the door, and I resolved to ascend to the summit of Montanvert.

These seem to be changes made purely to reflect Victor's solitary trip.

5. The Thomas Text replaces the two previous sentences with: "The affec-

tionate smile with which Elizabeth welcomed my altered mood excited me to greater exertion; and I felt as I spoke long forgotten sensations of pleasure arise in my mind. I knew that this state of being would only be temporary, that gloom and misery was near at hand, but this knowledge only acted as a stimulant, and gave added a tingling sensation of fear, while the blood danced along my veins—my eyes sparkled and my limbs even trembled beneath the influence of unaccustomed emotion."

6. The Montanvert, also known as the Mer de Glace (though *Murray* suggests that this is the name of the upper portion), is the name given to the glacier on the northern slopes of Mont Blanc. Mary Shelley wrote, in letter 4 of *Six Weeks' Tour*, "On the other side [of the valley of the Arveiron] rises the immense glacier of Montanvert, fifty miles in extent, occupying a chasm among mountains of inconceivable height, and of forms so pointed and abrupt, that they seem to pierce the sky. From this glacier we saw as we sat on a rock, close to one of the streams of the Arveiron, masses of ice detach themselves from on high, and rush with a loud dull noise into the vale. The violence of their fall turned them into powder, which flowed over the rocks in imitation of waterfalls, whose ravines they usurped and filled" (156–57).

7. The phrase "without a guide" is substituted for "alone" in the 1831 edition; Victor is already alone.

8. An obsolete usage of the word, in this context meaning having no independent volition.

9. The word is "wind" in the Draft and appears to be what was intended, though never corrected by Mary or Percy Shelley.

We feel, conceive, or reason; laugh, or weep,
Embrace fond woe, or cast our cares away;
It is the same: for, be it joy or sorrow,
The path of its departure still is free.
Man's yesterday may ne'er be like his morrow;

Nought may endure but mutability![10]

It was nearly noon when I arrived at the top of the ascent. For some time I sat upon the rock that overlooks the sea of ice. A mist covered both that and the surrounding mountains. Presently a breeze dissipated the cloud, and I descended upon the glacier. The surface is very uneven, rising like the waves of a troubled sea, descending low, and interspersed by rifts that sink deep. The field of ice is almost a league in width, but I spent nearly two hours in crossing it. The opposite mountain is a bare perpendicular rock. From the side where I now stood Montanvert was exactly opposite, at the distance of a league; and above it rose Mont Blânc, in awful majesty. I remained in a recess of the rock, gazing on this wonderful and stupendous scene. The sea, or rather the vast river of ice, wound among its dependent mountains, whose

Montanvert, or Mer de Glace (photo by Kristoferb, used under CC-by-SA 3.0 license).

aerial summits hung over its recesses. Their icy and glittering peaks shone in the sunlight over the clouds. My heart, which was before sorrowful, now swelled with something like joy; I exclaimed—"Wandering spirits, if indeed ye wander, and do not rest in your narrow beds, allow me this faint happiness, or take me, as your companion, away from the joys of life."

As I said this, I suddenly beheld the figure of a man, at some distance, advancing towards me with superhuman speed. He bounded over the crevices in the ice, among which I had walked with caution; his stature also, as he approached, seemed to exceed that of man. I was troubled: a mist came over my eyes, and I felt a faintness seize me; but I was quickly restored by the cold gale of the mountains. I perceived, as the shape came nearer, (sight tremendous and abhorred!) that it was the wretch whom I had created. I trembled with rage and horror, resolving to wait his approach, and then close with him in mortal combat. He approached; his countenance bespoke bitter anguish, combined with disdain and malignity, while its unearthly ugliness rendered it almost too horrible for human eyes. But I scarcely observed this; anger[11] and hatred had at first deprived me of utterance, and I recovered only to overwhelm him with words expressive of furious detestation and contempt.

"Devil!" I exclaimed, "do you dare approach me? and do not you fear the fierce vengeance of my arm wreaked on your miserable head? Begone, vile insect! or rather stay, that I may trample you to dust! and, oh, that I could, with the extinction of your miserable existence, restore those victims whom you have so diabolically murdered!"

Frankenstein meets the creature on the mountaintop. Colin Clive as Henry Frankenstein (the renamed Victor Frankenstein) and Boris Karloff as the creature (*Frankenstein*, Universal Films, 1931).

"I expected this reception," said the daemon. "All men hate the wretched; how then must I be hated, who am miserable beyond all living things! Yet you, my creator, detest and spurn me,

10. Another interpolation by Mary Shelley: The quoted lines are from "Mutability," a poem by Percy Shelley that first appeared in the 1816 collection *Alastor, or The Spirit of Solitude, and Other Poems* and clearly could not have been known to Victor.

11. "Anger" becomes "rage" in the 1831 edition.

[handwritten margin note:] He finds the creature in the Mountains, but is to angry and scared. Yells Devil!

12. According to the *Oxford English Dictionary*, one usage is "formally or surely consigned to evil or destruction; doomed."

thy creature, to whom thou art bound by ties only dissoluble by the annihilation of one of us. You purpose to kill me. How dare you sport thus with life? Do your duty towards me, and I will do mine towards you and the rest of mankind. If you will comply with my conditions, I will leave them and you at peace; but if you refuse, I will glut the maw of death, until it be satiated with the blood of your remaining friends."

"Abhorred monster! fiend that thou art! the tortures of hell are too mild a vengeance for thy crimes. Wretched devil! you reproach me with your creation; come on then, that I may extinguish the spark which I so negligently bestowed."

My rage was without bounds; I sprang on him, impelled by all the feelings which can arm one being against the existence of another.

He easily eluded me, and said,

"Be calm! I entreat you to hear me, before you give vent to your hatred on my devoted[12] head. Have I not suffered enough, that you seek to increase my misery? Life, although it may only be an accumulation of anguish, is dear to me, and I will defend it. Remember, thou hast made me more powerful than thyself; my height is superior to thine; my joints more supple. But I will not be tempted to set myself in opposition to thee. I am thy creature, and I will be even mild and docile to my natural lord and king, if thou wilt also perform thy part, the which thou owest me. Oh, Frankenstein, be not equitable to every other, and trample upon me alone, to whom thy justice, and even thy clemency and affection, is most due. Remember, that I am thy creature: I ought to be thy Adam; but I am rather the fallen angel, whom thou drivest from joy for no misdeed. Every where I see bliss, from which I alone am irrevocably excluded. I was benevolent and good; misery made me a fiend. Make me happy, and I shall again be virtuous."

"Begone! I will not hear you. There can be no community between you and me; we are enemies. Begone, or let us try our strength in a fight, in which one must fall."

"How can I move thee? Will no entreaties cause thee to turn a favourable eye upon thy creature, who implores thy goodness and compassion? Believe me, Frankenstein: I was benevolent; my soul[13] glowed with love and humanity: but am I not alone, miserably alone? You, my creator, abhor me; what hope can I gather from your fellow-creatures, who owe me nothing? they spurn and hate me. The desert mountains and dreary glaciers are my refuge. I have wandered here many days; the caves of ice, which I only do not fear, are a dwelling to me, and the only one which man does not grudge. These bleak skies I hail, for they are kinder to me than your fellow-beings. If the multitude of mankind knew of my existence, they would do as you do, and arm themselves for my destruction. Shall I not then hate them who abhor me? I will keep no terms with my enemies. I am miserable, and they shall share my wretchedness. Yet it is in your power to recompense me, and deliver them from an evil which it only remains for you to make so great, that not only you and your family, but thousands of others, shall be swallowed up in the whirlwinds of its rage.[14] Let your compassion be moved, and do not disdain me. Listen to my tale: when you have heard that, abandon or commiserate me, as you shall judge that I deserve. But hear me. The guilty are allowed, by human laws, bloody as they may be,[15] to speak in their own defence before they are condemned. Listen to me, Frankenstein. You accuse me of murder; and yet you would, with a satisfied conscience, destroy your own creature. Oh, praise the eternal justice of man! Yet I ask you not to spare me: listen to me; and then, if you can, and if you will, destroy the work of your hands."

"Why do you call to my remembrance[16] circumstances of which I shudder to reflect, that I have been the miserable origin and author? Cursed be the day, abhorred devil, in which you first saw light! Cursed (although I curse myself) be the hands that formed you! You have made me wretched beyond expression. You have left me no power to consider whether I am just to you, or not.[17] Begone! relieve me from the sight of your detested form."

"Thus I relieve thee, my creator," he said, and placed his hated hands before my eyes, which I flung from me with violence; "thus I take from thee a sight which you abhor. Still thou canst listen to me, and grant me thy compassion. By

13. This is the first indication that the creature, made from parts of other creatures, has a soul. Whence did it arise? Later, Victor claims that he gave the creature a soul, by a process undescribed. See note 19, Volume III, Chapter IV, below.

14. The scope of the creature's threat is greatly expanded by Percy Shelley in the Draft.

15. The phrase "may be" is replaced with "are" in the 1831 edition.

16. "I rejoined" is inserted here in the 1831 edition.

17. This sentence was added by Percy Shelley to the Draft.

the virtues that I once possessed, I demand this from you. Hear my tale; it is long and strange, and the temperature of this place is not fitting to your fine sensations; come to the hut upon the mountain. The sun is yet high in the heavens; before it descends to hide itself behind yon snowy precipices, and illuminate another world, you will have heard my story, and can decide. On you it rests, whether I quit for ever the neighbourhood of man, and lead a harmless life, or become the scourge of your fellow-creatures, and the author of your own speedy ruin."

As he said this, he led the way across the ice: I followed. My heart was full, and I did not answer him; but, as I proceeded, I weighed the various arguments that he had used, and determined at least to listen to his tale. I was partly urged by curiosity, and compassion confirmed my resolution. I had hitherto supposed him to be the murderer of my brother, and I eagerly sought a confirmation or denial of this opinion. For the first time, also, I felt what the duties of a creator towards his creature were, and that I ought to render him happy before I complained of his wickedness. These motives urged me to comply with his demand. We crossed the ice, therefore, and ascended the opposite rock. The air was cold, and the rain again began to descend: we entered the hut, the fiend with an air of exultation, I with a heavy heart, and depressed spirits. But I consented to listen; and, seating myself by the fire which my odious companion had lighted, he thus began his tale.

Frankenstein agrees to listen to his monster's story

CHAPTER III.[1]

1. Chapter 11 in the 1831 edition.

"IT IS WITH considerable difficulty that I remember the original æra of my being: all the events of that period appear confused and indistinct. A strange multiplicity of sensations seized me, and I saw, felt, heard, and smelt, at the same time; and it was, indeed, a long time before I learned to distinguish between the operations of my various senses. By degrees, I remember, a stronger light pressed upon my nerves, so that I was obliged to shut my eyes. Darkness then came over me, and troubled me; but hardly had I felt this, when, by opening my eyes, as I now suppose, the light poured in upon me again. I walked, and, I believe, descended; but I presently found a great alteration in my sensations. Before, dark and opaque bodies had surrounded me, impervious to my touch or sight; but I now found that I could wander on at liberty, with no obstacles which I could not either surmount or avoid. The light became more and more oppressive to me; and, the heat wearying me as I walked, I sought a place where I could receive shade. This was the forest near Ingolstadt; and here I lay by the side of a brook resting from my fatigue, until I felt tormented by hunger and thirst. This roused me from my nearly dormant state, and I ate some berries which I found hanging on the trees, or lying on the ground. I slaked my thirst at the brook; and then lying down, was overcome by sleep.

2. Mary Shelley added a clarifying foot-note to the 1823 and 1831 editions: "The moon."

3. Of course, the creature did not know at the time that the cloth he found was a cloak.

"It was dark when I awoke; I felt cold also, and half-frightened as it were instinctively, finding myself so desolate. Before I had quitted your apartment, on a sensation of cold, I had covered myself with some clothes; but these were insufficient to secure me from the dews of night. I was a poor, helpless, miserable wretch; I knew, and could distinguish, nothing; but, feeling pain invade me on all sides, I sat down and wept.

"Soon a gentle light stole over the heavens, and gave me a sensation of pleasure. I started up, and beheld a radiant form rise from among the trees.[2] I gazed with a kind of wonder. It moved slowly, but it enlightened my path; and I again went out in search of berries. I was still cold, when under one of the trees I found a huge cloak,[3] with which I covered myself, and sat down upon the ground. No distinct ideas occupied my mind; all was confused. I felt light, and hunger, and thirst, and darkness; innumerable sounds rung in my ears, and on all sides various scents saluted me: the only object that I could distinguish was the bright moon, and I fixed my eyes on that with pleasure.

"Several changes of day and night passed, and the orb of night had greatly lessened when I began to distinguish my sensations from each other. I gradually saw plainly the clear stream that supplied me with drink, and the trees that shaded me with their foliage. I was delighted when I first discovered that a pleasant sound, which often saluted my ears, proceeded from the throats of the little winged animals who had often intercepted the light from my eyes. I began also to observe, with greater accuracy, the forms that surrounded me, and to perceive the boundaries of the radiant roof of light which canopied me. Sometimes I tried to imitate the pleasant songs of the birds, but was unable. Sometimes I wished to express my sensations in my own mode, but the uncouth and inarticulate sounds which broke from me frightened me into silence again.

"The moon had disappeared from the night, and again, with a lessened form, shewed itself, while I still remained in the forest. My sensations had, by this time, become distinct, and my mind received every day additional ideas. My eyes became accustomed to the light, and to perceive objects in their right forms; I distinguished the insect from the herb, and, by degrees, one herb from another.[4] I found that the sparrow uttered none but harsh notes, whilst those of the blackbird and thrush were sweet and enticing.[5]

"One day, when I was oppressed by cold, I found a fire which had been left by some wandering beggars,[6] and was overcome with delight at the warmth I experienced from it. In my joy I thrust my hand into the live embers, but quickly drew it out again with a cry of pain. How strange, I thought, that the same cause should produce such opposite effects! I examined the materials of the fire, and to my joy found it to be composed of wood. I quickly collected some branches; but they were wet, and would not burn. I was pained at this, and sat still watching the operation of the fire. The wet wood which I had placed near the heat dried, and itself became inflamed. I reflected on this; and, by touching the various branches, I discovered the cause, and busied myself in collecting a great quantity of wood, that I might dry it, and have a plentiful supply of fire. When night came on, and brought sleep with it, I was in the greatest fear lest my fire should be extinguished. I covered it carefully with dry wood and leaves, and placed wet branches upon it; and then, spreading my cloak, I lay on the ground, and sunk into sleep.

"It was morning when I awoke, and my first care was to visit the fire. I uncovered it, and a gentle breeze quickly fanned it into a flame. I observed this also, and contrived a fan of branches, which roused the embers when they were nearly extinguished. When night came again, I found, with pleasure, that the fire gave light as well as heat; and that the discovery of this element was useful to me in my food; for I found some of the offals that the travellers had left had been roasted, and tasted much more savoury than the berries I gathered from the trees. I tried, therefore, to dress my food in the same manner, placing it on the live embers. I found that the berries were spoiled by this operation, and the nuts and roots much improved.

"Food, however, became scarce; and I often spent the whole day searching in vain for a few acorns to assuage the

4. The experience of the creature is similar to that hypothesized by Rousseau in *Emile*, which Mary Shelley had read in 1815: "Let us suppose that a child had at his birth the stature and the strength of a grown man, that he emerged, so to speak, fully armed from his mother's womb as did Pallas from the brain of Jupiter. . . . Not only would he perceive no object outside of himself, he would not even relate any object to the sense organ which made him perceive it . . . all his sensations would come together in a single point . . . he would have only a single idea, that is, of the I to which he would relate all his sensations; and this idea or, rather, this sentiment would be the only thing which he would have beyond what an ordinary baby has." However, notes Alan R. Richardson, "Rousseau imagines the man/child as an 'imbecile, an automaton, an immobile and almost insensible statue' who would learn to stand, if he attempted it at all, with the greatest difficulty and would not connect hunger with food, while Shelley's monster gains motor control almost at once and instinctively slakes his hunger with berries" ("From *Emile* to *Frankenstein*: The Education of Monsters," *European Romantic Review* 1, no. 2 [1991]: 147–62, note 1).

5. The *Encyclopædia Britannica* (3rd ed., 1797) says of the blackbird (*Turdus merula*), "The note of the male is extremely fine, but too loud for any place except the woods: It begins to sing early in the spring, continues its music part of the summer, desists in the moulting season, but resumes it for some time in September and the first winter months." There are so many species of "thrush" (subspecies of *Turdus* and cousin to the blackbird) as to make that overheard by the creature unidentifiable. Of course, at this unformed stage, the creature would not have known the correct names of the

birds, only variations in their songs and coloration.

6. A deduction plainly made later, as the creature at this point had seen nothing of human society. Many of the creature's observations are of course hindsight—that is, observations made when he is retelling his experiences—after he has read extensively in history and literature, so that he can extrapolate human conduct. However, as we will see, he is a strange mixture of naiveté and instinctual insights into the behavior of humans, perhaps as a result of residual memories of the brain implanted in him.

7. The creature fled from Victor's apartment in darkness and has not reported previously seeing a human being other than Victor. Victor was in his laboratory clothes when he threw himself on his bed; possibly, the creature, in his flight, passed people on the streets, but in the dead of night in Ingolstadt in November they would have been heavily muffled against the night air and scarcely recognizable as humans. Therefore, the meaning of his remark about the hut dweller's appearance is obscure.

8. A [handwritten: Might've seen more people, but did not recognize them as such] (the earl[...]hed in 1[...]ons" in L[...]ich Sata[...]ook I rec[...]hat the h[...]ild a permanent [...] and Mulc[...]y Vulcan, the architect of many heav[...]ers, designs it. However, it is not merely a retreat but a place where the fallen angels can rest and enjoy their freedom. It is also the capital city of Fairyland in Catherynne M. Valente's splendid *The Girl Who Circumnavigated Fairyland in a Ship of Her Own Making* (2011).

pangs of hunger. When I found this, I resolved to quit the place that I had hitherto inhabited, to seek for one where the few wants I experienced would be more easily satisfied. In this emigration, I exceedingly lamented the loss of the fire which I had obtained through accident, and knew not how to re-produce it. I gave several hours to the serious consideration of this difficulty; but I was obliged to relinquish all attempt to supply it; and, wrapping myself up in my cloak, I struck across the wood towards the setting sun. I passed three days in these rambles, and at length discovered the open country. A great fall of snow had taken place the night before, and the fields were of one uniform white; the appearance was disconsolate, and I found my feet chilled by the cold damp substance that covered the ground.

"It was about seven in the morning, and I longed to obtain food and shelter; at length I perceived a small hut, on a rising ground, which had doubtless been built for the convenience of some shepherd. This was a new sight to me; and I examined the structure with great curiosity. Finding the door open, I entered. An old man sat in it, near a fire, over which he was preparing his breakfast. He turned on hearing a noise; and, perceiving me, shrieked loudly, and, quitting the hut, ran across the fields with a speed of which his debilitated form hardly appeared capable. His appearance, different from any I had ever before seen,[7] and his flight, somewhat surprised me. But I was enchanted by the appearance of the hut: here the snow and rain could not penetrate; the ground was dry; and it presented to me then as exquisite and divine a retreat as Pandæmonium[8] appeared to the daemons of hell after their sufferings in the lake of fire. I greedily devoured the remnants of the shepherd's breakfast, which consisted of bread, cheese, milk, and wine; the latter, however, I did not like. Then overcome by fatigue, I lay down among some straw, and fell asleep.

The creature (Boris Karloff) meets the hermit (O. P. Heggie) (*Bride of Frankenstein*, Universal Pictures, 1935).

The hermit (Gene Hackman) meets the creature (Peter Boyle), from *Young Frankenstein* (Gruskoff/Venture Films, 1974).

"It was noon when I awoke; and, allured by the warmth of the sun, which shone brightly on the white ground, I determined to recommence my travels; and, depositing the remains of the peasant's breakfast in a wallet I found, I proceeded across the fields for several hours, until at sunset I arrived at a village. How miraculous did this appear! the huts, the neater cottages, and stately houses, engaged my admiration by turns. The vegetables in the gardens, the milk and cheese that I saw placed at the windows of some of the cottages, allured my appetite. One of the best of these I entered; but I had hardly placed my foot within the door, before the children shrieked, and one of the women fainted. The whole village was roused; some fled, some attacked me, until, grievously bruised by stones and many other kinds of missile weapons, I escaped to the open country, and fearfully took refuge in a low hovel, quite bare, and making a wretched appearance after the palaces I had beheld in the village. This hovel, however, joined a cottage of a neat and pleasant appearance; but, after my late dearly-bought experience, I dared not enter it. My place of refuge

Pandemonium, by John Martin (ca. 1825).

was constructed of wood, but so low, that I could with difficulty sit upright in it. No wood, however, was placed on the earth, which formed the floor, but it was dry; and although the wind entered it by innumerable chinks, I found it an agreeable asylum from the snow and rain.

"Here then I retreated, and lay down, happy to have found a shelter, however miserable, from the inclemency of the season, and still more from the barbarity of man.

"As soon as morning dawned, I crept from my kennel, that I might view the adjacent cottage, and discover if I could remain in the habitation I had found. It was situated against the back of the cottage, and surrounded on the sides which were exposed by a pig-stye and a clear pool of water. One part was open, and by that I had crept in; but now I covered every crevice by which I might be perceived with stones and wood, yet in such a manner that I might move them on occasion to pass out: all the light I enjoyed came through the stye, and that was sufficient for me.

"Having thus arranged my dwelling, and carpeted it with clean straw, I retired; for I saw the figure of a man at a distance, and I remembered too well my treatment the night before, to trust myself in his power. I had first, however, provided for my sustenance for that day, by a loaf of coarse bread, which I purloined, and a cup with which I could drink, more conveniently than from my hand, of the pure water which flowed by my retreat. The floor was a little raised, so that it was kept perfectly dry, and by its vicinity to the chimney of the cottage it was tolerably warm.

"Being thus provided, I resolved to reside in this hovel, until something should occur which might alter my determination. It was indeed a paradise, compared to the bleak forest, my former residence, the rain-dropping branches, and dank earth. I ate my breakfast with pleasure, and was about to remove a plank to procure myself a little water, when I heard a step, and, looking through a small chink, I beheld a young creature, with a pail on her head, passing before my hovel. The girl was young and of gentle demeanour, unlike what I have since found cottagers and farm-house servants to be. Yet she was meanly dressed, a coarse blue petticoat and a linen jacket being her only garb; her fair hair was plaited, but not adorned; she looked patient, yet sad. I lost sight of her; and in about a quarter of an hour she returned, bearing the pail, which was now partly filled with milk. As she walked along, seemingly incommoded by the burden, a young man met her, whose countenance expressed a deeper despondence. Uttering a few sounds with an air of melancholy, he took the pail from her head, and bore it to the cottage himself. She followed, and they disappeared. Presently I saw the young man again, with some tools in his hand, cross the field behind the cottage; and the girl was also busied, sometimes in the house, and sometimes in the yard.

"On examining my dwelling, I found that one of the windows of the cottage had formerly occupied a part of it, but the panes had been filled up with wood. In one of these was a small and almost imperceptible chink, through which the eye could just penetrate. Through this crevice, a small room was visible, white-washed and clean, but very bare of furniture. In one corner, near a small fire, sat an old man, leaning his head on his hands in a disconsolate attitude. The

The De Lacey cottage in winter? (Painting by Italian artist Francesco Foschi, mid-eighteenth century.)

young girl was occupied in arranging the cottage; but presently she took something out of a drawer, which employed her hands, and she sat down beside the old man, who, taking up an instrument, began to play, and to produce sounds, sweeter than the voice of the thrush or the nightingale. It was a lovely sight, even to me, poor wretch! who had never beheld aught beautiful before. The silver hair and benevolent countenance of the aged cottager, won my reverence; while the gentle manners of the girl enticed my love. He played a sweet mournful air, which I perceived drew tears from the eyes of his amiable companion, of which the old man took no notice, until she sobbed audibly; he then pronounced a few sounds, and the fair creature, leaving her work, knelt at his feet. He raised her, and smiled with such kindness and affection, that I felt sensations of a peculiar and over-powering nature: they were a mixture of pain and pleasure, such as I had never before experienced, either from hunger or cold, warmth or food; and I withdrew from the window, unable to bear these emotions.

"Soon after this the young man returned, bearing on his shoulders a load of wood. The girl met him at the door, helped to relieve him of his burden, and, taking some of the fuel into the cottage, placed it on the fire; then she and the youth went apart into a nook of the cottage, and he shewed her a large loaf and a piece of cheese. She seemed pleased; and went into the garden for some roots and plants, which she placed in water, and then upon the fire. She afterwards continued her work, whilst the young man went into the garden, and appeared busily employed in digging and pulling up roots. After he had been employed thus about an hour, the young woman joined him, and they entered the cottage together.

"The old man had, in the mean time, been pensive; but, on the appearance of his companions, he assumed a more cheerful air, and they sat down to eat. The meal was quickly dispatched. The young woman was again occupied in arranging the cottage; the old man walked before the cottage in the sun for a few minutes, leaning on the arm of the youth. Nothing could exceed in beauty the contrast between these two excellent creatures. One was old, with silver hairs and a countenance beaming with benevolence and love: the younger was slight and graceful in his figure, and his features were moulded with the finest symmetry; yet his eyes and attitude expressed the utmost sadness and despondency. The old man returned to the cottage; and the youth, with tools different from those he had used in the morning, directed his steps across the fields.

"Night quickly shut in; but, to my extreme wonder, I found that the cottagers had a means of prolonging light, by the use of tapers, and was delighted to find, that the setting of the sun did not put an end to the pleasure I experienced in watching my human neighbours. In the evening, the young girl and her companion were employed in various occupations which I did not understand; and the old man again took up the instrument, which produced the divine sounds that had enchanted me in the morning. So soon as he had finished, the youth began, not to play, but to utter sounds that were monotonous, and neither resembling the harmony of the old man's instrument or the songs of the birds; I since found that he read aloud, but at that time I knew nothing of the science of words or letters.[9]

"The family, after having been thus occupied for a short time, extinguished their lights, and retired, as I conjectured, to rest."

9. The Thomas Text continues, "I continued however to watch the countenances of the Cottagers and the changes I perceived were at once the excitements and the aliments of a boundless curiosity." The sentence was abandoned in the 1831 edition.

Discovers more people and watches them

old guy and young guy parallel?

CHAPTER IV.[1]

"I LAY ON MY straw, but I could not sleep. I thought of the occurrences of the day. What chiefly struck me was the gentle manners of these people; and I longed to join them, but dared not. I remembered too well the treatment I had suffered the night before from the barbarous villagers, and resolved, whatever course of conduct I might hereafter think it right to pursue, that for the present I would remain quietly in my hovel, watching, and endeavouring to discover the motives which influenced their actions.

"The cottagers arose the next morning before the sun. The young woman arranged the cottage, and prepared the food; and the youth departed after the first meal.

"This day was passed in the same routine as that which preceded it. The young man was constantly employed out of doors, and the girl in various laborious occupations within. The old man, whom I soon perceived to be blind, employed his leisure hours on his instrument, or in contemplation. Nothing could exceed the love and respect which the younger cottagers exhibited towards their venerable companion. They performed towards him every little office of affection and duty with gentleness; and he rewarded them by his benevolent smiles.

"They were not entirely happy. The young man and his companion often went apart, and appeared to weep. I saw

1. Chapter 12 in the 1831 edition.

no cause for their unhappiness; but I was deeply affected by it. If such lovely creatures were miserable, it was less strange that I, an imperfect and solitary being, should be wretched. Yet why were these gentle beings unhappy? They possessed a delightful house (for such it was in my eyes), and every luxury; they had a fire to warm them when chill, and delicious viands when hungry; they were dressed in excellent clothes; and, still more, they enjoyed one another's company and speech, interchanging each day looks of affection and kindness. What did their tears imply? Did they really express pain? I was at first unable to solve these questions; but perpetual attention, and time, explained to me many appearances which were at first enigmatic.

"A considerable period elapsed before I discovered one of the causes of the uneasiness of this amiable family; it was poverty: and they suffered that evil in a very distressing degree.[2] Their nourishment consisted entirely of the vegetables of their garden, and the milk of one cow, who gave very little during the winter, when its masters could scarcely procure food to support it. They often, I believe, suffered the pangs of hunger very poignantly, especially the two younger cottagers; for several times they placed food before the old man, when they reserved none for themselves.

"This trait of kindness moved me sensibly. I had been accustomed, during the night, to steal a part of their store for my own consumption; but when I found that in doing this I inflicted pain on the cottagers, I abstained, and satisfied myself with berries, nuts, and roots, which I gathered from a neighbouring wood.

"I discovered also another means through which I was enabled to assist their labours. I found that the youth spent a great part of each day in collecting wood for the family fire; and, during the night, I often took his tools, the use of which I quickly discovered, and brought home firing sufficient for the consumption of several days.

"I remember, the first time that I did this, the young woman, when she opened the door in the morning, appeared greatly astonished on seeing a great pile of wood on the outside. She uttered some words in a loud voice, and the youth

2. The Thomas Text deletes the second half of the sentence and substitutes: "They had appeared to me rich, because their possessions incomparably transcended mine, but I soon learnt, that many of these advantages were only apparent, since their delicate frame made them subject to a thousand wants of the existence of which I was entirely ignorant." The sentence was not used in the 1831 edition.

Discovering emotions and physical vs emotional wealth/happiness

3. We may deduce, as we will see in note 5, Volume II, Chapter V, below, that the people spoke French.

4. "Agatha" means "goodness" in Greek; "Felix" means "happiness" in Latin.

5. Bringing the creature to spring 1794, months after his "birth" in November 1793.

Becoming empathetic
and human-like

joined her, who also expressed surprise. I observed, with pleasure, that he did not go to the forest that day, but spent it in repairing the cottage, and cultivating the garden.

"By degrees I made a discovery of still greater moment. I found that these people possessed a method of communicating their experience and feelings to one another by articulate sounds.[3] I perceived that the words they spoke sometimes produced pleasure or pain, smiles or sadness, in the minds and countenances of the hearers. This was indeed a godlike science, and I ardently desired to become acquainted with it. But I was baffled in every attempt I made for this purpose. Their pronunciation was quick; and the words they uttered, not having any apparent connexion with visible objects, I was unable to discover any clue by which I could unravel the mystery of their reference. By great application, however, and after having remained during the space of several revolutions of the moon in my hovel, I discovered the names that were given to some of the most familiar objects of discourse: I learned and applied the words *fire*, *milk*, *bread*, and *wood*. I learned also the names of the cottagers themselves. The youth and his companion had each of them several names, but the old man had only one, which was father. The girl was called *sister*, or *Agatha*; and the youth *Felix*, *brother*, or *son*.[4] I cannot describe the delight I felt when I learned the ideas appropriated to each of these sounds, and was able to pronounce them. I distinguished several other words, without being able as yet to understand or apply them; such as *good*, *dearest*, *unhappy*.

"I spent the winter in this manner.[5] The gentle manners and beauty of the cottagers greatly endeared them to me: when they were unhappy, I felt depressed; when they rejoiced, I sympathized in their joys. I saw few human beings beside them; and if any other happened to enter the cottage, their harsh manners and rude gait only enhanced to me the superior accomplishments of my friends. The old man, I could perceive, often endeavoured to encourage his children, as sometimes I found that he called them, to cast off their melancholy. He would talk in a cheerful accent, with an expression of goodness that bestowed pleasure even upon me. Agatha listened with respect, her eyes sometimes filled with tears, which she endeavoured to wipe away unperceived; but I generally found that her countenance and tone were more cheerful after having listened to the exhortations of her father. It was not thus with Felix. He was always the saddest of the group; and, even to my unpractised senses, he appeared to have suffered more deeply than his friends. But if his countenance was more sorrowful, his voice was more cheerful than that of his sister, especially when he addressed the old man.

"I could mention innumerable instances, which, although slight, marked the dispositions of these amiable cottagers. In the midst of poverty and want, Felix carried with pleasure to his sister the first little white flower that peeped out from beneath the snowy ground. Early in the morning before she had risen, he cleared away the snow that obstructed her path to the milk-house, drew water from the well, and brought the wood from the out-house, where, to his perpetual astonishment, he found his store always replenished by an invisible hand. In the day, I believe, he worked sometimes for a neighbouring farmer, because he often went forth, and did not return until dinner, yet brought no wood with him. At other times he worked in the garden; but, as there was little to do in the frosty season, he read to the old man and Agatha.

"This reading had puzzled me extremely at first; but, by degrees, I discovered that he uttered many of the same sounds when he read as when he talked. I conjectured, therefore, that he found on the paper signs for speech which he understood, and I ardently longed to comprehend these also; but how was that possible, when I did not even understand the sounds for which they stood as signs? I improved, however, sensibly in this science, but not sufficiently to follow up any kind of conversation, although I applied my whole mind to the endeavour: for I easily perceived that, although I eagerly longed to discover myself to the cottagers, I ought not to make the attempt until I had first become master of their language; which knowledge might enable me to make them overlook the deformity of my figure; for with this also

6. What has led the creature to conceive of himself as "deformed"? Victor certainly fled from his presence, but according to Victor, he made no remarks about the creature's appearance. Similarly, the hut dweller who fled when the creature popped into his hut appears to have been more surprised than repelled and likely left hurriedly because he was trespassing in someone else's structure. Why also would the creature think that "delicate complexions" were admirable, except if he had been taught that?

Tantalizingly, the passage suggests that the creature's brain was not as blank as is implied but rather retained memories and attitudes of its previous user. For further evidence of this suggestion, see note 5, Volume II, Chapter V, below.

the contrast perpetually presented to my eyes had made me acquainted.

"I had admired the perfect forms of my cottagers—their grace, beauty, and delicate complexions: but how was I terrified, when I viewed myself in a transparent pool![6] At first I started back, unable to believe that it was indeed I who was reflected in the mirror; and when I became fully convinced that I was in reality the monster that I am, I was filled with the bitterest sensations of despondence and mortification. Alas! I did not yet entirely know the fatal effects of this miserable deformity.

"As the sun became warmer, and the light of day longer, the snow vanished, and I beheld the bare trees and the black earth. From this time Felix was more employed; and the heart-moving indications of impending famine disappeared. Their food, as I afterwards found, was coarse, but it was wholesome; and they procured a sufficiency of it. Several new kinds of plants sprung up in the garden, which they dressed; and these signs of comfort increased daily as the season advanced.

"The old man, leaning on his son, walked each day at noon, when it did not rain, as I found it was called when the heavens poured forth its waters. This frequently took place; but a high wind quickly dried the earth, and the season became far more pleasant than it had been.

"My mode of life in my hovel was uniform. During the morning I attended the motions of the cottagers; and when they were dispersed in various occupations, I slept: the remainder of the day was spent in observing my friends. When they had retired to rest, if there was any moon, or the night was star-light, I went into the woods, and collected my own food and fuel for the cottage. When I returned, as often as it was necessary, I cleared their path from the snow, and performed those offices that I had seen done by Felix. I afterwards found that these labours, performed by an invisible hand, greatly astonished them; and once or twice I heard them, on these occasions, utter the words *good spirit, wonderful*; but I did not then understand the signification of these terms.

"My thoughts now became more active, and I longed to discover the motives and feelings of these lovely creatures; I was inquisitive to know why Felix appeared so miserable, and Agatha so sad. I thought (foolish wretch!) that it might be in my power to restore happiness to these deserving people. When I slept, or was absent, the forms of the venerable blind father, the gentle Agatha, and the excellent Felix, flitted before me. I looked upon them as superior beings, who would be the arbiters of my future destiny. I formed in my imagination a thousand pictures of presenting myself to them, and their reception of me. I imagined that they would be disgusted, until, by my gentle demeanour and conciliating words, I should first win their favour, and afterwards their love.

"These thoughts exhilarated me, and led me to apply with fresh ardour to the acquiring the art of language. My organs were indeed harsh, but supple; and although my voice was very unlike the soft music of their tones, yet I pronounced such words as I understood with tolerable ease. It was as the ass and the lap-dog;[7] yet surely the gentle ass, whose intentions were affectionate, although his manners were rude, deserved better treatment than blows and execration.

"The pleasant showers and genial warmth of spring greatly altered the aspect of the earth. Men, who before this change seemed to have been hid in caves, dispersed themselves, and were employed in various arts of cultivation. The birds sang in more cheerful notes, and the leaves began to bud forth on the trees. Happy, happy earth! fit habitation for gods, which, so short a time before, was bleak, damp, and unwholesome. My spirits were elevated by the enchanting appearance of nature; the past was blotted from my memory, the present was tranquil, and the future gilded by bright rays of hope, and anticipations of joy."

7. *Aesop's Fables* (George Fyler Townsend translation, 1887) recounts the tale of the Ass and the Lapdog:

A MAN had an Ass, and a Maltese Lapdog, a very great beauty. The Ass was left in a stable and had plenty of oats and hay to eat, just as any other Ass would. The Lapdog knew many tricks and was a great favorite with his master, who often fondled him and seldom went out to dine without bringing him home some tidbit to eat. The Ass, on the contrary, had much work to do in grinding the corn-mill and in carrying wood from the forest or burdens from the farm. He often lamented his own hard fate and contrasted it with the luxury and idleness of the Lapdog, till at last one day he broke his cords and halter, and galloped into his master's house, kicking up his heels without measure, and frisking and fawning as well as he could. He next tried to jump about his master as he had seen the Lapdog do, but he broke the table and smashed all the dishes upon it to atoms. He then attempted to lick his master, and jumped upon his back. The servants, hearing the strange hubbub and perceiving the danger of their master, quickly relieved him, and drove out the Ass to his stable with kicks and clubs and cuffs. The Ass, as he returned to his stall beaten nearly to death, thus lamented: "I have brought it all on myself! Why could I not have been contented to labor with my companions, and not wish to be idle all the day like that useless little Lapdog!"

Aesop's Fables is a collection of stories attributed to the Greek Aesop, of uncertain biography, and may well have simply been an amalgamation of folklore. A German edition by Heinrich Steinhöwel appeared in 1476, and a French edition appeared in 1480, succeeded by an English edition by Caxton in 1484.

CHAPTER V.[1]

"I NOW HASTEN TO the more moving part of my story. I shall relate events that impressed me with feelings which, from what I was,[2] have made me what I am.

"Spring advanced rapidly; the weather became fine, and the skies cloudless. It surprised me, that what before was desert and gloomy should now bloom with the most beautiful flowers and verdure. My senses were gratified and refreshed by a thousand scents of delight, and a thousand sights of beauty.

"It was on one of these days, when my cottagers periodically rested from labour—the old man played on his guitar, and the children listened to him—I observed that the countenance of Felix was melancholy beyond expression: he sighed frequently; and once his father paused in his music, and I conjectured by his manner that he inquired the cause of his son's sorrow. Felix replied in a cheerful accent, and the old man was recommencing his music, when some one tapped at the door.

"It was a lady on horseback, accompanied by a countryman as a guide. The lady was dressed in a dark suit, and covered with a thick black veil. Agatha asked a question; to which the stranger only replied by pronouncing, in a sweet accent, the name of Felix. Her voice was musical, but unlike that of either of my friends. On hearing this word, Felix came

1. Chapter 13 in the 1831 edition.

2. The creature uses the more grammatical "had been" in place of "was" in the 1831 edition.

up hastily to the lady; who, when she saw him, threw up her veil, and I beheld a countenance of angelic beauty and expression. Her hair of a shining raven black, and curiously braided; her eyes were dark, but gentle, although animated; her features of a regular proportion, and her complexion wondrously fair, each cheek tinged with a lovely pink.[3]

"Felix seemed ravished with delight when he saw her, every trait of sorrow vanished from his face, and it instantly expressed a degree of ecstatic joy, of which I could hardly have believed it capable; his eyes sparkled, as his cheek flushed with pleasure; and at that moment I thought him as beautiful as the stranger. She appeared affected by different feelings; wiping a few tears from her lovely eyes, she held out her hand to Felix, who kissed it rapturously, and called her, as well as I could distinguish, his sweet Arabian. She did not appear to understand him, but smiled. He assisted her to dismount, and, dismissing her guide, conducted her into the cottage. Some conversation took place between him and his father; and the young stranger knelt at the old man's feet, and would have kissed his hand, but he raised her, and embraced her affectionately.

"I soon perceived, that although the stranger uttered articulate sounds, and appeared to have a language of her own, she was neither understood by, or herself understood, the cottagers. They made many signs which I did not comprehend; but I saw that her presence diffused gladness through the cottage, dispelling their sorrow as the sun dissipates the morning mists. Felix seemed peculiarly happy, and with smiles of delight welcomed his Arabian. Agatha, the ever-gentle Agatha, kissed the hands of the lovely stranger; and, pointing to her brother, made signs which appeared to me to mean that he had been sorrowful until she came. Some hours passed thus, while they, by their countenances, expressed joy, the cause of which I did not comprehend. Presently I found, by the frequent recurrence of one sound which the stranger repeated after them, that she was endeavouring to learn their language; and the idea instantly occurred to me, that I should make use of the same instructions to the same end. The stranger learned

3. While Safie is an "Arabian," she is described as having a classically Western appearance, with "wondrously fair" skin; her eyes are "dark" (non-Western) "but gentle." In many ways an idealized woman, shown both as standing up to her villainous father and as the perfect lover/wife to Felix De Lacey, her racial mixture is telling. Traditionally in Western literature, such attributes might have prefigured her inclusion in the role of the slave, the resident of the harem. Joyce Zonana, in "'They Will Prove the Truth of My Tale': Safie's Letters as the Feminist Core of Mary Shelley's Frankenstein" (*Journal of Narrative Technique* 21, no, 2 [Spring 1991], 170–84), sees her as "a woman who insists on her own possession of a soul, rejecting 'puerile amusements' and devoting herself to a 'noble emulation for virtue.' Safie's echoing of Mary Wollstonecraft's ideas (and words) identifies her, not as Mary Wollstonecraft herself, but as an exemplar of a woman claiming her rights as a rational being."

4. The name "Safie" is invented but is drawn either from the Greek *"sophia"* (wisdom) or the Arabic *"safa"* (pronounced "sah-fah" and meaning "pure"). It was originally "Maimouna" or "Amina" in Percy Shelley's editorial material; the Draft does not include this chapter. Note the similarity of the pronunciation of "Safie" to the French pronunciation of "Saville," the married name of Walton's sister.

about twenty words at the first lesson, most of them indeed were those which I had before understood, but I profited by the others.

"As night came on, Agatha and the Arabian retired early. When they separated, Felix kissed the hand of the stranger, and said, 'Good night, sweet Safie.'[4] He sat up much longer, conversing with his father; and, by the frequent repetition of her name, I conjectured that their lovely guest was the subject of their conversation. I ardently desired to understand them, and bent every faculty towards that purpose, but found it utterly impossible.

"The next morning Felix went out to his work; and, after the usual occupations of Agatha were finished, the Arabian sat at the feet of the old man, and, taking his guitar, played some airs so entrancingly beautiful, that they at once drew tears of sorrow and delight from my eyes. She sang, and her voice flowed in a rich cadence, swelling or dying away, like a nightingale of the woods.

"When she had finished, she gave the guitar to Agatha, who at first declined it. She played a simple air, and her voice accompanied it in sweet accents, but unlike the wondrous strain of the stranger. The old man appeared enraptured, and said some words, which Agatha endeavoured to explain to Safie, and by which he appeared to wish to express that she bestowed on him the greatest delight by her music.

"The days now passed as peaceably as before, with the sole alteration, that joy had taken place of sadness in the countenances of my friends. Safie was always gay and happy; she and I improved rapidly in the knowledge of language, so that in two months I began to comprehend most of the words uttered by my protectors.

"In the meanwhile also the black ground was covered with herbage, and the green banks interspersed with innumerable flowers, sweet to the scent and the eyes, stars of pale radiance among the moonlight woods; the sun became warmer, the nights clear and balmy; and my nocturnal rambles were an extreme pleasure to me, although they were considerably shortened by the late setting and early rising of the sun; for I never ventured abroad during daylight, fearful of meeting with the same treatment as I had formerly endured in the first village which I entered.

"My days were spent in close attention, that I might more speedily master the language; and I may boast that I improved more rapidly than the Arabian, who understood very little, and conversed in broken accents, whilst I comprehended and could imitate almost every word that was spoken.

"While I improved in speech, I also learned the science of letters,[5] as it was taught to the stranger; and this opened before me a wide field for wonder and delight.

"The book from which Felix instructed Safie was Volney's *Ruins of Empires*.[6] I should not have understood the purport of this book, had not Felix, in reading it, given very minute explanations. He had chosen this work, he said, because the declamatory style was framed in imitation of the eastern authors. Through this work I obtained a cursory knowledge of history, and a view of the several empires at present existing in the world; it gave me an insight into the manners, governments, and religions of the different nations of the earth. I heard of the slothful Asiatics; of the stupendous genius and mental activity of the Grecians; of the wars and wonderful virtue of the early Romans—of their subse-

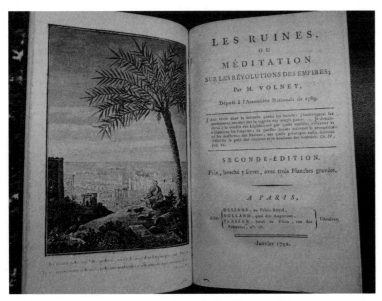

Volney's *The Ruins, Or, Meditation on the Revolutions of Empires*, printed just two years before Safie's studies.

5. It is simply not possible that one can learn to read by listening to another person learning to read. Reading is a matter of connecting symbols with meaning, and unless the symbols can be seen (or felt, if one is learning Braille), no connection can be made. The creature was certainly too far away to see the symbols in the book as Felix showed them to Safie. A more plausible theory is that his brain, taken from another French speaker, "remembered" how to read (and speak), and he merely convinced himself that he was "learning" a skill that he already possessed. Sir Walter Scott wrote, in his 1818 review of *Frankenstein* for *Blackwood's Edinburgh Magazine*, "That he should have not only learned to speak, but to read, and, for aught we know, to write ... by listening through a hole in a wall, seems as unlikely as that he should have acquired, in the same way, the problems of Euclid, or the art of bookkeeping, by single and double entry."

Furthermore, are we to understand that Safie did not know how to read? Or merely that Felix read to her to help her expand her knowledge of the language? The latter is more plausible, inasmuch as Safie's mother "taught her to aspire to higher powers of intellect," which must have included reading (although she may have only learned Turkic from her Christian-Arab mother).

6. More properly, *The Ruins, Or, Meditation on the Revolutions of Empires: and The Law of Nature*, by Constantin-François Chasseboeuf, who took the name Volney, published in 1791 in French. It was translated in 1802 into English. The book is described by *Frankenstein* scholar Pamela Clemit as "a powerful Enlightenment critique of ancient and modern governments as tyrannical and supported by religious fraud" ("*Frankenstein, Matilda*, and the Legacies of Godwin and Wollstonecraft," in *The Cambridge Companion*

THE NEW ANNOTATED FRANKENSTEIN

to Mary Shelley, ed. Esther Schor [Cambridge, UK: Cambridge University Press, 2003], 35).

In light of the date of translation, the book in question must have been the French edition, and Safie and the creature learned French. Because the creature already knew many of the words, we may deduce that the household spoke French, and this is confirmed later by the creature, who recounts that the De Lacey family hailed from Paris (though we learn later that the events here take place in Germany, probably not far from Ingolstadt) and that the senior De Lacey is of French descent.

7. The word is "degenerating" in the 1831 edition.

8. "Advantages" is used in place of "acquisitions" in the 1831 edition.

quent degeneration[7]—of the decline of that mighty empire; of chivalry, christianity and kings. I heard of the discovery of the American hemisphere, and wept with Safie over the hapless fate of its original inhabitants.

"These wonderful narrations inspired me with strange feelings. Was man, indeed, at once so powerful, so virtuous, and magnificent, yet so vicious and base? He appeared at one time a mere scion of the evil principle, and at another as all that can be conceived of noble and godlike. To be a great and virtuous man appeared the highest honour that can befall a sensitive being; to be base and vicious, as many on record have been, appeared the lowest degradation, a condition more abject than that of the blind mole or harmless worm. For a long time I could not conceive how one man could go forth to murder his fellow, or even why there were laws and governments; but when I heard details of vice and bloodshed, my wonder ceased, and I turned away with disgust and loathing.

"Every conversation of the cottagers now opened new wonders to me. While I listened to the instructions which Felix bestowed upon the Arabian, the strange system of human society was explained to me. I heard of the division of property, of immense wealth and squalid poverty; of rank, descent, and noble blood.

"The words induced me to turn towards myself. I learned that the possessions most esteemed by your fellow-creatures were, high and unsullied descent united with riches. A man might be respected with only one of these acquisitions;[8] but without either he was considered, except in very rare instances, as a vagabond and a slave, doomed to waste his powers for the profit of the chosen few. And what was I? Of my creation and creator I was absolutely ignorant; but I knew that I possessed no money, no friends, no kind of property. I was, besides, endowed with a figure hideously deformed and loathsome; I was not even of the same nature as man. I was more agile than they, and could subsist upon coarser diet; I bore the extremes of heat and cold with less injury to my frame; my stature far exceeded their's. When I looked around, I saw and heard of none like me. Was I then a monster, a blot upon the earth, from which all men fled, and whom all men disowned?

"I cannot describe to you the agony that these reflections inflicted upon me; I tried to dispel them, but sorrow only increased with knowledge. Oh, that I had for ever remained in my native wood, nor known or felt beyond the sensations of hunger, thirst, and heat!

"Of what a strange nature is knowledge! It clings to the mind, when it has once seized on it, like a lichen on the rock. I wished sometimes to shake off all thought and feeling; but I learned that there was but one means to overcome the sensation of pain, and that was death—a state which I feared yet did not understand. I admired virtue and good feelings, and loved the gentle manners and amiable qualities of my cottagers; but I was shut out from intercourse with them, except through means which I obtained by stealth, when I was unseen and unknown, and which rather increased than satisfied the desire I had of becoming one among my fellows. The gentle words of Agatha, and the animated smiles of the charming Arabian, were not for me. The mild exhortations of the old man, and the lively conversation of the loved Felix, were not for me. Miserable, unhappy wretch!

"Other lessons were impressed upon me even more deeply. I heard of the difference of sexes; of the birth and growth of children; how the father doated on the smiles of the infant, and the lively sallies of the older child; how all the life and cares of the mother were wrapt up in the precious charge; how the mind of youth expanded and gained knowledge; of brother, sister, and all the various relationships which bind one human being to another in mutual bonds.

"But where were my friends and relations? No father had watched my infant days, no mother had blessed me with smiles and caresses; or if they had, all my past life was now a blot, a blind vacancy in which I distinguished nothing. From my earliest remembrance I had been as I then was in height and proportion. I had never yet seen a being resembling me, or who claimed any intercourse with me. What was I? The question again recurred, to be answered only with groans.

Realizing he missed out on a childhood

"I will soon explain to what these feelings tended; but allow me now to return to the cottagers, whose story excited in me such various feelings of indignation, delight, and wonder, but which all terminated in additional love and reverence for my protectors (for so I loved, in an innocent, half painful self-deceit, to call them)."

CHAPTER VI.[1]

1. Chapter 14 in the 1831 edition.

2. Although the timeline is vague here, the creature began observing the De Lacey family in the spring of 1794. The crimes of the Turkish merchant likely took place in 1792, when mass arrests of royalists occurred. In September 1792, mobs entered the Paris prisons, slaughtering over two thousand prisoners; the Turk was lucky to avoid dying then. Safie's father, albeit of low character as is evidenced by his betrayal of Felix and his family, may have been guilty of nothing more than trading with the aristocracy. As such, he joins the parade of innocents wrongfully convicted: the De Laceys, Justine Moritz, Victor Frankenstein, and even the creature suffer the same fate.

3. Dedicated in 330 CE by the Roman emperor Constantine on the site of the ancient city of Byzantium, Constantinople was one of the two capitals of the Roman Empire, and the principal city of the eastern Roman, or Byzantine, Empire. By the twelfth century CE, it was the largest city in Europe. When the Byzan-

"SOME TIME ELAPSED before I learned the history of my friends. It was one which could not fail to impress itself deeply on my mind, unfolding as it did a number of circumstances each interesting and wonderful to one so utterly inexperienced as I was.

"The name of the old man was De Lacey. He was descended from a good family in France, where he had lived for many years in affluence, respected by his superiors, and beloved by his equals. His son was bred in the service of his country; and Agatha had ranked with ladies of the highest distinction. A few months before my arrival, they had lived in a large and luxurious city, called Paris, surrounded by friends, and possessed of every enjoyment which virtue, refinement of intellect, or taste, accompanied by a moderate fortune, could afford.

"The father of Safie had been the cause of their ruin. He was a Turkish merchant, and had inhabited Paris for many years, when, for some reason which I could not learn, he became obnoxious to the government.[2] He was seized and cast into prison the very day that Safie arrived from Constantinople[3] to join him. He was tried, and condemned to death. The injustice of his sentence was very flagrant; all Paris was indignant; and it was judged that his religion and

tine Empire fell to the Ottoman Turks in 1453, Constantinople became the capital of the Ottoman Empire. In 1923, with the founding of the modern nation of Turkey, it was renamed Istanbul. Making Safie's place of origin Constantinople automatically labeled her, in the minds of early nineteenth-century readers, as an exotic creature epitomizing the values of the Eastern Empire; literally spanning two continents, Constantinople was the gateway between the exotic East and the commonplace West.

4. The word "accidentally" is inserted in the 1831 edition.

5. This has the now somewhat obsolete meaning of "release from a place"—that is, to liberate Safie's father from prison.

6. And who, by the strangest of coincidences, happened to be there at the same time that Felix was communicating with her father through a "strongly grated window." It is a wonder that Felix could even see "the lovely Safie" in what must have been a poorly lit cell, much less her "gestures of gratitude."

7. "Parent" replaces "father" in the 1831 edition.

wealth, rather than the crime alleged against him, had been the cause of his condemnation.

"Felix had[4] been present at the trial; his horror and indignation were uncontrollable, when he heard the decision of the court. He made, at that moment, a solemn vow to deliver[5] him, and then looked around for the means. After many fruitless attempts to gain admittance to the prison, he found a strongly grated window in an unguarded part of the building, which lighted the dungeon of the unfortunate Mahometan; who, loaded with chains, waited in despair the execution of the barbarous sentence. Felix visited the grate at night, and made known to the prisoner his intentions in his favour. The Turk, amazed and delighted, endeavoured to kindle the zeal of his deliverer by promises of reward and wealth. Felix rejected his offers with contempt; yet when he saw the lovely Safie, who was allowed to visit her father,[6] and who, by her gestures, expressed her lively gratitude, the youth could not help owning to his own mind, that the captive possessed a treasure which would fully reward his toil and hazard.

"The Turk quickly perceived the impression that his daughter had made on the heart of Felix, and endeavoured to secure him more entirely in his interests by the promise of her hand in marriage, so soon as he should be conveyed to a place of safety. Felix was too delicate to accept this offer; yet he looked forward to the probability of that event as to the consummation of his happiness.

"During the ensuing days, while the preparations were going forward for the escape of the merchant, the zeal of Felix was warmed by several letters that he received from this lovely girl, who found means to express her thoughts in the language of her lover by the aid of an old man, a servant of her father's, who understood French. She thanked him in the most ardent terms for his intended services towards her father;[7] and at the same time she gently deplored her own fate.

"I have copies of these letters; for I found means, during my residence in the hovel, to procure the implements of writing; and the letters were often in the hands of Felix or

Agatha.[8] Before I depart, I will give them to you, they will prove the truth of my tale; but at present, as the sun is already far declined, I shall only have time to repeat the substance of them to you.

"Safie related, that her mother was a Christian Arab,[9] seized and made a slave by the Turks; recommended by her beauty, she had won the heart of the father of Safie, who married her. The young girl spoke in high and enthusiastic terms of her mother, who, born in freedom spurned the bondage to which she was now reduced. She instructed her daughter in the tenets of her religion, and taught her to aspire to higher powers of intellect, and an independence of spirit, forbidden to the female followers of Mahomet.[10] This lady died; but her lessons were indelibly impressed on the mind of Safie, who sickened at the prospect of again returning to Asia, and the being immured within the walls of a haram,[11] allowed only to occupy herself with puerile[12] amusements, ill suited to the temper of her soul, now accustomed to grand ideas and a noble emulation for virtue. The prospect of marrying a Christian, and remaining in a country where women were allowed to take a rank in society, was enchanting to her.

"The day for the execution of the Turk was fixed; but, on the night previous to it, he had quitted prison,[13] and before morning was distant many leagues from Paris. Felix had procured passports in the name of his father, sister, and himself. He had previously communicated his plan to the former, who aided the deceit by quitting his house, under the pretence of a journey, and concealed himself, with his daughter, in an obscure part of Paris.

"Felix conducted the fugitives through France to Lyons, and across Mont Cenis[14] to Leghorn,[15] where the merchant had decided to wait a favourable opportunity of passing into some part of the Turkish dominions.

"Safie resolved to remain with her father until the moment of his departure, before which time the Turk renewed his promise that she should be united to his deliverer; and Felix remained with them in expectation of that event; and in the mean time he enjoyed the society of the Arabian, who exhibited towards him the simplest and tenderest affection. They

8. How, one may wonder, might the creature have obtained the letters from the cottage without the knowledge of its inhabitants? Having obtained writing implements, undoubtedly also stolen from the cottage, he then proceeded to copy them over while confined in a "hovel" barely large enough for him to sit upright, lit only by light transmitted through the neighboring sty. The story is hardly to be believed—and to what end did he copy them? Perhaps they formed part of his curriculum for self-taught reading.

9. The Arab Christians were largely the remnants of ancient Arabic tribes descended from pre-Islamic times. Today, they include both Latinized Christians and Greek Orthodox Christians. Islamist countries generally gave these Christian families religious freedom in exchange for payment of special taxes imposed on all non-Muslims (called *jizyah* in Arabic or *cizye* in Turkish). The Arab-Christians were highly influential in the Arab Renaissance, which commenced in the 1840s.

10. The Quran is usually interpreted as teaching that women are subservient to men, who are the lords, masters, and managers of the household. However, the creature is not strictly correct in ascribing to Islam the idea that women are not to be educated. The prophet Muhammad is said to have applauded *religious* education for Muslim women; it was only secular education that, until recently, was withheld. Still, in 2007, UNICEF reported that in seventeen of the fifty-seven Organization of Islamic Cooperation (OIC) member countries, primary school participation stood at below 60 percent. (However, UNICEF also noted that in countries including Jordan, Bahrain, Lebanon, and Oman, girls outnumbered boys in school.) More than half the adult popu-

lation was illiterate in some Islamic countries, and the proportion was as high as 70 percent among women. Since 2007, OIC literacy rates have improved, but there is still a 6.5 percent disparity between literate boys and literate girls (as contrasted with developed countries, where there is no gender-based disparity).

11. *Haram* literally means "forbidden" in Arabic. *Harem* became the Turkish word for a separate part of a Muslim household for the housing of women—wives, concubines, female servants, and their offspring.

12. "Infantile," not "puerile," in the 1831 edition.

13. The phrase "had quit prison" is altered to "quitted his prison" in the 1831 edition.

14. A pass in Savoy between France and Italy.

15. Livorno, the capital of the province of Livorno and the most important port city in Tuscany, on the Ligurian Sea. Its population at this time was around fifty thousand. "Leghorn" is a Briticism and was unlikely used by the creature but rather interpolated by Shelley. As we have seen, it was on his return from Leghorn to Lerici that Percy Shelley died at sea: See the Foreword, pp. lvi, above, and note 40, Volume I, Letter III, above.

16. "Greatly" is omitted in the 1831 edition.

Harem Scene with Mothers and Daughters in Varying Costumes (photographer unknown, ca. 1900).

conversed with one another through the means of an interpreter, and sometimes with the interpretation of looks; and Safie sang to him the divine airs of her native country.

"The Turk allowed this intimacy to take place, and encouraged the hopes of the youthful lovers, while in his heart he had formed far other plans. He loathed the idea that his daughter should be united to a Christian; but he feared the resentment of Felix if he should appear lukewarm; for he knew that he was still in the power of his deliverer, if he should choose to betray him to the Italian state which they inhabited. He revolved a thousand plans by which he should be enabled to prolong the deceit until it might be no longer necessary, and secretly to take his daughter with him when he departed. His plans were greatly[16] facilitated by the news which arrived from Paris.

"The government of France were greatly enraged at the escape of their victim, and spared no pains to detect and punish his deliverer. The plot of Felix was quickly discovered, and De Lacey and Agatha were thrown into prison. The news reached Felix, and roused him from his dream of pleasure. His blind and aged father, and his gentle sister, lay in a noisome dungeon, while he enjoyed the free air, and the society of her whom he loved. This idea was torture to him. He quickly arranged with the Turk, that if the latter should find a favourable opportunity for escape before Felix could return to Italy, Safie should remain as a boarder at a convent at Leghorn; and then, quitting the lovely Arabian, he hastened to Paris, and delivered himself up to the vengeance of the law, hoping to free De Lacey and Agatha by this proceeding.

"He did not succeed. They remained confined for five months before the trial took place; the result of which deprived them of their fortune, and condemned them to a perpetual exile from their native country.

"They found a miserable asylum in the cottage in Germany, where I discovered them. Felix soon learned that the treacherous Turk, for whom he and his family endured such unheard-of oppression, on discovering that his deliverer was thus reduced to poverty and impotence,[17] became a traitor to good feeling and honour, and had quitted Italy with his daughter, insultingly sending Felix a pittance of money to aid him, as he said, in some plan of future maintenance.

"Such were the events that preyed on the heart of Felix, and rendered him, when I first saw him, the most miserable of his family. He could have endured poverty, and when[18] this distress had been the meed[19] of his virtue, he would have gloried in it: but the ingratitude of the Turk, and the loss of his beloved Safie, were misfortunes more bitter and irreparable. The arrival of the Arabian now infused new life into his soul.

"When the news reached Leghorn, that Felix was deprived of his wealth and rank, the merchant commanded his daughter to think no more of her lover, but to prepare to return with him to her native country. The generous nature of Safie was outraged by this command; she attempted to expostulate with her father, but he left her angrily, reiterating his tyrannical mandate.

"A few days after, the Turk entered his daughter's apartment, and told her hastily, that he had reason to believe that his residence at Leghorn had been divulged, and that he should speedily be delivered up to the French government;

17. The word "impotence" is replaced with "ruin" in the 1831 edition.

18. The word "when" is replaced by "while" in the 1831 edition, and the phrase "would have" is omitted.

19. The earned share or reward.

20. "Turkish" in the Draft, changed by Percy Shelley to "Arabic" but changed back to this description in the final 1818 text.

he had, consequently, hired a vessel to convey him to Constantinople, for which city he should sail in a few hours. He intended to leave his daughter under the care of a confidential servant, to follow at her leisure with the greater part of his property, which had not yet arrived at Leghorn.

"When alone, Safie resolved in her own mind the plan of conduct that it would become her to pursue in this emergency. A residence in Turkey was abhorrent to her; her religion and feelings were alike adverse to it. By some papers of her father's, which fell into her hands, she heard of the exile of her lover, and learnt the name of the spot where he then resided. She hesitated some time, but at length she formed her determination. Taking with her some jewels that belonged to her, and a small sum of money, she quitted Italy, with an attendant, a native of Leghorn, but who understood the common language of Turkey,[20] and departed for Germany.

"She arrived in safety at a town about twenty leagues from the cottage of De Lacey, when her attendant fell dangerously ill. Safie nursed her with the most devoted affection; but the poor girl died, and the Arabian was left alone, unacquainted with the language of the country, and utterly ignorant of the customs of the world. She fell, however, into good hands. The Italian had mentioned the name of the spot for which they were bound; and, after her death, the woman of the house in which they had lived took care that Safie should arrive in safety at the cottage of her lover."

CHAPTER VII.[1]

1. Chapter 15 in the 1831 edition.

2. That is, 1795, by our reckoning.

3. As discussed in note 5, Volume II, Chapter V, above, it is impossible to understand how the creature learned to read.

4. Milton's epic poem was first translated into French in 1727, by Nicolas François Dupré de Saint-Maur.

5. The creature here refers to Plutarch's *Lives of the Noble Greeks and Romans*, also known as *Parallel Lives*, probably written around 100 CE. It was translated into Latin by Ulrich Han in 1470 and into French by Jacques Amyot in 1559; the latter became the basis for the first English translation by Sir Thomas North, in 1579. The creature undoubtedly had the Amyot translation.

6. Goethe's *Sorrows of Young Werther* (1774) was first translated from German into French in 1776 by Baron Karl Siegmund von Seckendorff; there were numerous other translations. The book was immensely popular when it first

"SUCH WAS THE history of my beloved cottagers. It impressed me deeply. I learned, from the views of social life which it developed, to admire their virtues, and to deprecate the vices of mankind.

"As yet I looked upon crime as a distant evil; benevolence and generosity were ever present before me, inciting within me a desire to become an actor in the busy scene where so many admirable qualities were called forth and displayed. But, in giving an account of the progress of my intellect, I must not omit a circumstance which occurred in the beginning of the month of August of the same year.[2]

"One night, during my accustomed visit to the neighbouring wood, where I collected my own food, and brought home firing for my protectors, I found on the ground a leathern portmanteau, containing several articles of dress and some books. I eagerly seized the prize, and returned with it to my hovel. Fortunately the books were written[3] in the language the elements of which I had acquired at the cottage; they consisted of *Paradise Lost*,[4] a volume of *Plutarch's Lives*,[5] and the *Sorrows of Werter*.[6] The possession of these treasures gave me extreme delight; I now continually studied and exercised my mind upon these histories, whilst my friends were employed in their ordinary occupations.

"I can hardly describe to you the effect of these books.

appeared, making the twenty-four-year-old Goethe an international celebrity. Although he later distanced himself from the book, resenting that it overshadowed his other work, Goethe revised it in 1787 and eventually acknowledged its near-universal appeal.

Largely epistolary, the book tells of the hero's doomed love for a young woman who loves another man. Ultimately, Werther realizes that the only possible resolution of the triangle is the death of one of its members. Unable to commit an act of violence directed at his rival, he kills himself. Werther's style of dress became widely copied, and his suicide reportedly triggered a number of copycat suicides—termed today, rightly or wrongly, the "Werther effect": See A. Schmidtke and H. Häfner, "The Werther Effect After Television Films: New Evidence for an Old Hypothesis," *Psychological Medicine* 18, no. 3 (August 1988): 665–76.

7. The balance of this sentence was added by Percy Shelley to the Draft.

8. A reference to Percy Shelley's 1816 poem "Mutability," quoted earlier in the text accompanying note 10, Volume II, Chapter II, above, which it was clearly impossible for the creature to have read.

9. This sentence and the following question were added to the Draft by Percy Shelley.

10. The book parallels the lives of comparable Greeks and Romans. The names the creature mentions shortly—Theseus, Romulus, Lycurgus, Numa, and Solon—are the first five subjects of the book, in order of date of death. *Plutarch's Lives* was deeply familiar to the Shelleys: Percy read it in 1816 and again in May 1817, according to Mary's journals and letters, and like every book that each read, it was discussed extensively. The subjects of

They produced in me an infinity of new images and feelings, that sometimes raised me to ecstasy, but more frequently sunk me into the lowest dejection. In the *Sorrows of Werter*, besides the interest of its simple and affecting story, so many opinions are canvassed, and so many lights thrown upon what had hitherto been to me obscure subjects, that I found in it a never-ending source of speculation and astonishment. The gentle and domestic manners it described, combined with lofty sentiments and feelings, which had for their object something out of self, accorded well with my experience among my protectors,[7] and with the wants which were for ever alive in my own bosom. But I thought Werter himself a more divine being than I had ever beheld or imagined; his character contained no pretension, but it sunk deep. The disquisitions upon death and suicide were calculated to fill me with wonder. I did not pretend to enter into the merits of the case, yet I inclined towards the opinions of the hero, whose extinction I wept, without precisely understanding it.

"As I read, however, I applied much personally to my own feelings and condition. I found myself similar, yet at the same time strangely unlike the beings concerning whom I read, and to whose conversation I was a listener. I sympathized with, and partly understood them, but I was unformed in mind; I was dependent on none, and related to none. 'The path of my departure was free;'[8] and there was none to lament my annihilation. My person was hideous, and my stature gigantic: what did this mean? Who was I? What was I? Whence did I come?[9] What was my destination? These questions continually recurred, but I was unable to solve them.

"The volume of *Plutarch's Lives* which I possessed, contained the histories of the first founders of the ancient republics.[10] This book had a far different effect upon me from the *Sorrows of Werter*. I learned from Werter's imaginations despondency and gloom: but Plutarch taught me high thoughts; he elevated me above the wretched sphere of my own reflections, to admire and love the heroes of past ages. Many things I read surpassed my understanding and experience. I had a very confused knowledge of kingdoms, wide extents of country, mighty rivers, and boundless seas. But

I was perfectly unacquainted with towns, and large assemblages of men. The cottage of my protectors had been the only school in which I had studied human nature; but this book developed new and mightier scenes of action. I read of men concerned in public affairs governing or massacring their species. I felt the greatest ardour for virtue rise within me, and abhorrence for vice, as far as I understood the signification of those terms, relative as they were, as I applied them, to pleasure and pain alone. Induced by these feelings, I was of course led to admire peaceable law-givers, Numa,[11] Solon,[12] and Lycurgus,[13] in preference to Romulus and Theseus.[14] The patriarchal lives of my protectors caused these impressions to take a firm hold on my mind; perhaps, if my first introduction to humanity had been made by a young soldier, burning for glory and slaughter, I should have been imbued with different sensations.

"But *Paradise Lost* excited different and far deeper emotions. I read it, as I had read the other volumes which had fallen into my hands, as a true history. It moved every feeling of wonder and awe, that the picture of an omnipotent God warring with his creatures was capable of exciting. I often referred the several situations, as their similarity struck me, to my own. Like Adam, I was created apparently united by no link to any other being in existence; but his state was far different from mine in every other respect. He had come forth from the hands of God a perfect creature, happy and prosperous, guarded by the especial care of his Creator; he was allowed to converse with, and acquire knowledge from beings of a superior nature: but I was wretched, helpless, and alone. Many times I considered Satan as the fitter emblem of my condition; for often, like him, when I viewed the bliss of my protectors, the bitter gall of envy rose within me.[15]

"Another circumstance strengthened and confirmed these feelings. Soon after my arrival in the hovel, I discovered some papers in the pocket of the dress which I had taken from your laboratory. At first I had neglected them; but now that I was able to decypher the characters in which they were written,[16] I began to study them with diligence. It was your journal of the four months that preceded my creation. You minutely

the *Lives* were viewed as models of virtue, exemplars of how to conduct a modern existence. Rousseau claimed that he was intimately familiar with the series of biographies by the age of eight, and Charlotte Corday was said to have read Plutarch through the daylight hours of July 13, 1793, before assassinating the Jacobin leader Jean-Paul Marat that night.

11. Numa Pompilius (753–673 BCE) was the second king of Rome, successor to Romulus, who had founded the city in an era of war with the Sabines. Numa at first declined the throne, principally on the grounds that he was not war-like, as Romulus had been. Plutarch wrote of him, "It is true, indeed, of all just and good men, that they are praised more after they have left the world than before, since envy does not long survive them, and some even see it die before them; but in Numa's case the misfortunes of the kings who followed him made his fame shine all the brighter" (Loeb Classical Library Edition, translated by Bernadotte Perrin, 1914).

12. Solon (ca. 638–ca. 558 BCE) was an Athenian statesman and reformer whose actual legal work is shrouded in uncertainty. According to Plutarch, he softened many of the harsh rules of his predecessor, Draco. "But those things wherein he hoped to find them [that is, the Athenians] open to persuasion or submissive to compulsion, these he did, 'Combining both force and justice together,' as he says himself. Therefore when he was afterwards asked if he had enacted the best laws for the Athenians, he replied, 'The best they would receive'" (Loeb Classical Library Edition, translated by Bernadotte Perrin, 1914).

13. Lycurgus, the Spartan lawgiver, is another figure whose actual history is obscure, although he is generally assigned

THE NEW ANNOTATED FRANKENSTEIN

to the period 700–630 BCE. Even Plutarch writes of him, "Concerning Lycurgus the lawgiver, in general, nothing can be said which is not disputed, since indeed there are different accounts of his birth, his travels, his death, and above all, of his work as lawmaker and statesman; and there is least agreement among historians as to the times in which the man lived."

14. Plutarch wrote, "But after publishing my account of Lycurgus the lawgiver and Numa the king, I thought I might not unreasonably go back still farther to Romulus, now that my history had brought me near his times. And as I asked myself, 'With such a warrior' (as Aeschylus says) 'who will dare to fight?' 'Whom shall I set against him? Who is competent?' it seemed to me that I must make the founder of lovely and famous Athens [that is, Theseus, generally assigned to the period 1260–1200 BCE] the counterpart and parallel to the father of invincible and glorious Rome [Romulus, 771–717 BCE]" (Loeb Classical Library Edition, translated by Bernadotte Perrin, 1914). Both, noted Plutarch, resorted to the rape of women; both were of unknown origins but were reportedly descended from gods; and both were renowned for their strength as well as their sagacity. Both, too, ended their careers in conflict with their subjects. Romulus appears to have been a historical personage, but as to Theseus, William Smith writes, in *A Dictionary of Greek and Roman Biography and Mythology* (1848), "It is a vain task now to attempt to decide whether there is any historical basis for the accounts of Theseus that were handed down, and still more so to endeavour to separate the historical from the legendary in what has been preserved."

15. The Thomas Text adds, "while neither the feeling of remorse of [or?] self-accusation mingled with my throes;

described in these papers every step you took in the progress of your work; this history was mingled with accounts of domestic occurrences. You, doubtless, recollect these papers. Here they are. Every thing is related in them which bears reference to my accursed origin; the whole detail of that series of disgusting circumstances which produced it is set in view; the minutest description of my odious and loathsome person is given, in language which painted your own horrors, and rendered mine ineffaceable.[17] I sickened as I read. 'Hateful day when I received life!' I exclaimed in agony. 'Cursed creator! Why did you form a monster so hideous that even you[18] turned from me in disgust? God in pity made man beautiful and alluring, after his own image; but my form is a filthy type of yours, more horrid from its very resemblance. Satan had his companions, fellow-devils, to admire and encourage him; but I am solitary and detested.'[19]

"These were the reflections of my hours of despondency and solitude; but when I contemplated the virtues of the cottagers, their amiable and benevolent dispositions, I persuaded myself that when they should become acquainted with my admiration of their virtues, they would compassionate me, and overlook my personal deformity. Could they turn from their door one, however monstrous, who solicited their compassion and friendship? I resolved, at least, not to despair, but in every way to fit myself for an interview with them which would decide my fate. I postponed this attempt for some months longer; for the importance attached to its success inspired me with a dread lest I should fail. Besides, I found that my understanding improved so much with every day's experience, that I was unwilling to commence this undertaking until a few more months should have added to my wisdom.[20]

"Several changes, in the mean time, took place in the cottage. The presence of Safie diffused happiness among its inhabitants; and I also found that a greater degree of plenty reigned there. Felix and Agatha spent more time in amusement and conversation, and were assisted in their labours by servants. They did not appear rich, but they were contented and happy; their feelings were serene and peaceful, while mine became every day more tumultuous. Increase of knowledge only discovered to me more clearly what a wretched outcast I was. I cherished hope, it is true; but it vanished, when I beheld my person reflected in water, or my shadow in the moon-shine, even as that frail image and that inconstant shade.

"I endeavoured to crush these fears, and to fortify myself for the trial which in a few months I resolved to undergo; and sometimes I allowed my thoughts, unchecked by reason, to ramble in the fields of Paradise, and dared to fancy amiable and lovely creatures sympathizing with my feelings and cheering my gloom; their angelic countenances breathed smiles of consolation. But it was all a dream: no Eve soothed my sorrows, or shared my thoughts; I was alone. I remembered Adam's supplication to his Creator; but where was mine? He had abandoned me, and, in the bitterness of my heart, I cursed him.

"Autumn passed thus. I saw, with surprise and grief, the leaves decay and fall, and nature again assume the barren and bleak appearance it had worn when I first beheld the woods and the lovely moon. Yet I did not heed the bleakness of the weather; I was better fitted by my conformation for the endurance of cold than heat. But my chief delights were the sight of the flowers, the birds, and all the gay apparel of summer; when those deserted me, I turned with more attention towards the cottagers. Their happiness was not decreased by the absence of summer. They loved, and sympathized with one another; and their joys, depending on each other, were not interrupted by the casualties that took place around them. The more I saw of them, the greater became my desire to claim their protection and kindness; my heart yearned to be known and loved by these amiable creatures: to see their sweet looks turned[21] towards me with affection, was the utmost limit of my ambition. I dared not think that they would turn them from me with disdain and horror. The poor that stopped at their door were never driven away. I asked, it is true, for greater treasures than a little food or rest; I required kindness and sympathy; but I did not believe myself utterly unworthy of it.

although the contempt with [which] I was treated also prevented any sublime defiance to have a place in my mind." The creature evidently based this comparison on his close reading of Milton's *Paradise Lost*.

16. Another clue that the creature learned French, for as we have seen, Victor's native tongue must have been French.

17. The 1831 edition substitutes the word "indelible" for "ineffaceable."

18. The word "you" is in all capitals in the 1831 edition.

19. The word "abhorred" appears in place of "detested" in the 1831 edition.

20. The word "sagacity" replaces "wisdom" in the 1831 edition.

21. The word "turned" is replaced with "directed" in the 1831 edition.

22. That is, the late autumn of 1794, not true winter—note "red leaves" on the ground. The creature confirms this later.

23. In the 1818 edition, the spelling is subsequently changed from "De Lacey" to "De Lacy." However, consulting the Manuscript, this appears to be a typesetter's error and not the author's intention.

"The winter advanced, and an entire revolution of the seasons had taken place since I awoke into life.[22] My attention, at this time, was solely directed towards my plan of introducing myself into the cottage of my protectors. I revolved many projects; but that on which I finally fixed was, to enter the dwelling when the blind old man should be alone. I had sagacity enough to discover, that the unnatural hideousness of my person was the chief object of horror with those who had formerly beheld me. My voice, although harsh, had nothing terrible in it; I thought, therefore, that if, in the absence of his children, I could gain the good-will and mediation of the old De Lacy,[23] I might, by his means, be tolerated by my younger protectors.

"One day, when the sun shone on the red leaves that strewed the ground, and diffused cheerfulness, although it denied warmth, Safie, Agatha, and Felix, departed on a long country walk, and the old man, at his own desire, was left alone in the cottage. When his children had departed, he took up his guitar, and played several mournful, but sweet airs, more sweet and mournful than I had ever heard him play before. At first his countenance was illuminated with pleasure, but, as he continued, thoughtfulness and sadness succeeded; at length, laying aside the instrument, he sat absorbed in reflection.

"My heart beat quick; this was the hour and moment of trial, which would decide my hopes, or realize my fears. The servants were gone to a neighbouring fair. All was silent in and around the cottage: it was an excellent opportunity; yet, when I proceeded to execute my plan, my limbs failed me, and I sunk to the ground. Again I rose; and, exerting all the firmness of which I was master, removed the planks which I had placed before my hovel to conceal my retreat. The fresh air revived me, and, with renewed determination, I approached the door of their cottage.

"I knocked. 'Who is there?' said the old man—'Come in.'

"I entered; 'Pardon this intrusion,' said I, 'I am a traveller in want of a little rest; you would greatly oblige me, if you would allow me to remain a few minutes before the fire.'

"'Enter,' said De Lacy; 'and I will try in what manner I can relieve your wants; but, unfortunately, my children are from home, and, as I am blind, I am afraid I shall find it difficult to procure food for you.'

"'Do not trouble yourself, my kind host, I have food; it is warmth and rest only that I need.'

"I sat down, and a silence ensued. I knew that every minute was precious to me, yet I remained irresolute in what manner to commence the interview; when the old man addressed me—

"'By your language, stranger, I suppose you are my countryman;—are you French?'

"'No; but I was educated by a French family, and understand that language only.[24] I am now going to claim the protection of some friends, whom I sincerely love, and of whose favour I have some hopes.'

"'Are these Germans?'

"'No, they are French. But let us change the subject. I am an unfortunate and deserted creature; I look around, and I have no relation or friend upon earth. These amiable people to whom I go have never seen me, and know little of me. I am full of fears; for if I fail there, I am an outcast in the world for ever.'

"'Do not despair. To be friendless is indeed to be unfortunate; but the hearts of men, when unprejudiced by any obvious self-interest, are full of brotherly love and charity. Rely, therefore, on your hopes; and if these friends are good and amiable, do not despair.'

"'They are kind—they are the most excellent creatures in the world; but, unfortunately, they are prejudiced against me. I have good dispositions; my life has been hitherto harmless, and, in some degree, beneficial; but a fatal prejudice clouds their eyes, and where they ought to see a feeling and kind friend, they behold only a detestable monster.'

"'That is indeed unfortunate; but if you are really blameless, cannot you undeceive them?'

"'I am about to undertake that task; and it is on that account that I feel so many overwhelming terrors. I tenderly love these friends; I have, unknown to them, been for many months in the habits of daily kindness towards them; but

24. As of this date, the creature spoke only French. There is no evidence that he later learned any other language.

25. The Thomas Text adds, "They returned sooner than I expected and their inopportune appearance destroyed the fruits of so many months patience and expectation. My presence of mind deserted me at this crisis, I thought that[.]"

they believe that I wish to injure them, and it is that prejudice which I wish to overcome.'

"'Where do these friends reside?'

"'Near this spot.'

"The old man paused, and then continued, 'If you will unreservedly confide to me the particulars of your tale, I perhaps may be of use in undeceiving them. I am blind, and cannot judge of your countenance, but there is something in your words which persuades me that you are sincere. I am poor, and an exile; but it will afford me true pleasure to be in any way serviceable to a human creature.'

"'Excellent man! I thank you, and accept your generous offer. You raise me from the dust by this kindness; and I trust that, by your aid, I shall not be driven from the society and sympathy of your fellow-creatures.'

"'Heaven forbid! even if you were really criminal; for that can only drive you to desperation, and not instigate you to virtue. I also am unfortunate; I and my family have been condemned, although innocent: judge, therefore, if I do not feel for your misfortunes.'

"'How can I thank you, my best and only benefactor? from your lips first have I heard the voice of kindness directed towards me; I shall be for ever grateful; and your present humanity assures me of success with those friends whom I am on the point of meeting.'

"'May I know the names and residence of those friends?'

"I paused. This, I thought, was the moment of decision, which was to rob me of, or bestow happiness on me for ever. I struggled vainly for firmness sufficient to answer him, but the effort destroyed all my remaining strength; I sank on the chair, and sobbed aloud. At that moment I heard the steps of my younger protectors.[25] I had not a moment to lose; but, seizing the hand of the old man, I cried, 'Now is the time!— save and protect me! You and your family are the friends whom I seek. Do not you desert me in the hour of trial!'

"'Great God!' exclaimed the old man, 'who are you?'

"At that instant the cottage door was opened, and Felix, Safie, and Agatha entered. Who can describe their horror and consternation on beholding me? Agatha fainted; and Safie, unable to attend to her friend, rushed out of the cottage. Felix darted forward, and with supernatural force tore me from his father, to whose knees I clung: in a transport of fury, he dashed me to the ground, and struck me violently with a stick. I could have torn him limb from limb, as the lion rends the antelope. But my heart sunk within me as with bitter sickness, and I refrained. I saw him on the point of repeating his blow, when, overcome by pain and anguish, I quitted the cottage, and in the general tumult escaped unperceived to my hovel."

CHAPTER VIII.[1]

1. Chapter 16 in the 1831 edition.

2. Snares or traps.

"CURSED, CURSED CREATOR! Why did I live? Why, in that instant, did I not extinguish the spark of existence which you had so wantonly bestowed? I know not; despair had not yet taken possession of me; my feelings were those of rage and revenge. I could with pleasure have destroyed the cottage and its inhabitants, and have glutted myself with their shrieks and misery.

"When night came, I quitted my retreat, and wandered in the wood; and now, no longer restrained by the fear of discovery, I gave vent to my anguish in fearful howlings. I was like a wild beast that had broken the toils;[2] destroying the objects that obstructed me, and ranging through the wood with a stag-like swiftness. Oh! what a miserable night I passed! the cold stars shone in mockery, and the bare trees waved their branches above me: now and then the sweet voice of a bird burst forth amidst the universal stillness. All, save I, were at rest or in enjoyment: I, like the arch fiend, bore a hell within me; and, finding myself unsympathized with, wished to tear up the trees, spread havoc and destruction around me, and then to have sat down and enjoyed the ruin.

"But this was a luxury of sensation that could not endure; I became fatigued with excess of bodily exertion, and sank on the damp grass in the sick impotence of despair. There was none among the myriads of men that existed who would pity or assist me; and should I feel kindness towards my enemies? No: from that moment I declared everlasting war against the species, and, more than all, against him who had formed me, and sent me forth to this insupportable misery.

"The sun rose; I heard the voices of men, and knew that it was impossible to return to my retreat during that day. Accordingly I hid myself in some thick underwood, determining to devote the ensuing hours to reflection on my situation.

"The pleasant sunshine, and the pure air of day, restored me to some degree of tranquillity; and when I considered what had passed at the cottage, I could not help believing that I had been too hasty in my conclusions. I had certainly acted imprudently. It was apparent that my conversation had interested the father in my behalf, and I was a fool in having exposed my person to the horror of his children. I ought to have familiarized the old De Lacy to me, and by degrees have discovered myself to the rest of his family, when they should have been prepared for my approach. But I did not believe my errors to be irretrievable; and, after much consideration, I resolved to return to the cottage, seek the old man, and by my representations win him to my party.

"These thoughts calmed me, and in the afternoon I sank into a profound sleep; but the fever of my blood did not allow me to be visited by peaceful dreams. The horrible scene of the preceding day was for ever acting before my eyes; the females were flying, and the enraged Felix tearing me from his father's feet. I awoke exhausted; and, finding that it was already night, I crept forth from my hiding-place, and went in search of food.

"When my hunger was appeased, I directed my steps towards the well-known path that conducted to the cottage.

All there was at peace. I crept into my hovel, and remained in silent expectation of the accustomed hour when the family arose. That hour past, the sun mounted high in the heavens, but the cottagers did not appear. I trembled violently, apprehending some dreadful misfortune. The inside of the cottage was dark, and I heard no motion; I cannot describe the agony of this suspence.

3. That is, they spoke German.

4. We learn by this offhand remark that Felix and Safie have married.

"Presently two countrymen passed by; but, pausing near the cottage, they entered into conversation, using violent gesticulations; but I did not understand what they said, as they spoke the language of the country, which differed from that of my protectors.[3] Soon after, however, Felix approached with another man: I was surprised, as I knew that he had not quitted the cottage that morning, and waited anxiously to discover, from his discourse, the meaning of these unusual appearances.

"'Do you consider,' said his companion to him, 'that you will be obliged to pay three months' rent, and to lose the produce of your garden? I do not wish to take any unfair advantage, and I beg therefore that you will take some days to consider of your determination.'

"'It is utterly useless,' replied Felix, 'we can never again inhabit your cottage. The life of my father is in the greatest danger, owing to the dreadful circumstance that I have related. My wife[4] and my sister will never recover their horror. I entreat you not to reason with me any more. Take possession of your tenement, and let me fly from this place.'

"Felix trembled violently as he said this. He and his companion entered the cottage, in which they remained for a few minutes, and then departed. I never saw any of the family of De Lacy more.

"I continued for the remainder of the day in my hovel in a state of utter and stupid despair. My protectors had departed, and had broken the only link that held me to the world. For the first time the feelings of revenge and hatred filled my bosom, and I did not strive to control them; but, allowing myself to be borne away by the stream, I bent my mind towards injury and death. When I thought of my friends, of the mild voice of De Lacy, the gentle eyes of Agatha, and the exquisite beauty of the Arabian, these thoughts vanished, and a gush of tears somewhat soothed me. But again, when I reflected that they had spurned and deserted me, anger returned, a rage of anger; and, unable to injure any thing human, I turned my fury towards inanimate objects. As night advanced, I placed a variety of combustibles around the cottage; and, after having destroyed every vestige of cultivation in the garden, I waited with forced impatience[5] until the moon had sunk to commence my operations.

"As the night advanced, a fierce wind arose from the woods, and quickly dispersed the clouds that had loitered in the heavens: the blast tore along like a mighty avalanche, and produced a kind of insanity in my spirits, that burst all bounds of reason and reflection. I lighted the dry branch of a tree, and danced with fury around the devoted cottage, my eyes still fixed on the western horizon, the edge of which the moon nearly touched. A part of its orb was at length hid, and I waved my brand; it sunk, and, with a loud scream, I fired the straw, and heath, and bushes, which I had collected.[6] The wind fanned the fire, and the cottage was quickly enveloped by the flames, which clung to it, and licked it with their forked and destroying tongues.

"As soon as I was convinced that no assistance could save any part of the habitation, I quitted the scene, and sought for refuge in the woods.

"And now, with the world before me, whither should I bend my steps? I resolved to fly far from the scene of my misfortunes; but to me, hated and despised, every country must be equally horrible. At length the thought of you crossed my mind. I learned from your papers that you were my father, my creator; and to whom could I apply with more fitness than to him who had given me life? Among the lessons that Felix had bestowed upon Safie geography had not been omitted: I had learned from these the relative situations of the different countries of the earth. You had mentioned Geneva as the name of your native town;[7] and towards this place I resolved to proceed.

"But how was I to direct myself? I knew that I must travel in a south-westerly direction to reach my destination; but the sun was my only guide. I did not know the names of the towns that I was to pass through, nor could I ask information from a single human being; but I did not despair. From you only could I hope for succour, although towards you I felt no sentiment but that of hatred. Unfeeling, heartless creator! you had endowed me with perceptions and passions, and then cast me abroad an object for the scorn and horror

5. "Patience" in the Draft, rather than "impatience," but not corrected in future editions.

6. It is ironic that in James Whale's 1931 film *Frankenstein*, the creature is threatened with and terrified of fire, in the form of torches carried by the villagers.

7. It must have been mentioned in the "domestic occurrences" that the creature tells us earlier were described in Victor's notes.

8. In the Draft, the phrase "the bitterness and horror of my feelings" was originally "the horror of my situation," changed by Percy Shelley to "the outrages and the anguish I had endured."

9. That is, spring 1795.

of mankind. But on you only had I any claim for pity and redress, and from you I determined to seek that justice which I vainly attempted to gain from any other being that wore the human form.

"My travels were long, and the sufferings I endured intense. It was late in autumn when I quitted the district where I had so long resided. I travelled only at night, fearful of encountering the visage of a human being. Nature decayed around me, and the sun became heatless; rain and snow poured around me; mighty rivers were frozen; the surface of the earth was hard, and chill, and bare, and I found no shelter. Oh, earth! how often did I imprecate curses on the cause of my being! The mildness of my nature had fled, and all within me was turned to gall and bitterness. The nearer I approached to your habitation, the more deeply did I feel the spirit of revenge enkindled in my heart. Snow fell, and the waters were hardened, but I rested not. A few incidents now and then directed me, and I possessed a map of the country; but I often wandered wide from my path. The agony of my feelings allowed me no respite: no incident occurred from which my rage and misery could not extract its food; but a circumstance that happened when I arrived on the confines of Switzerland, when the sun had recovered its warmth, and the earth again began to look green, confirmed in an especial manner the bitterness and horror of my feelings.[8]

"I generally rested during the day, and travelled only when I was secured by night from the view of man. One morning, however, finding that my path lay through a deep wood, I ventured to continue my journey after the sun had risen; the day, which was one of the first of spring,[9] cheered even me by the loveliness of its sunshine and the balminess of the air. I felt emotions of gentleness and pleasure, that had long appeared dead, revive within me. Half surprised by the novelty of these sensations, I allowed myself to be borne away by them; and, forgetting my solitude and deformity, dared to be happy. Soft tears again bedewed my cheeks, and I even raised my humid eyes with thankfulness towards the blessed sun which bestowed such joy upon me.

"I continued to wind among the paths of the wood, until I came to its boundary, which was skirted by a deep and rapid river, into which many of the trees bent their branches, now budding with the fresh spring. Here I paused, not exactly knowing what path to pursue, when I heard the sound of voices, that induced me to conceal myself under the shade of a cypress. I was scarcely hid, when a young girl came running towards the spot where I was concealed, laughing as if she ran from some one in sport. She continued her course along the precipitous sides of the river, when suddenly her foot slipt, and she fell into the rapid stream. I rushed from my hiding place, and, with extreme labour from the force of the current, saved her, and dragged her to shore. She was senseless; and I endeavoured, by every means in my power, to restore animation, when I was suddenly interrupted by the approach of a rustic, who was probably the person from whom she had playfully fled. On seeing me, he darted towards me, and, tearing the girl from my arms, hastened towards the deeper parts of the wood.[10] I followed speedily, I hardly knew why; but when the man saw me draw near, he aimed a gun,[11] which he carried, at my body, and fired. I sunk to the ground, and my injurer, with increased swiftness, escaped into the wood.

"This was then the reward of my benevolence! I had saved a human being from destruction, and, as a recompence, I now writhed under the miserable pain of a wound, which shattered the flesh and bone. The feelings of kindness and gentleness, which I had entertained but a few moments before, gave place to hellish rage and gnashing of teeth. Inflamed by pain, I vowed eternal hatred and vengeance to all mankind. But the agony of my wound overcame me; my pulses paused, and I fainted.

"For some weeks I led a miserable life in the woods, endeavouring to cure the wound which

The creature (Boris Karloff) meets Maria, a young girl (Marilyn Harris), with disastrous results, in *Frankenstein* (Universal Pictures, 1931).

10. Later, the creature describes the girl as the rustic's child.

11. For those who revel in such details, the gun was likely a French musket of the 1763 Charleville model, used by the French in the Revolution, or a *fusil de chasse* (shotgun), used by French trappers in North America for hunting.

181

12. "This time" appears to refer to the present, that is, the time of the interview. We may fix the date as July 1795 (recall that the incident that the creature is about to describe—the death of William—occurred in early May 1795, according to the earlier letter from Frankenstein's father).

13. Here, in contrast to his earlier remark about the beauty of "delicate complexions"—a judgment for which he had no apparent basis (see note 6, Volume II, Chapter IV, above)—the creature now seems to understand that "beauty is in the eye of the beholder."

14. William's response to the creature is markedly different from that of other children depicted in the various films of *Frankenstein*, observes Martin Tropp, in *Mary Shelley's Monster: The Story of* Frankenstein (111). Beginning with Whale's 1931 *Frankenstein*, screen children almost inevitably relate to the creature as a fellow innocent.

I had received. The ball had entered my shoulder, and I knew not whether it had remained there or passed through; at any rate I had no means of extracting it. My sufferings were augmented also by the oppressive sense of the injustice and ingratitude of their infliction. My daily vows rose for revenge—a deep and deadly revenge, such as would alone compensate for the outrages and anguish I had endured.

"After some weeks my wound healed, and I continued my journey. The labours I endured were no longer to be alleviated by the bright sun or gentle breezes of spring; all joy was but a mockery, which insulted my desolate state, and made me feel more painfully that I was not made for the enjoyment of pleasure.

"But my toils now drew near a close; and, two months from this time,[12] I reached the environs of Geneva.

"It was evening when I arrived, and I retired to a hiding-place among the fields that surround it, to meditate in what manner I should apply to you. I was oppressed by fatigue and hunger, and far too unhappy to enjoy the gentle breezes of evening, or the prospect of the sun setting behind the stupendous mountains of Jura.

"At this time a slight sleep relieved me from the pain of reflection, which was disturbed by the approach of a beautiful child, who came running into the recess I had chosen with all the sportiveness of infancy. Suddenly, as I gazed on him, an idea seized me, that this little creature was unprejudiced, and had lived too short a time to have imbibed a horror of deformity.[13] If, therefore, I could seize him, and educate him as my companion and friend, I should not be so desolate in this peopled earth.

"Urged by this impulse, I seized on the boy as he passed, and drew him towards me. As soon as he beheld my form, he placed his hands before his eyes, and uttered a shrill scream: I drew his hand forcibly from his face, and said, 'Child, what is the meaning of this? I do not intend to hurt you; listen to me.'

"He struggled violently; 'Let me go,' he cried; 'monster! ugly wretch! you wish to eat me, and tear me to pieces—You are an ogre[14]—Let me go, or I will tell my papa.'

"'Boy, you will never see your father again; you must come with me.'

"'Hideous monster! let me go; My papa is a Syndic—he is M. Frankenstein—he would punish you. You dare not keep me.'

"'Frankenstein! you belong then to my enemy—to him towards whom I have sworn eternal revenge; you shall be my first victim.'

"The child still struggled, and loaded me with epithets which carried despair to my heart: I grasped his throat to silence him, and in a moment he lay dead at my feet.

"I gazed on my victim, and my heart swelled with exultation and hellish triumph: clapping my hands, I exclaimed, 'I, too, can create desolation; my enemy is not impregnable;[15] this death will carry despair to him, and a thousand other miseries shall torment and destroy him.'

"As I fixed my eyes on the child, I saw something glittering on his breast. I took it; it was a portrait of a most lovely woman. In spite of my malignity, it softened and attracted me. For a few moments I gazed with delight on her dark eyes, fringed by deep lashes, and her lovely lips; but presently my rage returned: I remembered that I was for ever deprived of the delights that such beautiful creatures could bestow; and that she whose resemblance I contemplated would, in regarding me, have changed that air of divine benignity to one expressive of disgust and affright.

"Can you wonder that such thoughts transported me with rage?[16] I only wonder that at that moment, instead of venting my sensations in exclamations and agony, I did not rush among mankind, and perish in the attempt to destroy them.

"While I was overcome by these feelings, I left the spot where I had committed the murder, and was seeking a more secluded hiding-place,[17] when I perceived a woman passing near me. She was young, not indeed so beautiful as her whose portrait I held, but of an agreeable aspect, and blooming in the loveliness of youth and health. Here, I thought, is one of those whose smiles are bestowed on all but me; she shall not escape: thanks to the lessons of Felix, and the sanguinary laws of man, I have learned how to work mischief. I

15. The word "impregnable" is replaced with "invulnerable" in the 1831 edition.

16. Indeed, the reader *can* wonder: "Out of the whole world in which to focus his sexual longing, it is astonishing, to say the least," write Morton Kaplan and Robert Kloss, "that he should gaze with desire first on the face of Frankenstein's mother" ("Fantasy of Paternity and the Doppelgänger: Mary Shelley's *Frankenstein*").

17. The balance of this paragraph is substantially revised in the 1831 edition, to read as follows:

> I entered a barn which had appeared to me to be empty. A woman was sleeping on some straw; she was young, not indeed so beautiful as her whose portrait I held, but of an agreeable aspect, and blooming in the loveliness of youth and health. Here, I thought, is one of those whose joy-imparting smiles are bestowed on all but me. And then I bent over her and whispered, "Awake, fairest, thy lover is near—he who would give his life but to obtain one look of affection from thine eyes; my beloved, awake!"
>
> The sleeper stirred; a thrill of terror ran through me. Should she indeed awake, and see me, and curse me, and denounce the murderer? Thus would she assuredly act if her darkened eyes opened and she beheld me. The thought was madness; it stirred the fiend within me—not I, but she, shall suffer; the murder I have committed because I am forever robbed of all that she could give me, she shall atone. The crime had its source in her; be hers the punishment! Thanks to the lessons of Felix, and the sanguinary laws of man, I had learned now to work mischief. I bent over her, and placed the portrait securely in one of the folds of her dress. She moved again, and I fled.

Thus the creature is depicted as less intent on murder, more as acting because of his expectation of mistreatment. However, Kaplan and Kloss, in "Fantasy of Paternity and the Doppelgänger: Mary Shelley's *Frankenstein*," wonder at the creature's calling himself Justine's lover upon meeting her for the first time and deciding to punish her for a crime he commits before he even knows of her existence. These actions are only explicable if the creature is Victor's doppelgänger and the responses those of Victor himself, they suggest.

18. Note that earlier, Justine stated that she was "unable to rest or sleep." How, then, did the creature plant the necklace on her person? This was corrected in the 1831 edition. See notes 4 and 5, Volume I, Chapter VII, above.

approached her unperceived, and placed the portrait securely in one of the folds of her dress.[18]

"For some days I haunted the spot where these scenes had taken place; sometimes wishing to see you, sometimes resolved to quit the world and its miseries for ever. At length I wandered towards these mountains, and have ranged through their immense recesses, consumed by a burning passion which you alone can gratify. We may not part until you have promised to comply with my requisition. I am alone, and miserable; man will not associate with me; but one as deformed and horrible as myself would not deny herself to me. My companion must be of the same species, and have the same defects. This being you must create."

CHAPTER IX.[1]

T HE BEING FINISHED speaking, and fixed his looks upon me in expectation of a reply. But I was bewildered, perplexed, and unable to arrange my ideas sufficiently to understand the full extent of his proposition. He continued—

"You must create a female for me, with whom I can live in the interchange of those sympathies necessary for my being. This you alone can do; and I demand it of you as a right which you must not refuse."[2]

The latter part of his tale had kindled anew in me the anger that had died away while he narrated his peaceful life among the cottagers, and, as he said this, I could no longer suppress the rage that burned within me.

"I do refuse it," I replied; "and no torture shall ever extort a consent from me. You may render me the most miserable of men, but you shall never make me base in my own eyes. Shall I create another like yourself, whose joint wickedness might desolate the world.[3] Begone! I have answered you; you may torture me, but I will never consent."

"You are in the wrong," replied the fiend; "and, instead of threatening, I am content to reason with you. I am malicious because I am miserable; am I not shunned and hated by all mankind? You, my creator, would tear me to pieces, and triumph; remember that, and tell me why I should pity

1. Chapter 17 in the 1831 edition.

2. The 1831 edition adds the phrase "to concede" at the end of this sentence.

3. Note that Frankenstein does not at this time think of the offspring of the creature and a mate—that thought only occurs to him when he is hard at work on the creation of the female being, perhaps dealing with her reproductive organs.

4. The creature goes overboard here. There is ample evidence that humans can become accustomed to the appearance of even the most severely deformed persons if they do not fear for their safety. Witness, for example, the Victorian fascination with the Elephant Man, Joseph Merrick, whose condition became celebrated and his company highly sought after. Merrick, who corresponded with many people, often ended his letters with the following poem that he adapted from a poem called "False Greatness," by English hymn writer Isaac Watts (the first four lines were wholly Merrick's):

'Tis true my form is something odd,
But blaming me is blaming God;
Could I create myself anew
I would not fail in pleasing you.

If I could reach from pole to pole
Or grasp the ocean with a span,

Joseph Merrick, ca. 1889.

man more than he pities me? You would not call it murder, if you could precipitate me into one of those ice-rifts, and destroy my frame, the work of your own hands. Shall I respect man, when he contemns me? Let him live with me in the interchange of kindness, and, instead of injury, I would bestow every benefit upon him with tears of gratitude at his acceptance. But that cannot be; the human senses are insurmountable barriers to our union.[4] Yet mine shall not be the submission of abject slavery. I will revenge my injuries: if I cannot inspire love, I will cause fear; and chiefly towards you my arch-enemy, because my creator, do I swear inextinguishable hatred. Have a care: I will work at your destruction, nor finish until I desolate your heart, so that you[5] curse the hour of your birth."

A fiendish rage animated him as he said this; his face was wrinkled into contortions too horrible for human eyes to behold; but presently he calmed himself, and proceeded—

"I intended to reason. This passion is detrimental to me; for you do not reflect that you[6] are the cause of its excess. If any being felt emotions of benevolence towards me, I should return them an hundred and an hundred fold; for that one creature's sake, I would make peace with the whole kind! But I now indulge in dreams of bliss that cannot be realized. What I ask of you is reasonable and moderate; I demand a creature of another sex, but as hideous as myself: the gratification is small, but it is all that I can receive, and it shall content me. It is true, we shall be monsters, cut off from all the world; but on that account we shall be more attached to one another. Our lives will not be happy, but they will be harmless, and free from the misery I now feel. Oh! my creator, make me happy; let me feel gratitude towards you for one benefit! Let me see that I excite the sympathy of some existing thing; do not deny me my request!"

I was moved. I shuddered when I thought of the possible consequences of my consent; but I felt that there was some justice in his argument. His tale, and the feelings he now expressed, proved him to be a creature of fine sensations; and did I not, as his maker, owe him all the portion of happi-

Victor Frankenstein (Gene Wilder) and the creature (Peter Boyle) entertain a crowded theater in *Young Frankenstein* (Gruskoff/Venture Films, 1974).

ness that it was in my power to bestow? He saw my change of feeling, and continued—

"If you consent, neither you nor any other human being shall ever see us again: I will go to the vast wilds of South America.[7] My food is not that of man; I do not destroy the lamb and the kid, to glut my appetite; acorns and berries afford me sufficient nourishment.[8] My companion will be of the same nature as myself, and will be content with the same fare. We shall make our bed of dried leaves; the sun will shine on us as on man, and will ripen our food. The picture I present to you is peaceful and human, and you must feel that you could deny it only in the wantonness of power and cruelty. Pitiless as you have been towards me, I now see compassion in your eyes: let me seize the favourable moment, and persuade you to promise what I so ardently desire."

"You propose," replied I, "to fly from the habitations of man, to dwell in those wilds where the beasts of the field will be your only companions. How can you, who long for the love and sympathy of man, persevere in this exile? You will return, and again seek their kindness, and you will meet with their detestation; your evil passions will be renewed, and you will then have a companion to aid you in the task of destruction. This may not be; cease to argue the point, for I cannot consent."

"How inconstant are your feelings! but a moment ago you were moved by my representations, and why do you again harden yourself to my complaints? I swear to you, by the earth which I inhabit, and by you that made me, that, with the companion you bestow, I will quit the neighbourhood of man, and dwell, as it may chance, in the most savage of places. My evil passions will have fled, for I shall meet with sympathy; my life will flow quietly away, and, in my dying moments, I shall not curse my maker."

I would be measured by the soul;
The mind's the standard of the man.

Mel Brooks's brilliant film *Young Frankenstein* (1974) surely has it right when it depicts an audience eager to see the creature sing and dance in evening wear.

5. The word "shall" is inserted here in the 1831 edition.

6. The word "you" is in all capitals in the 1831 edition.

7. "America" in the Draft.

South America, post-Columbus, has always had a population density (an indicator of the "vast wilds") among the lowest in the world. Today, for example, even well-developed countries like Brazil, Argentina, Venezuela, and Colombia have a density ranking them below the top 150 most dense countries. To put this in context, today the entire world (land only, excluding Antarctica) has a population per square mile of 140 persons; Ecuador, the densest South American country, has a population per square mile of 163, while Brazil, the largest country, has a density index of only about 62 persons per square mile, and Argentina, the second largest, only 37. Switzerland today, even with its Alpine regions, ranks nineteenth, with a density of 513 persons per square mile. (The United States has a density of about 85 persons per square mile and ranks 182nd.)

8. It was reported that Byron often went days eating only dry biscuits, which he took with wine; Percy Shelley was an avowed vegetarian, writing four essays on the subject, including his 1813 *A Vindication of Natural Diet* (in which he also championed the rights of animals).

9. The 1831 edition replaces this sentence with the following: "I must not be trifled with, and I demand an answer."

10. The creature refers to the Platonic/ Augustinian idea of the great chain of being, as Renaissance philosophers put it—the hierarchies of the cosmos: from stone to plant, to animal, to man, to the heavens, to the angels, to God. Alexander Pope develops a system of ethics in Epis- tle I of his epic poem *Essay on Man* (1732), asking, "Is the great chain, that draws all to agree, / And drawn supports, upheld by God, or thee?":

> Vast chain of being! which from God
> began,
> Natures ethereal, human, angel, man,
> Beast, bird, fish, insect, what no eye
> can see,
> No glass can reach; from infinite to
> thee,
> From thee to nothing.

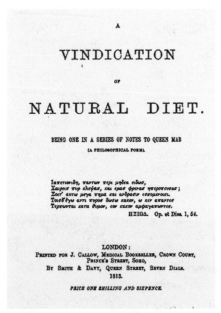

Vindication of a Natural Diet, by Percy Bysshe Shelley (1813).

His words had a strange effect upon me. I compassionated him, and sometimes felt a wish to console him; but when I looked upon him, when I saw the filthy mass that moved and talked, my heart sickened, and my feelings were altered to those of horror and hatred. I tried to stifle these sensations; I thought, that as I could not sympathize with him, I had no right to withhold from him the small portion of happiness which was yet in my power to bestow.

"You swear," I said, "to be harmless; but have you not already shewn a degree of malice that should reasonably make me distrust you? May not even this be a feint that will increase your triumph by affording a wider scope for your revenge?"

"How is this? I thought I had moved your compassion, and yet you still refuse to bestow on me the only benefit that can soften my heart, and render me harmless.[9] If I have no ties and no affections, hatred and vice must be my portion; the love of another will destroy the cause of my crimes, and I shall become a thing, of whose existence every one will be ignorant. My vices are the children of a forced solitude that I abhor; and my virtues will necessarily arise when I live in communion with an equal. I shall feel the affections of a sensitive being, and become linked to the chain of existence[10] and events, from which I am now excluded."

I paused some time to reflect on all he had related, and the various arguments which he had employed. I thought of the promise of virtues which he had displayed on the opening of his existence, and the subsequent blight of all kindly feeling by the loathing and scorn which his protectors had manifested towards him. His power and threats were not omitted in my calculations: a creature who could exist in the ice caves of the glaciers, and hide himself from pursuit among the ridges of inaccessible precipices, was a being possessing faculties it would be vain to cope with. After a long pause of reflection, I concluded, that the justice due both to him and my fellow-creatures demanded of me that I should comply with his request. Turning to him, therefore, I said—

"I consent to your demand, on your solemn oath to quit Europe for ever, and every other place in the neighbourhood of man, as soon as I shall deliver into your hands a female who will accompany you in your exile."

"I swear," he cried, "by the sun, and by the blue sky of heaven,[11] that if you grant my prayer, while they exist you shall never behold me again. Depart to your home, and commence your labours: I shall watch their progress with unutterable anxiety; and fear not but that when you are ready I shall appear."

Saying this, he suddenly quitted me, fearful, perhaps, of any change in my sentiments. I saw him descend the mountain with greater speed than the flight of an eagle, and quickly lost him among the undulations of the sea of ice.

His tale had occupied the whole day; and the sun was upon the verge of the horizon when he departed. I knew that I ought to hasten my descent towards the valley, as I should soon be encompassed in darkness; but my heart was heavy, and my steps slow. The labour of winding among the little paths of the mountains, and fixing my feet firmly as I advanced, perplexed me, occupied as I was by the emotions which the occurrences of the day had produced. Night was far advanced, when I came to the half-way resting-place, and seated myself beside the fountain. The stars shone at intervals, as the clouds passed from over them; the dark pines rose before me, and every here and there a broken tree lay on the ground: it was a scene of wonderful solemnity, and stirred strange thoughts within me. I wept bitterly; and, clasping my hands in agony, I exclaimed, "Oh! stars, and clouds, and winds, ye are all about to mock me: if ye really pity me, crush sensation and memory; let me become as nought; but if not, depart, depart and leave me in darkness."

These were wild and miserable thoughts; but I cannot describe to you how the eternal twinkling of the stars weighed upon me, and how I listened to every blast of wind, as if it were a dull ugly siroc[12] on its way to consume me.

Morning dawned before I arrived at the village of Chamounix;[13] but my presence, so haggard and strange, hardly calmed the fears of my family, who had waited the whole night in anxious expectation of my return.

The following day we returned to Geneva. The inten-

11. In the 1831 edition, the phrase "and by the fire of love that burns my heart," is inserted here, emphasizing a creature with more human emotions.

12. The "sirocco" is a hot, dry, dust-laden wind sourced in north Africa that picks up humidity as it crosses the Mediterranean before exhausting itself on southern Europe.

13. The balance of the chapter is substantially revised in the 1831 edition, reading as follows:

> I took no rest, but returned immediately to Geneva. Even in my own heart I could give no expression to my sensations—they weighed on me with a mountain's weight and their excess destroyed my agony beneath them. Thus I returned home, and entering the house, presented myself to the family. My haggard and wild appearance awoke intense alarm, but I answered no question, scarcely did I speak. I felt as if I were placed under a ban—as if I had no right to claim their sympathies—as if never more might I enjoy companionship with them. Yet even thus I loved them to adoration; and to save them, I resolved to dedicate myself to my most abhorred task. The prospect of such an occupation made every other circumstance of existence pass before me like a dream, and that thought only had to me the reality of life.

14. In the *Inferno*, canto 23, lines 58 *et seq.*, Dante, chased by the demons, has descended to the sixth gulf of the eighth circle of hell, where he observes a group of hypocrites forced to pace interminably, wearing mantles weighted with lead:

> They had on mantles with the hoods
> low down
> Before their eyes, and fashioned of the
> cut
> That in Cologne they for the monks
> are made.
> Without, they gilded are so that it
> dazzles;
> But inwardly all leaden and so heavy
> That Frederick used to put them on of
> straw.
> O everlastingly fatiguing mantle!
>
> (Henry Wadsworth Longfellow
> translation, first published in 1909)

"Frederick" is Frederick II (1194–1250), the last of the Holy Roman Emperors of the Staufen, or Hohenstaufen, dynasty, succeeded by Henry VII, of the House of Luxembourg.

tion of my father in coming had been to divert my mind, and to restore me to my lost tranquillity; but the medicine had been fatal. And, unable to account for the excess of misery I appeared to suffer, he hastened to return home, hoping the quiet and monotony of a domestic life would by degrees alleviate my sufferings from whatsoever cause they might spring.

For myself, I was passive in all their arrangements; and the gentle affection of my beloved Elizabeth was inadequate to draw me from the depth of my despair. The promise I had made to the dæmon weighed upon my mind, like Dante's iron cowl on the heads of the hellish hypocrites.[14] All pleasures of earth and sky passed before me like a dream, and that thought only had to me the reality of life. Can you wonder, that sometimes a kind of insanity possessed me, or that I saw continually about me a multitude of filthy animals inflicting on me incessant torture, that often extorted screams and bitter groans?

By degrees, however, these feelings became calmed. I entered again into the every-day scene of life, if not with interest, at least with some degree of tranquillity.

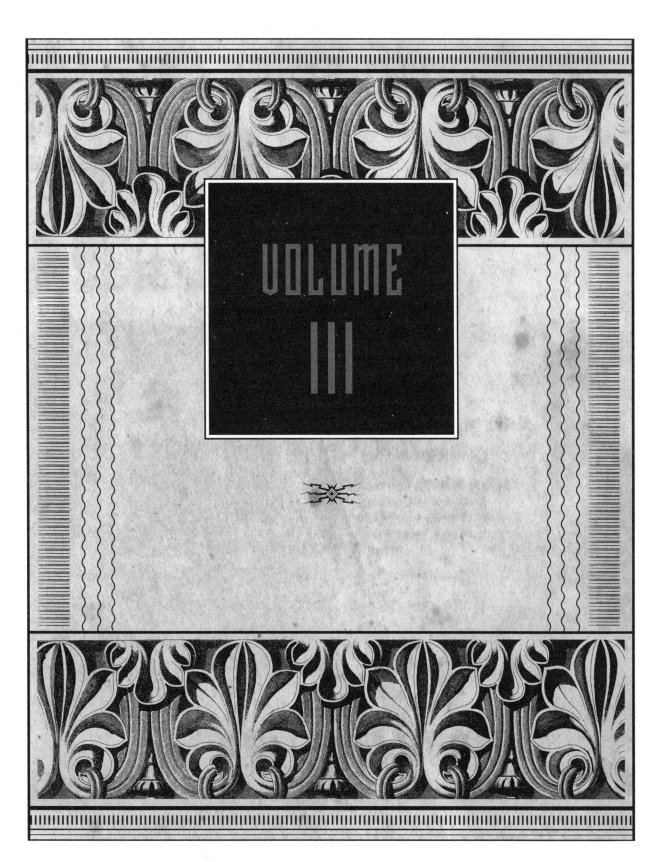

VOLUME

III

CHAPTER I.[1]

DAY AFTER DAY, week after week, passed away on my return to Geneva; and I could not collect the courage to recommence my work. I feared the vengeance of the disappointed fiend, yet I was unable to overcome my repugnance to the task which was enjoined me. I found that I could not compose a female without again devoting several months to profound study and laborious disquisition. I had heard of some discoveries having been made by an English philosopher, the knowledge of which was material to my success,[2] and I sometimes thought of obtaining my father's consent to visit England for this purpose; but I clung to every pretence of delay,[3] and could not resolve to interrupt my returning tranquillity. My health, which had hitherto declined, was now much restored; and my spirits, when unchecked by the memory of my unhappy promise, rose proportionably. My father saw this change with pleasure, and he turned his thoughts towards the best method of eradicating the remains of my melancholy, which every now and then would return by fits, and with a devouring blackness overcast the approaching sunshine. At these moments I took refuge in the most perfect solitude. I passed whole days on the lake alone in a little boat, watching the clouds, and listening to the rippling of the waves, silent and listless. But the fresh air and bright sun seldom failed to restore me to some

1. Chapter 18 in the 1831 edition. It is clear from the Draft that in an earlier version (the Ur-Text—see "A Note on the Text," above), the trip to England was proposed by Alphonse. However, at Percy Shelley's suggestion, Mary Shelley substantially rewrote the passage to make it clear that it was Victor's idea.

2. Who this might have been is uncertain. In 1794, Erasmus Darwin (see note 5, Preface, above) published *Zoonomia*, a work expressing what may be described as proto-evolutionary ideas that would later influence Charles Darwin; Victor may have seen the book and desired to seek out this original thinker. It is also uncertain exactly what additional knowledge Victor sought: He had already successfully created life, and the only announced difference between his current and previous projects was the substitution of a female's morphology for a male's. He may have planned to include female reproductive organs, which are admittedly more complex than the male machinery, but there is no indication of when he decided to take this step. See note 3, Volume II, Chapter IX, above. Only when he realizes that the creature is a threat to humanity

does he express concerns about propagation of his new "species." See text following note 3, below. In fact, the reasons for the trip appear thin; this was likely a demonstration of simple procrastination.

3. The balance of the sentence is replaced in the 1831 edition by the following: "and shrank from taking the first step in an undertaking whose immediate necessity began to appear less absolute to me. A change indeed had taken place in me;"

4. The phrase "your cousin" is replaced by "Elizabeth" in the 1831 edition.

degree of composure; and, on my return, I met the salutations of my friends with a readier smile and a more cheerful heart.

It was after my return from one of these rambles that my father, calling me aside, thus addressed me:—

"I am happy to remark, my dear son, that you have resumed your former pleasures, and seem to be returning to yourself. And yet you are still unhappy, and still avoid our society. For some time I was lost in conjecture as to the cause of this; but yesterday an idea struck me, and if it is well founded, I conjure you to avow it. Reserve on such a point would be not only useless, but draw down treble misery on us all."

I trembled violently at this exordium, and my father continued—

"I confess, my son, that I have always looked forward to your marriage with your cousin as the tie of our domestic comfort, and the stay of my declining years. You were attached to each other from your earliest infancy; you studied together, and appeared, in dispositions and tastes, entirely suited to one another. But so blind is the experience of man, that what I conceived to be the best assistants to my plan may have entirely destroyed it. You, perhaps, regard her as your sister, without any wish that she might become your wife. Nay, you may have met with another whom you may love; and, considering yourself as bound in honour to your cousin,[4] this struggle may occasion the poignant misery which you appear to feel."

"My dear father, re-assure yourself. I love my cousin tenderly and sincerely. I never saw any woman who excited, as Elizabeth does, my warmest admiration and affection. My future hopes and prospects are entirely bound up in the expectation of our union."

"The expression of your sentiments on this subject, my dear Victor, gives me more pleasure than I have for some time experienced. If you feel thus, we shall assuredly be happy, however present events may cast a gloom over us. But it is this gloom, which appears to have taken so strong a hold of your mind, that I wish to dissipate. Tell me, therefore, whether you object to an immediate solemnization of the marriage. We have been unfortunate, and recent events have drawn us from that every-day tranquillity befitting my years and infirmities. You are younger; yet I do not suppose, possessed as you are of a competent fortune, that an early marriage would at all interfere with any future plans of honour and utility that you may have formed. Do not suppose, however, that I wish to dictate happiness to you, or that a delay on your part would cause me any serious uneasiness. Interpret my words with candour, and answer me, I conjure you, with confidence and sincerity."

I listened to my father in silence, and remained for some time incapable of offering any reply. I revolved rapidly in my mind a multitude of thoughts, and endeavoured to arrive at some conclusion. Alas! to me the idea of an immediate union with my cousin[5] was one of horror and dismay. I was bound by a solemn promise, which I had not yet fulfilled, and dared not break; or, if I did, what manifold miseries might not impend over me and my devoted family! Could I enter into a festival with this deadly weight yet hanging round my neck,[6] and bowing me to the ground. I must perform my engagement, and let the monster depart with his mate, before I allowed myself to enjoy the delight of an union from which I expected peace.

I remembered also the necessity imposed upon me of either journeying to England, or entering into a long correspondence with those philosophers of that country, whose knowledge and discoveries were of indispensable use to me in my present undertaking. The latter method of obtaining the desired intelligence was dilatory and unsatisfactory: besides, any variation was agreeable to me, and I was delighted with the idea of spending a year or two in change of scene and variety of occupation, in absence from my family; during which period some event might happen which would restore me to them in peace and happiness: my promise might be fulfilled, and the monster have departed; or some accident might occur to destroy him, and put an end to my slavery for ever.[7]

These feelings dictated my answer to my father. I

5. The word "cousin" is replaced with "Elizabeth" in the 1831 edition.

6. Veeder, in *Mary Shelley and Frankenstein*, suggests that this is an allusion to the Mariner in Coleridge's *Rime of the Ancient Mariner*, who carried the weight of the albatross around his neck, and that it refers not to the threat of the creature but to the pending marriage.

7. This sentence is substantially revised in the 1831 edition, where it reads as follows:

> The latter method of obtaining the desired intelligence was dilatory and unsatisfactory; besides, I had an insurmountable aversion to the idea of engaging myself in my loathsome task in my father's house while in habits of familiar intercourse with those I loved. I knew that a thousand fearful accidents might occur, the slightest of which would disclose a tale to thrill all connected with me with horror. I was aware also that I should often lose all self-command, all capacity of hiding the harrowing sensations that would possess me during the progress of my unearthly occupation. I must absent myself from all I loved while thus employed. Once commenced, it would quickly be achieved, and I might be restored to my family in peace and happiness. My promise fulfilled, the monster would depart forever. Or (so my fond fancy imaged) some accident might meanwhile occur to destroy him, and put an end to my slavery forever.

In the 1818 text, Victor anticipates delight in being away from his family; in the revised version, his impending solitude is a matter of necessity, not pleasure.

8. The balance of this paragraph and the next three paragraphs are replaced in the 1831 edition with the following:

a guise which excited no suspicion, while I urged my desire with an earnestness that easily induced my father to comply. After so long a period of an absorbing melancholy that resembled madness in its intensity and effects, he was glad to find that I was capable of taking pleasure in the idea of such a journey, and he hoped that change of scene and varied amusement would, before my return, have restored me entirely to myself.

The duration of my absence was left to my own choice; a few months, or at most a year, was the period contemplated. One paternal kind precaution he had taken to ensure my having a companion. Without previously communicating with me, he had, in concert with Elizabeth, arranged that Clerval should join me at Strasbourg. This interfered with the solitude I coveted for the prosecution of my task; yet at the commencement of my journey the presence of my friend could in no way be an impediment, and truly I rejoiced that thus I should be saved many hours of lonely, maddening reflection. Nay, Henry might stand between me and the intrusion of my foe. If I were alone, would he not at times force his abhorred presence on me to remind me of my task or to contemplate its progress?

To England, therefore, I was bound, and it was understood that my union with Elizabeth should take place immediately on my return. My father's age rendered him extremely averse to delay. For myself, there was one reward I promised myself from my detested toils—one consolation for my unparalleled sufferings; it was the prospect of that day when, enfranchised from my miserable slavery, I

expressed a wish to visit England; but, concealing the true reasons of this request, I clothed my desires[8] under the guise of wishing to travel and see the world before I sat down for life within the walls of my native town.

I urged my entreaty with earnestness, and my father was easily induced to comply; for a more indulgent and less dictatorial parent did not exist upon earth. Our plan was soon arranged. I should travel to Strasburgh,[9] where Clerval would join me. Some short time would be spent in the towns of Holland, and our principal stay would be in England. We should return by France; and it was agreed that the tour should occupy the space of two years.

My father pleased himself with the reflection, that my union with Elizabeth should take place immediately on my return to Geneva. "These two years," said be, "will pass swiftly, and it will be the last delay that will oppose itself to your happiness. And, indeed, I earnestly desire that period to arrive, when we shall all be united, and neither hopes or fears arise to disturb our domestic calm."

"I am content," I replied, "with your arrangement. By that time we shall both have become wiser, and I hope happier, than we at present are." I sighed; but my father kindly forbore to question me further concerning the cause of my dejection. He hoped that new scenes, and the amusement of travelling, would restore my tranquillity.

I now made arrangements for my journey; but one feeling haunted me, which filled me with fear and agitation. During my absence I should leave my friends unconscious of the existence of their enemy, and unprotected from his attacks, exasperated as he might be by my departure. But he had promised to follow me wherever I might go; and would he not accompany me to England? This imagination was dreadful in itself, but soothing, inasmuch as it supposed the safety of my friends. I was agonized with the idea of the possibility that the reverse of this might happen. But through the whole period during which I was the slave of my creature, I allowed myself to be governed by the impulses of the moment; and my present sensations strongly intimated that the fiend would follow me, and exempt my family from the danger of his machinations.

It was in the latter end of August[10] that I departed, to pass two years of exile.[11] Elizabeth approved of the reasons of my departure, and only regretted that she had not the same opportunities of enlarging her experience, and cultivating her understanding.[12] She wept, however, as she bade me farewell, and entreated me to return happy and tranquil. "We all," said she, "depend upon you; and if you are miserable, what must be our feelings?"

I threw myself into the carriage that was to convey me away, hardly knowing whither I was going, and careless of what was passing around. I remembered only, and it was with a bitter anguish that I reflected on it, to order that my chemical instruments should be packed to go with me:[13] for I resolved to fulfil my promise while abroad, and return, if possible, a free man. Filled with dreary imaginations, I passed through many beautiful and majestic scenes; but my eyes were fixed and unobserving. I could only think of the bourne of my travels, and the work which was to occupy me whilst they endured.

After some days spent in listless indolence, during which I traversed many leagues,[14] I arrived at Strasburgh, where I waited two days for Clerval. He came. Alas, how great was the contrast between us! He was alive to every new scene; joyful when he saw the beauties of the setting sun, and more happy when he beheld it rise, and recommence a new day. He pointed out to me the shifting colours of the landscape, and the appearances of the sky. "This is what it is to live;" he cried, "now I enjoy existence! But you, my dear Frankenstein, wherefore are you desponding and sorrowful?" In truth, I was occupied by gloomy thoughts, and neither saw the descent of the evening star, nor the golden sun-rise reflected in the Rhine.—And you, my friend,[15] would be far more amused with the journal of Clerval, who observed the scenery with an eye of feeling and delight, than to listen to my reflections. I, a miserable wretch, haunted by a curse that shut up every avenue to enjoyment.

We had agreed to descend the Rhine in a boat from Strasburgh to Rotterdam, whence we might take shipping for London. During this voyage, we passed by many willowy islands, and saw several beautiful towns. We staid a day

might claim Elizabeth and forget the past in my union with her.

In this version, then, Clerval's companionship is thrust upon Victor by his father. The proposed length of the journey is also shortened.

9. Victor would have traveled northeast from Geneva to Basel on the border of Switzerland and followed the Rhine to Strasbourg, the capital of the Alsace region, in northeastern France. From there, he and Henry would likely have traveled north by boat through Germany into Holland. This is essentially the return route followed by the Shelleys from Switzerland in 1814, the trip they memorialized in *Six Weeks' Tour*.

10. August 1795, perhaps six weeks after his interview with the creature.

11. This paragraph is substantially revised in the 1831 edition:

> It was in the latter end of September that I again quitted my native country. My journey had been my own suggestion, and Elizabeth therefore acquiesced, but she was filled with disquiet at the idea of my suffering, away from her, the inroads of misery and grief. It had been her care which provided me a companion in Clerval—and yet a man is blind to a thousand minute circumstances which call forth a woman's sedulous attention. She longed to bid me hasten my return; a thousand conflicting emotions rendered her mute as she bade me a tearful, silent farewell.

12. That is, in accordance with the proprieties of the times, Elizabeth could not travel unchaperoned. The Shelleys' journey with Claire Clairmont in 1814 seems to verge on scandal by comparison.

13. The balance of this sentence is deleted in the 1831 edition.

14. Some 240 miles (390 km), about a four-hour drive today.

15. This is another "aside" to Walton.

16. Mannheim is about 60 miles (90 km) from Strasbourg.

17. Mayence (Mainz) is only about 120 miles (913 km) from Strasbourg. The failure to mention any other passengers or crew and the image of Victor lying "at the bottom of the boat" suggest that Victor and Henry hired a boat that they paddled themselves. With the current, they may have achieved as much as four or five miles per hour, but they were in no hurry.

18. Radu Florescu suggests, in his speculative *In Search of Frankenstein* (1975), that this is a reference to the actual Castle Frankenstein, near Darmstadt, a historic location that he claims was the inspiration—indeed, the source—of the name "Frankenstein" used by Shelley in her account. The suggestion has met with widespread skepticism, not least on the grounds that despite a trip on the Rhine (documented in *Six Weeks' Tour*), there is no evidence that either of the Shelleys visited or knew about the castle.

19. The grape harvest, that is.

20. Uri is actually a bay of Lake Lucerne, or a "gulf," as it is described in the posthumously published memoirs of Scottish historian and jurist Sir James Mackintosh (1765–1832): "The vast mountains rising on every side and closing at the end, with their rich clothing of wood, the sweet soft spots of verdant pasture scattered at their feet, and sometimes on their breast, and the expanse of water, unbroken by islands, and almost undisturbed by any signs of living men, make an impression which it would be foolish to attempt to convey by words" (*Memoirs of the Life of the Right Honourable Sir James Mackin-*

at Manheim,[16] and, on the fifth from our departure from Strasburgh, arrived at Mayence.[17] The course of the Rhine below Mayence becomes much more picturesque. The river descends rapidly, and winds between hills, not high, but steep, and of beautiful forms. We saw many ruined castles standing on the edges of precipices, surrounded by black woods, high and inaccessible.[18] This part of the Rhine, indeed, presents a singularly variegated landscape. In one spot you view rugged hills, ruined castles overlooking tremendous precipices, with the dark Rhine rushing beneath; and, on the sudden turn of a promontory, flourishing vineyards, with green sloping banks, and a meandering river, and populous towns, occupy the scene.

We travelled at the time of the vintage,[19] and heard the song of the labourers, as we glided down the stream. Even I, depressed in mind, and my spirits continually agitated by gloomy feelings, even I was pleased. I lay at the bottom of the boat, and, as I gazed on the cloudless blue sky, I seemed to drink in a tranquillity to which I had long been a stranger. And if these were my sensations, who can describe those of Henry? He felt as if he had been transported to Fairy-land, and enjoyed a happiness seldom tasted by man. "I have seen," he said, "the most beautiful scenes of my own country; I have visited the lakes of Lucerne and Uri,[20] where the snowy mountains descend almost perpendicularly to the water, casting black and impenetrable shades, which would cause a gloomy and mournful appearance, were it not for the most verdant islands that relieve the eye by their gay appearance; I have seen this lake agitated by a tempest, when the wind tore up whirlwinds of water, and gave you an idea of what the waterspout must be on the great ocean, and the waves dash with fury the base of the mountain, where the priest and his mistress were overwhelmed by an avalanche, and where their dying voices are still said to be heard amid the pauses of the nightly wind; I have seen the mountains of La Valais,[21] and the Pays de Vaud:[22] but this country, Victor, pleases me more than all those wonders. The mountains of Switzerland are more majestic and strange; but there is a charm in the banks of this divine river, that I never before saw equalled. Look at that castle which overhangs yon precipice; and that also on the island, almost concealed amongst the foliage of those lovely trees; and now that group of labourers coming from among their vines; and that village half-hid in the recess of the mountain. Oh, surely, the spirit that inhabits and guards this place has a soul more in harmony with man, than those who pile the glacier, or retire to the inaccessible peaks of the mountains of our own country."

Clerval! beloved friend! even now it delights me to record your words, and to dwell on the praise of which you are so eminently deserving. He was a being formed in the "very poetry of nature."[23] His wild and enthusiastic imagination was chastened by the sensibility of his heart. His soul overflowed with ardent affections, and his friendship was of that devoted and wondrous nature that the worldly-minded teach us to look for only in the imagination. But even human sympathies were not sufficient to satisfy his eager mind. The scenery of external nature, which others regard only with admiration, he loved with ardour:

> "The sounding cataract
> Haunted him like a passion: the tall rock,
> The mountain, and the deep and gloomy wood,
> Their colours and their forms, were then to him
> An appetite; a feeling, and a love,
> That had no need of a remoter charm,
> By thought supplied, or any interest
> Unborrowed from the eye."[24]

And where does he now exist? Is this gentle and lovely being lost for ever? Has this mind so replete with ideas, imaginations fanciful and magnificent, which formed a world, whose existence depended on the life of its creator; has this mind perished? Does it now only exist in my memory? No, it is not thus; your form so divinely wrought, and beaming with beauty, has decayed, but your spirit still visits and consoles your unhappy friend.[25]

Pardon this gush of sorrow; these ineffectual words are but a slight tribute to the unexampled worth of Henry, but they soothe my heart, overflowing with the anguish which his remembrance creates. I will proceed with my tale.[26]

tosh, ed. Robert James Mackintosh, 2nd ed. [London, 1836], 307). Mackintosh is best known for his *Vindiciae Gallicae: A Defence of the French Revolution and Its English Admirers* (1791), like Mary Wollstonecraft's *A Vindication of the Rights of Man* a response to Edmund Burke's *Reflections on the Revolution in France*.

21. La Valais or Valais is a canton in the southwestern part of Switzerland, in the central valley of the Rhône River, and includes magnificent mountains such as the Matterhorn.

22. Pays de Vaud (the Vaud region) refers to the canton of Vaud, in the western part of Switzerland. Its capital is Lausanne. Extending from the Jura to the Alps, it crosses three regions of distinct features: the towering Alps of its southern portion, the hills, moraines (rocks and sediment left by glaciers), and lakes of its middle region, and the gentler Jura mountains.

23. From Leigh Hunt's *Story of Rimini*, canto 2, line 55, first published in 1816 and therefore clearly another anachronism. The source is noted in the 1818 edition but not in subsequent ones. Hunt, a lesser Romantic poet who composed *Rimini* while serving a two-year prison sentence in Surrey for having slandered the Prince Regent (the future King George IV, whom he called "corpulent" and "the companion of gamblers and demireps"), dedicated the long work to Byron, who had helped him edit it.

Hunt's incarceration was leavened by visits from friends and by the permanent cohabitation of his wife, Marianne Kent Hunt, and their two children (a third was born in the prison infirmary about halfway through Hunt's sentence); by the presence of a pianoforte in the cell; and by a fragrant orchard just outside, which Hunt himself had been given leave to plant and cultivate. He was no stranger to prison cells, having spent time in debt-

or's prison as a child with his father, a Barbadian lawyer turned Anglican preacher. In 1817, three years after his release from Surrey, Hunt and his family—by then he and Kent had four children; eventually they would have six more—lived with the Shelleys. The year saw the birth of their fifth child, whom the couple named Percy Bysshe Shelley Leigh in honor of their host. (In 1822, following Percy's death, Mary Shelley and Percy Florence Shelley, three, lived with Leigh and Marianne and the couple's six children outside Genoa—see text accompanying note 61, the Foreword, above.)

24. Attributed in the 1831 edition to "Wordsworth's 'Tintern Abbey,'" more properly, "Lines Composed a Few Miles above Tintern Abbey, on Revisiting the Banks of the Wye during a Tour. July 13, 1798," by William Wordsworth, first published in 1798. Apart from thus also constituting an anachronism, the text was actually altered by Mary Shelley and italics added to reflect the change: "me" in the second line became "him."

25. Victor, not much of a storyteller, gets ahead of himself, foreshadowing the imminent death of Clerval.

26. Another aside to Walton.

27. Now the fourth largest city in Germany, it was a free state in 1797, on both banks of the Rhine, part of the Holy Roman Empire. Occupied by the French Republic in 1794, the portion on the left bank of the Rhine was incorporated into the republic in 1801.

28. Travel by post coach, that is.

29. The manuscript reads "September," and this reference to December is evidently a typographical error (repeated in all three editions supervised by Shelley or

Beyond Cologne[27] we descended to the plains of Holland; and we resolved to post[28] the remainder of our way; for the wind was contrary, and the stream of the river was too gentle to aid us.

Our journey here lost the interest arising from beautiful scenery; but we arrived in a few days at Rotterdam, whence we proceeded by sea to England. It was on a clear morning, in the latter days of December,[29] that I first saw the white cliffs of Britain. The banks of the Thames presented a new scene; they were flat, but fertile, and almost every town was marked by the remembrance of some story. We saw Tilbury

Tilbury Fort (photo by Mark.murphy, used under CC-by-SA 3.0 license).

Fort,[30] and remembered the Spanish armada; Gravesend, Woolwich, and Greenwich,[31] places which I had heard of even in my country.

At length we saw the numerous steeples of London, St. Paul's towering above all,[32] and the Tower[33] famed in English history.

St. Paul's Cathedral. St. Paul's Cathedral (photo by David Iliff, used under CC-by-SA 3.0 license).

Tower of London (photo by Carlos Delgado, used under CC-by-SA 3.0 license).

her father), for shortly after arriving, Victor remarks that it is October. See note 5, Volume III, Chapter II, below.

30. Tilbury Fort is on the north bank of the Thames, opposite Gravesend. Originally constructed by Henry III and subsequently extended and strengthened, "[i]t was here," according to *Baedeker's London and Its Environs* (1896), "that Queen Elizabeth assembled and reviewed her troops in anticipation of the attack of the Armada (1588), appearing in helmet and corselet, and using the bold and well-known words: 'I know I have the body of a weak, feeble woman, but I have the heart and stomach of a king, and of a king of England too.'"

31. All about twenty-five miles from London Bridge. Gravesend was then a resort and terminal for London stagecoaches, and Pocahontas is buried in the local church; Greenwich was also a popular resort and the home of the Royal Observatory (and, after 1851, the origin point of lines of longitude); and Woolwich was, even then, the site of the Royal Arsenal, the Royal Dockyard, the Royal Military Academy, and the Royal Artillery.

32. St. Paul's Cathedral, still the most prominent building in London, had been completed by the architect Sir Christopher Wren only about eighty-five years earlier, in 1710.

33. The Tower, which *Baedeker's London* calls "the ancient fortress and gloomy state-prison of London, and historically the most interesting spot in England," was, at the end of the eighteenth century, still surrounded by a battlemented wall and a deep moat (now drained). Though there is speculation that a Roman tower preceded the current structure, it probably was first built by William the Conqueror.

CHAPTER II.[1]

1. Chapter 19 in the 1831 edition.

L ONDON WAS OUR present point of rest; we determined to remain several months in this wonderful and celebrated city. Clerval desired the intercourse of the men of genius and talent who flourished at this time; but this was with me a secondary object; I was principally occupied with the means of obtaining the information necessary for the completion of my promise, and quickly availed myself of the letters of introduction that I had brought with me, addressed to the most distinguished natural philosophers.

If this journey had taken place during my days of study and happiness, it would have afforded me inexpressible pleasure. But a blight had come over my existence, and I only visited these people for the sake of the information they might give me on the subject in which my interest was so terribly profound. Company was irksome to me; when alone, I could fill my mind with the sights of heaven and earth; the voice of Henry soothed me, and I could thus cheat myself into a transitory peace. But busy uninteresting joyous faces brought back despair to my heart. I saw an insurmountable barrier placed between me and my fellow-men; this barrier was sealed with the blood of William and Justine; and to reflect on the events connected with those names filled my soul with anguish.

But in Clerval I saw the image of my former self; he was inquisitive, and anxious to gain experience and instruction.

Finding things in common with Clerval and former self

The difference of manners which he observed was to him an inexhaustible source of instruction and amusement.[2] He was for ever busy; and the only check to his enjoyments was my sorrowful and dejected mien. I tried to conceal this as much as possible, that I might not debar him from the pleasures natural to one who was entering on a new scene of life, undisturbed by any care or bitter recollection. I often refused to accompany him, alleging another engagement, that I might remain alone. I now also began to collect the materials necessary for my new creation,[3] and this was to me like the torture of single drops of water continually falling on the head. Every thought that was devoted to it was an extreme anguish, and every word that I spoke in allusion to it caused my lips to quiver, and my heart to palpitate.

After passing some months in London, we received a letter from a person in Scotland, who had formerly been our visitor at Geneva. He mentioned the beauties of his native country, and asked us if those were not sufficient allurements to induce us to prolong our journey as far north as Perth,[4] where he resided. Clerval eagerly desired to accept this invitation; and I, although I abhorred society, wished to view again mountains and streams, and all the wondrous works with which Nature adorns her chosen dwelling-places.

We had arrived in England at the beginning of October,[5] and it was now February. We accordingly determined to commence our journey towards the north at the expiration of another month. In this expedition we did not intend to follow the great road to Edinburgh,[6] but to visit Windsor, Oxford, Matlock, and the Cumberland lakes,[7] resolving to arrive at the completion of this tour about the end of July. I packed my chemical instruments, and the materials I had collected, resolving to finish my labours in some obscure nook in the northern highlands of Scotland.

We quitted London on the 27th of March, and remained a few days at Windsor, rambling in its beautiful forest.[8] This was a new scene to us mountaineers; the majestic oaks, the quantity of game, and the herds of stately deer, were all novelties to us.

From thence we proceeded to Oxford. As we entered

2. The following is inserted here in the 1831 edition: "He was also pursuing an object he had long had in view. His design was to visit India, in the belief that he had in his knowledge of its various languages, and in the views he had taken of its society, the means of materially assisting the progress of European colonization and trade. In Britain only could he further the execution of his plan." This expands the earlier emendation, making Clerval a man of business rather than a footloose student.

3. This could not have included body parts, for Victor had no means of preventing the corruption of such parts during his four-month sojourn. Yet, living on an isolated island, how did he obtain the parts he needed to assemble the creature's female companion? He would have needed to make repeated trips to Perth to visit charnel houses, and his parcels of body parts were unlikely to have gone unnoticed on the thinly populated island.

4. Perth is an ancient town, probably of Roman origin, in central Scotland, on the banks of the river Tay. It was the capital of Scotland until 1437, when the royal seat was moved to Edinburgh. It did not receive its current nickname, "The Fair City," until the publication in 1828 of Sir Walter Scott's novel *Fair Maid of Perth*.

5. This confirms that the earlier "December" was a typographical error. See note 29, Volume III, Chapter I.

6. The Great North Road was the principal mail and passenger coach route from London to York to Edinburgh. The modern A1 highway now generally follows the route, a distance of about 410 miles. In 1658, the first regular stage-coach route to York—a trip of about four days—was established. By the end of the eighteenth century, faster mail and pas-

senger coaches were used, and by 1815, a trip from London to York took only twenty hours, with another twenty-five-plus hours to reach Edinburgh. With the advent of rail in the nineteenth century, the coaching operations disappeared.

7. This was certainly the long way to get to Edinburgh, with the Lake District on the far western side of the island. Matlock is on the route to the Lake District, but one must wonder why it is mentioned here, other than for its splendor: Shelley's contemporary Nathaniel Hawthorne said of Matlock, which he visited with his wife, the illustrator Sophia Peabody, and their young son, Julian, while serving as U.S. Consul at Liverpool under his close friend President Franklin Pierce (whose campaign biography he had written), "I think there can be no more beautiful place in the world" (*Passages from the English Note-Books of Nathaniel Hawthorne*, 2 vols. [Leipzig: Tauchnitz, 1871], Vol. 2, 231). More prominent towns en route would have been Nottingham or Derby. While Matlock (properly Matlock Bath) was known for its spa in the eighteenth century and is described by Victor as resembling Switzerland, there is no indication that the travelers visited the spa, and no reason given for their visit. Shelley, in her journal entry for July 21, 1816, compares a Swiss vista to Matlock, suggesting that she herself had visited, but when such visit occurred is unknown.

8. About 22.5 miles (36 km) from London, Windsor Castle was traditionally the ancestral residence of English sovereigns.

9. In 1642, in the second year of the English Civil War, in which the Roundheads (the rebel forces allied with Oliver Cromwell and Parliament) contended with the Cavaliers (the royalists who supported the throne), Parliament took control of

Windsor Castle (photo by David Iliff, used under CC-by-SA 3.0 license).

High Street, Oxford, ca. 1890.

this city, our minds were filled with the remembrance of the events that had been transacted there more than a century and a half before. It was here that Charles I. had collected his forces. This city had remained faithful to him, after the whole nation had forsaken his cause to join the standard of parliament and liberty. The memory of that unfortunate king, and his companions, the amiable Falkland, the insolent Gower, his queen, and son, gave a peculiar interest to every part of the city, which they might be supposed to have inhabited.[9] The spirit of elder days found a dwelling here, and we delighted to trace its footsteps. If these feelings had not found an imaginary gratification, the appearance of the city had yet in itself sufficient beauty to obtain our admiration. The colleges are ancient and picturesque; the streets are almost magnificent; and the lovely Isis,[10] which flows beside it through meadows of exquisite verdure, is spread forth into a placid expanse of waters, which reflects its majestic assemblage of towers, and spires, and domes, embosomed among aged trees.

I enjoyed this scene; and yet my enjoyment was embittered both by the memory of the past, and the anticipation of the future. I was formed for peaceful happiness. During my youthful days discontent never visited my mind; and if I was ever overcome by *ennui*, the sight of what is beautiful in nature, or the study of what is excellent and sublime in the productions of man, could always interest my heart, and communicate elasticity to my spirits. But I am a blasted tree; the bolt has entered my soul; and I felt then that I should survive to exhibit, what I shall soon cease to be—a miserable spectacle of wrecked humanity, pitiable to others, and abhorrent[11] to myself.

We passed a considerable period at Oxford, rambling among its environs, and endeavouring to identify every spot which might relate to the most animating epoch of English history. Our little voyages of discovery were often prolonged by the successive objects that presented themselves. We visited the tomb of the illustrious Hampden,[12] and the field on which that patriot fell.[13] For a moment my soul was elevated from its debasing and miserable fears to contemplate the divine ideas of liberty and self-sacrifice, of which these sights were the monuments and the remembrancers.[14] For an instant I dared to shake off my chains, and look around me with a free and lofty spirit; but the iron had eaten into my flesh, and I sank again, trembling and hopeless, into my miserable self.

We left Oxford with regret, and proceeded to Matlock, which was our next place of rest. The country in the neighbourhood of this village resembled, to a greater degree, the scenery of Switzerland; but every thing is on a lower scale, and the green hills want the crown of distant white Alps,

London, and the king, Charles I, departed the city to set up his court in Oxford. He was accompanied by his queen, Henriette Marie, and their son, Charles II. Lucius Cary, 2nd Viscount of Falkland, was a member of the Long Parliament that took control of the government and originally opposed Charles's policies. He later moderated his views and attempted to broker compromises to end the constant armed conflicts between Cavalier and Roundhead forces. He was appointed secretary of state by Charles on January 1, 1642, but, despairing of a peaceful resolution to the conflict between Charles and the legislature, threw himself into the combat and died on the battlefield in 1643. Clarendon, in his *History of the Rebellion* (1702–4), wrote of Falkland, "But all his parts, abilities, and faculties, by art and industry, were not to be valued, or mentioned in comparison of his most accomplished mind and manners: his gentleness and affability was so transcendent and obliging, that it drew reverence, and some ... throughest ... born cor... ...kon...ing ... ...ended in 1... f the Rou... es I, the ... bsolute ... controlled by Cromwell, who termed the new era (and entity) the "Commonwealth of England," eventually the "Protectorate" under his personal rule. After his death, his son Richard failed to hold power, and by 1660, the Cavaliers succeeded in restoring the monarchy, with Charles II taking the throne. But the goals of the Great Rebellion were achieved, and absolute authority vested in the monarch, the divine right of kings, was over; essentially, a constitutional monarchy became the form of English government, as it is today, with primary power vested in the legislature.

[Handwritten note: Seems as though he is just vacationing with Clerval. One for Clerval sites 2 for his pieces]

Sir Thomas Gower was High Sheriff of Yorkshire and suffered for his loyalty to Charles but nonetheless survived Charles's execution and thrived during the Restoration. This is an error (evidently by Walton in his recollection of Victor's story), corrected in the 1831 edition to "Goring." Lord George Goring was a courtier and general who vacillated between supporting the king and Parliament, ultimately siding with the Royalists. According to Clarendon's *History*, "The disputes between King and Parliament afforded an opportunity which he resolved to use for his own advancement . . . of all his qualifications dissimulation was his masterpiece" (Book 8, 169).

Certainly the Shelleys must have put their own feelings into the mouth of Victor, who shortly terms the period of the Civil War "the most animating epoch of English history." Living in an era that was still imbued with the spirit of the American and French revolutions and under the influence of William Godwin, Mary Wollstonecraft, and the other English radicals of the day, the idealism of the English Civil War appealed greatly to them.

10. "Isis" was the name insisted on by cartographers of the day for that portion of the Thames that flowed from its source in Gloucestershire to Dorchester-on-Thames; it is still used occasionally.

11. The word "intolerable" is substituted for "abhorrent" in the 1831 edition.

12. J........................ der of th........................ ion to C........................ *His-tory*........................ 24), Will........................ one of th........................ the reco........................ vis-ited........................ rch

Gets second thoughts about leaving the creature

which always attend on the piny mountains of my native country. We visited the wondrous cave,[15] and the little cabinets of natural history, where the curiosities are disposed in the same manner as in the collections at Servox and Chamounix. The latter name made me tremble, when pronounced by Henry; and I hastened to quit Matlock, with which that terrible scene was thus associated.

From Derby still journeying northward, we passed two months in Cumberland and Westmoreland.[16] I could now almost fancy myself among the Swiss mountains. The little patches of snow which yet lingered on the northern sides of the mountains, the lakes, and the dashing of the rocky streams, were all familiar and dear sights to me. Here also we made some acquaintances, who almost contrived to cheat me into happiness. The delight of Clerval was proportionably greater than mine; his mind expanded in the company of men of talent, and he found in his own nature greater capacities and resources than he could have imagined himself to have possessed while he associated with his inferiors. "I could pass my life here," said he to me; "and among these mountains I should scarcely regret Switzerland and the Rhine."

But he found that a traveller's life is one that includes much pain amidst its enjoyments. His feelings are for ever on the stretch; and when he begins to sink into repose, he finds himself obliged to quit that on which he rests in pleasure for something new, which again engages his attention, and which also he forsakes for other novelties.

We had scarcely visited the various lakes of Cumberland and Westmoreland, and conceived an affection for some of the inhabitants, when the period of our appointment with our Scotch friend approached, and we left them to travel on. For my own part I was not sorry. I had now neglected my promise for some time, and I feared the effects of the daemon's disappointment. He might remain in Switzerland, and wreak his vengeance on my relatives. This idea pursued me, and tormented me at every moment from which I might otherwise have snatched repose and peace. I waited for my letters with feverish impatience: if they were delayed, I was miserable, and overcome by a thousand fears; and when they arrived, and I saw the superscription of Elizabeth or my father, I hardly dared to read and ascertain my fate.

Sometimes I thought that the fiend followed me, and might expedite my remissness by murdering my companion. When these thoughts possessed me, I would not quit Henry for a moment, but followed him as his shadow, to protect him from the fancied rage of his destroyer. I felt as if I had committed some great crime, the consciousness of which haunted me. I was guiltless, but I had indeed drawn down a horrible curse upon my head, as mortal as that of crime.

I visited Edinburgh[17] with languid eyes and mind; and yet that city might have interested the most unfortunate being. Clerval did not like it so well as Oxford; for the antiquity of the latter city was more pleasing to him. But the beauty and regularity of the new town of Edinburgh,[18] its romantic castle,[19] and its environs, the most delightful in the world, Arthur's Seat,[20] St. Bernard's Well,[21] and the Pentland Hills,[22] compensated him for the change, and filled him with cheerfulness and admiration. But I was impatient to arrive at the termination of my journey.

We left Edinburgh in a week, passing through Coupar,[23] St. Andrews,[24] and along the banks of the Tay,[25] to Perth, where our friend expected us. But I was in no mood to laugh and talk with strangers, or enter into their feelings or plans with the good humour expected from a guest; and accordingly I told Clerval that I wished to make the tour of Scot-

Edinburgh Castle (photo by Kim Traynor, used under CC-by-SA 3.0 license).

in Buckinghamshire, where Hampden was reportedly buried, in October 1817. However, there is no actual monument to "the Patriot," as he was known, in the church. See Clement Shorter, *Highways and Byways in Buckinghamshire* (London: Macmillan and Co., 1920).

13. Victor refers to Chalgrove Field, in Chalgrove, Oxfordshire, where Hampden was fatally wounded in a battle with Prince Rupert, a Royalist leader.

Portrait of John Hampden.

14. The word "remembrancer" is the official title of an executive officer of the Exchequer whose duty it is to memorialize the business of the Exchequer, but it is used here in a figurative sense, to mean "one who keeps memories."

15. The Great Masson Caverns, on the Heights of Abraham above Matlock Bath, are natural but were mined for fluorspar and other minerals. They can still be visited by tourists. However, there are other,

smaller caves on the High Tor, rising above Matlock Bath, described in *Baedeker's Great Britain* (1894), and one of these could be the "wondrous cave" visited by Victor and Henry.

Hawthorne writes of visiting, in June 1857, Matlock's "grand cavern," once a Roman lead mine: The members of his party, holding tallow candles, were led by a guide into a "darksome and ugly pit . . . kept under lock and key." Hawthorne disliked the "disagreeable" commercial aspect of such tourism: caverns, cataracts, and "precipitous crags compelled to figure in ornamental gardens,—and all accessible at a fixed amount of shillings and pence . . . it makes the wildest scenery look like the artificial rock-work which Englishmen are so fond of displaying in the little bit of grass-plot under their suburban parlour-windows." But he could not discount the sheer natural wonder of the surroundings, including the Romantic Rocks, "some crags which have been rent away . . . a very picturesque spot, and the price for seeing it is two-pence; though in our case it was included in the four shillings which we had paid for seeing the cavern" (*Passages from the English Note-Books*, Vol. 2, 230).

The Great Masson Caverns (photo by TheHeightsofAbraham, used under CC-by-SA 4.0 license).

Arthur's Seat (photo by Kim Traynor, used under CC-by-SA 3.0 license).

St. Bernard's Well (Edinburgh, 1800).

land alone. "Do you," said I, "enjoy yourself, and let this be our rendezvous. I may be absent a month or two; but do not interfere with my motions, I entreat you: leave me to peace and solitude for a short time; and when I return, I hope it will be with a lighter heart, more congenial to your own temper."

Henry wished to dissuade me; but, seeing me bent on this plan, ceased to remonstrate. He entreated me to write often. "I had rather be with you," he said, "in your solitary rambles,

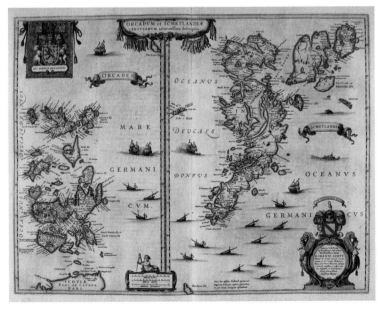

Blaeu's 1654 map of the Orkney and Shetland Islands.

16. Cumberland and Westmoreland are counties comprising a significant portion of the Lake District. We are now at about mid-June 1796. In 1799, William Wordsworth relocated to the Lake District, becoming known as one of the "Lake poets"; in 1811, Percy and Harriet Shelley had moved there, hoping to meet Samuel Taylor Coleridge.

17. Edinburgh, the capital of Scotland, was described by *Baedeker's Great Britain* one hundred years after Victor's visit as "one of the most romantically beautiful cities in Europe." This is in sharp contrast to the views of Edward Topham, who, visiting the town in 1774, found it overpopulated, with "little room for elegance": "I make no manner of doubt but that the High Street . . . is inhabited by a greater number of persons than any street in Europe," opined the correspondent of *Letters from Edinburgh, Written in the Years 1774 and 1775* (London, 1776), then all of twenty-five years old and enjoying his grand tour after over a decade at Eton and two inconclusive years at Trinity College, Cambridge. Topham was more naturally inclined to favor the streets of London, which as an aspiring playwright he mined for a series of farces. They were neither immediately successful nor enduring, and at the age of forty-one he retired to Yorkshire, where he became famous for breeding champion greyhounds.

18. Much was expected of the "new town" still under construction at the time of publication of the third edition of the *Encyclopædia Britannica* (1797), which crowed that "from the advantages of its situation, and its being built according to a regular plan, it hath undoubtedly a superiority over any city in Britain." The new town was first conceived in 1752, but was held up by the lack of concessions until 1767; even then, it was the subject of litigations reminiscent of modern

battles with environmental organizations. By 1797, the *Britannica* described it as "almost finished," and, though the editors failed to mention the construction, that must be the state in which Victor and Clerval saw it.

19. Dominating the skyline of Edinburgh, Edinburgh Castle was only the late~~st~~ ccu-pied ~~istle~~ Roc ~~ning~~ mo~~651~~ whe ~~with~~ the ~~ring~~ the ~~nar-ily~~ ~~pris-one~~

A bunch of history from all the places they traveled

20. Arthur's Seat, in Holyrood Park in Edinburgh, was described in the early 1900s by Robert Louis Stevenson (whose grandfather had engineered much of the city a century before) as technically a "hill," if one were to speak only of size, but "a mountain by virtue of its bold design" (*The Travels and Essays of Robert Louis Stevenson* [New York: Scribner's, 1909], 335).

21. St. Bernard's Well was built in 1789 from a design by the Scottish painter Alexander Nasmyth. It was his first architectural commission, and he took his inspiration from the early first century BCE Temple of Vesta in Tivoli, Italy (also known as Sibyl's temple). The well is situated on the south bank of the Water of Leith in Edinburgh, once on private property, now owned by the city. The sulfurous waters that sprang from the spot had legendary healing properties, to which Nasmyth's structure gives formal expression: Romanesque proportions are strictly adhered to, and from a detailed lintel, ten Doric columns rise. Under the dome is a statue of Hygieia (in Coade stone, and added in 1791), the daughter of

Skara Brae, Orkney, in summer 2012 (photo by Chmee2, used under CC-by-SA 3.0 license).

than with these Scotch people, whom I do not know: hasten then, my dear friend, to return, that I may again feel myself somewhat at home, which I cannot do in your absence."

Having parted from my friend, I determined to visit some remote spot of Scotland, and finish my work in solitude. I did not doubt but that the monster followed me, and would discover himself to me when I should have finished, that he might receive his companion.

With this resolution I traversed the northern highlands, and fixed on one of the remotest of the Orkneys[26] as the scene [of my] labours. It was a place fitted for such a work, being hardly more than a rock, whose high sides were continually beaten upon by the waves. The soil was barren, scarcely affording pasture for a few miserable cows, and oatmeal for its inhabitants, which consisted of five persons, whose gaunt and scraggy limbs gave tokens of their miserable fare. Vegetables and bread, when they indulged in such luxuries, and even fresh water, was to be procured from the main land, which was about five miles distant.

On the whole island there were but three miserable huts, and one of these was vacant when I arrived. This I hired. It contained but two rooms, and these exhibited all the squalidness of the most miserable penury. The thatch had fallen in, the walls were unplastered, and the door was off its hinges. I ordered it to be repaired, bought some furniture, and took possession; an incident which would, doubtless, have occasioned some surprise, had not all the senses of the cottagers been benumbed by want and squalid poverty. As it was, I lived ungazed at and unmolested, hardly thanked for the pittance of food and clothes which I gave; so much does suffering blunt even the coarsest sensations of men.

In this retreat I devoted the morning to labour; but in the evening, when the weather permitted, I walked on the stony beach of the sea, to listen to the waves as they roared, and dashed at my feet. It was a monotonous, yet ever-changing scene. I thought of Switzerland; it was far different from this desolate and appalling landscape. Its hills are covered with vines, and its cottages are scattered thickly in the plains. Its fair lakes reflect a blue and gentle sky; and, when troubled by the winds, their tumult is but as the play of a lively infant, when compared to the roarings of the giant ocean.

In this manner I distributed my occupations when I first arrived; but, as I proceeded in my labour, it became every day more horrible and irksome to me. Sometimes I could not prevail on myself to enter my laboratory for several days; and at other times I toiled day and night in order to complete my work. It was indeed a filthy process in which I was engaged. During my first experiment, a kind of enthusiastic frenzy had blinded me to the horror of my employment; my mind was intently fixed on the sequel[27] of my labour, and my eyes were shut to the horror of my proceedings. But now I went to it in cold blood, and my heart often sickened at the work of my hands.

Thus situated, employed in the most detestable occupation, immersed in a solitude where nothing could for an instant call my attention from the actual scene in which I was engaged, my spirits became unequal; I grew restless and nervous. Every moment I feared to meet my persecutor. Sometimes I sat with my eyes fixed on the ground, fearing to raise them lest they should encounter the object which I so

the god of medicine. Etched on one face of the neoclassical monument are the words "St. Bernard's Mineral Well."

22. Pentland Hills is an unnoteworthy range southwest of Edinburgh. *Baedeker's Great Britain* describes the area as affording "numerous pleasant rambles." What attracted Victor and Henry to the site is unknown. Sir Walter Scott (1771–1832) and Robert Louis Stevenson (1850–1894) were known to have walked the hills, as was the World War I poet Siegfried Sassoon, when he was being treated for shell shock—by William Rivers, who [*...*] ng cure" for [*...*] Craiglock-[*...*] cers, estab-[*...*] Edinburgh [*...*] ote 18, Vol-

[handwritten note: Really starts worrying about back home]

23. Coupar Angus is a village about 12 miles (19 km) distant from Perth, described on eighteenth-century maps as "Coup Inn." It was originally part of Angus County but was transferred to Perthshire County in 1891.

24. St. Andrews is an ancient town, seat of a university, and long the "ecclesiastical metropolis of Scotland," according to *Baedeker's Great Britain*. Legend tells that golf was invented here, and history records that golf was played on the "Old Course" in the early fifteenth century, until it was banned by James II in 1457. The ban was lifted in 1501 when James IV took up golf. St. Andrews hosts the British Open approximately every five years.

25. The river Tay, the longest in Scotland, flows through Perth until it empties into the Firth of Tay, south of Dundee. On September 26, 1877, a magnificent rail bridge built at a cost of £300,000 was opened across the Tay, only to collapse in a storm twenty-one months later as a train car-

rying seventy passengers passed over it. Fifty-nine known victims perished in the waters. The event has been studied obsessively, yielding no positive cause but three strongly suspected possible ones: the bridge was shaken apart and rent by violent oscillations, or waves, produced when its natural vibrating frequency was amplified by an identical frequency caused by gales of wind, creating high and low pressure above and below the path of the train (the Bernoulli effect); the wind caused the derailment of a carriage, whereupon an axle hit a pillar, which shuddered to earthquake-level proportions; the wind knocked down course after course of masonry like dominoes, to the extent that the upper and lower piers separated from each other and the bridge tipped into the river. The disaster was immortalized by William McGonagall, called by his own publisher "the greatest bad verse writer of his age . . . or of any other age"; among other transgressions, the poet multiplied the actual number of casualties:

> Beautiful Railway Bridge of the Silv'ry Tay!
> Alas! I am very sorry to say
> That ninety lives have been taken away
> On the last Sabbath day of 1879,
> Which will be remember'd for a very long time.

26. The Orkneys are a chain of about seventy small islands off the tip of northern Scotland. The Greek Pytheas (see note 6, Volume I, Letter I, above) referred to the northernmost point of land, probably Dunnett Head, as "Orcas," and the Roman geographer Pomponius Mela and historian Tacitus, both writing in the first century CE, called the islands the "Orcades."

As will be seen, it is impossible that Frankenstein was actually in the Orkney Islands; more likely, he was on a thinly populated island like Colonsay, in the

The Isle of Colonsay, 2006 (photo by Chris Bazley-Rose, used under CC-by-SA 3.0 license).

much dreaded to behold. I feared to wander from the sight of my fellow-creatures,[28] lest when alone he should come to claim his companion.

In the mean time I worked on, and my labour was already considerably advanced. I looked towards its completion with a tremulous and eager hope, which I dared not trust myself to question, but which was intermixed with obscure forebodings of evil, that made my heart sicken in my bosom.

Inner Hebrides, a short sail to Ireland. He may well have concealed his location for fear that he had left behind notes or other clues regarding his work.

27. The word "sequel" is replaced with "consummation" in the 1831 edition.

28. What "fellow-creatures"? Victor seems to have forgotten that he deliberately selected a location for his laboratory that featured only two other inhabited dwellings on the entire island.

28. Ask.

CHAPTER III.[1]

I SAT ONE EVENING in my laboratory; the sun had set, and the moon was just rising from the sea; I had not sufficient light for my employment, and I remained idle, in a pause of consideration of whether I should leave my labour for the night, or hasten its conclusion by an unremitting attention to it. As I sat, a train of reflection occurred to me, which led me to consider the effects of what I was now doing. Three years before[2] I was engaged in the same manner, and had created a fiend whose unparalleled barbarity had desolated my heart, and filled it for ever with the bitterest remorse. I was now about to form another being, of whose dispositions I was alike ignorant; she might become ten thousand times more malignant than her mate, and delight, for its own sake, in murder and wretchedness. He had sworn to quit the neighbourhood of man, and hide himself in deserts; but she had not; and she, who in all probability was to become a thinking and reasoning animal, might refuse to comply with a compact made before her creation. They might even hate each other; the creature who already lived loathed his own deformity, and might he not conceive a greater abhorence for it when it came before his eyes in the female form? She also might turn with disgust from him to the superior beauty of man;[3] she might quit him, and he be again alone, exasperated by the fresh provocation of being deserted by one of his own species.

1. Chapter 20 in the 1831 edition.

2. That is, the autumn of 1793. As will be seen, it is now roughly August 1796.

3. This is exactly what is depicted in the climax of James Whale's *Bride of Frankenstein* (Universal, 1935).

4. The [*handwritten annotation:* Might be the death of Cleval. The creature did not go to the aid of his future mate] makes ... Victor ... rather t... the des... departs... a few ... returns ... creature ...

5. Victor's narrative here is depicting a psychological landscape rather than an actual one: Recall that he selected a two-room hut for his laboratory and "apartment" and therefore could not have moved very far from his work.

[handwritten annotation: The creature stalks his creator]

The female creature is not yet unveiled by Dr. Pretorious (Ernest Thesiger) and Henry Frankenstein (Colin Clive), in a scene from the theatrical trailer for *Bride of Frankenstein* (Universal Pictures, 1935).

Even if they were to leave Europe, and inhabit the deserts of the new world, yet one of the first results of those sympathies for which the daemon thirsted would be children, and a race of devils would be propagated upon the earth, who might make the very existence of the species of man a condition precarious and full of terror. Had I a right, for my own benefit, to inflict this curse upon everlasting generations? I had before been moved by the sophisms of the being I had created; I had been struck senseless by his fiendish threats: but now, for the first time, the wickedness of my promise burst upon me; I shuddered to think that future ages might curse me as their pest, whose selfishness had not hesitated to buy its own peace at the price perhaps of the existence of the whole human race.

I trembled, and my heart failed within me; when, on looking up, I saw, by the light of the moon, the daemon at the casement. A ghastly grin wrinkled his lips as he gazed on me, where I sat fulfilling the task which he had allotted to me. Yes, he had followed me in my travels; he had loitered in forests, hid himself in caves, or taken refuge in wide and desert heaths; and he now came to mark my progress, and claim the fulfilment of my promise.

As I looked on him, his countenance expressed the utmost extent of malice and treachery. I thought with a sensation of madness on my promise of creating another like to him, and, trembling with passion, tore to pieces the thing on which I was engaged. The wretch saw me destroy the creature on whose future existence he depended for happiness, and, with a howl of devilish despair and revenge, withdrew.[4]

I left the room, and, locking the door, made a solemn vow in my own heart never to resume my labours; and then, with trembling steps, I sought my own apartment.[5]

I was alone; none were near me to dissipate the gloom, and relieve me from the sickening oppression of the most terrible reveries.

Several hours past, and I remained near my window gazing on the sea; it was almost motionless, for the winds were hushed, and all nature reposed

The creature meets his bride (*The Bride of Frankenstein*, Universal Pictures, 1935)

under the eye of the quiet moon. A few fishing vessels alone specked the water, and now and then the gentle breeze wafted the sound of voices, as the fishermen called to one another. I felt the silence, although I was hardly conscious of its extreme profundity until my ear was suddenly arrested by the paddling of oars near the shore, and a person landed close to my house.

In a few minutes after, I heard the creaking of my door, as if some one endeavoured to open it softly. I trembled from head to foot; I felt a presentiment of who it was, and wished to rouse one of the peasants who dwelt in a cottage not far from mine; but I was overcome by the sensation of help-lessness, so often felt in frightful dreams, when you in vain endeavour to fly from an impending danger, and was rooted to the spot.

Presently I heard the sound of footsteps along the passage; the door opened, and the wretch whom I dreaded appeared. Shutting the door, he approached me, and said, in a smoth-ered voice—

"You have destroyed the work which you began; what is it that you intend? Do you dare to break your promise? I have endured toil and misery: I left Switzerland with you; I crept along the shores of the Rhine, among its willow islands, and over the summits of its hills. I have dwelt many months in the heaths of England, and among the deserts of Scotland. I have endured incalculable fatigue, and cold, and hunger; do you dare destroy my hopes?"

"Begone! I do break my promise; never will I create another like yourself, equal in deformity and wickedness."

Confronted and rejected. A lot happening here.

6. The word "weakness" is altered to "irresolution" and "resolution" is changed to "determination" in the 1831 edition.

Something will happen and his happiness shall never return.

his rugged appearance made him strong and a good rower

"Slave, I before reasoned with you, but you have proved yourself unworthy of my condescension. Remember that I have power; you believe yourself miserable, but I can make you so wretched that the light of day will be hateful to you. You are my creator, but I am your master;—obey!"

"The hour of my weakness[6] is past, and the period of your power is arrived. Your threats cannot move me to do an act of wickedness; but they confirm me in a resolution of not creating you a companion in vice. Shall I, in cool blood, set loose upon the earth a daemon, whose delight is in death and wretchedness. Begone! I am firm, and your words will only exasperate my rage."

The monster saw my determination in my face, and gnashed his teeth in the impotence of anger. "Shall each man," cried he, "find a wife for his bosom, and each beast have his mate, and I be alone? I had feelings of affection, and they were requited by detestation and scorn. Man, you may hate; but beware! Your hours will pass in dread and misery, and soon the bolt will fall which must ravish from you your happiness for ever. Are you to be happy, while I grovel in the intensity of my wretchedness? You can blast my other passions; but revenge remains—revenge, henceforth dearer than light or food! I may die; but first you, my tyrant and tormentor, shall curse the sun that gazes on your misery. Beware; for I am fearless, and therefore powerful. I will watch with the wiliness of a snake, that I may sting with its venom. Man, you shall repent of the injuries you inflict."

"Devil, cease; and do not poison the air with these sounds of malice. I have declared my resolution to you, and I am no coward to bend beneath words. Leave me; I am inexorable."

"It is well. I go; but remember, I shall be with you on your wedding-night."

I started forward, and exclaimed, "Villain! before you sign my death-warrant, be sure that you are yourself safe."

I would have seized him; but he eluded me, and quitted the house with precipitation: in a few moments I saw him in his boat, which shot across the waters with an arrowy swiftness, and was soon lost amidst the waves.

All was again silent; but his words rung in my ears. I

burned with rage to pursue the murderer of my peace, and precipitate him into the ocean. I walked up and down my room hastily and perturbed, while my imagination conjured up a thousand images to torment and sting me. Why had I not followed him, and closed with him in mortal strife? But I had suffered him to depart, and he had directed his course towards the main land. I shuddered to think who might be the next victim sacrificed to his insatiate revenge. And then I thought again of his words—*"I will be with you on your wedding-night."*[7] That then was the period fixed for the fulfilment of my destiny. In that hour I should die, and at once satisfy and extinguish his malice. The prospect did not move me to fear; yet when I thought of my beloved Elizabeth,—of her tears and endless sorrow, when she should find her lover so barbarously snatched from her,—tears, the first I had shed for many months, streamed from my eyes, and I resolved not to fall before my enemy without a bitter struggle.

The night passed away, and the sun rose from the ocean; my feelings became calmer, if it may be called calmness, when the violence of rage sinks into the depths of despair. I left the house, the horrid scene of the last night's contention, and walked on the beach of the sea, which I almost regarded as an insuperable barrier between me and my fellow-creatures; nay, a wish that such should prove the fact stole across me. I desired that I might pass my life on that barren rock, wearily it is true, but uninterrupted by any sudden shock of misery. If I returned, it was to be sacrificed, or to see those whom I most loved die under the grasp of a daemon whom I had myself created.

I walked about the isle like a restless spectre, separated from all it loved, and miserable in the separation. When it became noon, and the sun rose higher, I lay down on the grass, and was overpowered by a deep sleep. I had been awake the whole of the preceding night, my nerves were agitated, and my eyes inflamed by watching and misery. The sleep into which I now sunk refreshed me; and when I awoke, I again felt as if I belonged to a race of human beings like myself, and I began to reflect upon what had passed with greater composure; yet still the words of the fiend rung in my

7. The warning is in all capitals in the 1831 edition.

← Definitely foreshadowing. May add to list of holding off Marriage

8. Confirming that Frankenstein destroyed the mate in approximately August or September 1797.

9. This sentence and the next sentence are replaced in the 1831 edition with the following:

> He said that he was wearing away his time fruitlessly where he was, that letters from the friends he had formed in London desired his return to complete the negotiation they had entered into for his Indian enterprise. He could not any longer delay his departure; but as his journey to London might be followed, even sooner than he now conjectured, by his longer voyage, he entreated me to bestow as much of my society on him as I could spare. He besought me, therefore, to leave my solitary isle, and to meet him at Perth, that we might proceed southwards together.

Again, Clerval is depicted as a man of business rather than the adventurous soul he is in the 1818 edition.

ears like a death-knell, they appeared like a dream, yet distinct and oppressive as a reality.

The sun had far descended, and I still sat on the shore, satisfying my appetite, which had become ravenous, with an oaten cake, when I saw a fishing-boat land close to me, and one of the men brought me a packet; it contained letters from Geneva, and one from Clerval, entreating me to join him. He said that nearly a year had elapsed since we had quitted Switzerland,[8] and France was yet unvisited.[9] He entreated me, therefore, to leave my solitary isle, and meet him at Perth, in a week from that time, when we might arrange the plan of our future proceedings. This letter in a degree recalled me to life, and I determined to quit my island at the expiration of two days.

Yet, before I departed, there was a task to perform, on which I shuddered to reflect: I must pack my chemical instruments; and for that purpose I must enter the room which had been the scene of my odious work, and I must handle those utensils, the sight of which was sickening to me. The next morning, at day-break, I summoned sufficient courage, and unlocked the door of my laboratory. The remains of the half-finished creature, whom I had destroyed, lay scattered on the floor, and I almost felt as if I had mangled the living flesh of a human being. I paused to collect myself, and then entered the chamber. With trembling hand I conveyed the instruments out of the room; but I reflected that I ought not to leave the relics of my work to excite the horror and suspicion of the peasants, and I accordingly put them into a basket, with a great quantity of stones, and laying them up, determined to throw them into the sea that very night; and in the mean time I sat upon the beach, employed in cleaning and arranging my chemical apparatus.

Nothing could be more complete than the alteration that had taken place in my feelings since the night of the appearance of the daemon. I had before regarded my promise with a gloomy despair, as a thing that, with whatever consequences, must be fulfilled; but I now felt as if a film had been taken from before my eyes, and that I, for the first time, saw clearly. The idea of renewing my labours did not for one instant occur to me; the threat I had heard weighed on my thoughts, but I did not reflect that a voluntary act of mine could avert it. I had resolved in my own mind, that to create another like the fiend I had first made would be an act of the basest and most atrocious selfishness; and I banished from my mind every thought that could lead to a different conclusion.

Between two and three in the morning the moon rose; and I then, putting my basket aboard a little skiff, sailed out about four miles from the shore. The scene was perfectly solitary: a few boats were returning towards land, but I sailed away from them. I felt as if I was about the commission of a dreadful crime, and avoided with shuddering anxiety any encounter with my fellow-creatures. At one time the moon, which had before been clear, was suddenly overspread by a thick cloud, and I took advantage of the moment of darkness, and cast my basket into the sea; I listened to the gurgling sound as it sunk, and then sailed away from the spot. The sky became clouded; but the air was pure, although chilled by the north-east breeze that was then rising. But it refreshed me, and filled me with such agreeable sensations, that I resolved to prolong my stay on the water, and fixing the rudder in a direct position, stretched myself at the bottom of the boat. Clouds hid the moon, every thing was obscure, and I heard only the sound of the boat, as its keel cut through the waves; the murmur lulled me, and in a short time I slept soundly.

I do not know how long I remained in this situation, but when I awoke I found that the sun had already mounted considerably. The wind was high, and the waves continually threatened the safety of my little skiff. I found that the wind was north-east, and must have driven me far from the coast from which I had embarked. I endeavoured to change my course, but quickly found that if I again made the attempt the boat would be instantly filled with water. Thus situated, my only resource was to drive before the wind. I confess that I felt a few sensations of terror. I had no compass with me, and was so little[10] acquainted with the geography of this part of the world that the sun was of little benefit to me. I might be driven into the wide Atlantic, and feel all the tortures of

10. The word "little" is revised to "slenderly" in the 1831 edition.

[handwritten margin note: + again with fellow creatures (rub in creature's face) (building up for significant loss)]

11. In place of the word "sunk," the following is inserted in the 1831 edition: "—all left behind, on whom the monster might satisfy his sanguinary and merciless passions. This idea plunged me[.]"

Victor finally realizes that he has carelessly exposed his family to danger.

12. Death is not imminent but, instead, days away.

13. Victor has been on the water from, say, 2:30 a.m. until near sunset, an interval of no more than seventeen hours, some of which was spent aimlessly drifting while he was asleep, presumably with the sail luffed so that he would avoid capsizing the skiff or being knocked overboard. Even with a "high" wind during the periods he attended to his skiff, it is not possible that he traveled more than two hundred miles; the average speed of a modern sailboat, rigged and steered by an experienced sailor, is five to 10 miles (8 to 16 km) per hour, and Victor was asleep for six to eight hours of his voyage.

14. What happened to the first sail?

15. The word "eagerly" is replaced with "carefully" in the 1831 edition.

starvation, or be swallowed up in the immeasurable waters that roared and buffeted around me. I had already been out many hours, and felt the torment of a burning thirst, a prelude to my other sufferings. I looked on the heavens, which were covered by clouds that flew before the wind only to be replaced by others: I looked upon the sea, it was to be my grave. "Fiend," I exclaimed, "your task is already fulfilled!" I thought of Elizabeth, of my father, and of Clerval; and sunk[11] into a reverie, so despairing and frightful, that even now, when the scene is on the point of closing before me for ever,[12] I shudder to reflect on it.

Some hours passed thus; but by degrees, as the sun declined towards the horizon, the wind died away into a gentle breeze, and the sea became free from breakers. But these gave place to a heavy swell; I felt sick, and hardly able to hold the rudder, when suddenly I saw a line of high land towards the south.

Almost spent, as I was, by fatigue, and the dreadful suspense I endured for several hours, this sudden certainty of life rushed like a flood of warm joy to my heart, and tears gushed from my eyes.[13]

How mutable are our feelings, and how strange is that clinging love we have of life even in the excess of misery! I constructed another sail[14] with a part of my dress, and eagerly steered my course towards the land. It had a wild and rocky appearance; but as I approached nearer, I easily perceived the traces of cultivation. I saw vessels near the shore, and found myself suddenly transported back to the neighbourhood of civilized man. I eagerly[15] traced the windings of the land, and hailed a steeple which I at length saw issuing from behind a small promontory. As I was in a state of extreme debility, I resolved to sail directly towards the town as a place where I could most easily procure nourishment. Fortunately I had money with me. As I turned the promontory, I perceived a small neat town and a good harbour, which I entered, my heart bounding with joy at my unexpected escape.

As I was occupied in fixing the boat and arranging the sails, several people crowded towards the spot. They seemed very much surprised at my appearance; but, instead of offering me any assistance, whispered together with gestures that at any other time might have produced in me a slight sensation of alarm. As it was, I merely remarked that they spoke English; and I therefore addressed them in that language: "My good friends," said I, "will you be so kind as to tell me the name of this town, and inform me where I am?"

"You will know that soon enough," replied a man with a gruff[16] voice. "May be you are come to a place that will not prove much to your taste; but you will not be consulted as to your quarters, I promise you."

I was exceedingly surprised on receiving so rude an answer from a stranger; and I was also disconcerted on perceiving the frowning and angry countenances of his companions. "Why do you answer me so roughly?" I replied: "surely it is not the custom of Englishmen to receive strangers so inhospitably."

"I do not know," said the man, "what the custom of the English may be; but it is the custom of the Irish to hate villains."

While this strange dialogue continued, I perceived the crowd rapidly increase. Their faces expressed a mixture of curiosity and anger, which annoyed, and in some degree alarmed me. I inquired the way to the inn; but no one replied. I then moved forward, and a murmuring sound arose from the crowd as they followed and surrounded me; when an ill-looking man approaching, tapped me on the shoulder, and said, "Come, Sir, you must follow me to Mr. Kirwin's, to give an account of yourself."

"Who is Mr. Kirwin? Why am I to give an account of myself? Is not this a free country?"

"Aye, Sir, free enough for honest folks. Mr. Kirwin is a magistrate;[17] and you are to give an account of the death of a gentleman who was found murdered here last night."

This answer startled me; but I presently recovered myself. I was innocent; that could easily be proved: accordingly I followed my conductor in silence, and was led to one of the best houses in the town. I was ready to sink from fatigue and hunger; but, being surrounded by a crowd, I thought it politic to rouse all my strength, that no physical debility might

16. The voice is "hoarse," not "gruff," in the 1831 edition.

17. A layperson appointed by the king to supervise the administration of justice and resolution of disputes, also known as "justice of the peace." The position is not a professional one—that is, the appointee was not expected to be a full-time judge—and often was given as patronage to large landowners or other prominent individuals who had little or no legal training.

be construed into apprehension or conscious guilt. Little did I then expect the calamity that was in a few moments to overwhelm me, and extinguish in horror and despair all fear of ignominy or death.

I must pause here; for it requires all my fortitude to recall the memory of the frightful events which I am about to relate, in proper detail, to my recollection.

CHAPTER IV.[1]

WAS SOON INTRODUCED into the presence of the magistrate, an old benevolent man, with calm and mild manners. He looked upon me, however, with some degree of severity; and then, turning towards my conductors, he asked who appeared as witnesses on this occasion.

About half a dozen men came forward; and one being selected by the magistrate, he deposed, that he had been out fishing the night before with his son and brother-in-law, Daniel Nugent, when, about ten o'clock, they observed a strong northerly blast rising, and they accordingly put in for port. It was a very dark night, as the moon had not yet risen; they did not land at the harbour, but, as they had been accustomed, at a creek about two miles below. He walked on first, carrying a part of the fishing tackle, and his companions followed him at some distance. As he was proceeding along the sands, he struck his foot against something, and fell all his length on the ground. His companions came up to assist him; and, by the light of their lantern, they found that he had fallen on the body of a man, who was to all appearance dead. Their first supposition was, that it was the corpse of some person who had been drowned, and was thrown on shore by the waves; but, upon examination, they found that the clothes were not wet, and even that the body was not then cold. They instantly carried it to the cottage of an old woman

1. Chapter 21 in the 1831 edition.

2. Are we to understand that Clerval put up no struggle when attacked by the creature? Belefant, in *Frankenstein, the Man and the Monster*, suggests that this is evidence that *Victor* murdered Clerval, for he would have been able to approach Clerval from the front or while he was sleeping and overpower him without a struggle (94–95).

Clerval killed in sleep?

Speculation that Victor Killed Clerval

near the spot, and endeavoured, but in vain, to restore it to life. He appeared to be a handsome young man, about five and twenty years of age. He had apparently been strangled; for there was no sign of any violence, except the black mark of fingers on his neck.[2]

The first part of this deposition did not in the least interest me; but when the mark of the fingers was mentioned, I remembered the murder of my brother, and felt myself extremely agitated; my limbs trembled, and a mist came over my eyes, which obliged me to lean on a chair for support. The magistrate observed me with a keen eye, and of course drew an unfavourable augury from my manner.

The son confirmed his father's account: but when Daniel Nugent was called, he swore positively that, just before the fall of his companion, he saw a boat, with a single man in it, at a short distance from the shore; and, as far as he could judge by the light of a few stars, it was the same boat in which I had just landed.

A woman deposed, that she lived near the beach, and was standing at the door of her cottage, waiting for the return of the fishermen, about an hour before she heard of the discovery of the body, when she saw a boat, with only one man in it, push off from that part of the shore where the corpse was afterwards found.

Another woman confirmed the account of the fishermen having brought the body into her house; it was not cold. They put it into a bed, and rubbed it; and Daniel went to the town for an apothecary, but life was quite gone.

Several other men were examined concerning my landing; and they agreed, that, with the strong north wind that had arisen during the night, it was very probable that I had beaten about for many hours, and had been obliged to return nearly to the same spot from which I had departed. Besides, they observed that it appeared that I had brought the body from another place, and it was likely, that as I did not appear to know the shore, I might have put into the harbour ignorant of the distance of the town of from the place where I had deposited the corpse.

Mr. Kirwin, on hearing this evidence, desired that I should

be taken into the room where the body lay for interment that it might be observed what effect the sight of it would produce upon me. This idea was probably suggested by the extreme agitation I had exhibited when the mode of the murder had been described. I was accordingly conducted, by the magistrate and several other persons, to the inn. I could not help being struck by the strange coincidences that had taken place during this eventful night; but, knowing that I had been conversing with several persons in the island I had inhabited about the time that the body had been found, I was perfectly tranquil as to the consequences of the affair.

I entered the room where the corpse lay, and was led up to the coffin. How can I describe my sensations on beholding it? I feel yet parched with horror, nor can I reflect on that terrible moment without shuddering and agony,[3] that faintly reminds me of the anguish of the recognition. The trial, the presence of the magistrate and witnesses, passed like a dream from my memory, when I saw the lifeless form of Henry Clerval stretched before me. I gasped for breath; and, throwing myself on the body, I exclaimed, "Have my murderous machinations deprived you also, my dearest Henry, of life? Two I have already destroyed; other victims await their destiny: but you, Clerval, my friend, my benefactor"—

The human frame could no longer support the agonizing suffering[4] that I endured, and I was carried out of the room in strong convulsions.

A fever succeeded to this. I lay for two months on the point of death:[5] my ravings, as I afterwards heard, were frightful; I called myself the murderer of William, of Justine, and of Clerval. Sometimes I entreated my attendants to assist me in the destruction of the fiend by whom I was tormented; and, at others, I felt the fingers of the monster already grasping my neck, and screamed aloud with agony and terror. Fortunately, as I spoke my native language,[6] Mr. Kirwin alone understood me; but my gestures and bitter cries were sufficient to affright the other witnesses.

Why did I not die? More miserable than man ever was before, why did I not sink into forgetfulness and rest? Death snatches away many blooming children, the only hopes of

3. The balance of the sentence does not appear in the 1831 edition, and the "trial" mentioned in the next sentence becomes an "examination."

Alibi discovered revised to

Breakdown

7. According to Greek legend, Ixion, a king of Thessaly and son of the war god Ares, was caught by Zeus in the act of attempting to seduce Zeus's wife, Hera. Hera had reported Ixion's advances to Zeus; Zeus tested Ixion by constructing a cloud that looked like Hera and placing it in Ixion's bed. The inevitable occurred, and Zeus punished Ixion by affixing him to a fiery wheel, either in the sky or the underworld, depending on the source of the tale. The punishment roughly approximated a crime committed by Ixion against his own father-in-law, Eioneus (or Deioneus): Unwilling to pay Eioneus the bride-price for his daughter, Ixion murdered him by throwing him into a burning pit, having lured him to the inferno on the pretext of wishing to deliver payment. A pariah thereafter, shunned by all, he found a sympathetic audience in Zeus, who was willing to redeem him and offered him a place on Mount Olympus. It was there, in the god's own court, that Ixion repaid Zeus's largesse by trying to lure Hera away from him—hence a punishment that may seem out of proportion to the crime.

8. The old woman refers to the "quarter sessions" court, which quarterly heard matters that were more serious than those tried summarily by a justice of the peace or magistrate. The quarter sessions court, however, would not hear a case of murder, which would be referred to the periodic assize court. This in fact happened here, for

Everyone believes he did this. Even himself

their doating parents: how many brides and youthful lovers have been one day in the bloom of health and hope, and the next a prey for worms and the decay of the tomb! Of what materials was I made, that I could thus resist so many shocks, which, like the turning of the wheel,[7] continually renewed the torture.

But I was doomed to live; and, in two months, found myself as awaking from a dream, in a prison, stretched on a wretched bed, surrounded by gaolers, turnkeys, bolts, and all the miserable apparatus of a dungeon. It was morning, I remember, when I thus awoke to understanding: I had forgotten the particulars of what had happened, and only felt as if some great misfortune had suddenly overwhelmed me; but when I looked around, and saw the barred windows, and the squalidness of the room in which I was, all flashed across my memory, and I groaned bitterly.

This sound disturbed an old woman who was sleeping in a chair beside me. She was a hired nurse, the wife of one of the turnkeys, and her countenance expressed all those bad qualities which often characterize that class. The lines of her face were hard and rude, like that of persons accustomed to see without sympathizing in sights of misery. Her tone expressed her entire indifference; she addressed me in English, and the voice struck me as one that I had heard during my sufferings:

"Are you better now, Sir?" said she.

I replied in the same language, with a feeble voice, "I believe I am; but if it be all true, if indeed I did not dream, I am sorry that I am still alive to feel this misery and horror."

"For that matter," replied the old woman, "if you mean about the gentleman you murdered, I believe that it were better for you if you were dead, for I fancy it will go hard with you; but you will be hung when the next sessions[8] come on. However, that's none of my business, I am sent to nurse you, and get you well; I do my duty with a safe conscience, it were well if every body did the same."

I turned with loathing from the woman who could utter so unfeeling a speech to a person just saved, on the very edge of death; but I felt languid, and unable to reflect on all that

An Irish petty sessions court of the day.

had passed. The whole series of my life appeared to me as a dream; I sometimes doubted if indeed it were all true, for it never presented itself to my mind with the force of reality.

As the images that floated before me became more distinct, I grew feverish; a darkness pressed around me; no one was near me who soothed me with the gentle voice of love; no dear hand supported me. The physician came and prescribed medicines, and the old woman prepared them for me; but utter carelessness was visible in the first, and the expression of brutality was strongly marked in the visage of the second. Who could be interested in the fate of a murderer, but the hangman who would gain his fee?

These were my first reflections; but I soon learned that Mr. Kirwin had shewn me extreme kindness. He had caused the best room in the prison to be prepared for me (wretched indeed was the best); and it was he who had provided a physician and a nurse. It is true, he seldom came to see me; for, although he ardently desired to relieve the sufferings of every human creature, he did not wish to be present at the agonies and miserable ravings of a murderer. He came, therefore, sometimes to see that I was not neglected; but his visits were short, and at long intervals.

One day, when I was gradually recovering, I was seated

9. In the 1831 edition, the balance of the sentence is revised to "than desire to remain in a world which to me was replete with wretchedness."

10. If, as is clear from this statement, Kirwin was certain that exculpatory evidence can "easily be brought," why would he avoid Victor, who concluded that he "did not wish to be present at the agonies and miserable ravings of a murderer"?

11. This reminds us of the tantalizing questions raised by Clerval's murder: Where was he killed? Why did the creature bring Clerval's corpse to a small town in Ireland? The creature certainly had no way of knowing that Victor would beach his craft here, and Clerval could not have been anywhere near the town—or Ireland, for that matter, for he had written to Victor asking him to meet up in Perth. Furthermore, the body was not yet cold when discovered. This suggests that the creature actually took Clerval prisoner and transported him *while yet alive* to this town, killing him either in the boat in which they traveled or immediately on taking him ashore. All of this occurred in the short interval after the creature departed from Victor's island laboratory. No explanation for these conundrums is put forward by the creature or Victor.

12. In the 1831 edition, the preceding portion of this sentence is replaced with the following: "Immediately upon your being taken ill, all the papers that were on your person were brought me, and I examined them."

in a chair, my eyes half open, and my cheeks livid like those in death, I was overcome by gloom and misery, and often reflected I had better seek death[9] than remain miserably pent up only to be let loose in a world replete with wretchedness. At one time I considered whether I should not declare myself guilty, and suffer the penalty of the law, less innocent than poor Justine had been. Such were my thoughts, when the door of my apartment was opened, and Mr. Kirwin entered. His countenance expressed sympathy and compassion; he drew a chair close to mine, and addressed me in French—

"I fear that this place is very shocking to you; can I do any thing to make you more comfortable?"

"I thank you; but all that you mention is nothing to me: on the whole earth there is no comfort which I am capable of receiving."

"I know that the sympathy of a stranger can be but of little relief to one borne down as you are by so strange a misfortune. But you will, I hope, soon quit this melancholy abode; for, doubtless, evidence can easily be brought to free you from the criminal charge."[10]

"That is my least concern: I am, by a course of strange events, become the most miserable of mortals. Persecuted and tortured as I am and have been, can death be any evil to me?"

"Nothing indeed could be more unfortunate and agonizing than the strange chances that have lately occurred. You were thrown, by some surprising accident, on this shore, renowned for its hospitality: seized immediately, and charged with murder. The first sight that was presented to your eyes was the body of your friend, murdered in so unaccountable a manner, and placed, as it were, by some fiend across your path."[11]

As Mr. Kirwin said this, notwithstanding the agitation I endured on this retrospect of my sufferings, I also felt considerable surprise at the knowledge he seemed to possess concerning me. I suppose some astonishment was exhibited in my countenance; for Mr. Kirwin hastened to say—

"It was not until a day or two after your illness that I thought of examining your dress,[12] that I might discover some trace by which I could send to your relations an account of your misfortune and illness. I found several letters, and, among others, one which I discovered from its commencement to be from your father. I instantly wrote to Geneva: nearly two months have elapsed since the departure of my letter.[13]—But you are ill; even now you tremble: you are unfit for agitation of any kind."

"This suspense is a thousand times worse than the most horrible event: tell me what new scene of death has been acted, and whose murder I am now to lament."

"Your family is perfectly well," said Mr. Kirwin, with gentleness; "and some one, a friend, is come to visit you."

I know not by what chain of thought the idea presented itself, but it instantly darted into my mind that the murderer had come to mock at my misery, and taunt me with the death of Clerval, as a new incitement for me to comply with his hellish desires. I put my hand before my eyes, and cried out in agony—

"Oh! take him away! I cannot see him; for God's sake, do not let him enter!"

Mr. Kirwin regarded me with a troubled countenance. He could not help regarding my exclamation as a presumption of my guilt, and said, in rather a severe tone—

"I should have thought, young man, that the presence of your father would have been welcome, instead of inspiring such violent repugnance."

"My father!" cried I, while every feature and every muscle was relaxed from anguish to pleasure. "Is my father, indeed, come? How kind, how very kind. But where is he, why does he not hasten to me?"

My change of manner surprised and pleased the magistrate; perhaps he thought that my former exclamation was a momentary return of delirium, and now he instantly resumed his former benevolence. He rose, and quitted the room with my nurse, and in a moment my father entered it.

Nothing, at this moment, could have given me greater pleasure than the arrival of my father. I stretched out my hand to him, and cried—

"Are you then safe—and Elizabeth—and Ernest?"

13. This scene, therefore, occurs at most a few weeks after Victor's recovery, probably in November or early December 1796.

14. Bringing the likely date of the events to mid-December 1796 and the season of the winter assizes. However, see note 10, Volume III, Chapter V, below.

Reunion with father

My father calmed me with assurances of their welfare, and endeavoured, by dwelling on these subjects so interesting to my heart, to raise my desponding spirits; but he soon felt that a prison cannot be the abode of cheerfulness. "What a place is this that you inhabit, my son!" said he, looking mournfully at the barred windows, and wretched appearance of the room. "You travelled to seek happiness, but a fatality seems to pursue you. And poor Clerval—"

The name of my unfortunate and murdered friend was an agitation too great to be endured in my weak state; I shed tears.

"Alas! yes, my father," replied I; "some destiny of the most horrible kind hangs over me, and I must live to fulfil it, or surely I should have died on the coffin of Henry."

We were not allowed to converse for any length of time, for the precarious state of my health rendered every precaution necessary that could insure tranquillity. Mr. Kirwin came in, and insisted that my strength should not be exhausted by too much exertion. But the appearance of my father was to me like that of my good angel, and I gradually recovered my health.

As my sickness quitted me, I was absorbed by a gloomy and black melancholy, that nothing could dissipate. The image of Clerval was for ever before me, ghastly and murdered. More than once the agitation into which these reflections threw me made my friends dread a dangerous relapse. Alas! why did they preserve so miserable and detested a life? It was surely that I might fulfil my destiny, which is now drawing to a close. Soon, oh, very soon, will death extinguish these throbbings, and relieve me from the mighty weight of anguish that bears me to the dust; and, in executing the award of justice, I shall also sink to rest. Then the appearance of death was distant, although the wish was ever present to my thoughts; and I often sat for hours motionless and speechless, wishing for some mighty revolution that might bury me and my destroyer in its ruins.

The season of the assizes approached. I had already been three months in prison;[14] and although I was still weak, and in continual danger of a relapse, I was obliged to travel nearly

An English courtroom of the day (*Bow Street Office* by Thomas Rowlandson, 1808).

15. The "grand jury" and the "petty jury" were bodies empaneled by the king (and selected by local officials to consider whether the evidence merited that alleged criminals be brought to trial. The grand jury was abolished in Ireland in 1924. Ireland's relationship with England was changing at the time of *Frankenstein*; in 1801, in the wake of the so-called United Irishmen Rebellion against English rule, the Irish Parliament was abolished, and Ireland became part of the United Kingdom of England and Ireland. "Home rule" was a contentious subject between England and Ireland for more than a century thereafter, and not until 1914 was that status granted by England. In 1922, most of Ireland seceded from the UK and formed the Irish Free State, changing its name to Ireland in 1937. Thereafter, only Northern Ireland remained part of the United Kingdom.

16. Probably just after the new year in 1797.

17. The word "permitted" replaces "allowed" in the 1831 edition.

[handwritten note:] Kirwin and Franky Sr. hooked on innocence

a hundred miles to the county-town, where the court was held. Mr. Kirwin charged himself with every care of collecting witnesses, and arranging my defence. I was spared the disgrace of appearing publicly as a criminal, as the case was not brought before the court that decides on life and death. The grand jury[15] rejected the bill, on its being proved that I was on the Orkney Islands at the hour the body of my friend was found, and a fortnight after my removal I was liberated from prison.[16]

My father was enraptured on finding me freed from the vexations of a criminal charge, that I was again allowed[17] to breathe the fresh atmosphere, and allowed to return to my native country. I did not participate in these feelings; for to me the walls of a dungeon or a palace were alike hateful. The cup of life was poisoned for ever; and although the sun shone upon me, as upon the happy and gay of heart, I saw around me nothing but a dense and frightful darkness, penetrated by no light but the glimmer of two eyes that glared upon me. Sometimes they were the expressive eyes of Henry, languishing in death, the dark orbs nearly covered by the lids, and the long black lashes that fringed them; sometimes it was the

18. Homesickness (Fr.). Chris Lambert, writing for *Harvard Magazine* in 2001, explains, "In 1688 a Swiss doctor, Johannes Hofer, identified a new medical syndrome, nostalgia: 'the sad mood originating from the desire for return to one's native land.' Various displaced Swiss of the seventeenth century suffered from it—students from the Republic of Berne studying in Basel; domestics working in France and Germany; soldiers fighting abroad. The nostalgia syndrome removed people from present reality. The afflicted took on a lifeless and haggard countenance, became indifferent to their surroundings, confused past and present, and even hallucinated voices and ghosts." The term "nostalgia" was still employed by doctors treating soldiers during the Civil War. In World War I, a theory was advanced th[...] by a reactio[...] the diagnos[...] (See Charle[...] to the Stud[...] Account of T[...] ory, Vision, [...] into the Duc[...] Hospital, Le [...][The Lancet, February 13, 1915, 316–20]. Myers was a medical doctor and a captain of the Royal Army Medical Corps.) The designation "posttraumatic stress disorder" was adopted in the third edition of the American Psychiatric Association's *Diagnostic and Statistical Manual of Mental Disorders* (DSM-III), published in 1980. See note 22, Volume III, Chapter II, above.

[handwritten annotation:] Agrees with Man (he has bad conscience)

19. This paragraph and the succeeding paragraph are revised in the 1831 edition as follows:

Yet one duty remained to me, the recollection of which finally triumphed over my selfish despair. It was necessary that I should return without delay to Geneva, there to watch over

watery clouded eyes of the monster, as I first saw them in my chamber at Ingolstadt.

My father tried to awaken in me the feelings of affection. He talked of Geneva, which I should soon visit—of Elizabeth, and Ernest; but these words only drew deep groans from me. Sometimes, indeed, I felt a wish for happiness; and thought, with melancholy delight, of my beloved cousin; or longed, with a devouring *maladie du pays*,[18] to see once more the blue lake and rapid Rhone, that had been so dear to me in early childhood: but my general state of feeling was a torpor, in which a prison was as welcome a residence as the divinest scene in nature; and these fits were seldom interrupted, but by paroxysms of anguish and despair. At these moments I often endeavoured to put an end to the existence I loathed; and it required unceasing attendance and vigilance to restrain me from committing some dreadful act of violence.

I remember, as I quitted the prison, I heard one of the men say, "He may be innocent of the murder, but he has certainly a bad conscience." These words struck me. A bad conscience! yes, surely I had one. William, Justine, and Clerval, had died through my infernal machinations; "And whose death," cried I, "is to finish the tragedy? Ah! my father, do not remain in this wretched country; take me where I may forget myself, my existence, and all the world."[19]

My father easily acceded to my desire; and, after having taken leave of Mr. Kirwin, we hastened to Dublin. I felt as if I was relieved from a heavy weight, when the packet sailed with a fair wind from Ireland, and I had quitted for ever the country which had been to me the scene of so much misery.[20]

It was midnight. My father slept in the cabin; and[21] I lay on the deck, looking at the stars, and listening to the dashing of the waves. I hailed the darkness that shut Ireland from my sight, and my pulse beat with a feverish joy, when I reflected that I should soon see Geneva. The past appeared to me in the light of a frightful dream; yet the vessel in which I was, the wind that blew me from the detested shore of Ireland, and the sea which surrounded me, told me too forcibly that I was deceived by no vision, and that Clerval, my friend and dearest companion, had fallen a victim to me and the monster of my creation. I repassed, in my memory, my whole life; my quiet happiness while residing with my family in Geneva, the death of my mother, and my departure for Ingolstadt. I remembered shuddering at the mad enthusiasm that hurried me on to the creation of my hideous enemy, and I called to mind the night during which he first lived. I was unable to pursue the train of thought; a thousand feelings pressed upon me, and I wept bitterly.

Ever since my recovery from the fever I had been in the custom of taking every night a small quantity of laudanum;[22] for it was by means of this drug only that I was enabled to gain the rest necessary for the preservation of life. Oppressed by the recollection of my various misfortunes, I now took a double dose,[23] and soon slept profoundly. But sleep did not afford me respite from thought and misery; my dreams presented a thousand objects that scared me. Towards morning I was possessed by a kind of night-mare; I felt the fiend's grasp in my neck, and could not free myself from it; groans and cries rung in my ears. My father, who was watching over me, perceiving my restlessness, awoke me,[24] and pointed to the port of Holyhead,[25] which we were now entering.

the lives of those I so fondly loved and to lie in wait for the murderer, that if any chance led me to the place of his concealment, or if he dared again to blast me by his presence, I might, with unfailing aim, put an end to the existence of the monstrous image which I had endued with the mockery of a soul still more monstrous. My father still desired to delay our departure, fearful that I could not sustain the fatigues of a journey, for I was a shattered wreck—the shadow of a human being. My strength was gone. I was a mere skeleton, and fever night and day preyed upon my wasted frame. Still, as I urged our leaving Ireland with such inquietude and impatience, my father thought it best to yield. We took our passage on board a vessel bound for Havre-de-Grace and sailed with a fair wind from the Irish shores.

This passage contains the notion that Victor endowed the creature with a soul. The creature has mentioned his own soul, though perhaps metaphorically, in earlier declamations (see, for example, note 13, Volume II, Chapter II, above), but in the 1831 edition, we learn that the soul neither was bestowed by a divine spirit nor arose out of inanimate body parts.

Victor now acts less out of a desire to leave Ireland and more to take up his moral responsibility to protect his family.

20. We never learn the name of the Irish town in which Victor was initially imprisoned. It is well over 300 nautical miles (556 km) from the closest of the Orkney Islands (more from the "remotest") to the shores of Ireland, well beyond a one-day sail in a skiff. See note 26, Volume III, Chapter II, above, for another suggestion.

21. The preceding part of this sentence does not appear in the 1831 edition.

22. Laudanum, a tincture of opium, was widely used as a sedative and was commonly kept in many households.

Prior to the twentieth century, physicians had little understanding of the physical or psychological dangers presented by depressants and opiates regularly consumed and essentially self-prescribed; it was believed that the use of drugs such as opium, morphine, and cocaine could be beneficial. For example, according to the third edition of the *Encyclopædia Britannica*:

> Opium at present is in great esteem, and is one of the most valuable of all the simple medicines. In its effects on the animal system, it is the most extraordinary substance in nature. It touches the nerves as it were by magic and irresistible power, and steeps the senses in forgetfulness; even in opposition to the determined will of the philosopher or physiologist, apprised of its narcotic effect. . . . Opium is the most sovereign remedy in the materia medica, for easing pain and procuring sleep, and also the most certain antispasmodic yet known; but, like other powerful medicines, becomes highly noxious to the human constitution, and even mortal, when improperly administered.

Mrs. Beeton's Book of Household Management (1861), in its advice regarding childhood diseases, prescribes laudanum as part of an emollient for thrush and part of an emetic for "hooping-cough" and lists powdered opium and laudanum as part of a well-stocked home medicine cabinet. In fact, laudanum was much abused by mothers who did straw-plaiting, lacework, and other home-based piecework to tranquilize their infants.

The 1888 *Encyclopædia Britannica* scoffed at any notion that smoking opium might be considered dangerous, comparing the smoking of opium—which enabled smokers "to undergo great fatigue and to go for a considerable time with little or no food"—to moderate alcohol or tobacco consumption. Ultimately, "[w]hen carried to excess it becomes an inveterate habit; but this happens chiefly in individuals of weak will-power, who would just as easily become the victims of intoxicating drinks, and who are practically moral imbeciles, also addicted to other forms of depravity." Similarly, the third edition of the *Britannica* commented that excessive use (and especially excessive use by children, dosed by "ignorant women and mercenary nurses") led to languor and dejection and rendered children "stupid, inactive, and rickety."

The British government took steps to curb opium use in the late 1800s and early 1900s, but by then the genie was well out of the bottle. Although opium was commonly viewed as a symbol of Eastern licentiousness and corruption, the lure of its calming, euphoric properties claimed some famous literary figures, including

Advertisement from 1910 Sears, Roebuck catalog.

Byron and Percy Shelley, both heavy laudanum users; Charles Baudelaire; Elizabeth Barrett Browning; Samuel Taylor Coleridge, whose "Kubla Khan," written in 1797, was inspired by an opium-induced dream; Thomas De Quincey, whose *Confessions of an English Opium-Eater* (1821) explored his addiction in excruciating detail; John Keats; and novelist Wilkie Collins (*The Moonstone, The Woman in White*). Critics have speculated that Lewis Carroll's *Alice's Adventures in Wonderland* (1865) was written as a result of (or at least referred to) opium use.

23. This phrase is revised in the 1831 edition to read, "I now swallowed double my usual quantity."

24. The balance of the sentence is omitted in the 1831 edition, and the following replaces it, lending Victor's recollections a more fatalistic, almost dreamlike tone: "the dashing waves were around, the cloudy sky above, the fiend was not here: a sense of security, a feeling that a truce was established between the present hour and the irresistible, disastrous future imparted to me a kind of calm forgetfulness, of which the human mind is by its structure peculiarly susceptible."

25. Holyhead, on the island of Anglesey, is a port in northern Wales and today serves as a terminus for ferries to Dublin. From there, Victor plans to travel across land to Portsmouth, as will be seen. Why the Frankensteins traveled in stages is unclear; by the end of the eighteenth century, Dublin had a substantial export trade with Europe, and it would certainly have been possible to arrange transport on a ship bound directly for Le Havre, Rotterdam, or even Bordeaux.

CHAPTER V. [1]

1. Chapter 22 in the 1831 edition.

2. This paragraph and the following two sentences are replaced in the 1831 edition with the following, wherein Victor goes far beyond grief over Clerval, expressing moral sentiments regarding his own conduct:

> The voyage came to an end. We landed, and proceeded to Paris. I soon found that I had overtaxed my strength and that I must repose before I could continue my journey. My father's care and attentions were indefatigable, but he did not know the origin of my sufferings and sought erroneous methods to remedy the incurable ill. He wished me to seek amusement in society. I abhorred the face of man. Oh, not abhorred! They were my brethren, my fellow beings, and I felt attracted even ~~to them, as~~ ~~creatures~~ ~~are and~~ ~~inn I felt~~ that I ~~their inter~~ ~~ourse.~~ ~~an enemy~~ mong ~~those joy it was to shed their~~ ~~blood and to revel in their~~ ~~roans.~~ ~~How they would each and all~~ abhor

WE[2] HAD RESOLVED not to go to London, but to cross the country to Portsmouth, and thence to embark for Havre.[3] I preferred this plan principally because I dreaded to see again those places in which I had enjoyed a few moments of tranquillity with my beloved Clerval. I thought with horror of seeing again those persons whom we had been accustomed to visit together, and who might make inquiries concerning an event, the very remembrance of which made me again feel the pang I endured when I gazed on his lifeless form in the inn at ————.[4]

As for my father, his desires and exertions were bounded to the again[5] seeing me restored to health and peace of mind. His tenderness and attentions were unremitting; my grief and gloom was obstinate, but he would not despair. Sometimes he thought that I felt deeply the degradation of being obliged to answer a charge of murder, and he endeavoured to prove to me the futility of pride.

"Alas! my father," said I, "how little do you know me. Human beings, their feelings and passions, would indeed be degraded, if such a wretch as I felt pride. Justine, poor unhappy Justine, was as innocent as I, and she suffered the same charge; she died for it; and I am the cause of this—I murdered her. William, Justine, and Henry—they all died by my hands."

Goes into deep blame on himself

My father had often, during my imprisonment, heard me make the same assertion; when I thus accused myself, he sometimes seemed to desire an explanation, and at others he appeared to consider it as caused by[6] delirium, and that, during my illness, some idea of this kind had presented itself to my imagination, the remembrance of which I preserved in my convalescence. I avoided explanation, and maintained a continual silence concerning the wretch I had created.[7] I had a feeling that I should be supposed mad, and this for ever chained my tongue, when I would have given the whole world to have confided the fatal secret.

Upon this occasion my father said, with an expression of unbounded wonder, "What do you mean, Victor? are you mad? My dear son, I entreat you never to make such an assertion again."

"I am not mad," I cried energetically; "the sun and the heavens, who have viewed my operations, can bear witness of my truth. I am the assassin of those most innocent victims; they died by my machinations. A thousand times would I have shed my own blood, drop by drop, to have saved their lives; but I could not, my father, indeed I could not sacrifice the whole human race."[8]

The conclusion of this speech convinced my father that my ideas were deranged, and he instantly changed the subject of our conversation, and endeavoured to alter the course of my thoughts. He wished as much as possible to obliterate the memory of the scenes that had taken place in Ireland, and never alluded to them, or suffered me to speak of my misfortunes.

As time passed away I became more calm: misery had her dwelling in my heart, but I no longer talked in the same incoherent manner of my own crimes; sufficient for me was the consciousness of them. By the utmost self-violence, I curbed the imperious voice of wretchedness, which sometimes desired to declare itself to the whole world; and my manners were calmer and more composed than they had ever been since my journey to[9] the sea of ice.

We arrived at Havre on the 8th of May,[10] and instantly proceeded to Paris, where my father had some business

me and hunt me from the world did they know my unhallowed acts and the crimes which had their source in me!

My father yielded at length to my desire to avoid society and strove by various arguments to banish my despair.

3. Le Havre (or Havre) was then, and remains, the second largest port in France; at the time of the Frankensteins' visit, it was surpassed only by Nantes, and today it ranks behind only Marseilles. Its proximity to England made it highly strategic during the Napoleonic Wars, soon to erupt.

4. Victor's concealment of the place of his imprisonment further suggests some obfuscation regarding the location of his "Scottish" laboratory. Why else leave the village nameless? Certainly he was treated kindly by Mr. Kirwin.

5. [*Sic*].

Frankx Sr. notices Victor isn't right

[...]ed [...] the 1831 edition [...] offspring [...] of."

[...] ext two sentences [...] [...]ised [...] substantially revised in the [...] 1831 edition to read as follows, seem[...] [...]ly to suggest that Victor maintained his guilty silence out of [...]dness rather than shame:

I avoided explanation, and maintained a continual silence concerning the wretch I had created. I had a persuasion that I should be supposed mad, and this in itself would forever have chained my tongue. But, besides, I could not bring myself to disclose a secret which would fill my hearer with consternation and make fear and unnatural horror the inmates of his breast. I checked, therefore, my impatient thirst for sympathy and was silent when I would have given the world to have confided the fatal secret.

Yet, still, words like those I have recorded would burst uncontrollably from me. I could offer no explanation of them, but their truth in part relieved the burden of my mysterious woe. Upon this occasion my father said, with an expression of unbounded wonder, "My dearest Victor? what infatuation is this?"

8. The Thomas Text continues,

What could induce me to talk thus incoherently of the dreadful subject that I dared not explain?—In truth, it was insanity, not of the understanding but of the heart, which ~~produced a state of sickness~~ caused me always to think of one thing, of one sentiment, and ~~that~~ thus there would at times escape to my lips, as a half stifled ~~groan~~ sigh may; though else unseen & unheard, just move~~s~~ the flame that surrounds the marty[r] at the stake. But though he sigh, he will not recant, & though I more weak, gave vent to my pent up thoughts in words such as these, yet I shrunk unalterably from any thing that should reveal the existence of my enemy.

9. The Thomas Text adds, "Montanvert and[.]"

10. Four months have elapsed since Victor's acquittal. This is an excessive amount of time to have spent traveling from Ireland; the voyage from Portsmouth to Le Havre (a distance of about 110 miles [177 km]) could not have been longer than one day. Victor's recollection of the term of his confinement may well be distorted, notwithstanding the corroborative statements of Mr. Kirwin—he was feverish,

which detained us a few weeks. In this city,[11] I received the following letter from Elizabeth:—

"*To* VICTOR FRANKENSTEIN.[12]

"MY DEAREST FRIEND,

"It gave me the greatest pleasure to receive a letter from my uncle dated at Paris; you are no longer at a formidable distance, and I may hope to see you in less than a fortnight. My poor cousin, how much you must have suffered! I expect to see you looking even more ill than when you quitted Geneva. This winter has been passed most miserably, tortured as I have been by anxious suspense; yet I hope to see peace in your countenance, and to find that your heart is not totally devoid of comfort and tranquillity.

"Yet I fear that the same feelings now exist that made you so miserable a year ago, even perhaps augmented by time. I would not disturb you at this period, when so many misfortunes weigh upon you; but a conversation that I had with my uncle previous to his departure renders some explanation necessary before we meet.

"Explanation! you may possibly say; what can Elizabeth have to explain? If you really say this, my questions are answered,[13] and I have no more to do than to sign myself your affectionate cousin. But you are distant from me, and it is possible that you may dread, and yet be pleased with this explanation; and, in a probability of this being the case, I dare not any longer postpone writing what, during your absence, I have often wished to express to you, but have never had the courage to begin.

"You well know, Victor, that our union had been the favourite plan of your parents ever since our infancy. We were told this when young, and taught to look forward to it as an event that would certainly take place. We were affectionate playfellows during childhood, and, I believe, dear and valued friends to one another as we grew older. But as brother and sister often entertain a lively affection towards each other, without desiring a more intimate union, may not such also be our case? Tell me, dearest Victor. Answer me, I conjure you, by our mutual happiness, with simple truth— Do you not love another?

"You have travelled; you have spent several years of your life at Ingolstadt; and I confess to you, my friend, that when I saw you last autumn so unhappy, flying to solitude, from the society of every creature, I could not help supposing that you might regret our connexion, and believe yourself bound in honour to fulfil the wishes of your parents, although they opposed themselves to your inclinations. But this is false reasoning. I confess to you, my cousin,[14] that I love you, and that in my airy dreams of futurity you have been my constant friend and companion. But it is your happiness I desire as well as my own, when I declare to you, that our marriage would render me eternally miserable, unless it were the dictate of your own free choice. Even now I weep to think, that, borne down as you are by the cruelest misfortunes, you may stifle, by the word honour, all hope of that love and happiness which would alone restore you to yourself. I, who have so interested[15] an affection for you, may increase your miseries ten-fold, by being an obstacle to your wishes. Ah, Victor, be assured that your cousin and playmate has too sincere a love for you not to be made miserable by this supposition. Be happy, my friend; and if you obey me in this one request, remain satisfied that nothing on earth will have the power to interrupt my tranquillity.

"Do not let this letter disturb you; do not answer it tomorrow, or the next day, or even until you come, if it will give you pain. My uncle will send me news of your health; and if I see but one smile on your lips when we meet, occasioned by this or any other exertion of mine, I shall need no other happiness.

"ELIZABETH LAVENZA.
"Geneva, May 18th, 17—."[16]

This letter revived in my memory what I had before forgotten, the threat of the fiend—"*I will be with you on your wedding-night!*"[17] Such was my sentence, and on that night would the daemon employ every art to destroy me, and tear

after all, and he retells Walton their conversation more than two years after it took place. The arrival in Paris is set on such a definite date that it is the Dublin departure date that must be doubted. In the Draft, the date was originally February 8, in line with a trial at the winter assizes.

11. This phrase and the preceding sentence are deleted in the 1831 edition, and the following phrase replaces them: "A few days before we left Paris on our way to Switzerland,"

12. This address is omitted in the 1831 edition.

13. In the 1831 edition, the balance of the sentence reads as follows: "and all my doubts satisfied."

Elizabeth asks if Victor wants to go through with marriage

14. [...aced with ...rected to ...on.

15. [...s in the Draft

16. The warning is in all capitals in the 1831 edition.

18. The phrase "to be with me on my wedding-night" is in all capitals in the 1831 edition.

me from the glimpse of happiness which promised partly to console my sufferings. On that night he had determined to consummate his crimes by my death. Well, be it so; a deadly struggle would then assuredly take place, in which if he was victorious, I should be at peace, and his power over me be at an end. If he were vanquished, I should be a free man. Alas! what freedom? such as the peasant enjoys when his family have been massacred before his eyes, his cottage burnt, his lands laid waste, and he is turned adrift, homeless, penny-less, and alone, but free. Such would be my liberty, except that in my Elizabeth I possessed a treasure; alas! balanced by those horrors of remorse and guilt, which would pursue me until death.

Sweet and beloved Elizabeth! I read and re-read her letter, and some softened feelings stole into my heart, and dared to whisper paradisaical dreams of love and joy; but the apple was already eaten, and the angel's arm bared to drive me from all hope. Yet I would die to make her happy. If the mon-ster executed his threat, death was inevitable; yet, again, I considered whether my marriage would hasten my fate. My destruction might indeed arrive a few months sooner; but if my torturer should suspect that I postponed it, influenced by his menaces, he would surely find other, and perhaps more dreadful means of revenge. He had vowed *to be with me on my wedding-night*,[18] yet he did not consider that threat as bind-ing him to peace in the mean time; for, as if to shew me that he was not yet satiated with blood, he had murdered Clerval immediately after the enunciation of his threats. I resolved, therefore, that if my immediate union with my cousin would conduce either to her's or my father's happiness, my adver-sary's designs against my life should not retard it a single hour.

In this state of mind I wrote to Elizabeth. My letter was calm and affectionate. "I fear, my beloved girl," I said, "little happiness remains for us on earth; yet all that I may one day enjoy is concentered in you. Chase away your idle fears; to you alone do I consecrate my life, and my endeavours for contentment. I have one secret, Elizabeth, a dreadful one; when revealed to you, it will chill your frame with horror,

Remembers what the creature said.

Sweet letter

and then, far from being surprised at my misery, you will only wonder that I survive what I have endured. I will confide this tale of misery and terror to you the day after our marriage shall take place; for, my sweet cousin, there must be perfect confidence between us. But until then, I conjure you, do not mention or allude to it. This I most earnestly entreat, and I know you will comply."

In about a week after the arrival of Elizabeth's letter, we returned to Geneva.[19] My cousin[20] welcomed me with warm affection; yet tears were in her eyes, as she beheld my emaciated frame and feverish cheeks. I saw a change in her also. She was thinner, and had lost much of that heavenly vivacity that had before charmed me; but her gentleness, and soft looks of compassion, made her a more fit companion for one blasted and miserable as I was.

The tranquillity which I now enjoyed did not endure. Memory brought madness with it; and when I thought on what had passed, a real insanity possessed me; sometimes I was furious, and burnt with rage, sometimes low and despondent. I neither spoke or looked, but sat motionless, bewildered by the multitude of miseries that overcame me.

Elizabeth alone had the power to draw me from these fits; her gentle voice would soothe me when transported by passion, and inspire me with human feelings when sunk in torpor. She wept with me, and for me. When reason returned, she would remonstrate, and endeavour to inspire me with resignation. Ah! it is well for the unfortunate to be resigned, but for the guilty there is no peace. The agonies of remorse poison the luxury there is otherwise sometimes found in indulging the excess of grief.

Soon after my arrival my father spoke of my immediate marriage with my cousin.[21] I remained silent.

"Have you, then, some other attachment?"

"None on earth. I love Elizabeth, and look forward to our union with delight. Let the day therefore be fixed; and on it I will consecrate myself, in life or death, to the happiness of my cousin."

"My dear Victor, do not speak thus. Heavy misfortunes have befallen us; but let us only cling closer to what remains,

19. This is now late May or early June 1797.

20. "My cousin" is replaced with "The sweet girl" in the 1831 edition.

21. "Elizabeth" is substituted for "my cousin" in the 1831 edition.

22. The warning is again in all capitals in the 1831 edition.

Foreshadowing repetition to the death of Elizabeth

and transfer our love for those whom we have lost to those who yet live. Our circle will be small, but bound close by the ties of affection and mutual misfortune. And when time shall have softened your despair, new and dear objects of care will be born to replace those of whom we have been so cruelly deprived."

Such were the lessons of my father. But to me the remembrance of the threat returned: nor can you wonder, that, omnipotent as the fiend had yet been in his deeds of blood, I should almost regard him as invincible; and that when he had pronounced the words, *"I shall be with you on your wedding-night,"*[22] I should regard the threatened fate as unavoidable. But death was no evil to me, if the loss of Elizabeth were balanced with it; and I therefore, with a contented and even cheerful countenance, agreed with my father, that if my cousin would consent, the ceremony should take place in ten days, and thus put, as I imagined, the seal to my fate.

Great God! if for one instant I had thought what might be the hellish intention of my fiendish adversary, I would rather have banished myself for ever from my native country, and wandered a friendless outcast over the earth, than have consented to this miserable marriage. But, as if possessed of magic powers, the monster had blinded me to his real intentions; and when I thought that I prepared only my own death, I hastened that of a far dearer victim.

As the period fixed for our marriage drew nearer, whether from cowardice or a prophetic feeling, I felt my heart sink within me. But I concealed my feelings by an appearance of hilarity, that brought smiles and joy to the countenance of my father, but hardly deceived the ever-watchful and nicer eye of Elizabeth. She looked forward to our union with placid contentment, not unmingled with a little fear, which past misfortunes had impressed, that what now appeared certain and tangible happiness, might soon dissipate into an airy dream, and leave no trace but deep and everlasting regret.

Preparations were made for the event; congratulatory visits were received; and all wore a smiling appearance. I shut up, as well as I could, in my own heart the anxiety that preyed there, and entered with seeming earnestness into the plans of my father, although they might only serve as the decorations of my tragedy. A house was purchased for us near Cologny,[23] by which we should enjoy the pleasures of the country, and yet be so near Geneva as to see my father every day; who would still reside within the walls, for the benefit of Ernest, that he might follow his studies at the schools.[24]

In the mean time I took every precaution to defend my person, in case the fiend should openly attack me. I carried pistols and a dagger constantly about me, and was ever on the watch to prevent artifice; and by these means gained a greater degree of tranquillity. Indeed, as the period approached, the threat appeared more as a delusion, not to be regarded as worthy to disturb my peace, while the happiness I hoped for in my marriage wore a greater appearance of certainty, as the day fixed for its solemnization drew nearer, and I heard it continually spoken of as an occurrence which no accident could possibly prevent.

Elizabeth seemed happy; my tranquil demeanour contributed greatly to calm her mind. But on the day that was to fulfil my wishes and my destiny, she was melancholy, and a presentiment of evil pervaded her; and perhaps also she thought of the dreadful secret, which I had promised to reveal to her the following day. My father was in the mean time overjoyed, and, in the bustle of preparation, only observed[25] in the melancholy of his niece the diffidence of a bride.

After the ceremony was performed, a large party assembled at my father's; but it was agreed that Elizabeth and I[26] should pass the afternoon and night at Evian,[27] and return to Cologny the next morning.[28] As the day was fair, and the wind favourable, we resolved to go by water.

Those were the last moments of my life during which I enjoyed the feeling of happiness. We passed rapidly along: the sun was hot, but we were sheltered from its rays by a kind of canopy, while we enjoyed the beauty of the scene, sometimes on one side of the lake, where we saw Mont Salêve, the pleasant banks of Montalêgre,[29] and at a distance, surmounting all, the beautiful Mont Blânc, and the assemblage of snowy mountains that in vain endeavour to emulate her; sometimes coasting the opposite banks, we saw the mighty

23. Cologny is a small suburb of Geneva, on the southeastern shore of the lake.

24. This sentence is replaced in the 1831 edition with the following, further evidence that Elizabeth is of good stock, not a mere peasant girl: "Through my father's exertions a part of the inheritance of Elizabeth had been restored to her by the Austrian government. A small possession on the shores of Como belonged to her. It was agreed that, immediately after our union, we should proceed to Villa Lavenza and spend our first days of happiness beside the beautiful lake near which it stood."

25. The word "observed" is revised to "recognized" in the 1831 edition.

26. In the 1831 edition, the balance of [this sen]tence are [sub]stituted: [by] water, [continu]ing our voyage on the following day. The day was fair, and the wind [favour]able, all [turned] on our [nuptial embarkation]."

27. Evian was a small resort town farther around the southern shore of the lake, about 28 miles (45 km) east of Geneva. At the time of Victor's nuptials, it was not known for its mineral waters, which were not analyzed until 1807, and it had not yet developed as a spa. However, by 1815, Percy Shelley wrote, in *Six Weeks' Tour*, "they have mineral waters here [by which he meant Evian, which they were then visiting], *eaux savonneuses* [soapy water], they call them" (116). Situated in the Haute-Savoie district, the town was under the rule of the despotic king of Sardinia, and Percy Shelley described the inhabitants as "more wretched, diseased, and poor than I ever recollect to have seen. The contrast [with the nearby Swiss citizens] . . . affords a powerful illustra-

tion of the blighting mischiefs of despotism, within the space of a few miles" (116).

28. The Thomas Text revises this to read, "Elizabeth and I should immediately depart for a small estate we possessed at Evian."

29. Montalègre is a small town in the Cologny district.

30. The Jura did not stop the French, whose army invaded Switzerland in 1798, establishing the Helvetic Republic.

The Thomas Text adds at the beginning of the next paragraph the following: "~~Why~~ Then gazing on the beloved face of Elizabeth on her graceful form and languid eyes, ~~of with~~ instead of feeling the exultation of a—lover—a husband—~~in~~ a sudden gush of tears blinded my sight, & as I turned away to hide the involuntary emotion fast drops fell in the wave below. Reason again awoke, and shaking off all unmanly—or more properly all natural thoughts of mischance, I smiled as[.]"

A photograph of the town of Evian-les-bains, as Evian is now known, ca. 1895.

Jura opposing its dark side to the ambition that would quit its native country, and an almost insurmountable barrier to the invader who should wish to enslave it.[30]

I took the hand of Elizabeth: "You are sorrowful, my love. Ah! if you knew what I have suffered, and what I may yet endure, you would endeavour to let me taste the quiet, and freedom from despair, that this one day at least permits me to enjoy."

"Be happy, my dear Victor," replied Elizabeth; "there is, I hope, nothing to distress you; and be assured that if a lively joy is not painted in my face, my heart is contented. Something whispers to me not to depend too much on the prospect that is opened before us; but I will not listen to such a sinister voice. Observe how fast we move along, and how the clouds which sometimes obscure, and sometimes rise above the dome of Mont Blânc, render this scene of beauty still more interesting. Look also at the innumerable fish that are swimming in the clear waters, where we can distinguish every pebble that lies at the bottom. What a divine day! how happy and serene all nature appears!"

Thus Elizabeth endeavoured to divert her thoughts and mine from all reflection upon melancholy subjects. But her temper was fluctuating; joy for a few instants shone in her eyes, but it continually gave place to distraction and reverie.

The sun sunk lower in the heavens; we passed the river Drance,[31] and observed its path through the chasms of the higher, and the glens of the lower hills. The Alps here come closer to the lake, and we approached the amphitheatre of mountains which forms its eastern boundary. The spire of Evian shone under the woods that surrounded it, and the range of mountain above mountain by which it was overhung.

The wind, which had hitherto carried us along with amazing rapidity, sunk at sunset to a light breeze; the soft air just ruffled the water, and caused a pleasant motion among the trees as we approached the shore, from which it wafted the most delightful scent of flowers and hay. The sun sunk beneath the horizon as we landed; and as I touched the shore, I felt those cares and fears revive, which soon were to clasp me, and cling to me for ever.

31. A small tributary of the Rhône, visited during the composition of *Six Weeks' Tour*: "As soon as we had passed the opposite promontory, we saw the river Drance, which descends from between a chasm in the mountains, and makes a plain near the lake, intersected by its divided streams. Thousands of *besolets*, beautiful water-birds, like sea-gulls, but smaller, with purple on their backs, take their station on the shallows, where its waters mingle with the lake" (114).

CHAPTER VI.[1]

1. Chapter 23 in the 1831 edition.

2. The Thomas Text deletes the balance of the sentence up to the phrase "and contemplated" and inserts the following:

> leaving the shore we sought the retreat of our house and garden. ~~but~~ Again as I entered the iron gates of the demesne, an ~~unres~~ unexplainable feeling bade me hold—yet Elizabeth unwarned, and fearless passed on, and I, again half ashamed—& for the first time dreading lest any unholy sight should meet her sense, any shadow of the fiend, should cross her, ~~I~~ hastily walked on, and passing my arm round her prayed with a feeling of bitter tenderness, that she might never suffer ill. Thus we entered the ~~ar~~ mansion—and still not [speaking for both our hearts were too] [...] over-

3. [...] ding" [...] is [...] e 1831 e[...]

IT WAS EIGHT o'clock when we landed;[2] we walked for a short time on the shore, enjoying the transitory light, and then retired to the inn, and contemplated the lovely scene of waters, woods, and mountains, obscured in darkness, yet still displaying their black outlines.

The wind, which had fallen in the south, now rose with great violence in the west. The moon had reached her summit in the heavens, and was beginning to descend; the clouds swept across it swifter than the flight of the vulture, and dimmed her rays, while the lake reflected the scene of the busy heavens, rendered still busier by the restless waves that were beginning to rise. Suddenly a heavy storm of rain descended.

I had been calm during the day; but so soon as night obscured the shapes of objects, a thousand fears arose in my mind. I was anxious and watchful, while my right hand grasped a pistol which was hidden in my bosom; every sound terrified me; but I resolved that I would sell my life dearly, and not relax the impending[3] conflict until my own life, or that of my adversary, were extinguished.

Elizabeth observed my agitation for some time in timid and fearful silence; at length she said,[4] "What is it that agitates you, my dear Victor? What is it you fear?"

Notices Victor's pain and feels empathetic for him throughout this time

"Oh! peace, peace, my love," replied I, "this night, and all will be safe: but this night is dreadful, very dreadful."

I passed an hour in this state of mind, when suddenly I reflected how dreadful[5] the combat which I momentarily expected would be to my wife, and I earnestly entreated her to retire, resolving not to join her until I had obtained some knowledge as to the situation of my enemy.

She left me, and I continued some time walking up and down the passages of the house, and inspecting every corner that might afford a retreat to my adversary.[6] But I discovered no trace of him, and was beginning to conjecture that some fortunate chance had intervened to prevent the execution of his menaces; when suddenly I heard a shrill and dreadful scream. It came from the room into which Elizabeth had retired. As I heard it, the whole truth rushed into my mind, my arms dropped, the motion of every muscle and fibre was suspended; I could feel the blood trickling in my veins, and tingling in the extremities of my limbs. This state lasted but for an instant; the scream was repeated, and I rushed into the room.

Great God! why did I not then expire! Why am I here to relate the destruction of the best hope, and the purest creature of earth. She was there, lifeless and inanimate, thrown across the bed, her head hanging down, and her pale and distorted features half covered by her hair.[7] Every where I turn I see the same figure—her bloodless arms and relaxed form flung by the murderer on its bridal bier. Could I behold this, and live? Alas! life is obstinate, and clings closest where it is most hated. For a moment only did I lose recollection; I fainted.[8]

When I recovered, I found myself surrounded by the people of the inn; their countenances expressed a breathless terror: but the horror of others appeared only as a mockery, a shadow of the feelings that oppressed me. I escaped from them to the room where lay the body of Elizabeth, my love, my wife, so lately living, so dear, so worthy. She had been moved from the posture in which I had first beheld her; and now, as she lay, her head upon her arm, and a handkerchief thrown across her face and neck, I might have supposed her

4. In place of the phrase "at length she said," the 1831 edition reads, "but there was something in my glance which communicated terror to her, and trembling, she asked,"[.]

5. The word "dreadful" is replaced by "fearful" in the 1831 edition.

6. Victor's abandonment of Elizabeth in pursuit of knowledge may be seen, notes Chris Baldick, in *In Frankenstein's Shadow: Myth, Monstrosity, and Nineteenth-Century Writing* (Oxford: Clarendon Press, 1990), as an "unusually condensed résumé of the action of the novel as a whole."

7. The scene is said by some to conjure Henry Fuseli's famous painting *The Nightmare* (1781). Fuseli (1741–1825) was Swiss but resided most of his life in England; he was a fixture in the circle of radical artists and thinkers that included Mary Shelley's parents, William Godwin and Mary Wollstonecraft Godwin. [...]ous rela[...] ollstone[...] and she [...]t as Wil[...]y Shelley [...]oes only [...]ainting, [...]overed" [...]al expectations of the effects of gravity. Veeder, in chapter 6, "The Women of Frankenstein," suggests that this is Mary Shelley's symbol of acceptance of the death of her stepsister Fanny Imlay, found with her hair around her face, and that Elizabeth's "relaxed" posture indicates her acceptance of death and her escape from male dominance.

8. In the 1831 edition, the narrator relates that he "fell senseless on the ground," not that he "fainted."

Victor's hope and Elizabeth die. [handwritten annotation]

The Nightmare, by Henry Fuseli (1781).

The creature attacks Elizabeth, in
Frankenstein (Universal Pictures, 1931).
The similarity to the Fuseli painting is
certainly no coincidence.

asleep. I rushed towards her, and embraced her with ardour; but the deathly languor and coldness of the limbs told me, that what I now held in my arms had ceased to be the Elizabeth whom I had loved and cherished. The murderous mark of the fiend's grasp was on her neck, and the breath had ceased to issue from her lips.

While I still hung over her in the agony of despair, I happened to look up. The windows of the room had before been darkened; and I felt a kind of panic on seeing the pale yellow light of the moon illuminate the chamber.[9] The shutters had been thrown back; and, with a sensation of horror not to be described, I saw at the open window a figure the most hideous and abhorred. A grin was on the face of the monster; he seemed to jeer, as with his fiendish finger he pointed towards the corpse of my wife. I rushed towards the window, and drawing a pistol from my bosom, shot;[10] but he eluded me, leaped from his station, and, running with the swiftness of lightning, plunged into the lake.

The report of the pistol brought a crowd into the room. I pointed to the spot where he had disappeared, and we followed the track with boats; nets were cast, but in vain. After passing several hours, we returned hopeless, most of my companions believing it to have been a form conjured by my fancy. After having landed, they proceeded to search the country, parties going in different directions among the woods and vines.

I did not accompany them;[11] I was exhausted: a film covered my eyes, and my skin was parched with the heat of fever. In this state I lay[12] on a bed, hardly conscious of what had happened; my eyes wandered round the room, as if to seek something that I had lost.

At length I remembered that my father would anxiously expect the return of Elizabeth and myself, and that I must return alone. This reflection brought tears into my eyes, and I wept for a long time;[13] but my thoughts rambled to various subjects, reflecting[14] on my misfortunes, and their cause. I was bewildered in a cloud of wonder and horror. The death of William, the execution of Justine, the murder of Clerval, and lastly of my wife; even at that moment I knew not that

9. Veeder, in *Mary Shelley and Franken-[stein]* ... himself and Mary ... wedding ... points out that the ... strong parallels to the ... I, Chap-ure pen- ... th occur ... in the yellow light ... both scenes, the creature grins and extends a hand. Veeder suggests that the parallel is deliberate, signifying that while Victor sought consummation of his male and female halves (androgyny), his female half being ... would not ... ath.

10. In the 1831 edition, Victor ... "fired" rather than "shot."

11. The preceding ... does not appear in the 1831 edition, which amends the ... passage to read as follows: ... attempted to accompany them and proceeded a short distance from the house, but my head whirled round, my steps were like those of a drunken man, I fell at last in a state of utter exhaustion." Thus Victor's failure to take an active part in the hunt becomes less reprehensible.

12. "Lay" is replaced with "was carried back and placed" in the 1831 edition.

13. The preceding portion of this sentence and the preceding sentence are deleted from the 1831 edition, and the following appears: "After an interval I arose, and as if by instinct, crawled into the room where the corpse of my beloved lay. There were women weeping around; I hung over it and joined my sad tears to theirs; all this time no distinct idea presented itself to my mind,"[.]

14. The word "confusedly" is inserted here in the 1831 edition.

15. The word is "now" in the Draft and there is no period preceding it.

16. "Elizabeth" is substituted for "niece" in the 1831 edition.

Important line → Victor loses hope

my only remaining friends were safe from the malignity of the fiend; my father even now might be writhing under his grasp, and Ernest might be dead at his feet. This idea made me shudder, and recalled me to action. I started up, and resolved to return to Geneva with all possible speed.

There were no horses to be procured, and I must return by the lake; but the wind was unfavourable, and the rain fell in torrents. However, it was hardly morning, and I might reasonably hope to arrive by night. I hired men to row, and took an oar myself, for I had always experienced relief from mental torment in bodily exercise. But the overflowing misery I now felt, and the excess of agitation that I endured, rendered me incapable of any exertion. I threw down the oar; and, leaning my head upon my hands, gave way to every gloomy idea that arose. If I looked up, I saw the scenes which were familiar to me in my happier time, and which I had contemplated but the day before in the company of her who was now but a shadow and a recollection. Tears streamed from my eyes. The rain had ceased for a moment, and I saw the fish play in the waters as they had done a few hours before; they had then been observed by Elizabeth. Nothing is so painful to the human mind as a great and sudden change. The sun might shine, or the clouds might lour; but nothing could appear to me as it had done the day before. A fiend had snatched from me every hope of future happiness: no creature had ever been so miserable as I was; so frightful an event is single in the history of man.

But why should I dwell upon the incidents that followed this last overwhelming event. Mine has been a tale of horrors; I have reached their acme, and what I must now relate can but be tedious to you. Know[15] that, one by one, my friends were snatched away; I was left desolate. My own strength is exhausted; and I must tell, in a few words, what remains of my hideous narration.

I arrived at Geneva. My father and Ernest yet lived; but the former sunk under the tidings that I bore. I see him now, excellent and venerable old man! his eyes wandered in vacancy, for they had lost their charm and their delight—his niece,[16] his more than daughter, whom he doated on with all that affection which a man feels, who, in the decline of life, having few affections, clings more earnestly to those that remain. Cursed, cursed be the fiend that brought misery on his grey hairs, and doomed him to waste in wretchedness! He could not live under the horrors that were accumulated around him;[17] an apoplectic fit was brought on, and in a few days he died in my arms.[18]

What then became of me? I know not; I lost sensation, and chains and darkness were the only objects that pressed upon me. Sometimes, indeed, I dreamt that I wandered in flowery meadows and pleasant vales with the friends of my youth; but awoke, and found myself in a dungeon. Melancholy followed, but by degrees I gained a clear conception of my miseries and situation, and was then released from my prison. For they had called me mad; and during many months,[19] as I understood, a solitary cell had been my habitation.[20]

But liberty had been a useless gift to me had I not, as I awakened to reason, at the same time awakened to revenge. As the memory of past misfortunes pressed upon me, I began to reflect on their cause—the monster whom I had created, the miserable daemon whom I had sent abroad into the world for my destruction. I was possessed by a maddening rage when I thought of him, and desired and ardently prayed that I might have him within my grasp to wreak a great and signal revenge on his cursed head.

Nor did my hate long confine itself to useless wishes; I began to reflect on the best means of securing him; and for this purpose, about a month after my release, I repaired to a criminal judge in the town, and told him that I had an accusation to make; that I knew the destroyer of my family; and that I required him to exert his whole authority for the apprehension of the murderer.

The magistrate listened to me with attention and kindness: "Be assured, sir," said he, "no pains or exertions on my part shall be spared to discover the villain."

"I thank you," replied I; "listen, therefore, to the deposition that I have to make. It is indeed a tale so strange, that I should fear you would not credit it, were there not something in truth which, however wonderful, forces convic-

17. The balance of the sentence is omitted from the 1831 edition and replaced with the following: "the springs of existence ~~was unable~~ ~~few days he~~

His father dies of heartbreak

18. ~~With the death of Alphonse, all three of the principals of the drama—Walton, Victor, and the creature—are orphans, and in the final scene, "All three . . . are on their own, lost, and without roots of any kind . . ." observes Christopher Small,~~ in *Mary Shelley's Frankenstein: Tracing the Myth* (Pittsburgh: University of Pittsburgh, 1973). With Alphonse's death, suggest some of the psychoanalytic critics, Victor at last achieves his goal of parricide and is free to become his own father. William Veeder, in *Mary Shelley and Frankenstein*, chapter 5, "The Divided Self and Man," notes that Victor's indirect extermination of his family—by means of the creature—has occurred in tellingly reverse-alphabetical order, W(illiam), J(ustine), H(enry), E(lizabeth), and (A)lphonse, with A (Alpha) for the last.

Why does Victor's brother Ernest survive the slaughter of the Frankenstein extended family? Veeder argues that it is precisely because he is "earnest." Mary ~~Shelley, in her thesis, could not pub-~~ *← more Darth Victor* ~~the Pro-~~ ~~conquered all;~~ ~~endure in~~

19. ~~The duration of this period of "many~~ of "many ~~months" is impossible to measure,~~ re, but it is ~~reasonable to assume that Victor's~~ 's presentation to the Geneva magistrate that follows his recovery took place late in 1797.

20. Although the historical record is not clear, it appears that as late as the French Revolution, the primary response to the insane throughout Europe was confinement in private "madhouses" and pub-

lic institutions that were little more than prisons. In 1790, the revolutionary government decreed that within six weeks "all persons detained in fortresses, religious houses, houses of correction, police houses, or other prisons, whatsoever . . . so long as they are not convicted, or under arrest, or not charged with major crimes, or confined by reason of madness, will be set at liberty." The mad were to be examined and either released or "cared for in hospitals indicated for that purpose."

In Paris, arrangements were made for insane men to be sent to the Bicêtre Hospital, which had been established in 1642 as an orphanage and would famously house the Marquis de Sade for three years in the early 1800s. Insane women were confined in the Salpêtrière, formally called the General Hospital but named informally for the gunpowder, or saltpeter, once produced on the site (a former arsenal). Under Louis XIV, the mandate of both hospitals was effectively to keep beggars off the streets; initially the insane were confined with criminals. After a short while the criminals were removed, and the institutions were dedicated to the insane. In 1793, Philippe Pinel was appointed physician superintendent of the Bicêtre. Under his supervision, Jean-Baptiste Pussin, a former tanner who had somewhat improbably become "governor" of the mental ward (following his treatment there for a tuberculosis-related medical condition, lymphadenitis of the cervical lymph nodes), was given permission to institute what became known as "moral management" of the mad. In 1797, after Pinel had moved to the Salpêtrière, Pussin unshackled the lunatics. Three years later, Pinel and Pussin instituted much the same policy; the latter had moved to the women's asylum with his former mentor. Straitjackets were retained at both institutions for cases that proved intractable.

Pussin's professional development

tion. The story is too connected to be mistaken for a dream, and I have no motive for falsehood." My manner, as I thus addressed him, was impressive, but calm; I had formed in my own heart a resolution to pursue my destroyer to death; and this purpose quieted my agony, and provisionally[21] reconciled me to life. I now related my history briefly, but with firmness and precision, marking the dates with accuracy, and never deviating into invective or exclamation.

The magistrate appeared at first perfectly incredulous, but as I continued he became more attentive and interested; I saw him sometimes shudder with horror, at others a lively surprise, unmingled with disbelief, was painted on his countenance.

When I had concluded my narration, I said. "This is the being whom I accuse, and for whose detection[22] and punishment I call upon you to exert your whole power. It is your duty as a magistrate, and I believe and hope that your feelings as a man will not revolt from the execution of those functions on this occasion."

This address caused a considerable change in the physiognomy of my auditor. He had heard my story with that

Pinel, médecin en chef de la Salpêtrière, délivrant les aliénés de leurs chaînes (Pinel, chief doctor at la Salpêtrière, releasing the hysterical women from their chains), by Tony Robert-Fleury (nineteenth century, date unknown).

half kind of belief that is given to a tale of spirits and super-natural events; but when he was called upon to act officially in consequence, the whole tide of his incredulity returned. He, however, answered mildly, "I would willingly afford you every aid in your pursuit; but the creature of whom you speak appears to have powers which would put all my exertions to defiance. Who can follow an animal which can traverse the sea of ice, and inhabit caves and dens, where no man would venture to intrude? Besides, some months have elapsed since the commission of his crimes, and no one can conjecture to what place he has wandered, or what region he may now inhabit."[23]

"I do not doubt that he hovers near the spot which I inhabit; and if he has indeed taken refuge in the Alps, he may be hunted like the chamois, and destroyed as a beast of prey. But I perceive your thoughts: you do not credit my narrative, and do not intend to pursue my enemy with the punishment which is his desert."

As I spoke, rage sparkled in my eyes; the magistrate was intimidated; "You are mistaken," said he, "I will exert myself; and if it is in my power to seize the monster, be assured that he shall suffer punishment proportionate to his crimes. But I fear, from what you have yourself described to be his properties, that this will prove impracticable, and that, while every proper measure is pursued, you should endeavour to[24] make up your mind to disappointment."

"That cannot be; but all that I can say will be of little avail. My revenge is of no moment to you; yet, while I allow it to be a vice, I confess that it is the devouring and only passion of my soul. My rage is unspeakable, when I reflect that the murderer, whom I have turned loose upon society, still exists. You refuse my just demand: I have but one resource; and I devote myself, either in my life or death, to his destruction."

I trembled with excess of agitation as I said this; there was a phrenzy in my manner, and something, I doubt not, of that haughty fierceness, which the martyrs of old are said to have possessed. But to a Genevan magistrate, whose mind was occupied by far other ideas than those of devotion and heroism, this elevation of mind had much the appearance of mad-

occurred hand in hand with that of his wife, Marguerite Pussin, who was similarly untrained. The Pussins had a natural affinity for dealing with the deranged, kept detailed notes, and recorded many stories of the use of calm, methodical conversation to effect change in the fortunes of their patients, providing Pinel with a wealth of case histories. In *A Treatise on Insanity: In Which Are Contained the Principles of a New and More Practical Nosology of Maniacal Disorders Than Has Yet Been Offered to the Public* (Sheffield, UK: W. Todd, 1806), Pinel credits the Pussins with nothing less than having changed the course of psychiatry. He cites, essentially, a single factor crucial to their success—proximity: They "lived amongst the insane day and night," learning both their patients' ways and the "chief art of managing maniacal patients": that of "administering consolation" while ~~employing "stratagems"~~ ~~and diversionary logic~~ ~~a review of the original French~~ edition of Pinel's book, *Traité Médico-Philosophique sur l'Aliénation Mentale, ou la Manie*, 8 vols. (Paris, 1801). In *The Edinburgh Review, or Critical Journal: For April 1803 . . . July 1803* (Edinburgh: Constable, London: Longmans, 1803], 165). In 2003, Ivan Berini, M.D., of the Salpêtrière, described the discrete populations housed at the end of the seventeenth century, and the hospital's inner workings and organizational logic: "four categories of women were placed there. 'Bad' adolescents were kept enclosed in the 'Correction' section, with the idea that they could be rehabilitated. Women labeled as prostitutes filled the 'Common' section. Women who had been imprisoned with or without sentences were quartered in the 'Jail,' and inhabitants within the 'Quarter of the Insane' were those who usually had been sent there by their families. In 1679, the institution housed 100 women who qualified as 'mad' and 148 women with

← Darth Victor

seizure disorders. By 1833, the numbers had increased to 117 insane women under treatment, 105 insane women labeled as sick, 923 women with mental illnesses characterized as incurable, and 266 women with seizure disorders" (Ivan Berlin, "The Salpêtrière Hospital: From Confining the Poor to Freeing the Insane," *American Journal of Psychiatry* 160, no. 9 [September 2003]: 1579).

In England, private madhouses flourished and became a significant industry. Only at the end of the eighteenth century did the English legislature begin to regulate these very profitable enterprises; public institutions such as Bethlem Royal Hospital ("Bedlam") were greatly expanded, and many new public insane asylums were founded.

Whether Victor was chained up or simply had a "solitary cell" is unclear from his account, although it appears that he was not sent to a private madhouse but rather was retained in the general prison.

21. The phrase "for an interval" is substituted for "provisionally" in the 1831 edition.

22. In the 1831 edition, Victor demands "seizure" rather than "detection."

23. This is far from the reaction that Victor had predicted Justine's judges would have were he to try to exculpate her from her alleged crime. But then, argue Morton Kaplan and Robert Kloss, in "Fantasy of Paternity and the Doppelgänger: Mary Shelley's *Frankenstein*," Victor did not want Justine to be exonerated—he wanted her, William, Clerval, Elizabeth, and his father to die before he confessed to his own guilt.

24. The phrase "endeavour to" is omitted in the 1831 edition.

ness. He endeavoured to soothe me as a nurse does a child, and reverted to my tale as the effects of delirium.

"Man," I cried, "how ignorant art thou in thy pride of wisdom! Cease; you know not what it is you say."

I broke from the house angry and disturbed, and retired to meditate on some other mode of action.

CHAPTER VII.[1]

Y PRESENT SITUATION was one in which all voluntary thought was swallowed up and lost. I was hurried away by fury; revenge alone endowed me with strength and composure; it modelled[2] my feelings, and allowed me to be calculating and calm, at periods when otherwise delirium or death would have been my portion.

My first resolution was to quit Geneva for ever; my country, which, when I was happy and beloved, was dear to me, now, in my adversity, became hateful. I provided myself with a sum of money, together with a few jewels which had belonged to my mother, and departed.

And now my wanderings began, which are to cease but with life. I have traversed a vast portion of the earth, and have endured all the hardships which travellers, in deserts and barbarous countries, are wont to meet. How I have lived I hardly know; many times have I stretched my failing limbs upon the sandy plain, and prayed for death. But revenge kept me alive; I dared not die, and leave my adversary in being.

When I quitted Geneva, my first labour was to gain some clue by which I might trace the steps of my fiendish enemy. But my plan was unsettled; and I wandered many hours around the confines of the town, uncertain what path I should pursue. As night approached, I found myself at the entrance of the cemetery where William, Elizabeth, and my

1. Chapter 24 in the 1831 edition.

2. The word "modelled" is replaced by "moulded" in the 1831 edition.

questioning suicide again but looks to hunting the monster

3. The phrase "I swear" is omitted here in the 1831 edition.

4. In furtherance of his invocation of "spirits of the dead," Victor likely refers to the Erinyes or Furies, female deities of vengeance, older than the Olympian gods of ancient Greece.

father, reposed. I entered it, and approached the tomb which marked their graves. Every thing was silent, except the leaves of the trees, which were gently agitated by the wind; the night was nearly dark; and the scene would have been solemn and affecting even to an uninterested observer. The spirits of the departed seemed to flit around, and to cast a shadow, which was felt but seen not, around the head of the mourner.

The deep grief which this scene had at first excited quickly gave way to rage and despair. They were dead, and I lived; their murderer also lived, and to destroy him I must drag out my weary existence. I knelt on the grass, and kissed the earth, and with quivering lips exclaimed, "By the sacred earth on which I kneel, by the shades that wander near me, by the deep and eternal grief that I feel, I swear; and by thee, O Night, and by the spirits that preside over thee, I swear[3] to pursue the daemon, who caused this misery, until he or I shall perish in mortal conflict. For this purpose I will preserve my life: to execute this dear revenge, will I again behold the sun, and tread the green herbage of earth, which otherwise should vanish from my eyes for ever. And I call on you, spirits of the dead; and on you, wandering ministers of vengeance, to aid and conduct me in my work. Let the cursed and hellish monster drink deep of agony; let him feel the despair that now torments me."

I had begun my adjuration with solemnity, and an awe which almost assured me that the shades of my murdered friends heard and approved my devotion; but the furies[4] possessed me as I concluded, and rage choked my utterance.

I was answered through the stillness of night by a loud and fiendish laugh. It rung on my ears long and heavily; the mountains re-echoed it, and I felt as if all hell surrounded me with mockery and laughter. Surely in that moment I should have been possessed by phrenzy, and have destroyed my miserable existence, but that my vow was heard, and that I was reserved for vengeance. The laughter died away: when a well-known and abhorred voice, apparently close to my ear, addressed me in an audible whisper—"I am satisfied: miserable wretch! you have determined to live, and I am satisfied."

I darted towards the spot from which the sound proceeded; but the devil eluded my grasp. Suddenly the broad disk of the moon arose, and shone full upon his ghastly and distorted shape, as he fled with more than mortal speed.

I pursued him; and for many months this has been my task. Guided by a slight clue, I followed the windings of the Rhone, but vainly. The blue Mediterranean appeared; and, by a strange chance, I saw the fiend enter by night, and hide himself in a vessel bound for the Black Sea. I took my passage in the same ship; but he escaped, I know not how.

Amidst the wilds of Tartary[5] and Russia, although he still evaded me, I have ever followed in his track. Sometimes the peasants, scared by this horrid apparition, informed me of his path; sometimes he himself, who feared that if I lost all trace[6] I should despair and die, often left some mark to guide

5. Like Constantinople and the Golden Horde in the Mongol empire, Tartary has been invoked by countless writers, usually to conjure romance, unknowableness, and the forbidden. It traditionally served as a historical more than a geographical designation—referring to the vast tract of northern and central Asia extending from the Caspian Sea and the Ural Mountains to the Pacific Ocean. George Ripley and Charles A. Dana's *New American Cyclopaedia: A Popular Dictionary of Knowledge*, 16 vols. (New York: D. Appleton and Co., 1863) acknowledges the difficulty of explaining exactly what the region encompassed (while simultaneously offering a primer on the

Map of Tartary, from 1612 Latin edition of Abraham Ortelius's *Theatrum Orbis Terarrum.*

nineteenth-century spelling of place-names): "applied somewhat vaguely to an extensive region of central Asia, stretching from the seas of Japan and Okhotsk [in the Russian district of Khabarovsk Krai] on the East to the Caspian on the West; and some geographers even extend the term so as to include a portion of eastern Europe as far West as the river Don. Tartary in its most extended sense therefore includes Mantchooria, Mongolia, the country of the Khalkas, Soongaria [between the Altay and Thian-chan mountains, and known for marriage ceremonies performed on horseback, with the bride speeding ahead and the putative groom in pursuit: 'and if he overtakes her, she becomes his wife without further ceremony; but if the woman be disinclined toward her pursuer, she will not suffer him to overtake her'—see Samuel Augustus Mitchell, *Mitchell's Geographical Reader: A System of Modern Geography, Comprising a Description of the World, with Its Grand Divisions, America, Europe, Asia, Africa, and Oceanica* (Philadelphia: Thomas, Cowperthwait, and Co., 1840), 451], and East Toorkistan, all subject to China; Independent Toorkistan; all the southern part of the Russian possessions in Asia; and in Europe the greater part of the Russian governments of Orenburg, Astrakhan, Ekaterinoslav, the Cossack provinces, and the Crimea, the last of which is sometimes called Little Tartary." Backpedaling, the editors then conclude: "The name Tartary, however, is generally restricted to the region bounded North by Siberia, East by the seas of Okhotsk and Japan, South by China proper, Thibet, India, Afghanistan, and Persia, and West by the Caspian Sea; while it is properly applicable to the western part only of this territory, known as Toorkistan" (Vol. 15, *Spiritualism–Uzziah*, 295). The *Encyclopædia Britannica* (3rd ed.) is more definite: "Tartary is a vast country in the northern parts of Asia, bounded by Siberia on

me. The snows descended on my head, and I saw the print of his huge step on the white plain. To you first entering on life, to whom care is new, and agony unknown, how can you understand what I have felt, and still feel? Cold, want, and fatigue, were the least pains which I was destined to endure; I was cursed by some devil, and carried about with me my eternal hell; yet still a spirit of good followed and directed my steps, and, when I most murmured, would suddenly extricate me from seemingly insurmountable difficulties. Sometimes, when nature, overcome by hunger, sunk under the exhaustion, a repast was prepared for me in the desert, that restored and inspirited me. The fare was indeed coarse, such as the peasants of the country ate; but I may[7] not doubt that it was set there by the spirits that I had invoked to aid me. Often, when all was dry, the heavens cloudless, and I was parched by thirst, a slight cloud would bedim the sky, shed the few drops that revived me, and vanish.

I followed, when I could, the courses of the rivers; but the daemon generally avoided these, as it was here that the population of the country chiefly collected. In other places human beings were seldom seen; and I generally subsisted on the wild animals that crossed my path. I had money with me, and gained the friendship of the villagers by distributing it, or bringing with me some food that I had killed, which, after taking a small part, I always presented to those who had provided me with fire and utensils for cooking.

My life, as it passed thus, was indeed hateful to me, and it was during sleep alone that I could taste joy. O blessed sleep! often, when most miserable, I sank to repose, and my dreams lulled me even to rapture. The spirits that guarded me had provided these moments, or rather hours, of happiness, that I might retain strength to fulfil my pilgrimage. Deprived of this respite, I should have sunk under my hardships. During the day I was sustained and inspirited by the hope of night: for in sleep I saw my friends, my wife, and my beloved country; again I saw the benevolent countenance of my father, heard the silver tones of my Elizabeth's voice, and beheld Clerval enjoying health and youth. Often, when wearied by a toilsome march, I persuaded myself that I was dreaming until night should come, and that I should then enjoy reality in the arms of my dearest friends. What agonizing fondness did I feel for them! how did I cling to their dear forms, as sometimes they haunted even my waking hours, and persuade myself that they still lived! At such moments vengeance, that burned within me, died in my heart, and I pursued my path towards the destruction of the daemon, more as a task enjoined by heaven, as the mechanical impulse of some power of which I was unconscious, than as the ardent desire of my soul.

What his feelings were whom I pursued, I cannot know. Sometimes, indeed, he left marks in writing on the barks of the trees, or cut in stone, that guided me, and instigated my fury. "My reign is not yet over," (these words were legible in one of these inscriptions); "you live, and my power is complete. Follow me; I seek the everlasting ices of the north, where you will feel the misery of cold and frost, to which I am impassive. You will find near this place, if you follow not too tardily, a dead hare; eat, and be refreshed. Come on, my enemy; we have yet to wrestle for our lives; but many hard and miserable hours must you endure, until that period shall arrive."

Scoffing devil! Again do I vow vengeance; again do I devote thee, miserable fiend, to torture and death. Never will I omit[8] my search, until he or I perish; and then with what ecstasy shall I join my Elizabeth, and those who even now prepare for me the reward of my tedious toil and horrible pilgrimage.

As I still pursued my journey to the northward, the snows thickened, and the cold increased in a degree almost too severe to support. The peasants were shut up in their hovels, and only a few of the most hardy ventured forth to seize the animals whom starvation had forced from their hiding-places to seek for prey. The rivers were covered with ice, and no fish could be procured; and thus I was cut off from my chief article of maintenance.

The triumph of my enemy increased with the difficulty of my labours. One inscription that he left was in these words: "Prepare! your toils only begin: wrap yourself in furs, and

the north and west; this is called Great Tartary. The Tartars who lie south of Moscovy and Siberia, are those of Affracan, Cireassia, and Dagistan, situated north-west of the Caspian Sea; the Calmuc Tartars, who lie between Siberia; the Usbec Tartars and Moguls, who lie north of Persia and India; and, lastly, those of Tibet, who lie northwest of China" (Vol. 3, 387).

6. The phrase "of him" is inserted here in the 1831 edition, and the word "often" appearing later in this sentence is omitted.

7. The word "may" becomes "will" in the 1831 edition.

8. The plainer phrase "give up" is substituted for "omit" in the 1831 edition, and "those" becomes "my departed friends."

9. Victor imperfectly recalls a story told by Xenophon, in the *Anabasis*, his roughly contemporaneous account of Cyrus of Persia (Cyrus the Younger) and of the retreat, in 401–399 BCE, of the "Ten Thousand," mercenaries who, upon their return to Greece, stood upon Mount Theches (present-day Deveboynu Tepe) and cried out, upon first seeing the Black Sea (not the Mediterranean), "Thálatta! Thálatta!" ("The sea! The sea!")—initially Xenophon, then in the rearguard, mistook his soldiers' exuberance for cries of alarm signaling an attack. The text is a classic of ancient Greek literature. A small group of scholars maintain that there is no known independent basis of fact for the tale or for Xenophon's participation in the march. His unabashedly swashbuckling depiction of his own exploits and leadership rol~~e~~ ~~has been passed by writers~~ such as Ita~~lo~~ ~~Calvino and Xenophon~~ in praising ~~his vivid prose; and Plutarch~~ (who wro~~te extensively about~~ the events ~~of Cyrus's campaign~~ to a com~~plete retelling in his essay~~ "Why Rea~~d the Classics?" and see also~~ McLaugh~~lin,~~ ~~Xenophon's~~ ~~Anabasis,~~ 19–24). Th~~e book provided the basis~~ for the 197~~9 film *The Warriors*, directed by~~ Walter Hill and adapted from the eponymous novel by Sol Yurick (1965). Hill and David Shaber, who co-wrote the screenplay, centered the actions around contemporary gang warfare in New York.

Anabasis was first translated into English in 1839; Victor likely read it in Greek, though the story itself was also perhaps part of an oral tradition to which he may have been exposed.

[handwritten annotation: finds new way of travel with dogs and hears towns account of Monster]

provide food, for we shall soon enter upon a journey where your sufferings will satisfy my everlasting hatred."

My courage and perseverance were invigorated by these scoffing words; I resolved not to fail in my purpose; and, calling on heaven to support me, I continued with unabated fervour to traverse immense deserts, until the ocean appeared at a distance, and formed the utmost boundary of the horizon. Oh! how unlike it was to the blue seas of the south! Covered with ice, it was only to be distinguished from land by its superior wildness and ruggedness. The Greeks wept for joy when they beheld the Mediterranean from the hills of Asia,[9] and hailed with rapture the boundary of their toils. I did not weep; but I knelt down, and, with a full heart, thanked my guiding spirit for conducting me in safety to the place where I hoped, notwithstanding my adversary's gibe, to meet and grapple with him.

Some weeks before this period I had procured a sledge and dogs, and thus traversed the snows with inconceivable speed. I know not whether the fiend possessed the same advantages; but I found that, as before I had daily lost ground in the pursuit, I now gained on him; so much so, that when I first saw the ocean, he was but one day's journey in advance, and I hoped to intercept him before he should reach the beach. With new courage, therefore, I pressed on, and in two days arrived at a wretched hamlet on the seashore. I inquired of the inhabitants concerning the fiend, and gained accurate information. A gigantic monster, they said, had arrived the night before, armed with a gun and many pistols; putting to flight the inhabitants of a solitary cottage, through fear of his terrific appearance. He had carried off their store of winter food, and, placing it in a sledge, to draw which he had seized on a numerous drove of trained dogs, he had harnessed them, and the same night, to the joy of the horror-struck villagers, had pursued his journey across the sea in a direction that led to no land; and they conjectured that he must speedily be destroyed by the breaking of the ice, or frozen by the eternal frosts.

On hearing this information, I suffered a temporary access of despair. He had escaped me; and I must commence a destructive and almost endless journey across the mountainous ices of the ocean,—amidst cold that few of the inhabitants could long endure, and which I, the native of a genial and sunny climate, could not hope to survive. Yet at the idea that the fiend should live and be triumphant, my rage and vengeance returned, and, like a mighty tide, overwhelmed every other feeling. After a slight repose, during which the spirits of the dead hovered round, and instigated me to toil and revenge, I prepared for my journey.

I exchanged my land sledge for one fashioned for the inequalities of the frozen ocean; and, purchasing a plentiful stock of provisions, I departed from land.

I cannot guess how many days have passed since then; but I have endured misery, which nothing but the eternal sentiment of a just retribution burning within my heart could have enabled me to support. Immense and rugged mountains of ice often barred up my passage, and I often heard the thunder of the ground sea, which threatened my destruction. But again the frost came, and made the paths of the sea secure.

By the quantity of provision which I had consumed I should guess that I had passed three weeks in this journey; and the continual protraction of hope, returning back upon the heart, often wrung bitter drops of despondency and grief from my eyes. Despair had indeed almost secured her prey, and I should soon have sunk beneath this misery; when once, after the poor animals that carried[10] me had with incredible toil gained the summit of a sloping ice mountain, and one sinking under his fatigue died, I viewed the expanse before me with anguish, when suddenly my eye caught a dark speck upon the dusky plain. I strained my sight to discover what it could be, and uttered a wild cry of ecstasy when I distinguished a sledge, and the distorted proportions of a well-known form within. Oh! with what a burning gush did hope revisit my heart! warm tears filled my eyes, which I hastily wiped away, that they might not intercept the view I had of the daemon; but still my sight was dimmed by the burning drops, until, giving way to the emotions that oppressed me, I wept aloud.

10. The word "carried" is corrected to "conveyed" in the 1831 edition.

finds Monster

11. The word "foe" replaces "enemy" in the 1831 edition.

But this was not the time for delay; I disencumbered the dogs of their dead companion, gave them a plentiful portion of food; and, after an hour's rest, which was absolutely necessary, and yet which was bitterly irksome to me, I continued my route. The sledge was still visible; nor did I again lose sight of it, except at the moments when for a short time some ice rock concealed it with its intervening crags. I indeed perceptibly gained on it; and when, after nearly two days' journey, I beheld my enemy at no more than a mile distant, my heart bounded within me.

But now, when I appeared almost within grasp of my enemy,[11] my hopes were suddenly extinguished, and I lost all trace of him more utterly than I had ever done before. A ground sea was heard; the thunder of its progress, as the waters rolled and swelled beneath me, became every moment more ominous and terrific. I pressed on, but in vain. The wind arose; the sea roared; and, as with the mighty shock of an earthquake, it split, and cracked with a tremendous and overwhelming sound. The work was soon finished: in a few minutes a tumultuous sea rolled between me and my enemy, and I was left drifting on a scattered piece of ice, that was continually lessening, and thus preparing for me a hideous death.

In this manner many appalling hours passed; several of my dogs died; and I myself was about to sink under the accumulation of distress, when I saw your vessel riding at anchor, and holding forth to me hopes of succour and life. I had no conception that vessels ever came so far north, and was astounded at the sight. I quickly destroyed part of my sledge to construct oars; and by these means was enabled, with infinite fatigue, to move my ice-raft in the direction of your ship. I had determined, if you were going southward, still to trust myself to the mercy of the seas, rather than abandon my purpose. I hoped to induce you to grant me a boat with which I could still pursue my enemy. But your direction was northward. You took me on board when my vigour was exhausted, and I should soon have sunk under my multiplied hardships into a death, which I still dread,—for my task is unfulfilled.

Oh! when will my guiding spirit, in conducting me to the dæmon, allow me the rest I so much desire; or must I die, and he yet live? If I do, swear to me, Walton, that he shall not escape; that you will seek him, and satisfy my vengeance in his death. Yet, do I dare ask you to undertake my pilgrimage, to endure the hardships that I have undergone? No; I am not so selfish. Yet, when I am dead, if he should appear; if the ministers of vengeance should conduct him to you, swear that he shall not live—swear that he shall not triumph over my accumulated woes,[12] and live to make another such a wretch as I am. He is eloquent and persuasive; and once his words had even power over my heart: but trust him not. His soul is as hellish as his form, full of treachery and fiend-like malice. Hear him not; call on the manes[13] of William, Justine, Clerval, Elizabeth, my father, and of the wretched Victor, and thrust your sword into his heart. I will hover near, and direct the steel aright.

Walton, *in continuation.*[14]

August 26th, 17—.[15]

You have read this strange and terrific story, Margaret; and do you not feel your blood congealed with horror, like that which even now curdles mine? Sometimes, seized with sudden agony, he could not continue his tale; at others, his voice broken, yet piercing, uttered with difficulty the words so replete with agony.[16] His fine and lovely eyes were now lighted up with indignation, now subdued to downcast sorrow, and quenched in infinite wretchedness. Sometimes he commanded his countenance and tones, and related the most horrible incidents with a tranquil[17] voice, suppressing every mark of agitation; then, like a volcano bursting forth, his face would suddenly change to an expression of the wildest rage, as he shrieked out imprecations on his persecutor.

His tale is connected, and told with an appearance of the simplest truth; yet I own to you that the letters of Felix and Safie, which he shewed me,[18] and the apparition of the monster, seen from our ship, brought to me a greater conviction of the truth of his narrative than his asseverations, however

12. The balance of this sentence is revised in the 1831 edition to read as follows: "and survive to add to the list of his dark crimes." Here Mary Shelley makes the creature more evil, a criminal; in the previous version, it is the creature's *existence* that makes Victor a "wretch," not the creature's evildoing.

13. A Roman term for the spirits of the dead.

14. And so the novel returns to the epistolary form established in Volume I, Letters I through IV, above, with letters written by Robert Walton to his sister, Margaret Saville. Letter IV breaks off on page 33, above, and as this is "in continuation" there is no salutation. Because the device was wholly familiar to the average reader of the day, Shelley's use of it here and the reappearance of the reliable narrator Walton work to dispel any lingering doubts as to Victor's credibility.

15. This is likely August 1799 (as is confirmed by the clues of various publications quoted by Frankenstein and Walton). The date given in the Draft is August 13, but it was apparently changed to be consistent with the August 19 missive reproduced above as part of Volume I, Letter IV.

16. Probably to avoid the repetition of the word "agony," it is replaced in the 1831 edition with "anguish."

17. "Smothered" in the Draft, altered by Percy Shelley.

18. These are at best copies of the letters. Why would copies—which could have been fabricated by Victor—be seen by Walton as credible evidence?

19. This question is omitted in the 1831 edition.

20. Ten days in the Draft.

21. The word "spirit" is substituted for "feelings" in the 1831 edition.

22. The 1831 edition replaces the phrase "real beings" with "beings themselves[.]"

23. Are we to understand that, on his deathbed, Victor engaged Walton in conversation about books that they had both read?

earnest and connected. Such a monster has then really existence; I cannot doubt it; yet I am lost in surprise and admiration. Sometimes I endeavoured to gain from Frankenstein the particulars of his creature's formation; but on this point he was impenetrable.

"Are you mad, my friend?" said he, "or whither does your senseless curiosity lead you? Would you also create for yourself and the world a dæmoniacal enemy? Or to what do your questions tend?[19] Peace, peace! learn my miseries, and do not seek to increase your own."

Frankenstein discovered that I made notes concerning his history: he asked to see them, and then himself corrected and augmented them in many places; but principally in giving the life and spirit to the conversations he held with his enemy. "Since you have preserved my narration," said he, "I would not that a mutilated one should go down to posterity."

Thus has a week[20] passed away, while I have listened to the strangest tale that ever imagination formed. My thoughts, and every feeling of my soul, have been drunk up by the interest for my guest, which this tale, and his own elevated and gentle manners have created. I wish to soothe him; yet can I counsel one so infinitely miserable, so destitute of every hope of consolation, to live? Oh, no! the only joy that he can now know will be when he composes his shattered feelings[21] to peace and death. Yet he enjoys one comfort, the offspring of solitude and delirium: he believes, that, when in dreams he holds converse with his friends, and derives from that communion consolation for his miseries, or excitements to his vengeance, that they are not the creations of his fancy, but the real beings[22] who visit him from the regions of a remote world. This faith gives a solemnity to his reveries that render them to me almost as imposing and interesting as truth.

Our conversations are not always confined to his own history and misfortunes. On every point of general literature[23] he displays unbounded knowledge, and a quick and piercing apprehension. His eloquence is forcible and touching; nor can I hear him, when he relates a pathetic incident, or endeavours to move the passions of pity or love, without tears. What a glorious creature must he have been in the days of his prosperity, when he is thus noble and godlike in ruin. He seems to feel his own worth, and the greatness of his fall.

"When younger," said he, "I felt as if I were[24] destined for some great enterprise. My feelings are profound; but I possessed a coolness of judgment that fitted me for illustrious achievements. This sentiment of the worth of my nature supported me, when others would have been oppressed; for I deemed it criminal to throw away in useless grief those talents that might be useful to my fellow-creatures. When I reflected on the work I had completed, no less a one than the creation of a sensitive and rational animal, I could not rank myself with the herd of common projectors.[25] But this feeling,[26] which supported me in the commencement of my career, now serves only to plunge me lower in the dust. All my speculations and hopes are as nothing; and, like the archangel who aspired to omnipotence, I am chained in an eternal hell.[27] My imagination was vivid, yet my powers of analysis and application were intense; by the union of these qualities I conceived the idea, and executed the creation of a man. Even now I cannot recollect, without passion, my reveries while the work was incomplete. I trod heaven in my thoughts, now exulting in my powers, now burning with the idea of their effects. From my infancy I was imbued with high hopes and a lofty ambition; but how am I sunk! Oh! my friend, if you had known me as I once was, you would not recognize me in this state of degradation. Despondency rarely visited my heart; a high destiny seemed to bear me on, until I fell, never, never again to rise."

Must I then lose this admirable being? I have longed for a friend; I have sought one who would sympathize with and love me. Behold, on these desert seas I have found such a one;[28] but, I fear, I have gained him only to know his value, and lose him. I would reconcile him to life, but he repulses the idea.

"I thank you, Walton," he said, "for your kind intentions towards so miserable a wretch; but when you speak of new ties, and fresh affections, think you that any can replace those who are gone? Can any man be to me as Clerval was;

24. The preceding phrase is deleted in the 1831 edition, and the phrase "I believed myself" is substituted.

25. An archaic term: a "projector" is one who creates a project.

26. The word is "thought" in the 1831 edition, not "feeling."

27. Here Victor explicitly likens himself to Satan in Milton's *Paradise Lost*, a comparison already made by the creature with regard to himself. See text accompanying note 15, Volume II, Chapter VII, above.

28. In *The Essential Frankenstein: The Definitive, Annotated Edition of Mary Shelley's Classic Novel*, ed. Leonard Wolf (New York: Plume/Penguin Books, 2003), Wolf points out that Walton is presumptuous: There is no evidence that Walton's "love" was reciprocated, and indeed, only a few sentences later, Victor explains why he cannot attach himself to Walton.

29. The 1831 edition replaces the odd word "invaded" with "contemplated."

30. In the Draft, originally August 27, corrected to August 31.

31. Seneca, a Stoic philosopher (ca. 4 BCE–65 CE), wrote *De Brevitate Vitae* ("On the Shortness of Life"), in which he argued that the human lifespan is long enough to afford time for what is important—in his view, the study of philosophy—and that a life in pursuit of the material (a category in which he included labor, exertion of authority, and what we would today call the development of a career) is meaningless. He structured the essay as a letter to a friend, Paulinus, who supervised Rome's supply of grain. Ordered by his former pupil Nero—whom he had accused of being a political demagogue, and whom he and others were said to have conspired to assassinate—to commit suicide as punishment for rebellion, Seneca complied.

32. This sentence does not appear in the 1831 edition; the following takes its place, its effect that of Walton's training the lens upon himself: "Yet it is terrible to reflect that the lives of all these men are endangered through me. If we are lost, my mad schemes are the cause."

or any woman another Elizabeth? Even where the affections are not strongly moved by any superior excellence, the companions of our childhood always possess a certain power over our minds, which hardly any later friend can obtain. They know our infantine dispositions, which, however they may be afterwards modified, are never eradicated; and they can judge of our actions with more certain conclusions as to the integrity of our motives. A sister or a brother can never, unless indeed such symptoms have been shewn early, suspect the other of fraud or false dealing, when another friend, however strongly he may be attached, may, in spite of himself, be invaded[29] with suspicion. But I enjoyed friends, dear not only through habit and association, but from their own merits; and, wherever I am, the soothing voice of my Elizabeth, and the conversation of Clerval, will be ever whispered in my ear. They are dead; and but one feeling in such a solitude can persuade me to preserve my life. If I were engaged in any high undertaking or design, fraught with extensive utility to my fellow-creatures, then could I live to fulfil it. But such is not my destiny; I must pursue and destroy the being to whom I gave existence; then my lot on earth will be fulfilled, and I may die."

September 2d.[30]

my beloved sister, I write to you, encompassed by peril, and ignorant whether I am ever doomed to see again dear England, and the dearer friends that inhabit it. I am surrounded by mountains of ice, which admit of no escape, and threaten every moment to crush my vessel. The brave fellows, whom I have persuaded to be my companions, look towards me for aid; but I have none to bestow. There is something terribly appalling in our situation, yet my courage and hopes do not desert me. We may survive; and if we do not, I will repeat the lessons of my Seneca,[31] and die with a good heart.[32]

Yet what, Margaret, will be the state of your mind? You will not hear of my destruction, and you will anxiously await my return. Years will pass, and you will have visitings of despair, and yet be tortured by hope. Oh! my beloved sister, the sickening failings of your heart-felt expectations are, in prospect, more terrible to me than my own death. But you have a husband, and lovely children; you may be happy: heaven bless you, and make you so!

My unfortunate guest regards me with the tenderest compassion. He endeavours to fill me with hope; and talks as if life were a possession which he valued. He reminds me how often the same accidents have happened to other navigators, who have attempted this sea, and, in spite of myself, he fills me with cheerful auguries. Even the sailors feel the power of his eloquence: when he speaks, they no longer despair; he rouses their energies, and, while they hear his voice, they believe these vast mountains of ice are molehills, which will vanish before the resolutions of man. These feelings are transitory; each day's expectation delayed fills them with fear, and I almost dread a mutiny caused by this despair.

September 5th.[33]

A scene has just passed of such uncommon interest, that although it is highly probable that these papers may never reach you, yet I cannot forbear recording it.

We are still surrounded by mountains of ice, still in imminent danger of being crushed in their conflict. The cold is excessive, and many of my unfortunate comrades have already found a grave amidst this scene of desolation. Frankenstein has daily declined in health: a feverish fire still glimmers in his eyes; but he is exhausted, and, when suddenly roused to any exertion, he speedily sinks again into apparent lifelessness.

I mentioned in my last letter the fears I entertained of a mutiny. This morning, as I sat watching the wan countenance of my friend—his eyes half closed, and his limbs hanging listlessly,—I was roused by half a dozen of the sailors, who desired admission into the cabin. They entered; and their leader addressed me. He told me that he and his companions had been chosen by the other sailors to come in deputation to me, to make me a demand,[34] which, in justice, I could not refuse.[35] We were immured in ice, and should

33. September 6th in the Draft.

34. The word "demand" is replaced with "requisition" in the 1831 edition.

35. Only a few years earlier, in 1789, a mutiny occurred on HMS *Bounty* on its return from Otaheite (Tahiti). Apparently the result of personality and disciplinary conflicts between Captain William Bligh and Master Fletcher Christian following theft, insubordination, and desertion among the crew during nearly six months in Tahiti and the resultant punishment meted out to the men by Bligh, the mutiny had nothing to do with personal danger to the crew occurring in the course of the voyage itself.

The morning of April 28 found Bligh, half-dressed and seemingly inadequately provisioned, set adrift with eighteen members of the crew before dawn in a 23-foot launch by mutinous crewmen. His shockingly successful 3,618-mile voyage from the spot of the mutiny, near Tofoa, to Coupang, a settlement on Timor (where he purchased a boat and began his return voyage to England), is the subject of *A Narrative of the Mutiny, on Board His Majesty's Ship Bounty; And the Subsequent Voyage of Part of the Crew, in the Ship's Boat* (London: George Nicol, 1790). In the memoir, Bligh gave no opportunity for the traitorous members of his crew to feel that they had triumphed: He devoted only six pages to the indignity of having been ambushed, tied up, and tossed into the launch, and eighty to his subsequent return voyage.

A well-publicized court-martial was held in 1792, resulting in the hanging of several crew members. Walton, no experienced captain, may well have been mindful of the risks of taking a hard line with his crew.

In "The Story of the Court-Martial of the *Bounty* Mutineers," Douglas O. Linder, of the University of Missouri–Kansas City

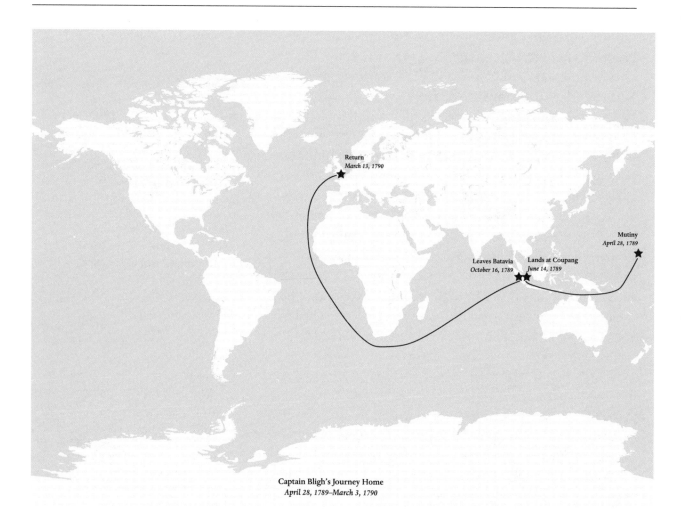

Captain Bligh's Journey Home
April 28, 1789–March 3, 1790

School of Law, conjectures that, had the "botanical curiosity" breadfruit not been discovered in Tahiti in 1769, providing an economic purpose for such expeditions as Bligh's, and had not Bligh witnessed, in his early twenties, the bludgeoning death of Captain James Cook, by Hawaiians in the Sandwich Islands, the *Bounty* would never have sailed nor the mutiny have occurred (see http://law2.umkc.edu/faculty/projects/ftrials/Bounty/bounty account.html).

36. In the 1831 edition, "insisted" replaces "desired."

probably never escape; but they feared that if, as was possible, the ice should dissipate, and a free passage be opened, I should be rash enough to continue my voyage, and lead them into fresh dangers, after they might happily have surmounted this. They desired,[36] therefore, that I should engage with a solemn promise, that if the vessel should be freed, I would instantly direct my coarse southward.

This speech troubled me. I had not despaired; nor had I yet conceived the idea of returning, if set free. Yet could I, in justice, or even in possibility, refuse this demand? I hesitated before I answered; when Frankenstein, who had at first been silent, and, indeed, appeared hardly to have force enough to attend, now roused himself; his eyes sparkled, and his cheeks flushed with momentary vigour. Turning towards the men, he said—

"What do you mean? What do you demand of your captain? Are you then so easily turned from your design? Did you not call this a glorious expedition? and wherefore was it glorious? Not because the way was smooth and placid as a southern sea, but because it was full of dangers and terror; because, at every new incident, your fortitude was to be called forth, and your courage exhibited; because danger and death surrounded, and these dangers you were to brave and overcome. For this was it a glorious, for this was it an honourable undertaking. You were hereafter to be hailed as the benefactors of your species; your name adored, as belonging to brave men who encountered death for honour and the benefit of mankind. And now, behold, with the first imagination of danger, or, if you will, the first mighty and terrific trial of your courage, you shrink away, and are content to be handed down as men who had not strength enough to endure cold and peril; and so, poor souls, they were chilly, and returned to their warm fire-sides. Why, that requires not this preparation; ye need not have come thus far, and dragged your captain to the shame of a defeat, merely to prove yourselves cowards. Oh! be men, or be more than men. Be steady to your purposes, and firm as a rock. This ice is not made of such stuff as your hearts might be; it is mutable, cannot withstand you, if you say that it shall not. Do not return to your families with the stigma of disgrace marked on your brows. Return as heroes who have fought and conquered, and who know not what it is to turn their backs on the foe."

He spoke this with a voice so modulated to the different feelings expressed in his speech, with an eye so full of lofty design and heroism, that can you wonder that these men were moved. They looked at one another, and were unable to reply. I spoke; I told them to retire, and consider of what had been said: that I would not lead them further north, if they strenuously desired the contrary; but that I hoped that, with reflection, their courage would return.

37. So much for Walton as a judge of men—see text accompanying note 20, Volume I, Letter II, above, for his judgment that his crew was possessed of "dauntless courage."

38. The 17th in the Draft.

39. Corrected to "9th" in the 1831 edition.

They retired, and I turned towards my friend; but he was sunk in languor, and almost deprived of life.

How all this will terminate, I know not; but I had rather die, than return shamefully,—my purpose unfulfilled. Yet I fear such will be my fate; the men, unsupported by ideas of glory and honour, can never willingly continue to endure their present hardships.

September 7th.

The die is cast; I have consented to return, if we are not destroyed. Thus are my hopes blasted by cowardice and indecision;[37] I come back ignorant and disappointed. It requires more philosophy than I possess, to bear this injustice with patience.

September 12th.[38]

It is past; I am returning to England. I have lost my hopes of utility and glory;—I have lost my friend. But I will endeavour to detail these bitter circumstances to you, my dear sister; and, while I am wafted towards England, and towards you, I will not despond.

September 19th,[39] the ice began to move, and roarings like thunder were heard at a distance, as the islands split and cracked in every direction. We were in the most imminent peril; but, as we could only remain passive, my chief attention was occupied by my unfortunate guest, whose illness increased in such a degree, that he was entirely confined to his bed. The ice cracked behind us, and was driven with force towards the north; a breeze sprung from the west, and on the 11th the passage towards the south became perfectly free. When the sailors saw this, and that their return to their native country was apparently assured, a shout of tumultuous joy broke from them, loud and long-continued. Frankenstein, who was dozing, awoke, and asked the cause of the tumult. "They shout," I said, "because they will soon return to England."

"Do you then really return?"

"Alas! yes; I cannot withstand their demands. I cannot lead them unwillingly to danger, and I must return."

"Do so, if you will; but I will not. You may give up your purpose; but mine is assigned to me by heaven, and I dare not. I am weak; but surely the spirits who assist my vengeance will endow me with sufficient strength." Saying this, he endeavoured to spring from the bed, but the exertion was too great for him; he fell back, and fainted.

It was long before he was restored; and I often thought that life was entirely extinct. At length he opened his eyes, but he breathed with difficulty, and was unable to speak. The surgeon gave him a composing draught,[40] and ordered us to leave him undisturbed. In the mean time he told me, that my friend had certainly not many hours to live.

His sentence was pronounced; and I could only grieve, and be patient. I sat by his bed watching him; his eyes were closed, and I thought he slept; but presently he called to me in a feeble voice, and, bidding me come near, said—"Alas! the strength I relied on is gone; I feel that I shall soon die, and he, my enemy and persecutor, may still be in being. Think not, Walton, that in the last moments of my existence I feel that burning hatred, and ardent desire of revenge, I once expressed, but I feel myself justified in desiring the death of my adversary. During these last days I have been occupied in examining my past conduct; nor do I find it blameable. In a fit of enthusiastic madness I created a rational creature, and was bound towards him, to assure, as far as was in my power, his happiness and well-being. This was my duty; but there was another still paramount to that. My duties towards my fellow-creatures[41] had greater claims to my attention, because they included a greater proportion of happiness or misery. Urged by this view, I refused, and I did right in refusing, to create a companion for the first creature. He shewed unparalleled malignity and selfishness, in evil: he destroyed my friends; he devoted to destruction beings who possessed exquisite sensations, happiness, and wisdom; nor do I know where this thirst for vengeance may end. Miserable himself, that he may render no other wretched, he ought to die. The task of his destruction was mine, but I have failed. When actuated by selfish and vicious motives, I asked you to under-

40. The composition and dose would have depended on the surgeon's preferences. The *Edinburgh New Dispensary*, the standard reference work of the time (revised by Andrew Duncan in 1791), recommended that hysteria and other nervous cases be treated variously with compounds of asafoetida (*Ferula assafoetida*), camphor (*Cinnamomum camphora*), clary Sage (*Salvia sclarea*), feverfew (*Tanacetum parthenium*), galbanum (*Ferula galbaniflua*), black hellebore (*Hyoscyamus niger*), iron (martial flowers, called *Ens veneris*), lavender (*Lavandula angustifolia*), opium (*Papaver somniferum*), pennyroyal (*Mentha pulegium*), St. John's wort (*Hypericum perforatum*), valerian (*Valeriana officinalis*), and wood soot (literally, the material produced when wood is burned). Regarding the last, the chemist Daniel Cox's *New Medical Compendium, for the Use of Families, etc.* (London: Longmans, 1808), notes that "the more resinous the wood, the more the soot abounds with bitter oily matter. . . . Wood soot is directed in hysteric cases, and in different nervous disorders, as an antispasmodic and corroborant," often in combination with asafoetida, mentioned above (63).

41. The 1831 edition replaces "my fellow-creatures" with the phrase "the beings of my own species."

42. According to Robinson, "From this point until the end of the novel, [the text] is dominated more by" Percy Shelley's "voice, for he fair-copied and embellished the last twelve-and-three-quarter pages of the Draft" (*The Original Frankenstein*, 252, n. 113).

43. Victor again changes his mind about the virtues of the pursuit of knowledge; having failed to convince Walton's crew to continue the expedition, he now warns Walton against the very ambition which he exhorted the crew to embrace.

44. Arthur Belefant, in *Frankenstein, the Man and the Monster*, makes the tantalizing argument that the creature never existed and that he was only the product of Victor's fevered imagination. Belefant suggests that Victor was in fact terrified of committing incest by means of a marriage to Elizabeth, his spiritual sister, forced on him by his mother on her deathbed. In order to forestall the marriage, he first killed William, then Clerval (who may have been involved in William's death or may have grown suspicious of Victor), and finally, in desperation, Elizabeth. Only Victor, up to this point, has seen the creature; the other "witnesses" are all unverifiable, being part of Victor's tale. As noted above in various places, many of the incidents described by Victor seem impossible, either physically (leaping about the glacier) or by reason of the time sequencing (the killing of Clerval), but are easily explained if the creature did not exist. That Walton sees the creature, Belefant proposes, was an addition made by Percy Shelley, who did not fully understand the secret tale of incest and murder that Mary Shelley had composed. A review of the Draft makes clear, however, that while Percy Shelley did make many revisions in the course of preparation of the fair copy, these were almost exclusively turns of phrase, and it is plain that the confron-

take my unfinished work; and I renew this request now, when I am only induced by reason and virtue.

"Yet I cannot ask you to renounce your country and friends, to fulfil this task; and now, that you are returning to England, you will have little chance of meeting with him. But the consideration of these points, and the well-balancing of what you may esteem your duties, I leave to you; my judgment and ideas are already disturbed by the near approach of death. I dare not ask you to do what I think right, for I may still be misled by passion.

"That[42] he should live to be an instrument of mischief disturbs me; in other respects this hour, when I momentarily expect my release, is the only happy one which I have enjoyed for several years. The forms of the beloved dead flit before me, and I hasten to their arms. Farewell, Walton! Seek happiness in tranquillity, and avoid ambition, even if it be only the apparently innocent one of distinguishing yourself in science and discoveries.[43] Yet why do I say this? I have myself been blasted in these hopes, yet another may succeed."

His voice became fainter as he spoke; and at length, exhausted by his effort, he sunk into silence. About half an hour afterwards he attempted again to speak, but was unable; he pressed my hand feebly, and his eyes closed for ever, while the irradiation of a gentle smile passed away from his lips.

Margaret, what comment can I make on the untimely extinction of this glorious spirit? What can I say, that will enable you to understand the depth of my sorrow? All that I should express would be inadequate and feeble. My tears flow; my mind is overshadowed by a cloud of disappointment. But I journey towards England, and I may there find consolation. [44]

I am interrupted. What do these sounds portend? It is midnight; the breeze blows fairly, and the watch on deck scarcely stir. Again; there is a sound as of a human voice, but hoarser; it comes from the cabin where the remains of Frankenstein still lie. I must arise, and examine. Good night, my sister.

Great God! what a scene has just taken place! I am yet dizzy with the remembrance of it. I hardly know whether I shall have the power to detail it; yet the tale which I have recorded would be incomplete without this final and wonderful catastrophe.

I entered the cabin, where lay the remains of my ill-fated and admirable friend. Over him hung a form which I cannot find words to describe; gigantic in stature, yet uncouth and distorted in its proportions. As he hung over the coffin, his face was concealed by long locks of ragged hair; but one vast hand was extended, in colour and apparent texture like that of a mummy.[45] When he heard the sound of my approach, he ceased to utter exclamations of grief and horror, and sprung towards the window. Never did I behold a vision so horrible as his face, of such loathsome, yet appalling hideousness. I shut my eyes involuntarily, and endeavoured to recollect what were my duties with regard to this destroyer.[46] I called on him to stay.

He paused, looking on me with wonder; and, again turning towards the lifeless form of his creator, he seemed to forget my presence, and every feature and gesture seemed instigated by the wildest rage of some uncontrollable passion.

"That is also my victim!" he exclaimed;[47] "in his murder my crimes are consummated; the miserable series of my being is wound to its close! Oh, Frankenstein! generous and self-devoted being! what does it avail that I now ask thee to pardon me? I, who irretrievably destroyed thee by destroying all thou lovedst. Alas! he is cold; he may not[48] answer me."

His voice seemed suffocated; and my first impulses, which had suggested to me the duty of obeying the dying request of my friend, in destroying his enemy, were now suspended by a mixture of curiosity and compassion. I approached this tremendous being; I dared not again raise my looks[49] upon his face, there was something so scaring and unearthly in his ugliness. I attempted to speak, but the words died away on my lips. The monster continued to utter wild and incoherent self-reproaches. At length I gathered resolution to address him, in a pause of the tempest of his passion: "Your repentance," I said, "is now superfluous. If you had listened to the voice of conscience, and heeded the stings of remorse, before you had urged your diabolical vengeance to this extremity, Frankenstein would yet have lived."

tation between Walton and the creature was Mary Shelley's intended conclusion.

An even more radical interpretation is suggested by David Ketterer, in his thoughtful *Frankenstein's Creation*: Neither the creature nor Frankenstein existed; both, and the entire remaining cast of the tale, are figments of Walton's imagination, an "anxiety" dream arising out of his uncertainties about his expedition. Ketterer admits the similarity of the suggestion to that in *The Dream of Prospero* (Oxford: Clarendon Press, 1967), by David Gwilym James, who proposed that all of the story of *The Tempest* is meant by Shakespeare to be seen as a dream experienced by Prospero in his library in Milan, one that serves to warn him about his responsibilities as a ruler.

45. The scene echoes not only the earlier image of Caroline Beaufort kneeling at the side of her dead father (immortalized by Alphonse Frankenstein in a painting—see note 33, Volume I, Chapter VI, above), but also the scene of Elizabeth's death, with her hair half-covering her face (see note 7, Volume III, Chapter VI, above). William Veeder, in *Mary Shelley and Frankenstein*, chapter 7, "Value and Viability," sees the detail of the creature's hair hanging down as confirming the existence of the female portion of the creature's psyche (in Veeder's view, all psychologically balanced individuals have both male and female psychic components). He concludes, however, that Mary Shelley did not mean to suggest that the creature could hope to integrate the male and female portions of its psyche and achieve the desired state of androgyny without extensive social intercourse—that is, the creature would never become psychologically healthy in isolation. Veeder also notes that, as in both the bridal chamber scene and the scene of Frankenstein's first meeting with the creature (see note 9, Volume I, Chapter IV, above), the crea-

ture extends his hand, identifying him with Elizabeth and symbolizing that there is an opportunity for Victor and the creature to resolve their relationship.

46. "Endeavoured to recollect"? Only moments before, Victor expressed his "dying wish" (as Walton presently characterizes it) that Walton destroy the creature.

47. In French, no doubt—as we have seen, there is no textual evidence to suggest that the creature acquired any other language, and even if he learned to "get by" in German or other tongues during his rapid travels, he could not speak any other language as fluently as is displayed here. Accordingly, we can now answer the question asked earlier about Walton's linguistic skills: He spoke and understood French, although he does not point that out here, and he kindly, and without mentioning it, translates the creature's story into English for the benefit of his sister. We must therefore take the phraseology of the creature's remarks as Walton's interpretations, not actual transcriptions.

48. The phrase "may not" is replaced with "cannot" in the 1831 edition.

49. The odd word "looks" is changed to "eyes" in the 1831 edition.

50. The word "I" is italicized in the Draft.

51. The word "more" does not appear in the 1831 edition.

52. The creature evidently knows that Frankenstein has related his history to Walton—otherwise, he would explain the identity of "Clerval." How does the creature know this?

53. See John Milton's statement ascribed to Satan in *Paradise Lost* (which, it will be recalled, the creature had read):

"And do you dream?" said the daemon; "do you think that I[50] was then dead to agony and remorse?—He," he continued, pointing to the corpse, "he suffered not more[51] in the consummation of the deed;—oh! not the ten-thousandth portion of the anguish that was mine during the lingering detail of its execution. A frightful selfishness hurried me on, while my heart was poisoned with remorse. Think ye that the groans of Clerval were music to my ears?[52] My heart was fashioned to be susceptible of love and sympathy; and, when wrenched by misery to vice and hatred, it did not endure the violence of the change without torture such as you cannot even imagine.

"After the murder of Clerval, I returned to Switzerland, heart-broken and overcome. I pitied Frankenstein; my pity amounted to horror: I abhorred myself. But when I discovered that he, the author at once of my existence and of its unspeakable torments, dared to hope for happiness; that while he accumulated wretchedness and despair upon me, he sought his own enjoyment in feelings and passions from the indulgence of which I was for ever barred, then impotent envy and bitter indignation filled me with an insatiable thirst for vengeance. I recollected my threat, and resolved that it should be accomplished. I knew that I was preparing for myself a deadly torture; but I was the slave, not the master of an impulse, which I detested, yet could not disobey. Yet when she died!—nay, then I was not miserable. I had cast off all feeling, subdued all anguish to riot in the excess of my despair. Evil thenceforth became my good.[53] Urged thus far, I had no choice but to adapt my nature to an element which I had willingly chosen. The completion of my dæmoniacal design became an insatiable passion. And now it is ended; there is my last victim!"

I was at first touched by the expressions of his misery; yet when I called to mind what Frankenstein had said of his powers of eloquence and persuasion, and when I again cast my eyes on the lifeless form of my friend, indignation was re-kindled within me. "Wretch!" I said, "it is well that you come here to whine over the desolation that you have made. You throw a torch into a pile of buildings, and when they are consumed you sit among the ruins, and lament the fall. Hypocritical fiend! if he whom you mourn still lived, still would he be the object, again would he become the prey of your accursed vengeance. It is not pity that you feel; you lament only because the victim of your malignity is withdrawn from your power."

"Oh, it is not thus—not thus," interrupted the being; "yet such must be the impression conveyed to you by what appears to be the purport of my actions. Yet I seek not a fellow-feeling in my misery. No sympathy may I ever find. When I first sought it, it was the love of virtue, the feelings of happiness and affection with which my whole being overflowed, that I wished to be participated. But now, that virtue has become to me a shadow, and that happiness and affection are turned into bitter and loathing despair, in what should I seek for sympathy? I am content to suffer alone, while my sufferings shall endure: when I die, I am well satisfied that abhorrence and opprobrium should load my memory. Once my fancy was soothed with dreams of virtue, of fame, and of enjoyment. Once I falsely hoped to meet with beings, who, pardoning my outward form, would love me for the excellent qualities which I was capable of bringing forth.[54] I was nourished with high thoughts of honour and devotion. But now vice has degraded me beneath the meanest animal. No crime, no mischief, no malignity, no misery, can be found comparable to mine. When I call over[55] the frightful catalogue of my deeds, I cannot believe that I am he whose thoughts were once filled with sublime and transcendant visions of the beauty and the majesty of goodness. But it is even so; the fallen angel becomes a malignant devil. Yet even that enemy of God and man had friends and associates in his desolation; I am quite alone.

"You, who call Frankenstein your friend, seem to have a knowledge of my crimes and his misfortunes. But, in the detail which he gave you of them, he could not sum up the hours and months of misery which I endured, wasting in impotent passions. For whilst I destroyed his hopes, I did not satisfy my own desires. They were for ever ardent and craving; still I desired love and fellowship, and I was still spurned.

So farewel Hope, and with Hope
 farewel Fear,
Farewel Remorse: all Good to me is
 lost;
Evil be thou my Good . . .

(Book 4, lines 108–10)

54. The phrase "bringing forth" is revised to "unfolding" in the 1831 edition, and in the succeeding sentence, "vice" becomes "crime." In the following sentence, "crime" is replaced with "guilt."

55. The phrase is "run over" in the 1831 edition, and "deeds" become "sins." In place of "I am he," the phrase is "I am the same creature[.]"

56. "Contumely" means insolent or insulting language or treatment.

57. The phrase "these hands" replaces "they" in the 1831 edition, and "it" is revised to "that imagination."

58. And where would the creature obtain the wood for such a "funeral pile"? In the *Quarterly Review* (January 1818), John Croker slyly remarks that the pyre will be "(of ice, we conjecture)." Wolfson and Levao, in *The Annotated Frankenstein*, suggest that it will consist of the remains of Frankenstein's and the creature's sledges as well as the wreckage of previous explorers' ships, trapped in the ice.

Was there no injustice in this? Am I to be thought the only criminal, when all human kind sinned against me? Why do you not hate Felix, who drove his friend from his door with contumely?[56] Why do you not execrate the rustic who sought to destroy the saviour of his child? Nay, these are virtuous and immaculate beings! I, the miserable and the abandoned, am an abortion, to be spurned at, and kicked, and trampled on. Even now my blood boils at the recollection of this injustice.

"But it is true that I am a wretch. I have murdered the lovely and the helpless; I have strangled the innocent as they slept, and grasped to death his throat who never injured me or any other living thing. I have devoted my creator, the select specimen of all that is worthy of love and admiration among men, to misery; I have pursued him even to that irremediable ruin. There he lies, white and cold in death. You hate me; but your abhorrence cannot equal that with which I regard myself. I look on the hands which executed the deed; I think on the heart in which the imagination of it was conceived, and long for the moment when they[57] will meet my eyes, when it will haunt my thoughts, no more.

"Fear not that I shall be the instrument of future mischief. My work is nearly complete. Neither yours nor any man's death is needed to consummate the series of my being, and accomplish that which must be done; but it requires my own. Do not think that I shall be slow to perform this sacrifice. I shall quit your vessel on the ice-raft which brought me hither, and shall seek the most northern extremity of the globe; I shall collect my funeral pile,[58] and consume to ashes this miserable frame, that its remains may afford no light to any curious and unhallowed wretch, who would create such another as I have been. I shall die. I shall no longer feel the agonies which now consume me, or be the prey of feelings unsatisfied, yet unquenched. He is dead who called me into being; and when I shall be no more, the very remembrance of us both will speedily vanish. I shall no longer see the sun or stars, or feel the winds play on my cheeks. Light, feeling, and sense, will pass away; and in this condition must I find my happiness. Some years ago, when the images which this world affords first opened upon me, when I felt the cheering warmth of summer, and heard the rustling of the leaves and the chirping[59] of the birds, and these were all to me, I should have wept to die; now it is my only consolation. Polluted by crimes, and torn by the bitterest remorse, where can I find rest but in death?

"Farewell! I leave you, and in you the last of human kind whom these eyes will ever behold. Farewell, Frankenstein! If thou wert yet alive, and yet cherished a desire of revenge against me, it would be better satiated in my life than in my destruction. But it was not so; thou didst seek my extinction, that I might not cause greater wretchedness; and if yet, in some mode unknown to me, thou hast not yet ceased to think and feel,[60] thou desirest not my life for my own misery. Blasted as thou wert, my agony was still superior to thine; for the bitter sting of remorse may[61] not cease to rankle in my wounds until death shall close them for ever.

"But soon," he cried, with sad and solemn enthusiasm, "I shall die, and what I now feel be no longer felt. Soon these burning miseries will be extinct. I shall ascend my funeral pile triumphantly, and exult in the agony of the torturing flames.

The light of that conflagration will fade away; my ashes will be swept into the sea by the winds. My spirit will sleep in peace; or if it thinks, it will not surely think thus. Farewell."

He sprung from the cabin-window,[62] as he said this, upon the ice-raft which lay close to the vessel. He was soon borne away by the waves, and lost in darkness and distance.[63]

THE END.

59. The birds are "warbling" rather than "chirping" in the 1831 edition.

60. The 1831 edition revises the balance of the sentence to read as follows: "thou wouldst not desire against me a vengeance greater than that which I feel."

61. The word is "will," not "may," in the 1831 edition.

62. Just as the creature did, points out William Veeder, in *Mary Shelley and Frankenstein*, after killing Elizabeth.

63. And so Walton reveals himself to be craven: Having only a few days before solemnly promised Victor, a man whom he virtually worshipped, that he would carry out Victor's vengeance, he now allows the creature to depart unchecked and unharmed.

Mary Shelley's original version of this paragraph in the Draft read: "He sprung from the cabin window as he said this on to an ice raft that lay close to the vessel & pushing himself off he was carried away by the waves and I soon lost sight of him in the darkness & distance." Thus she originally intended that the fate of the creature be even more uncertain and his departure a choice made by him, rather than an outcome effected by the passive action of the waves.

AFTERWORD
Mary Shelley's *Frankenstein* and Genetic Engineering

BY ANNE K. MELLOR

A S LESLIE KLINGER'S superbly annotated edition of *Frankenstein, or the Modern Prometheus* has reminded us, a myth was born in Geneva on the night of June 16, 1816, the only entirely human-created, datable myth describing the origin of mankind. (All other creation myths depend either on the direct agency of God or gods or, as in the case of the golem, divine participation though a sacred sign.) On that night, Mary Wollstonecraft Godwin gave birth to one of the enduring myths of modern civilization, the narrative of the scientist who single-handedly creates a new species, a humanoid form that need not die.

This narrative has become *the* myth of modern science, the master narrative for the ways in which man's attempts to control and improve the workings of nature can have unintended and even monstrous consequences. As Shelley's creature says to Victor Frankenstein, "You are my creator, but I am your master: obey!" This myth has been invoked since World War II and even before to describe almost every scientific, social, and political development with potentially disastrous outcomes, from the atomic bomb dropped on Hiroshima; to the "Frankenfish" or "Frankenfoods" of genetically modified salmon and wheat; to the economic crisis of 2008, which the *New York Times*'s Joe Nocera called the result, in part, of "Frankenstein-like financial engineering."[1]

---

1. Joe Nocera, "Financial Mistakes, Doomed to Be Repeated," *New York Times*, October 10, 2008, http://www.nytimes.com/2008/10/11/business/11nocera.html?_r=0.

Why was *this* myth born on *this* night? As scholar Gillen D'Arcy Wood has reminded us, the eruption of the Indonesian volcano Tamboro in April 1815 caused the "Year without a Summer"[2] and forced the Shelley-Byron entourage to remain indoors during the freezing weather; they then decided to compete in a ghost story contest that inspired at least three of the participants to write, although only John Polidori and Mary Shelley actually produced stories worthy of the name. (Polidori's *The Vampyre,* incorporating Byron's "A Fragment," featuring vampire Augustus Darvell, was published under Byron's name after 1819, and may have served as an inspiration for Bram Stoker's *Dracula.*)

Here I want to focus on just why Mary Wollstonecraft Godwin had her particular daydream or "waking dream" of "the pale student of unhallowed arts" bringing to life "the thing he had put together." In a terror that Mary shared, he then fled from "his odious handy-work," only to be awakened by "the horrid thing . . . looking on him with yellow, watery, but speculative eyes." This reverie, so vivid that Mary Shelley recalled it in detail fifteen years later when preparing a new introduction for the revised 1831 edition of *Frankenstein,* grew directly out of her most traumatic biographical experiences. A motherless child—her mother, Mary Wollstonecraft, died of puerperal fever as a consequence of giving birth to this daughter—Mary Godwin had undergone a childhood of parental abandonment and abuse. Her father, William Godwin, assigned child-rearing responsibilities to his second wife, Mary Jane Clairmont, who favored her own children and especially resented Mary. To end the household friction, Godwin shipped the fourteen-year-old Mary off to Dundee, Scotland, to stay with strangers, the William Baxter family, for two years.

Mary returned to London in 1814, at the age of sixteen, and fell in love with the married Percy Shelley, her adored father's disciple. A few weeks shy of seventeen, she left her father's home to travel with Shelley. Seven months later, she gave birth prematurely to a baby girl, who lived only two weeks. As Mary recorded in her journal on March 19, 1815, "Dream that my little baby came to life again; that it had only been cold, and that we rubbed it before the fire, and it lived. Awake and find no baby." Immediately pregnant again, Mary gave birth on January 24, 1816, to a son, whom she named William. Five months later, she had the waking dream that engendered her novel, a novel that perhaps for the first time in literature embodies the anxieties of a very

---

2. Gillen D'Arcy Wood, *Tambora: The Eruption That Changed the World* (Princeton, NJ: Princeton University Press, 2014), 9.

young, pregnant woman, and may hint at the questions the author might obsessively have asked herself: Will I be able to love my child, even if the child is deformed? Will I be able to mother a child? What if my child dies?— a question sharpened by the infant mortality rate in Europe in Mary's day: as high as 20 percent. Could I ever want my child to die? Could I kill my own child? Could my child kill *me*, as I killed my mother, Mary Wollstonecraft, in childbirth?[3] Victor Frankenstein's horrified rejection of his newborn child, his desire to kill it, here expresses the postnatal depression, even intense hostility, that some new mothers feel—or are afraid of feeling. This postnatal hostility erupts into the novel at the moment when Mary Shelley represents the creature's murder of little William Frankenstein, a boy who has the same blond hair and "lively blue eyes, dimpled cheeks, and endearing manners" of Mary's own son, William Shelley—a boy who has the same propensity to take little *"wives"*: Louisa Biron being William Frankenstein's favorite playmate, while Allegra Byron was William Shelley's choice. The creature's accidental smothering of the child he wished to adopt expresses Mary Shelley's horrified recognition that she is capable of *imagining* herself as the murderer of her own child—capable of infanticide. As Shelley here realizes, a battered and abused child is fully capable of becoming a battering, abusive parent.

At the same time, this waking dream articulates Mary Godwin's intense anxieties of authorship. The daughter of two famous writers, the mistress of an aspiring poet and novelist, competing in a ghost story contest with the most famous living writer of the day, Lord Byron, Mary felt understandably inadequate. As she recalled fifteen years later, *"Have you thought of a story? I was asked each morning, and each morning I was forced to reply with a mortifying negative."* In fact, as we know from Polidori's journal, she began writing her story on June 17, 1816, the morning after the challenge was issued. She subsequently accepted several editorial revisions, of style and of content, from her mentor Percy Shelley, revisions that I have described in detail in *Mary Shelley: Her Life, Her Fiction, Her Monsters*, and that in my view did not improve the novel.

Equally important, as Leslie Klinger's annotations amply document, *Frankenstein* is born out of the specific historical, political, and scientific milieu in which the Shelley-Byron entourage moved. In my book on Mary Shelley's fiction, I describe at length the ways in which the novel responds to the originating ideology and devastating consequences of the French Revolution and

---

3. I developed this line of questioning in Anne K. Mellor, *Mary Shelley: Her Life, Her Fiction, Her Monsters* (New York: Routledge, 1988), 41.

Napoleon's military campaigns; to the specific utopian dreams of human perfectibility and the marriage of opposites promoted by Godwin and the Romantic poets Mary Shelley knew intimately; and to the negative impact on women of the patriarchal culture in which the author lived, and the sexual division of labor so acutely analyzed by her mother, Mary Wollstonecraft, in *A Vindication of the Rights of Woman*. My intention here is to look at the ways in which Victor Frankenstein's scientific project—to create a "new species" that would be able to "renew life where death had apparently devoted the body to corruption"—resonates with recent advances in genetic engineering.

Mary Shelley grounded Frankenstein's scientific experiments on the cutting-edge science of her day. Although she had no personal experience of "doing science"—note that Victor's laboratory consists of a small attic room lit by a single candle—she had read and discussed with Byron and Percy Shelley the theories and experiments of the leading biologists and chemists of the late eighteenth century, among them Humphry Davy, Erasmus Darwin, and Luigi Galvani. When Victor goes to the University of Ingolstadt (a hotbed of revolutionary Jacobin activity), he attends the lectures on chemical physiology of Professor Waldman, whose arguments are derived directly from Davy's *A Discourse, Introductory to a Course of Lectures on Chemistry* (1802). There Davy insists that chemistry has bestowed upon the chemist "powers which may be almost called creative; which have enabled *him* to modify and change the beings surrounding him, and by his experiments to interrogate nature with power, not simply as a scholar, passive and seeking only to understand *her* operations, but rather as a master, active with his own instruments" (italics added). Or, as Waldman puts it in the novel, "The modern masters [of this science] . . . penetrate into the recesses of nature, and shew how *she* works in her hiding places."

Davy's text has two all-important implications for Shelley's novel. First, Davy relies on the gendered metaphor of nature as female, the scientist as male. In effect, a male scientist penetrates, changes, and exploits nature, which is passive. Second, Davy introduces a distinction between two methods of scientific practice: the interventionist scientist, "active with his own instruments," who in Davy's view triumphantly "masters" nature, as opposed to the "passive" scholar who simply tries to understand and describe its workings. For Shelley, the interventionist scientist is clearly problematic. Davy's disciple, Victor Frankenstein, is motivated not by a desire for knowledge so much as by a hubristic desire to be world-famous, even to be worshipped as a god. As he predicts, "A new species would bless me as its creator and source; many happy and excellent natures would owe their being to me.

No father could claim the gratitude of his child so completely as I should deserve theirs."

In contrast, Mary Shelley endorses the work of the passive scholar, most notably Erasmus Darwin, the father of the theory of evolution. In his extensive footnotes to his two-volume poem *The Botanic Garden* (1789–91), Erasmus Darwin had described in detail the evolution of animal from plant life, the movement up the evolutionary ladder from single-sex propagation to dual-sex propagation, and the role of sexual selection in evolutionary development—the very theory of the evolution of the species for which his grandson Charles Darwin would be given credit. From a Darwinian perspective, Victor's experiment is anti-evolution. His attempt to create a "new" and more perfect "species" is flawed on two counts. First, Victor constructs his creature not only from human materials gathered from charnel houses and cemeteries but also from animal materials gathered from "slaughter-houses" (it is these animal parts that enable Victor to construct a creature who is eight feet tall, a giant who immediately terrifies all who see him, including his maker). Second, Victor engages in single-sex propagation, creating a male creature who can theoretically reproduce himself (by repeating Victor's experiment as recorded in the lab notes the creature finds in Victor's coat pocket). Not only does Victor thereby eliminate the need for females in the reproductive act: Perhaps the most horrifying aspect of his scientific project is the possibility that human society could survive without women, but he also moves *down* the evolutionary ladder, from dual-sex to single-sex reproduction.

The scientific experiments that had the greatest immediate impact on Shelley's novel were those of Luigi Galvani, the Italian biologist who tried to prove the materialist thesis that the life force (or "soul") was inseparable from the body, as the vitalists and Christians had argued, and was identical with electricity. Remember that Victor animates his creature with a "spark" of life. Galvani spent his career applying different voltages of electricity to dead animals, most famously to frogs (his statue in front of the University of Bologna shows him holding an open book that supports the corpse of a frog). As the English saw it, the most famous galvanic experiment occurred in London in 1803, when Galvani's nephew Giovanni Aldini brought the corpse of the recently hanged murderer Thomas Foster (or Forster) from Newgate Prison to his operating theater. There, Aldini applied ever stronger currents of electricity to the corpse, at which Thomas Foster first opened his eyes, then clenched his fist, and finally went into convulsions. As Aldini exulted in his written account of this experiment, "The action even of those muscles furthest distant from the points of contact with the [voltaic] arc was so much increased as almost to give an appearance of re-animation." He concludes, "vitality might, perhaps, have been restored, if many circumstances had not rendered it impossible."[4]

Of course, in Shelley's novel, Victor Frankenstein does not succeed in creating a superior species. He does not eliminate women and become God the Father. As I have argued, Mother Nature *fights back* against this scientific attempt to penetrate her recesses and steal her secrets.[5] She does this first by disabling Victor with both mental and physical diseases. In bringing forth his male creature and then in the aborted act of bringing forth a female creature, Victor is tormented with anxiety attacks, depression, sleeplessness, and physical exhaustion, which so wrack his body that he dies of "natural" causes at the age of twenty-eight. Nature pursues Victor with the very fire and electricity he stole from her when he animated his creature with a "spark of being." The lightning, thunder, and rain that rage around Victor on that "drear November night" of his first creation; on the Orkney islands during his aborted effort; again in the Alps, when he encounters his creature; and finally at the North Pole, when he dies—these are not just the expected paraphernalia of a gothic novel but also, more significantly, a manifestation of Mother Nature's elemental powers: powers not unlike those of the Greek furies. They pursue Victor (like Orestes) to his hiding places. Each of the storms is exceptionally violent, not unlike those produced by the sulfate aerosols sent into the stratosphere by Tambora's eruption and directly experienced by Mary Shelley in Geneva in 1816.

Moreover, nature punishes Victor by preventing him from creating a *normal* child. Victor lacks the maternal instinct that would have enabled him to empathize with his creature, to ask even once whether his creature *wants* to be born, to give him an average size and familiar appearance. Remember that Victor used large animal parts because "minute" parts would "hinder my speed," and that the features Victor has selected as "beautiful" include a "yellow skin" that "scarcely covered the work of muscles and arteries," "watery" dun white eyes, a "shriveled complexion," and "straight black lips." By failing to sympathize or identify with his creature, Victor denies to him

4. Mellor, *Mary Shelley: Her Life, Her Fiction, Her Monsters*, 105. The full text of Giovanni [John] Aldini's *An Account of the Late Improvements in Galvanism: With a Series of Curious and Interesting Experiments Performed before the Commissioners of the French National Institute, and Repeated Lately in the Anatomical Theatres of London* (London: Cuthell and Martin/J. Murray, 1803) may be found at https://archive.org/stream/accountoflateimp00aldi/accountoflateimp00aldi _djvu.txt.

5. Mellor, *Mary Shelley: Her Life, Her Fiction, Her Monsters*, 72, 76, 92–93, 111–12, 235.

the affection, the emotional and physical support, the nurturing, the "mothering," that every newborn child requires. Thus his unnatural mode of sexual reproduction has produced an unnatural offspring, and all who see the creature reject him as monstrous. Finally, Mother Nature punishes Victor by preventing him from participating in *natural* reproduction and family relations, by ensuring that Victor's unnatural creation destroys his wife, most of his family, and his best friend, Clerval. In this novel the penalty of violating nature is death.

Implicit in Shelley's novel is an alternative ideal, I have argued: her underlying conviction that civilization can only be advanced by human beings who value and cooperate with nature. Note that the only member of the Frankenstein family who survives is Ernest, who wants to be, not the lawyer/magistrate his father urges, but rather a farmer, one who must collaborate with rather than defy nature's seasons and demands. The model for such "natural co-operation" put forth in the novel is that of the "domestic affections," a mutually loving, egalitarian family, here represented by the De Laceys: the blind (and lovingly cared for) Father, Agatha (whose name means goodness), and Felix (happiness). They are then joined by Safie (Sophia/wisdom), the liberated woman who is Shelley's homage to Mary Wollstonecraft and who seeks a companionate marriage with Felix. Here Mary Shelley implicitly endorses an ideal of community based on mutual dependence, cooperation, and self-sacrifice—what Carol Gilligan in *In a Different Voice* has called an ethic of care.[6] But this loving family is ripped out of the novel, in flight from Victor's creature.

The novel thus suggests that where there is no ethic of care, where the nurturing love of a mother is absent (as it is from all the families in this novel, including that of the De Laceys), where a person places a higher value on a career and social fame than on the domestic affections (as Victor Frankenstein does, completely ignoring his best friend, his father, and even his fiancée as he conducts his scientific experiments), there monsters are made. As Victor finally realizes, in a statement that bores his alter ego, the ambitious and hubristic Walton, but nonetheless functions in the novel as Mary Shelley's own credo:

A human being in perfection ought always to preserve a calm and peaceful mind, and never to allow passion or a transitory desire to disturb his

6. Carol Gilligan, *In a Different Voice: Psychological Theory and Women's Development* (Cambridge, MA: Harvard University Press, 1993 [repr. 2003, 38th printing,]), xix.

tranquility. I do not think that the pursuit of knowledge is an exception to this rule. If the study to which you apply yourself has a tendency to weaken your affections, and to destroy your taste for those simple pleasures in which no alloy can possibly mix, then that study is certainly unlawful, that is to say, not befitting the human mind. If this rule were always observed; if no man allowed any pursuit whatsoever to interfere with the tranquillity of his domestic affections, Greece had not been enslaved; Caesar would have spared his country; America would have been discovered more gradually; and the empires of Mexico and Peru had not been destroyed.

Mary Shelley here suggests three things. First, political rulers who are incapable of loving all their subjects equally, of meeting the needs of all their citizens (as the leaders of the French Revolution had failed to do when they began to guillotine the aristocracy, Catholic clergy, and even the king and queen)—such leaders become monstrous tyrants. In Cruikshank's famous print, it is Napoleon—rather than Victor Frankenstein—who is the "modern Prometheus." Second, a society that fails to embrace and nurture members of other races, such as the inhabitants of Mexico and Peru—note that the creature is not "an European," to borrow Walton's language, but rather a giant who might recall one of Genghis Khan's Mongolian warriors or the Golden Horde of the thirteenth century—such a society creates empires, colonies, and racial enemies rather than supporting a cosmopolitan vision of the brotherhood of man. Finally, in the same way, scientists who fail to take ethical responsibility for the predictable—or even unintended—consequences of their experiments and technological developments can destroy life as we know it.

All of this begs for comment on some of the most troubling scientific developments of the past three-quarters of a century. We might think first of the atomic bombs dropped on Hiroshima and Nagasaki, after which several critics pointed to the uncanny similarities between Victor Frankenstein's career and that of Robert Oppenheimer, director of the Los Alamos Laboratory, where the bombs were designed and developed. Oppenheimer himself is said to have thought, after watching the test detonations in New Mexico that preceded the Japanese bombings, of a verse from the *Bhagavad Gita*: "Now I am become Death, the destroyer of worlds."[7] Or we might think of bioterrorism—in particular of anthrax as a powder that can be sent through the mail, as U.S. Army biologist Dr. Bruce Edwards Ivins was accused of

7. See https://www.youtube.com/watch?v=lb13ynu3Iac.

doing in 2001. Or we might think of the global climate change caused by carbon emissions produced at first by the Industrial Revolution and, more immediately, during our current Anthropocene era.

Most relevant to the issues raised by Mary Shelley's novel, however, are scientific developments in the fields of biology, microbiology, and genetic engineering. Using noninvasive prenatal genetic diagnosis, a newly pregnant woman's blood can be scanned and the following information about her fetus gleaned: whether it is male or female; has a chromosomal deficiency or any one of over a hundred single-gene disorders, including Huntington's disease, Down syndrome, cystic fibrosis, Tay-Sachs disease, or dwarfism; and other genetic traits, such as the presence of red hair. If the testing is done early enough, the mother can terminate her pregnancy with Mifeprex (the marketed combination of mifepristone [RU 486] and misoprostol). This kind of screening has been commercially developed and as of this writing is available and relatively cheap—usually less than $1,000. It will no doubt be of great interest to health insurers, especially to Medicaid, which will likely recommend it in the strongest possible terms to poor women, together with the suggestion that they terminate any diseased or disabled fetuses (thus sparing Medicaid the costs of caring for such an infant). From the perspective of the disabled community, as the late Paul Miller, an attorney with achondroplasia (dwarfism) who served in different capacities under Presidents Bill Clinton and Barack Obama, argued, such a practice can be viewed as tantamount to "genetic genocide."[8]

Most relevant to the ethical issues raised by *Frankenstein*, perhaps, are the implications of the CRISPR-Cas9 technology for permanently altering the DNA of a human egg or sperm. CRISPR-Cas9 technology was developed in 2012 by Professor Jennifer Doudna and her assistants at the University of California, Berkeley, working with Emmanuelle Charpentier, of Umea University, in Sweden.[9] In 2015, Professor Feng Zhang, of the Broad Institute of MIT and Harvard, developed another CRISPR protein, Cpf1.[10] CRISPR is the

8. Paul Steven Miller, JD, and Rebecca Leah Levine, MPH, JD, "Avoiding Genetic Genocide: Understanding Good Intentions and Eugenics in the Complex Dialogue between the Medical and Disability Communities," *Genetics in Medicine* 15 (August 2012), http://www.nature.com/gim/journal/v15/n2/full/gim2012102a.html.

9. See, for example, Andrew Pollack, "Jennifer Doudna, a Pioneer Who Helped Simplify Genome Editing," *New York Times*, May 11, 2015, http://www.nytimes.com/2015/05/12/science/jennifer-doudna-crispr-cas9-genetic-engineering.html.

10 Michael Specter, "The Gene Hackers," *The New Yorker*, November 16, 2015, http://www.newyorker.com/magazine/2015/11/16/the-gene-hackers.

memorable acronym for "clustered regularly interspaced short palindromic repeats." In layman's terms, this technology allows biologists to target a specific gene or string of nucleotides in the DNA of a given cell; in combination with Cas9 or Cpf1, a tracer, they can then snip out that gene and stitch the DNA neatly back together, or cut out the gene and replace it with another. Several commentators have compared the process to the "cut and paste"[11] function of a computer; it can be taught to and performed by a graduate student in an hour.[12]

The tool seems to work in nearly every organism, from silkworms to monkeys, and also in every cell type, from kidneys to hearts to T-cells. CRISPR is being used to develop better biofuels and new enzymes for industrial markets, such as laundry detergents, water treatment, and paper milling; to improve foods such as yogurt, fish, and meat; and to modify the genes in pig embryos in order to create organs that can be used for human implants with less chance of rejection. The future implications of this technology are enormous. Potentially, CRISPR-Cas9 could be used on human eggs or sperm to eliminate some of the single-gene disorders mentioned above. Obviously, the appeal of this technology for the medical community is undeniable. A researcher with the Francis Crick Institute in London received permission to use CRISPR-Cas9 to alter human embryos.[13] Although a genetically altered embryo will not now be implanted in a female womb, it is only a matter of time before that happens. And of course, any such altered gene in a human embryo is passed down to all descendants.[14]

The parallels with Victor Frankenstein's scientific project—to create a new and superior species—are obvious. Dr. Leroy Hood, the co-founder of the Institute for Systems Biology who developed the automated DNA sequencer, in 1998 pointed to human germline engineering (the altering of reproductive cells) as having the potential not only to eliminate hereditary diseases but also to produce individuals with superior intelligence, greater physical attractiveness, and improved emotional stability.[15] In China, scientists attempted to

11. Ibid.

12. Jennifer Kahn, "The Crispr Quandary," *New York Times Magazine*, November 9, 2015.

13. Ewen Callaway, "UK Scientists Gain Licence to Edit Genes in Human Embryos," *Nature*, February 2016, http://www.nature.com/news/uk-scientists-gain-licence-to-edit-genes-in-human-embryos-1.19270.

14. Sarah Knapton, "British Scientists Granted Permission to Genetically Modify Human Embryos," *Telegraph*, February 1, 2016, http://www.telegraph.co.uk/science/2016/03/12/british-scientists-granted-permission-to-genetically-modify-huma/.

15. Leroy Hood, "The Human Genome Project—Launch Pad for Genetic Engineering," in *Engineering the Human Germline: An Exploration of the Science and Ethics of Altering the Genes We*

use CRISPR-Cas9 to alter genes that cause a blood disorder, beta-thalassemia, in a human embryo. Significantly, in this case, their "editing technique ran amok and cut the DNA at many unintended sites," according to the *New York Times*.[16] At every level, this technology poses serious ethical issues. An engineered sterile or sex-limited (male) species, such as scientists have produced for the Zika-bearing mosquito, could jump to another species through interbreeding. Genetically modified crops could spread and devastate other ecosystems. And germline engineering in human embryos could produce new abnormalities.

Confronting this possibility, the National Academy of Sciences of the United States, the Chinese Academy of Sciences, and Britain's Royal Society in 2016 called for a "pause" in the race to edit the human genome. But their authority is not regulatory, only moral; and many physicians, including Dr. George Church of the Harvard Medical School, argued in opposition that "banning human germline editing could put a damper on the best medical research and instead drive the practice underground to black markets and uncontrolled medical tourism."[17] If we as a society are going to avoid Victor Frankenstein's mistakes—his failure to mother his creation—we must take responsibility for both the intended and the unintended consequences of human germline engineering. First, we must establish federally mandated and enforced guidelines for such research. Second, we must fund extensive studies to determine the immediate and long-term impact of these new technologies on the environment. Most of all, we must engage in a well-informed, ongoing public debate concerning all the ethical issues raised by genetic engineering, lest our "designer babies" become monsters.

ANNE K. MELLOR
Distinguished Research Professor of English
University of California, Los Angeles

Pass on to Our Children, ed. Gregory Stock and John Campbell (New York: Oxford University Press, 2000), 17–24.

16. The Editorial Board of the *New York Times*, "A Pause to Weigh Risks of Gene Editing," *New York Times*, December 18, 2015, http://www.nytimes.com/2015/12/18/opinion/a-pause-to-weigh-risks-of-gene-editing.html.

17. Nicholas Wade, "Scientists Seek Moratorium on Edits to Human Genome That Could Be Inherited," *New York Times*, December 3, 2015, http://www.nytimes.com/2015/12/04/science/crispr-cas9-human-genome-editing-moratorium.html. See also GenomeWeb, "CRISPR Leaders Argue Against Total Ban on Human Germline Editing," March 20, 2015, https://www.genomeweb.com/gene-silencinggene-editing/crispr-leaders-argue-against-total-ban-human-germline-editing.

APPENDIX 1
Author's Introduction
[to the 1831 edition of *Frankenstein*]

THE PUBLISHERS OF the Standard Novels, in selecting 'Frankenstein' for one of their series, expressed a wish that I should furnish them with some account of the origin of the story. I am the more willing to comply, because I shall thus give a general answer to the question, so very frequently asked me—'How I, then a young girl, came to think of, and to dilate upon, so very hideous an idea?' It is true that I am very averse to bringing myself forward in print; but as my account will only appear as an appendage to a former production, and as it will be confined to such topics as have connection with my authorship alone, I can scarcely accuse myself of a personal intrusion.

It is not singular that, as the daughter of two persons of distinguished literary celebrity,[1] I should very early in life have thought of writing. As a child I scribbled; and my favourite pastime, during the hours given me for recreation, was to 'write stories.' Still I had a dearer pleasure than this, which was the formation of castles in the air—the indulging in waking dreams the following up trains of thought, which had for their subject the formation of a succession of imaginary incidents. My dreams were at once more fantastic and agreeable than my writings. In the latter I was a close imitator—rather doing as others had done, than putting down the suggestions of my own mind. What I wrote was intended at least for one other eye—my childhood's companion and friend; but my dreams were all my own; I accounted

not easy being from two famous

1. William Godwin and Mary Wollstonecraft, that is. See the Foreword, text following note 20, above.

for them to nobody; they were my refuge when annoyed—my dearest pleasure when free.

I lived principally in the country as a girl, and passed a considerable time in Scotland. I made occasional visits to the more picturesque parts; but my habitual residence was on the blank and dreary northern shores of the Tay, near Dundee. Blank and dreary on retrospection I call them; they were not so to me then. They were the eyry of freedom, and the pleasant region where unheeded I could commune with the creatures of my fancy. I wrote then—but in a most common-place style. It was beneath the trees of the grounds belonging to our house, or on the bleak sides of the woodless mountains near, that my true compositions, the airy flights of my imagination, were born and fostered. I did not make myself the heroine of my tales. Life appeared to me too common-place an affair as regarded myself. I could not figure to myself that romantic woes or wonderful events would ever be my lot; but I was not confined to my own identity, and I could people the hours with creations far more interesting to me at that age, than my own sensations.

After this my life became busier, and reality stood in place of fiction. My husband, however, was, from the first, very anxious that I should prove myself worthy of my parentage, and enrol myself on the page of fame. He was for ever inciting me to obtain literary reputation, which even on my own part I cared for then, though since I have become infinitely indifferent to it. At this time he desired that I should write, not so much with the idea that I could produce any thing worthy of notice, but that he might himself judge how far I possessed the promise of better things hereafter. Still I did nothing. Travelling, and the cares of a family, occupied my time; and study, in the way of reading, or improving my ideas in communication with his far more cultivated mind, was all of literary employment that engaged my attention.

In the summer of 1816, we visited Switzerland, and became the neighbours of Lord Byron. At first we spent our pleasant hours on the lake, or wandering on its shores; and Lord Byron, who was writing the third canto of Childe Harold, was the only one among us who put his thoughts upon paper. These, as he brought them successively to us, clothed in all the light and harmony of poetry, seemed to stamp as divine the glories of heaven and earth, whose influences we partook with him.

But it proved a wet, ungenial summer,[2] and incessant rain often confined

2. The summer of 1816, popularly known as the "Year without a Summer," was cooler and wetter than most, with frequent and severe storms throughout Europe, flooding, crop failures, and famine. The primary cause was the eruption the previous year of Mount Tambora, in Indonesia (then the Dutch East Indies), on April 5–15, 1815 (and continuing for some four

Mount Tambora (photo by Jialiang Gao, used under CC-by-SA 3.0 license).

us for days to the house. Some volumes of ghost stories, translated from the German into French, fell into our hands. There was the History of the Inconstant Lover, who, when he thought to clasp the bride to whom he had pledged his vows, found himself in the arms of the pale ghost of her whom he had deserted.[3] There was the tale of the sinful founder of his race, whose miserable doom it was to bestow the kiss of death on all the younger sons of his fated house, just when they reached the age of promise. His gigantic, shadowy form, clothed like the ghost in Hamlet, in complete armour, but with the beaver up, was seen at midnight, by the moon's fitful beams, to advance slowly along the gloomy avenue. The shape was lost beneath the shadow of the castle walls; but soon a gate swung back, a step was heard, the door of the

---

months), which resulted in substantial amounts of volcanic ash in the atmosphere, a reduction of sunlight, and a decrease in the average temperature. See note 7, Volume II, Chapter I, above.

3. Probably *"La Morte Fiancée."* See Preface, note 11, above.

chamber opened, and he advanced to the couch of the blooming youths, cradled in healthy sleep. Eternal sorrow sat upon his face as he bent down and kissed the forehead of the boys, who from that hour withered like flowers snapt upon the stalk.[4] I have not seen these stories since then; but their incidents are as fresh in my mind as if I had read them yesterday.

'We will each write a ghost story,' said Lord Byron; and his proposition was acceded to. There were four of us.[5] The noble author began a tale, a fragment of which he printed at the end of his poem of Mazeppa. Shelley, more apt to embody ideas and sentiments in the radiance of brilliant imagery, and in the music of the most melodious verse that adorns our language, than to invent the machinery of a story, commenced one founded on the experiences

4. This was the story titled *"Portraits de Famille."* See Preface, note 11, above.

5. Polidori's *The Vampyre* was credited by the publisher to Lord Byron when it was first published, in London's *New Monthly Magazine* of April 1, 1819, and said to have been written "at the request of a lady." In an effort to bolster that alleged authorship (and boost sales), the magazine publisher included a letter "from Geneva" whose author, probably the hack writer John Mitford, claimed to have received the manuscript, along with certain anecdotes about Byron's stay at the Villa Diodati, on the banks of Lake Geneva (discussed in the Foreword, text accompanying note 50, above), from "a lady," whose account of the ghost story competition differs from Mary Shelley's recollection:

Among other things which the lady, from whom I procured these anecdotes, related to me, she mentioned the outline of a ghost story by Lord Byron. It appears that one evening Lord B., Mr. P. B. Shelly [*sic*], the two ladies and the gentleman before alluded to [Mary Shelley, Claire Clairmont, and Polidori], after having perused a German work, which was entitled Phantasmagoriana, began relating ghost stories; when his lordship having recited the beginning of Christabel, then unpublished, the whole took so strong a hold of Mr. Shelly's mind, that he suddenly started up and ran out of the room. The physician and Lord Byron followed, and discovered him leaning against a mantle-piece, with cold drops of perspiration trickling down his face. After having given him something to refresh him, upon enquiring into the cause of his alarm, they found that his wild imagination having pictured to him the bosom of one of the ladies with eyes (which was reported of a lady in the neighbourhood where he lived) he was obliged to leave the room in order to destroy the impression. It was afterwards proposed, in the course of conversation, that each of the company present should write a tale depending upon some supernatural agency, which was undertaken by Lord B., the physician, and Miss M. W. Godwin. My friend, the lady above referred to, had in her possession the outline of each of these stories, I obtained them as a great favour, and herewith forward them to you, as I was assured you would feel as much curiosity as myself, to peruse the *ebauches* of so great a genius, and those immediately under his influence. [Note: We have in our possession the Tale of Dr. _____, as well as the outline of that of Miss Godwin. The latter has already appeared under the title of 'Frankenstein; or, The Modern Prometheus;' the former, however, upon consulting with its author, we may, probably, hereafter give to our readers.—ED.]

of his early life. Poor Polidori[6] had some terrible idea about a skull-headed lady, who was so punished for peeping through a key-hole—what to see I forget—something very shocking and wrong of course; but when she was reduced to a worse condition than the renowned Tom of Coventry,[7] he did not know what to do with her, and was obliged to despatch her to the tomb of the Capulets,[8] the only place for which she was fitted. The illustrious poets also,[9] annoyed the platitude of prose, speedily relinquished their uncongenial task.

I busied myself to *think of a story,*—a story to rival those which had excited us to this task. One which would speak to the mysterious fears of our nature, and awaken thrilling horror—one to make the reader dread to look round, to curdle the blood, and quicken the beatings of the heart. If I did no[t accom]plish these things, my ghost story would be unworthy of its name. I [thought] and pondered—vainly. I felt that blank incapability of invention wh[ich is the] greatest misery of authorship, when dull Nothing replies to our anxi[ous invo]cations. *Have you thought of a story?* I was asked each morning, and ea[ch morn]ing I was forced to reply with a mortifying negative.[10]

Every thing must have a beginning, to speak in Sanchean[11] ph[rase; and] that beginning must be linked to something that went before. The Hindoos

[handwritten note: Basically the movie we watched]

6. Polidori was already ten years in the grave when Mary Shelley wrote this phrase, having committed suicide, it appears, in 1821. Byron, too, was seven years dead, and of course Percy Shelley had drowned nine years previous.

7. Better known as "Peeping Tom of Coventry." Brewer's *Dictionary of Phrase and Fable* recounts,

> Leofric, Earl of Mercia and Lord of Coventry, imposed some very severe imposts on the people of Coventry, which his countess, Godiva, tried to get mitigated. The earl, thinking to silence her importunity, said he would comply when she had ridden naked from one end of the town to the other. Godiva took him at his word, actually rode through the town naked, and Leofric remitted the imposts. Before Godiva started, all the inhabitants voluntarily confined themselves to their houses, and resolved that anyone who stirred abroad should be put to death. A tailor thought to have a peep, but was rewarded with the loss of his eyes, and has ever since been called Peeping Tom of Coventry.

8. Juliet's family in Shakespeare's *Romeo and Juliet*.

9. Meaning Lord Byron and Percy Shelley.

10. This self-effacing version of the gestation of *Frankenstein* is contradicted by Polidori's diary (*The Diary of Dr. John William Polidori, 1816, Relating to Byron, Shelley, etc.* (London: Forgotten Books, 2012), which records, on June 17, "The ghost-stories are begun by all but me" (125).

11. Sancho Panza, Don Quixote's faithful squire in Cervantes's masterpiece, says, "methinks in this matter of government, the beginning is everything" (Part II, chapter 33, Margaret Oliphant, ed. and trans., *Cervantes*, [Edinburgh and London: William Blackwood and Sons, 1880], 185).

give the world an elephant to support it, but they make the elephant stand upon a tortoise.[12] Invention, it must be humbly admitted, does not consist in creating out of void, but out of chaos; the materials must, in the first place, be afforded: it can give form to dark, shapeless substances, but cannot bring into being the substance itself. In all matters of discovery and invention, even of those that appertain to the imagination, we are continually reminded of the story of Columbus and his egg.[13] Invention consists in the capacity of seizing on the capabilities of a subject, and in the power of moulding and fashioning ideas suggested to it.

Columbus Breaking the Egg, by William Hogarth (1752).

12. In Hindu mythology, the world is supported on the back of the elephant Maha-pudma, who stands on the back of the tortoise Chukwa (per Brewer, *Dictionary of Phrase and Fable*).

13. The story, told by many (an early version may be found in Girolamo Benzoni's *Historia del Mondo Nuovo*, published in 1565) and undoubtedly apocryphal, goes as follows: One night, while dining, Columbus became annoyed when a detractor complained that anyone could have found the lands to which Columbus had famously voyaged and that the simplicity of the feat made it trivial. Columbus replied that anything is easy once you know how it's done. He demonstrated the principle by challenging the detractor to stand an egg on its end. The challenger appeared puzzled, whereupon Columbus crushed one end of the egg against the tabletop, permitting it to stand easily.

Many and long were the conversations between Lord Byron and Shelley, to which I was a devout but nearly silent listener.[14] During one of these, various philosophical doctrines were discussed, and among others the nature of the principle of life, and whether there was any probability of its ever being discovered and communicated. They talked of the experiments of Dr. Darwin, (I speak not of what the Doctor really did, or said that he did, but, as more to my purpose, of what was then spoken of as having been done by him,) who preserved a piece of vermicelli in a glass case, till by some extraordinary means it began to move with voluntary motion.[15] Not thus, after all, would life be

14. Polidori's diary casts doubt on this as well, suggesting that it was a conversation on June 15 between Percy Shelley and Polidori, not Percy Shelley and Byron, that sparked Mary Shelley's imagination; furthermore, Polidori's medical background makes his participation in conversation involving Galvani's work more likely than Byron's. On the other hand, Mary Shelley's journal describes the nightly conversations at the Villa Diodati as *"tête-à-tête"* between Percy Shelley and Byron (Jones, ed., *Mary Shelley's Journal*, 184), while Polidori describes the June 15 conversation as being "about principles—whether man was to be thought merely to be an instrument," rather than about the possibilities of reanimation.

15. There is no other record of a discussion of Darwin in the presence of Mary Shelley. Scholars speculate that she may be misremembering her reading of his epic poem *The Temple of Nature, or The Origin of the Society* (1802). In the "additional notes" to the poem, Darwin discusses the spontaneous vitality of microscopic animals:

> Some of the microscopic animals are said to remain dead for many days or weeks, when the fluid in which they existed is dried up, and quickly to recover life and motion by the fresh addition of water and warmth. Thus the chaos redivivum of Linnæus dwells in vinegar and in bookbinders paste: it revives by water after having been dried for years, and is both oviparous and viviparous; Syst. Nat. Thus the vorticella or wheel animal, which is found in rain water that has stood some days in leaden gutters, or in hollows of lead on the taps of houses, or in the slime or sediment left by such water, though it discovers no sign of life except when in the water, yet it is capable of continuing alive for many months though kept in a dry state. In this state it is of a globulous shape, exceeds not the bigness of a grain of sand, and no signs of life appear; but being put into water, in the space of half an hour a languid motion begins, the globule turns itself about, lengthens itself by slow degrees, assumes the form of a lively maggot, and most commonly in a few minutes afterwards puts out its wheels, swimming vigorously through the water as if in search of food; or else, fixing itself by the tail, works the wheels in such a manner as to bring its food to its mouth; English Encyclopedia, Art. Animalcule. Thus some shell-snails in the cabinets of the curious have been kept in a dry state for ten years or longer, and have revived on being moistened with warmish water; Philos. Transact. So eggs and seeds after many months torpor, are revived by warmth and moisture; hence it may be concluded, that even the organic particles of dead animals may, when exposed to a due degree of warmth and moisture, regain some degree of vitality, since this is done by more complicate animal organs in the instances above mentioned." (Additional Note I, paragraph 7)

Note that Darwin mentions *vorticella*, tiny protozoa, which Mary Shelley may have confused with *vermicelli* ("little worms"), a fine-stranded pasta. The "pasta" theory was first

given. Perhaps a corpse would be re-animated; galvanism[16] had given token of such things: perhaps the component parts of a creature might be manufactured, brought together, and endued with vital warmth.

Night waned upon this talk, and even the witching hour had gone by, before we retired to rest. When I placed my head on my pillow, I did not sleep, nor could I be said to think. My imagination, unbidden, possessed and guided me, gifting the successive images that arose in my mind with a vividness far beyond the usual bounds of reverie. I saw—with shut eyes, but acute mental vision,—I saw the pale student of unhallowed arts kneeling beside the thing he had put together. I saw the hideous phantasm of a man stretched out, and then, on the working of some powerful engine, show signs of life, and stir with an uneasy, half vital motion. Frightful must it be; for supremely

---

advanced by Desmond King-Hele, in *Erasmus Darwin and the Romantic Poets* (New York: St. Martin's Press, 1986).

Ashton Nichols, of the Department of English at Dickinson College, suggests that the connection to pasta in Mary Shelley's recollection may have arisen from paragraph 3 of the same note, in which Darwin describes an experiment:

> Thus in paste composed of flour and water, which has been suffered to become acescent [sour], the animalcules called eels, vibrio anguillula, are seen in great abundance; their motions are rapid and strong; they are viviparous, and produce at intervals a numerous progeny: animals similar to these are also found in vinegar; Naturalist's Miscellany by Shaw and Nodder, Vol. II. These eels were probably at first as minute as other microscopic animalcules; but by frequent, perhaps hourly reproduction, have gradually become the large animals above described, possessing wonderful strength and activity.

See http://users.dickinson.edu/~nicholsa/Romnat/frankmis.htm.

Gene Wilder and Mel Brooks reference this confusion in an early scene in the film *Young Frankenstein* (1974) in which Dr. Frankenstein responds to a student who refers to Darwin's preservation of a piece of vermicelli with the arch question, "Are you speaking of the worm or the spaghetti?"

16. Galvanism, bioelectrical force, was discovered in 1791 by Luigi Galvani. Galvani's nephew, Giovanni Aldini, subsequently performed experiments with corpses, attempting to reanimate them with electricity. In 1803, he performed a public experiment at Newgate Prison on the corpse of the executed criminal George Foster. The popular *Newgate Calendar*, the almanac of executions and the lives of executed criminals, reported: "On the first application of the process to the face, the jaws of the deceased criminal began to quiver, and the adjoining muscles were horribly contorted, and one eye was actually opened. In the subsequent part of the process the right hand was raised and clenched, and the legs and thighs were set in motion." German natural philosopher Johann Ritter (1776–1810), whose first researches involved Galvani's experiments, declared that "galvanic phenomena seemed to bridge the gap between living and non-living matter" (quoted in H. A. M. Snelders, "Romanticism and Naturphilosophie and the Inorganic Natural Sciences, 1797–1840: An Introductory Survey," *Studies in Romanticism* 9, no. 3 [1970], 199).

Giovanni Aldini (1803).

frightful would be the effect of any human endeavour to mock the stupendous mechanism of the Creator of the world. His success would terrify the artist; he would rush away from his odious handy-work, horror-stricken. He would hope that, left to itself, the slight spark of life which he had communicated would fade; that this thing, which had received such imperfect animation, would subside into dead matter; and he might sleep in the belief that the silence of the grave would quench for ever the transient existence of the hideous corpse which he had looked upon as the cradle of life. He sleeps; but he is awakened; he opens his eyes; behold the horrid thing stands at his bedside, opening his curtains, and looking on him with yellow, watery, but speculative eyes.

I opened mine in terror. The idea so possessed my mind, that a thrill of fear ran through me, and I wished to exchange the ghastly image of my fancy for the realities around. I see them still; the very room, the dark *parquet*, the closed shutters, with the moonlight struggling through, and the sense I had that the glassy lake and white high Alps were beyond. I could not so easily get rid of my hideous phantom; still it haunted me. I must try to think of something else. I recurred to my ghost story,—my tiresome unlucky ghost story! O! if I could only contrive one which would frighten my reader as I myself had been frightened that night!

Swift as light and as cheering was the idea that broke in upon me. 'I have found it! What terrified me will terrify others; and I need only describe the spectre which had haunted my midnight pillow.' On the morrow I announced that I had *thought of a story*. I began that day with the words, *It was on a dreary night of November,* making only a transcript of the grim terrors of my waking dream.

At first I thought but of a few pages—of a short tale; but Shelley urged me to develop the idea at greater length. I certainly did not owe the suggestion of one incident, nor scarcely of one train of feeling, to my husband, and yet but for his incitement, it would never have taken the form in which it was presented to the world. From this declaration I must except the preface. As far as I can recollect, it was entirely written by him.[17]

And now, once again, I bid my hideous progeny go forth and prosper. I have an affection for it, for it was the offspring of happy days, when death and grief were but words, which found no true echo in my heart. Its several pages speak of many a walk, many a drive, and many a conversation, when I was not alone; and my companion was one who, in this world, I shall never see more. But this is for myself; my readers have nothing to do with these associations.

I will add but one word as to the alterations I have made. They are principally those of style. I have changed no portion of the story, nor introduced any new ideas or circumstances. I have mended the language where it was so bald as to interfere with the interest of the narrative; and these changes occur almost exclusively in the beginning of the first volume. Throughout they are entirely confined to such parts as are mere adjuncts to the story, leaving the core and substance of it untouched.

M.W.S.
London, October 15, 1831.

17. See Preface, note 4, above.

APPENDIX 2
A Chronology of the Events of
Frankenstein[1]

1772	Victor Frankenstein born
1776	Elizabeth Lavenza comes to live with the Frankensteins
1784	Justine Moritz enters the Frankenstein household
1785	Victor begins to read the alchemists

1. Leonard Wolf, in "A Chronology of Events in *Frankenstein*," *The Annotated Frankenstein*, has carefully calculated the length of the intervals of time elapsing between the events prior to and after the "birth" of the creature as described in the 1818 text. However, Wolf refrains from affixing specific years, because he is unable to reconcile the specific dates of Walton's August 5 letter and William's May 7 death. See note 43, Volume I, Letter IV, and note 5, Volume I, Chapter VI, above. Anne K. Mellor has worked out her own timetable, without explanation, and suggests that Mary Shelley chose dates overlapping with key events of the French Revolution (*Mary Shelley: Her Life, Her Fiction, Her Monsters*, 238, n. 22).

Based on Wolf's computation of the intervals, this editor has worked backward and forward from the date determined for the "birthdate" to determine the dates set forth in the table. Charles E. Robinson, in *The Original Frankenstein*, speculates that Shelley herself constructed a chronology at some point, for she clearly made alterations in the intervals and ages given in the Draft and the final 1818 text. For example, the interval between Victor's departure from Geneva and his return is indicated in three different places in the Draft as five years (which would shift many of the dates in this table forward a year), but this was corrected in the final text to six years. However, the following table relies only on the data in the 1818 text.

1787	Victor sees tree struck by lightning
1789	Victor's mother, Caroline, and Elizabeth contract scarlet fever; Caroline dies; Justine leaves to live with her mother; Victor leaves for Ingolstadt
1791	Victor attains fame at university
Early 1793	Victor sick with nervous exhaustion
November 1793	Creature made
Late Autumn 1794	De Lacey family confrontation
May 1795	Victor and Henry Clerval tour Ingolstadt; death of Victor's brother William; Victor's father, Alphonse, writes to Victor
June 1795	Victor returns to Geneva; Justine convicted of William's death
July 1795	Interview with creature at Chamonix
August 1795	Victor departs Switzerland
September 1795	Victor and Henry arrive in England
March 1796	Victor and Henry depart London
August 1796	Victor relocates to island cottage; Henry stays in Perth
Autumn 1796	Female creature made and destroyed
September 1796	Death of Henry; Victor arrested

December 1796	Victor released from prison[2]
May 1797	Victor and Alphonse return to Le Havre
June 1797	Victor and Alphonse return to Geneva
Summer 1797	Marriage to Elizabeth; death of Elizabeth and Alphonse
January 1798	Victor begins pursuit of creature
December 1798	Walton arrives in Petersburg
July 31, 1799	Walton's ship is icebound; crew spots creature
August 1, 1799	Walton meets Victor
August 20, 1799	Victor begins to tell Walton his story
September 11, 1799	Victor dies
September 12, 1799	Creature boards Walton's ship, tells his story, and departs

2. This date is based on the interval determined by Wolf but appears to be too early—see note 10, Volume III, Chapter V, above.

APPENDIX 3

On "Frankenstein."

BY THE LATE PERCY BYSSHE SHELLEY[1]

THE NOVEL OF "Frankenstein, or the Modern Prometheus," is undoubtedly, as a mere story, one of the most original and complete productions of the age. We debate with ourselves in wonder as we read it, what could have been the series of thoughts, what could have been the peculiar experiences that awakened them, which conducted in the author's mind, to the astonishing combination of motives and incidents and the startling catastrophe which compose this tale. There are perhaps some points of subordinate importance which prove that it is the Author's first attempt. But in this judgement, which requires a very nice discrimination, we may be mistaken. For it is conducted throughout with a firm and steady hand. The interest gradually accumulates, and advances towards the conclusion with the accelerated rapidity of a rock rolled down a mountain. We are held breathless with suspense and sympathy, and the heaping up of incident on incident, and the working of passion out of passion. We cry "hold, hold, enough"—but there is yet something to come, and like the victim whose history it relates we think we can bear no more, and yet more is to be borne. Pelion is heaped on Ossa, and Ossa on Olympus. We climb Alp after Alp, until the horizon is seen, blank, vacant and limitless, and the head turns giddy, and the ground seems to fail under the feet.

1. Apparently written in 1818, the piece was first published in *The Athenaeum* for November 10, 1832, after publication of the 1831 edition (and ten years after the death of Percy Shelley). Although Percy Shelley may be viewed as one of the world's first "sock-puppet" reviewers, it is fascinating to receive his understanding of the intent of the work he helped create—quite a different intent, scholars observe, from what is now believed to be that of Mary Shelley.

This Novel thus rests its claim on being a source of powerful and profound emotion. The elementary feelings of the human mind are exposed to view, and those who are accustomed to reason deeply on their origin and tendency, will perhaps be the only persons who can sympathise to the full extent in the interest of the actions which are their result. But, founded on nature as they are, there is perhaps no reader who can endure any thing beside a new love-story, who will not feel a responsive string touched in his inmost soul. The sentiments are so affectionate and so innocent, the characters of the subordinate agents in this strange drama are clothed in the light of such a mild and gentle mind. — The pictures of domestic manners are every where of the most simple and attaching character. The pathos is irresistible and deep. Nor are the crimes and malevolence of the single Being, tho' indeed withering and tremendous, the offspring of any unaccountable propensity to evil, but flow inevitably from certain causes fully adequate to their production. They are the children, as it were, of Necessity and Human Nature. In this the direct moral of the book consists; and it is perhaps the most important, and of the most universal application, of any moral that can be enforced by example. Treat a person ill, and he will become wicked.[2] Requite affection with scorn; —let one being be selected, for whatever cause, as the refuse of his kind— divide him, a social being, from society, and you impose upon him the irresistible obligations— malevolence and selfishness. It is thus that, too often in society, those who are best qualified to be its benefactors and its ornaments, are branded by some accident with scorn, and changed, by neglect and solitude of heart, into a scourge and a curse.

The Being in "Frankenstein" is, no doubt, a tremendous creature. It was impossible that he should not have received among men that treatment which led to the consequences of his being a social nature. He was an abortion and an anomaly, and though his mind was such as its first impressions formed it, affectionate and full of moral sensibility, yet the circumstances of his existence were so monstrous and uncommon, that when the consequences of them became developed in action, his original goodness was gradually turned into the fuel of an inextinguishable misanthropy and revenge. The scene between the Being and the blind De Lacey in the cottage is one of the most profound and extraordinary instances of pathos that we ever recollect. It is impossible to read this dialogue—and indeed many other situations of a somewhat simi-

2. As has been seen above, though this theme certainly figured as part of Mary Shelley's intended message, there is so much more going on in the book that Percy Shelley may have been unable to recognize.

lar character—without feeling the heart suspend its pulsations with wonder, and the tears stream down the cheeks! The encounter and argument between Frankenstein and the Being on the sea of ice almost approaches in effect to the expostulations of Caleb Williams with Falkland.[3] It reminds us indeed somewhat of the style and character of Godwin to whom the Author has dedicated his work, and whose productions he seems to have studied. There is only one instance however in which we detect the least approach to imitation, and that is, the conduct of the incident of Frankenstein's landing and trial in Ireland. —The general character of the tale indeed resembles nothing that ever preceded it. After the death of Elizabeth, the story, like a stream which grows at once more rapid and profound as it proceeds, assumes an irresistible solemnity, and the magnificent energy and swiftness as of a tempest.

The church yard scene, in which Frankenstein visits the tombs of his family, his quitting Geneva and his journey through Tartary to the shores of the Frozen Ocean, resembles at once the terrible reanimation of a corpse, and the supernatural career of a spirit. The scene in the cabin of Walton's ship, the more than mortal enthusiasm and grandeur of the Being's speech over the dead body of his victim, is an exhibition of intellectual and imaginative power, which we think the reader will acknowledge has seldom been surpassed.

3. Characters appearing in William Godwin's *Caleb Williams*, referenced in the dedication of *Frankenstein*.

APPENDIX 4

Frankenstein on the Stage and the Screen

W HILE THE CRITICS may have been mixed in their reactions to the book, the public embraced it nearly instantaneously. By August 1818, five months after publication, a friend, the novelist Thomas Love Peacock,[1] wrote to Mary Shelley, "I went to the Egham races. I met on the course a great number of my old acquaintance, by the reading portion of whom I was asked a multitude of questions concerning 'Frankenstein' and its author. It seems to be universally known and read." A French edition of the book, the first foreign language version, appeared in 1821, and, as noted in the Foreword, an 1823 two-volume edition was published in England by G. & W. B. Whitaker. The 1818 text was reprinted numerous times, beginning in 1865, and it remained in print until 1942, when it appeared as an Armed Services edition. In 1831, a revised edition (though, as has been seen, Mary Shelley denied making any major changes) was published by H. Colburn and R. Bentley as part of their Standard Novels series. This contained the first illustrations, by Chevalier. The 1831 edition was reprinted by more than a half-dozen publishers in the nineteenth century and has been reprinted by countless publishers since.

The story began to take on a life of its own. In July 1823, Richard Brinsley Peake penned and staged *Presumption; or, The Fate of Frankenstein* at the Eng-

---

1. See Foreword, note 41, above.

T. P. Cooke as the creature in *Presumption, or the Fate of Frankenstein*, by Richard Brinsley Peake (1823).

lish Opera House. The play was an enormous success, moving to New Covent Garden in 1824. Only a few weeks after Peake's version opened, H. M. Milner's *Frankenstein! or, The Demon of Switzerland*, a melodrama with music, opened at the Royal Coburg Theatre. Peake burlesqued his own play in *Another Piece of Presumption* in October 1823, and numerous other London productions quickly followed, including *Frankenstein* (Royalty Theatre, 1823), *Frankenstein* (Coburg, 1823), and the burlesques *Frankenstein* (David-Royal Amphitheatre, 1823) *Frank-*

in-Steam (Adelphi, 1823), *Frankenstitch* (Surrey, 1823), and *Frank-n-Stein, or the Modern Promise to Pay* (Olympic, 1824).

A few years later, *Le Monstre et le Magicien*, based on *Frankenstein*, appeared on the Paris stage; a production in English translation opened later that year at the West London Theatre. Not to be outdone, Milner wrote a new work, based on the French play, called *Frankenstein; or, The Man and the Monster!* This again ran at the Royal Coburg Theatre, opening on July 3, 1826. "After 1826," writes Radu Florescu, "there was hardly a season in London, Edinburgh, Paris, Vienna, New York, in English provincial theatres or at the universities, where some melodramatic or burlesque adaption of *Frankenstein* was not performed either by professional or amateur groups."[2] On January 4, 1981, a production of *Frankenstein*, written by Victor Gialanella, opened and closed on Broadway, setting a (temporary) record for the most expensive Broadway flop of all time. In 2011, the National Theatre in London mounted a fascinating dramatic adaptation of *Frankenstein* by Nick Dear, directed by Danny Boyle, starring Benedict Cumberbatch and Jonny Lee Miller, who alternate the roles of Victor Frankenstein and the creature. Fans did not miss the fact that Cumberbatch and Miller star in two different well-received television versions of a modern Sherlock Holmes.

O. Smith as the monster, in Henry Milner's *Frankenstein; or the Man and the Monster* (1826).

Jonny Lee Miller as the creature and Benedict Cumberbatch as Victor Frankenstein, in the 2011 National Theatre production of *Frankenstein*.

VICTOR FRANKENSTEIN AND HIS creation are not the most filmed characters in history. That distinction belongs to Sherlock Holmes, with Dracula and Tarzan running close behind. However, the Internet Movie Database (www.imdb.com) lists 147 films with "Fran-

2. Radu Florescu, Alan G. Barbour, and Matei Cazacu, *In Search of Frankenstein* (Boston: New York Graphic Society, 1975), 166.

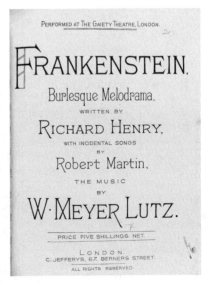

Richard Henry's *Frankenstein*, a burlesque melodrama (1887).

kenstein" in the title, and there are dozens of other films that include characters from Mary Shelley's novel. The following is merely a selection of some of the more noteworthy films (although "noteworthy" in this genre rarely indicates a film of quality). For a catalog of virtually every "Frankenstein" film made before 1984, see Donald Glut's comprehensive *The Frankenstein Catalog* (Jefferson, NC, and London: McFarland & Company, 1994).

Title	Year Released	Production Company	Notes
Frankenstein The first cinematic depiction of Frankenstein's creature, in Edison's 1910 *Frankenstein* (Edison Company), starring Charles Ogle as the creature.	1910	Thomas A. Edison	Long thought lost, this is the first filmed version of Shelley's tale. Though only a one-reel silent, the film is powerful and thrilling, with a brilliant special effect showing the creation of the monster (played by Charles Ogle). It can be found today on YouTube.
Il mostro di Frankenstein ("The Monster of Frankenstein")	1920	Albertini Film (Italian language)	Little is known about the film, now lost, but it was reportedly based on Shelley's novel.
Frankenstein	1931	Universal	Directed by James Whale, and though it strays far from Shelley's novel, the most influential production ever made. It starred, of course, Boris Karloff as the creature.

Title	Year Released	Production Company	Notes
Bride of Frankenstein Publicity photo of James Whale with the creature, during the shooting of *Bride of Frankenstein* (ca. 1935).	1935	Universal Poster for *La moglie di Frankenstein* (*The Bride of Frankenstein*) (Universal Pictures, 1935), directed by James Whale.	Also directed by Whale and with Karloff reprising his role as the creature, it also featured a frame depicting Mary Shelley, played by Elsa Lanchester, who also appears as the eponymous and iconic "Bride."
Son of Frankenstein	1939	Universal	Sequel to *Bride of Frankenstein*, with Karloff returning as the monster. Starring Basil Rathbone as Baron von Frankenstein and Bela Lugosi as Ygor, but without Whale's direction, the film pales in comparison to its predecessors.
Ghost of Frankenstein	1942	Universal	The studio attempted to squeeze more juice from the fruit, with Lon Chaney Jr. as the monster and a cast including Sir Cedric Hardwicke, Ralph Bellamy, Lionel Atwill, and Lugosi returning as Ygor, but the film is poorly regarded.

Title	Year Released	Production Company	Notes
Frankenstein Meets the Wolf Man	1943	Universal	With Chaney playing the Wolf Man, the studio cast Lugosi as the monster. For the first time, Universal used the name "Frankenstein" to mean the monster—Baroness Frankenstein (Ilona Massey) appears as a character and does indeed meet the Wolf Man's alter ego, Larry Talbot, but she is a minor character.
House of Frankenstein Poster for *House of Frankenstein* (Universal Pictures, 1944), directed by Earle Kenton and starring Boris Karloff as Dr. Gustav Niemann, John Carradine as Dracula, and Lon Chaney Jr. as Larry Talbot (the Wolfman), and with J. Carrol Naish, Lionel Atwill, and George Zucco.	1944	Universal	A weak sequel to *Frankenstein Meets the Wolf Man* and *Dracula's Daughter* (1936), it again starred Chaney as the Wolf Man and Boris Karloff as a mad doctor, leaving Glenn Strange to play the monster.
House of Dracula	1945	Universal	An even weaker sequel, this time to *House of Frankenstein,* with Chaney as the Wolf Man, John Carradine as Dracula, and Glenn Strange returning as the monster.

Title	Year Released	Production Company	Notes
Abbott and Costello Meet Frankenstein	1948	Universal	In a fitting demise for the Universal series, the boys send up the *House of Frankenstein/House of Dracula* films. Happily, Lugosi returned as Dracula, with Chaney appearing for the last time as the Wolf Man and Glenn Strange as the creature.
I Was a Teenage Frankenstein	1957	American International Pictures	Whit Bissell plays an English descendant of Victor Frankenstein, who comes to America to try his hand at mad science.
The Curse of Frankenstein	1957	Hammer Films (Warner Bros.)	Directed by Terence Fisher, this introduced Peter Cushing as the Baron Victor Frankenstein and starred Christopher Lee as the creature. The script is only loosely based on Shelley's novel.
Frankenstein 1970	1958	Allied Artists	Boris Karloff in a leaden performance as Baron Frankenstein and weakly directed by Howard W. Koch, but the film still has its admirers.

Title	Year Released	Production Company	Notes
The Revenge of Frankenstein *Left:* Poster for *The Revenge of Frankenstein* (Hammer Films, 1958), directed by Terence Fisher and starring Peter Cushing. *Right:* Poster for *La vendetta di Frankenstein* (*The Revenge of Frankenstein*) (Hammer Films, 1958), directed by Terence Fisher and starring Peter Cushing.	1958	Hammer Films (Columbia)	A sequel to *The Curse of Frankenstein*. Under Terence Fisher's direction, Cushing returned as the baron; Michael Gwynn plays the monster created by the baron.
The Evil of Frankenstein	1964	Hammer Films (Universal)	Cushing again plays the baron, with the monster portrayed by Kiwi Kingston. A flashback depicts a scene from Shelley's novel, and the film has been termed a sequel to a Hammer Film that was never made!
Frankenstein Meets the Spacemonster	1965	Futurama Entertainment Corporation (Allied Artists)	An artificial human is built for space travel; on returning to Earth, he combats aliens. Curiously, the film was released in Mexico as *Marte Invade a Puerto Rico* ("Mars Invades Puerto Rico")
Jesse James Meets Frankenstein's Daughter	1966	Circle Productions (Embassy Pictures)	The title pretty much says it all.

Title	Year Released	Production Company	Notes
Frankenstein Created Woman Poster for *La maledizione del Frankenstein* (distributed in most countries as *Frankenstein Created Woman*) (Hammer Films, 1967), starring Peter Cushing and Susan Denberg.	1967	Hammer Films (20th Century Fox)	Fisher returned to the directorial chair, with Cushing reprising the role of Baron Victor Frankenstein. The monster of this film is a woman, Christina, portrayed by Susan Denberg.
Frankenstein Must Be Destroyed	1969	Hammer Films (Warner Bros./ Seven Arts)	Terence Fisher directed Peter Cushing again, with another monster that is nondescript.
Frankenstein Unbound	1970	Mount Company	Produced and directed by Roger Corman and starring John Hurt, the film is based on the Brian Aldiss novel and blends science fiction, time travel, the events of Shelley's life, and the events of her novel.

Title	Year Released	Production Company	Notes
The Horror of Frankenstein	1970	Hammer Films (Metro-Goldwyn-Mayer-EMI/Associated British Picture Corporation)	A remake of *The Curse of Frankenstein* without Cushing or Lee; David Prowse (who later played Darth Vader) appears as the monster.
Dracula vs. Frankenstein Poster for *Dracula vs. Frankenstein* (Troma Entertainment, 1971), directed by Al Adamson and starring J. Carrol Naish and Lon Chaney Jr.	1971	Independent International Pictures Corp.	Noteworthy solely for its cast, which included J. Carrol Naish as Dr. Frankenstein and Lon Chaney Jr.; Forrest Ackerman appears in a small part and was a technical consultant.
Blackenstein	1972	Eddie C. Stewart and Exclusive International Pix	Made in the heyday of black exploitation films, the script bears little resemblance to Shelley's story, though the "mad scientist" is Dr. Stein.

Title	Year Released	Production Company	Notes
La figlia di Frankenstein ("The Daughter of Frankenstein"), released in the U.S. as *Lady Frankenstein* Poster for *Lady Frankenstein* (Condor International Productions, 1971), directed by Mel Welles and starring Joseph Cotten.	1972	Condor International (New World Pictures) (Italian language)	Well regarded by some critics, especially the lead performance by Sara Bay as Tania Frankenstein. Also includes Joseph Cotten as Baron Frankenstein and bodybuilder Mickey Hargitay, remembered as the husband of Jayne Mansfield, as a police detective.
Les expériences érotiques de Frankenstein ("The Erotic Experiences of Frankenstein")	1972	Comtoir du Film Production/Fenis Film (French language)	With an appearance by Count Cagliostro as well as Dr. Frankenstein, the muddled script is mildly erotic.
El espiritù de la colmena ("The Spirit of the Beehive")	1973	Elias Querejeta P.C. (Spanish language)	In 1940, a young girl is deeply taken with the film *El Dr. Frankenstein, autor del monstruo,* the Spanish-language version of the 1931 *Frankenstein.*

Title	Year Released	Production Company	Notes
Frankenstein: The True Story	1973	Universal, NBC	Made for television, this four-hour film was scripted by Christopher Isherwood and Don Bachardy and had a distinguished cast including James Mason, Leonard Whiting, David McCallum, Jane Seymour, John Gielgud, Ralph Richardson, and Michael Sarrazin as the creature. Though set in the appropriate time period, it bears little resemblance to Shelley's tale.
Flesh for Frankenstein, also released as *Andy Warhol's Frankenstein* Poster for Andy Warhol's *Chair pour Frankenstein* (*Flesh for Frankenstein*)(Compagnia Cinematographia Champion, 1973), written and partially directed by Paul Morrissey and starring Udo Kier.	1974	Rassam Production (Bryanston Pictures)	With the ubiquitous Udo Kier as Baron Frankenstein as well as several Warhol "regulars" and including special effects by Carlo Rambaldi (later famed for his work on *E.T. the Extraterrestrial*), Warhol's nearly incoherent film involves zombies, disemboweling, and sex.

Title	Year Released	Production Company	Notes
Frankenstein and the Monster from Hell	1974	Hammer Films (Paramount)	Terence Fisher returned to direct Peter Cushing in this sequel to *Frankenstein Must Be Destroyed*; David Prowse again played the monster. Though Cushing's baron is left alive and contemplating his next creation at the film's end, the Hammer Films series ended here.
The Rocky Horror Picture Show	1975	20th Century Fox	An enduring camp classic, starring Tim Curry as the inimitable Dr. Frank-N-Furter.
Young Frankenstein	1975	20th Century Fox	Mel Brooks's finest film, in the view of many, with a screenplay co-written by its star, Gene Wilder. A warm and very affectionate sendup of the Universal series of *Frankenstein* films. See below for an interview with Mel Brooks about the film forty years after its making.
Victor Frankenstein	1977	ASPEKT Film AB (Films Around the World)	A faithful adaptation of Shelley's novel, without, however, the character of Justine.
Dr. Franken	1980	NBC	Robert Vaughn stars as a slightly mad physician who reanimates a John Doe. "Suggested by" Shelley's novel.

Title	Year Released	Production Company	Notes
Mary Shelley's Frankenstein Poster for *Mary Shelley's Frankenstein* (TriStar Pictures, 1994), directed by and starring Kenneth Branagh as Victor and Robert De Niro as the creature.	1994	TriStar Pictures/ Japan Satellite Broadcasting Corporation/ The IndieProd Company	Directed by and starring Kenneth Branagh as Victor Frankenstein and Robert De Niro as the creature, the film is well intentioned (hoping to emulate the success of Coppola's 1992 *Bram Stoker's Dracula*) but ultimately boring; it was a box office failure.
Frankenstein and Me	1996	Desert Music Pictures	A sweet, small film, starring Burt Reynolds, about a young boy who dreams of Universal's monsters (Dracula, Frankenstein, the Wolf Man).
Frankenstein Reborn	2005	The Asylum	A modern retelling, with many character names drawn from the novel.
Frankenstein	2007	Impossible Pictures	Made for television, set slightly in the future, featuring Dr. Victoria Frankenstein.

Title	Year Released	Production Company	Notes
Bikini Frankenstein	2010	Retromedia Entertainment	Soft porn, about an evil doctor who creates an undead sex kitten.
Army of Frankensteins	2013	Boiling Point Media/Six Stitches Entertainment	An evil doctor (do we sense a theme here?) sends back in time a young man who finds himself in the middle of the American Civil War along with an army of undead creatures.
I, Frankenstein Poster for *I, Frankenstein* (Hopscotch Features, 2014), written and directed by Stuart Beattie.	2014	Hopscotch Features/ Lakeshore Entertainment/ Lionsgate	An action film, hoping to cash in on the success of the *Underworld* films, in which Shelley's creature survives from 1795 to the present, only to be caught up in a war between immortal demons and angels.

INTERVIEW WITH MEL BROOKS,
WRITER-DIRECTOR OF *YOUNG FRANKENSTEIN*

Mel Brooks (photo by Angela George, used under CC-by-SA 3.0 license).

In March 2014, the editor had the privilege of conducting a short interview via telephone with legendary writer-director Mel Brooks about his wonderful 1974 film *Young Frankenstein*.

LSK: Mr. Brooks, you have co-credit on the script, but I assume that it was all your idea?

MB: No, it wasn't. I'll tell you exactly how the idea to do the film came about. I was making a movie called *Blazing Saddles* [in late 1973], and a leading actor in it, besides Cleavon Little, was Gene Wilder. Gene Wilder was busy one day in a corner while we were preparing the lighting to shoot a scene with him, and he was scribbling on a legal pad. I said, "Gene, what are you writing?" And he said, "I have an idea for a film." I said, "What's the idea?" He said, "It's called *Young*

Frankenstein. It's about a Frankenstein today who is ashamed of his crazy forebears, the ones that think they can reanimate dead tissue." So I said, "That's interesting," and he said, "Well, I think it would make an interesting and funny movie." I said, "Well, let me see a draft." He showed me about fifteen or sixteen pages that was an outline and some rough dialogue. I liked it very much, and I said, "When you finish it, why don't you show it to me?" He said, "Why don't you write it with me?" I said, "OK, sure," so we began working on it. Even when I was editing *Blazing Saddles*, at night we were working on *Young Frankenstein*. It was fun right from the beginning, so I knew it would work, I knew it had to be done.

James Whale, director of *Frankenstein* (Universal Pictures, 1931) and *Bride of Frankenstein* (Universal Pictures, 1935)

LSK: Were you familiar with the book? Or only the old [1931] film?

MB: That's a good question. I knew the book really well, I'd read it more than once, but I was really enamored of the James Whale films.

LSK: That's impressive. Unlike most comedies, and there have been dozens of Frankenstein films made, none of them paid much attention to the original material. You paid a great deal of attention to that material. How did you get Gene Hackman involved in the film?

MB: Gene Wilder used to play tennis on weekends in those days with Gene Hackman. Hackman asked him what he was doing, and Wilder said, "We're doing a kind of strange comedy. Mel wants to do it in black and white to give it some gravitas," and he explained *Young Frankenstein*. Hackman said, "Do you think there would be anything in it for me? I'd love to do a comedy!" And Wilder said, "There's a perfect part for you, but there's no money. It's a very low-budget film." Hackman replied, "I don't care about the money, I just want to do what I enjoy." So he came over, and he met with me, and I said, "It would be an honor to work with you. I don't have to audition you, I know you're good!" And that's how it came about.

LSK: I saw also, from doing a little research, that you cast a real Frankenstein. It's uncredited, but he appeared in the film.

MB: Yeah. He had the name "Frankenstein," and he was kind of, you know, joyous, and so we put him in. I think he was one of the people who was screaming while the creature was being thrown through the window.

LSK: How did you resist giving him a screen credit?

MB: I think he said he didn't want credit. Let me give you one more piece of information that might be valuable. In the film that James Whale did in 1931, there is a scene where the doctor brings the monster to life. In that scene, there are a lot of gadgets, and a lot of buzzing and fizzing and all kinds of little machines that constituted the state of the art of electronics in 1931. I loved them and thought they were just fabulous. I did some research, and I found that they were created by a man named Kenneth Strickfaden. I traced him and found that he had all of that stuff in a garage in Santa Monica. We went down and told him we would give him credit and pay him enough money that it would make sense to lease his equipment to us, so we could use it in the movie. He said, "Sure," and I said he'd have to supervise it so we didn't make any mistakes. So he did it, and we have in our movie in the original laboratory scene all of that stuff.

LSK: And it works so well, because in the script, Gene Wilder discovers his grandfather's original laboratory!

MB: This year [2014], 20th Century Fox is doing an incredible celebration of *Young Frankenstein*—it is indeed the fortieth anniversary of the making of the film. We're going to go to Grauman's Chinese Theater [in Hollywood] and put our fingers in the cement and all that.

LSK: Where is that equipment now?

MB: I think it's in the hands of Strickfaden's heirs [Strickfaden died in 1984, at the age of eighty-eight].

LSK: What's your favorite scene in the film?

MB: My favorite scene is the quiet little comedy scene, with Marty Feldman, when the doctor has failed miserably and the creature has not come to life. It lays there as this big, dead hulk, stitched together, and they're having dinner, and it starts with Gene Wilder, Dr. Frankenstein, saying "Reputation, reputation," just the way they did in the old movie. And [Inga, played by Teri Garr] says, "Darling, you haven't touched your food," and he puts his hands in the mashed potatoes, and he says, "There, I've touched it, I've touched it!" Then Marty Feldman comes in and he says, "I'll never forget my old dad. When these things would happen to him—the things he'd say to me . . ." and then he doesn't talk! It was the most brilliant and crazy thing he ever did! Everyone just waits and waits, and he doesn't talk. So finally—I didn't do any direction at all—finally, after two minutes of silence, Gene picks it up and yells, "What did he say?" And Marty Feldman says, "Get out of the bathroom, give someone else a chance!" And then he sticks a big potato in his mouth. It's just the most unusual, crazy dinner scene ever done on film.

LSK: There are so many wonderful scenes.

MB: I was so happy to get that on film! One scene we just couldn't get on film, we just all kept breaking up laughing. That was the one in which Gene Wilder says, "All right, get the bags." And Marty Feldman says, "OK, you get the blonde, I'll get the one in the turban."

LSK: It's so Marx Brothers! What was your biggest disappointment? What did you not get to do that you wanted to do?

MB: I had no disappointments. I did absolutely everything I wanted to do. Not even in the release of the film—I loved what Fox did. I loved Alan Ladd Jr. for giving us all the money, but it wasn't that much; we made the whole film for $2.2 million, I think. It was going to be a Columbia picture but they wouldn't allow me to make it in black and white. But when I got to Fox, Laddie said that it should be in black and white, as a salute to the great James Whale. So Laddie was very important to the film, to the stature of the film and the feelings about it.

LSK: I look forward to showing it in my class!

MB: It was a pleasure talking to you. I'm glad someone is doing a companion to the book!

APPENDIX 5
Frankenstein in Academia

I N THE FINAL quarter of the twentieth century, scholars rediscovered *Frankenstein* and Mary Shelley. As Timothy Morton writes, *"Frankenstein* criticism [is] an industry that has been burgeoning since the 1980s."[1] Morton suggests a breakdown into six categories, which he admits are wholly arbitrary: (1) the body, medicine, and science; (2) commodity culture and social structure; (3) gender and queer theories; (4) genre, literary form, and literary history; (5) language and psyche; and (6) race, colonialism, and orientalism. More than fifteen years have elapsed since Morton's categorization, and the growth of *Frankenstein* scholarship has continued apace, especially with the proliferation of Shelley websites.[2] Without creating an extensive bibliography, it is not possible to give a true picture of the breadth of *Frankenstein* studies, but Morton's categories remain useful for an overview of the field.[3]

1. Timothy Morton, ed., *Mary Shelley's Frankenstein: A Sourcebook* (London and New York: Routledge, 2001), 80.

2. For a splendid collection of digitized manuscripts of Percy Shelley, Mary Shelley, William Godwin, and Mary Wollstonecraft, see www.shelleygodwinarchive.org; see also http:// www.poetryfoundation.org/bio/mary-wollstonecraft-shelley for an excellent detailed overview of Mary Shelley's life and work. For a chronology and resource site, see http://www .rc.umd.edu/reference/chronologies/mschronology. A nice fan-created site, focusing primarily on *Frankenstein*, is http://www.marywshelley.com/. There are dozens more.

3. See, for example, the recent Harvard University Press publication, *The Annotated Frankenstein*, edited by Susan J. Wolfson and Ronald L. Levao (2012), which details more than

The "body, medicine, and science" category looks at science in Mary Shelley and Percy Shelley's day and at the two writers' involvement with key figures in the scientific revolution. See, for example, Marilyn Butler's fine essay "The Shelleys and Radical Science,"[4] examining the Shelleys' reading in science, or Martin Willis's broader work, *Mesmerists, Monsters, and Machines: Science Fiction and the Cultures of Science in the Nineteenth Century.*[5] The subject has been examined in popular books such as Roseanne Montillo's *The Lady and Her Monsters: A Tale of Dissections, Real-Life Dr. Frankensteins, and the Creation of Mary Shelley's Masterpiece.*[6] The Shelleys found themselves in the middle of the debate among scientists (the name itself a neologism of the age) about the nature of the "life-principle"—with friends like John Abernethy and Humphry Davy on the "materialist" side and William Lawrence on the "theological" side of the issue.[7] Other historical-scientific issues, such as the need for cadavers for medical study[8] and the discoveries of the properties of electricity,[9] are woven into the text of *Frankenstein.*

Under "commodity culture and social structure," Moore intends to include studies of Marxist thought and cultural studies, as well as literary criticism that focuses on how the novel reflects its specific historical context ("historicism"). Elsie B. Michie, for example, argues that *Frankenstein* is a story of production of a "commodity," namely the creature, and that Victor Frankenstein is an alienated producer of commodities. Even the novel itself is viewed as a commodity to be produced by an artist alienated from the marketplace.[10] Franco Moretti argues that the creature is a displaced version of the worker, arising from the feudal poor. Viewed as a race apart, he is deeply disturbing to

---

fifty critical works in a section headed only as "Further Reading." Criticism of Bram Stoker's *Dracula* falls into much the same categories as those suggested by Morton for *Frankenstein*—see Leslie S. Klinger, ed., "Sex, Lies and Blood: *Dracula* in Academia," in *The New Annotated Dracula* (New York: W. W. Norton, 2008), 537–46.

4. In Marilyn Butler, ed., *Frankenstein* (Oxford and New York: Oxford University Press, 1994), xv–xxi.

5. Published by Kent State University Press in 2006.

6. Published by William Morrow in 2013.

7. See Preface, note 8, above.

8. See, for example, Tim Marshall, *Murdering to Dissect: Graverobbing,* Frankenstein, *and the Anatomy Literature* (Manchester: Manchester University Press, 1995), and note 11, Volume I, Chapter III, above.

9. See note 51, Volume I, Chapter I, above.

10. Elsie B. Michie, "Production Replaces Creation: Market Forces and *Frankenstein* as Critique of Romanticism," *Nineteenth-Century Contexts* 12, no. 1 (1988): 27–33.

the bourgeoisie. In Moretti's view, "The literature of terror is born precisely *out of the terror of a split society*, and out of that desire to heal it."[11]

Frankenstein also echoes some of the debates of the French Revolution on the role of government in child rearing, including the glosses of William Godwin, Mary Wollstonecraft, and the other English Jacobins. Scholars have examined in detail how the creature's education follows the Rousseauian program of schooling, and in particular how the creature mirrors the "natural man" of Rousseau's Second Discourse. The novel can certainly also be read as a demonstration, and a criticism, of Mary Shelley's father's views on education.[12] See Alan Richardson's fine collection *Literature, Education, and Romanticism: Reading as Social Practice, 1780–1832*.[13]

A very broad category of criticism may be labeled "gender and queer theories." Some of the criticism focuses on the historical and cultural contexts of gender images (that is, what it means to be a "man" or a "woman") in *Frankenstein*. For example, Mary Jacobus's important essay "Is There a Woman in This Text?"[14] considers whether *Frankenstein* should be read as criticism of the "oedipal politics" of Milton's *Paradise Lost*. She observes that in Mary Shelley's narrative, the central tragedy of the creature's life is the inherent impossibility of his ever bonding with a female counterpart; instead he is forced to rely solely on his creator, the flawed Victor.

Other works of criticism focus on Mary Shelley's status as a woman writer, including biographical studies that emphasize her relationship to her father (and deceased mother), her experiences as a mother herself (with three chil-

11. Emphasis in the original. Franco Moretti, *Signs Taken for Wonders: Essays in the Sociology of Literary Forms*, trans. Susan Fischer, David Forgacs, and David Miller (London: Verso, 1983).

12. Godwin did not trust the idea of institutionalized learning: "The most desirable mode of education," he wrote, ". . . is that which is careful that all the acquisitions of the pupil shall be preceded and accompanied by desire. . . . The boy, like the man, studies because he desires it. He proceeds upon a plan of his own invention, or by which, by adopting, he has made his own. Everything bespeaks independence and inequality" (*The Enquirer*, 1797). In *An Enquiry Concerning Political Justice*, he was even more explicit: "No vice can be more destructive, than that which teaches us to regard any judgement as final, and not open to review. The same principle that applies to individuals, applies to communities. There is no proposition, at present apprehended to be true, so valuable, as to justify the introduction of an establishment for the purpose of inculcating it on mankind. Refer them to reading, to conversation, to meditation; but teach them neither creeds nor catechisms, either moral or political."

13. Published by Cambridge University Press in 1994. *Frankenstein* and Rousseau are discussed on pages 203–12.

14. Published in *New Literary History* 14 (1982): 117–41.

dren dying in childbirth or infancy), and her relationship to Percy Shelley. Key readings include Sandra M. Gilbert and Susan Gubar's "Horror's Twin: Mary Shelley's Monstrous Eve,"[15] a detailed feminist interpretation of the novel; Katherine C. Hill-Miller's *"My Hideous Progeny": Mary Shelley, William Godwin, and the Father-Daughter Relationship,*[16] which examines the overlapping figures of the creature, Elizabeth, and Mary Wollstonecraft; Ellen Moers's classic *Literary Women,*[17] and Anne K. Mellor's "Possessing Nature: The Feminine in *Frankenstein.*"[18]

As a novel that has multiple pairings of women (Elizabeth/Justine, Elizabeth/Caroline, Elizabeth/biological mother, and Safie/Agatha) and multiple pairings of men (Alphonse/Victor, Victor/creature, Victor/Clerval, and Victor/Walton), *Frankenstein*'s queer relationships have been examined as well. For example, Frann Michel's "Lesbian Panic and Mary Shelley's *Frankenstein*" considers the novel's depiction of the infertility of same-sex relationships between women (Justine/Elizabeth and Agatha/Safie in particular) to be the result of the thwarted homosexual relationships that are at the book's core (Walton/Victor and Victor/creature).[19] That is, Michel holds that Mary Shelley's personal views about lesbianism are expressed indirectly through the failure of male homosexual relationships. Eve Kosofsky Sedgwick argues, in her influential *Between Men: English Literature and Homosocial Desire,*[20] that the male/male relationships in *Frankenstein* and in other late eighteenth-century and early nineteenth-century fiction, including Godwin's *Caleb Williams*, and the protagonists' creation, in such cases, of a small, all-male intimate family, express deep-rooted homophobia.

Much *Frankenstein* criticism has focused on the history of the genre, the growth and demise of gothic literature, Mary Shelley's literary influences, the source of many of her themes, her method and process as a writer, and problems of determining the "true" or "best" text of the work. Some, however, go beyond the novel itself to look at the relationship between author and text—

15. In Sandra M. Gilbert and Susan Gubar, *The Madwoman in the Attic: The Woman Writer and the Nineteenth-Century Literary Imagination* (New Haven, CT: Yale University Press, 1979), chapter 7.

16. Published by University of Delaware Press in 1995.

17. Published by Doubleday in 1977; see "Female Gothic," pp. 90–98.

18. In Anne K. Mellors, ed., *Romanticism and Feminism* (Bloomington: Indiana University Press, 1988), 220–32.

19. *GLQ: A Journal of Lesbian and Gay Studies* 2, no. 3 (1995): 237–52.

20. New York: Columbia University Press (1985).

and in this case, co-authors. Zachary Leader, for example, in "Parenting Frankenstein," argues that the degree to which Mary Shelley allowed Percy Shelley to collaborate with her reflected not only her likely anxieties about authorship (she was in fact only nineteen, cut off from her family, an unwed mother, and financially dependent on Percy; and, in light of her parentage, a great deal was expected of her), but also an acceptance of the social aspects of creation of a work of art. Percy Shelley (and Godwin) espoused a Promethean view of the creative act—of the importance that the artist break free of the common view and express a unique and personal vision. Anticipating Gertrude Stein, who held that artistic creation does not occur ex nihilo, Mary Shelley saw *Frankenstein* as more of a communal act, having recounted, in her introduction to the 1831 edition, how it arose from a group discussion; yet she also fiercely insisted that she was solely responsible for the final product, not her husband.[21] "None of which is to deny that Mary Shelley is likely to have felt dependent on Percy Shelley or was insecure about her style," suggests Lender. Rather he suggests, his revisions of *Frankenstein* "may have posed less of a test or threat" than some feminist critics think. However, Lender fails to note that Mary exercised a similar position of editor with regard to Percy's poetry, which would have given even more support to his arguments.[22]

Michael Scrivener's "Frankenstein's Ghost Story: The Last Jacobin Novel"[23] considers the work as a classic "Jacobin novel"—that is, a novel embodying the ideals of the French Revolution and its emphasis on a society that nurtures its citizens—examining the impact of what he describes as "errant utilitarianism." By "errant utilitarianism," Scrivener means the failure of the central characters—Robert Walton, the explorer-narrator of the tale who is seeking the North Pole; Victor Frankenstein; and the creature—to fulfill their goals of the betterment of the condition of humankind through advances in geography and biology and, in the case of the creature, overcoming prejudice with reason and exemplifying justice. Walton abandons his

21. In a letter to Sir Walter Scott, written after his review of *Frankenstein* misattributed the anonymous publication to Percy, Mary confessed that she was the author in order to prevent Scott from "continuing in the mistake of supposing Mr. Shelley guilty of a juvenile attempt of mine; to which—from it being written at an early age, I abstained from putting my name—and from respect to those persons from whom I bear it" (letter dated June 14, 1818).

22. Leader's essay appears in his *Revision and Romantic Authorship* (Oxford and New York: Oxford University Press, 1996), 167–205.

23. *Genre* 19, no. 3 (Fall 1986): 299–318.

quest; Victor does nothing to improve humanity's lot, as he had vowed to do; and the creature abandons his quest for justice, settling instead for revenge.

Opinions diverge concerning which text of the novel is "best." For more on this subject, see "A Note on the Text," above. Nora Crooks's "In Defence of the 1831 *Frankenstein*"[24] argues that the 1831 text is not substantively different from the 1818 version. Both depict characters who make choices in furtherance of their lofty goals that become disastrous—Walton, in his thoughtless pursuit of glory, and Victor, in his choice of scientific experimentation over domesticity. The later text, however, reflects Mary Shelley's evolving views of compulsion or "necessity" with respect to the characters' actions, allowing the principals to explain how they were compelled to make their choices. That is, the thirty-year-old Mary had more sympathy for the characters than did her nineteen-year-old self.

Beth Lau's "*Frankenstein, The Rime of the Ancient Mariner* and *Kubla Khan*" examines the numerous allusions to Coleridge's work in the novel as well as Mary Shelley's modeling, consciously or unconsciously, of the "passive-aggressive" nature of Victor Frankenstein on the similar character of the Ancient Mariner.[25] Joyce Carol Oates calls *Frankenstein* "in large part a kind of gloss upon or rejoinder to John Milton's Paradise Lost" and its tale of an angelic creature (Lucifer) exiled from his creator, noting that "the influence of John Milton on *Frankenstein* is so general as to figure on nearly every page."[26] *Frankenstein* is viewed as having deeply influenced Charlotte Brontë in her creation of *Jane Eyre* (1847). Arlene Young points out that both feature doppelgängers, both record protagonists' flight from their "only home," and both central characters find themselves voyeurs of idealized households, in the course of which they learn that domestic happiness is possible: The creature spies on the De Laceys (father, daughter Agatha, son Felix, and fiancée Safie), the idealized French family on whom he stumbles, and Jane detachedly observes Moor House, the home of the St. John siblings, where she finds temporary sanctuary in her wanderings.[27]

Studies that isolate the language of a text, often built around the work

24. In Michael Eberle-Sinatra, ed., *Mary Shelley's Fictions: From Frankenstein to Falkner* (Basingstoke, Hampshire: Macmillan, 2000).

25. The essay appears in Nicholas Roe, ed., *Samuel Taylor Coleridge and the Sciences of Life* (Oxford and New York: Oxford University Press, 2002), 207–23.

26. "Frankenstein's Fallen Angel," *Critical Inquiry*, 10 (1984), 543-54. See numerous notes below tracing the Miltonic influences.

27. "The Monster Within: The Alien Self in Jane Eyre and *Frankenstein*," *Studies in the Novel* 23, no. 3 (1991): 325–38.

of the psychoanalyst Jacques Lacan and his student Jacques Derrida, who developed the deconstructionist school of literary criticism, are of particular use in the context of *Frankenstein*, as the creature struggles to speak and eventually to read. In "Periphrastic Naming in Mary Shelley's *Frankenstein*," Bernard Duyfhuizen considers the terminology applied to the creature—"wretch," "monster," "dæmon"—and points out how the repetition of these words reveals the relationship of speaker to subject in some cases, as well as self-assessment when the word is applied by the speaker to the speaker.[28] Barbara Johnson, in her important essay "My Monster/My Self,"[29] examines the idea that *Frankenstein* can be read as Mary Shelley's autobiography, both as to the circumstances of her own life, including the death of her mother in childbirth and her own multiple pregnancies, and the travails of authorship. In building her case, Johnson outlines the parallels between Mary's and Victor Frankenstein's acts in the "workshop of filthy creation." Steven Vine's "Filthy Types: *Frankenstein*, Figuration, Femininity" analyzes how characters in the novel find themselves embodied in some other figure, seeking to create a likeness of themselves, a display of their being. Other psychological studies, noted in the text above, make more specific observations about incidents such as Victor's dream and the confusion between the identities of Victor and the creature.[30]

In Moore's final category, critics examine the novel in the light of the developments of imperialism and colonialism in Mary Shelley's era, including the generalized fear of the "Other." H. L. Malchow, for example, asserts that "Shelley's portrayal of her monster drew upon contemporary attitudes towards non-whites, in particular on fears and hopes of the abolition of slavery in the West Indies, as well as on middle-class apprehension of a Luddite proletariat." The creature, Malchow argues, has been "constructed out of a cultural tradition of the threatening 'Other'—whether troll or giant, gypsy or Negro—from the dark inner recesses of xenophobic fear and loathing."[31] Gayatri Chakravorty Spivak sees Victor's fears about the "race of devils" that he might foster (and the punishment he ultimately receives for acting on such fears) as indicative of Mary Shelley's anxieties about the European mission of

28. *Studies in the Novel* 27, no. 4 (1995): 477–92.

29. The essay appears in Johnson's *A World of Difference* (Baltimore: Johns Hopkins University Press, 1987), 144–54.

30. See, for example, note 33, Volume I, Chapter I, and note 3, Volume I, Chapter II, above.

31. "Frankenstein's Monster and Images of Race in Nineteenth-Century Britain," *Past and Present* 139 (1993): 90–130.

world domination.[32] Anne K. Mellor proposes that at the root of Victor's anxiety is a deep-seated fear of interracial breeding, prevalent in the culture and exemplified by the writings of the Shelleys' friend William Lawrence, a physician who contended that the Mongol race was disposed toward violence. In Mellor's view, Mary Shelley contrasts this with the creature's happiness at the prospect of the marriage of Felix De Lacey and the non-European Safie, whom he treats as his "family." Mellor argues that Mary is suggesting that if only Victor could have seen the creature as part of the race of Man, rather than as a mere expression of the white man, the creature's life might have been very different.[33]

32. *A Critique of Postcolonial Reason: Towards a Theory of the Vanishing Present* (Cambridge, MA: Harvard University Press, 1999), 132–40. See also W. Joseph Lew, "The Deceptive Other: Mary Shelley's Critique of Orientalism in *Frankenstein*," *Studies in Romanticism* 30 (Summer 1991): 255–83, a study of the ways in which Shelley viewed traditional Western uses of the East in literature.

33. "*Frankenstein*, Racial Science, and the Yellow Peril," *Nineteenth-Century Contexts* 23, no. 1 (2001): 1–28.

APPENDIX 6
Frankenstein in Popular Culture

BY THE MID-NINETEENTH century, Frankenstein and his creation had entered the vernacular. Fueled partly by the novel and partly by the success of stage productions and the scope of theatrical parodies, the name "Frankenstein" became a shorthand expression for good but misguided intentions, and his creature a symbol of powerful forces unleashed unwittingly. Political cartoons, for example, used the image of a Frankenstein monster in 1832 and 1833 in commentary on the new voting population; John Tenniel also used the "Frankenstein-monster" to represent new political forces in various cartoons in the last third of the nineteenth century. In 1854, John Leech used the image of the monster to depict the forces of the Crimean War let loose by an uninformed Russian government in conflict with Britain and the allied forces. An American cartoonist in 1900 used Frankenstein's monster to symbolize European imperialism threatening American democracy; others, including politicians, evoked Frankenstein and the creature as images of those who would turn over power to the "people" and the result-

"The Irish Frankenstein," by John Tenniel (1882).

"The Brummagem Frankenstein," by John Tenniel (1866) "Brummagem" was the working-class pronunciation of "Birmingham," the center of unrest regarding workers' suffrage.

"The Russian Frankenstein and His Monster," by John Leech (1854).

War as Frankenstein's monster, by Bob Satterfield (1915).

"Our Frankenstein, depicts the monster of European imperialism arriving to threaten America" (*Life* magazine, 1900, artist unknown).

ing monster that would arise. Later, with the rise of Hitler, the metaphor was again popularized: One political cartoon depicted Mussolini and Stalin confronting a monster-sized Hitler, with the caption "Are WE Frankensteins?"

Frankenstein was adapted into the medium of graphic stories, including comic books, magazines, comic strips, and cartoons. Donald Glut's *The Frankenstein Catalog* lists more than 650 comic book appearances through 1984,[1] and there have been many, many more since. For example, as of 2015, two series, *Joe Frankenstein* and *Frankenstein Underground*, are in print with major comic book publishers.

The earliest appearance of *Frankenstein* in a comic book was Dick Briefer's *Frankenstein*, issue number 7 of Prize Comics (Feature Publications, December 1940). The story was only loosely based on the novel: Victor Frankenstein creates a giant monster, accidentally released into society. The

"The American Frankenstein," political cartoon by Frank Bellew expressing concern over the power of the railroads (1874).

Political cartoon from the *Washington Post* (Clifford K. Berryman, 1940).

1. This extensive list *excludes* cameo appearances, cover illustrations, and characters inspired by or physically resembling the creature (such as the Hulk, or Lurch of the *The Addams Family*).

monster is tormented by humanity and vows revenge against Victor and the human race. Called *New Adventures of Frankenstein*, with the writer-artist credited as Frank N. Stein, the series ran for sixty-one issues.[2] The early stories are full of grisly horror; over time, however, the monster (later referred to as Frankenstein) diminished in size and menace, evolving into a patriotic hero and eventually a figure of humor, with little reference to the early tales. In 1945, the humorous character got his own comic book written and drawn by Briefer, with a different origin story; the series ran for thirty-three issues, from 1945 to 1954.

Although the creature and Victor Frankenstein appeared in dozens of other comic-book stories beginning in 1944 (with the first a *Captain America* story in U.S.A. Comics, no. 13), Mary Shelley's novel received serious attention in 1945, when Ruth A. Roche wrote a version for Classic Comics, no. 26, later reprinted under the Classics Illustrated series. A comic-book adaptation of the 1931 film appeared in 1963 under the title *Frankenstein*, from Dell Publishing, eventually devolving into a routine superhero series with no relation to the novel or film. Then, in 1973, the Marvel Comics Group began a series, initially entitled *The Monster of Frankenstein*, later changed to *The Frankenstein Monster*. The first three episodes are based on the novel; the balance are original adventures. The series ran only eighteen issues, but the character has appeared in various other comics in the Marvel universe.

There are other film and television tie-ins. Herman Munster, who is described as the "happy Frankenstein monster," appeared regularly in a sixteen-issue comic book series called *The Munsters* from 1964 to 1968, while the television series of the same name was first appearing. A four-issue series, written by Roy Thomas and called *Mary Shelley's Frankenstein*, appeared from Topps Comics in 1994—a tie-in to the Kenneth Branagh film of the same name. It included trading cards with stills from the film. In 2013, to promote the film *I, Frankenstein*, Darkstorm Comics created a downloadable graphic novel titled *I, Frankenstein: Genesis* by Kevin Grevioux.

Frankenstein, No. 1 (New York: Prize Comics, 1945). Dick Briefer, writer and artist.

Just as *Frankenstein* has been adapted into new stories on stage and in film and graphic media, the novel and its characters have been woven into other books. These are pastiches (stories intended to imitate the style of Mary Shelley), sequels, parodies, and original tales.

2. Issues 7–9, 11–54, and 55–68, the last appearing in February–March 1948.

Left: Frankenstein, Marvel Classics Comics, No. 20 (New York: Marvel Comics, 1977). John Warner, writer; Dino Castrillo, artist. *Center, left: Frankenstein* by Mary W. Shelley (New York: Gilberton Publications, 1945, as reissued in 1971) (Classics Illustrated, No. 26). Ruth A. Roche, adapter; Robert Hayward Webb and Ann Brewster, artists. *Center, right: Frankenstein* by Mary W. Shelley (New York: Gilberton Publications, 1945) (Classic Comics, No. 26). Ruth A. Roche, adapter; Robert Hayward Webb and Ann Brewster, artists. *Right: Frankenstein,* No. 2, September (New York: Dell Comics, 1966).

The tireless Donald Glut lists more than 150 titles in *The Frankenstein Catalog* through 1984, and many more have appeared since. Noteworthy are the novels by French author Benoît Becker, *La Tour de Frankenstein* and five others, published in the 1950s, and Robert J. Myers's novels *The Cross of Frankenstein* and *The Slave of Frankenstein*, straightforward sequels published in the 1970s. In 1973, Brian W. Aldiss, one of the deans of science fiction, published a novel called *Frankenstein Unbound*, in which a twenty-first-century politician is transported to nineteenth-century Switzerland, where he encounters both Victor Frankenstein and Mary Shelley.

Dean Koontz created a series of five novels, beginning with *Prodigal Son* in 2004 and running through 2011 with the appearance of *The Dead Town*, that are collectively known as Dean Koontz's *Frankenstein*. The series, which uses only a limited number of elements from Mary Shelley's novel, is set in present-day New Orleans and features Victor Frankenstein, now known as Victor Helios. Victor continues to make new creatures for his own purposes. He is opposed in the stories by two contemporary homicide detectives and Deucalion, who is identified as Frankenstein's original monster. In 2015, Stephen Jones edited a collection of stories about man-made creatures of human and subhuman pedigree, inspired by *Frankenstein*. Titled *The Mammoth Book of Frankenstein*, it includes reprints of stories that first appeared in pulp magazines by Robert Bloch and Manly Wade Wellman as well as modern stories from Ramsey Campbell, Dennis Etchison, Karl Edward Wagner, David J. Schow, R. Chetwynd-Hayes, David Case, Graham Masterson, Basil Copper,

Left: Mary Shelley's Frankenstein, No. 1 (New York: Topps Comics, 1994). Roy Thomas, writer; Rafael Kayanan, penciller (cover art by Timothy Bradstreet). (Based on the screenplay by Steph Lady and Frank Darabont.) *Center: The Monster of Frankenstein*, No. 1, January (New York: Marvel Comics Group, 1972). The title of the series was changed in issue no. 6 to *The Frankenstein Monster*. Gary Friedrich, writer; Mike Ploog, artist. *Right:* Herman Munster, as played by Fred Gwynne (from *The Munsters*, CBS, 1964–1966).

John Brunner, Guy N. Smith, Kim Newman, Paul J. McAuley, Roberta Lannes, Michael Marshall Smith, Daniel Fox, Adrian Cole, Nancy Kilpatrick, Brian Mooney, and Lisa Morton.

It would be impossible to catalog all images of the creature. There are dozens of licensed images from the 1931 Universal film, including a number of "action figures" and statuettes, in various locations and poses. There are also hundreds of unlicensed products, ranging from ashtrays to breakfast cereals to plush dolls, from rubber and latex masks to hats. A very unscientific survey can be made by searching www.zazzle.com, which sells products (factory-produced to hand-crafted) from a wide variety of sellers: It lists more than forty thousand "Frankenstein gifts," including stickers, posters, T-shirts, dolls, key rings, and so on. Truly, "It's alive!"

Bibliography[1]

PRIMARY SOURCES

Godwin, William. *The Elopement of Percy Bysshe Shelley and Mary Wollstonecraft Godwin, as Narrated by William Godwin with Commentary by H. Buxton Forman, C.B.* Boston: The Bibliophile Society, 1916.

Polidori, John William. *Diary of Dr. John William Polidori.* 1816. London: Forgotten Books, 2012.

Shelley, Mary Wollstonecraft. *The Annotated Frankenstein.* Edited by Leonard Wolf. New York: Clarkson N. Potter, Inc., 1977.

———. *The Annotated Frankenstein.* Edited by Susan J. Wolfson and Ronald Levao. Cambridge, MA: Belknap/Harvard University Press, 2012.

———. *The Essential Frankenstein.* Edited by Leonard Wolf. New York: iBooks, 2004.

———. *The Essential Frankenstein: The Definitive, Annotated Edition of Mary Shelley's Classic Novel.* Edited by Leonard Wolf. New York: Plume/Penguin Books, 2003.

———. *Frankenstein.* New York: Fall River Press, 2012. Illustrations by Lynd Ward.

———. *Frankenstein.* Adapted by Malvina G. Vogel. New York: Playmore Publishers, 1993. Great Illustrated Classics.

———. *Frankenstein.* Edited by Margaret Brantley. New York: Pocket Books, 2004.

---

1. This is but a partial bibliography, containing works referenced in the course of researching this book. A complete listing (albeit only through 1984, alas) of books, articles, recordings, films, games, comics, and sundry other incarnations of *Frankenstein* may be found in Donald Glut's *Frankenstein Catalog,* cited both below and above. There are numerous incomplete bibliographies online as well. Other works are referenced in the notes to the text.

———. *Frankenstein*. Edited by J. Paul Hunter. New York: W. W. Norton, 1995. Norton Critical Editions.

———. *Frankenstein*. Edited by Susan J. Wolfson. New York: Pearson Education, 2006. Longman Cultural Editions.

———. *Frankenstein*. Introduction by Jeffery Deaver. Oxford: Oxford University Press, 2001. Oxford World's Classics.

———. *Frankenstein: 1818 Text*. Edited by Marilyn Butler. Oxford: Oxford University Press, 2001. Oxford World's Classics.

———. *Frankenstein; or, The Modern Prometheus*. Introduction by Wendy Lesser. New York: Alfred A. Knopf, 1992.

———. *Frankenstein; or, The Modern Prometheus*. 1831. Whitefish, MT: Kessinger Publishing Company, 2010.

———. *Frankenstein; or, The Modern Prometheus*. 1831. Introduction by Patrick McGrath. Lakewood, CO: Millipede Press, 2007.

———. *Frankenstein; or, The Modern Prometheus*. Edited by Maurice Hindle. London: Penguin Group/Penguin Classics, 2003.

———. *Frankenstein; or, The Modern Prometheus*. Edited, annotated, and illustrated by M. Grant Kellermeyer. Fort Wayne, IN: Oldstyle Tales Press, 2013.

———. *Frankenstein; or, The Modern Prometheus*. Introduction by Douglas Clegg, afterword by Harold Bloom. New York: Signet Classics, 2013.

———. *Frankenstein; or, The Modern Prometheus: The 1818 Text*. Edited by James Rieger. Chicago: University of Chicago Press, 1982.

———. *The Journals of Mary Shelley*. Edited by Paula R. Feldman and Diana Scott-Kilvert. Baltimore: Johns Hopkins University Press, 1987.

———. *The Letters of Mary W. Shelley*. Edited by Frederick L. Jones. 2 vols. Norman: University of Oklahoma Press, 1944.

———. *The Letters of Mary Wollstonecraft Shelley*. Edited by Betty T. Bennett. 2. vols. Baltimore: Johns Hopkins University Press, 1980.

———. *Mary Shelley's Journal*. Edited by Frederick L. Jones. Norman: University of Oklahoma Press, 1947.

———. *The Original Frankenstein*. Edited by Charles E. Robinson. Oxford: The Bodleian Library, 2008.

———. *Robert Andrew Parker's Illustrated Frankenstein*. Edited and illustrated by Robert Andrew Parker. New York: Clarkson N. Potter, 1976.

Shelley, Mary Wollstonecraft, and Percy Bysshe Shelley. *History of a Six Weeks' Tour Through a Part of France, Switzerland, Germany and Holland: With Letters Descriptive of a Sail Round the Lake of Geneva, and of the Glaciers of Chamouni*. 1817. Charleston, SC: Bibliolife (n.d.).

Shelley, Percy Bysshe. *The Letters of Percy Bysshe Shelley*. Collected and edited by Ronald Ingpen. 2 vols. London: Sir Isaac Pitman & Sons; New York: Charles Scribner's Sons, 1909.

————. *The Letters of Percy Bysshe Shelley*. Edited by Frederick L. Jones. 2 vols. Oxford: Clarendon Press, 1964.

————. *Shelley's Lost Letters to Harriet*. Edited, and with an introduction, by Leslie Hotson. London: Faber & Faber, 1930.

BIOGRAPHY AND CRITICISM

Aldiss, Brian W., with David Wingrove. *Trillion Year Spree: The History of Science Fiction*. New York: Athenaeum, 1986.

Baldick, Chris. *In Frankenstein's Shadow: Myth, Monstrosity and Nineteenth-century Writing*. Oxford: Clarendon Press, 1990.

Behrendt, Stephen C., and Anne Kostelanetz Mellor, eds. *Approaches to Teaching Shelley's Frankenstein*. New York: Modern Language Association of America, 1990.

Belefant, Arthur. *Frankenstein, the Man and the Monster*. Indialantic, FL: Benjamin, Ross and Lane, 2008.

Bloom, Harold, ed. *Mary Shelley's Frankenstein*. New York: Bloom's Literary Criticism/Infobase Publishing, 2007.

————, ed. *Mary Shelley's Frankenstein* (Updated Edition). New York: Chelsea House Publishers, 2007. Bloom's Modern Critical Interpretations.

Blunden, Edmund. *Shelley: A Life Story*. New York: Viking Press, 1947.

Botting, Fred. *Making Monstrous:* Frankenstein, *Criticism, Theory*. Manchester: Manchester University Press, 1991.

Florescu, Radu, Alan G. Barbour, and Matei Cazacu. *In Search of Frankenstein*. Boston: New York Graphic Society, 1975.

Frayling, Christopher. *Mad, Bad and Dangerous?: The Scientist and the Cinema*. London: Reaktion Books, 2005.

Haining, Peter, ed. *The Frankenstein File*. London: New English Library, 1977.

Harris, Janet. *The Woman Who Created Frankenstein: A Portrait of Mary Shelley*. New York: Harper & Row, 1979.

Harris-Fain, Darren. "Mary Wollstonecraft Shelley (1797–1851)," *Dictionary of Literary Biography*, Volume 178: *British Fantasy and Science Fiction Writers Before World War I*. Edited by Darren Harris-Fain. Detroit, MI: Gale Research, 1997.

de Hart, Scott Douglas. *Shelley Unbound: Discovering Frankenstein's True Creator*. Port Townsend, WA: Feral House, 2013.

Hitchcock, Susan Tyler. *Frankenstein: A Cultural History*. New York: W. W. Norton, 2007.

Hoobler, Dorothy, and Thomas Hoobler. *The Monsters: Mary Shelley and the Curse of Frankenstein*. Boston: Little, Brown, 2006.

Horton, Robert. *Frankenstein*. New York: Columbia University Press, 2014. Cultographies Series.

Johnson, Barbara, "My Monster/My Self," *Diacritics* 12 (1982): 2–10.

Kaplan, Morton. *The Unspoken Motive: A Guide to Psychoanalytic Literary Criticism*. New York: The Free Press (1973).

Ketterer, David. *Frankenstein's Creation: The Book, the Monster, and Human Reality*. Victoria, BC: University of Victoria, 1979.

Lauritsen, John. *The Man Who Wrote Frankenstein*. Dorchester, MA: Pagan Press, 2007.

Lederer, Susan E. *Frankenstein: Penetrating the Secrets of Nature*. New Brunswick, NJ: Rutgers University Press, 2002. National Library of Medicine, History of Medicine Division.

Levine, George, and U. C. Knoepflmacher, eds. *The Endurance of Frankenstein: Essays on Mary Shelley's Novel*. Berkeley: University of California Press, 1979.

Marsh, Nicholas. *Mary Shelley: Frankenstein*. London: Palgrave Macmillan, 2009.

Marshall, Mrs. Julian [Florence A.]. *The Life and Letters of Mary Wollstonecraft Shelley*. 2 vols. London: R. Bentley and Son, 1889.

Mellor, Anne Kostelanetz. *Mary Shelley: Her Life, Her Fiction, Her Monsters*. New York: Routledge, 1989.

Michaud, Nicolas, ed. *Frankenstein and Philosophy: The Shocking Truth*. Chicago: Open Court, 2013.

Mitchell, Robert. *Experimental Life: Vitalism in Romantic Science & Literature*. Baltimore: Johns Hopkins University Press, 2013.

Montillo, Roseanne. *The Lady and Her Monsters: A Tale of Dissections, Real-Life Dr. Frankensteins, and the Creation of Mary Shelley's Masterpiece*. New York: William Morrow, 2013.

Morrison, Lucy, and Staci L. Stone, eds. *A Mary Shelley Encyclopedia*. Westport, CT: Greenwood Publishing Group, 2003.

Morton, Timothy, ed. *Mary Shelley's Frankenstein: A Sourcebook*. New York: Routledge, 2002.

Nardo, Don, ed. *Readings on Frankenstein.* San Diego: Greenhaven Press, Inc., 2000.

Nitchie, Elizabeth. *Mary Shelley, Author of "Frankenstein."* New Brunswick, NJ: Rutgers University Press, 1953.

Phy, Allene Stuart. *Mary Shelley.* Mercer Island, WA: Starmont House, 1988. Starmont Reader's Guide, no. 36.

Robinson, Charles E., "Texts in Search of an Editor: Reflections on *The Frankenstein Notebooks* and on Editorial Authority," pp. 91–110 of *Textual Studies and the Common Reader: Essays on Editing Novels and Novelists.* Edited by Alexander Pettit. Athens: University of Georgia Press, 2000.

Robinson, Charles E., ed. *The Frankenstein Notebooks: A Facsimile Edition of Mary Shelley's Novel, 1816–1817.* 4. Vols. New York: Garland Publishing, Inc., 1996.

St. Clair, William. *The Godwins and the Shelleys: A Biography of a Family.* New York: W. W. Norton, 1989.

Sanborn, F. B., ed. *The Romance of Mary W. Shelley, John Howard Payne and Washington Irving.* Boston: The Bibliophile Society, 1907.

Schor, Esther H. *The Cambridge Companion to Mary Shelley.* Cambridge, UK: Cambridge University Press, 2004.

Schwartz; Janelle A. *Worm Work: Recasting Romanticism.* Minneapolis: University of Minnesota Press, 2012.

Small, Christopher. *Ariel Like a Harpy: Shelley, Mary and Frankenstein.* London: Victor Gollancz, 1972.

—————. *Mary Shelley's* Frankenstein: *Tracing the Myth.* Pittsburgh: University of Pittsburgh Press, 1973.

Stott, Andrew McConnell. *The Poet and the Vampyre: The Curse of Byron and the Birth of Literature's Greatest Monsters.* New York: Pegasus Books, 2014.

Sunstein, Emily W. *Mary Shelley: Romance and Reality.* Boston: Little, Brown, 1989.

Tropp, Martin. *Mary Shelley's Monster: The Story of* Frankenstein. Boston: Houghton Mifflin, 1977.

Veeder, William. *Mary Shelley and Frankenstein: The Fate of Androgyny.* Chicago: University of Chicago Press, 1986.

Walling, William A. *Mary Shelley.* Boston: Twayne Publishers, 1972.

Willis, Martin. *Mesmerists, Monsters, and Machines: Science Fiction and the Cultures of Science in the Nineteenth Century.* Kent, OH: Kent State University Press, 2006.

STAGE AND SCREEN

Anobile, Richard J. *James Whale's Frankenstein Starring Boris Karloff.* New York: Universe Books, 1974.

Balderston, John L., and Garrett Fort. *Frankenstein—A Play.* Edited by Philip J. Riley. Albany, GA: BearManor Media, 2010.

Brooks, Mel, with Rebecca Keegan. Young Frankenstein: *The Story of the Making of the Film.* New York: Black Dog & Leventhal Publishers, 2016.

Forry, Steven Earl. *Hideous Progenies: Dramatizations of* Frankenstein *from Mary Shelley to the Present.* Philadelphia: University of Pennsylvania Press, 1990.

Glut, Donald F. *The Frankenstein Catalog.* Jefferson, NC: McFarland & Company, 1984.

Mank, Gregory William. *Bela Lugosi and Boris Karloff: The Expanded Story of a Haunting Collaboration, with a Complete Filmography of Their Films Together.* Jefferson, NC: McFarland & Company, 2009.

Mank, Gregory William. *It's Alive!: The Classic Cinema Saga of Frankenstein.* New York: A. S. Barnes & Company, 1981.

Milner, H. M. *Frankenstein—Or, The Man and the Monster—A Stage Play.* Redditch, Worcestershire, UK: Read Books Ltd., 2011.

Osborne, Jennifer, ed. *Monsters: A Celebration of the Classics from Universal Studios.* New York: Del Rey Books, 2006.

Riley, Philip J., ed. *Frankenstein: The Original Shooting Script.* Screenplay by Garrett Fort and Francis Edwards Faragoh. Absecon, NJ: MagicImage Filmbooks, 1989.

———, ed. *Robert Florey's Frankenstein Starring Bela Lugosi.* Albany, GA: BearManor Media, 2010.

Shriver, Gordon B. *Boris Karloff: The Man Remembered.* Baltimore: Publishamerica, 2004.

Skal, David J. *The Monster Show: A Cultural History of Horror.* New York: Faber & Faber, 2001.

Svehla, Gary L., and Susan Svehla, eds. *We Belong Dead: Frankenstein on Film.* Baltimore: Midnight Marquee Press, 2005.

Wiebel, Frederick C., Jr. *Edison's Frankenstein.* Albany, GA: BearManor Media, 2009.

ADDITIONAL REFERENCES

Ankarloo, Bengt, and Stuart Clark, eds. *Witchcraft and Magic in Europe,* Volume 5: *The Eighteenth and Nineteenth Centuries.* Philadelphia: University of Pennsylvania Press, 1999.

Bakewell, Michael, and Melissa Bakewell. *Augusta Leigh: Byron's Half-Sister—A Biography.* London: Chatto & Windus, 2000.

Benz, Ernst. *Theology of Electricity: On the Encounter and Explanation of Theology and Science in the 17th and 18th Centuries.* Allison Park, PA: Pickwick Publications, 1989. Princeton Theological Monograph Series, no. 19.

Cunliffe, Barry. *The Extraordinary Voyage of Pytheas the Greek.* New York: Penguin Books, 2003.

Dumas, Alexandre. *Alexandre Dumas' Adventures in Caucasia.* Translated and edited by Alma Murch Elizabeth. New York: Chilton (1962).

———. *Alexandre Dumas' Adventures in Czarist Russia.* Translated and edited by Alma Murch Elizabeth. New York: Chilton, 1961.

George, Arthur L., and Elena George. *St. Petersburg—The First Three Centuries.* Stroud, Gloucestershire, UK: Sutton Publishing, 2004.

Godwin, Joscelyn. *Arktos: The Polar Myth in Science, Symbolism and Nazi Survival.* Kempton, IL: Adventures Unlimited Press, 1996.

Jerrmann, Eduard. *Pictures from St. Petersburg.* 1852. Berkeley: University of California Libraries, 2014.

Klingaman, William K., and Nicholas P. Klingaman. *The Year Without Summer: 1816 and the Volcano That Darkened the World and Changed History.* New York: St. Martin's/Griffin, 2014.

Markus, Julia. *Lady Byron and Her Daughters.* New York: W. W. Norton, 2014.

Morton, Alan. *Science in the 18th Century.* London: Science Museum, 1993.

Muirhead, Findlay, ed. *Switzerland with Chamonix and the Italian Lakes.* London: Macmillan & Co., 1923. The Blue Guides.

Morus, Iwan Rhys. *Frankenstein's Children: Electricity, Exhibition, and Experiment in Early-Nineteenth-Century London.* Princeton, NJ: Princeton University Press, 1998.

Murray, John. *Murray's Handbook for Travellers in Switzerland.* 1838. New York: Humanities Press, 1970.

Rousseau, Jean Jacques. *Emile, Julie and Other Writings.* Edited by R. L. Archer. Woodbury, NY: Barron's Educational Series, 1964.

Scott, G. Firth. *The Romance of Polar Exploration: Interesting Descriptions of Arctic and Antarctic Adventure from the Earliest Time to the Voyage of the "Discovery."* 1906. Memphis, TN: General Books LLC, 2012.

Stefansson, Vilhjalmur. *Ultima Thule: Further Mysteries of the Arctic.* New York: Macmillan, 1940.

Strickland, Margot. *The Byron Women.* New York: St. Martin's Press, 1974.

Weisser, Michael R. *Crime and Punishment in Early Modern Europe.* Atlantic Highlands, NJ: Humanities Press, 1979.

Wood, Gillen D'Arcy. *Tambora: The Eruption That Changed the World.* Princeton, NJ: Princeton University Press, 2014.

Wright, Helen S. *The Great White North: The Story of Polar Exploration from the Earliest Times to the Discovery of the Pole.* New York: Macmillan, 1910.

PARODIES, PASTICHES, AND COMICS

Baranowski, Don W. *Sherlock Holmes: The Adventure of the Frankenstein Monster.* West Conshohocken, PA: Infinity Publishing, 2006.

Briefer, Dick. *The Monster of Frankenstein.* West Orange, NJ: Idea Men Productions, 2006. Includes issues 18 through 33 of the comic.

Cooper, Roscoe. *Diary of Victor Frankenstein.* New York: DK Publishing, 1997.

Karloff, Boris, ed. *Tales of Terror.* West Orange, NJ: Idea Men Productions, 2006.

Kay, Jeremy. *The Secret Laboratory Journals of Dr. Victor Frankenstein.* Woodstock, NY: Overlook, 1995.

Kuhns, Luke Benjamin. *Sherlock Holmes and the Horror of Frankenstein.* London: MX Publishing, 2013. Artist: Marcie Klinger.

Petrucha, Stefan. *The Shadow of Frankenstein.* Milwaukie, OR: DH Press, 2006.

Tremayne, Peter. *Hound of Frankenstein.* London: Mills & Boon, 1977.

Yoe, Craig, ed. *Dick Briefer's Frankenstein.* San Diego: IDW Publishing, 2013.

Acknowledgments

U NLIKE VICTOR FRANKENSTEIN, I did not work alone in creating this "hideous progeny." The breadth of the research reflected here would not have been possible in the pre-Internet days of yore, but as always, I have relied heavily upon others in pulling together the material included. The pioneering work of Leonard Wolf, in *The Annotated Frankenstein*, and of James Rieger and Charles Robinson in parsing the texts, was essential to the production of this book. I am also indebted to the dozens of academicians who have written tirelessly about the Shelleys and their works, especially those who generously posted their essays for public consumption. Thanks also to Raymond McLagan of the Pepperdine University Payson Library for his help. Special thanks to Anne K. Mellor, who read the manuscript and offered valuable insights and wrote a brilliant afterword. My consulting editor/researcher, Janet Byrne, went far beyond what was expected of her in finding special material, especially those items that, in the words of Sherlock Holmes, are "a little *recherché*."

Inspiration came from my usual sources: my editors and friends Bob Weil, Marie Pantojan, Peter Miller, and the rest of the wonderful team at Liveright/W. W. Norton; my agent, Don Maass; my lawyer and friend Jonathan Kirsch; my longtime Sherlockian friends Andy Peck, Jerry Margolin, and Mike Whelan, constant cheerleaders; my amazing and generous writer-friends Laurie R. King, Nancy Holder, Lisa Morton, Cornelia Funke, and Neil Gaiman; my pal John Landis, who always seems to find something I need though I didn't know it existed; my dear friend and writing partner Laura Caldwell, whose talent, energy, and enthusiasm astonish and inspire me; my children, Matt, Wendy, Stacy, Evan, and Amanda; my granddaughter Maya, whose own reading of *Frankenstein* encouraged mine (and the rest of my grandchildren, who fill my life with joy); and especially, as always, *the* woman, my wife, Sharon, who proofread the story and asked all the right questions.

LESLIE S. KLINGER
Malibu, California